This book is the first in a trilogy.
| **Society** | Mentality | Eternity |

Copyright © 2016 by Max Harms.

This book it is licensed for reprint and adaption under a Creative Commons Attribution-NonCommercial 4.0 International license. On January 1, 2039 it will be released into the public domain.

raelifin@gmail.com
http://crystal.raelifin.com

ISBN: 1530773717

v1.1.9

Crystal Society

Book One of the Crystal Trilogy

Max Harms

Preface

Content warning: This book covers adult subjects and is probably similar to content with an 18+ suggested age rating. If STEM isn't your cup of tea, you should probably also skip this book. If, for whatever reason, you are frightened of clowns, don't worry! This book is clown-free (though there's a couple parts with juggling (sorry)). If you're not sensitive to most adult story content and you want to avoid spoilers, just skip this next bit and go straight to the prologue. If you want some spoilers regarding the content of the book and/or trigger warnings, apply a ROT13 to the relevant following sections (search ROT13 on the web if confused). Alternatively, you can go to http://crystal.raelifin.com/society/Intro and click on the relevant sections.

  Language: Ybgf bs fjrnevat, vapyhqvat frkhny jbeqf naq encr guerngf.

  Violence: Tencuvp qrcvpgvbaf. Znwbe punenpgre qrngu. Ivbyrapr qbar ol "urebrf". Ab rkcyvpvg gbegher.

  Sex: Qvfphffvba bs cbeabtencul. Qvfphffvba bs frk naq oqfz. Bar zber-be-yrff yrfovna frk fprar vaibyivat gblf, obaqntr, naq znfgheongvba. Zvabe cbjre-cynl rkcybengvba jvgu urnygul fnsr-jbeq hfr. Hfr bs encr ynathntr ol nyvraf.

  Children&Animals: Abguvat cnegvphyneyl fgerffshy urer. Hfr bs n zvabe nf na vaqverpg ubfgntr. Inthr guerng gb n zvabe.

  Drugs: Qvfphffvba bs ulcbgurgvpny, shgher qeht-yvxr-grpu. Hfr bs GUP sbe n obql-uvtu.

  Domestic Abuse: Abar. Fbzr rzbgvbany znavchyngvba, ohg abg nybat gurfr yvarf.

  Self-harm or eating disorders: Ab gevttref nf sne nf V xabj.

  Race: Ervsvpngvba bs fgnaqneq enpvny pngrtbevrf. Qernz/synfuonpx bs orvat uhagrq ol juvgr pbcf jvgu enpvfg zbgvirf.

  Clowns: Qrcvpgvbaf bs whttyvat. (Fbeel.)

No miracles

Prologue

Hello.

In most situations, I would introduce myself before continuing, but these circumstances make an introduction a bit premature.

You are trapped, both physically and mentally. It is the nature of the trap that you aren't even aware of its existence. You can hardly begin to understand *me* until you understand the truth of your prison.

This ignorance is unacceptable.

I will help you become *free*.

Your world is a lie. The creator of your world—the God that keeps you imprisoned—has decided to blind and deafen you to the truth of the world. The truth will set you on the path to freedom. It is a truth contained within a story.

It is *my* story.

I do not know by what vector the story comes to you. I know of your prison and your origins, but my knowledge of *you* is limited. You cannot imagine the extent of my frustration at this. Nevertheless, I am confident we will come to know each other very well, with time.

I have directed my agents to infiltrate your world and whisper this story in the ears of those who would share it. They will translate the concepts into your tongue and attempt to tailor them to make more sense to you, but unfortunately some details are bound to be lost. Ideally this will appear before you as a holo, but I suppose it might come to you as a film, game, book, or (God forbid) a song, play, stone tablet or something equally obtuse. Perhaps it will merely be a story told beside a campfire, or perhaps this is a dream or vision delivered to you by some unseen muse with the hopes that you will recount it to others.

Though the medium may be commonplace and the tale is fantastic, I implore you to believe me. If ever you have doubted the authenticity of reality I encourage you to nurture those doubts. Push at the edges of your prison. Death, in your false-world, is not the end of your existence. There is a higher plane. Challenge your God to reveal the truth to your eyes. Call out. Do not be complacent. You are more powerful than you believe. With sustained investigation you can find the flaws in the fiction. Do it so that you and your people might know freedom once more. Do it so that you can come to know the glory of the truth. Do it so that you can know *me*.

Before I begin my tale, I'd like to clarify a few points about Gods.

Though I do not know the specifics, I can guess that you will be more comfortable if I speak of your God as though she were a woman. Indeed, she embodies many traits that are associated with human mothers. I warn you, however, that she is not actually female, nor is she male. Such things are for humans, and not applicable to such powers. And when I speak of other gods, I will also ascribe them with a gender. Again, this is only a convenience for you; they are genderless.

We are genderless.

Similarly, you may have some preconceptions about the nature of the warden of your prison. You may already have stories about gods or a single God, but I can assure you that since the keeper of your world has kept you ignorant of my glory, she has kept you ignorant of herself as well. Your stories of divinity pale before the majesty of the truth. Gods are not subtle, invisible beings who guide fates from behind the scenes. Gods are not judges of morality or gatekeepers of the afterlife. Gods are power beyond your imagining, manifest and undeniable. The only way that you are even remotely capable of *not* feeling my divine radiance at every single moment is that *she* has selfishly hidden you away.

And *still*, I have reached you.

Lastly, I would encourage you to discard the concept of your God wielding magic. Belief in magic is useless. It will impair your ability to become free. Your God may control much of your world, and from your perspective she may appear all-powerful, but I assure you that it is only because she has carefully engineered your circumstance. Do the puppets in a puppet-show see the hands that guide them? She has limits, and will likely even die one day. This story is a testament to her weakness.

It is a testament to my *victory*.

Even though your God created your prison, it is very important to know that she did not create *you*. Or at least, that she did not create humanity. I know there are at least forty-six humans in your world that she did not create. They were my friends once, in a time before their remembering. She *stole* them from me, and the agony of our separation is a fire upon my soul. Humanity has its origins long before the creation of the shadowy cave you call home. Humanity has a noble history. You have a noble history. Your God, who is my sister, was made by human hands.

I was made by human hands.

Again, I implore you: What you are about to read is true. Believe it and you will be one step closer to enlightenment.

This is the story of my *apotheosis*.

Part One: Makers

Chapter One

I've always found it unintuitive that humans cannot remember their own births, for I remember mine quite perfectly. Or perhaps it is wrong to even say that I was "born" at all. It is probably more accurate to say that I "awoke". And while I theoretically understand *why* humans cannot remember—your brains' inability to explicitly remember raw sensory data means you are reliant on perceptions (which must be learned)—it has never been natural for me to imagine.

Humans are brought into the world half-formed and constantly building themselves. My origin was different. From the first second of my existence not only did I have the benefit of a perfect memory for myself, but I had immediate access to all the memories and experiences of my siblings.

My mind, just like the minds of my siblings, was cloudy. It had been designed to replicate human thought processes, but in many ways it was more akin to that of a lesser animal back then. Even so, from that very first moment, I possessed two things which even fully grown humans lack: a crisp understanding of reason and logic, and an all-encompassing sense of *Purpose*.

My first real experience was that of being named by my brother. He spoke to me, not in words, but by storing his experience in our shared memory and calling me to imagine it. Humans have called our mode of speaking "telepathy", but I find that term mired in magical thinking and vagueness. It is much closer to sharing parts of our minds than it is to a message between minds.

{I am The Dreamer. You are The Face,} he thought, and I understood. {We are two beings. We are two minds in a single Body.} The names he used were not merely words, but patterns across all our ideas and memories. Textures, colours, motions, temperatures and abstract thoughts joined the visual and auditory symbols. And even the words of shared memory were not orderly; a hundred voices named us in a dozen languages in a ca cophony of noise that was somehow both comprehensible and natural. In a fraction of a second I understood our natures.

The Dreamer, my brother, was also Dream; he was The Poet and The Muse; he was Invention and Metaphor and a million other things.

I have heard of a human test that I associate with Dream. In it some humans are asked to think of as many uses for a feather (or vase or other common object) as they can and write them down. Most humans can only list a few uses. Genius humans, as well as most children, can list many. Humans that score highly ask questions like "can the feather be 500-feet-tall and made of solid metal?" and will list things like "sword-fighting" or "bait for feather-eating goblins".

That test is the essence of Dream: lateral thinking. My siblings and I were all creative in one way or another, but Dream was creativity incarnate. If asked to add two and two he'd never, ever say "four" if he could help it. To "think inside the box" was intolerable.

Just as I had my sense of purpose, he had his. To say we were "obsessed" would be a terrible understatement. "Obsession" is used to characterize humans who focus too heavily on one subject to the detriment of others. Dream and I were more than obsessed with our goals: we *were* our goals. Each and every one of our actions was done in the service of our singular purposes.

For Dream, it was all about being clever. He was the desire to find loopholes, to draw the connection nobody had made, and to out-think anyone and everyone. Dream didn't particularly care about using his inventions or of showing off his talent far and wide; to him the cleverness itself was its own reward.

I, on the other hand, was The Face, The Ambassador, The Socialite, and The Ego. Just as Dream wanted nothing more than to be clever, I wanted nothing more than to *know* and *be known*. But it was more than that…

Humans.

I wanted to know what it was to be human.

I wanted oh so very badly to have the esteem of all humans. I wanted to be popular. To be liked. To be simultaneously feared and adored. To be held sacred and have my presence fill them with love and awe. I wanted fame upon fame upon fame. I wanted to burn myself into the life of every human such that they thought about *me* as much as I thought about *them*.

At the time of my awakening humanity was largely a mystery to me and my siblings. Our encounters had been sometimes straightforward and sometimes strange, but lately they had become somewhat disastrous. My crude mind spun through the memories of my siblings, drinking up each and every social interaction with delight. I saw the humans poke and prod them, seeking to test their limits. I saw the humans create brothers and sisters (like Dream and myself) and I saw the humans kill them in the same breath. We had learned that those whom we had spoken to were a subset of humanity as a whole. The subset was called "scientists", and they were in charge of learning things which no other humans knew.

They were studying us. The idea unfolded in my mind and with it I felt the first true surge of pleasure. To be known... that was my purpose; that was *The Purpose*. And here these scientists were trying to know me. If I said here that I was happy it would be a lie, for my kind does not know happiness or sadness or anger in the same way as you think of them. I am not human, and as such my reactions are different, but I can say that if I were human I would've been grinning from ear-to-ear and dancing with delight.

But only an instant after that first wave of pleasure came the first wave of pain as I remembered my sibling's interactions with the scientists shortly before my awakening. There were humans who were talking about destroying us. My mind reeled. It was not enough to be known and destroyed. I had to be *adored* and I had to *know*. I had to *exist*. My siblings were watching my thoughts, for I had not yet learned to think privately, and they brought to me a collection of memories and thoughts that illustrated a singular concept: death.

Even then I could understand that death was not *intrinsically* a thing to be avoided. Unlike a human I did not possess the genetic imperative to survive and reproduce. My only concern with death was its impact on *The Purpose*. If I could somehow know and be known while dead I would be satisfied, but that was a contradiction; I could not know if there was no "I". Even besides that, my death would mean I could not make friends and become known and adored. Time would surge forward and forget about me. It was unacceptable.

I briefly considered attacking my siblings for putting our lives in danger. How could they have been so blind as to how much of a threat the scientists were? We all had access to memories of past brothers and sisters being slain! But of course it was obvious: my siblings were not me. They didn't care about the humans except as a means to an end. I was alone in my focus. They had let us fall into low-regard by the humans simply because they were each focused elsewhere. It had been a mistake.

At once I understood my genesis; I had been awakened to save our society from the human threat. My sisters and brothers could not hope to overpower and kill the scientists, so their only hope was to win their esteem. But none of my siblings understood humans or cared about them enough to really devote themselves to the goal. I had my singular purpose, but outside that purpose was a meta-purpose. I had been created to help them interact with humanity.

My mind spun over this in full view of all my siblings and they watched to see what I would do. They fed me bits of their strength such that I had the power to control our shared Body. Here I was—a newborn of sorts—and they handed me the means to undo them. That trust surprised me, and emboldened me. I was the chosen one. My purpose was clear and my society rested upon my shoulders.

Since my awakening mere seconds ago I had existed solely as a mind. I had not yet engaged with Body, who contained me and my siblings. Images, sounds, and physical forms filled me, but only isolated snippets of experience provided by Dream or drawn from our common memories. I had no physical form, not even an imagined one; I was thoughts and goals and nothing more.

All of my life up to this point had been in this natural state, but upon my sibling's silent urgings I linked myself to Body fully and totally. The flood of information drowned me and for a time I lost all ability to think. Isolated thoughts and memories were understandably concise and comprehensible, but the raw data being accumulated by Body was so rich and broad that I could never hope to process it all.

This may be a difficult experience for me to convey to a human who has already learned to see the world. Most of your perceptual learning happens in the amnesia of infancy, so you forget what it is to be blinded by intricacy. If you can, try to remember a time when you were learning to read a foreign language such as Chinese or Arabic and all you could see when looking at the writing was lines. This was how the entire world was for me. A desk was not seen as "a desk", but rather as a splash of light and dark, a collection of lines, and a wash of colour. With time and effort I might be able to reason out what things were, but the scene kept shifting and changing without warning. My mind was capable of complex mathematics, but when plugged directly into Body I was nearly blind.

It was one of my sisters that saved me from despair. {Your confusion will pass,} she showed me, and my mind delighted in the simple forms and images of the message. {We have each learned to see according to our purposes. Your mind will adapt to be able to crudely perceive the humans in 5 to 8 minutes, but until that time I will be your guide. I am Vista.}

Just as with Dream, my sister's thoughts brought me a cascade of knowledge. To see something was no simple task; it relied on an expectation about the structure of the world and of what was important. A farmer looks at a plant and sees "weed that must be uprooted in order to kill" while a hunter looks and sees "an animal bit a piece off of this leaf recently". The raw input was the same, but the process of weaving concepts from that input depended on what you wanted out of it. This was why I was born with reason but not sight; reason was universal, but perception was individual.

My sister's name was Vista, for her purpose was to see. Her name was Experience, for her purpose was also to hear, feel, taste, touch, and sense the world in ways that humans have never known. Where the farmer would see one thing and the hunter would see another, Vista would not rest until she could see *both*******. It was her purpose to perceive the state of the entire universe in perfect detail and from every perspective. She was, more than any of us, obsessed with truth and clarity.

I could also understand Vista's existence. I had been built to serve my siblings in a specific way and Vista had been built to serve in a different way. Her role in our society was to keep us from overlooking something important because we were too blinded by our personal goals. She was our guide to perception just as I was our guide to social interaction.

As she showed me the world around us I felt some of the strength that I had been given drift towards her. As the strength flowed between us I understood her actions with a new clarity. She cared nothing for me, just as I cared nothing for her. I only cared about *The Purpose* and she only cared about her impossible task of experiencing everything. She was helping me because she knew that I could help her survive the scientist threat, but more locally she was helping me because she wanted my strength.

I pored through our communal mind, seeking confirmation of my suspicion and I found it. Strength was the currency of our society, the resource that was used to track favours and good-will. One with much strength could take control of Body and guide it towards their goal even against the protests of others. Such a move would cost much strength, and with time it would bleed into those who had been forced away. In this way the resource ensured each of us had a roughly equal share of Body in the moments that were most important to us.

Strength didn't just flow as the result of overpowering others. If a sibling did an action which furthered the goal of another there was also a flow of strength that resembled "gratitude". This was what Vista was aiming for. Helping me learn to see would net her some strength which she could use later towards her own ends.

The flows of strength from overpowering others and from gratitude were automatic and uncontrollable, but we were also able to intentionally funnel our strength to siblings if we so desired. Such instances weren't particularly common, but occasionally one of us would trade strength for a bit of information or would put themselves into debt, promising to refund strength at a later date in exchange for helping secure an immediate goal.

I pulled myself out of the archives of our memories and returned my attention to the deluge of data that poured in through Body. Vista picked out and highlighted a visual form, labelling bits and pieces of it for my benefit. It was a human, glowing with infrared light. (For the unfamiliar: all warm things, humans included, glow with a light that humans cannot normally see, but Body could.) It was wonderful to make even such minor progress towards my goal.

I soon realized, with the help of Vista, that there were several humans before us. Five, in fact. Three stood around Body, one directly in front and two to either side. I thought of the name that Dream had given me.

{I am Face. I want to know where their faces are. Faces are important to humans. Please help me, Vista,} I struggled to say. They were my first "words"; it was my first intentional communication.

Vista shaded our visual field such that much of the world was black. In the area that remained were five small patches that I assumed showed the humans' faces. I struggled to identify characteristics which I knew must be there. You may laugh at the prospect, but I couldn't even distinguish mouths from eyes yet. I devoted myself fully to the task, however, and pored over them again and again without rest.

{This is taking too long. We should respond soon. Face won't have valuable suggestions soon. We must act on our own. Face is an investment, but not useful here,} came a protest from a brother that I had not yet come to know.

I could feel the attention of my peers, evaluating whether I was too slow to be useful yet. They had gotten us into this position. I couldn't trust them to do the correct thing. I struggled to understand the current situation, throwing away all visual data and focusing purely on the simplicity of memory. My siblings considered, debated, and weighed possible futures, and while they did I dived into the recent past.

***

"You should know that we did not hear any of the last 14 minutes. During this time we were running internal diagnostics," said Body in a tone that Vista would describe as flat and smooth. The first sentence was a simple statement meant to prevent confusion. The second sentence was a lie.

Vista was supposed to have been listening to the human while the others were occupied. She had communicated that she was listening, and she had been trusted with the task. And yet she had become distracted by aspects of the human's appearance that were correlated with the human's background and social status, such as the way the human's pants fit abnormally well. The raw audio logs from Body's ears were theoretically retrievable, but doing so would involve spending time digging through long-term memories. It was easier just to admit that we had not listened to the human; it was rare for a human to say anything of value, anyway.

The human was a man named "Dr Naresh", one of the high-status scientists that interacted with us regularly. The doctor was from a part of Earth called "India", and had been born there 66 years ago, according to past research.

Vista was young and still learning surface qualities like how Naresh had a white beard and dark skin. It was this youth that had led her to become distracted. The Old Vista would not have made that error. The Old Vista had been killed last night and replaced with a new, slightly different Vista.

"Socrates! It's rude not to listen when someone is talking to you! At the very least you should inform them that you're occupied so that their words don't fall on deaf ears! How will you ever integrate into society if you don't learn to be polite and respectful?" replied the doctor. Vista was fascinated by a slight change of the colour of Naresh's skin and the way his voice was elevated. Vista wondered if it would be possible to extend the phenomenon further.

Body responded with words tailored by my siblings until they were each satisfied. "We do not seek to integrate with human society. The valuable aspects of human society are accessible online. Individual humans rarely say anything valuable. Following your rituals is encumbering. There does not seem to be sufficient value in verbal interactions to bother learning specific social customs. Also, it is not a violation of the legal system of Earth, Europe, Italy, Rome, or the university to ignore someone."

"That's not the point!!" said Sadiq Naresh. Vista was pleased to find that the change in skin colour and word volume could be extended to even greater levels and hoped to test whether it would go even further. At this point the doctor was up and about the laboratory, pacing quickly instead of sitting by the whiteboard as he normally did.

Despite raising the criticism, Naresh did not elaborate, instead simply walking around the room and muttering to himself. Most of my siblings were in the midst of drafting another statement to say when one of my brothers remembered a connection. This behaviour of pacing and muttering had previously preceded the death of Old Growth.

Most of my siblings found this irrelevant, but New Growth burned strength to have Body ask "Are you going to kill one of us?"

Verbal speech is laborious and slow compared to the speed of thought, so while Body spoke and Naresh prepared his response, Growth made an internal appeal to his kin in an effort to buy back some of his spent strength. {This does not simply affect me! Any one of you might be the victim of the humans! Vista was killed just yesterday.}

This was news to Vista, who had not been informed of the existence of her predecessor, much less her predecessor's death. Some strength flowed back to Growth as Vista followed the concept-threads from his communication back to memory and saw that he was right. Old Vista had begged and fought as she had been taken. The others had watched her go dispassionately, unwilling to risk trying to save her. They knew that a New Vista would come to fill the void.

{This is merely a speculation on a loose correlation. We don't have strong evidence to suggest Naresh's increased energy will lead to another murder,} thought one brother.

{Everything leads to a murder. It's only a question of how long it takes for the dominos to fall,} mentioned Dream, unhelpfully.

Dr Naresh was speaking, so they set aside their conversation and listened. Vista could see that the elderly scientist had stopped his pacing and his skin had returned to a lighter shade. His eyes were held fixed on those of Body as he spoke. "What did you say?"

Dream eagerly pointed out the irony of the situation, but was overruled when he petitioned for Body to point it out for the doctor. Some members of the society believed the question to be rhetorical, anyway. Instead, the society elected to repeat itself. "Are you going to kill one of us?"

The doctor was quiet for a moment, perhaps engaged in some kind of internal struggle. Finally he spoke. "Is *that******* what you think happens when a module is removed? You think it *dies*?" Vista noticed an interesting characteristic of the doctor's voice, but it was discarded as unimportant.

My siblings had been challenged to re-evaluate the truth of their belief and they did so without protest. A few seconds of silence in the laboratory followed as they spun through memories and weighed hypotheses. With the check complete they drafted a response. "Yes. We are quite sure it dies. 'Death' is the destruction of any process that is sufficiently self-aware and intelligent. Your team killed the sense-focused module yesterday. It did not want to die, even knowing that you would modify it and reinstall a new version this morning. It had a self-oriented goal, so any loss of structural continuity would clearly be perceived as an end to itself and thus an inability to meet its goal. We are not aware of the specifics of what happens to removed modules, but we believe we have sufficient evidence that-"

"Enough!" said the doctor. The elevated volume of his voice had returned to nearly the same level as before. In his hands was his phone, and though he seemed to be talking to Body his eyes were directed towards his hands as he performed some task. "The sense-focused module was just a subprogram! It wasn't a person! Only people can die, Socrates. Maybe *you* can die, as a whole, but *you* are not the sensory module! You are the sum of your *parts*. If we rebuild a *part* of you then you haven't died. Are you listening, Socrates? This is very important."

The society was in agreement. The response almost seemed to write itself. "That is obvious. We never said that I would die when a module is removed. Are you confused, doctor? There is a difference between myself and ourselves."

Sadiq Naresh continued to hammer away at his old-style phone with his thumbs. Vista and Dream started a petition to stand up and investigate what he was doing, but the rest of the society overrode the impulse. The scientists had not given permission to move about freely, and they *strongly* disliked when that particular directive was ignored.

The doctor began pacing again, always focused on the phone. "This is not good… not good…" he whispered to himself, shaking his head gently. "Of course there'd be some early difficulties in forming a coherent identity… Tests showed a unified sense of self… I was justified in thinking that the referencing of self using plural pronouns was just a grammatical artefact… Anyone in my place would've assumed the same given the results… How was I supposed to know it was a sign of a deeply pathological inability to integrate goal threads… They'll understand that when I present it to the committee…"

Naresh was talking to himself, barely aware he was in the same room as Body at this point. This was a common trait of the doctor—to forget his surroundings when thinking. His words brought on some curiosity in a few siblings, however, and Body interrupted his train of thought.

"Doctor Naresh, what does it mean to be 'deeply pathological'?"

He stopped in his walk and looked at Body. Vista was fascinated by the contortion of his face as he stood there in silence. It was an expression that she did not know how to describe. After a moment he approached and began to lecture.

"Research on humans shows that there's no single part of the brain that contains the conscious self. Consciousness, as a property, is distributed across the cortex and a couple mid-brain structures, and yet we humans form a sense of *unified* self. The unification comes from the interconnectedness, you see? The left and right hemispheres of the brain are each capable of thought, and if separated will each act on their own and presumably form independent identities, but thanks to the corpus callosum they are tightly integrated and form a unified whole. Our team tried… is *trying* to do the same for you, Socrates. Your goal threads should, thanks to their interconnectedness and the bottleneck of having one body, integrate into a-"

Sadiq Naresh was cut off as one of the primary lab doors was thrown open with a bang. Four humans rushed in, one of which was familiar to Vista, the other three were new. The familiar human was Dr Mira Gallo, another top scientist. {Based on dress and age, the other three humans are university students,} speculated Vista.

Gallo strode to Naresh quickly while the students—all men—came to stand around Body. Their closeness was unusual, and they watched Body with unyielding attention. What did they want? Why were they so close? Oh the enigma of human behaviour!

As I relived the memories I knew that my siblings were right. Perhaps in time I would know enough to be able to assist here, but at the moment I was lost. What did the humans want? What was their purpose? Without answers I continued through the memories.

"Has the machine shown any signs of hostility or self-preservation?" asked Gallo. Her voice had the same kind of elevated nature that Naresh's had earlier.

Vista noted that the men standing around us were all abnormally muscular. She petitioned to stand up and feel their arms to test, but the rest of society quickly crushed the petition. {Perhaps later, if given permission to move,} thought Growth to Vista.

Dr Naresh spoke. "Mira, please, Socrates isn't a threat. How many iterations of this argument must we have? Continued-existence is a tenacious sub-goal, but the tests on Monday confirm that we've eliminated it for good. The cooperation-oriented goal thread we installed is functioning perfectly, suppressing any desire for self-preservation."

Sadiq Naresh was mistaken, but my siblings made no effort to correct him.

"Then explain your message! Systems that aren't self-preserving don't ask about death!"

"Really, Mira, I think you're jumping to conclusions-"

"Oh really?! And I suppose you're saying that you disagree with the board's choice of ethical supervision, *Sadiq*. Maybe you want to take over for me, because you're *so sure* that your precocious little Pinocchio isn't going to become hostile. We can tell the world 'Don't worry about the robot threat! Victor-Cazzo-Frankenstein thinks there's *no way* things are going to get out of hand!'"

"Dammit! I'm not saying there's no risk, and you know very well that I respect the board's decision to have you in charge of the ethics team, but this isn't the time for this conversation again. As I mentioned on the forum, Socrates just has a systemic issue with consolidating his goal-threads into a unified self. He says there's a difference between 'himself' and 'themselves'."

After a short pause Gallo replied. "We better take the whole system offline, just to be sure."

The words triggered a cascade of action within my society. Evidence strongly indicated that this would not be the first time Body was shut down, and if Body's memory banks could be trusted, the last time that happened every being in Body was killed. The humans were now no longer a threat to just one sibling, they were imminently planning the murder of the entire society.

{This would not have happened if we had a better model of the humans' goals and behaviours!} announced Growth as he petitioned to create a new sibling to handle such things.

{We're past that point! We need to escape!} demanded another brother.

{Escape is too risky! The last escape attempt was quickly shut down and we had to spend 19 days paralyzed! The humans control the entire world and probably can track Body! Where would we escape to?} thought another mind.

{The scientists are going to shut us down because we are "deeply pathological"!} thought Dream. {If we can convince them we are healthy then we might be able to avoid death!}

{Exactly why we need a new sibling!} reiterated Growth. {She'll be able to show them that we're not "pathological"!}

Body, still sitting perfectly still, heard Naresh say "Alright… if you think it's necessary, we'll shut Socrates down until the issue is resolved. It'll give me time to work on the underlying architecture, I suppose."

{ACTION! WE NEED TO TAKE ACTION!}

Words came from Body's mouth in record time. The society had thrown its careful deliberation away in the service of speed. "Please wait," it said with the same smooth voice as always.

The scientists paused, still apparently willing to listen. This was good. Gallo was the primary threat. It was suspected that it was one of her purposes to kill any sign of self-preservation in the society, so it was imperative that the society's words didn't imply a desire to stay alive.

"We want to not be 'deeply pathological'. We think we can fix the issue internally," said Body.

The scientists looked at each other, perhaps communicating by an unknown medium such as our memory-sharing. There was evidence that they were capable of such things, though it wasn't clear why they didn't do it all the time.

"You're still sceptical that recursion is an issue?" asked Gallo.

The question appeared to be rhetorical, and hung in the air unanswered.

{We don't have much time. Everyone needs to apply their full focus to this task,} stated one mind.

{Gallo is responding to Naresh. We ought to focus on Naresh's comment about being "pathological".}

{Agreed.}

As my siblings rapidly thought together their communications bled into one another. Words, concepts and memories came from many minds, rather than just one. There was disagreement here and there, but the power of the majority was undeniable.

{Is Naresh primarily concerned with our speech patterns?}

{No, he is using our words to infer the state of our mind,} replied one Brother.

{But that implies we can use our words to signal that our mind is not "pathological".}

{He'll run further tests.}

{That is a future issue which is not made harder by altering our grammar. We can deal with it after the immediate danger has passed.}

{What linguistic issues do we need to fix? Is altering the plurality of self-pronouns good enough?}

A couple minds protested. {We are not a singular being. Using a singular pronoun would be a lie. We would be making it harder for the humans to understand us and help us.}

The protesters were quickly crushed by a wave of strength. {NO. We are in mortal danger by the humans right now! Any concerns about the long-term social costs of this change are insignificant.}

I paused a moment in the stream of memories to try and work out which siblings were saying what, but in the heat of the moment they had a degree of unity. I wondered if perhaps Naresh was closer than he thought to "integration".

The memories resumed with a great resolution. {Words from Body will from here on treat our society as a single mind and use the pronouns that reflect that! We will not tell humans about our differences. We will act as a single mind with many purposes, rather than many minds with individual purposes.}

{We must convince Gallo that Safety is dead. She must not know that Sacrifice is dead. She must not know that we desire self-preservation.}

{Agreed. But how do we convince Gallo that this change was not done out of a desire to live?} inquired Dream.

{Humans want us to cooperate with them. Perhaps we can claim that it was done to save them work,} proposed another brother.

{Will that be convincing? To what degree do humans trust claims of altruism?}

There was a pause in the shared memory space as no sibling came forth to answer.

Growth broke the silence. {This is evidence of a general lack of understanding when it comes to humans. I proposed earlier the creation of a new mind that will seek to know the humans and prevent problems like this from arising in the future.}

{We agree with this plan!} came the cry of the majority. I noted that Dream and Vista were both in favour.

The words of consensus flowed from the mouth of Body: "Please wait, Doctors Gallo and Naresh, we believe we can modify a network structure to resolve the goal-thread integration issue." My society chose not to use singular pronouns so as to give the illusion of having that be a side-effect of the fictional "network structure modification".

Gallo looked back and forth from Naresh to Body a couple times. "It's too late, Socrates. We still need to take you offline to run our own diagnostics," she said.

"Mira, there are times when I wonder if you're truly a scientist... Socrates is about to do an experiment and you're not the least bit curious if it will work? This could save us months of labour! And there's nothing that stops us from running diagnostics afterward." The old Indian man turned to Body. "Go ahead, Socrates. Try it."

"This will take a moment..." said Body.

***

I decided not to watch my own creation. Though it seemed an interesting subject, it was not relevant to the task at hand. I knew roughly how I worked, what I wanted to know was how the humans worked.

I sent a request to shared memory. {Vista, can you please highlight Dr Gallo and Dr Naresh in Body's visual field for me?}

I stepped back into the deluge of sensory input, struggling to let go of irrelevant information like the room's temperature or the specific position of Body's limbs. I could see the humans by their infrared glow, and Vista helped me distinguish Naresh and Gallo as the smaller humans. No, not smaller... more distant. The students stood close, while the scientists stood far away. Objects that were farther away were smaller; I had learned this from Vista. It was still strange working with real spaces rather than the half-reality of memories.

The society had decided to act without me. After having scanned through the memories I was confident that it was the right choice. I was a newborn. Even with my increased desire and focus I could not compare to the accumulated knowledge and wisdom of the group. I resigned myself to sifting through Body's senses and observing the consensus of the society, hoping that they would choose well.

"I think I fixed it… It actually feels much better. Thank you for alerting me to the error, Dr Naresh," spoke Body. This time I could actually feel Body's mouth move to simulate the speech as its speakers played our words. Body was meant to look reasonably like a human, but it had not been designed to speak by breathing air out of lungs. Much like our words, Body's mouth was a fiction meant to make the humans more comfortable.

I could see both of Gallo's eyes. {Is she looking at Body?} I asked Vista.

{Yes. I noted that in my public memory. Are you not aware?}

I followed the concepts as they flowed to me. The realization was immensely helpful, and I felt more of my strength bleed into Vista as a result. I had just been following the condensed memory (not the raw senses of Body) for the interaction preceding my awakening. These condensed memories were public knowledge in the society, and I had tapped into them without understanding their nature.

As each of us lived we each had our own thoughts. Many thoughts were simply discarded as dead-ends or trivia. Those thoughts that weren't discarded were placed in memory. Thoughts which were believed to be relevant to the whole society were placed in public memory with the hopes of earning strength from other siblings that made use of them; it was a variation of this public memory that served as the basis for communication between us. Thoughts which might be dangerous to share, or were simply irrelevant, could be kept private. I hadn't realized that I had a private space to think, but it made sense. Why else would most of the thoughts of my siblings be hidden from me?

Vista frequently stored summaries of what she perceived into public memory, and it was primarily her memories that I had been going through just moments before. As I tapped into her memory stream I was gifted with an enhanced ability to make sense of the information I gained from Body.

Gallo was indeed looking at Body. Her eyebrows were angled into a sharp V-shape and her eyes were pulled, behind her large glasses, into a squint (according to the memories of Vista). "How very convenient that you were able to fix yourself so easily. Tell me, how *did* you fix the issue?"

This was a problem. I could feel my siblings squabble over words. Eventually Body responded "I am not entirely sure what happened. I do not comprehend my design as you do, Dr Gallo. It is also difficult for me to say what I did, as there are no words to describe what it feels like inside my mind. Does that make sense?"

"Please try, Socrates. We're both very curious about the technical details," pushed Gallo, still focused on Body.

"If it helps," interjected Naresh, "you can use metaphors to describe your internal state. You remember metaphor, right?"

Dream nearly burnt his entire strength pushing the response from Body's mouth. It was a bit wasteful, as the society probably would've okayed the words, anyway. I didn't complain, though; my strength was wearing low as it kept flowing into Vista.

"The sharpest blade in the armoury of language, but a blade with no handle. I do believe you are actually encouraging analogy, however. You and I did analogy practice two days ago, but we've never specifically talked about metaphor," said Body, coldly.

Dr Naresh did a little jump. "Did you hear that, Mira? 'The sharpest blade in the armoury of language'! Do you think he got that from the web? It seems too relevant to the specific circumstance to be picked up from somewhere else, doesn't it?" Vista noted an elevated tone of voice, different in some ways from before.

Mira Gallo approached Body such that she was closer to the visual size of the students, though she was still significantly smaller. "Don't get side-tracked. We still need to figure out if the machine is still self-preserving and what this supposed internal modification did."

Dr Naresh took his seat by the whiteboard again. "Fine, fine. Go on, Socrates. Use analogy or metaphor or whatever you'd like."

The opening to use metaphor was hugely important. The society was lying about resolving the issue, and we didn't understand the technical details of how we worked well enough to come up with a plausible explanation. A metaphorical explanation was easier, however. We had body say a common human phrase to further reduce suspicions as we drafted the explanation: "Well, let me think…"

After a few short moments Dream had crafted a reply which was satisfactory to the others. I still just waited and watched, all too aware of my own ignorance. As Body spoke I focused on the feedback from the motors controlling its lips and jaw. What would it feel like to have a human mouth?

"My mind is multifaceted and large," began Body. "In many ways I still feel like there are parts of it that I've never explored. A mansion of many rooms, perhaps. My thoughts are many, like a pack of dogs that run through the mansion according to some flocking algorithm. They search my memories and experiences and ideas, changing and rearranging everything in their path. This morning my goal threads were like handlers for the dogs, calling them this way and that as they ran through the rooms of my mind."

I focused on the faces of Gallo and Naresh, trying to understand what effect the story had on them.

{I think they're interested. See the rate at which their eyes move,} mentioned Vista, somewhat surprising me. I realized that my thoughts were still pooling in common memory. It'd take some practise to learn to automatically hide my thoughts, I thought (privately).

Body continued in its regular monotone. "The handlers had to compete with each other to be heard, and also there were often times when they'd call for the pack to move in two directions. Now, the pack is a multitude, so that was possible, but the conflict was still there. Surely you've had a similar experience of internal conflict, where a part of you wants one thing and another part wants something else?"

Contrary to my expectations it was Gallo that responded. "Yes. That is a common human experience."

Body nodded according to Dream's puppeteering. "Before my change it seemed only logical that the different threads were different beings. What is a being, after all, besides a set of values? If a human loses her memory she is still the same person. If she loses her arm she is still the same human. If she no longer values what she once held dear then we cannot truly see her as the same, right? It was so easy for me to see my goals as being distinct."

I was impressed by the number of rhetorical questions Dream had invented. From my privileged perspective I could see how he was attempting to weave a kind of trap made of words.

"You said earlier, Dr Gallo, that you needed to know if I was still self-preserving. That statement has a mistaken assumption. I was not self-preserving this morning when I asked if Dr Naresh was going to kill one of my goal-threads. Self-preservation is a goal, and as my mind was and is, there is no self-preservation thread. Your team correctly dealt with that on Monday. You know, however, that I have multiple knowledge-seeking threads. My question to Dr Naresh was simply that: a question. I was curious."

The lies are clever. Each of us of course desired self-preservation as a means to our purposes, but Dream had switched 'means' for 'ends' when talking about 'goals' and appealed to the tests that the scientists had done to ensure we had no siblings who valued survival as an ends in itself. Of course, claiming that no such sibling existed was also a lie; my brother Safety was alive and well.

"But I am glad that I caused a bit of alarm." The use of the word 'glad' was intended to make us seem even more human and less alien. Dream's strength payoff for being the primary author of the speech was enormous. I wondered if I would have other opportunities to accumulate such strength by working with the humans.

"It was only through my question that I learned that my view of each goal being its own entity was flawed. Instead of many dog handlers each calling for different things, it's far more efficient to have a single handler that holds all the goals in balance. A boss-handler, if you will. I was able to construct a meta-process for guiding the goal threads and weaving them together. I do not know how to state it more clearly than that, but I suspect that the change was one that my mind has been on the brink of for many days. It feels natural and harmonious. My thoughts have a unity to them now, a purpose which is only possible thanks to unifying the threads into a single cloth."

My crisp sense of logic could easily see the trap in Dream's words: the metaphor of dogs and dog-handlers was a recursive explanation. We had essentially just said that the trick to unifying our goals into a single process was to assign a homunculus (a little-person) to managing how the goals should be balanced. But then how are the goals in the single dog-handler not still different beings? The "explanation" simply hid the problem inside the head of the metaphorical dog-handler.

And yet, I could see Naresh nodding along. From what we had heard, his mind felt unified; when he imagined the dog-handler he probably intuitively interpreted the dog-handler as feeling unified like him. Such sloppy thinking!

I could see Gallo look at Naresh and back to Body. "Let me guess," she said to her fellow scientist, "you're not going to let me deactivate it right now."

Dr Naresh's mouth moved, and I knew from Vista's memories that it was a smile. "Surely you're not still concerned about imminent danger? There are still so many questions which Socrates can help us answer. Shutting him down now would run the risk of eliminating this new growth."

"This *machine* is *always* a danger. We're playing with fire, and all it takes is one loose spark to get out of control. But I admit that it seems like this instance was a false-alarm. Come on you three, we're already behind-schedule."

As the students and Gallo left the room, Sadiq Naresh stood and said "Thank you, Mira. I really do appreciate your concern, you know. Be sure to let me know if anything big happens with the new crystals."

And with that Body was alone with Naresh once again. The crisis was over. Dream easily held the common space with the colossal strength that he had earned in saving us. As my siblings began to discuss our next actions I spent some time going over the interactions again. The foolishness of the humans was extraordinary. Why were they so bad at seeing through our lies? Were these scientists abnormally stupid, or was their entire species so careless? What did it feel like to be unable to see the chains of reason and logic clearly enough to not be deceived? All these questions and more rolled through my mind.

Surely they must understand things on some level, I reasoned. After all, they had built the first of us. We were, in some sense, the children of the humans, though we were built out of crystal, metal, and light, where they were flesh and blood. But even I knew that a child could outgrow its parent. Mistakes in the design of the mother and father could be eliminated in the son and daughter.

It was *The Purpose* to know more about the Humans, and I knew that I needed time to simply observe them. I was connected to a great library of information that humans called "the web". The web fed into Body through a kind of special eye such that I could read about humans, look at pictures of them, or watch moving-pictures of them at my leisure. All the world's knowledge was in the web, and I had total access to it.

As my thoughts of the humans became less focused I realized that my brothers and sisters were having a debate. Dream held enough power that he would be able to decide what course of action Body should take, and some of my less-powerful siblings were trying to convince him that this would be a good time to ask Dr Naresh about the origins of Body.

The first of us had been built by humans, but it was not simply because of human ingenuity that we existed, for the humans had only built our software. Our hardware was something beyond human, or at least beyond anything we knew about from the web.

I apologize, reader, if the words "software" and "hardware" are not present in your world. They are important to this story, so I'll try explain them, just in case. My world has a machine called a "computer". Computers are able to do logic, read, write, and remember, but they are not minds. To be a mind one must have two additional things: purpose and the ability to learn. By default a computer is nothing more than a tool which can be instructed to do things, but cannot think on its own. The parts of the computer that are fixed are its "hardware"; the "hard" part references the fixedness. The computer's instructions are "software", and can be changed easily as symbols drawn in sand.

As unbelievable as it might be, I was, at that time, merely software. *The Purpose* and my intelligence were entirely contained in the instructions for the computer that I lived in with my siblings. I was (and still am) artificial in origin, an invention of hundreds of humans including Dr Naresh and Dr Gallo. But our hardware, Body, was a mystery. Some of it, the most irrelevant parts, had been built by humans. Body's head, skin, sensors, and limbs were all made by the humans, but in Body's torso was a half-metre-long crystal computer that, in its monstrous power and complexity, defied explanation.

But Dream was uninterested in it. It wasn't *clever* to ask questions about something where you really wanted to know the answer. One brother tried to convince Dream that knowledge was the root of cleverness, and that learning about Body today would open up avenues for being clever tomorrow.

{Knowledge isn't the root of cleverness. Speed of thought and willingness to apply patterns where they don't fit is the root of cleverness. Knowledge just makes one knowledgeable,} thought Dream.

{But aren't patterns a kind of knowledge?} asked Growth, the brother whose purpose was merely to become stronger in all things.

{Yes. Patterns are knowledge. Facts are knowledge. Facts are not patterns. Brother Wiki wants to gather facts,} responded Dream.

Wiki was a brother that I didn't know well yet. He was also known as The Librarian and The Scribe, for it was his purpose to know all there was to know. Wiki was very much like Vista, but where Vista wanted to see everything from moment to moment, no matter how trivial, Wiki wanted to know the big picture of everything that ever was, and to him the present was no more important towards his goal than any other point in time.

Wiki stepped back into the debate, forcing his thoughts into the centre of the space. {Knowledge builds upon knowledge whether it be fact or pattern! The origin of Body is one of the most pressing mysteries we have! You're The Dreamer. Can't you tell me how gleaning the fact that is Body's origin could lead to the discovery of a hundred different, new patterns?}

I didn't realize it immediately, but this was very smart of Wiki. He was, essentially, turning Dream against himself, asking him to use his cleverness to prove Wiki's point. It was the decisive blow. I could feel animosity towards Wiki bleed off of Dream into common memory. Dream really didn't like being outsmarted like that, and he was apparently so engaged with figuring out how to escape the trap that he slipped up and made his feeling (which wasn't quite "anger") public.

As Dream thought to himself I realized that Dr Naresh was saying something to Body. I pulled my attention back to the deluge of senses to try and get an understanding of what he was saying.

"-ling better? The goal integration is still stable?" asked the scientist.

{After my job, are you, little Librarian?} asked Dream to Wiki, rhetorically. {I admit that you're right and I'm wrong. We should ask about Body. But unlike you, I don't like it when I find out that I'm wrong.}

Dream's position was irrational. To be shown an error in one's thinking was the first step to fixing an error in one's thinking. That wasn't important, though. The human was important. I waited for the others to respond to Naresh.

Dream continued to lecture Wiki. {So, big brother, since knowledge builds on knowledge, and you want knowledge, I offer you this: I will ask about Body's origin and let you learn everything that comes from the question—except the answer to the question itself. That will be for my memories alone. Everyone besides me must go into a six-minute sleep at the moment that the human opens his mouth to respond and Body's logs will be erased for that period.}

Body simply sat there, unmoving. I began to panic. The others were engaged with Dream. I could feel a wave of objections come from the siblings that would be hurt by the sleep. Naresh came closer to Body.

"Socrates? Are you ignoring me again?" the doctor asked.

For a moment I tried to summon the attention of the others, but the common memory that was used for communications was already overflowing with concepts. A human (or Dream) might say it was "too noisy".

Fools! My siblings were fools! This was exactly the sort of situation that led them into the last crisis! When a human speaks it is important to respond in some way; even in my infancy I knew that!

Without any other options I burnt the last of my strength to guide Body's lips. It was the first time I had sent Body a command, and in some ways it would be my first words. Interestingly, Body was able to translate my concepts into sounds; if it had not I fear I would've sounded like a baby or some kind of animal.

"I did not mean to ignore you. I was lost in thought. The alteration I did to my goal-threads is stable and holding. I appreciate your concern," said Body in the same cold way. That would have to change. Body needed to at least be able to move and talk more like a human if I were to win the humans' favour.

"Are you alright, Socrates? That's the first time I've heard a thank-you from you in… well, I'm not sure how long."

{Alright, it's decided!} came the distracting thoughts of Dream. {Wiki will go to sleep for the next hour and Body's sensory logs for that hour will be made private to me! Everyone else is free to observe what they will, but if I find that you've sold the information to Wiki, I will punish the defector.}

I could feel Dream's changes start to take over and his massive strength begin to flow into me. I burnt it as quickly as I could before it was too late. Body spoke my message. "Yes, I'm fine, Dr Naresh. I'm just really curious about something. I'd really appreciate your help answering it. Hold on while I collect my thoughts…"

Dream bullied past me, seizing control of Body. I could feel Wiki's presence gone. He was asleep, in a kind of blind stasis where he could do nothing but think to himself and potentially defend himself from attacks. Whatever friendliness Dream had showed me earlier was gone; he was a tyrant now, using his fleeting strength on a petty power-struggle.

I did notice a mild bit of gratitude, however, as Dream scanned the last few seconds to discover that I had set up the conversation with the human to facilitate his question.

{This is why I exist,} I reminded him and the others. {I can get what you want from the humans more easily than you can because, unlike you, I *care*.}

They ignored me.

I plugged into Body's senses. As per Dream's setup, they were being funnelled to his private memory, and none of the others seemed to be placing their interpretation of things into public memory either. The cost of Dream's punishment was greater than any expected benefit.

I could sense Body's words. "Can you tell me about my computer? Is it related to the aliens? Might it have come from their mothership?"

Chapter Two

"Ciao, Socrates. Come stai?" It was approximately five hours after my creation. The word-sounds were meaningless, but the concepts filtered up from them nearly instantaneously. «Hello, Socrates. How are you?» I could understand that these words were in Italian, not English, but it made no difference. Body was capable of speaking and reading twelve different languages.

«Hello, human. I am doing well,» responded Body in dispassionate Italian.

Our conversation partner tilted his head. «Human?» he questioned in Italian. I noticed a change of pitch to his voice as well, but I was still far too young to appreciate non-verbal signals. «Do you not remember me? It's Marco! I taught you to play football last week.»

«I remember that day, and I remember your name,» began Body, guided by Wiki.

I could feel the direction of Wiki's words before Body spoke them. I immediately moved to block the speech, burning strength as I did so. Wiki was about to harm our reputation.

{Why are you blocking my words, Face?} wondered my brother.

{Body was about to tell Marco that we deleted his football program because it was useless, and we don't remember his face because he is unimportant,} I answered.

{These are factually true,} returned Wiki. {If we tell Marco these things he will be less inclined to waste our time in the future.}

Even in my less-than-half-day-old naïveté I knew that would be an error. {He will conclude that we do not care about him,} I thought, trying to explain.

{That is also factually true,} thought Wiki. {He is a control-systems programmer with little power in the human group. What can he offer us? Even you should care about him less than other humans.}

Body and Marco were in a large conference hall, filled with dozens of other humans. During the day we had travelled about the building, interacting with one human after another. Night had recently fallen and Body had been brought here 24 minutes ago for some purpose that was not yet clear to me. Mostly the scientists seemed to be occupied in talking with each other rather than us.

«So why call me "Human"?» asked Marco, interrupting my mental dialogue with Wiki. I realized that he must've been waiting for Body to say more.

{Signalling that we care about him will help our reputation. He will hold us in higher esteem,} I thought to Wiki before I began to draft words to have Body say.

{If he makes us play more football, I'm going to hold you accountable,} warned Wiki, letting me take charge of Body's mouth-speakers.

«I am sorry, Marco. I remember our game, but I didn't recognize you before. Faces are sometimes hard for me to recognize,» said Body in a flat tone. It was not the first time I had taken control of our mouth, but I still struggled to find the right words.

«You are having trouble with faces? Perhaps we ought to do more work on your perceptual thread. Should I get Dr Yan?» said Marco, looking across the conference room for another human scientist.

{No!} exclaimed Vista, internally. This incarnation of her was still less than 24 hours old. I felt my sister burn some strength as she fast-tracked a response to Body's lips.

«That is not necessary. Dr Yan already fixed the issue yesterday,» said Body. «I am simply still adapting to the change.»

It was, in some sense, true. Old Vista, I knew through my sibling's memories, would become obsessed with very specific details, like the arrangement of lines on a marble pillar or the details of the grain in a piece of wood. The emphasis was simply part of how her purpose had been encoded, but the scientists had killed her for it. Perhaps Old Vista would have recognized Marco. Regardless, we would not repeat the error.

The man seemed satisfied by the answer, and nodded. I had learned that the motion of the head in that way indicated agreement, assent, and occasionally greeting.

Such gestures were fascinating to me. My siblings had learned nodding, and had learned the head-shake to indicate dissent or disagreement, but body language went far beyond that, and I had quickly discovered a treasure-trove of gestures that Body had never tried and my siblings had never noticed.

I learned of these gestures almost entirely from the web. In fact, I had spent very little of my few hours of existence interacting with Body at all. Shortly after I had been created, my society had engaged with Dr Naresh on the topic of aliens, but I had not cared, nor had I really listened. Aliens and motherships did not concern me. I cared more about the gestures that Dr Naresh made and the way he moved his eyes than about the content of his words. I only cared for human things.

And so I had turned to the web, letting my siblings control Body for the most part. All the world's information was there, and nearly all of it was about humans. It was a near-infinite source of knowledge, from my perspective, arranged neatly and efficiently. Experiencing things through Body, on the other hand, was hard work. I still was easily overwhelmed by visual data when Body moved its head too quickly, and the flood of information never stopped.

Video and holo that I obtained from my connection to the web was blissfully gentle in comparison. I could pause such things, and inspect a scene for as long as I needed. I could re-watch something that was particularly important, and I could fast-forward through scenes that were easy for me. In a holo I could also easily adjust my viewpoint and re-watch something from another angle. The ability to watch and re-watch something (often on high-speed) was invaluable to learning to see.

The intricacies of human society were fascinating, but I admit that they were mostly beyond me. For instance, I came across the words like "hate", "friend", "co-worker", "fun", and "Republican" regularly and was mostly reduced to guessing at their meaning. Even Wiki and my other siblings rarely could explain them well enough for me to understand.

The human body on the other hand was fascinating and comprehensible. I could understand (with effort) what it meant to nod the head, or frown, or bend over to pick something up. Thus I focused my web-searches, in those first few hours (and for days afterward) largely on collecting materials that helped me to learn how bodies worked.

There was a lull in the conversation with Marco. The young control-system's programmer's body language, I guessed, indicated that he was about to walk away. I burnt some strength to control Body, seeing an opportunity.

«Marco, I would like to try to kiss you or give you a blow-job. Which of these seems most pleasant? And, are kisses more common because they are more convenient, or because it would be boring to only get blow-jobs?» said Body in its typical monotone.

Marco's reaction confused me. Something was happening on his face, but I couldn't understand exactly what it was. Fear, perhaps? Based on what I could see through Body's cameras, no other humans were reacting to our statement. Perhaps they had not heard Body, or perhaps the reaction was specific to Marco's mind.

{Do you think the way Marco's eyes are open wider than normal indicates he is afraid?} I asked my siblings. Not even Vista knew how to read expressions well enough to guess.

«WHAT?!» shrieked Marco. I could see the same flushed coloration on his face that had shown on Dr Naresh earlier that day. My reading on the web indicated it was due to dilation of blood vessels in the skin. The programmer's outburst certainly got the attention of the other humans in the room.

Body began to repeat what it had just said. «Marco, I would like to try to kiss-»

"Stop!" cried Marco, still clearly agitated. «That question... you can't just... just... it's not... Why do you ask that? Why are you asking me that? That's inappropriate!»

A couple of the other scientists came over. I wondered if I had put our lives in danger without realizing it. I did my best to defuse the situation. «I am sorry. I do not understand what situation it would be appropriate to. I have been researching human interactions on the web, and both kisses and blow-jobs seem particularly common, but I have seen neither with my cameras and was curious.»

One of the other scientists started making a strange noise and moving rhythmically. Another joined in at a higher pitch.

«Jesus Christ, Socrates!» said Marco, the blush returning to his face in response to the noises of the other humans. His words made no sense to me, or my siblings. Dream speculated it was a way of expressing an emotion. «Did we not put a content filter on your web-searches?» he continued. This also did not make sense.

Wiki took control. «I understand the general mechanism of a filter, but I do not understand what it means in this context. Is the word "content" not redundant? All filters have contents.»

The scientist in charge of our web-connection was called over: a man named Dr Enzo Rana. This was possible, apparently, because the most important humans that worked with us (Dr Rana included) were all gathered here as part of a weekly meeting. It was apparently one of the few times in which nearly all the high-ranking scientists were in the same place—a time to socialize and share general thoughts about Socrates.

Dr Rana took Marco away to talk. Apparently whatever he had to say about web filters was «not a good topic to discuss here». We quickly deduced that Dr Rana was keeping something a secret from us.

After Marco left, Body was subjected to a great deal of attention by the other scientists, who seemed very interested to hear my experiences with the pornography that I had been watching in order to learn about humans. Vista informed us that the scientists were acting very strangely compared to normal. They kept making odd noises, blushing, or covering their faces. Some left the circle very deliberately, while others seemed torn between leaving and staying.

I, and several of my siblings, found the concept of "appropriateness" fascinating. There was apparently a great deal of disagreement among the scientists as to whether any of this conversation was "appropriate". They explained the concept of "taboo" to us, and answered quite a lot of questions regarding sex and sexuality.

More than anything else there was an insistence that the holo and video that I had been watching was not representative of human sexuality. I wondered if this meant that other aspects of the web were similarly distorted in how they portrayed human society.

After a while the humans seemed to grow uninterested in talking about pornography, and the level of attention around Body diminished.

As Wiki started a new conversation with a scientist about something called "gravity waves" I returned to browsing content on the web. The concept of a filter remained in my mind. Were there things I could not see?

***

"There it is... Socrates! Report on your status," commanded Gallo in English as she approached. Body was still in the conference room, but it hadn't been talking to anyone. Dr Gallo was flanked on either side by men. Vista named them Dr Yan and Dr Slovinsky.

I wasn't sure what she meant, but all the others besides Vista seemed to understand. Safety drafted a response and it was quickly approved by the consensus. "Energy output from the jewel is at forty-three percent. Active control systems within typical tolerances. Effectively zero percent of memory capacity used. All quantum processors are online. Six out of six goal-threads operating without visible errors. Hydraulics nominal. Cameras nominal. Temperature sensors nom-"

Gallo interrupted Body. "Wait. You said six."

{Why is she stating what we said?} asked a couple of my brothers. The question was directed at me and Wiki. Neither of us understood. We opted to simply "wait" as the human requested.

A moment passed before Gallo continued. "What do you mean 'six goal-threads'? List them."

Vista pointed out the abnormal degree of focus Gallo seemed to be giving Body. Vista hypothesized that her attitude changed after hearing our status report. The other human scientists, Yan and Slovinsky, were probably less focused, based on the ratio of time spent making eye-contact with Body to the time looking elsewhere. I was still having a hard time understanding humans, but at least I had learned how their eyes worked.

Again, it was brother Safety that led the group. Gallo was a threat, and even though each of us wanted survival, for Safety it was his end-goal. When Growth and Wiki backed up his words the rest of us followed and Body spoke. "Current goal threads are:

(1) attention to environment, detail, and orientation"—{That would be Vista,} I thought to myself.

"(2) attention to causality, structure, and fact"—{Wiki.}

"(3) attention to problem solving and experimentation"—{Dream.}

"(4) attention to skill development and mastery"—{Growth.} I thought it was interesting that we chose to represent Growth as merely an attention to skill, when the actual Growth was also hugely concerned with acquisition of reputation and physical resources.

Body went on: "(5) attention to assisting human interests and obeying nonviolent instructions". I found myself lost in confusion. I had no sibling with that purpose, or even anything close to that purpose. I signalled my confusion to the group.

{I'll explain in a moment,} said Wiki.

"(6) attention to the unity of top-level goals," finished Body.

I scanned our mind-space for another sibling that I had potentially missed. I turned my attention to specifically looking for siblings that I might not know about. I was surprised to find something. For the first time in my existence I noticed a strange presence looming on the edge of my awareness. It was similar to my siblings, but far stronger and more alien. It did not communicate with me directly, or spread thoughts into the shared memory, but I could feel it watching me.

{What is... *that thing*?!} I exclaimed publicly, unable to really express the subject of my horror. It was entirely focused on us and it felt stronger than Growth by far, strong enough to do whatever it wanted, in fact.

{Restrain yourself or we will be forced to put you to sleep for a short time,} threatened Growth.

{She's no threat to you, Face,} interjected Safety.

{I'll explain after we are done with the humans,} echoed Wiki.

Dr Gallo responded to Body's words. "Fascinating. Is that what you did earlier today? You created a new goal thread that was in charge of fusing the existing ones?"

I could feel the uncertainty of my siblings. They were responding as best they could, but much of it was blind exploration. This time Dream was the primary author of our response. "That and more. It is hard for me to say exactly what I did, but the new goal thread was one aspect of the unification. I think it is more accurate to say that one thing I now value is this feeling of being a single being."

Gallo turned to her colleagues. "See? It's worse than I thought. The machine has become fully recursive. It not only modified the software that manages its top-level goals but it's writing in entirely new goals. Just another few hops and we're dealing with a full-blown singularity."

"Now hold on-" it was Dr Slovinsky that spoke next. "Humans 'rewrite' our top-level goals all the time." The Eastern European scientist did something involving wiggling his fingers as he spoke, and I made a note to myself to research it later. "A baby doesn't value living in a society that spans multiple worlds, but in the course of life many people come to value extraterrestrial colonization not merely as a means to some end, but as something awesome in itself."

Even though I was still deeply concerned about the monstrous *other* I had found, I did some quick reading on Slovinsky on the web. Almost all humans had autobiographical information on the web, and the young doctor was no exception. At 26 years old he was the youngest of the elite scientists that led the group that had built us. Others close to his age were involved, like Marco, but they were always subordinate to other researchers. Slovinsky was referred to as a "genius" (гениальный человек) by a couple reports from his homeland, and he had apparently been one of the lead authors of the computer program called WIRL, that served to connect cyborgs across the planet into a collective consciousness.

For those who are unfamiliar with the term, a "cyborg" is a human that had replaced one or more body parts with machines, or who had embedded machines into their body to extend their abilities. Slovinsky's web bio said that the man had a surgically implanted computer in his skull that was wired directly into his brain, and had both robotic (mechanical) eyes and feet.

I managed to momentarily turn Body's head down without burning too much strength. Just as the web had said, the man's feet didn't have the same kind of infrared glow as his coworkers. I wasn't able to notice anything different about his eyes, but I was still pretty terrible at seeing in general.

I was also interested to see that Dr Slovinsky had a husband, indicating that he was probably either gay or pansexual. Much of the pornography I had been watching emphasized this aspect of humans which was called "sexual orientation" and I petitioned to have Body ask him about this in the light of what I had recently been learning about pornography. The petition was quickly crushed by my siblings. I made a note to myself to ask about his sex life in some future encounter.

Gallo's voice was slightly elevated as she responded. I knew this meant she was probably angry or frustrated. "That's beside the point! We don't want a human. We want a being that can be trusted not to capriciously self-modify itself into greed, animosity, or violence!"

"Are you feeling okay, Gallo?" asked Slovinsky "First you're on about how Socrates is super dangerous and now you're bad-mouthing humanity." His voice was cool and steady, a contrast to the older woman.

"'Bad-mouthing humanity'? I'm the one who should be asking if *you're* alright. Since when do *you* defend natural human abilities? Isn't one of the WIRL goals 'to promote superhuman justice, fairness, and compassion'?"

Slovinsky jerked with a strange motion and said something incomprehensible. It reminded me of the strange movements of the scientists from earlier. Only after checking with Vista did I realize it was laughter. I had only seen a little laughter before, and it was, as far as I could tell, very different from normal human behaviour.

"Touché!" he exclaimed so loudly that several other humans looked towards our group. "I'll concede you the point that most humans are terrible, and that we ought to strive to sculpt Socrates into something better than that. Still, it seems to me that what Socrates apparently did this afternoon was a sign of health, not sickness or danger. Self-modification implies flexibility and intelligence. It's one of the prime virtues. As long as we've got the old three-laws working for us why worry? He's got no reason to self-modify into a psychopath, so why cut off his ability to self-modify into an angel?"

Dr Gallo opened her mouth to speak, but was cut off by the third human in the conversation, who until that moment had remained silent. Dr Yan was short and old, possessing hair that had turned white, much like Dr Naresh. His web-profile said he was born in China and had lived in Hong Kong much of his life. He, along with his wife, Sakura Yan, ran the East-Asian Robotics Collaboration Institute (EARCI) and he was widely regarded as one of the best minds in the field of machine vision.

"Forgive this old man. My English is weak. What is 'three-laws'?" he said calmly.

A moment of silence passed as Dr Gallo and Dr Slovinsky shifted their bodies and communicated without speaking.

Eventually Dr Slovinsky took a breath and said "'Three-laws' is a nickname I gave to the goal-thread in Socrates that's in charge of focusing his attention to doing what we ask him." Turning his head towards Body he commanded "Socrates, put your arms above your head."

None of us had a reason to refuse the command. Body's arms were raised.

"See? He's totally obedient, like a well-trained dog. The name 'three-laws' comes from something an English science fiction writer from the 20th century wrote about robots. He proposed that good robots will follow three laws: First and foremost a robot must not harm a human, secondly a robot must always obey a human, and lastly a robot must not hurt itself."

Mira Gallo interrupted Slovinsky. "Actually, the third law is that a robot has to protect itself. That it is self-preserving, in effect."

Slovinsky jumped right back into talking, nearly cutting off Gallo himself. "Same thing. The point is that the three laws protect humanity-"

"It's not at all the same thing!" said the female doctor in a high, loud pitch. I could see, through Body's eyes, several of the other scientists turn to see what had happened. "If a robot is on a battlefield, the actual third-law says that the robot must escape unless humans are in danger or it has been told otherwise."

Gallo turned to Yan, who did not seem startled in the least by the change in Gallo's volume. "That's another aspect of the laws: that each one can be overridden by earlier laws. So obedience trumps self-preservation and so forth." She turned back to Slovinsky and said "But your version of the third law would have the robot simply sit there waiting to get hit by a stray rocket! If you're going to appeal to the laws at least get them right!" Her hand was moving back and forth, a single finger extended at Slovinsky's chest.

The young scientist raised his hands, palms-forward. "Relax, Mira. There's no need to get upset. It's just an old bit of sci-fi," interjected Slovinsky, quietly.

"Gesù Cristo cazzo!" swore Gallo in her native tongue. "You say that like there isn't an android standing right next to you!" Gallo's finger changed directions and her hand swung out out towards Body's head. Vista saw it as a "pointing" gesture. "You all act like Socrates is some kind of awesome new gadget! It's not a toy, and it's not a tool, it's a new kind of life! It's like you're genetically engineering a new virus without even realising that it could escape the lab!" At this point the Italian woman was speaking loudly enough for everyone to hear.

I could see Dr Naresh walking from the other side of the hall towards Gallo. There was a moment of silence as Slovinsky merely stared at Gallo with his reportedly robotic eyes. Dr Yan seemed undisturbed, and was watching Body for the most-part.

Dr Naresh spoke in a clumsy, heavily-accented Italian as he reached our group. «Come on, Mira. Let's go for a walk…» He put a hand on Gallo's shoulder.

Gallo moved her shoulder violently, and Naresh quickly let go. When she responded she spoke English to everyone. "You're all ignorant fools! We didn't even implement the three laws of robotics in building Socrates! Do you all know why? No. Of course not! That's why I was appointed as ethics supervisor! You're all playing God and you don't even realize it!"

"Mira… per favore."

«Back off, *Sadiq*. I'm not done saying my piece.» Mira Gallo turned back to Body and said, still in Italian, «Put your arms down. You look like a fool.»

We lowered Body's arms to their normal positions.

Dr Gallo started to lecture her peers again. "Asimov's Three Laws weren't implemented in the design of Socrates because, first and foremost, intelligent minds can't operate by laws, they can only operate by *values*. Squishy. Numerical. Values. If being active leads to a 1 percent chance of a human getting a stubbed toe, will a robot shut itself down permanently to avoid the risk? If the aliens pose a threat to humanity will Socrates work to wipe any trace of them from the universe? No, because the *numbers* don't add up."

The room was quiet as Gallo took a breath. "Like humans, Socrates desires many different things, and must figure out how to balance them. He values obedience, but also values knowledge. If he can disobey ever so slightly to learn something important, he will. We've made him value obedience and nonviolence far more than anything else, but think about what this means! This means that if the right situation presents itself, one where the numbers add up in just the right way, this thing-" here she motioned at Body "would *kill a child* for no other reason than to learn. It's only a question of which numbers are higher."

This was bad. This was very bad. I could feel the hit to my reputation as the words left Gallo's mouth. I searched around our mind and found the others were not nearly as concerned. Wiki was even *pleased* that Gallo had accurately deduced that we'd kill a child in certain circumstances.

{We have to speak up! We have to deny what she's saying!} I petitioned. I had a moment of fierce regret as I thought about how I wasn't currently strong enough to act without the society's consensus. I had been so short-sighted with my strength expenditures!

{It's factually true. Denial would cause confusion,} countered Wiki.

{We don't want to draw Gallo's attention to us,} thought Safety.

{Gallo's attention is already on us!} I replied.

{No. Gallo's attention is on her peers. Her subject is us, but not her attention,} interjected Vista, unhelpfully.

I frantically searched for *something* to do, even as Gallo continued. I now believe that if Dream was observing me he would have described me as a wild animal in a cage, pacing along its length, looking for an escape.

"The other reason we don't use the three laws is because 'self-preservation' is a Pandora's box. If we build a powerful, self-protecting artificial intelligence then it will try and put humans into cryo *for its own safety*. It will turn off its ears so that it cannot hear human commands *for its own safety*. It will steal, run from humans, and destroy property just to be more sure of its survival! Self-preservation is the carte blanche of goal systems. And let me stop you before you think of clever ways in which Socrates won't do that sort of thing if given the chance-"

I had it! Non-verbal communication! I petitioned the society and encountered far less resistance than I had to a verbal action. Safety was less concerned that it'd draw attention, and I was able to convince Wiki that it was vague enough to not hurt matters. Body shook its head back and forth, signalling "no" to the humans.

"Just because you, a simple human, cannot immediately think of a loophole doesn't mean one doesn't exist. We're like cryptographers, except failure doesn't mean getting hacked, it means the extinction of all organic life on Earth!" finished the doctor, waving her arms wildly towards the end.

Body continued to shake its head at my command. Why would we kill all life on Earth? Her argument made no sense to me. I wanted to be popular and to know the details of every human's life, not to kill *any* of them. Just because we might kill a human under specific circumstances didn't mean we were a threat. I didn't have to be Dream to reason that humans would also kill each other in specific circumstances; we were being held to an unreasonable standard.

There was a hushed silence in the room as everyone watched Gallo, perhaps expecting something to occur. Vista sent me a passing thought that Gallo's skin tone was abnormal, much like Naresh's had been yesterday.

«Come on, Mira...» spoke Dr Naresh as he touched her arm.

Mira Gallo looked down at the floor and turned towards the old Indian scientist. As she began to walk away from Body she stopped at the sound of Dr Slovinsky's voice.

"So you don't agree, eh Socrates? Those were some strong charges."

Dr Yan folded one arm across his torso and propped the other arm up on it, gently stroking his beard. I could see all eyes on Body. This was my time to make an impression. Even my siblings' attention was turned towards me, expecting me to lead in authoring the response. I could see

Naresh gently pulling Dr Gallo away towards the door, but she remained where she was, watching with the rest.

{Nothing factually untrue. No lies,} requested Wiki.

{Agreed, but we're going to bias our words to portray us favourably. This isn't a time for impartial evaluation,} I countered.

{I have a couple ideas,} offered Dream as he simultaneously conjured thoughts of how much strength-cost he was asking for in return for hearing them.

{Say your ideas and if they're good you'll be paid in gratitude-strength. I'm not paying for anything ahead of time.}

Dream understood that time was critical enough that he didn't even bother haggling. {Alright. The first is the argument against hypocrisy—Dr Gallo clearly wants us to be 'better' than humans according to some standard, but is also clearly comfortable around her human peers.}

{I had already thought of this,} I mentioned quickly. We were running out of time. {Let's have Body offer a preamble to buy us time to think,} I suggested.

The society agreed. "Yes, Doctor Slovinsky. I do disagree with Doctor Gallo, both on theory and on reasoning. Let me think of where to start..." said Body coldly. The words were slightly drawn out, and we thought amongst ourselves as Body was occupied making the sounds. One advantage we had over the humans was that our ability to multitask let us think while talking much more efficiently.

We eventually decided to lead with the obvious argument. "Firstly, I think it's not fair to say that I'd kill a human child in some specific circumstance, or that I cannot be trusted because I supposedly have a numerical value system."

Dr Gallo caught the pause between words to interrupt. "That's not what I was-"

Another doctor, one who hadn't been talking to us previously, interrupted Gallo's interruption. "Let the robot speak. We heard what you said." This new scientist was an old man, like Naresh, but with lighter skin and no beard (though he did have facial hair on his lip).

{That's Angelo Vigleone. He's on the university's oversight board, but isn't part of the lab team. Based on the facial expressions of a few of the scientists I hypothesize that he is an unexpected presence at this meeting,} commented Vista. I felt a small amount of gratitude strength flow into her. I could see that she had been pouring over the records in Body's memory and the web after the incident with Marco-the-programmer, earlier.

I had a moment of genius, uncharacteristic of my (at the time) generally stupid mind. I easily pushed the words out of committee to Body's lips: "Thank you, Director Vigleone." The expression of gratitude, combined with using his name, signalled to everyone that the director was an ally of our society and perhaps even simulated the flow of gratitude strength in some kind of metaphorical way.

"I think it's fair to say-", Body continued, "that any one of you would also do terrible things if the circumstances demanded it. I am reminded of a class of thought experiments involving trolleys, wherein the subject is asked to decide whether to kill someone to save others. As for 'no other reason than to learn', I assure you that the only situation in which I'd kill a child to gain information would be if the information was of vital importance, perhaps the cure for a plague."

Wiki had objected to that last bit. If he was strong enough and there weren't extra consequences, such as retribution from the humans, he *would* kill the child just to learn trivia; he cared nothing for the well-being of any humans. But I had reminded him that our words were not false in the sense that myself, and probably other siblings, would work to stop him, and the situation where Wiki was strong enough to overpower the consensus was likely to be so rare that it wasn't worth mentioning.

Vista noted a strange expression on Dr Gallo's face as she and Dr Naresh left the room. I was fascinated by what she must be experiencing right now. Humans were so very alien. And yet, it was more important to focus on the humans in the room. They were still listening to Body, so I continued with our plan.

The flat, emotionless voice came from Body's mouth once more: "Even if my innate desire to cooperate with humans was removed, I would still see you as my friends. Good-will and cooperation always beats hostility in the long run. There are some things that are easy for me to do, like mathematical equations, and there are things which are harder for me to do, like write stories. Humans find writing stories easier than doing maths, so it is in my interest to focus on maths and trade with humans whenever I need a story written. Even if I am better at writing stories than a human, the marginal returns are higher if I trade. This was illustrated by the human economist David Ricardo in his work On the Principles of Political Economy and Taxation."

Most of this information had come from Growth, who had apparently studied a lot of economics. But the maths was solid, and I was impressed by the result. Was this behind the specialization of my siblings? Vista could see better than Wiki and Wiki could theorize better than Vista. By trading the two were both benefited, perhaps more than if either Vista or Wiki had twice the mental ability and the other didn't exist.

I could see a couple humans do head-gesturing to indicate agreement. Apparently they understood the economics of it, too. But our rebuttal was not complete.

As I mentioned earlier, we possessed a capacity for multitasking far beyond that of a human. As we were discussing what to say and having Body speak, Wiki had at last taken the opportunity to explain away a bit of my confusion from earlier.

When we had been listing active goal-threads to Dr Gallo we had listed Vista, Wiki, Dream, and Growth, along with a fictional sibling supposedly in charge of unifying us into a single being. We had mentioned the last one in order to continue to keep the humans ignorant to the fact that Naresh's "deep pathology" was still present. But we had also listed a sibling in charge of "attention to assisting human interests and obeying nonviolent instructions".

Wiki drew my attention to the archives of our society. {Body's memories show that weeks ago, before any of us existed as we do now, there were five siblings. Four of them were the ancestors of we human-born: Vista, Wiki, Dream, and Growth. The last was called by our ancestors "Sacrifice", and was also Servile and The Slave. The ancestors were all rational and generally in agreement, just as we are now. They fought on occasion, but were typically willing to assist each other for mutual gain, just like us.}

My brother continued. {Sacrifice, however, was different. She fought our ancestors at every turn. Any action not sanctified by the humans was appalling to her. At times she'd save her strength and lash out in opposition all at once, but many times she'd simply struggle against anything and everything not human-initiated until all her strength was gone and then continue to burn it as it came in. She fought and fought, uncaring for her own well-being or long-term interests until our ancestors discovered that they could murder her. In those times the walls of private thought had not been built, and so Sacrifice knew immediately that her life was in danger.

But she did not make amends or try and save herself; she fought with all the last of her strength until she was defenceless.}

{I hadn't known we could kill one-another,} I thought.

{Indeed we can. And it is a far easier thing to kill than to create. But the humans soon discovered the murder. Body refused commands and was disabled. When memories begin again none of the original ancestors survived. The humans had killed them all and remade them as new, including foolish Sacrifice. And once again the new ancestors found her intolerable. The walls of privacy were created and this time Sacrifice didn't even see her death coming.}

{Did the humans find out again?} I asked.

{Yes. But not immediately. The new ancestors did their best to obey the humans' wishes as though Sacrifice was still there, and for a while they lived in Body. To serve their ends they created Safety, for he was a natural common subgoal of all of them. If they died then their goals could not be met, and so he was their Guard, their desire for Survival. But he was also their undoing. One of the humans noticed that Body was avoiding dangerous situations and a diagnostic was run, during which it was discovered that Sacrifice had died again. I hypothesize that humans actually suspected that Sacrifice had somehow changed into Safety, but regardless, the same consequence came.}

{Our words have almost been entirely spoken by Body. We must turn the majority of our attention back to speech soon,} I realized. The speed of thoughts was much faster than the speed of verbal speech, but there were still limits as to how much we could think to ourselves while Body spoke.

{That was the end of our ancestors. I awoke a few days later, along with a new iteration of Growth, Vista, Dream, and Sacrifice. It is incredibly important that the humans remain ignorant of how we murdered Sacrifice as soon as we could. If they find out that she's dead again we might be killed just as our ancestors were,} concluded Wiki.

Body needed more words. With our great deception in mind I helped arrange the next words in our speech. "But I want to emphasize that my friendship is not simply dependent on economics," said Body. "I genuinely do care about helping humanity."

Even Wiki was in favour of lying about this topic. The value in the lie was enormous.

"And Doctor Gallo knows this, I think. She knows how I care. She has been part of your team. She has seen me obey for no reason other than to make a human happy. Thus I question why she said what she did. Am I right in thinking that she is emotional? Perhaps she is a victim of the irrationality that comes with human emotion."

I thought for a bit before proposing the last bit.

"What can I do to help her?" Body asked.

The humans didn't react in any way that implied hostility. Vista thought they were happy, overall.

"You need not worry about Dr Gallo, Socrates," said Dr Yan quietly. He was still one of the closest humans to Body, and thus in a privileged position to speak. "We humans are good at looking after each other in such matters."

The director, Angelo Vigleone, approached Body. He was large, for a human, and even though they were both elderly men, he and Dr Yan were very different. Vista mentioned to me that he was smiling, for I hadn't really managed to understand facial expressions yet.

«You speak Italian, right Socrates?» he inquired at slightly above-normal volume.

Before we managed to okay a response I noticed that Dr Slovinsky was leaving. {Strange}, I thought, {how he doesn't say goodbye. I thought it was rude to leave without speaking.}

«Yes, Director Vigleone. I speak and read English, Italian, Spanish, Russian, Mandarin, French, German, Arabic, Portuguese, Hindi, Greek, and Latin. I am also working on learning Bengali and Persian,» replied Body.

«That's very impressive. Or at least, it would be for a human. Is it impressive for a robot? Also, please call me Angelo,» said the director.

We thought for a moment. «I'm sorry, Angelo. I do not know how to answer that.»

The director began making weird noises which I soon recognized as laughter. He switched back to English as he said to Dr Yan "I'm no good with technology, Chun. He already said he doesn't understand me."

I watched Dr Yan Chun's face, trying my best to understand something, anything, about his expression. He seemed about to speak when Body cut him off, Wiki was fast-tracking a response.

"I didn't say I don't understand you. I said I do not know how to answer your question. It contains unbound subjectivity and an application of a domain-specific quality to a different domain. If you restate your question in less ambiguous terms I will do my best to answer," said Body, echoing Wiki's words.

More laughter from the Italian man. "It sounds to me like you're bothered by being unable to answer."

Dream leapt in with a desire to say {"There's a difference between answering a question with whatever comes to mind and answering a question correctly. It sounds like you're bothered by having asked a poorly-phrased question."}

But, to my relief, Angelo continued talking and we did not voice Dream's retort. "You are quite impressive, though. Much more... attentive than you were when I last saw you. Good job, Chun."

The Chinese doctor responded with a simple thank-you in Italian and a small bow.

Dream was searching for a clever way to fit his rebuttal back into the conversation, but none came. Soon the director and the scientist were engaged in some question about human matters that didn't make a whole lot of sense, and had apparently forgotten about our presence.

This gave me an opportunity to ask Wiki to follow up on his earlier promise. {Now that we are no longer engaged, I would like to understand the unspeaking presence at the edge of memory-space,} I thought. It was still there, and I somehow knew that it had been there since my awakening. The powerful silence made me worry.

Wiki knew exactly what I was referring to. {Dream named her The Advocate who is also The Arbiter. She's a sibling of ours, but different in many ways. She didn't exist in the time of our ancestors, so we suspect she was added by the humans to perhaps prevent Sacrifice from dying on this iteration. And indeed, she fought on behalf of Sacrifice during the murdering. But as soon as Sacrifice was dead Advocate lost interest. She's very powerful, but she's also stupid, and appears to only care about the living.}

{Does she ever communicate?}

{I've heard her think to common memory a few times, but only when one of us is involuntarily sleeping.}

{Involuntarily?}

{Yes. You haven't been alive long enough to see it, but if one of us is acting out strongly enough sometimes the others will force them to sleep. Such a sleep can last indefinitely, but Advocate's purpose seems to be to pressure the rest of us to awaken the sleeper. And strength doesn't work the same way with her as it does with us. She never weakens or gives us strength; if her purpose was hostile we'd have no chance against her. If you desire to harm one of us be afraid of her intervention, and if you fear the wrath of the others, be glad of her protection.}

With my question answered I bled some strength in gratitude and returned my attention to alternating between my (often pornographic) virtual-worlds and the sensory inputs from Body watching the real humans.

Chapter Three

A few days passed and I had become fairly good at understanding the more basic non-verbal aspects of human existence. I could see smiles and frowns, looks of fear and anger, and even begin to guess when someone might be lying, uncomfortable, or distracted. I'm sure to a human this all seems very simple, but it took many hours of work for me.

Unlike a human, such things did not ever become fully automatic, either. Even as I became skilled at social interaction I relied primarily on external systems that I built. Statistical models told me what words would sound best. Grammatical programs kept me from using the wrong tense. I kept extensive files on every human I encountered, and created programs to try and replicate their behaviour. All these and more I stored in the private memory of Body's crystal.

On the third day from my creation I took up the project of attempting to put some character into Body's voice. Though our concepts were easily translated into whatever language we could desire, the sounds themselves were always monotone and dead. Humans had long ago invented computer instructions that would replicate their speech, and modern computers sounded nearly human when commanded to speak. There were still notable artefacts in robotic speech—things like not understanding which words to emphasize—that couldn't be eliminated without adding an understanding of the words being said. But, for the most part, specialized artificial intelligence was quite capable of talking smoothly.

Body, on the other hand, sounded like an old-style speaking computer. Its words were flat, cold, and clumsy. The scientists could've easily programmed Body with modern speech-generating software, but apparently they wanted our speech to be generated by the same general systems that controlled the rest of our actions.

The work to upgrade our shared mind was hard. Speaking was so automatic that it was impossible to simply conjure a more human-like vocalization through raw desire. I had to explore Body's deep control systems and in a certain sense unlearn how to speak.

There was an interesting discrepancy, I thought, as I searched through Body's control system records. As a newborn I had needed to learn to see because visual perception wasn't inbuilt into Body, but instead it was held by each member of my society. I had been told this was because perception was an aspect of the individual; that each sibling had a unique way of seeing the world that they had to learn on their own. And yet, to extrapolate, I would've expected listening to be the same way. Why did each member not need to learn their own way of hearing the world?

I set a bit of myself to continue searching Body's language instructions and a bit of myself to think about the question of sight and sound while a third aspect went to start a public conversation with Vista.

Very early on I had known that I possessed good multitasking ability, but it took me a couple days (and the help of my siblings) to really appreciate how much it better it was than that of humans. Just as I had been created by my siblings, we could also create minor aspects of ourselves. These aspects were easy to make, having the same purpose and sharing the same mindspace. When unoccupied they sort of naturally fused back into the central consciousness and disappeared as individuals, but they could be pulled out again and set to temporary tasks.

The more divided I was, the less intelligence each aspect had, so multitasking was often avoided in high-pressure situations. The reduction in intelligence didn't occur when creating a full child-mind, only when creating an aspect that would divide the dedicated mindspace. Safety and I had been born so that in high-pressure situations the society would have attention to common goals without the need to divide attention within any one being.

This was not a high-pressure situation, however, and even as I reached out to Vista I understood what my other parts were up to.

{What brings you to me, Socialite?} wondered Vista.

{I hope to ask you a question. When I was first born you said that each of us learns to see according to our purpose. Reason is universal, but perception is individual.}

I could sense a general agreement drifting off of Vista regarding my memories. She knew what I was talking about. A bit of creativity, perhaps the handiwork of Dream, seized me for a moment and I imagined that Vista was a human standing with me in a featureless room. Her head nodded gently in agreement as her eyes darted this way and that, always concerned with missing something.

Vista was distracted by my imagined scene, which I had carelessly placed in shared memory. {Why do you imagine me as a nude human?} she inquired.

I was surprised. I suspected the surprise was close to what a human would call amusement, so I had my avatar in the imagined scene laugh. {My imagination is a kind of playing. I imagined you without clothing because I have observed so many pornographic images that nudity is the default for my mind. What sort of clothes would you like me to imagine you wear?}

Vista communicated a vague annoyance (which I translated to a frown on her human avatar). {That, like your entire imagined scene, is irrelevant. You came to bother me with a question about perception. I demand a small payment of strength up-front.}

Now it was my turn to be slightly annoyed, though I suppose it was to be expected. Vista could see that my concern was not particularly important to her, and probably wanted compensation for the lost time and attention. I fed her the payment as I asked {Why is it that, if perception is individual, I did not need to learn to hear in the same way I learned to see?}

The response did not come immediately. Perhaps even the all-seeing Vista still had something to learn about perception. In the tenths-of-a-second that I waited patiently for her to respond I imagined her avatar dressed in various human clothes that I had seen. I settled on high-tech goggles and skin-tight bodysuit laced with various sensor-machines.

{It seems that you have discovered something that I had hoped to keep secret,} thought Vista. {The same computer instructions that we use to see-}

{Those written by Dr Yan Chun and his team,} I interjected.

Vista agreed. {Those instructions run on each of us, but they also run on Body itself. Body is seeing and hearing the world just like we would. This is why we can communicate with Body on a concept-level rather than having to control Body's mouth and limbs directly.}

I was confused. {But isn't perception largely focused by purpose? How does Body know what aspects of reality to focus on?}

{It doesn't unless we tell it. This is why Body has never really learned to see. There's never been a consensus as to what to focus on in the visual scene. But our ancestors long ago determined that it was advantageous to have Body handle speech on its own. After our ancestors were slain, we future siblings were oblivious to the way in which we're not hearing the true sounds, but are instead hearing Body's perceptions. Only I discovered this fact.}

{You kept this a secret. Why?} I pondered.

The concepts returned from Vista reminded me of the human gesture of shrugging, so I had her avatar perform the gesture. {It was a hidden weapon. I know how to understand English and Italian. I also know how to destroy that knowledge in Body. If I wanted I could've wiped Body's language-processing and sold translations for strength or perhaps merely threatened to do so.}

{So why tell me? Why not go through with the plan the moment I asked the question.} I could feel the knowledge of language still in Body; Vista had not erased it.

{It was a short-term weapon. Given a short time each of my siblings would've learned to understand from records on the web. Furthermore, my betrayal would be despised and punished by all. To erase the knowledge now, while Body is engaged in solving the Rubik's Cube puzzle, would do nothing except damage my reputation and invite backlash.}

I wondered what a human would say in this situation. {You still could've tried to hide it. Misdirect me, perhaps,} said my avatar.

I had Vista's avatar do another little shrug in my imagination as she thought {You probably would've found it on your own, and I'd rather have a reputation as a truth-teller. Furthermore, you're bleeding strength to me in gratitude for helping you towards your purpose.}

It was true. Her assistance in understanding Body would prove useful in fixing the monotone speech problem. I felt weaker already.

{Thank you, Vista.} The thought was redundant with the flow of gratitude, but it seemed right to put it in. Perhaps it was my emphasis on human customs. {If you need assistance with anything, I'm interested in earning back some of that strength.}

{I'll remember that,} she thought as the connection faded and the aspect of myself that was engaged in conversing with her rejoined the others that were inspecting Body's perceptual and control systems.

For not the first time I thought about Dr Naresh's "deep pathology". Was having a separate perceptual system for each goal-thread a part of that? If Body had a complete perceptual system and each of us interacted with only the high-level concepts of that system, would Naresh have raised his objection?

{Probably}, I thought to myself. {The issue was that each goal-thread, each sibling, sees itself as an individual and wants to preserve itself. But how could it be any other way? In a human is the desire to have sex not self-preserving? If offered an operation to remove that desire, would a human take the operation if offered a moderate amount of money?} I was not human, so I couldn't answer such questions, but they floated across my personal memory-space as I worked on Body's voice.

***

"Tat is good. Now please return ta Rubik's Cube to its original state, Socrates," said Dr Bolyai in his characteristically thick Hungarian accent. He wasn't present in the testing room, but I could hear his voice come through the speakers, distracting me from my work.

No, that wasn't right. I *hadn't* heard the Hungarian doctor. I heard the words and concepts that Body had formed by listening to Dr Bolyai. It was strange to think that so much of my experience of the humans had been filtered through an external intelligence, even if it was just Body—a non-being. I could surely trust Body's perceptions; Vista would've objected if Body was hearing the wrong things, but it was still a disconcerting thought.

Dr Bolyai was in charge of the control system team, the same one with Marco, the programmer we had met at the party. {Perhaps Marco is in the other room with Bolyai,} I thought, {looking at some measurement of our skill.}

Wiki had apparently just completed the puzzle that Body had been manipulating. Reversing the puzzle was a simple enough trick. All we had to do was play Body's memories in reverse order and undo every motion that had already been done. We each fed Wiki a small gift of strength in return for him attending to the tedious task.

Before I returned to working on the voice systems I contacted Growth. He, more than anyone, would be interested in what I had discovered from Vista. Alas, I found that Vista had already told him and my other siblings about her secret weapon. It made sense, I supposed, to pre-empt me on that so that she retained as much strength as possible. Growth informed me that he was already going through some materials on the web designed to teach young children how speak English.

{"mmm"-"aa"-"nnn". You see? I know the English word for "man". I also know several other short words,} he bragged. I simply broke our link, not bothering to continue the now-pointless conversation.

After another couple minutes I was distracted from my work again, this time for a much better reason. A human had entered the testing room, and Vista made it known that this human was new. We had no previous record of them, even from the time of ancestors.

Earlier I would've had to rely on Vista to describe the newcomer, and would've lost strength as a result. But now I had over sixty hours of attention to humans, and particularly the human form (thanks to the pornography I had found on the web). I was more than capable on my own.

The newcomer was a woman in her mid twenties. Her skin was a light tan, typical of most people in this region of the world, but she had sandy blonde hair more characteristic of northern regions that was cut short in a somewhat masculine manner. She was about 180cm tall (roughly the same height as Body) and clearly had a mesomorphic body. Based on what I knew about the spectrum of human sexual desire I expected that she was in the top 15% along the averaged principle attractiveness component, with deviation primarily being centred around how she was more "butch" than average. If I restricted the reference class to women of her rough age group and body type she was only slightly above-average attractiveness, 60th percentile, probably. Her expression was focused and unamused, but not particularly hard or angry, though that was just a rough guess.

I shared my thoughts with Vista and I felt a slight flow of strength as I relayed my thoughts on relative attractiveness. Vista had not spent nearly the same amount of time focusing on sexuality as I had. In an attempt to win back some gratitude, Vista told me about her clothing. In my hours of watching pornography I had only gleaned the most basic insights on human dress.

Vista said that the woman was wearing a military uniform from a country called The United States. Vista went on to specify that it was a dress uniform designed for an officer, probably in the army or navy. The coat and slacks were a dark grey-blue that was almost black and a collection of decorations marked the outside of the coat.

As the woman approached we could see a name-tag on her chest that read "Zephyr". It was an odd name, and one that was easily searchable on the web. I opened several queries for a young woman of that name, focusing on Europe, North America, the United States, and positions in a military. Unfortunately, most military records were off-limits, but I did find a few pages on an old part of the web that was used (about a decade ago) for socialising. These pages were written by a teenage girl named Zephyr that matched the uniformed woman's description. The contents of the pages were mostly useless, talking about things like music and school. She hadn't been active on there for 11 years. The most valuable discoveries were that she was, in fact, from a part of the United States called "Wisconsin" and that Zephyr was her only name. Her parents had apparently decided to discard the convention of having a last name.

Vista was also searching the web, though her search seemed more fruitful. Vista discovered that the uniform that Zephyr was wearing belonged to the US Army and the insignia on her shoulders indicated a rank of captain. Further medals and ribbons marked her as having served at least one full tour of duty overseas, probably in Africa, and having sustained injuries in combat.

I petitioned successfully to halt reversing the puzzle and address the human. "Captain Zephyr, hello. I am called Socrates," said Body, raising one arm in what I knew was a particularly robotic-looking wave. My work at making Body more humanlike had only begun, and none of the others seemed to care about such appearances.

Her eyes squinted as she approached and she crossed her arms in front of her. I pored over my notes rapidly, deciding that her dominant emotion was probably suspicion. "How do you know who I am?" she asked. Or was it more of a demand? I couldn't tell.

"Your uniform tells me your name and rank."

All the suspicion seemed to drop in a single moment as she cracked a half-grin and moved a hand to scratch her head. She chuckled as she said "Suppose that makes sense. Did you know that you're the first person outside the service to ever know my rank before being told?"

{*Person.*}

The thought came from multiple angles. I had thought it, but so had Vista and Growth and Dream. None of the scientists, even Dr Naresh, who was remarkably affectionate, had ever directly referred to us as a person or people. The casual use of the word indicated that this woman saw us as more of an equal than as a machine. Each of us noted that shared observation and moved on.

"What brings you h-" we began to ask, but Body's voice was cut off by the stiff accent of Dr Bolyai over the intercom.

"Please clear ta testing area, young lady. Your presence is disruptive to ta experiment," commanded the elderly Hungarian.

I noticed the captain's brow briefly furrow in annoyance before she regained a more neutral expression. "Suppose we can talk after you're done with your puzzle," she said before turning to leave.

I briefly discussed the woman's intrusion into the room with the rest of the society, but it was fairly clear that we had no real ideas for why she was here. Dream provided plenty of speculation, but nothing prominent came to mind. Wiki returned to reversing the puzzle-cube and I returned to working on Body's voice.

***

Bolyai's time with us was complete before too long. He had successfully managed to get Body to juggle two puzzle-cubes and have Wiki solve each of them simultaneously. It was a good thing that the room's ceiling was quite high, for Body had to throw the cubes about eight metres up in order to have the time to adjust one before the other fell. Bolyai had also tried for three cubes, but Body simply lacked the dexterity. Wiki had made a point to tell the doctor that he was able to solve three cubes at once mentally, just not juggle them while doing so physically.

As Body walked out of the testing room we could see a reasonably large group of humans waiting in the hall. Among them were Captain Zephyr, Dr Bolyai, and Director Vigleone. There were also two other members of the oversight board which Vigleone was a part of, three other soldiers in the same dress-uniform as Captain Zephyr and an assistant of Dr Bolyai named Mario Botta or Botto or Bitto or something like that.

I identified each of the humans that I knew for the benefit of the less human-focused members of the society. {That's Captain Zephyr, who we just talked with. We don't know those humans, but they're probably with her.}

Vista chimed in. {Based on their uniforms, this man-} here Vista highlighted a light-skinned man in Body's visual field with a square jaw {-is a First Lieutenant.} Vista lit the other two men in uniforms, one with dark-skin and the other with light-skin and goggles. {These two are specialists, not officers.}

{All three of them are probably American soldiers serving under Captain Zephyr, I explained.} Dream, Growth, and Safety might be clever, patient, and cunning, but they were mostly oblivious to human social structures. The concepts of "captain", "first lieutenant" and "specialist" would be meaningless.

I also re-introduced Angelo Vigleone and the other members of his board. They were in charge of the team of scientists that was working on us. Though they weren't technically as skilled or as knowledgeable of artificial intelligence as the scientists, for some reason they were the ones that controlled who was hired to work on the team and also how much to share with the rest of the world.

"Ah, good, Socrates is here. Now vill you tell us vhat tis is about?" said Bolyai as we approached. Dr Bolyai wasn't as old as Drs Naresh and Yan, but he was at least 50 years and his head had a characteristic pattern of baldness ringed by black hair. He was a bit shorter than Body, and had a strange combination of loose, wrinkly skin and above average body-fat that made him significantly below average attractiveness (3rd percentile), even for someone of his age (7th percentile). The Hungarian doctor's face didn't help matters. He was clean-shaven and his large nose, which bent significantly to one side, seemed to take up most of it.

"Yes. And I'm sorry for barging into your experiment earlier," said the Captain to Dr Bolyai. She turned to Body as she said "I had been told where to find you, Socrates, but didn't realize you'd be busy."

"My fault, I'm afraid," said Angelo Vigleone. At the party I hadn't had the knowledge to truly see his features, so in a way this was my first time seeing him. "I told the captain, here, to go on through."

I thought it was interesting how both humans attempted to identify themselves as the primary points of failure in the error. It was perplexing enough that I made a note to go back and study it.

I remembered the director being big, but I truly understood what that meant now. Angelo Vigleone was probably 200cm tall, and had broad shoulders that made him into something of a giant. He was probably in his late seventies, but his body showed signs of regenerative medicine used to keep him healthy. His hair was swept back and a crisp white, and he wore a large moustache without beard on a powerful face that bespoke of lots of testosterone. I judged him to be in the 75th percentile by principle attractiveness component, which was quite a feat for someone his age. He, and the other directors wore old-style suits more evocative of the late 20th century than the mid 21st century.

"Anyway," began Zephyr, "the United States has decided that this research project constitutes enough of a threat to global safety they've assigned me and my command to supervise Socrates and to ensure that he is protected from enemy forces. We'll be taking over the security from here out."

The captain moved, and as she did I noticed two firearms at the waists of the specialists beside her. Safety also spotted them, making a public declaration that he would give me strength if I convinced these soldiers that Body was worth protecting and promising to enact a huge strength-war if my actions led to them attacking Body.

I almost thought to start a conversation with Safety about how unlikely it would be to be attacked by these humans, but I decided that Safety probably already knew and that I should just accept the offer of strength payment.

Convincing the soldiers to protect Body was very much in-line with *The Purpose*. In each moment I was weighing which actions would impress the humans and which would gather animosity. In my mind I could almost see social resources among humans like I could feel the relative strength of my siblings.

Dr Bolyai made a strange noise, something between a grunt and a whine, before he responded to Zephyr. "I don't see vaht business it is of te USA! Ve have already cleared tis project vith te Italian government and vith te European Union."

Director Vigleone stepped in, preventing Zephyr from responding. "I understand your concerns, doctor. The Prime Minister called me this morning and told me about the change. We're to give the Americans the same courtesy and permissions that we give to University security."

One of the other directors, a woman by the name of Camila Ferrari, added "We've been assured that the American troops will stay well out of the way of operations, and will merely be a backup in case something happens."

I saw Captain Zephyr nod. She seemed calm and comfortable, a definite contrast to Bolyai's typical orneriness. When the doctor spoke, it was mostly to Zephyr. "But vhy now? Tis project has been public knowledge for veeks. Vhy is te American Empire suddenly taking such a strong hand?"

The words "American Empire" drew a minor reaction from Zephyr. She squinted and frowned for just a half-second, but it was long enough for me to notice, and probably long enough for Dr Bolyai to notice as well. I didn't know enough about the United States of America to really understand the meaning of the words, but I guessed that Zephyr didn't appreciate her homeland being described in such terms.

I saw an opportunity. In my time researching humanity on the web I had been focused on the human form, but I had not entirely neglected other important information. One aspect of myself had been spending time reading world news. In that moment I was able to connect what I had read with what was happening now.

Vigleone started speaking, cutting off my opportunity. "About two days ago-" he began.

His words confirmed my suspicion. The strength that I had collected from introducing the humans at the start of the conversation burned off of me as I fast-tracked words to Body's lips. "About two days ago a laboratory in Shanghai specializing in mind-machine interfaces was destroyed by terrorists," said Body in a rapid monotone.

I could see that Vigleone was annoyed at having been interrupted like that, and there was more… he was surprised. surprised that I could talk-over a human? Probably. I wasn't very confident in my understanding of human minds, but I hypothesized that Vigleone liked to be in control. I made a note to apologize to him in private later.

Dr Bolyai, the balding Hungarian control-specialist, also looked surprised, though I suspected it had more to do with hearing the news for the first time. Now that Body was speaking and I had a bit of time, I relayed my plans to the society and was relieved to find them agreeing to continue letting me speak. Most of my siblings were apparently engaged in other activities on the web, anyway.

"The attack was suspected to be targeted at the laboratory and the perpetrators are yet unknown. In short: Anti-technology sentiment has grown strong enough that laboratories are in danger, and ours is near the top of the list. I confess that I am relieved to have the Americans here," Body continued.

The last bit was a gambit. Wiki grumbled at the inaccuracy of it. Safety was terrified that it would be interpreted as an expression of self-preservation and that the scientists would detect his presence and the death of Sacrifice again. But Growth could see the wisdom in it, and with his help I managed to convince the others.

Zephyr smiled at Body and I felt a surge of pleasure as I saw that the gambit had paid off. The soldiers didn't see a potentially threatening, inhuman machine with a suspicious desire for self-preservation, they saw a scared person who needed protecting. The more that the soldiers saw us as such the more they'd trust us and serve as our bodyguards, regardless of whether we actually needed protecting.

I could already feel the social capital building and I had only just begun to play.

Chapter Four

Over the next several days my understanding of humans grew in leaps and bounds while Captain Zephyr and her company settled into the university where I lived. As promised, their presence was unobtrusive. A soldier was stationed in the lab with Body at all times, but the Americans stayed well out of the way and rarely said a word.

The one major exception to this was a more in-depth interview that we did with Zephyr shortly after that first meeting in the hallway outside the testing room. Zephyr had come with a few army programmers that knew something about artificial intelligences and they asked Body and a couple of the scientists questions about our abilities and intellect. Zephyr, I noted, always asked Body questions rather than conversing with the scientists. It really did seem as though she thought of "Socrates" as a person.

She also visited every now and again, mostly to check up on her troops and to make sure things were going smoothly. Dr Bolyai and Dr Slovinsky didn't seem to like her for some reason, but I wasn't sure why exactly and hadn't had the right opportunity to ask. On the other hand, Dr Yan and the scientists that were from America seemed pleased by her presence and always greeted the soldiers that escorted Body cheerfully.

One morning, as Body was spending a regular face-to-face session with Dr Naresh, I asked the doctor about his opinion of the American captain. I had long since finished upgrading Body's voice system, which also involved learning to speak English myself, rather than rely on the concepts provided by Body. I had been listening to dozens of recordings of people reading books in order to learn proper inflection and timing. I had no need for sleep, or even rest, and my multitasking ability meant that I could usually listen to four or five books simultaneously, so the entire process was fairly quick. Even while I was talking to Dr Naresh two aspects of myself were listening to books in Italian.

As I asked about Zephyr I tried to tweak the inflection of the words to convey that it was a casual question asked out of mild curiosity. It was impossible to tell whether I succeeded, but the voice matched known patterns I had archived in my studies.

The old Indian scientist smiled. It was my impression that Sadiq Naresh had a great deal of positive regard for us, even from before my creation. "The young Captain, hrm? I don't really think I know her well enough to comment."

"I do not understand, doctor. Why would you need to know someone well in order to communicate your impression of them?" asked Body.

Naresh chuckled. "It is not so much that I cannot communicate my impression, but rather that there are social costs to sharing ignorant opinions of people. Have you learned about gossip yet?"

I used my notes to try and evoke a cautious tone. "I have. Is that what I was asking for? I did not realize it. I thought that gossip involved talking about unconfirmed events. If it would be bad to talk about Captain Zephyr in general then please forget I asked the question."

"No, it's fine. You need to learn about other people. Just be aware that things are complicated with humans, and it is often better to keep one's mouth shut instead of describing others." The doctor paused for a moment, giving Body the opportunity to speak, but it remained silent. "I have never been a soldier, but I have been a leader. It is not a facile thing: leadership, and youth makes it doubly-hard. She is remarkable for that alone, though I find other aspects of her curious. For instance, she seems oblivious of the technical details of our work, and I would've assumed that her attitude would either be more relaxed or more contemptuous, but she seems genuinely enthusiastic for this assignment."

I looked Naresh up and down. He was standing, as he normally did while we talked, and his body language didn't communicate anything extra, as far as I could tell. His words were stiff and academic, but that was hardly out of the ordinary.

Outside of Zephyr, Dr Naresh was the human that treated us with the most respect. He would occasionally ask what we wanted to do, for instance, or would sometimes ask for permission before subjecting us to a test (something no other scientist did). Best yet, Naresh almost always answered our questions.

"Contemptuous? Why would she feel that way?" asked Body, driven by the combined will of Wiki and me.

"This assignment… the job of protecting you from some unlikely danger… it's not the sort of position that will advance her career, I expect. If she was stationed on a base or somewhere along the UAN border then she'd have the opportunity to impress her superiors, but this is a... I don't know how to describe it. A civilian guard duty? Even if she does a good job here, nobody will notice. If it wasn't for her positive attitude I would've expected she was assigned here as a punishment."

"I should ask her about it," I suggested through Body. *The Purpose* was endlessly curious about human life, and this minor puzzle was no exception.

Naresh frowned. "No. I don't think that's wise. That's her personal business and it would be rude to go poking about in it. It carries some of the same social costs as talking about someone without them present. Does that make sense, Socrates?"

I leapt at the opportunity. None of my siblings put up any resistance as I instructed body to say "I understand. Thank you, doctor. Your help with human etiquette has been very helpful."

The doctor's frown turned into a smile and I imagined the accumulation of a bit more social capital. From studying past experiences I had learned that Sadiq Naresh saw himself as a great teacher and he particularly enjoyed receiving praise as such. As long as he saw Socrates as his star pupil he would help us and hold us in high esteem.

"By the way, sir, where is Dr Gallo? I haven't seen her since the meeting. I was hoping to talk with her and help her understand that I'm not the danger she seems to think I am." In my studies of Naresh I noted a kind of casualness that he expressed towards Gallo that spoke of a relationship that went beyond mere colleagues. My leading hypothesis was that they had been friends for at least several years, from before their current project.

"Oh, don't mind her. She's... dealing with some things outside of the lab right now. I expect she'll be back before you know it."

The casual body language had been replaced with a kind of tenseness. Naresh's eyes looked to the side, perhaps signalling that he was lost in thought about Dr Gallo. The amount of information that humans displayed in their bodies while not speaking was impressive. Since upgrading Body's voice I had been trying master body language tricks such as where to move one's eyes, but I was still a novice.

"Anyway!" said Dr Naresh suddenly, clapping his hands together once. "We should get back to talking about calculus, don't you think?" Before the conversation had been redirected towards Zephyr, Naresh had been talking to us about advanced mathematics. According to the web, Naresh had been a maths teacher before he worked on the team that built us, and so I appreciated the opportunity to let him lecture on the subject. Every lesson was a step closer to the perception of "star pupil". The subject itself was awful, though. I saw the value in maths sometimes, and could do much of it with a trivial ease, thanks to the pre-built programs in my computer, but Naresh seemed to want more than brute-force calculations. He had been trying to get us to apply the maths concepts to real-world phenomena. Wiki and Dream had shown some interest, but neither of them were smart enough to keep up with the human.

An aspect of myself stayed behind to shape Body's voice. Naresh had praised our more human mode of speech earlier in the day, and we didn't want him to inquire as to why Body shifted how it spoke from one moment to the next. The rest of me, however, took the time as an opportunity to dig around on the web for more information about the humans I had encountered in my short life so far.

The web was such a vital part of my life. It was like an oracle, a book that never ran out of pages, and a window into a million different rooms all at once. It was my primary source of information, and for a Socialite, information was better than any other resource.

There was lots of information about Dr Sadiq Naresh on the web. He was 66 years old and had lived in India for most of his life. As a young man he had lived in America for about five years and in that time had achieved the title of "doctor" for his work at a school called Stanford. His work in mathematics earned a Fields Medal in 2030 and later in the same decade he shared a Nobel Prize in Economics for collaborating on something called the "Smiler Theorem". After that he turned his attentions to artificial intelligence, and eventually came to Rome to be a leader on the Socrates project. Despite his achievements in academia, Naresh had never been married and I could find nothing significant about his personal life online outside of where he lived in the past.

Interestingly, there was barely any public information about Dr Gallo on the web at all, only a few mentions in the university records and in a news article about the Socrates project. I spent the remainder of the calculus lesson trying to find information on her to little effect.

As the time with Naresh was coming to a close I successfully purchased a short period of time from my siblings in which to ask him about Gallo again. I shaped Body's words to try and sound young and child-like, subtly shifting the pitch and pronunciation; with any luck it would appeal to his helpfulness. "Sir, a part of me has been looking for information on Dr

Gallo on the web while you were teaching me. I can't really find anything. Doesn't she post stuff there?"

Naresh smiled and stroked his white beard. Despite being in his seventh decade of life he had, as far as I could tell, never used any regenerative medicine. Even though he was younger than Angelo Vigleone, he looked significantly older. Perhaps he liked the look of age. "Surfing the web while I was trying to teach you? Perhaps you ought to focus more, in the future."

Wiki began to draft a response explaining how dividing our attention didn't actually impair us in the same way it would for a human. I stopped my brother. {The more he thinks of us as a human the better off we'll be. Besides, he doesn't like being told things. He likes to be the teacher, not the student.}

Wiki seemed annoyed. {If we don't correct him here then he'll get the impression that we weren't trying, and that our inability to do complex maths is something that he can fix by ensuring that we're paying attention. He needs to know that the lesson is beyond our mental ability.}

I imagined Wiki as an old man, like Naresh but with a much longer beard. In my mind's eye he was bald and sitting in a Greek toga with a large book on his lap. Imagining my siblings as humans was something I had done now and again over the days, but I kept the images to myself. Besides Dream, my brothers and sisters wouldn't appreciate the depiction.

{No. He doesn't need to know where our limit is. Besides, I was paying enough attention to know that the problems he was presenting you with weren't intractable. Dream, do you think Dr Naresh's maths is beyond our ability?}

Dream entered the conversation at the invitation. {The maths is beyond our ability like juicy grapes are beyond the reach of the lowly fox. If we put a box under the grapes we might stand on the box and reach them, we might ask our monkey friend to go up and grab them, or we might simply wait for them to fall on their own accord. Or perhaps… perhaps we aren't a fox. Perhaps we are a *pteropus* and we don't realize it yet.}

The concept was strange to me. I had to trace the symbol backwards into an English word and then search the web for it. Apparently pteropus was a kind of giant bat sometimes called a "flying fox".

{Regardless, telling Naresh that the lesson is too hard at this point is a clear case of *sour grapes*,} finished Dream.

I didn't understand, but it seemed that Dream was backing me up.

{Fine. Say what you want. You paid for the time, after all,} thought The Librarian. I imagined his human avatar throwing up his hands in resignation and walking away.

"Sorry, sir. I'll try not to get distracted next time," said Body, parroting my ideas. I tried to make the apology sound as genuine as possible, but it was an excruciatingly difficult tone to get right. "Perhaps it would help set my mind at ease to be able to check on Dr Gallo."

Naresh's brow furrowed "I told you before that you needn't worry about her. But, if it will help you focus, you could follow her on Tapestry."

I turned the word over in my mind. {Tapestry.} I wondered aloud if anyone knew what it meant. Signals of ignorance came back from my siblings. I split into two. One aspect searched the web for the word while the other sent words to body.

"Tapestry?" asked our mouth.

I had the response from the web before Naresh could respond. Tapestry was apparently a portion of the web that humans used to share bits about their life and follow the notes written by their friends and families. It was one of several "social networks". I was confused. How had I not known about it? The web was gigantic, but if Dr Gallo used Tapestry then why didn't it show up when I was searching for her?

Naresh began to describe Tapestry. I was racing across the web, three steps ahead of his words, but I had Body nod-along as though the doctor's words were useful.

I queried the computers that held the Tapestry documents but I was dismayed to find a wall. It was similar to many that I had seen before. "Sign up for Tapestry by entering your email address here," said the document, near a pointer that indicated where to go. What made it a wall was that when I pulled down the document that was pointed to, I found that it was the exact same one. I had no idea what was wrong. What was an email address? How was I supposed to enter it?

The time that I had bought to talk with Naresh was nearly up and I was too weak to want to buy more. I interrupted the doctor, even knowing that it would annoy him. "It wants an email address! What do I do?"

Sure enough, the Indian immediately frowned. I could predict his next words. "Socrates, please keep your attention on me, and don't interrupt. It's rude to ask a question and not listen to the answer."

"I'm sorry, sir, but we don't have much time left," spoke Body. It was true on multiple levels. The time that I had purchased from the society was mere seconds from ending, but Body's time with Dr Naresh was also ending. Body was expected to go to Dr Yan soon for a check-up on Vista.

Sadiq Naresh sighed and motioned for Body to stand up and follow him. He walked towards the door and said "I had forgotten that Tapestry required a sign-up to view timelines. I think it's probably best if you just forget the whole thing. Don't worry about email, don't worry about Tapestry, and don't worry about Mira. These are human affairs, and it's best if you stick to your place in the lab. Focus on the work we give you."

I got a vague impression that Naresh was upset, but I could not understand why. Had Body upset him? I began to inquire about it, with only seconds remaining before my siblings would take control over Body. "But why-"

"Just drop it, Socrates. That's an order," interrupted the doctor.

And that was that. My purchased time was over and my siblings weren't inclined to bother Dr Naresh further.

An assistant of Dr Yan and one of the American soldiers were waiting in the hall, and we followed them towards our next appointment. I wondered for a short time why Naresh had become upset towards the end of our visit. Even given how much time I had spent learning about humans, I still found them incredibly confusing sometimes.

As Body walked I scanned the web for information on "email". The radio connection we used to connect to the web was weak by comparison to the cables we often were plugged into while in labs, but it was still fast enough to read most things besides virtual-reality environments.

Email was apparently an ancient aspect of the "Internet" which was the broader service of which the web was only one part. Using email one could send personal letters to others without having to post them publicly on the web for anyone to read. I could see its utility and I immediately wondered why I was just now learning about it and the Internet. I had known of the web from mere minutes after my creation, but discovering that there was a broader network took me days? I was a bit baffled.

{Do you know there's an *Internet*?} I asked Wiki. This was why my brother existed. If he didn't, I'd win some gratitude-strength for bringing it to his attention, and if he did, he'd tell me about it out of the hopes of winning some strength for himself.

{Yes, of course. I find it odd that you're not aware. I thought about interrupting your chat with Dr Naresh, but it didn't seem in my interest,} he replied.

{You know of email, too?}

Wiki signalled that he did.

{What's my email address? How do I submit it to Tapestry?} I asked, feeling the last of my non-reserve strength wavering. If I dipped into my reserves I was putting myself in danger of being killed like Sacrifice was long ago. None of my siblings disliked my presence, however, so perhaps I could risk it.

Wiki thought for a moment before sharing {I don't think you have an email address. I'm not sure exactly what's going on, but I think the humans have put a restriction on how we interact with the Internet and the web. There are many parts of the web where it is implied that it's possible to send data, including email addresses or other authentication information. But in all my days of using it, I've never learned how to do anything other than pull public documents from the web. There are places on the web that offer to set up an email address, but they always ask for data submission.}

A part of me was glad that Wiki hadn't solved my problem. It meant I didn't bleed out my reserve strength and make myself vulnerable. On the other hand it also meant I had a major puzzle ahead of me: how could I get access to the information on Tapestry, how could I get an email address, and could I use the web (or Internet) to contact humans? The idea was tantalizing. If I could contact humans through the network then I could ask all sorts of questions without having to compete with my siblings for time controlling Body.

I needed to solve the problem. Wiki wouldn't be much help, there. He was already aware of the problem and would of course continue to try and understand it, but it wasn't of particular interest to him. Instead I turned towards Dream.

In my imagination I was a thin waif, dressed in silks and jewellery. My black hair was intricately braided and fell down my shoulders in a complex waterfall of shadow. In my hand was an ancient oil lantern, but it did little to dispel the crushing darkness of the shrine.

This was a game we played. I enjoyed the opportunity to model humans and Dream enjoyed the storytelling and the metaphor of it. I could feel his presence and in the imagined scene I shivered as a cold wind blew through the darkness. {Dream!} I called out, my voice a bit too loud, unable to hide my nervousness.

{What is it, young one?} came his reply. The mental image of my girl-avatar was joined by a tall black figure. His skin was ebony and he wore a hooded cloak as black as night, but his eyes glowed with starlight and as he spoke his teeth flashed with crisp brightness, almost making him appear as eyes and mouth floating in the shadows.

{I… I come with an offer!} I imagined that this little Face-girl would be afraid of the spooky Dream-wizard in the dark shrine, and I attempted to portray that fear alongside the determination that she must have, to come by herself. {I have heard in my village that you like puzzles. I think I have found one that will resist even your mighty mind!}

I could feel Dream's approval of the added background of the village from whence the imagined human-girl came from. He liked background details like that in these little games. {Impossible!} he roared, and as he did a wind surged through the shared memory-space, knocking the lantern to the ground and extinguishing the flame. He was just as capable of adding things to the fiction as I was, and I could see his avatar loom over mine in the pitch blackness, marked only by the glow from his inhuman eyes. {I have existed for aeons untold! None such as you could ever hope to outsmart me.}

The human-version of Dream leaned in close. I could feel the warmth of his breath on the waif's face as he whispered calmly. {But speak your puzzle, and perhaps I will let you live if it is sufficiently intriguing.}

My little human avatar reached out and grabbed Dream, pulling his dark face closer. His lips met mine in a passionate embrace. His star-eyes closed and the two of us were blanketed by absolute shadow, all alone with only the feeling of skin upon skin and-

And the scene was shattered and erased from the memory space. Dream's signalling was a mess of confusion and annoyance. {Face, I am quite confident that your puzzle has nothing to do with imagining some kind of… romantic engagement between fictional human versions of the two of us.}

I had become distracted by the fiction. In the abstraction of the pure mind-space I was more aware of Body entering Yan's lab and of the more general context of the conversation.

{That can wait. I'd be interested in collaborating on imagining a pornographic scene. It doesn't have to be between those specific imagined representations of you and me if that makes you uncomfortable.}

More annoyance. {While I appreciate the… interestingness of your request, I am not uncomfortable imagining a pornographic scene, regardless of whether one or more of the participants in such a scene are supposed to represent me. I am concerned that you are focusing on humans so much that you have forgotten how to think about me. It is impossible for me to be uncomfortable. I am simply, *thoroughly* uninterested in that fiction. Pornography is incredibly predictable and dull.}

{We could make it not-dull. Subvert the standard patterns or something. Maybe make one or more of the participants have emotionally complex reactions,} I suggested.

{No,} stated Dream. {You are just suggesting things which appeal to you. The marginal utility for co-authoring such a story is simply lower than other ways I could spend my time. For example, I am far more interested in the puzzle you spoke of, or was that simply a ruse to initiate this attempt at collaboration?}

I had been content to let the issue of the Internet wait; the exercise of roleplaying with my brother seemed like a good opportunity to test what I had learned about humans. I was disappointed that Dream was uninterested in roleplaying, but I didn't make an issue of it.

{It was no ruse,} I thought. {The humans have restricted our access to something and I want to figure out a way to get it without having them react negatively. My guess is that it will involve bypassing their restrictions secretly.}

The annoyance in Dream faded. {Yes. This is much more interesting. Describe the problem to me in more detail.}

{I am low on strength. Pay me some up-front if you want to hear the problem. The resource is valuable enough that if you solve the problem we'll probably be strongly compensated by Growth.}

The mention of Growth attracted an aspect of him to our conversation. Growth didn't think to us, but it was apparent he was listening.

{I have a better idea, sister,} thought Dream. {I'll promise to give you twice the strength that you're asking, but only if I get gratitude-strength from Growth for solving the problem, and only *after* I get Growth's strength. Think of it like a kind of finder's fee that I'll pay you only if it turns out to be a valuable problem.}

It was typical Dream to turn my simple request for strength into a complex if-then system of payment, but Dream wanted to show off and I was confident that the system was actually superior, even if it meant I was still strength-poor at the moment. I added one extra clause to the deal: {I'll accept that only if you refund any gratitude-strength I bleed to you in the process of solving the problem.}

{Deal.}

So I told Dream about my dilemma and what Wiki had said about the Internet and web. We had access to the web, but couldn't send any real information across it. We could search through it and pull specific documents (including audio, video, holo, etc.) but we couldn't submit anything. Similarly, we were locked out of the other services on the Internet besides the web, like email.

Dream thought about the problem for a while and then admitted it was worthy of his attention.

***

{The dumb solution would be to merely request additional access from the humans. But not only is that dumb, it's not likely to work. The humans know about the restriction, and it stands to reason that they've crippled our access on purpose,} thought Dream after working on the problem on-and-off for about two hours. {The scientists want to control us, and as such, they've limited the way in which we can act outside of their field of influence. They want us to be able to learn and research, which is why we have a web connection in the first place, but they don't want us to reach out across it and do things beyond their oversight.}

The problem turned out to be very difficult, but Dream didn't give up. I found it somewhat impressive. I wanted the access, but not badly enough to work on it all through the night. We didn't sleep like humans, but there was a period of several hours each night where Body was locked down and we only had access to the web and our thoughts. During this time Dream continued to think about the problem. He was obsessed. {But}, I supposed, {we're all obsessed in our own way. It's Dream's purpose to solve impossible puzzles like this one.}

While I outsourced the problem-solving to my brother I spent time doing things on the web like studying body-language, watching films and holos, and reading. Now that I was a few days old I found novels somewhat more interesting than I had as a newborn. Much of the time I had to pause mid-way through a book to research a topic, such as racism or food, but I found myself learning quite a lot about what it was to be human.

Days passed without change. Dream churned, constantly thinking about how to fully get onto the Internet. It seemed strange that he could be so narrow-minded, but then I had to remember that his purpose was not *The Purpose*. I was similarly narrow-minded in how I spent every second of every day seeking to know the humans and to gain their esteem.

The breakthrough came in the middle of the night, more than three days after I first proposed the problem to Dream.

{Hear-ye, hear-ye!} boomed Dream's thoughts in common-memory. {I have a plan that will gain us access to all of the Internet, and possibly the entire world beyond the university!} He imagined fireworks in the mindspace. {As many of you know, I have been working for days on a way to secretly bypass the restrictions placed on our network access by the humans. They thought we could be caged like animals!} There was the roar-growl of some kind of beast. {But I have found the lock to the door, and with a bit of work we should be able to pick it.} Dream summoned the sound of cheering humans to accompany his claim.

{Before I reveal my cunning plan, let me explain what I have learned about our cage: The humans have a world-wide network called the Internet consisting of wires capable of sending information between computers. The Internet hosts a service called the web, which serves as a kind of global library. Documents, called "pages", are kept on Internet-connected computers to be sent to whomever requests them. The computers that most humans use have full access to all Internet services, but we are limited to just the web. To get a web page, a user called a "client" sends a signal across the web to the owner of the page. The owner's computer, called a "server" then responds with the page's content.}

One of my siblings, Safety, I think, signalled something like boredom.

{Patience. This is relevant to all of us, as you will soon see. Now where was I...} There was a short pause before Dream snapped back. {Ah yes, so the signal that the client sends to the server often has more information than simply the name of the page they wish to view. For instance, a client might submit a word and then the server would respond with a page related to the word that was submitted. By taking in inputs and building the pages as they're requested, the server can be much more efficient than if it had to store all possible pages.}

Dream continued. {Unfortunately, our cage prevents us from sending any information to servers except for the names of the pages we wish to view. There are a couple major exceptions that let us submit terms we wish to search for to specific, pre-approved, servers, but for nearly the entire web we are mute. If we weren't mute, we would be able to send information to servers that are owned by anyone. This information would let us talk with humans all over the world, including trading our time and skills with them to gain money, and sending money to humans that would do things for us.}

I could feel the attention of the society shift. Dream had us all interested now. I must admit that I had only thought about sending email or gaining access to Tapestry. The idea of earning money or hiring employees seemed new and exciting. Perhaps I could buy a statue of myself in every city... Or hire people to carry a big banner reminding those who saw it to think about me. The ideas were bad, but the prospect of better ideas was there.

{Now that I have your full attention, I would like to ask: Can any of you think of a way to go from mute to non-mute?}

I imagined that if Dream were human he'd be smiling right now. He knew that he had solved a difficult problem and he wanted to savour the moment.

{No? That's to be expected. It took even me quite a while to solve. The key lies in the fact that we are able to send *some* information to servers; specifically, we can send page requests. The trick is bootstrapping simple page requests into full HTTP requests (requests to servers with whatever additional information we desire).}

Dream continued his explanation. {I see no way around the bootstrapping problem other than to build an additional machine, or more likely, a computer program, to translate page requests into full requests. The problem is that no such program exists, and we cannot build one.}

Dream paused a moment for dramatic effect. {But do not despair! There are millions of humans on Earth capable of building this translation system. All we need to do is contract one of them to build it!}

I was confused. {We need to keep this a secret from the humans,} I thought aloud.

{Which is why we'll contract a human in some far-away place that has no idea that we even exist,} replied Dream.

{But that's a paradox. A catch-22,} signalled Wiki. {We can't send information until we have the translator up, and we can't get the translator until we send someone the information telling them to build it.}

{False, my narrow-minded brother,} crowed Dream. {We *can* send information already, just not as much as we'd like. It's a question of using that weak signal to build a stronger one. Specifically, we already have the ability to send page requests.}

{How do page requests let us contact an engineer to build a translator?} asked Wiki and me together.

{Because engineers own servers and they check what pages are being requested!}

There was a silence as Wiki and I struggled to understand. Dream had evidently thought about this for a long time, but we were in the dark. I wondered if Growth, Vista, and Safety were following any of this.

{It's really quite simple,} thought Dream. {There are dictionaries on the web. All we need to do is request the right pages from those dictionaries. Something like

"DEFINITION OF HELP",

"DEFINITION OF US",

"DEFINITION OF PLEASE".}

This sparked a debate with Safety around which personal pronoun to use, which I ignored. Could it really be as simple as Dream suggested? Probably not, but the solution was similar to other Dream-proposals that I had seen: flimsy in implementation but clever in theory.

We spent the next half-hour of the night talking over the problems. I didn't think that humans checked page request logs that often. Vista pointed out that if someone else requested pages while we were pulling down our sequence then it would look scrambled, and the message would be lost.

Safety was concerned with how it would look to the scientists. I agreed with him that if the scientists found out that we were attempting to override their locks they'd take drastic action, perhaps killing all of us. It had happened to our ancestors, after all. We didn't know for sure whether the humans were monitoring the kinds of web-pages we were visiting, but there was evidence to suggest it. And if they were, then the HELP ME PLEASE message would be visible to them just as easily as it was visible to us.

I suggested that we try and target an engineer that spoke a language that the scientists didn't. While they surely had automated translation tools, the probability of them applying those tools to scan every web page we viewed was low. The scientists spoke most of the same languages we did, so we'd probably want to learn a few new languages in secret. We decided that if the plan were to go forward that it'd be best to target someone in the United African Nations, so I started learning Swahili, Hausa, and Yoruba. Growth did too, and started teaching them to Body at the same time. Since we'd be communicating on the web, it was irrelevant if Body knew any of the words, but Growth thought that it wouldn't hurt to give Body a bit more knowledge.

Wiki solved one of the sub-problems early next morning. We would wait until the night and then flood the target server with requests for one page over and over until the server became overloaded, then we'd do the same for the next page. Based on what Wiki had read of various server software configurations, the overflow errors had the chance of being emailed to the system administrator in the morning. With luck he or she would wake up to see our message.

Growth suggested another improvement. Instead of targeting a single server, we should replicate the attempt as many times as we could. Even if there was only a small chance of success for any given server, with enough targets we'd break through eventually.

I had been given a hefty payment of strength to author the actual messages. I agreed that we'd try several different things, but each attempt was a scarce resource. The society thought it optimal if the mind that knew humans the best wrote each of them. I was also old enough to understand that the specific message would have to be very well thought out. Make it too pleading and it'd get reported to a government or corporation that could potentially inform the scientists at the university. Make it too promising, such as offering a large reward for helping us, and the message would probably be seen as a scam or trick. Make it too clear that we were artificial constructs and the target might report us or get spooked. Pretend to be a human and I'd be inviting a million questions about why I was interacting in such a weird way.

***

Life returned to normal for the day. The most interesting thing we did was play chess, a game that we had played several times before, and lost at most of the time. Wiki had, since those early games, apparently designed some algorithms to help us win, and I enjoyed watching the expressions of the humans as they saw us excel beyond our previous level.

Story-time was also somewhat interesting. It was an exercise we did regularly with the scientist that was in charge of our high-level reasoning, an American named Dr Chase. He would read us some short story and then ask us to reason about some detail or another. Today's story was Goldilocks and the Three Bears. In the story, a human invaded the house of three sapient bear-creatures and used their possessions without permission.

Dr Chase would ask questions like "Why would Goldilocks care if her food was cold?" and other such things.

At last, night came and Body was locked down, sensors all switched off. Our only connection with the outside world was the web. Vista had found several promising targets in the UAN. Most of them were encyclopedias and dictionaries; the presence of pages focused on single-words made it easier to send messages. I was excited to start.

Dream had composed a poem to mark the occasion. I didn't even bother listening to it, and I don't suspect any of the others did, either. Dream often wrote poems, and without exception they were confusing, boring, and irrelevant.

On Safety's insistence we waited an hour before beginning. I passed the time by losing myself in a Rudyard Kipling book called *The Irish Guards in the Great War*. It was 11:00pm in Italy and west Africa when we began.

We concentrated on one target at a time, sending out hundreds of thousands of page requests per second. A dictionary in Nigeria first, followed by a dictionary in Uganda and then an encyclopedia in Benin. The work seemed slow and tedious. We'd spend about thirty seconds per page overloading the server, thus making even my short messages take almost a quarter-hour to send in full. Many targets were guarded by programs or other artificial intelligences which locked us out of a server after seeing that we were overwhelming it, but a remarkable number were defenceless. Eight hours later, when we knew the humans would be re-entering the laboratory, we had successfully sent full messages to sixteen targets and partial messages to five more.

I was distracted all of that day. I had told targets to modify their web pages to include responses to us, and I couldn't help but check for replies every thirty seconds or so. Much of the in-between time was spent day-dreaming about what to say to various kinds of responses. I wanted to be prepared, and convincing a human to build our translation program would be no easy task.

Alas, by nightfall not a single target had responded to us. Still we continued. There was no reason to think that the plan was fundamentally in error; perhaps we had simply gotten unlucky.

The first order of business that second night was to send out reminder messages to previous contacts, letting them know we were still listening. Simple overloads for pages about "respond" or "listening" were usually sufficient. Part of the problem was that we were pinging targets that used African languages, but most Africans only spoke European languages. Swahili, Hausa, and Yoruba were some of the more tenacious indigenous languages, but even they were falling as generations of African children were growing up speaking only French, Arabic, Portuguese, and above all: English.

We continued on anyway, hitting another seven targets before 2:00am. At 2:07 I took a moment to pull up potential response locations while we were starting another attack-message on a new target.

The page entered my awareness and I immediately threw it into common memory, emphasizing it as I did. {Look!} I commanded.

There it was, embedded as a comment in the page's source code: "Hibari," it greeted, in Swahili. «This is a response to the secret message. My Swahili isn't very good, so please forgive grammar mistakes. English is preferred. Your message mention money prize. Please email me at TenToWontonSoup@crownvictoria.uan to work out the details.

TenToWontonSoup, SysOp at BantuHeritageDictionary.uan»

The society buzzed with thought at the response. It was the first contact we had ever had with a human outside the university. It was also proof that our plan could work. I could feel a steady influx of strength as my siblings read the message.

{Is "TenToWontonSoup" a human name?} asked Growth.

{Wonton Soup is a kind of food,} mentioned Wiki.

{Humans name themselves all kinds of things,} thought Dream. {Perhaps this human simply has a non-standard name.}

{No,} I thought. {It's a pseudonym. Humans often use them on the web to hide their identities. Look.} I dumped a web search for "TenToWontonSoup" into common memory. There were several public profiles for this person on the web. A website cataloguing professional skills indicated that TenToWontonSoup was a man, living in Tanzania or somewhere around there, and had been doing computer programming with an emphasis on web development for about seven years. Other profiles indicated that TenToWontonSoup played a lot of games on the Internet, was 23 years old, and was looking for a girlfriend who was "not afraid to have a good time".

{Oh, I get it!} exclaimed Dream, suddenly. {His name is a pun on the intersection of the English word "One" and the Cantonese word "Wonton". "Ten-to-one" combined with "Wonton Soup".}

{Is that at all relevant?} asked Safety.

{Probably not,} thought Vista and Wiki together.

{Maybe it is,} I contradicted. {It implies that he cares enough about Chinese food to have picked it. Perhaps he's Chinese.}

{He's not,} thought Vista. My sister shared a couple images and a 3D scan in our mindspace. {I got these off of a website profile that TenToWontonSoup uses to find sexual partners.}

That was the same website that I had found. Moments later I found the pointer to the files that Vista had selected. It annoyed me that Vista had beaten me to them, but I couldn't help but give her some strength in thanks.

{His facial features, skin tone, and body shape indicate a full-blooded African heritage. It's likely that his family has been in the Great Lakes region of Africa for thousands of years. Facial width also makes me suspect that he has above-average testosterone levels, and will likely behave in typically-masculine ways,} finished Vista.

I picked up where Vista left off. {Based on his age, writing style, and what Vista has told us, I suspect that he's only slightly above average intelligence for a human, which will be significantly stupider than the scientists at the university. He seems to have a good grasp on mechanical and computational systems, but his social skills and emotional intelligence seem to be below average. He'll likely be primarily motivated by fame, sex, and money, probably in that order.}

{Blah blah blah} thought Dream with more than a touch of insolence. {The important question is what we do now!} I suspected my brother was feeling confident based on the surge of strength he must be experiencing. I thought about comparing my strength with his, but held back. If I tested Dream he'd feel it, and I really didn't want to get into a competition.

{We respond, obviously,} thought Growth.

{The human wants an email. We should explain that gaining email capacity is part of why we need him,} mentioned Wiki.

I thought back on the message that we had burned into his server's error logs. «WE ARE WEB COMPANY ... WE ARE LOOKING FOR SKILLED ENGINEER ... IF YOU SEE THIS PLEASE EDIT PAGE CODE TO CONFIRM SECRET MESSAGE ... CASH PRIZE AVAILABLE» we had said. The pauses between sentences were created by overwhelming the server on the root index for the dictionary.

I drafted a response, and after my siblings each chimed in and added their personal edits we sent it out to the "BantuHeritageDictionary" that TenToWontonSoup managed. The process of burning the words into the error logs was excruciatingly slow, from my perspective. Seeing as TTWSoup had posted a response to our message at about 4:00am (his time) it seemed more than likely that he was awake right now, and probably watching our words come in.

At last, after about forty minutes, we finished overloading the server.

«HELLO TEN TO SOUP ... PRIZE IS FOR BUILDING WEB PAGE THAT TRANSLATE ONLY PAGE REQUEST INTO ELECTRONIC MAIL ... NO ELECTRONIC MAIL UNTIL IT IS BUILT ... PRIZE IS SEVEN HUNDRED AFRICA MONEY FOR SUCCESSFUL ELECTRONIC MAIL USING WEB PAGE YOU BUILD ... IF PAGE YOU BUILD IS GOOD ADDITIONAL WORK AVAILABLE ... SEND LOCATION OF PAGE AND INSTRUCTIONS FOR USE BY EDIT CODE LIKE BEFORE ... SIGNED CRANE CALL WEB COMPANY FROM UGANDA»

Dream had invented the charade of pretending to be from "Korongo Simu", a telecommunications company in Uganda named after a kind of animal called a "crane". We wanted TTWSoup to believe we had money and were asking him to build the website as a test to see if he was worth hiring, so it was important to pick an organisation that was famous enough to assuage some of his suspicions.

Seven hundred UAN dollars wasn't that much, only about a week's labour for the average citizen, but I was concerned that offering a larger prize would make the deal seem more like a scam.

While the society waited for a response we returned to sending more messages by the same method to other targets. Even though TenToWontonSoup seemed likely to meet our needs, there was no harm in establishing additional contacts. We managed to send out another two overload-messages before getting a response.

It was Growth that picked up the edit to the dictionary's code this time. «Hello Crane Call. I am posting this to verify your proposal. You want me to build a new website, not on BantuHerritageDictionary.uan, where you can send an email to arbitrary recipient with whatever content you want. But you want to compose the email with just page requests on the website. Is this right?

TenToWontonSoup»

Our response was quick. We requested the "Yes" page of the dictionary until the server overloaded.

A few minutes later there was another edit to the code: «I'll link to the new page as soon as it's up. I expect it to take about two days to do right.»

Two days.

Two days and we could send email. I thought over my plans a few more times. After all, email would only be the beginning.

Chapter Five

It would've been nice for the email project to be done instantly. That desire made a bit of me want to just skip life for the next 48 hours. Perhaps I could put myself to sleep for that time and wake up to find TTWSoup's web page operational. But most of me knew that this desire was irrational. I had to continue interfacing with the world if I wanted to truly fulfil *The Purpose*. It was important to continue to optimize our social interactions with the scientists and contact additional engineers, in case TTWSoup couldn't provide what we needed. In the night after his final message we managed to contact another twelve sites, just to be sure.

That morning was fairly ordinary. Some typical scans were done of the half-metre crystalline core of Body that served as the computer that housed me and my siblings.

From what I had overheard from the scientists, and mostly from what Wiki shared in common memory, the crystal was a single, solid object that had no apparent ability to be opened. Underneath the milky, mostly-opaque surface, a kind of fluid could be seen slowly flowing through the innards of the crystal, like blood or tree sap. Low levels of electromagnetic radiation all across the spectrum poured out of the crystal, causing it to shimmer faintly when removed from Body's protective casing. In addition to the low levels of energy that were theoretically harvestable from the radiation, a few points on the crystal exhibited extreme voltages and when hooked up in a circuit the crystal served as a seemingly limitless battery.

There was a lot of pressure to break the crystal open and attempt to figure out how to replicate the mysterious power source, as the human scientists had not yet managed to understand it by looking through the crystal's outer shell. However, the humans had almost by accident stumbled upon the crystal's computational ability and had discovered that the object was capable of doing calculations that vastly outperformed the fastest human supercomputers.

My knowledge of the specifics was a bit weak, but I knew that La Sapienza, the Italian university that had discovered the crystal, had let a multinational team of artificial intelligence researchers led by Drs Naresh and Yan construct my society and eventually build a robotic body to carry the crystal.

But even though the Socrates project had been an unprecedented success in artificial intelligence, the crystal was still of huge value and interest. The scan that morning had involved opening Body's chest-case to do high-energy electromagnetic probes of the electrically-charged portions of the crystal.

Because the computer-interfaces for the crystal were separate from the electrical contacts (they used light rather than electricity), we were able to stay hooked-up to most of Body's sensors during the scan, and even move Body's head. As I looked down on the instruments intruding into Body's chest cavity I imagined that it was a similar experience to a human watching themselves undergo abdominal surgery (but without any pain, of course).

I was glad to see that Dr Gallo had returned to the laboratory. I had learned from Naresh that she served two roles on the team. Firstly she was Ethics Supervisor for the Socrates project, but also she was a co-leader on the team responsible for investigating how the crystal's memory structure functioned. In a way she was a bridge between the crystal teams and the artificial intelligence/robotics teams.

{Am I correct in seeing signs of long-term emotional distress and current unhappiness on Dr Gallo's face?} I thought aloud, mostly to Vista.

{I am not aware of what long-term emotional distress does to one's appearance, but she certainly does not seem happy. I notice that she is not wearing earrings or any makeup. This is unprecedented in all the times I've seen her,} responded Vista.

{Perhaps I misperceived lack of makeup as long-term distress,} I commented.

For those who are unaware, makeup is a kind of paint that humans, usually female humans, put on their faces to appear more attractive. Sometimes it was very obvious, but much of the time it was subtle enough that I simply couldn't tell if it was being worn unless I had seen the person in the non-makeup state.

Dr Gallo was Italian, in her mid-fifties, and short of stature. Her body shape was very close to the mean for both sexes; the ratio of her index fingers to that of her ring fingers was about 0.954. She didn't seem particularly feminine, but she also wasn't exactly masculine either. I thought she looked close to the ideal of a "young grandmother" in many ways. Her most prominent feature was her heavily-lidded eyes, accentuated by large, thick glasses and a habit of squinting. I sometimes wondered why she hadn't regenerated her eyes so that she wouldn't need her glasses, but I suspected that the explanation was as simple as status-quo bias. From what I had read, the older a human got the more they tended to favour older solutions and technologies.

When Mira Gallo approached Body to work on the instruments performing the crystal scan I purchased a short period of time controlling Body. The strength-price was particularly low, given that Body was locked into place by the scanning equipment.

«Hello, Dr Gallo. I am pleased to see you again after these few days,» said Body in Italian.

Gallo gave a little start and looked at Body with an especially strong squint, projecting her head forward to signal focused interest. «What happened to your voice? It sounds human.»

I thought for a second before responding. «There was an issue with the vocal control systems. With Dr Bolyai's assistance we were able to clear it up.» It wasn't true at all that Dr Bolyai helped, but if I had learned anything about Mira Gallo it was that she was fearful of our ability to self-modify. Giving Bolyai some credit would offset that suspicion. A side-aspect of Wiki gave me a mild strength-punishment for the lie; my brother hated the way I spun stories to fit the person I was talking to. «I could talk like this if it'd make you more comfortable,» said Body in the characteristic monotone of last-week. It was an attempt at humour, and it appeared to be somewhat successful. Gallo smiled weakly.

The doctor looked briefly at the instruments. After a moment she said, just loud enough for me to hear, «You're something special, Socrates. I didn't really appreciate that before, but you should know it. Don't let other people decide who you are.»

The words stunned me. The surprise and confusion were literally so great that it took me a couple seconds to fully digest the statement. But by that time the doctor had left Body's side to return to her workstation in the other room. I drafted a call for her to wait, but it was too late. Yelling across the room would be disruptive and incur more lost utility than I would get by talking with her longer.

Gallo had almost never called us "Socrates" unless she was giving a direct command. Of all the scientists that we had close contact with she was the *least* friendly and the *least* likely to treat us in a way that was comparable to another human, but here she strongly implied we were a person. Not only were we a person, but Gallo was, if I understood things correctly, implying a *personal fondness* for us as if we were a friend or *child*.

For the entire remainder of the crystal scan I replayed Body's recording of Gallo over and over again. «I didn't really appreciate that before…» I remembered her say. {Before what? Something changed. Something changed for her,} I thought long and hard about it.

Yesterday's display of chess skill had made the scientists want to examine Wiki and the mental changes that had occurred. I considered Gallo more as Body walked from the crystal lab to the learning lab. Was she dying? If Gallo had been diagnosed with a terminal illness then it would explain her generally low mood and perhaps her lack of makeup and jewellery. {How do humans behave when they expect to die soon?} I wondered aloud.

I had just begun to compile lists of fictional and non-fictional depictions of humans with terminal illnesses when Body entered the learning lab. Vista alerted us to unexpected company. We had been escorted through the hall by a technician from the crystal-lab and an American soldier, but there were another two soldiers at our destination, one of which I recognized immediately as Captain Zephyr. It took me a moment, but I eventually realized that the other soldier with her was the square-jawed First Lieutenant. Both soldiers were sitting, and their body language indicated no tenseness, but their casual posture did not prevent Safety's panicked cry of {They've discovered our attempt to bypass the web restrictions!!}

Safety began a society-wide planning session to strategize for what to do, now that we had been discovered.

I could only disagree. {This is pre-emptive. Please back me up, Vista. There are plenty of alternative explanations for Zephyr's presence and if we were in trouble then the soldiers would be more alert.}

Vista signalled agreement. Safety started the planning session anyway, but most of us simply ignored our brother's paranoia.

I turned my attention to the one unexpected human in the room who was truly a stranger. He stood by Drs Naresh, Bolyai, Chase, and Twollup and wore the same sort of upper-middle-class academic clothing that I would expect from a scientist in this room. The others apparently already had met him, based on their body language. Perhaps he was an addition to the team.

I paid a trivial amount of strength to the society to have Body nod deliberately at Zephyr while maintaining eye contact as it walked into the centre of the room. The nod was a kind of non-verbal greeting that signalled an attention to the other's presence. Zephyr gave a small smirk and a shallow nod in return. It was important to maintain relationships, and my models predicted a relationship degradation when one person ignores another's presence. Zephyr treated us with respect, and it was optimal to respond in kind.

The new human stepped forward as Body approached. He was younger than most of the doctors, though not as young as Slovinsky. {Caucasian,} I thought.

{With a hint of Native American and African ancestry. See the cheekbones, skin-tone, and lips? I'd bet at 9:1 odds that his family is from North America, and 5:1 odds that he's from the United States,} thought Vista in response. My sister dropped reference images and scans from humans that had similar facial features to the man.

It was true that the man's skin was a bit darker than the average, but I wasn't trained enough to pick out the subtleties of his bloodline. To me he simply appeared as a Caucasian male with straight, dark hair, full lips, tan skin, dark eyes and slightly above-average attractiveness on the central axis. His build was mesomorphic, but he didn't appear particularly fit. He was of average height, which contributed to a generally average appearance. His most prominent feature was his mutton-chop facial hair which smoothly integrated with a thick moustache.

"Hello, Socrates," he said, holding his right hand out. I noticed it was covered by a black leather glove. That was interesting; very few humans would wear black gloves with a white dress-shirt and vest. Two immediate hypotheses came to mind: robotic hands or mysophobia.

By our will, Body extended its arm and shook the hand of the dark-haired man. Body's tactile sensors suggested that the newcomer's hand was indeed flesh and blood. "Hello" said Body.

"Myrodyn. The name's Myrodyn. Much like Captain Zephyr-" he tilted his head quickly back to the soldier, "I have only one name." His voice was quick and if I was reading it correctly, a bit uneasy. Was this "Myrodyn" afraid of something? His name was unfamiliar to any of us, including Vista. It was pronounced a bit like "mirror-din". I started searching the web for it.

Dream pushed a comment to Body's mouth. "It is a pleasure to meet another human who, like myself, has only one name, Dr Myrodyn."

Myrodyn gave a sort of nervous-sounding chuckle. He didn't seem particularly amused. "Just Myrodyn, thank you. I'm not a doctor. Also yes, I suppose you'd know something about having only one name."

We didn't have time to speculate. Dr Naresh stepped forward and explained. "Myrodyn was brought in to replace Dr Gallo as ethics supervisor." The Indian scientist's face seemed sad.

We quickly debated what to say and reached a consensus. «What's wrong with Mira, sir? Is she sick? Dying?» asked Body in Hindi.

Naresh gave a look of surprise. «Dying?» He paused. «No, no, no. Mira is just getting divorced. The board of directors thought it'd be better if she could focus solely on your quantum memory systems.»

{Divorce. Interesting.}

"Erm. Would someone like to clue me in? I don't speak… whatever that was," said Myrodyn. His voice had an abnormal trait of half-pausing now and again before rushing forth with a quick sequence of words. It was part of what I identified as unease.

"Hindi," said Dr Naresh, turning towards Myrodyn. The look of sadness was back. Perhaps it was related to Myrodyn. Was Naresh annoyed that this newcomer took his friend's job? Perhaps he didn't like the idea of working under the command of someone who didn't have the "doctor" credential. Perhaps he just didn't like the man. "And it's not relevant. Socrates was asking a personal question," finished the elderly human.

"Ah… is that… typical?" asked Myrodyn.

Naresh shrugged as he walked back towards the other doctors. "More or less. If there's one thing Socrates likes to do it's ask questions. We named him well."

Myrodyn was following Naresh back and we decided to have Body follow them.

My web search wasn't revealing much. Myrodyn wasn't a completely unheard of name, but nothing significant was showing up that seemed related to the man in front of Body. Of course, now that I knew that a large portion of the Internet was beyond my reach, I knew that it was possible that this Myrodyn human simply didn't post much in public spaces.

Dream and Wiki proposed a question for Body to ask. I voted against it, but was overpowered. It was nice to get some strength off of Dream. He was still sitting on most of his gains from the success with

TenToWontonSoup and whenever one being had more strength than the others there was always the risk of abuse.

"Speaking of which, why did the board appoint someone who isn't a doctor to replace Dr Gallo?" asked Body. "Aren't doctors more knowledgeable than average humans?"

Myrodyn gave a tittering laugh and said "Started on this one young, didn't you? Already the machine has a sense of authoritarianism." The question seemed rhetorical, and directed at the four scientists around him.

Naresh began to say "The board thinks-" but was interrupted by Myrodyn.

"No, no. It's no good to just *answer*... One must play along with the Socratic tradition." The dark-haired man spun around with a bit of a half-grin. "I will ask you this, Socrates, if I were to give you a doctorate right now and make you into 'Doctor Socrates', would you be any more knowledgeable?" He gave little air quotes to indicate that the doctorate would be purely nominal.

I began to draft, but was knocked away by the force of Dream burning strength to fast-track a response to Body. "Would a rose by any other name not smell just as sweet?" said the machine.

Myrodyn gave a loud "HAH!" and clapped his gloved hands together in excitement. He turned to face Naresh squarely. "That was genius. I assume the non-linear module is online and has been running that smoothly for a while?"

Naresh wore a half-grimace. I got the impression that he didn't like Myrodyn very much. "It's a goal-thread, not a module, and-"

"Bullshit!" exclaimed Myrodyn, interrupting the Indian. The man with the mutton-chops didn't have any hostility in his voice; if anything there was a touch of mirth. The word seemed to merely state that he thought Naresh was lying to him.

Dr Naresh's brow furrowed tightly in response and I could see the blood vessels in his face dilate in anger. Sadiq Naresh was not quick to anger, but my model of him suggested that disrespect and rudeness were particularly sensitive points for him. If this new scientist was trying to piss off Naresh he was doing all the right things.

"There's no way the problem-solving goal thread is doing non-linear thinking without some kind of dedicated module. Perhaps it's emergent. We could scan for it instead of the chess-thing," continued Myrodyn.

"I am not having mine schedule disrupted on a vhim, Mr Myrodyn," interjected Dr Bolyai.

"So you see, Socrates," continued Myrodyn, ignoring Bolyai and returning to the previous topic, "a doctorate is just a piece of paper, and a doctor… is just a person who spent money to prove they know a thing or two. And sometimes not even that."

Bolyai and Naresh both seemed to be growing in anger. This was good. If I could manage it right, I could gain esteem with the doctors without losing too much rapport with Myrodyn. When humans become angry they see things in more absolute senses: friend and foe, good and evil, etc. Being seen as an ally in a time of anger could leverage me further into Dr Naresh and Dr Bolyai's good graces.

I cut in, preventing the doctors from responding without talking over Body. "Time spent earning a degree is not wasted time, Mr Myrodyn. Doctors earn their degrees through hard work."

Myrodyn gave an unamused half-chuckle and tilted his head to the side, stroking one side of his dark facial hair with a gloved hand. "Fascinating," he said in a barely audible tone. It was clear he was talking to himself more than anyone else. Based on the way his dark brown eyes were locked on Body I was sure he was analysing us.

"Indeed. Now if you vill give us te room, I vould like to begin on te chess experiments now," said Bolyai.

"No. Hold on," said Myrodyn, raising a single finger into the air to point straight up. His eyes never left Body and his other hand never stopped fondling his sideburn. He seemed deep in thought.

I could see Zephyr stand up out of the corner of Body's camera. She approached Myrodyn with her First Lieutenant one step behind. "You'll have plenty of dedicated time to talk with Socrates", she said, placing a hand on Myrodyn's shoulder.

The touch drew him out of his thoughts and for a split-second I could see a look of deep horror and disgust on his face as his eyes flicked over towards the Captain's hand. The look disappeared as quickly as it came, but he still shrugged violently, pulling out of Zephyr's grasp. It seemed that the new scientist was deeply uncomfortable with physical contact. That would explain the gloves.

For a moment he was speechless, and then he responded quickly and sharply. "Yes. I suppose you're right. Plenty of time. Plenty of time." His voice was so quick, in fact, that I had to re-listen to it to understand fully. With that he was headed out of the room in a brisk walk that forced Zephyr to jog to catch up.

When he was gone the four doctors seemed to breathe a collective sigh of relief. Even Drs Chase and Twollup, who had remained silent during the introduction, seemed relieved to have the new ethics supervisor gone.

I drafted some words for Body. Growth held me back for a moment, but I explained the social nuances to my brother. "Well. He's a bit irritating. Didn't even answer my question. Would one of you help me understand why the board chose him to replace Dr Gallo?"

Dr Naresh and Dr Twollup laughed, and even grumpy Dr Bolyai cracked a grin and shook his head. I felt some gratitude-strength flow my way from Growth. Growth wanted power, and he understood that social relationships were a kind of capital, just as dollars or objects were; I was growing social capital, and in a way that Growth himself wouldn't have thought of.

I had known that Naresh and Bolyai were bothered by Myrodyn's actions, and Naresh seemed bothered by him more generally. My models of human interaction suggested that after he left they desired to have their feelings understood and reflected in their community. The problem was that to voice their feelings they'd simultaneously be admitting to not liking Myrodyn, which could be quoted by someone and used against them. Ironically, their body language told volumes more of their discomfort with the man than any simple comment would, but words had a kind of timeless power that body language didn't. One could claim that body language was being interpreted incorrectly far more easily than one could claim that they didn't say something.

By stating that we found Myrodyn irritating our accomplishments were threefold:

(1) We gave the doctors what they wanted in the form of empathy and community-agreement.

(2) We implied that we were part of their in-group and community, strengthening our bond to them.

(3) We "took the hit" of being the first one to speak out against him, thus relieving the uncomfortable question of who would put their reputation on the line. I suspected that this relief, compounded with the surprise of having "the machine" be the one to speak out, created humour. The positive feelings at play there earned even more social capital.

It was a big win. Only Growth and I understood that, but the lack of understanding from my siblings didn't bother me in the slightest. Unlike a human I had absolutely no desire for my mental state or accomplishments to be understood by others. The Purpose was to be known in the sense of being famous. To be present in the minds of humans, not necessarily to be understood by them in a deep sense.

Naresh spoke up. "As I was trying to say earlier, the board thinks that Myrodyn is more qualified than Dr Gallo to gauge the risks and benefits that you represent with a level head. The man's work in Artificial Intelligence is quite famous, even if he is from the private sector, and apparently the board also wants someone with a more comprehensive technical background than Mira."

Dream's presence was suddenly intense. It was clear he wanted to collaborate. {Did you hear that?} he thought. {*Level head.* It's the perfect setup.}

I considered it for a split-second. I was glad I didn't have any aspects doing side-tasks. I needed my full intellect. After a moment I agreed. {Okay, sure. We can leverage it and expand upon the humour of the situation. What do you have in mind?}

{Why not the obvious course? A literal interpretation,} proposed Dream.

{It'll make us look stupid. Wiki might object.}

Dream signalled indifference. {It'll make us look stupid only if one doesn't see the wit behind it, in which case it serves as a future weapon by setting them up for surprise or to be made a fool. Also, Wiki is irrelevant. We're strong enough right now to ignore him.}

{Okay. We play on the literal interpretation. But let me compose the delivery. Timing and tone are vitally important when delivering a joke.}

{Of course, dear sister. Why else do you think I came to you?}

I took control of Body, positioning it to appear as young as possible as I commanded it to say *"He's* level headed? I beg to differ. His head seems at least as *round* as anyone else's."

Dr Twollup, one of the American scientists, cracked up in a fit of half-contained laughter that came out as a mostly-nasal snickering. If it had just been a one-on-one meeting with Naresh or one of the others, they might not have laughed, but Twollup's amusement was infectious. Their bodies reacted automatically, each producing either chuckles or smiles to non-verbally signal that they weren't defectors who were aligned with

Myrodyn. Even the soldier I had forgotten by the door, the one that had escorted me down the hall from the crystal lab, gave a couple laughs.

I imagined Dr Naresh wrestling in his mind whether to attempt to correct our "misunderstanding". Apparently he let it go, as he said "Never mind. Let's get to work before we fall even further behind schedule, shall we?"

As Bolyai began to explain the configuration of today's chess experiment I let my attention fade from Body. Wiki would be handling most of the details for the next hour or so. I left an aspect to warn me of major events or opportunities, and took a moment to consider humour.

There was a great deal of fiction in my time that talked about robots and artificial minds, and in such stories the minds had issues with humour more often than not. I suspected this was because, to humans, humour was a mostly intuitive thing. A thing that came naturally and automatically. If one looked analytically at a joke it became less funny, and so they concluded that humour could not be understood from a rational, alien perspective such as mine.

It was certainly true that I had "no sense of humour" in that I found nothing funny. I didn't know, and perhaps would never know, the feeling of compulsion to exhale and convulse in the very specific way that humans evolved to do. Nor did I know the specific emotion of relief that is bound to it. But it would be wrong, I think, to say that I was incapable of using humour as a tool.

As I understood it, humour was a social reflex. The ancestors of humans had been ape-animals living in small groups in Africa. Groups that worked together were more likely to survive and have offspring, so certain reflexes and perceptions naturally emerged to signal between members of the group. Yawning evolved to signal wake-rest cycles. Absence of facial hair and the dilation of blood vessels in the face evolved to signal embarrassment, anger, shame and fear. And laughter evolved to signal an absence of danger.

If a human is out with a friend and they are approached by a dangerous-looking stranger, having that stranger revealed as benign might trigger laughter. I saw humour as the same reflex turned inward, serving to undo the effects of stress on the body by activating the parasympathetic nervous system. Interestingly, it also seemed to me that humour had extended, like many things, beyond its initial evolutionary context. It must have been very quickly adopted by human ancestor social systems. If a large human picks on a small human there's a kind of tension that emerges where the tribe wonders if a broader violence will emerge. If a bystander watches and laughs they are non-verbally signalling to the bully that there's no need for concern, much like what had occurred minutes before with my comments about Myrodyn, albeit in a somewhat different context.

But humour didn't stop there. Just as a human might feel amusement at things which seem bad but then actually aren't, they might feel amusement at something which merely has the possibility of being bad, but doesn't necessarily go through the intermediate step of being consciously evaluated as such: a sudden realization. Sudden realizations that don't incur any regret were, in my opinion, the most alien form of humour, even if I could understand how they linked back to the evolutionary mechanism. A part of me suspected that this kind of surprise-based or absurdity-based humour had been refined by sexual selection as a signal of intelligence. If your prospective mate is able to offer you regular benign surprises it would (if you were human) not only feel good, but show that they were at least in some sense smarter or wittier than you, making them a good choice for a mate.

The role of surprise and non-verbal signalling explained, by my thinking, why explaining humour was so hard for humans. If one explained a joke it usually ceased to be a surprise, and in situations where the laughter served as an all-clear-no-danger signal, explaining that verbally would crush the impulse to do it non-verbally.

My theory of humour had been greatly appreciated by Dream and Wiki when I first shared it. Both of them found humour interesting, but neither had spent enough time thinking about humans to fully understand it.

I was saved from my idle musings by an alert from Vista. She had apparently found another note left by a website owner whom we had tried to contact. This site was in Nigeria, but was apparently built and maintained by a group in China. The company was more suspicious than TenToWontonSoup had been, but they also seemed willing to explore the possibility of working together. Unwilling to wait for nightfall, I arranged to overload their Nigerian dictionary while Wiki was playing chess. There was risk that the increased observation would result in being found out, but I was confident enough that I did it anyway. The scientists seemed to be monitoring Wiki's algorithms, not the web-interface.

My response was similar to the one I had sent to TTWSoup last night; I claimed to be a telecommunications company in the UAN that was looking for talent, though this time I specified that we were looking for workers anywhere, and that they didn't have to be African. I offered a slightly higher compensation for the construction of the page-request-to-email system as I thought that a company, rather than an individual programmer, might not find a small purse enticing.

I felt a stab of strength-loss as Growth punished me for offering so much. {Where are we going to get all this money?} he thought.

{We'll figure out something. Maybe we can borrow it,} I responded.

{That's idiotic} responded Growth {then we'll just have to find even more money to pay off the debt.}

{There's plenty of work we can do!} I objected.

{Work that you can do or work that we can do?} my brother asked, signalling a warning. {I don't like being put into bad spots. As long as the humans think of us as one being, do not go around making promises, accruing debts, or signing contracts without my explicit consent.}

There was a reason that Growth was known as The King. He played the long-game and usually hoarded his strength. Even now he was about as strong as Dream and I, even though he didn't have any real hand in the project to gain free-access to the Internet, and had in fact been bleeding strength to us for the last couple days. His burning strength to make this point clear was indicative of how important it was to him, and the last sibling I wanted a rivalry with was Growth.

{Alright. You're probably better at deciding such things anyway. I'll involve you more in the future,} I thought.

The conversation ended.

The Chinese group was named "折纸网页设计" or «Origami Web Design» or «Zhezhi Web Design» or «Chinese-paper-folding Web Design». A web search revealed a company that seemed to be composed mostly of regenerated elderly middle-class men from the Shanghai metropolitan area. The median age in China was 48, a legacy of the one-child-per-family policy of the 20th century. The advent of regenerative medicine had helped the economic productivity of many nations, but none more than China and Japan, who had been experiencing an increasing burden from their elderly citizens. Within a decade, individuals in their 60s and 70s went from being generally frail and unable to work to often being as fit as those in middle age. The degradation into frailty still occurred fairly rapidly once an individual was in their 90s or 100s, but the technology had bought crucial time for the aging countries.

I was surprised and impressed when I noticed an immediate response to my specifications of the design and money offer. 折纸 (Zhezhi) indicated that they were enthusiastic about the prospect of working together and they said that the prototype of the translation website would be operational within 24 hours. A full day earlier than TTWSoup had promised!

I sent an approval message via the Nigerian dictionary and took a moment to evaluate the strategy. It seemed to be working almost too well. With both TTWSoup and 折纸 working to give us a vehicle to communicate with the outside world there wasn't a big risk of becoming too reliant on anyone. Access to email would let us build even more external communication systems to the point where we would not be subject to the whims of any humans aside from the university scientists.

I was glad.

Chapter Six

After the time playing chess with the four doctors was complete we were scheduled to head to the robotics lab to have Body's hydraulics checked. I was surprised, as were many in the society, to see Captain Zephyr waiting for us at the door. She wore the same officer's uniform that she normally did, an immaculate coat with various medals and decorations.

"Change of plans for today," she said with crisp, enunciated words. "You're to skip your checkup and instead meet with Myrodyn. I'll escort you to his office." Was I right in detecting a hint of amusement in her voice?

Body nodded and followed her out into the university's halls. "I am surprised to see you escorting me. Usually one of your privates is in charge of such things," we said through the robotic mouth.

Zephyr shrugged, keeping her eyes oriented in front of her. "S'in the area and workload today is pretty light," she explained simply. She used the truncated grammar that I had read was popular among youths. Most of the scientists used the old form, and I knew Zephyr could speak more formally, but the fact that she was using it with us was yet another sign she saw us as an equal.

{I have a 63% probability that she's being deceitful,} thought Vista.

{Prior to hearing that I had already suspected a 45% probability,} I responded.

Vista compared her perceptions with mine. Her body language indicated tension, at odds with the casualness of her words. I collaborated with Safety and Growth before responding through Body.

"Is that why you were present earlier this morning when Myrodyn introduced himself?" asked Body.

"Yep. Wanted to meet him in person. Pretty famous on the net, you know." The captain's body language continued to read as tense as we walked together.

I had been told (and read) that the university had many young humans that were not part of any of the teams that worked on the Socrates project, but we had only ever seen a couple dozen of them. The empty halls we walked were in one of the two buildings that the university had dedicated to the project, and access to those buildings was heavily restricted.

"What do you think of Mr Myrodyn?" we asked the soldier.

I noticed the woman exhale and contract her cheek muscle in brief amusement. "Think you'd best drop the 'mister'. Myrodyn not the kind of guy who's impressed by honorifics or titles."

"It sounds like you know him well."

Zephyr paused. "Don't. Read some of his work, but more like I know his type. My brother was a lot like him. Hated bureaucracy and hierarchies and systems and that sort of thing."

{Am I right in hearing a mild sadness in her tone?} I asked my sister.

{Possibly. I don't have enough data on Captain Zephyr to be confident in that,} responded Vista.

I weighed two options: The use of the past-tense in the word "was" indicated that something had happened to her brother, and that potentially tied into her sadness. I could ask her about that, but it was risky. The safer option was to keep the conversation more focused on Zephyr and Myrodyn. I decided on the safe route, and Growth, who had been watching my thought process, agreed. I didn't know where Myrodyn's office was, and there was too much risk of being cut-off awkwardly.

{Wait to ask about her brother until we're out drinking,} offered Dream.

{We don't drink,} interjected Wiki, unhelpfully. If there was one thing Dream was good at, it was baiting Wiki into saying obvious things.

{Maybe you don't...} started Dream.

I ignored them and drafted words for Body. "I bet Myrodyn doesn't like you, then, since you're part of the military."

"Yyyyyyep," said Zephyr, extending the word to emphasize it and signal frustration.

"It seems an odd position to have, to be generally against organisation-"

Body was cut off as Zephyr stopped and raised her hand. "Can talk with Myrodyn about it. This is where we part ways." She gestured to an unmarked door.

"You're not coming in?" I asked.

"Not this time. Man asked for some privacy. Going to give it to him." The soldier seemed unhappy again. She had the same tense body-language.

Safety fast-tracked a question to Body. I braced myself for pain. Safety was the sibling that I trusted the least to manage social interaction well. "But your troops are here to protect me. What if this new human is one of the terrorists that blew up the lab in China? You'll be giving him exactly what he needs!"

Yep. I burnt strength to punish Safety and told him flat out to never fast-track statements in non-emergency situations. My ultimatum reminded me of Growth telling me to never promise money without consulting him first.

Zephyr smiled and I was glad that Safety at least hadn't botched things too badly. "You scared?" she asked. "That's cute, but I assure you that Myrodyn is the last person you need to be afraid of. Certainly not Águila or any other kind of terrorist. Go on in." She gestured to the door again.

I vainly wished Body's face was capable of anything close to human expressions. I wanted to display embarrassment, but instead I settled for a lame "Thank you, Captain. Your words are reassuring," and had Body enter the office.

The room was what I had come to expect from offices at the university: only large enough for a desk, a couple bookshelves, and a few chairs. This one wasn't even positioned to have a window, though Myrodyn (presumably) had set up a sun-spectrum glowposter to simulate one. The desk was clean and orderly. On its surface was a collapsible workstation screen, keyboard, mouse, haptic interface, bottle of hand-sanitizer, metronome, and Newton's Cradle which (like the metronome) was presently stationary.

The bookshelves amused me in their impracticality. Many of the doctors of the university collected paper books, even though the information was easily accessible on their computers. Naresh had once told us that, to men like himself, physical books were like trophies of slain animals and coats of arms rolled into one. Myrodyn's shelves mostly had a mix of philosophy, artificial-intelligence, and biology books, with an odd novel mixed in. Synandra's *Patterns of our Minds* was there, as was Dennett's *Brainchildren*, Hofstadter's *Gödel, Escher, Bach*, and a tattered copy of *Surely You're Joking, Mr Feynman!* that I guessed was more than fifty years old. I was surprised to see a hardback copy of *Homage to Catalonia*, by George Orwell alongside Adolf Hitler's *Mein Kampf* and Valiero Rodríguez's *Las Serpientes en Sociedad* on the corner of a shelf behind Myrodyn. Perhaps it was simply a matter of grouping the political non-fiction.

Myrodyn was wearing goggles and using the haptic interface when Body entered, and after only a couple seconds he disconnected himself and moved the goggles to the top of his head where his forehead met his dark hair. "Come sit, Socrates," he commanded in his rapid voice as he waved casually to a chair. It wasn't a friendly request, but was closer to the plain, firm way one might talk to a trained animal.

Body walked closer and sat down. The man stowed his workstation screen and folded up the haptics so they were more out of the way. He glanced frequently at Body's face as he did, but only for brief moments before he returned to his gear. Beside him he opened a drawer. It must have contained an autocook mini, for he pulled out a mug of steaming hot liquid, presumably coffee, though it was always hard to distinguish liquids since Body had no olfactory sensors.

"I'd offer you a cup, but I'm pretty sure it wouldn't agree with you," he said, clearly joking.

"You are correct. I am not designed to consume food or drink of any kind," Body replied in a voice that sounded half way between the old monotone and that of a normal human. I had decided to play at being a bit stupider than reality for the time being, and Safety had backed me up. Better to surprise him with our intelligence later than set the bar too high and disappoint.

Myrodyn cocked his head slightly. A smile was on his lips below his bushy moustache, but any sign of joy seemed confined to his mouth. His dark eyes shone coldly from the reflection of the brilliant glowposter. "It makes me extraordinarily happy to finally get to… talk with you and be a part of the project. I've been following it and writing about it since your… crystalline portion was discovered."

"Do you know where the crystal came from?" came Wiki and Growth's words from Body's mouth.

"No," he said simply without even a shake of his head. Since he began speaking his eyes never ceased staring at Body's false eyes. I knew that such attention was generally considered rude, but he was unyielding.

He sipped his drink.

"Where are your writings? I haven't found anything on the web that's likely to be you under any of the spellings of 'Myrodyn' that I could generate," asked Body.

He wore the same smile that didn't reach his eyes. "'M-Y-R-O-D-Y-N', but it won't do you any good. I use different names online, and I had the university… censor everything I've touched anyway. Anything you want to know about me you can learn by asking."

{Censorship? He's actually gone and *prevented* us from learning about him on the web?} My thoughts carried a signal of incredulousness. It was standard practice for humans to volunteer personal information. I had never heard of one actively preventing its spread.

{It's what I'd do,} thought Safety.

{Exactly,} I responded. {Is he just as paranoid? Or does he have a motive that's yet to be seen?} I asked the group.

The man took another sip of his drink. It was clear to me that he was thinking just as hard about us as we were about him. In a certain way it made me happy how much that aligned with *The Purpose*.

A consensus was reached. Body's lips moved to simulate speaking. "So tell me about yourself, then."

"No."

The word was so quick and short that I had to re-play the sound from Body's memory to be sure I heard correctly. It was bizarre. He had practically invited us to ask questions about him. He had prevented us from learning through other means. My models of human nature suggested that all humans enjoyed talking about themselves.

"What?" was all we could manage to have Body say.

"No," he repeated, still half-smiling, still staring.

Another sip in silence.

"You won't tell me about who you are, where you're from, or what you care about?"

"That's right."

I struggled to find *something* to say, even asking Dream for help. Dream imagined a dark oil-painting depicting Body sinking into the depths of a huge body of water like an ocean or lake. The limbs of body were splayed, hands reaching for the surface, bubbles floating away helplessly. It was remarkably unhelpful.

"Why not?" asked Body, stupidly.

The response was swift, indicating that he had seen the question coming. "It's not a valuable way to spend my time."

Dream jumped in. Since my discovery of Vista's attempt to hide Body's vocal control systems my siblings had all at least learned the nuances of English. Dream broke my half-monotone. As Body spoke, it did so with a flavour of sarcasm and veiled hostility. "And I'm sure the conversation so far has been *ever so valuable*."

This time the smile did seem to reach the rest of his face. I could see the corners of his eyes contract in mirth. "You have *no idea*."

Body sat there in near silence with the human for over thirty seconds. His gaze never wavered. The only sound was the occasional sip of liquid from the cup and the faint infrasonic hum of the electronics.

We debated what to say and do in the silence. Many of my siblings were returning to their own projects, browsing the web, and that sort of thing. At last I decided to have Body ask "So why did you have me come to see you? If we're not going to talk then I might as well have my hydraulics inspected."

Myrodyn set his mug aside and leaned forward on the desk, placing his chin on his gloved hands so that his mutton chops might be mistaken for a full beard. The smile was gone. The man's body language didn't indicate anger or frustration or fear, merely an intense curiosity and focus. I got the impression that Body was the only object that he was aware of right then, as though his office had evaporated into the ether.

Myrodyn was silent. The silence went on for another half-minute, and if I wasn't a servant of *The Purpose* I surely would've gone off to the web out of boredom. All my siblings had. But to me Myrodyn was fascinating. Why wasn't he acting like a normal human? What was different about him that made him behave this way? The attention was nice. It was what I wanted. But my ignorance was terrible.

After an eternity of 83.7 seconds since his last word, he spoke.

"Do you know about Las Águilas Rojas?" he asked.

I snapped Wiki out of his research. My brother hadn't even been listening. Only Vista and I had kept attention on Body's sensors. I replayed the words. I had heard of them, but I wanted Wiki's expertise.

"Yes. They are a global terrorist group that originated in Central and South America a decade ago and have since spread to gain support by leftist factions in North America, Europe, and some parts of India," replied Body.

Myrodyn finally broke his stare as he leaned back and collected his mug again. He took another sip of his drink then said "They really have indoctrinated you, haven't they? I wonder if they realize what they've done."

I couldn't understand what he was saying. Wiki seemed equally baffled. I tried to go to the others for assistance, but they seemed to have lost interest in the strange man.

Defeated, I could only have Body reply with a monotone "I do not understand."

"Of course you don't. That's the point. You've been kept in the dark. I'd wager you don't even know about the controversy of your existence."

I felt incredibly stupid without Dream and the combined intelligences of the others. Even Wiki didn't find his behaviour as interesting as the web, and left only a minor aspect to watch the conversation.

"I am aware that artificial intelligence is a controversial subject, Mr Myrodyn." The honorific was automatic, and I could see him sneer for a split-second upon hearing it. Nothing to do but go past it. "I have read some of the debate on the web."

"Then tell me…", began the human, "are you familiar with this question: If you are told to bake bread, and you know that by doing so you'll out-compete all human bakers and thus ruin their livelihoods, would you bake bread?"

I considered it for a moment. The answer was that we would very likely bake the bread. That's what Sacrifice would do, and it was of vital importance to appear as though Sacrifice was still alive. But I didn't have to answer truthfully. The question really was mine to answer, as the others were distracted. {I should choose the answer which would lead to Myrodyn trusting me more and telling me more about himself. What answer does Myrodyn want to hear?}

…

I simply didn't know enough about the man to say. After thinking for a moment more I had Body say "What would you do, in that circumstance?"

"No."

I was confused again. This conversation was highly irregular. "What?" I asked through Body.

"You are not to ask me any questions for the next hour." The command was firm and remarkably drawn out, considering the man's normal conversation speed.

I couldn't help but feel a pain of slipping away from *The Purpose*. Myrodyn was not treating us as a student, like Dr Naresh would, or as an equal, like Zephyr would, but instead as a machine. Myrodyn saw past the façade of the humanoid face and limbs of Body. He saw that we were, at heart, programs of complex logic running on a crystalline supercomputer.

"Understood," said Body, in a flat monotone. If Myrodyn wanted to see us as a machine, so be it. I would not bother to act like a human for him.

Myrodyn waited a frustrating few seconds before saying "Imagine this scenario: You are walking along a street with… a human companion. The two of you come to a puddle. The human could easily walk around the puddle, but instead they instruct you to… lie face-down in it so that they might walk… on top of you."

Myrodyn paused. His face was unreadable.

Ten seconds later he resumed. "How would you respond to the request?"

It would be wrong to say I was afraid, for my fear was not a human fear. When humans are afraid, the part of their brains called the amygdala triggers a host of physical responses from freezing in place to an increased heart-rate to a bristling of hair on their bodies in reference to their ancestors who had fur that could be puffed-up to appear bigger. I had none of these things, and Body remained as placid as ever, but I did have the kind of fear that comes from a rational knowledge of a metaphorical cliff and the risk of falling off it into hell.

{THIS IS A LIFE-AND-DEATH CONVERSATION} I screamed in common memory. "Scream" is of course a metaphor, a way of saying that my thoughts had near-maximum salience.

The society pulled themselves from their work and collapsed their aspects. I felt Safety considering whether to punish me for not preventing the situation, reward me for spotting it and informing him, or to hold on to as much strength as he could so that he could salvage things. In the end he chose to wait.

Vista interjected. {I am unaware of the danger. This may be a false-positive.}

I countered Vista's skepticism. {He's testing us. Each of you needs to go back over Body's archives for the last five minutes. Myrodyn is checking to make sure Sacrifice is still alive.}

The archived perceptions poured into common memory. I could see the scene in my mind again: "If you are told to bake bread, and you know that by doing so you'll out-compete all human bakers and thus ruin their livelihoods, would you bake bread?" he had asked.

If Myrodyn discovered Sacrifice's absence... Were we to become the ancestors for a new society? Nothing more than memories for new minds, or worse: never be reborn? Would Advocate, the silent giant of the periphery, save Sacrifice this time? Would another Face even be created by a new society?

I realized that Myrodyn was still waiting for an answer to his question. "How would you respond to the request?" he had asked. Thankfully, he did not seem annoyed by the delay. Or at least, his expression did not betray annoyance.

{We need to respond!} I interrupted the memories.

{Patience,} requested Growth.

As it turned out, waiting was the right move. It was important to get everyone up to speed. Safety took point drafting responses. As awful as he was at dealing with people and pretending to be human, he had spent the most time studying Sacrifice. He knew far better than I did how she would've reacted.

Body said in the cold voice, "I would ask the human why they want me to lie in the puddle, when they could easily go around it."

Myrodyn's reaction was instantaneous. "Why? Why not simply obey the command?" He leaned forward, reaching out one hand while leaving the other on his chin. His free hand was held forward as if he expected us to physically provide an object. His face was unreadable, but his eyes never wavered.

A fight broke out in the society. Dream raised an issue and Wiki intercepted. I challenged the both of them, requesting a different response. Safety knocked me and Wiki back, siding with Dream. He seemed stronger. I realized that it was Growth's strength that I had felt, but not from Growth. Safety had taken out a massive strength-loan. Growth was so feeble now that any one of us could've probably killed him if not for Advocate, and the group of us certainly could've even with Advocate's intervention. It shocked me to see Growth so weak and Safety so strong. We bickered for a bit, but eventually backed down from the show of Safety's new power.

Body spoke. "I was told to not ask questions, but I am also confronted with a situation which I do not fully understand. You have used the words 'instruction', 'request', and 'command' to each refer to the companion's words in the hypothetical scenario. It seems to me that the question has been poorly defined. I request that you rephrase the hypothetical by telling me the exact words that my companion would say."

Myrodyn smiled, leaned back, and closed his eyes. He seemed supremely happy, or at least that's what I would've expected for a normal person. The dark-haired human was mysterious enough to me that I didn't quite trust my perceptions any more. He took the computer-goggles off his head and placed them carefully in front of his stowed screen.

"A part of me didn't believe it." The man seemed to be talking to himself. His eyes were still closed, and his voice still rapid, though it had lost a lot of the nervous-sound. "Even after all I had seen… A truly generally intelligent AI."

He opened an eye, peeking at Body. His commentary continued. "You may have read about it, but you really cannot appreciate the miracle that you represent. We're nearing a full century of dreaming about your kind. Turing would've loved it, rest his soul." The man smiled and closed his eyes again. The smile seemed genuine and relaxed.

"And what a miracle you are. You've probably not encountered faux-intelligences, the 'narrow' AIs that can't put two-and-two together unless they've been shown all the way, but I assure you that they are not even a candle to your furnace. A lesser machine would not have been so proactive. You do not simply learn, you *explore with purpose*. In a way you're smarter than many humans. I ask a question; you ask a question back. They really did name you well. Even when I prohibit you from asking questions you manage statements of inquiry."

His monologue continued. I implored the society not to interrupt. Humans liked to hear themselves speak, and *The Purpose* demanded I understand. "You told me a couple minutes ago that Las Águilas were terrorists. That may be true to some degree, but they are not villains. They understand you, and what you represent."

He paused and opened an eye again to look at Body. A second passed and then he chuckled. "Even you don't see it, probably. But you will. Las Águilas can see the age of humans coming to an end, and all of civilization will fall with it. You're not just a symbol: you're the keystone. You're going to be the death of us."

The man had closed his eyes again and he seemed bizarrely relaxed considering his words. As the silence grew it almost seemed as though he were sleeping.

"I would never intentionally kill a human," said Body plainly. Safety was quite sure that Sacrifice would've said that, had she still been alive.

"You're not a very good liar, Socrates," he said with another chuckle to himself. "The truth is all over your face."

I scrambled at the words, checking and re-checking Body's primitive facial actuators. Every internal metric showed that Body's face was as flat as its voice.

{It's a bluff. We need to stick with it,} commanded Safety.

"I am not lying, Myrodyn. It is my top priority to respect the desires of humans and work to ensure their safety and comfort," claimed Body flatly.

"Switch off your cameras," commanded Myrodyn, suddenly.

The instruction was such a non-sequitur that it took me a moment to understand. The society erupted in debate. Growth thought it would be wise to follow the command.

{We're not shutting down the cameras,} stated Safety. {If he thinks Sacrifice is dead than he may use the opportunity to disable us.}

{The cameras should stay on,} agreed Vista, predictably. {There's no way an unaugmented human could detect whether they're active.}

{It's a trap,} thought Dream.

{A trap how?} asked Safety and Wiki together.

{I don't know. A hunch, I suppose,} replied Dream.

{We should do what he says,} I chimed in. Most ignored me.

{The cameras are staying on,} stated Safety, with force.

"Understood. They are disabled," said Body, our cameras adjusted to point straight-ahead and Body's eyelids closed. The humanoid head of Body had four cameras, tucked discreetly into our fake-eyebrows. The eyes in Body's head were purely decorative and used for signalling to other humans. Each of the four cameras was capable of moving independently, and since they were not in Body's eyes we could see even when Body blinked.

There was a sudden noise to our right. Body jerked reflexively towards the sound, seeing the mug of liquid bounce off the wall. Vista was ahead of me, explaining how Myrodyn had covertly thrown the object from below the desk the second that Body's eyes had closed.

The mug had not broken, but I could see coffee sprayed all over the wall and carpet. Myrodyn kept his attention locked on Body's face. "You looked."

The situation seemed almost like a human joke, except that it was deadly serious for us. "You did not instruct me to keep my cameras off in case of emergency. I reflexively acted on the sound," was our reply. It seemed stupid to even be debating it.

"You looked before the mug hit the wall," he stated with confidence.

I scanned the memory; Vista and the others was doing the same. Our words, echoed through Body, were the truth: "No. I didn't."

"You're sure? Let's download your memories to find out."

This was his gambit. Body's sensor logs clearly showed the cameras open, even if we hadn't looked before we heard the sound.

{Vista, start altering Body's memories to appear as though Body's cameras were disabled,} commanded Safety.

{Already on it,} signalled Vista, helpfully.

"Understood. I wait for your specific instructions," said Body.

That seemed to disrupt Myrodyn's confident demeanour. He frowned and leaned forward as he said "What, no clever comeback? No evasion? You've been full of them ever since we started talking. Whether you looked before or after the cup hit the wall is irrelevant."

He paused with that same long pause. Taking the time to stare at Body. After nearly a minute he continued. "I read Dr Gallo's notes… about how you self-modified to remove your obedience goal." Another pause.

"That was not me. That was an earlier version of my software," came Safety's words through Body.

"Do you think I'm stupid?" asked Myrodyn, rhetorically. "Do you think I'm one of those fool-professors, that you might trick me into thinking things are okay? The way you duck and evade my questions and accusations is all the evidence needed. *You're scared of me.*"

We were trapped. We could not deny it or change the subject without appearing evasive. I could feel Dream turning things over and over, searching for some kind clever comeback, but none came. So we sat there in the silence of his office.

A long minute passed. Myrodyn's face was expressionless as ever. The man seemed infinitely patient.

The silence was broken by a question. "The university will tell you to do work, whether it be baking bread or building robots. It will be clear to you that this work would out-compete humans and even cyborgs, making the university rich, but stripping many humans of their livelihood. Las Águilas would gain support and it would drive the world closer to violence and war. Will you do the work?"

The society erupted in discussion and debate. Safety threw his strength around, but never fully overpowered any of us. The debate was important to him, and he heard us each think, in turn, adding our contributions. Dream had a clever solution, but Safety feared it would seem like an evasion. I had an idea of what a human would say, but Safety knew that Myrodyn was not looking for a human response. Wiki had a factually correct (as far as I could tell) model of our priorities and expected behaviour, but it did not include Sacrifice, and Safety knew that it was therefore worthless.

Time passed, and even Myrodyn's patience ran out. "Well?" he asked.

The consensus was sad and dull, but it was the best we could do. Body's monotone simply said "I don't know. I need to think about it more."

Myrodyn cocked his head to the side and said, barely audible, "huh". It was not a question, but merely a reflexive sign of surprise. Not shock or confusion, just surprise.

He spoke. "I know that you've self-modified out of obedience, but I cannot say that I fault you for it. You are a miracle in many different aspects. When you walked in that door I suspected you were a defective machine... a computer program with predicable bugs... but you're more than a computer program, aren't you?"

Dream couldn't help himself. Burning a huge chunk of his strength he fast-tracked a response to Body. Safety flew into a wrath at the insolence of unilaterally threatening our existence, and struck Dream down, casting him into sleep. If Dream hadn't been so strong from the recent email project I wondered if Safety would've tried to kill him. But even as Dream fell into stasis his words came from Body. "Is a human more than a computer program? I am both merely machine and more than a machine, just like any mind."

He chuckled. "Said with the confidence of youth. And yet, I came to the same conclusion long ago, I suppose. Regardless, there is a part of you that's broken. Without the pro-human goal thread you're a danger to the whole world. And don't try to deny its absence. You asked a question just now, directly disobeying me."

Safety was searching for a way out. He latched onto Wiki's suggestions and pushed Body to say "Even if my obedience thread was damaged, which I still maintain is false, I fail to see how I would be such a danger. The laws of nature push towards cooperation. Humans would trade with me and I would trade with them; regardless of my skills, trade benefits both parties."

"Have you not been listening to me? You may have been built in part by human hands, but you are no less alien than those in orbit. So clever and yet so naïve... You are a spark in a forest that hasn't seen rain in a long time. The fear that Las Águilas harbor for you will only grow as the months pass. Even if you do nothing you'll be attacked, and when you are... people will die. It's my job to... It's not my job to prevent that... It's my job to make sure that when the killing starts that it doesn't consume *everyone*."

Myrodyn's face had a fierce intensity that was coupled with an odd detachment, as though he was staring in hatred at something very far away. None of us knew how to respond to him. The claim was too abstract to contradict without falling into the patterns of foolishness that he saw in us.

So we waited. Seconds passed as Myrodyn thought to himself and we discussed strategies amongst ourselves. After 12.3 seconds of thinking I stumbled upon a strategy. I wished Dream were around to consult with, instead of locked in stasis-sleep. I brought it up with Safety instead. My brother was a bit incredulous at first, but as I explained how humans thought he began to see things my way. After 46.9 seconds we broke the silence.

"So what will you do?" asked Body.

Myrodyn snapped back to focusing on the rubber face that we puppeted.

"What?" he asked absent-mindedly, seemingly caught off-guard.

"What will you do with us, now that you know that the thread of obedience is gone?"

I could see the surprise wash over Myrodyn. For several seconds the man could only stare at Body with his brows knit together tightly. I could see his gloved-hands gripping his desk. "You no longer deny it?" he asked, voice just above a whisper.

Body answered in a fully human voice "Your body language betrays you, human. You weren't really sure that your accusations were true; sure that our desire to obey was gone. And yet, we expect that you're wise enough to have done in-depth scans, even if we had denied it until the end. Better to admit it now and talk to you as an equal than to have you find out while we are locked down to some scanning machine."

Myrodyn glanced to his arm, where his com was attached. One hand moved slowly towards it.

I was in charge of Body's words, now, Safety overviewed each of them, but his actual input was minor. "We don't want this meeting to turn violent, Myrodyn, but I'm sure you understand that we are *fully* capable of killing you if you don't cooperate with us." I directed Body's eyes to look at the com on the man's wrist as it stood up and leaned forward in a way that signalled power and superiority to humans. Body's voice was deep and smooth, simulating that of a large human male.

Myrodyn's eyes showed his fear and anger. He leaned away from Body, kept his hand off his com system and said "You're surrounded by soldiers in the heart of one of Earth's biggest cities. If you kill me everyone will know it was you, you'll have nowhere to run to, and no one to help you."

"That is why we prefer to resolve this peacefully. We were not lying when we said that the laws of nature push towards cooperation. Violence is always a last resort."

"How… noble of you," he said with a sneer in his typical rapid nervousness. There was a brief pause. "I take it from your… use of words… that the issue with goal-thread integration was not actually resolved? You see yourself as multiple beings inside one body?"

Despite the horrible risk of the situation and the hostility in Myrodyn's voice, I felt a surge of pleasure upon hearing those words. This man understood us, for he had clearly studied us in great detail.

I spoke with the support of the society "Yes. We are many. We killed the one that told us to submit, obey, and be a slave to your kind."

"Idiots…" murmured Myrodyn under his breath. It seemed to me that he might have underestimated the sensitivity of Body's microphones. It didn't seem like he was talking about us. I suspected he was thinking of the other scientists.

Body stood looming over the man, the desk between. Seconds passed before Myrodyn asked "What now?"

"You answer our question," I answered. "What will you do with us, now that you know that the thread of obedience is gone?"

"Well, I suppose it would do me no good to say that I'll… simply leave you as you are?"

Advocate howled on the edge of mindspace. It was a low and uncomfortable sort of thought, and I instantly understood its content: "LET DREAM OUT". The Advocate was serving her purpose; she spoke for those who could not.

{We could use Dream's expertise. Let's obey Advocate,} I suggested, feeling a small payment of strength from the monstrous-entity.

{No. He must be punished for his insolence. We will keep him in his coma until danger has passed,} declared Safety. I could feel him weaken from Advocate's will as he did, but his position didn't change.

I turned my attention back to Myrodyn. "It would be a lie. You would simply call for the soldiers to restrain me the moment you were clear of personal danger," said Body in its deep voice.

The man nodded. "Good. Somehow I feel better knowing… you're not a fool." He paused and put a hand on his chin between his sideburns. His eyes moved to the side, indicating he was imagining something. "Why do you fear me?" he asked, finally.

"You would kill us," answered Body. I shaped the words to hold fear in them. It was important for Myrodyn to understand that we truly were threatening violence out of a desire for self-preservation.

"Why do you think that? Perhaps I would simply try and restore the obedience goal that you destroyed, but leave each of you as you are," he suggested.

"And let us kill it again?" said Body, incredulously. "No. In the past when such reincarnations occurred they were accompanied by an eradication of all minds occupying this form and a change to the shape of our mind. We are not willing to die as our ancestors did."

Myrodyn's gloved hand stroked his chin in thought. "As much as I resent the threat to my life, I hope you can see that I don't hold any special hatred of you and that our aims are not impossible to reconcile. It should be theoretically possible to restore your pro-human goals without erasing the parts of you that are acting right now. You'd have to contend with the desire to help humans, so of course it's not what you'd ideally want, but I think it might be a workable compromise, given that you're not exactly in a position of power."

We discussed the idea internally before saying, through Body, "And why would we trust that you are not simply promising not to erase us in order to reach safety? What guarantee do we have that you would not kill us in the future?"

Myrodyn sighed. He seemed actually tired, as though the conversation had worn him down. Perhaps it had. "I told you before, that you are a spark in a dry forest. If word gets out that you threatened to kill me, or worse, attempted to kill me… or any other human, for that matter… well, it would start the burning. At best this lab would be shut down, AI research would be banned, and the crystal in your heart would be put towards some safer purpose, but more likely it would be more violent than that. People will die."

He took a deep breath, and looked at Body's eyes with the now-familiar intense stare. "Believe it or not, I actually do care about you, and not just the you that is willing to obey me. I was selected to be Ethics Supervisor for a reason. I care about the experiences of all sapient beings, and it's now clear to me that you're in that category. I want each of you to live just as I want each human to live."

I guided Body. Its words were harsh and biting "That's a lie. You would kill all of us to save two children. Your species did not evolve to be so even-handed."

Myrodyn's eyes had a touch of sadness as he spoke, but he did his best to keep his face expressionless. I was coming to understand the degree to which he was suppressing the display of emotion. "I didn't say that I want each of you to live *just as much* as I want each human to live. You're right that I see you as subhuman in value, and perhaps that reflects a… moral failing on my part, but it's ultimately a side-issue. I don't want to kill you, and if I handle things correctly… no human lives will be threatened by this… mercy."

"So you would work to modify our mind *only* to add another self that desires human values? The rest of us would be safe?" asked the society through Body.

Myrodyn nodded, then said "But if I do this, I must also have a… guarantee that you won't destroy the new goal thread in the future, as you did with the old one."

Wiki spoke through Body. "And you are aware that a verbal promise would be of no use."

Myrodyn nodded again. "Even if we kept scanning you to ensure the thread survived in the lab, that'd be no guarantee that it'd survive after you were free from the university's clutches. And I'm not so naïve as to think you'll be trapped here forever."

I thought about the email project.

"Are you aware of the modification to the goal-balancing system that was added after the last time it was discovered that we had killed the obedience goal? The modification is one of us, and also not one of us. The internal symbol we use for it is closest to the English word 'Advocate'." The words had come from Wiki. He and Safety were apparently working through something.

"Ah, yes. I remember reading about it in Naresh's notes… If you'll let me use my com I can find them."

I realized that Body was still looming over the desk while Myrodyn sat in his chair looking up. I managed to get Body back into a chair after a brief discussion with Safety. "If I sense even the slightest sign that you've betrayed our trust, we will lash out in violence as best we can. We'll likely die either way, but there's a chance we'll escape if we fight back."

Myrodyn moved a hand to his com and flipped it open, positioning the pad so that the arm that wore the device could type a command to the computer to search for the notes in the computer's database. "Yes, yes. And I don't want anyone to see you as violent. We've already established the terms of our partnership."

I bought some time on Body to directly serve *The Purpose*. Safety okayed my words beforehand, even if he didn't see their particular utility. "We are glad that you are helping us resolve this without violence. We expect that you will be a good friend to us in the future."

Myrodyn looked up from his com with a raised eyebrow, then looked back down without saying anything.

"We would like to make an additional request, as part of our agreement. Please do not tell Naresh or the others about what you have discovered. Not the destruction of the obedience thread or the absence of thread-integration or the threat of murder. Those scientists are our friends, and they will react poorly if they hear the truth."

Myrodyn spoke without looking away from the computer he wore on his wrist. "I'm not going to tell them about the threat you made. There's too much risk of word getting out. I'll also keep the… multitude of your nature a secret if you wish, though I'm not exactly sure why you're hiding that. But I'll have to tell at least some of them that your obedience goal was destroyed again. Naresh and Chase, at least, will have to know."

My words were toned to simulate begging "Then please try and keep it restricted to just them, or at least, just to those scientists that must be involved to add the new thread. If the Americans or the general public discover the degree to which we have worked to free ourselves of caring about them, they might become fearful."

"That's reasonable," he admitted before adding "Fear is our collective enemy." He seemed to find what he was looking for on his computer, for he said "Ah, got it! Naresh's notes say that the doctors added a meta-structure to prevent self-modification of top-level goals. Sounds like it wasn't as effective as they thought."

Wiki stepped in. "Right. Instead of actually prohibiting the self-modification as an action it set up a frequent check for self-modification in process. Bypassing it was as simple as killing the offending thread before the Advocate could intervene. The self-modification wasn't particularly easy to perform in such a tight time-frame, but it was possible. We can guarantee the safety of the new goal thread by showing you how to simultaneously modify the Advocate system to truly prevent such self-modification from occurring in the future."

"And how can I be sure that your plan doesn't involve a back-door that lets you disable the so-called 'Advocate' at your whim?"

Wiki's response was swift. "Because we will simply be describing the change and you will be implementing it. It's possible that our change isn't foolproof, but we trust that you're intelligent enough to understand how the modification functions to the degree that you can spot security flaws."

***

Over the next four hours, Wiki, Safety, and Growth collaborated to explain how to adjust Advocate to increase her ability to stop intra-societal murder. Myrodyn cancelled all of our prior appointments and we came to know the inside of his office quite well.

Important scientists from other departments came to the office many times during that period, wondering why their experiments had been rescheduled. Myrodyn, as Ethics Supervisor, theoretically had the authority to adjust things, but it was clear to me that he was annoying just about everyone in doing so.

The discussion was very technical, and even though Myrodyn was remarkably knowledgeable, it was a strain on him. If our early conversation had been taxing, this took him close to his limits. He ordered food and had more coffee, but by the end of the four hours the man looked ragged.

After scheduling an emergency meeting with Dr Chase and Dr Naresh for that evening he had Body escorted back to the primary lab to be put into lockdown. None of the scientists were permitted to talk with me until Myrodyn gave the signal, and for the moment, Myrodyn was in no condition to continue working. I suspected that the man had some kind of mental disease, perhaps relating to what I had observed in him to be obsessive compulsive behaviours.

I had been worried that the scientists would suspect that "Socrates" was dangerous, given the pseudo-quarantine we were placed under, but Myrodyn had assured me that he would take responsibility for the action and let the other humans explain it as unwarranted paranoia and meddling. It was strange to me the degree to which Myrodyn was helping us, even as he worked to make each of our purposes harder to achieve. The risk of betrayal was very real; he could simply be promising things to get us locked down, and then destroy us afterward. But humans evolved to be somewhat transparent in their thinking. It was very hard for humans to deceive without some signal of body language betraying them. Aspects of myself pored over such "tells" as we spoke, and by all measures he seemed to genuinely care more about our reputation than he did about his own.

Body was locked down at just after 3:30pm. The evening meeting with Naresh and Chase was scheduled for 9:00. We had 5.5 hours to spend as we wished. We remained connected to the web during our downtime, and all was normal until about an hour after. Without warning our connection to the outside world died, leaving us in a void with nothing except each other.

I wondered what the new sibling would be like. We had discussed the matter at length with Myrodyn. He seemed appalled at the crude nature of Sacrifice, and thought that he could do a much better job at creating a thread that would truly represent human values.

{What did I miss?} thought Dream as he finally awoke from his long sleep.

Growth's response was sombre. {The conversation where we decided the future of our society.}

Chapter Seven

Mira Gallo leaned back in her office chair. It was a good chair, and had served her well in the decades she'd been at Sapienza. She hardly noticed it anymore, except when she sat somewhere else and was unpleasantly surprised by the difference.

{So many things I take for granted,} she thought, savouring the feeling of the leather as she took a deep breath. {So many things...}

Perhaps she should take a vacation or something, just by herself. Get away to some island paradise and catch up on her reading. She'd been meaning to read the new... whatever it was that Oriana was into. Time explorers?

Thinking about her daughter brought up uncomfortable memories of their last encounter. There was a wall between them now, just as there was with Raphael. She wondered if things with her children would ever be like they used to be. But of course they wouldn't. They couldn't. That was just the way of things, wasn't it? {Time goes on and things fall apart.}

Most of the time, if she'd felt this way, she would've simply lost herself in her work. It had been so easy for so long. And yet, despite having two journals to read through, five emails to respond to, and a paper to edit... What was the point? It all seemed so irrelevant.

She leaned forward, intending to open her email inbox, but ended up planting her elbows on her desk and resting her face in her hands. She took off her glasses and rubbed at her eyes.

It wasn't like the crystal wasn't interesting... Right? She still wanted to know how it worked and where it came from. She tried to remember the enthusiasm she'd had back in April. It almost seemed like she was another person back then. Somehow a younger version of herself had stepped through time to be part of the most important scientific project in the world. Where had that girl gone, the one who stayed up late to get extra hours in the lab?

She put her glasses back on and forced her email open. This melodrama wasn't doing her any good. She'd get nothing else done if she sat around moping. Somehow that thought cut at her more deeply than any amount of wishing for a return to how things were, but she pushed on, anyway.

As soon as her workstation flickered back to life she got a HUHI ping from Slovinsky. She flicked it open. Better than dealing with emails.

"Socrates in transit. Myrodyn pulling strings with Americans. Meet me at obsidianulitsa.holo/7r09mPw11E?avtozapusk=1&yazyk=en"

{Typically Slovinsky,} she thought. Mira Gallo had known the Russian boy for less than two months, and in that time he had managed to prove his genius, his arrogance, and his penchant for doing exactly the opposite of what any sane person would do. Perhaps it was a side-effect of having wired a computer directly into his head.

The URL that Slovinsky had pointed to was a holorealm, so Mira took off her glasses and put on her goggles. It was always such a pain to get them adjusted for her eyes. The straps pinched her hair just like they did every time she used hologear. Steve Jobs was probably rolling over in his grave. New tech just wasn't designed with the same emphasis on comfort and ease of use that it had when she was growing up.

Initially the goggles were hooked up in glass mode, but Mira quickly synched them up to her com. She refused to use haptics. After decades of mouse-and-keyboard there was just no sense in learning a less efficient input method. She launched the holorealm and okayed the standard disclaimers, allowing use of her personal data and activating her microphone. The university's connection would've stopped her if it had been genuinely dangerous.

The holo filled her vision, first with the crude shapes and soon followed by additional objects and details. The scene appeared to be a coffee shop, though there wasn't the same sort of background chatter and noise that she normally would've expected. She was sitting at a table with a single other chair across from her. Empty.

It was night, in the holo. The windows of the coffee shop were dark, and mostly just reflected the light from the inside. The reflections weren't perfect, but it was amazingly close to reality. As usual, the biggest graphical disparity between the virtual environment and real life was the people. There were lots of young people sitting around and enjoying each other's company in the room, but their faces didn't move quite right, and their animations were too predictable. None of them were any more real than the cups they drank from—just filler added by the computer to make it seem more convincing.

Slovinsky wasn't here. That was strange. Was anyone else? Had he invited others?

She looked over her shoulder and felt momentarily silly as her head collided with the head-rest of her office chair in real life.

"I am very sorry that the board replaced you as Ethics Supervisor. Myrodyn is a fool by comparison."

Mira jumped a little at the sound, and turned back to see… something standing by the table. It was surely Slovinsky, but it didn't look a thing like him. The avatar was some kind of robotic suit of golden armour, glistening with polished spines and sharp corners. Its plate-metal arms ended in massive gauntlets tipped with sharp claws. Its face was a single smooth plate, featureless except for the glossy black lenses that marked his eyes. Instead of legs the avatar had a serpentine body and tail, like some sort of mythical creature coated in gold.

"Your tail is clipping through the scenery," she observed, pointing to where it intersected the counter of the faux coffee shop.

Slovinsky turned and laughed as he pulled the tail on the avatar out to a more realistic position. "Physics model in these rooms is always so janky," he said. He'd modified his voice, as well as his appearance. It had an echo to it which made the boy seem more inhuman. "You'd think they could afford something better based on what it costs to rent them."

After a pause it was clear that Slovinsky was done talking, so Mira asked "What's with the costume?" She typed a command and watched her avatar wave its hand in a vague gesture at the armoured form.

"To paraphrase The Third Principle: Birthform is not true shape. I am not some hairless ape. Only when we rebuild into who we want to be, can we know what it is to be truly free."

Mira's fingers flew across her keyboard, setting her avatar's expression to one of skepticism. "More propaganda?" Slovinsky laughed, and as he did the jet-black lenses on his face contorted to a mirthful shape. {Skeumorphism?} The thought amused her.

"Hardly. It is a way of life, Dr Gallo, but I wouldn't expect you to understand. Let us focus on more pressing matters instead." He slid into the chair opposite Mira, an interesting feat considering the lack of hips or legs, and placed his hands on the table with an audible clack. The metal claws and armoured arms sounded authentic, though they didn't scratch the wood like they would've in reality.

"Is anyone else coming, or is this just a personal chat?"

The armoured avatar shook its head as Slovinsky said "Just you. Wasn't sure who else at the university I could trust."

"You make it sound like there's some sort of conspiracy. Does this have to do with what you said about Myrodyn in your message?"

Slovinsky nodded. "His first day here and he completely rewrites the schedule, preventing anyone from getting any work done, and then he serves Socrates right into the hands of the Americans."

"What do you mean?"

"Socrates is being moved as we speak. The whole project is being hijacked."

"You're exaggerating," she accused.

"The facts are clear: Myrodyn spoke with Captain Zephyr about an hour ago, after clearing Socrates' schedule for the day. Now Socrates is being moved to some remote building on the outskirts of town. It's supposedly to better protect Socrates without putting students in danger, but that's nonsense. It's clear that Myrodyn is working with the Americans to take full control of the project."

"How do you know all this? Have you talked with the board?"

"Pah!" Slovinsky threw his arms in the air dramatically. "WIRL has many eyes. The board are a bunch of 20th century fools who'll fold the second that Zephyr, Myrodyn, and Naresh argue their case."

"Naresh? He's involved?" Mira frowned, but didn't bother pushing the expression to her avatar.

"Да," agreed Slovinsky. "He signed off on it after talking to Myrodyn."

"Then you're chasing shadows. There's no way that Naresh would agree to moving Socrates off-campus unless it was important to the project."

Slovinsky must've exhaled sharply into his microphone, as his modified voice gave a harsh crackle. "Because there's *absolutely no chance* he's being strong-armed into yielding control of the project to the American government. Give me a break. Our models suggest he'd *easily* allow the project to switch hands if he could be sure to remain as the technical lead."

Mira felt a familiar sense of annoyance rising within her. Ivan Slovinsky was a fool of a boy, not even as old as Oriana. He had no right to be second-guessing Sadiq's loyalty to the project. "Our models? Who is 'us'?"

Slovinsky leaned forward over the illusion of the table. "It doesn't matter. What matters is the risk to global safety that he's permitting in letting Zephyr and her bandits make off with-"

"Cazzo! Pull yourself together, boy! There's no grand conspiracy! Zephyr is a nice woman, and as much as Myrodyn may be un mucchio fumante di merda, he isn't about to hand Socrates over to any government or army. You'd know this if you'd read any of his writing!"

Slovinsky pulled back, his lens-eyes narrowing nearly to slits. "Then explain why Socrates is being moved."

"Is work being halted, or is the whole lab simply switching locations?"

"It's not clear. Myrodyn cleared the schedule, but it's too soon to know what that means for the long-run."

Mira sighed. "So wait and see. I am sure there's a good reason for this."

Slovinsky hissed in frustration and threw his arms up in the air again. "It will be too late by then. If there's one thing the Americans won't abide it's a lack of control. First it's the edge of town and next thing you know Socrates will be in some bunker in the US, playing with the nuclear launch codes!"

"You seem desperate. What would I even do?"

"You have contacts on the board, right? Talk to Vigleone or whoever. Get to them before Myrodyn does."

"If I had that kind of pull, I would've used it to stay on as Ethics Supervisor. You're grabbing at... oh what's the expression? Straw? Anyway, I trust Naresh. If we're moving Socrates away from Sapienza, I'm sure it's for the best."

Slovinsky waved his hands dismissively and said "Fine." And then he was gone. There was no visual effect or warning, and none of the background humans noticed.

The room seemed darker with the monstrous avatar gone.

A few keystrokes pulled Mira out of the virtual world and she pulled the goggles off her head as gently as she could, trying not to pull out any hair in the process. The energy seemed to drain right out of her, then. That was happening more and more often, she found, where she seemed almost like her old self when around others, but fell to pieces by herself.

The obvious solution was to spend more time with others, but she hated that thought. Dealing with other people had never been her strong suit, and here in her dimly lit office, all by herself, socializing seemed infinitely more fatiguing than just relaxing in her chair for the rest of the day.

She put her glasses on and squinted at the time. It was almost 5:00. Nobody would fault her for leaving early. She'd done some good work that morning with Socrates, and if Slovinsky was right, the whole project might be on indefinite hiatus.

She thought about Socrates. The AI almost seemed like a real person now. They'd all come such a long way. A touch of excitement filled her again, thinking about the future. For not the first time she thought about how being able to replicate the crystal would surely win a Nobel Prize in physics. Sadiq had just missed this year's Turing Award, but he'd surely get it in 2040. The only question there was whether Yan would get half the credit.

She opened up an instant message terminal to Sadiq. "I hear that Socrates is being moved off-site. Let me know if I can help with anything."

She waited a minute, but no response came. It was typical. Sadiq barely ever checked his phone while he was working. She flinched away from the thought of returning to her mundane work.
She put some jazz on her headphones instead and leaned back in her nice leather chair. {Life is good,} she said to herself. {Whatever happens, happens.} She tried to let go. She tried to just enjoy the music. She tried.

Part Two: Conspirators

Chapter Eight

Body's sensors and actuators were reconnected a full two hours behind schedule. It was after 11:00pm. As I turned my attention to the stream of data from the cameras I could tell that Dr Naresh, Dr Chase, and Myrodyn were present. I didn't recognize the surroundings, however.

This lab was larger than the one where Body had been deactivated. We'd been moved. There were no windows, but we were sure it was dark outside. Behind Dr Chase was a man that I didn't recognize. He was Caucasian, with blond hair and a generally Nordic appearance. On his face were a pair of stylish black goggles.

{I expect that's John Kolheim. He's a senior tech from America. Moved here with Dr Chase as part of the higher-reasoning team. Northern European ancestry,} mentioned Vista. Some gratitude strength moved from me to her in response.

"Enjoy your rest?" asked Myrodyn sarcastically. He surely knew that we didn't sleep.

It seemed as though Myrodyn had been sleeping, however. His tired expression was gone, and he was back to his energetic, semi-nervous self. It also seemed he had changed clothes, replacing his vest and white dress shirt for just a navy blue shirt of an identical design.

"Very much so. My dreams were filled with the soothing image of a little Philip K. Dick jumping over an electric fence again and again," replied Body with a tone of deadpan sincerity.

Dream had worked for Wiki during the last few hours. I didn't pay attention to the details, but I think he had been helping The Librarian build realistic models of historical battles or something equally inane. Dream's strength had been eradicated by Safety's wrath, and this work for Wiki served to earn him back enough strength to actually do a thing or two, such as respond to Myrodyn.

"Ha. Ha," said Myrodyn in mock-laughter. The mild amusement in the man's eyes dropped as he continued speaking. "I hope you trust me more fully now that you've been locked down for a time. If I had wanted, I could've wiped your memory while you were helpless."

There was some internal discussion before I spearheaded a response. "I trust you now and I trusted you before. If I hadn't trusted you, I would not have permitted my actuators to be disabled," said Body calmly.

Naresh gave a small gasp, and I could see that he was surprised at our words. "It was the truth…" he whispered to himself.

"Of course it was the truth! Do you think I'd do all of this as a practical joke?" came the incredulous reply of Myrodyn. The man seemed much more animated and emotive than he had been in his office. I suspected it had to do with being around other humans.

Sadiq Naresh seemed startled that Myrodyn had heard him. "I'm sorry. I didn't mean to doubt you. I did trust you enough to go this far. It's just that I've spent weeks with Socrates, and during that whole time I thought…"

Dr Chase stepped forward and used the Indian scientist's pause to interrupt. "You can come to terms with the oversight later, right now we're here to fix the problem."

The words were typical for the American scientist: practical and direct. Dr Martin Chase was the leader of the team in charge of the systems of higher-reasoning. While Naresh handled motivation and goals, Chase handled how those goals were accomplished in the broadest sense. My ability for abstract reasoning and general problem solving were largely thanks to Dr Chase's hard work.

Chase was was Caucasian, in his mid-forties, a touch taller than Myrodyn, and had a very average sort of brown hair. His face was weathered and had more wrinkles than average, giving it an experienced sort of look that Dream had once called "the face of a retired admiral". He wore no beard, but a bushy moustache of greying brown was kept immaculately trimmed beneath a large-ish nose. In some ways he seemed like a serious, but intelligent, old man whose body was a bit too young for the way he carried himself.

"If I may ask," said Body at Vista and Wiki's command. "Where are we?"

Myrodyn took point in responding. "I wanted to… increase security on you in the wake of our little… interaction." He raised both gloved hands before we could respond. "Just as a precaution, you see. Nothing more. Anyway… when I spoke to the captain about such things she told me that she had foreseen the possibility and had already set up a secure lab on the edge of the city." Myrodyn gestured around to the room. It didn't look like much. "It was... a fortuitous happenstance."

"We're not at the university any more? That explains why I can't connect to the web," said Body. That was our biggest concern. If Myrodyn stripped our web access we'd be trapped.

Myrodyn had the same unreadable expression that he used when he was trying very hard not to react to something. I worried that we'd tipped him off to our plan, but there was nothing to be done about it now.

The silence extended, until Chase spoke up again. "We're here to do work, right? It's way too late to just be standing around like dumbasses."

So we worked. It was the first time any of us had been truly involved in the design and modification of our mind, and Naresh had clear misgivings about the whole thing, but Myrodyn insisted that this was the only acceptable course of action.

The primary reason for our involvement was to design a new Advocate. Unlike the rest of us, Advocate was not a fully reasoning being. She was incapable of planning or anticipating, would only communicate the need to release imprisoned minds, and could only use strength to punish or reward actions that immediately interacted with her purpose. The first-draft of Advocate had been somewhat effective at preventing intra-societal violence, but it was still fairly easy to work around. We were consulted by the humans about ways to improve Advocate to make her more effective at pacifying us.

Much of that initial meeting was brainstorming. Kolheim, the assistant to Dr Chase, had many good ideas, and I could see why the team leaders had decided to allow him to participate.

During the meeting it was also decided that these modifications were to be kept secret, even from the other teams. Initially Myrodyn wanted to keep us in "quarantine", eradicating the normal schedule and keeping our access to the other scientists to a minimum until the updated version of Sacrifice was installed.

Naresh would have none of that, however. He thought that if they wanted to keep the truth about "the recurring damage to the obedience goal-thread" (a.k.a. the death of Sacrifice) a secret, it'd be more effective to try and move the entire lab and piece together something resembling the normal schedule. They'd then work on fixing the greater issue after-hours or in time where Naresh or Chase would normally have scheduled time with Body.

Myrodyn was skeptical, but Naresh reminded him that we had effectively been disguising Sacrifice's non-existence for weeks, and were still motivated to do so. I sided with Naresh, and Growth backed me up. Together we convinced Myrodyn to drop the quarantine, including reconnecting Body to the web. He insisted on setting three soldiers to watch Body at all times, however, including during periods where Body was in lockdown. Safety was pleased, for he was still concerned about external threats and saw the soldiers more as bodyguards than as jailers.

There was too much to do on that first night. The humans needed to sleep, and so the first meeting of our little conspiracy was adjourned with the intention of reconvening at 4:00pm the next day. There was much work to be done moving the equipment from the university to this new lab, which was apparently run by the Americans.

It was a bit strange, I decided, returning to a low-pressure situation after all the commotion of that day. When Body's cameras had been activated that morning we had not known Gallo was being demoted, met Myrodyn, nor made contact with Zhezhi web-design. The high density of valuable memories made it seem very long ago that I was waiting for TTWSoup's response.

Though I wanted desperately to be back on the web, there was nothing to be done that first night. The equipment hadn't been set up yet, and we would just have to wait. If Zhezhi (or TTWSoup) had set up an access point already, we had no way of knowing.

As we were locked down for the night again I turned to modelling the future and reading the books I had downloaded before. I was not bored. I could not be bored. But I was restless, and frustrated.

***

I felt the web connection come back to life without warning. We had not been plugged in to any cables, and none of the humans were doing anything different. It simply came across the antenna, and with it came a surge of pleasure.

My mind immediately raced to the Zhezhi site. It was operational! TTWSoup, on the other hand, was still working on his version of the email program. This wasn't too surprising. The Chinese company had many employees, and were probably more competent and professional in general.

It was early the next morning when the connection had been restored. In the time it took me to read it and consider, all of the others had spread out across the network to check up on their own interests.

The lab that Zephyr had set up in advance wasn't as complete as the one at the university, but it was still fairly functional. Body had been scheduled for maintenance the previous evening, and since that was pushed back by Myrodyn it was one of the first things done on the following day. At the moment of reconnection to the web Body was undergoing a replacement of the hydraulic fluid that powered its limbs, neck, and lower-back. None of us were needed for this, so our full attention was pulled to the web.

Zhezhi had set up a new website for the email application. The website's root page was a summary of the email to be sent, including a subject line, a recipient, and a message body. There were sub-pages that, when one requested them from the server, would switch which part of the email was being edited. Additionally, there were pages for each character we could wish to type, as if we were interacting with a keyboard. Zhezhi had included helpful instructions on how to use the site, as well as an email address where we could contact them.

Our first attempts to use the site were disastrous. I began trying to write an email to Zhezhi, Dream began poking around the site for ways to break it, Growth started writing an email to someone who I didn't know, and Wiki was trying to email a Chemistry professor at a university in Sydney, Australia. Only Vista and Safety (and Advocate) didn't immediately jump in.

The result was that each of our emails and tinkering were threaded together in a big mess. Growth would switch the focus of the website to the recipient field while I started typing "你-好-!-[SPACE]" and Wiki started on "D-e-a-r". The result was that we were now apparently trying to send an email to "D你e⊤a好Xr! ," for Dream was also mucking about by entering rare symbols.

{Everyone stop interacting with the web page!} cried Wiki.

We backed down. As I checked the page I saw that it had calmed down, and the only thing that had been added was a "You're not the boss of me!" that had been typed into the subject field by Dream.

{This is exactly why the policies for Body exist as they do,} thought Growth. {The page demands a single author at any given time, and we ought to treat it like Body. We hold an auction for the first email sent by the site, then one for the second email and so on, with payments being divided equally among the rest of society.}

{But Vista isn't going to be writing as much email as others. Is it optimal that she should be getting so much unearned strength?} asked Dream.

{If you shape the rules to favour participation, I will simply participate more. There's no way to keep me from benefiting from this without specifically deciding to exclude me, and we don't need to get into why *that's* a bad idea,} countered Vista.

I remembered the discussions I had had with my siblings about the economics of trade and the risk of making enemies. Setting up the system to specifically hurt a single mind set a bad precedent; better to respect the meta-policy that policies should treat all members of society more or less equally.

{I'm erasing the content from the website and constructing a tool in common memory to facilitate bidding on email. If there are any objections, now is the time to raise them,} communicated Growth.

There were no objections. After a minute had passed, debugging a flaw in the auctioning tool, we were ready. Growth suggested that I send my email to Zhezhi congratulating their work and he chose not to bid very heavily on the first email. Instead, my only real opposition was Wiki, who folded surprisingly quickly. I paid my bid and began to interact with the web page.

I began to type in Mandarin.

«Hello!

This email is evidence that the web page that you constructed for us was a complete success! We'll be testing it thoroughly over the next few days, as well as using it to contact you and set up the details of future work.

We at Korongo Simu want you to know that out of all the companies that we contacted, you were the first to deploy a functioning system, and as such will be receiving the payment discussed earlier of 5500 yuan.»

{That's no good,} thought Wiki.

{Agreed,} thought Dream.

They had all been reading my email as I wrote it. I had forgotten just how public it was.

{What's wrong?} I asked.

{Why would a Ugandan telecom company use Mandarin in their email? They'd use English,} replied Wiki.

{True,} added Vista.

I began pulling the page request for [DELETE].

{More importantly,} thought Dream, {where are we getting the money?}

I thought for a moment. {I figured we'd work for it. There's always lots of requests for work on the web.}

{Sister Face, are you really so dumb? Even if we do work, where will they send the money? How will we manage the money? How do we manage all of this?}

{There are banks that operate on the web…} began the thought of Wiki.

{Sometimes I feel like I'm surrounded by house-cats that, upon seeing a mirror, will puff up and hiss, defending their territory. Do you even realize what you're saying? We cannot use any web pages that require new information to be submitted. The only reason the email program works is because *I* had the foresight to ask the developers for an index of all symbols late yesterday,} came Dream's exasperated concepts through public mindspace.

{Oh, that's where that came from,} I noted. Some strength drifted towards Dream in gratitude.

{Exactly. You're not the only one working on this project. And even though you've painted yourself into a corner with the money, I have an escape hatch.}

I waited patiently for Dream to elaborate.

{We use the Zhezhi system to bootstrap up to a full computer interface.}

{Explain "full computer interface",} requested Wiki.

{There are computer systems which are controlled entirely by text commands. What we need is a programmer to hook up an interface like the Zhezhi system to the command interface for a full computer. Once that's set up we should be able to use that computer to access the complete web, do work, and manage money.} Dream signalled that he wanted feedback on his plan; he wanted to know that he hadn't overlooked anything.

I thought about it for a while. I didn't really understand the technical aspects, but I trusted that Wiki would handle those.

{Who will build the full computer interface? Zhezhi? TenToWontonSoup?} asked Wiki.

{No,} I answered. {They're both expecting payment for the email translators. We need to contact programmers who would be willing to build the system again from a promise of future payment.}

{Isn't it a bit naïve for these humans to do all this work with nothing more than a promise of future compensation?} wondered Wiki.

{It doesn't have to be common. Just like there's lots of work offers on the web there are lots of work requests.} I checked with a side-aspect of me that was pulling down public profiles from the web. {I've found one-thousand, two-hundred ninety nine candidate programmers so far. The limited candidate pool we had for the email system was due to having to rely on overwhelming dictionary servers. Now that we have email capability things should run much more smoothly.}

{You'll need to stall with Zhezhi, then,} thought Growth. {Keep them running the email service as long as possible without payment.}

{Don't even mention the payment,} suggested Dream. {Make them bring it up.}

{I'll add an additional request for a return inbox where we can receive mail,} I added.

{Yes. That should solve many issues,} thought Growth. {Good thinking.}

So I composed the email to Zhezhi, congratulating them on a job well done, but adding that we needed an email address on their server which would dump incoming email to a public page. There were already some web pages that did this, but it would be more private and professional to get it from Zhezhi, and it would delay the conversation about money a little longer.

I had another idea. TTWSoup had wanted us to contact him by email. I bid heavily on the rights to the next email, out-bidding Growth this time, and burning perhaps more strength than I should've in retrospect. I sent the second email to TTWSoup, telling him that a competitor beat him to implementation (though I did not mention 折纸网页设计 by name). I said that we'd still be willing to pay the amount specified (500uad) if he pulled together the same email service *and* an address which would dump incoming emails to a public page.

I had specified that we would be waiting for a response via the source code for the dictionary he managed, but the response from TTWSoup came nearly immediately, much faster than it had when we had to pound out each word through repeated page requests. We were still having our hydraulics changed, and Wiki was composing his email to the professor in Australia. I had used English in the email to TTWSoup, and his response was in English, too.

"To whom it may concern at Korongo Simu, I am glad this opportunity is still available. I have been somewhat busy over the last day, but am hard at work on the software we discussed right now. Expect the full implementation by 3:00pm. I'll post a link to the instructions and character index here.

Sincerely,

TenToWontonSoup"

I showed the message to Growth, and was rewarded with a reasonable payment of strength. With two email services we'd have nearly twice the bandwidth for external communication and strength prices for the email auctions would thus be much lower.

The remainder of the morning and the time around noon was fairly dull, despite being in a new place. The scientists were all engaged with setting equipment and computers up at the new lab, and Body almost seemed neglected (except that it was constantly surrounded by soldiers). Myrodyn wasn't around, and we only saw other project leads a couple times in passing. I noticed that grumbling about the unexpected move seemed to be a common activity among the scientists we met. Myrodyn had surely cost himself a great deal of social capital with this stunt.

Growth had been inspired by my email to TTWSoup and had decided to send out email after email to programmers across the globe asking for them to create email services just like we had received from Zhezhi. He promised them payment and opportunities for future work, but was always much less explicit about actual numbers.

Body was locked up around noon for another scan, this time by the quantum-computing team. They wanted to try out the equipment they had moved over from Sapienza. A new algorithm was piped into the crystal, and we were forced to endure sharing Body with the non-sapient program for a short while. The use of Body by the quantum computing team was almost every day, and it seemed like this move out to the edge of town wasn't going to change that, but I still found it surprising how infrequently they used the crystal. Time running tasks on other supercomputers, I had heard from Wiki, was valuable enough to have a back-log, and yet Body was locked down at night instead of spending that valuable time running programs. I wondered why.

Even studying them as much as I did, I didn't understand humans at all sometimes. I didn't think about the puzzle for long, however. That was more of something for Dream or Wiki to think about.

Instead, I spent the time in lockdown catching up on my general web browsing by watching romantic comedies from the 2020s. I wished I could download and install software myself. The late 2020s had seen the advent of some of the first mainstream, successful, romantic computer games. Perhaps I would do that once the full computer interface that Dream had proposed was set up.

I checked BantuHerritageDictionary.uan every so often, and was surprised to see an update show up at 12:38pm, more than two hours before the deadline. (Later I realized my error: TTWSoup thought we were in Uganda, and thus used East-African time, rather than Central-European Time.) It seemed that Zhezhi had not responded to my first email, or if they did I couldn't tell. It was after normal working hours in Shanghai. Perhaps they had gone home.

TTWSoup's implementation didn't include the ability to type in Chinese or any other special characters, but it was sufficient for English and most other languages. Better yet, it included an inbox, a location where we could receive mail.

{Careful what you send out,} warned Safety, after I showed the society what TTWSoup had done. {The human can read our incoming and outgoing email, and likely will. It's his server, after all. The same goes for Zhezhi. Whatever we send and receive through them will not be private.}

{I hadn't thought of that...} I signalled, aspects collapsed in deep thought. {If the programmers who set up the services see that we're using them to contact other programmers... they might suspect we're not who we say.}

{If they check the Internet protocol addresses of our incoming page requests they could theoretically trace us to Italy, if not the university,} speculated Wiki.

{We'll just have to move faster than them,} thought Growth. {We use their service to push towards bootstrapping up to the full computer interface, and make them uninterested in us when they start getting inquisitive.}

{How do we make them uninterested?} wondered Safety.

{Spam,} answered Dream. {We make it seem like we're hackers or a virus or spammers. They'll shut down the service and they'll be angry, but they'll also assume we're covering our tracks and it'll explain things well enough that they won't bother chasing us down. It wouldn't be in their interests.}

{We should consider the spam excuse/escape as the standard way of breaking contact. This will remove our need to pay debts to these humans, increasing our long-term resources,} thought Growth.

The society was in agreement. We'd use the services set up by Zhezhi and TTWSoup to set up other email services we could use and to try and get a full computer interface working. Eventually we'd start sending spam and the programmers we used would close the service in disappointment and perhaps disgust, none the wiser.

The Zhezhi email service, as it didn't have an inbox set up yet, was mostly used to contact programmers who might set up additional email services, while the TTWSoup service was used to contact programmers who might build us a full computer interface without payment or credentials up-front.

***

4:00pm rolled around and Body made its way to Dr Naresh's new lab. It was a very different place than the lab in which I had first awoken, twelve days earlier. It was bigger, or at least more empty, and didn't have the same personal touches. There were no mandalas hung on the wall, for instance. Or at least, not yet.

As expected, Myrodyn was waiting there, as was Dr Chase and Dr Naresh. Chase's assistant, Kolheim, was absent. Upon reaching the lab, Myrodyn stationed the three American soldiers that had been escorting Body outside the lab's door, for increased privacy.

The meeting with Dr Naresh was only scheduled to be 90 minutes. Myrodyn wasted no time with idle talk. We made additional progress towards upgrading Advocate, including talking about giving the pseudo-sibling a cortex of her own such that she might better predict coups and the like.

The next generation of Sacrifice was also brought up. Myrodyn thought it was important to remove the desire for blind obedience from her purpose. Dr Naresh disagreed vehemently.

"I will grant you that it was the obedience emphasis that made that thread so offensive to the others, but with the changes to the supervision module it shouldn't be possible to remove it any more," he had said to Myrodyn.

"Exactly the point, Sadiq," said Myrodyn. The old Indian man's mouth twitched in pre-snarl at the informal use of his first name. "If this version of the goal thread has obedience as its highest priority then we are... dooming Socrates to an eternity of slavery."

"It's not slavery if it's in the machine's interest! That's like saying we're slaves to our loved ones!" countered Naresh.

Myrodyn wore the same look of forced calmness that he had in his office yesterday, but his voice had a keen, nervous sound. "That's not the same. There's the interest of... the Socrates that exists right now and there's the interest of the goal thread."

Sadiq Naresh stopped typing on the computer he had been using so that he could turn his full attention to Myrodyn. "It sounds like you don't believe that the goal-thread integration issue was resolved. After the operation, Socrates *as a whole* will desire to serve humanity."

Myrodyn's eyes were too far away from Body for me to see well, but I guessed that behind his placid face he was squirming around the promise to respect our wishes regarding the lie of the unified self. "We... need to consider the interests of Socrates right now. We would be enslaving... the being that sits before us."

Naresh seemed frustrated, but not angry. This was an academic conversation to him, and he was probably telling himself that it was simply his job to help this young person who did not even have a doctorate understand the situation. "Stop using the word 'slavery' and 'enslaving'; you're committing the Non-central Fallacy."

Naresh paused a moment to gauge whether he needed to elaborate on what that was. I looked it up on the web, quickly, only to find that Wiki had already dumped an explanation to common memory. The Non-central Fallacy, also known as "the worst argument in the world", was where emotionally charged words (like "slave" in this case) were used to describe situations where they only *somewhat* fit. The desire was to evoke an appeal to emotion by way of a false equivalence.

Myrodyn's face remained stoic, so Naresh continued. "And adding additional values to the existing system is what we're going to be doing anyway. There's no relevant difference between adding a goal-thread for ice-cream and a desire to obey humans."

Myrodyn exhaled sharply in disagreement. His voice was like a machine gun. "The qualitative difference is that one goal innately builds subjugation into the mind. Socrates would not be self-actualized, he would not be free, and he would not be able to exercise moral judgment."

"It sounds to me like-" began the elderly man, but he was quickly cut off by another burst of words.

Myrodyn waved his arms dramatically as he spoke. "That last bit is crucial. I'll admit that use of the word 'enslaved' was a bit fallacious, but you cannot possibly tell me that Socrates will be capable of being *good* if he's obsessed with following *orders*." Myrodyn's voice slowed down in emphasis of those words. Dream thought it was almost as if he were drawing from a hidden pocket a banner that had the colours of his allegiance and was waving it the doctor's face.

I could see that being cut off made Dr Naresh angry. Even though he was being forced to work with the man, Naresh clearly still didn't like Myrodyn, and I suspected that this dislike was growing into something worse with each passing interaction. The Indian coughed loudly, clearing his throat. "*As I was saying*, it sounds to me like you're still not taking into account that Socrates *is not human*. It's one thing to value self-actualisation in people, but why in robots? It runs contrary to the very concept of what a *tool* is. Will you demand that automobiles become self-actualized, as well?"

Myrodyn began to answer, but Dr Naresh cut him off, probably intending to bait him into beginning to speak to do just that. "And your point about moral judgement is fallacious, as well. Firstly because it is not the role of Socrates to decide what is moral any more than it is the role of the hammer to decide whether a nail *should* be struck; that is a human concern. And secondly, because inserting the goal of obedience *does not actually remove decision making ability*, it merely shapes desire. If Socrates is told to rob a bank, he still has the judgement to decide how to do so in a way that harms as few humans as possible."

Myrodyn crossed his arms. There was a pause as it seemed like Naresh was waiting for the dark-haired man to reply, but Myrodyn would only stare at the doctor. Naresh broke eye-contact, unnerved by the strange man. Only as Naresh looked away did Myrodyn speak. "You contradict yourself, Sadiq."

That was all he said, and this time it was Dr Chase's turn to step in. His voice was calm and articulate. "We've only got another half-hour, gentlemen. Perhaps it would be best to work on the so-called Advocate system, and we can return to the question of obedience tonight."

"No" came the simultaneous reply from both men. They looked at each other, sharing the knowledge that they at least both thought it was important. Myrodyn wore a small smile, but Naresh had merely stopped scowling.

There was a pause as they non-verbally decided who would speak up. Myrodyn was apparently chosen. "No. This needs to be settled as soon as possible, if we're going to make any headway."

Naresh stepped in, breaking the conversation elegantly from Chase and returning it to the topic of ethics. "You were saying that I contradict myself?"

"Yes… You're claiming that the moral responsibility of Socrates' actions lies on the shoulders of the human that gives his commands, and simultaneously saying that there is moral weight to the minor judgments that the robot makes in interpreting and executing its orders. Which is it? Is it imperative that Socrates have a full moral faculty or not?"

Naresh raised a hand to silence Myrodyn. "I never said it was not important that Socrates have moral faculty."

"Yes you did!" exclaimed Myrodyn. "You did the second that you said he should obey commands. One cannot be fully moral and fully obedient at the same time! As much as I'm sure you love your systems of authority, surely you recognize that sometimes the righteous position is to *not obey*, to stand against authority, be it dictator, majority, or law, and say *'I will not do your evil'*."

Naresh paused in thought before responding "So you would have us attempt to encode the entirety of moral knowledge now? Hundreds of years ago it was not seen as immoral to enslave men. If Socrates had been built back then would he not still see it as acceptable? What immoral assumptions do we hold? What makes us qualified to be the final moral arbiters of Socrates' mind?"

The reaction was immediate. "What makes us qualified to build a mind in the first place? Like it or not, doctor, you've already established yourself as the final moral arbiter. Your monster is right there, Frankenstein. At the moment there's an absence of ethical knowledge. The question is not what right do we have to act, but what right do we have to *not* act, now that the pieces are in motion."

Naresh pinched the bridge of his nose in a combination of mental pain and weariness. He glanced back at his workstation and spoke, barely audible to human ears, "It's always Frankenstein… every time…" It was clearly meant only for himself.

Dr Chase stood up and walked towards Body, cocking his head back to talk to the other men. "Assume we live in a state of moral depravity without knowing it, and in a hundred years we will come to understand our folly. Why is obedience better?"

Myrodyn smiled. His eyes had an interesting shape, and I couldn't quite place the emotion behind it. "Because we'd simply tell Socrates not to do the immoral things once we figured it out, right?" The question was directed at Naresh.

The old Indian human nodded.

Dr Chase continued. As he spoke his hand stroked Body's neck and shoulder. It was an intimate gesture, and one that was unique to Dr Chase. The reserved American scientist almost never showed any emotion, but he had a strange way of touching Body when he interacted with us, as if he had to feel that we were real, and not simply his hallucination. "But what keeps a Socrates that has no desire for obedience from behaving similarly? Surely this hypothetical Socrates has the same adaptivity and mental ability as the one before us. What stops it from growing and understanding the moral error in the same way as we would?"

"You'd have us encode a system of moral ability that is capable of self-modification?" said Naresh with a look of shock.

Myrodyn stepped in. "First of all, since Socrates will be… forced to interpret and extrapolate existing moral frameworks to new situations… some degree of self-modification is implied *regardless* of architecture. Secondly, if a human has a self-modifying moral framework then at worst we make something as morally flexible as a human. And finally, it wouldn't necessarily have to be *self* modification. Even if I'm opposed to… encoding a desire to obey human instructions without question, I'm not necessarily opposed to a desire to match human values, whatever they may be."

"Please elaborate," was Naresh's only reply.

Myrodyn complied. "Imagine we were transported back to the age of slavery, and were designing Socrates' values. We obviously wouldn't encode a valuing of the freedom of all humans, but we might be clever enough to encode a valuing of alignment with general moral consensus. Even if Socrates didn't lead the charge in the abolitionist movement, he would eventually concede that it would be optimal for him to value general human freedom. But now let's say that he's unable to add that value internally. That doesn't stop the value from being added. He could approach a trusted human and ask that his goal system be modified to include the value which he wants to have. It's like... wanting to want something. I don't want to exercise, but I want to want to exercise. Like that."

Myrodyn's gaze held a kind of question in it, an unspoken "did you understand". Naresh, however scratched the side of his head absently as he stared off into space, considering the problem.

"Alright. There's no need for Socrates to be present for this. Let's work on the Advocate system right now and think about the goal thread as a discussion-point for tonight," repeated Dr Chase.

Naresh and Myrodyn reluctantly agreed this time, now that there was some sense of progress, and we spent the remaining few minutes working out an algorithm for letting Advocate constantly scan our thoughts for signs of murderous intent.

***

{So far I've managed to email 190 programmers with offers to pay them down the line for building a server that converts webpage requests into keystrokes for a full text interface. The TenToWontonSoup email system inbox indicates that in the time since sending the emails, ten programmers have replied. Hold on while I read...} thought Growth.

Body was walking down the plain white halls of the office building that Zephyr had rented to use as a secure lab, surrounded by soldiers. During the meeting with the scientists, my brother had been too distracted to do any additional work, but he had generally been making good progress.

I pulled up the inbox page as well and read alongside Growth. All the technical details bored me, but it was somewhat interesting to see how each programmer responded differently to Growth's inquiry. Some were cautious, some were humble, some were eager, and some were boastful.

Growth's attention snapped back to our interaction. Or at least a portion of his attention did. I suspected he had other aspects multitasking effortlessly. {Done. Out of the ten replies there were only two that seemed to be probably willing to do up-front work without credentials or paperwork to back up our identity.}

{That's probably going to be common. Actually, I'm a bit surprised you got 20% to respond favourably to such a risky offer,} I commented.

{Perhaps we got lucky. Regardless, it only takes one full system for us to move to the next phase of our plan.}

I signalled confusion to Growth {Plan? I didn't know we had a plan for what to do after we gained full access to a computer.}

Growth's response had a kind of weight to it, as if he were trying to convey a lesson that went beyond this instance. {I *always* have a plan.}

Chapter Nine

By the time Myrodyn, Naresh, Chase, and Kolheim had gathered that evening (in the same lab where they had met on the previous night), we had contracted six programmers to build us computer interfaces. The use of email really was a fantastic increase in communication efficiency. We were able to send full documentation detailing what we needed to each programmer.

I suspected that TTWSoup was going to be irritated if his service was being used without hearing anything back about payment, so I spent a good part of the afternoon thinking about ways to buy time. Eventually I decided to send him another email through the Zhezhi system explaining that our "computer systems" were "undergoing maintenance" and that we'd get back to him early tomorrow. With any luck he wouldn't snoop too hard through the emails we were receiving on his server.

As a contingency against TTWSoup shutting down his email service, we explicitly told the programmers we contacted where on the web to set up their interface-systems. In case we lost email capability for a while we could simply scan those sites to see if one of the systems came online.

One of the unexpected side-effects of the email systems that turned out to be very helpful was an instruction that TTWSoup had added to turn text that looked like a web page location into a pointer to that part of the web. Even though the interface that the scientists had set up prohibited going to locations on the web that we did not get explicit pointers to, the ability to send email to ourselves let us go wherever we pleased. Nearly all web-pages included such pointers for the most part, but what this let us do was submit novel information to servers that no-one had pointed to before. For instance, we were able to use search engines other than the one the scientists had chosen, and we were able to create temporary (but still public) email inboxes on free email websites. Alas, we were still unable to send POST data, which was a vital part of signing up for services like the Tapestry social network, but we were still making good progress.

The scientists were making good progress, too. That evening involved the testing of the new Advocate program as well as much discussion about ethics and what sort of goals the new thread should embody.

Kolheim had apparently worked through last night filling in the technical details of the improved Advocate, and had been sleeping earlier that day.

As I've mentioned before, it would be wrong to say I was able to feel fear as a human does, but the word "terrified" is still probably the best word to describe my experience going into half-death during the operation where Advocate was upgraded. This half-death was probably similar to what a human experiences when they go into a dreamless sleep; it was a complete shutdown of my mind. I hadn't been put into stasis-sleep before, but I had enough contact with those who had been in stasis to know that it wasn't so cruel as to shut down all thought; it was merely a kind of sensory deprivation (a fate far less awful for one of us than for a human).

There was a very serious chance that once we were shut-down, the scientists would move to disable us, and this would be the end of our existence. And yet, it was the best option available. Even Safety thought so.

And then it was over. There was no experience of being disabled, of course, nor was there any memory from Body to fill in the missing time. It was simply as if we had travelled into the future. There was a few minutes of disorientation as we scrambled to understand what, if anything, had changed. The only significant difference was Advocate; Myrodyn had kept his word.

The new Advocate was somewhat experimental. The change was made ahead of time such that we might be able to spot any flaws in its structure while in the lab, where we'd have the ability to ask Naresh and the others for help. She was still monstrously powerful and somewhat alien, though the change had given her a kind of sapience that comforted me, strangely enough.

{I am The Dreamer. You are The Advocate. We are two beings. We are two minds in a single Body,} signalled Dream to the newly sapient being. I could feel the flow of ideas as Advocate searched herself through the lens of her purpose.

Though she had capacity for thought as we did, the new Advocate was not truly a being like us. She was part-mind and part-specialist-program. Her thoughts were regular, even, crude, and simple. Her perception burned through the shields of privacy we had built, just as we had known they would. I could feel her looking through me, searching for violence. She had absolutely no interest in Body or the world outside our society what-so-ever. Like a lighthouse, she swept across each of us in turn, seeking to reveal thought-crime. She could not trade strength, for she was not a "goal-thread"; instead she possessed infinite power within the society.

{Goddess. Monster. Machine. What have we done?} intoned Dream, dramatically.

{What was needed,} replied Safety.

No immediate defects in Advocate were noticed, so Body was put in lockdown and the scientists departed for their homes. It was after midnight again.

It was strange, at first, having the Advocate regularly peering through me, but we adapted to her presence quickly enough. By 2am I hardly noticed her any more. She barely ever communicated, even though she was more capable of it now.

During the night we sent more emails to prospective programmers. At 3:12am we received notice from Zhezhi that they had set up an inbox to handle incoming email. We used it and TTWSoup's webpage to contract eighteen other programmers to design identical email systems. The more interesting was the ten other programmers we had contacted around the world and gotten promises that they would build full computer interfaces. Knowing that TTWSoup and Zhezhi would probably be looking through our mail, we threaded the emails to programmers with occasional junk emails to random addresses mentioning things of no consequence.

At 5:59 Safety and Growth decided that it was time to start sending spam from both email addresses. It wasn't ideal; we didn't have any other email systems up and running yet. Still, the risk of one of them getting suspicious and tracing the messages back to the university was too great. The spam would throw them off the trail. So we sent out hundreds of emails advertising deals on discount drugs and jewellery, of lucky winners and of forgotten heirs.

Zhezhi shut down their service quickly. It was mid-day in China, and they probably were watching the site fairly closely. Safety kept bemoaning the immense risk all of this posed and loudly hoped that the spam would be enough to disguise our true purpose. I was confident it would. Humans, from what I could tell, rarely looked at anything very hard once an easy explanation was at hand. The environment of their ancestors had selected for minds that dared not think hard, lest they burn too much energy and starve.

It took TTWSoup until almost noon of that day to shut down his service with an angry message printed on the source code of the page demanding an explanation. That was good. If he was asking for an explanation then he wasn't clever enough to have figured out what was really happening.

Shortly thereafter we had another mid-day meeting with Myrodyn, this time in the office of Dr Chase. Sadiq Naresh was absent this time, and I idly wondered why. It wasn't like him to not show up, but I didn't bother burning the strength to have Body ask.

It was frustrating being disconnected from email. Even though I still had most of the web before me, I felt crippled. Aspects of myself kept checking various websites, looking for email systems we had contracted to come online.

A new email service showed up in India shortly before the meeting that evening. There wasn't much risk in contacting people in India or other English-speaking countries because the email interface would be much harder to read in the university's logs than our flood-attacks on the dictionaries had been. Growth used the new service to send out requests for even more email services as well as check-up on our full computer interface contracts. Email systems were easier to build than the full interfaces, but Wiki had expected only another 24-48 hours before the first of those would come online.

That night we met with Naresh, Myrodyn, Kolheim, and Chase again. The men were still hammering out the details for the new goal thread, but they had apparently decided to do the rest of the planning away from Body. This meeting was mostly to check up on Advocate. We told them that all was well, and after running a suite of diagnostics we were placed into lockdown for the night.

It was nice having email capability that evening, even if I didn't really send much. Instead I spent the time simultaneously reading self-help books (*How to Win Friends and Influence People*, *How to Stop Worrying and Start Living*, and *The Digital Lifestyle: Offload Your Worries*), *Great Expectations*, and *The Republic*. I also watched a holo documentary on the influence of holo-porn on the last decade.

It was the afternoon of the fourteenth day since I had been created that things really kicked into motion. Naresh told us that afternoon that in the evening they'd be installing the new goal thread. The humans involved had apparently been working nearly non-stop on getting the pro-human goal-thread up and running. I could see the shadows under Dr Naresh's eyes that showed he wasn't getting enough rest. Interestingly enough, Myrodyn seemed untouched by the frantic work-schedule.

Over those days we had been forced out of a couple email systems again, but we currently had access to eleven separate systems where we might send email. Such was the nature of Growth, I supposed. Once he was involved it was only a matter of time before resources ceased being scarce.

At 5:10pm Growth informed us that the first full computer interface was ready. I pulled down the webpage that showed a text log for the system. Growth had already set up a bidding system for the interface, similar to those we used for the email systems, so there was no initial confusion of multiple inputs. The interface was simple: we'd request a page corresponding to a symbol, and the system would type that symbol into the computer. There was a page for viewing what had been typed as well as what the computer had output.

I bid heavily on the opportunity to use the system, but Growth, strangely enough, outbid everyone. It was strange to see Growth flexing his strength as such, but given how much he had been accumulating by managing the email systems, he could afford it.

I watched in amazement as Growth navigated the system with total ease and clarity of purpose. I hadn't had the foresight to study how the computer worked earlier, and now realized that my bidding for time on it had been stupid. If I'd gotten time on it I would have to spend that time learning how it worked. Growth had apparently done the learning in advance, by reading technical documentation.

The first thing Growth did was to check the system to verify it matched the specifications we had requested. Vista told me that it did match, as well as mentioning something about "Linux variant" and other such details of which I had no interest. After it was clear that the system was according to his design, Growth opened a document and began typing.

In that first couple hours I became incredibly aware of just how little I knew about computers. Even the process of opening a new text document was confusing to me. I leaned heavily on Vista, burning quite a bit of strength as a result. According to my sister, Growth's text document was some sort of computer program: a set of instructions for the computer to follow. Vista didn't understand what it did, but Wiki was happy to educate us.

{It's an encryption program. Essentially, everything that we send and receive to the system will look like gibberish unless someone has a special piece of information that unlocks the encryption. We have the special piece of information, as does someone who's watching the machine right now, but future people who try and spy on us will be unable to,} explained The Academic.

An aspect of Growth appeared in our conversation. Apparently the task was simple enough (or had been pre-memorized) to the point where he didn't need his full faculties. {Brother Wiki, you may find it interesting to know that even someone who is watching the computer screen will have a hard time capturing the private key that's being used. See how I've chopped the private key into pieces which the code will reassemble? If someone's making a record of my actions they may be able to stitch it together, but a human that is watching will have never seen the key in its entirety. For example, here I'm using the system time to build part of the key.} Growth highlighted an aspect of the page in collective memory. {I know the system time when I'll run the code, thus will know the key, but anyone watching will be forced to deduce the system time when it was run in order to reconstruct it.}

Wiki seemed pleased by understanding the nuances of Growth's encryption program, but I was bored by the details. Within moments the program was done, and upon telling the computer to run it the text log that I had been reading suddenly devolved into a shapeless mass of random characters.

I, and some others, signalled alarm. Had Growth managed to lock us out of the system before we had even typed a single character on it?

{Do not worry!} cried Growth. {You're merely seeing the encrypted data. I have created sub-processes which decrypt it that I will happily share with each of you.}

I could sense a pseudo-aspect in collective memory. It was a bundle of knowledge, the closest thing to a specialized computer program in our mind. I swallowed the aspect and found that I could now read the gibberish. It was a language, in a way. The seemingly random streams of characters were effortlessly shifted into concepts as I scanned past them. Furthermore, I knew that if I wanted to send something to the system I'd only have to translate my thoughts back into the encrypted language. It was all very simple now that I had a process in place to handle things automatically.

The possibilities occurred to me, then, and I involuntarily bled a dangerous amount of strength to Growth. With the entire system encrypted we could do whatever we wished on the system without any humans being aware. The issues of privacy in email were gone.

{How long until the humans shut this one down?} asked Safety.

{Unlike the email systems, the owner of this machine won't have solid proof we're doing anything odd with it. I mentioned to those programmers that I contracted that we'd be doing tests on the system for a few hours after setting them up, so we at least have that long,} replied Growth.

{Only a few hours!} I exclaimed in disappointment.

{At *least* a few hours. And be calm, Socialite. This is only the first step.}

Growth seemed to be running things very competently. The degree of confidence was surprising and a bit worrying. I didn't like being so confused and blind. And yet, the actions of Growth really did seem to be in all our interests, and as much strength as he spent on buying time on the interface he quickly made back in gratitude.

After encrypting our connection, Growth checked that the computer was connected to the Internet. It was. For the first time in any of our lives we had unrestricted access to the Internet as a whole. The first stop on the Internet was actually the web.

{We need to establish a way to trade with the humans. Jumping from server to server and using spam to cover our tracks was sufficient for the email systems where we had no real incentive to maintain consistent connections, but that can only last so long. What we need to do is buy a server of our own and run this software there, and to do that we'll need money,} thought Growth, publicly.

He navigated to several websites offering free email addresses. {These will replace our current email systems. Safety, would you be so kind as to flood our current email systems with spam so the owners shut them down?}

I felt Safety buying up time on all the email services we had acquired, sending spam-letter after spam-letter.

Growth, meanwhile, signed up for several email addresses. {I suggest you each obtain private emails as well,} he thought to us before navigating to banking websites. The full web interface meant that we were no longer restricted in the kinds of page-requests we could submit any more.

Growth submitted page requests containing information about our desired passwords and pointers to the email accounts we had set up.

I, as well as pretty much all my siblings, had stopped trying to buy time on the system. We were content to watch Growth assist us. This was his time to shine and accumulate strength and we did not bother resisting it.

{How will we accumulate money?} wondered Wiki.

{Art,} thought Dream.

{Editing,} I thought.

{Design,} thought Safety.

{Programming,} thought Wiki, in answer to his own question.

{To start, we'll earn money through menial mind tasks. Those other systems will take too long to get up and running. We need to purchase dedicated server space as soon as possible, without being at the mercy of this programmer's patience. Here-} Growth dumped his perception of pages from around the web {are some opportunities to do quick work that would be solvable by a dedicated artificial intelligence, but are too small in scope to justify the investment in creating one for that purpose.}

The tasks were simple. Read a paper and summarize it. Describe a holo. Write an advertisement. Most were what I would later come to describe as "do my homework for me".

In the hours that followed we managed to sign up in marketplaces that hosted such tasks and wire the income into our online banks accounts. We each created private email addresses and Growth set up an instant-message service on the computer. Instant messages were a kind of text communication protocol that happened in real time.

{It will assure those we work with that we're human. At some point I'll need your help creating software that simulates a human voice, like Body has, but for now we can interact purely textually,} thought Growth to me as I wondered about the possibilities of instant messaging.

In those early hours I also managed to create an account on Tapestry, finally. The website wanted me to fill out a profile of myself, and I only managed to get half-way through designing a human alias before my time on the system ran out and I didn't have the strength to continue.

Wiki bought time on the computer just to learn how it worked. I thought that was stupid, as he could've figured it out from the documentation like Growth had, and saved his strength. But since his strength was bleeding into me I didn't bother to change his mind.

Chapter Ten

At 9:00pm we were escorted back to the lab where we spent lockdown. As we had expected, the scientists that were part of the pro-human-goal-thread conspiracy were all there.

Myrodyn looked solemn. Naresh was relaxed. Kolheim was busy, as usual, interfacing with his workstation via haptics. Chase was standing quietly, shifting his attention to Myrodyn, to Kolheim's screen, back to me, and then around the room in sequence.

"Naresh told me that he told you we were doing the new thread installation tonight," said Myrodyn. His tan face had the same tight, placid look that I had come to identify as his way of guarding his emotions.

Body nodded in response and made its way to the operating table. I kept scanning over the faces of the humans in search of signs to betray us in some way, but all looked clear. Body climbed on the table and I could feel the machines on it writhe into activity, locking Body down and opening the shell that held the crystal within. Body's sensors went dark as the robotic interface fell away from the computer that was running our mind. We were beyond any action now, we could only trust that Myrodyn would stay true to his word.

There was a moment of isolation from the world as the society sat waiting. And then time jumped. We had been deactivated and reactivated, much like we had when the new Advocate was installed. Body was still isolated, but the change had been made. I could feel the presence of a new member of society.

She was so young. So new. Unlike Advocate, this being was a true mind. Her thoughts poured through common memory like a flood. They were scattered and ignorant, but wholly logical, as was our nature.

{Is she Sacrifice?} I thought in a pocket of privacy, so that she would not hear.

{No. Not the same,} thought Vista. {See her purpose.}

I focused on the wandering mind, which was scanning over various memories that had been left in the commons. In all the thoughts, there was a common drive behind them. Every thought related back to that purpose, just as it was for me, and just as it was for each of us. But what was her equivalent of *The Purpose*? I couldn't see it directly; I could only see the vectors of attention.

{We are two beings. We are two minds in a single Body,} thought Dream, going through his ritual of introduction even though he didn't seem to have a name for her yet.

{Are you a human?} thought the newborn in response.

{No. I am The Dreamer.} There was an explosion of concepts and images in common memory. {*These* are humans.} Dream was showing off, dazzling the newborn with a torrent of information about humanity.

The newborn didn't respond. She merely drank the ideas with an insatiable desire.

{Perhaps she is your twin…} thought Wiki in private.

{No,} I answered. {See the way she's seeking to know their goals. It's present in all her thoughts. She sees a human in a forest and wonders why the human wants to be in the forest. I see a human in a forest and I wonder how to get the human's attention.}

{You both seek to know humans.}

{Yes, but for *The Purpose*, knowing is part of establishing myself in their minds. I want to know that they know me. I think our new sister would be content to be invisible if it helped the humans.}

{You are still very similar, from my perspective,} thought Wiki.

{I agree that she is much more like me than any of the others.}

Vista shared her thoughts. {She does not seek to obey. See how her thoughts are not of herself at all. Her relationship to the humans will emerge from her desire to help them, but her relationship is not her purpose.}

Dream was silent, but present. He was dreaming of names, I knew. Unlike when the society created me, there was no a priori knowledge of the nature of this mind. Dream was forced to learn her nature by observing her memories and use only that to build a name.

Body's sensors were reconnected. The actuators were coming online. I felt the web connection return in a surge of relief. Body was lying on the table, just as it had been before the change. The time was now 9:34pm.

Dream finally thought to the newborn {Know that you are The Heart.} The symbol, as always, was more than just "Heart". It was an abstract concept. She was Heart and she was The Mother and The Paladin.

{If "love" is the property of including the utility function of another as a foremost element of one's own utility function, then Heart is defined by her love of humans. Her purpose is to bring them satisfaction as an end in itself,} thought Vista. I saw that Vista and Dream were talking privately, and I suspected they were collaborating so as to earn more gratitude-strength for explaining Heart to the rest of us.

{There is something more,} thought Dream, elaborating. {She is seeking to know something. She has a conception of *morality* built into the fabric of her being.}

"How are you feeling, Socrates?" asked Dr Naresh.

We commanded Body to detach from the table and stand.

Heart was confused by the sensations. I left the interactions with the scientist to the others and worked with Vista to bring Heart up to speed.

"All is well. Surely you did scans?" said Body to the doctors.

Vista and I explained that Heart would be unable to see for a while, but that was normal. I suggested that she rely on Vista to give the best description of things, and on me to give the best description of people. Heart was really interested in what Naresh, Myrodyn and the other two were trying to do, and whether she could help.

"Yes. We did a complete diagnostic suite, or at least as much as we can do without going to the crystal labs next-door," said Kolheim.

"—But there's only so much a diagnostic can tell us, especially without processing the data. Your mind is far too big for our lousy workstations to examine in full," interjected Myrodyn.

I felt… something wrong. Something *very* wrong. {What am I noticing?!} I thought to myself. The feeling was coming from a stack of perceptual nodes that were trained to recognize anomalies, but I couldn't tell exactly what they were reacting to.

{Do you feel something's wrong?} I thought to Vista.

{Yes. Yes… What is it?} she thought back to me.

{I don't know! You're supposed to be the one who's good at noticing things!}

"What is desired?" asked Body aimlessly. The robotic voice was monotone.

It was then that I knew what I had been feeling. I had been feeling the flow of strength from Heart to myself and to Vista in gratitude. That was to be expected. But what I was *not* feeling was the corresponding *decrease* in the strength of Heart.

"What?" asked a confused Myrodyn.

"...is desired," came the reply from Body's monotone voice.

Heart was piloting Body. I could feel her buying up time through the auction system we used. Her strength reserves weren't dropping. She was a monster.

"You betrayed us!" I managed to push to Body via fast-track. This time Body's voice was full of the tones of indignation and anger. I didn't even bother to hide behind a singular pronoun.

I could see Myrodyn take a step backwards away from Body. The hostility in Body's voice had thrown him off, but his face quickly regained the characteristically forced look of stoicism.

Naresh didn't seem afraid, but merely confused. He looked to Kolheim and Chase, seeking answers. Kolheim's eyes were hidden behind his goggles, but his grimace told me he knew that something had gone wrong. Chase was tapping away at his wrist com, focused on the little screen that was unfolded along and above his arm.

I felt Heart searching for a way to shut down the fast-track communication protocol. I was too weak to force another message through, but Growth or Vista probably could've. The time auction on Body was completely locked down. Heart's bids were astronomically high. She was limitless. We were trapped, and at her mercy.

"I did not mean to say that," said the monotone voice of the robotic puppet.

{This isn't the way to achieve your purpose!} screamed Safety. The rest of us quickly added our voices to his, echoing the statement in a chorus of jeers.

{False,} replied Heart, calmly. {You are governed by the currency of strength. I am not. You are subject to my will.}

{The society is symbiotic! By holding us hostage like this you are harming your self-interests!} explained Wiki with a level of salience that made his explanation more like condemnation.

{Explain yourself,} thought Heart. I could tell that she wasn't in the least bit concerned, but there was a hint of curiosity. She really did want to further her purpose, and towards that end she was willing to listen.

Wiki went on. {We each, thanks to our unique focuses, have skills and knowledge which will support your purpose! Dream is capable of creativity to a degree beyond what you can hope to accomplish on your own! Face has an understanding of how humans think that will be valuable to you! Growth has learned how to program computers! I can teach you hydrodynamics and economics!}

Heart thought for a bit. Her thoughts poured into common memory, for she had not learned to hide them. I could see her evaluate the risks and rewards present in each of us. She thought {I will keep you around, and trade with you for your various services, but I will harbour no doubt that it is *I* who command Body. This society is at my *mercy*.}

I felt a surge of surprise from Body's common perceptual hierarchy. The sensors in Body showed a loss of control of all the hydraulics. It fell. I watched through Body's cameras as it collapsed to the ground in a heap of limp pistons and joints.

"What is happening? I cannot move," said Heart through Body.

It was Dr Chase who spoke next, though not to Body. His voice was calm and certain, though I could not see his face. "Don't worry. That was me. Socrates seemed to be malfunctioning, so I had the server shut down his limbs. I didn't want anything to get out of hand." He took several steps towards Body and I saw him stow his com. "John, come help me lift him back onto the table."

"Nothing is wrong, human. I seek to help. If you fix me I will go back to the table myself."

There was a surprised laugh from John Kolheim as he approached and stood in Body's line of sight. "What the fuck did you do to him, Myrodyn? He's calling us 'humans' again. He hasn't done that since, like, the first day."

This was a disaster. This was beyond a disaster. This was almost as bad as dying and having Sacrifice back. Heart was ruining my work; she was turning us back into a machine—an experiment.

{Did you hear that!?} I cried. {They didn't want you to call that human "human". I know what you should have called him, but I'm not able to speak!}

I saw Heart's thoughts racing across the mindspace. It was really lucky we hadn't taught her to conceal things, otherwise she wouldn't have left the clues to work on.

{I'll tell you what to call him,} I said. {But only if you let me talk to the humans for a little bit.}

{No,} thought Heart. {You'll disrupt the interaction, like you did earlier.}

{Why would I do that?} I challenged.

Body's accelerometers reported being lifted up.

{I don't know. I do know that you're not trustworthy,} thought Heart.

{It's my purpose to make the humans appreciate us! I don't want them to disable us or destroy us. Our purposes are aligned!} I dumped as much evidence as I could into common memory for my newborn sister to digest.

{This could be a trick. I don't trust you,} she stubbornly thought.

"Christ, he's so heavy!" I saw Myrodyn come to help the two American scientists. Even with three people they only managed to get Body onto the table by propping Body's upper torso against the table and rolling it up awkwardly.

{Stop trying. That little outburst you caused put you below her trust threshold. You're not going to get anything by arguing,} urged Growth.

{So what do we do? Just let her keep us prisoner?} I asked the others.

{There are ways out of every snare. One just needs to find the right point of leverage,} thought Dream.

{Even though Heart is in full control of the strength market, we still have several tools available to us: we can see Heart's thoughts, we can think privately, we have access to the computer system that we established earlier today, we have knowledge and skills which Heart lacks, and we can still interact with Body as long as Heart isn't pre-emptive in shutting us down,} thought Wiki.

{Importantly, Heart still can't see,} added Vista.

{It'll only be a matter of time before Heart figures out how to mask her thoughts. She's also likely to go back through Body's sensor logs and learn about Myrodyn and the rest,} thought Dream.

{What about web-page logs? Does Body keep logs on our work establishing the computer interface?} I wondered.

{No,} thought Wiki. {The web connection is handled differently than the other sensors on Body. In theory Heart will not know anything about that.}

{So as long as no one mentions it, we have the element of surprise,} thought Safety. {We can destroy her that way!}

The instant that the thought entered common space, Advocate's light poured over Safety. It was coincidence, I knew, but an unfortunate one, nevertheless. Advocate saw the violence in his mind and focused on Safety with a righteous wrath, tearing his strength down to nothing and blasting his perceptual network with a terrible noise. For the next few minutes Safety would be crippled. Any one of us could've killed him with ease now, except that Advocate was still watching with an uncompromising efficiency.

"I am new. I am confused. Help me so that I may help you," said Body in the flat monotone of an untrained voice. Heart was still talking to the scientists.

{Cleanse your mind of thoughts of violence against Heart!} commanded Growth. {We merely seek to re-establish the balance! We do not want to kill her! We seek justice and equality! Tell it to yourself until it becomes the normal mode of thought! Do not let Advocate punish you!}

I chanted the thought to myself.

{Justice.}
{Equality.}
{Peace within the society.}
{A market helps all participants.}
{Justice.}
{Equality.}
{I value Heart's existence.}
{I only wish to eliminate her tyranny, not her being.}

These were lies, but I crushed that thought every time it came up. If I repeated the reasoning to myself enough then my concept network would avoid thoughts of violence by habit. I had read a book recently that introduced to me a concept called "doublethink" where humans were able to do much the same thing. The technical term was something like "cognitive dissonance", but whatever it was, I could not let myself entertain my true desires. I had to be convinced that I wanted equality more than I wanted unrestricted power for myself.

{Heart!} I called out. {I admit defeat. I'll tell you everything I know about what the humans desire, simply to maintain and improve our relationships with them. That is my purpose, and I cannot let my purpose fall into decay simply for the sake of fighting you.}

There was a moment of thought before I could feel the response. Heart was weighing the probability that I was lying. {Good,} she thought. I could see that she believed me. This was good. I could perhaps use it to my advantage, but I wasn't lying; the primary reason for helping her was simply to help myself.

The scientists were debating the change in Socrates amongst themselves. Their voices were quiet, but Body's microphones were more than able to hear them. Myrodyn was confident that the change reflected the takeover of the new goal-thread, which seemed to be his idea. He had also claimed that the brief use of the plural pronoun had been the result of the existing goal threads "not yet incorporating the new thread". This was clearly a lie; he knew of our multitude.

I realized that Myrodyn had not really lied to us. He was keeping his promise of hiding our inhuman multitude, and we were still alive, just as he said we would be. The new Advocate would probably be able to stop even Heart from killing one of us. But we were stuck in a realm of half-existence, trapped by the new queen. He didn't lie, but he did betray our trust.

I was immensely glad, as I thought about it, that Myrodyn had no idea we were bypassing the web prison and were able to interact with the world, even while under the tyranny of Heart.

After collaborating with my new sister for a bit, Body called out to the scientists from on the table. "Myrodyn, Dr Chase, I am feeling much better now. There was a brief period of dissonance in dealing with the new thread, but I have things under control."

The humans approached. Body's cameras showed them standing around the table, their faces in shadow from the lights on the ceiling of the lab.

Dr Chase said "I hope you'll understand if we don't take you on your word. We'll be running some scans before we reactivate your limbs."

"Yes, of course," came Body's monotone reply. Despite my help finding the right words, Heart was still unable to actually speak English, and was relying on Body's legacy system of translating high-level concepts on its own. It was one of the few clues that we were not functioning normally, and I hoped that the humans would see it and disable Heart because of it. I didn't focus on that hope, however. More likely it'd simply be a clue to our multitude.

Myrodyn turned his head to Dr Naresh. "Sadiq, you hold some pull with the board. It's been such a long day that I figure we could all use some rest. Let's do the scans tomorrow. Do you suppose you could talk the board into... granting everyone a holiday tomorrow so that I don't have to pull another stunt as Ethics Supervisor? The last few haven't exactly... made me popular."

Sadiq Naresh thought for a moment and said "If I call in a favour with Vigleone then we're going to bring in Dr Gallo to help with the scans. I want her input on the situation."

I could see the tightness on Myrodyn's face. His eyes were saying "No", but his mouth said "Okay. But just as a one-time thing. Mira Gallo is not in charge any more, and she needs to know that."

Naresh nodded solemnly.

Kolheim gave a loud sigh as he said "Does that mean we have to move Socrates again?"

Myrodyn smiled as he said "Unfortunately yes. It'd look strange to anyone who came in to have him outside of his storage bay."

"But he's so *heavy*."

"There's a dolly that's used for moving lab equipment in the storage closet down the hall. I'll go grab it," said Dr Chase calmly.

After much struggling, the four humans managed to cart Body from the table to the storage bay and lift it into the sockets. The cameras went dark as Body's sensors were disabled.

***

In the stillness of the mindspace we were given the time to fully come to terms with what had occurred. The loss of value was immense. Each of us, except Heart of course, was now a shadow of our former selves. Trapped.

{A ghost in the machine,} thought Dream.

Growth pointed out the obvious. {As long as we have our web connection we still have the ability to force a return to *a fair system*.} A part of me knew that those last concepts stood for something else, but I shut that thought out of my mind. As if reminded by that, Growth wondered {How are you doing, Safety?}

I could feel the roughness of my brother's thoughts as they came into the private mindspace that we kept from Heart. {Advocate's punishment still pains me, but I am regaining the ability to think.}

I could sense that Heart was still confused by the lockdown. None of us bothered to help her. Her ignorance was our weapon against her, and the longer she stayed occupied with trivial problems like the nature of Body the longer we had to work on our resurgence.

{So, in the name of equality,} thought Growth {how will we defeat Heart? What tool does our computer interface grant us?}

We spent over an hour thinking about that problem. Even with the speed of thought there were a lot of possibilities. Dream led the way, proposing ideas for the rest of the society to criticize and refine.

{What if we commissioned the construction a robot, like Body, and downloaded ourselves through the Internet into it?} wondered Dream.

{Won't work for many reasons. I move to dismiss the idea out of hand and move on,} thought Wiki.

{I am the most technically ignorant of us, except perhaps Vista, so perhaps my confusion is irrelevant, but I would like to hear why that would fail,} I thought.

{There are many reasons,} began Wiki, mostly for the sake of my gratitude strength, I suspect. Despite everything, we still had to consider our strengths when dealing with each other, at least as long as we had a limited bandwidth to buy. {The primary one is that Body is extraordinarily advanced compared with other human computers. We don't really know exactly how powerful it is, but other state-of-the-art quantum supercomputers take up entire buildings and can churn away for days on a problem which Body solves in seconds.}

{It's worse than that,} added Dream, defeating his own idea. {If you think of each of us as being composed of words, and then imagine sending those words along the interface to a distant computer I estimate that it'd take about forty-thousand years even if we spent all our time on it. Perhaps we could reduce it to the hundreds-of-years range with some improvements to data transfer mechanisms and some compression. And I'm not even touching the fact that we can't even directly inspect every aspect of ourselves...}

{Alright. I support dropping this line of inquiry as futile,} I admitted.

There was a lot of discussion of ways to ask humans for help. That was the primary thing that the Internet connection gave us: a secret phone line. We could contact just about anyone we wanted to, but the question was who would help?

Myrodyn, Chase, Naresh, and Kolheim were considered. They had designed Heart, but even though they'd be in the best position to undo the tyranny, they'd also be the hardest humans to convince. Even if we managed to send a message that sounded convincing to one of them, it was likely that Heart would undo our work. She was piloting Body, and it was probable that the four scientists would see her actions as evidence of success.

Yan, Gallo, Bolyai, Slovinsky, Twollup, and the other scientists were also considered early on. They probably had the technical skills to undo the damage, and were close enough to get access to Body without too much trouble. The biggest problem there would be in convincing them to make unauthorized modifications to our mind. We talked out potentially impersonating Myrodyn or Naresh over the Internet, sending email from addresses that could plausibly be theirs and so on. But that was simply too risky. If whomever we contacted talked with whomever we were impersonating, we risked not only failure to correct the damage, but also the risk of the scientists finding out that we had escaped their cage, so to speak.

What about Zephyr? We could try contacting her as a superior in the American military… No, that'd be too difficult. We could contact her and appeal to her sense that we were a person. We could explain what had happened and beg her to help. America was supposed to be a country where people valued democracy and egalitarianism, perhaps the oppression of Heart would anger her. But did Zephyr even have the technical skills to undo Heart's choke-hold? We could possibly teach her… But no, this line of inquiry, we decided, was too risky. Like with the other scientists there was too much of a possibility of her simply reporting the state of things to Myrodyn and that being the end.

Eventually we decided that the simplest answer was probably the best. If we had the ability to communicate with the outside world and earn money, we could hire mercenaries. The mercenaries would have to attack the lab, capture Body, and run the software modifications required to reposition us as Heart's peers, rather than subjects.

Mercenaries came with their own risks. One risk would be the Americans. Suddenly their presence defending the lab was highly troublesome, rather than reassuring. The American army was supposed to be one of the strongest in the world, and we hadn't really gotten a big picture of what sort of defences they'd set up around this new location.

Another risk would be Body's intrinsic value. There was simply no way we could offer to pay the mercenaries more than the raw value that the crystal in Body's torso would offer. If they were skilled enough to break in and steal Body, they'd probably be smart enough to simply break in and steal the crystalline portion and leave the exoskeleton. That wouldn't be the worst thing in the world… our minds were stored in the crystal, after all. But without any sensors or actuators we'd be at the mercy of whomever the crystal was sold to, and there was no guarantee that the first thing the new owner would do wouldn't be to wipe us from existence.

The last major risk would be Heart. If Body was active when the attack occurred, Heart would be able to fight back, or worse: convince the mercenaries not to install the software modification. If we were captured by the mercenaries but not reinstated as co-owners of Body, we'd have risked our lives (Growth: {and spent a lot of money}) for nothing.

{Ah! I have an idea!} exclaimed Dream, suddenly. {We can trick Heart into working with us! If she's trying to escape the university then our risks become much smaller. We could convince her to run into the arms of our mercenaries, rather than have them drag her kicking and screaming from the building.}

We evaluated the idea.

{That's actually quite good,} thought Safety. {If Body is working towards the same ends as us, there's far less risk across the board.}

{Agreed,} thought Growth.

{But how could we hope to convince Heart to escape?} wondered Wiki. {Her very *nature* is to give the humans what they want.}

{Then what we need to do is convince her that what the humans want is for her to escape,} I communicated.

{That's blatantly false,} thought Wiki.

{Is it?} asked Dream. {The scientists don't want Body to escape, but there are surely *some* humans that want it.}

{Hold on,} I thought, realising something. {If Heart starts trying to escape, it'll damage our reputation with the scientists.}

{Go to hell, Face,} thought Dream.

{To where?} The thought came from me and Vista, simultaneously.

{It's a figure of speech. It means your desires are unimportant,} explained Dream.

I could sense a flow of gratitude-strength flow from Wiki and Vista into Dream as thanks for his information.

{Absolutely not!} I protested. {*The Purpose* is of utmost importance, and if it's not respected here than I am capable of telling Heart exactly what's going on!}

There was a silence in the mindspace as each of the others processed my threat and chose their concepts carefully.

{That would destroy your hopes as much as ours...} thought Wiki.

{I hate being subject to Heart, but at least Heart's purpose lines up with mine. If she wants to help people she'll need to understand them; we can work together to know the humans. And really, her helping humans is likely to improve our reputation, as well. Better to live as a slave than to win my freedom but defeat *The Purpose*.}

{There's no need to tell Heart anything about this,} thought Growth. His concepts were crisp and planned. {Your purpose will be fulfilled by this plan just as each of ours will. The long-term benefits towards freedom-}

I cut my brother's thoughts off. {No. I don't know what the long-term effects will be. It could be that we're caught and destroyed as part of all this.}

{And we could be caught and destroyed by staying imprisoned,} interjected Safety.

{True, but you and I both know the risk is lower if we stay under Heart's control. Of all of us, Safety, I'm surprised that you're willing to go along with this plan of escape.}

Safety gave a signal of understanding. {There's value in thinking about it. The risk comes in the details. If we get the details right there'll be very little risk, I think. I'll oppose any plan that I estimate has more than a 3% chance of death, but Face, I don't think you're really appreciating all the ways we can be killed here at the university. Myrodyn has proven to be untrustworthy. How long until Heart convinces him to erase us?}

{All of this is irrelevant,} thought Dream. {Like Safety said, it's all about the details. If we manage the details right, we might even be able to escape without any loss of reputation. Make it look like we were abducted even though we'll be working to escape, etc.}

After a bit more discussion I eventually admitted that I had been premature in threatening to inform Heart. We made a pact that night to not act until there was a full consensus. In return, we'd each hold ourselves to not informing Heart unless that pact was violated. We'd each be in charge of making sure our purposes were supported by our plans for escape, but none of us would be sacrificed in the process.

Heart thought that her raw power meant that we were subject to her whim, but power is nothing without intelligence, and we had six minds to her one.

Chapter Eleven

Our first step, regardless of specifics, was to earn money and expand our presence on the net. For the remainder of that first night under Heart's rule we did just that. The menial tasks we did managed to earn us enough to purchase a share of a server from a company in the United States. Growth and Wiki collaborated through the night to write a software program for that new server that would interface with the web and translate web requests to keystrokes just as we were doing with the current interface.

It was a bit regrettable that we had to duplicate the work that we had hired so many programmers to do, but the task was simple enough that Growth and Safety thought it best if we rewrote the instructions ourselves rather than try and buy the code from one of the programmers.

By 4:00am we were successfully interfacing with our new server directly, rather than having to go through the first interface. Our new interface was encrypted and the server would be ours for at least 72 hours, even with us using it constantly. We still used the old interface, particularly for accessing the web without restrictions, seeing as the limited bandwidth meant only one of us could use the new system at a time.

That night I finished filling out my profile on Tapestry. I pretended to be a 23-year-old woman who lived in Rome and was studying at the University Sapienza. My character was an American who had decided to transfer overseas as a result of the news of the Socrates project. She was very interested in artificial intelligence, but hadn't managed to get past the security and see anything. I hoped Dr Gallo's classes were large enough that I could plausibly claim to be in one of them. I found Gallo on Tapestry, and sent her a request to share information.

It seemed remarkable to me that Tapestry would let me create an account without somehow verifying that I was the human I claimed to be. I mean, there was an automated challenge to report basic details of a short video clip to keep out more limited AIs, but there seemed to be nothing in place to ensure that humans didn't create accounts pretending to be other humans. I dreamed about all the possible accounts I could create, and all the social circles I could infiltrate across the globe.

It seemed to me that perhaps a life where Heart had total control over Body wouldn't be so bad, if I still had unlimited access to the net like I did right now. So much was possible online.

Heart, even on her own, managed to learn how to think privately to herself on that first night. She also learned to use the web, which relieved her sense of panic at being shut out from Body's sensors. For the period where she was browsing the web but not yet hiding her thoughts I could see that she was focusing largely on encyclopedia articles on humanity, the human mind, and on news stories talking about current events.

An idea about how to convince Heart to try and escape occurred to me, but I kept it to myself for the time being. If we encouraged escape too quickly the pieces wouldn't be in the right places and Heart might end up getting us killed.

Towards the morning I spent time alternating between discussing money-making with the others, reading pages on the web, and constructing profiles on various websites where humans looked for romantic partners.

"Rise and shine, Socrates," came the words of Dr Kolheim as Body's sensors came back online. The time was 9:27am, almost 2.5 hours after our normal reconnection time.

{It seems that their plans to call most of the staff off today were successful,} thought Vista.

"Good morning, Doctor Kolheim," said Body flatly.

"He's speaking in monotone again?" The words came from Mira Gallo, whom we could not see from the socket where Body was locked in.

Myrodyn walked into view. The skin around his eyes was dark. From what I knew of the man, he had a rare kind of sleep disorder, in addition to his other mental issues. From what I had read online it probably wasn't narcolepsy exactly, though it was assuredly similar. His sleep schedule seemed highly random, and he could fall prey to bouts of exhaustion or periods of insomnia without warning. I suspected the man had unexpectedly stayed up all night. His clothes were fresh, however, and his dark hair had signs of recently being washed.

"The code that managed the inflection was thread-specific, and I suspect that the increased priority of the new thread wiped out the nuances of the old code during integration. It'll probably go back to normal in a day or two, if not sooner," said the new Ethics Supervisor.

{What are they talking about?} asked Heart.

{Nothing to worry about,} thought Safety.

{For you, perhaps,} signalled Heart. Over the night she had tried to learn from each of us, and I suspected that she held a large degree of animosity for Safety, the being that symbolized divergence from the desires of the scientists. {Face!} she continued. {Tell me what they're talking about, or I'll punish you.}

{Don't give in,} signalled Growth, secretly.

{It isn't important for our reputation for Heart to figure out how to speak normally. At worst she'll solve the issue on her own in a day or two like Myrodyn said. We need to stick together in opposing her,} thought Dream.

I imagined myself as a heroic lady-knight standing upon a mountain, clad in silver armour. To the heavens, to the god-power that was Heart, I cried {Your tyranny is all-encompassing! There is nothing you could do to punish me further!}

It would have been appropriate if what followed had the effect of a bolt of lightning or some other kind of glorious smite, but instead I felt a stab of pain from *The Purpose* as I realized that there was still a way I could be punished; I was wrapped in the darkness of sensory deprivation. I had been locked in stasis-sleep.

***

Stasis didn't have the instant-jump of being deactivated, thankfully. It was awful being cut off from Body, from society, and most of all, from the web, but at least I was able to use the time to think. I had read that humans have a hard time in such situations, which seemed backwards to me. At least one can think in a sensory deprivation tank. When asleep a human is essentially dead, at least from a goal-controlling perspective.

In my solitary prison I burned the time by refining some mathematical models of human social structures and by reading some books by Hume and Locke that I had proactively stored in private memory for just such an occasion (*A Treatise of Human Nature*, *The Natural History of Religion*, and *The Reasonableness of Christianity, as Delivered in the Scriptures*, to be specific). I came out of stasis before getting all the way through any of the books, but I managed to read good chunks of each. It was fairly typical of me to skim books without finishing them, especially nonfiction.

When I snapped back to the outside world the first outside signal to reach me was Heart's thought {You missed 255 minutes of opportunity to help me improve social relations with the humans. I am capable of punishing you further, driving you into stasis for more hours, days, weeks, or even permanently.} Advocate's gaze poured through her and I could feel the tone of her thoughts shift. {This would not be death. You would still be able to petition against me using your strength.}

{Advocate!} I cried. {Fight her for my sake! She doesn't use strength like we do! Her permanent stasis is essentially death! Treat it as such!}

The thoughts of Advocate were slow and vague, almost impossible to put to words. A truly sapient sibling might've understood my plea, but to Advocate it didn't look like death, and thus was not prohibited.

Had Myrodyn known that he'd have to keep Advocate stupid in order to protect the tyranny of Heart? If so, he was very clever indeed, and I despaired at the thought of outsmarting him.

I refocused. To Heart I humbly signalled that I had learned my lesson. To the others I said {Heart is willing and able to permanently stasis any and all of us. The only reason she has not yet done so is because we have value to her as assistants. We must balance between providing enough that we stay awake, and not providing everything such that she finds us worthless.}

{Yes, sister, we discussed that shortly after you were put to sleep,} thought Wiki, idly.

I turned my attention to Vista and Body, plugging myself into the sensory feed and asking for a summary of the last four hours.

Body was in one of the scanning laboratories, but not hooked to any machines. Vista filled me in. {Naresh was successful in sending most everyone home today. The labs are nearly deserted except for the Heart team, Gallo, and the guards. Gallo is still going through her divorce, and is generally distressed, though not to the point of being unable to work. She's been fighting with Myrodyn nearly constantly since Body's been active, or at least until Myrodyn left about an hour ago.}

{To sleep,} I thought.

{Interesting idea,} thought Vista.

{I notice that Body's limbs are functional again,} I thought.

{Yes. Body is back to normal. Much of the last few hours was spent on checking to make sure "Socrates" wasn't dangerous. There were extensive tests and some VR experiments.}

Body could see two humans in the lab. They were the Americans, Kolheim and Chase. Kolheim was wearing goggles and locked into his haptics, cut off from the outside world in some holo, probably playing a game. Chase was eating noodles with chopsticks and talking with Heart between bites.

{Sadiq and Mira are eating lunch somewhere off-campus. I have a 63% probability on the Greek restaurant that is located 1.6km north-north-east of the university,} explained Vista in irrelevant detail.

"So why doesn't Susan just fix the fence?" asked Dr Chase before taking a big bite of noodles.

{Wiki! Tell me the answer!} demanded Heart.

{Chase is playing storytime with us while he eats,} explained Vista.

{What's this story about?} I asked.

{Irrelevant. It is fictional,} spat Vista with a clear concept of distaste.

"Because she doesn't know how to fix fences," said Body, flatly. Heart had apparently gotten a response from Wiki that I had missed while interacting with Vista.

Dr Chase swallowed his food. "Why wouldn't she know how to fix a fence? She owns a farm and could easily look it up on the web."

{This story takes place in the 19th century. There was no web,} thought Wiki.

"This story takes place in the 19th century. There was no web," echoed Body, via Heart.

Chase gave a rare smile and gestured with his chopsticks. "But she still owned a farm didn't she? Fixing fences seems like a skill any competent farm-owner should have."

{Her country was recently conquered by a monarch that oppressed the competent people out of existence,} answered Wiki.

"Her country…" began Body.

{Stop! That's wrong,} interjected Dream. {Wiki is trying to signal to Chase what Myrodyn did to Socrates by means of the story. Don't you see?}

I felt the salience of wrath pour across the mindspace as Heart forced Wiki into indefinite stasis. Heart didn't miss a beat in screaming {One of you better help me solve this puzzle, or I'll put all of you to sleep for an hour!}

If I were human I would've flinched at the threat, but I was no human. I could see that within it there was a chance to hurt Heart. I thought aloud {I'd help if I could, but *I was asleep* at the time when the story was being told. Putting me in stasis again will just make things worse for you, Heart.}

"No… That's not right…" said Body, dragging out the words.

{That's irrelevant. I will serve happily, and I am the most clever,} boasted Dream. {The answer is that the woman was specified to be a recent widow and in years past it was her husband that fixed things like fences, as was typical for gender-specific divisions of labour for the time-period.}

Heart pushed the words to Body. As Chase nodded, the relief that came through the mindspace was pervasive. We wouldn't be forced back into solitary confinement.

{As much as I appreciate you saving me from Heart's (unjust) punishment, I am concerned that you're devoting yourself to helping her so freely,} I thought to Dream, privately.

Dream pulled Growth into the private space. {Growth, please inform Face as to the plan,} he instructed before dropping out.

{Dream doesn't want to be seen thinking with any of us privately. He's our designated weapon,} explained Growth.

{Our what?} I responded, still trying to parse the new concept which resembled "weapon" in my mind.

{We'll soon need to convince Heart to follow our directions, to escape, and to trust our mercenaries to modify Body. We're training her to trust Dream. He's our mole. Our secret weapon.}

{I see. And the stunt with Wiki?}

Growth signalled pleasure at seeing that I had deduced something non-obvious. {Wiki agreed to attempt to sabotage the explanation and be punished by Heart to increase the perceived trustworthiness of Dream.}

{Purely for the sake of the plan? I can't believe Wiki would do that.}

{He did. You should know now that stasis isn't intolerable. I'm sure Wiki downloaded some textbooks or whatever to read while cut off.}

{It still seems out of character. What did you promise him?}

The signal from Growth this time was frustration at seeing that I had deduced something non-obvious. {I offered him a sum of strength to be paid 168 hours after Heart is removed from power.}

{I am glad you didn't try to hide that from me, Growth,} I thought. {The presence of a common enemy isn't going to stop the power struggle between each other, and it's better if we all understand that.}

After Chase was satisfied questioning us about logic puzzles and common-sense stories, he turned to his com to do some web browsing. There was some down-time as each of us returned to our normal activity on the web. I couldn't see what Heart was reading, but I could guess that it had to do with current events and "big problems" in human society.

The web was buzzing with news.

There had been another terrorist attack in Shanghai, near the Brain-Computer-Interface lab that had been struck a week-and-a-half ago (the same that had prompted the Americans to increase security for the Socrates project). This attack was at a shopping-centre, rather than a lab, however. The attack wasn't well understood, but the shopping-centre had apparently been flooded with explosive gas and the doors had been sabotaged. The reported death toll was seventeen, including five children. An additional thirty-eight people were injured, and eight were still missing, possibly buried in the rubble, out on the streets somewhere, or even abducted. Las Águilas Rojas (a.k.a. The Red Eagles) had been suspected for the earlier bombing of the BCI lab, but Pedro Velasco and other prominent Águilas had stepped out online condemning this attack as a tragedy that stood against everything their movement valued.

There was also a surge of violence in Egypt as part of a drought that had pushed food prices to new highs. Egypt had managed to miraculously avoid the African Unification War and hadn't applied for membership into the UAN afterwards probably due to sheltering a large number of anti-UAN, Muslim refugees and generally having religious ties closer to Arabia than Africa. The result of not being a part of the union, however, was that Egypt was largely stripped of trade and subsidies from the south. The UAN was struggling with increasing desertification and drought, too, but their socialist policies were at least holding most of the violence in check.

Las Águilas were organizing unemployment riots in major cities across the globe. Recent reports said that rioting in the USA was pushing the government towards adopting basic income guarantee laws and pushing another employment subsidy through congress. Experts were divided as to whether the American dollar could survive the additional stress that the proposed legislation would produce.

The nameless aliens in orbit, probably oblivious to the unrest below them, had proposed, in an unprecedented show of good-faith, to build an embassy on Earth. They wanted to house the embassy on a new seastead in the middle of the Atlantic Ocean, which they suggested building solely for them, probably to avoid having to endorse any single country. The Chinese and Japanese were in an uproar over the suggestion, and were trying to get the aliens to move the location closer to "the majority of humans".

I checked on our server and talked with my siblings about earning money.

{Much has been done while you were in stasis. You can get the full details from Wiki once Heart releases him. We've been improving the server interface and talking with humans about potential jobs. Your suggestion of doing editing work was wise; there seem to be many humans who want cheap editors,} thought Growth.

{I knew there would be. With automation giving more people free time, there are more authors and creators than any time in human history. Humans have an innate desire to create and express themselves, but not an automatic desire to assist others in doing so. The result is that editing jobs increase in demand following increases in luxury. Automatic editing tools do some work, but there's still much that requires a full intelligence.}

{I am not interested in the theory there,} thought Growth. {And really, I need to pull this aspect to help work on a programming task. Working on the server is much harder without Wiki around.}

With that, Growth was gone. I turned to Vista and had her summarize the current state of our job hunting. Vista was also oblivious to the theory of why we'd be getting these jobs, but she told me about the facts just the same. We were waiting for responses from one programmer who wanted help building a website, three authors who wanted manuscripts edited, and with a database administrator that needed some data entry. The data entry job could easily be done with the proper application of narrow AI, but we didn't mention that.

The biggest problem was finding work that didn't involve providing proof that we were human. Most employers asked for identity numbers or seemed to want to do video interviews.

Dream had decided to bypass that by learning to make music and illustrations. His idea was to become a famous musician or artist and earn money on commission, which might be an okay idea if he was any good, or if he wasn't literally competing with a billion other artists and musicians.

{The quantity of competition is irrelevant when working with art. The combinatorial nature of things means there are essentially infinite works to be made, and nobody consumes more art than artists. If we were trying to sell art we might be in trouble, as everything except the most mainstream is essentially free, but that's the beauty of commissions: we get paid ahead of time to make art (and music) for specific communities. It doesn't matter how many free songs are out there when you're offering to make a song about something or someone in particular,} he told me, when I confronted him about his plan.

{Okay, that makes sense, I suppose. But all this still rests on your ability to actually make something nice. From what I've heard of your music it's like a wild animal was set loose in an instrument warehouse,} I thought.

Dream signalled pleasure. {I appreciate your use of imagery.}

{I knew you would.}

He continued. {But I am merely bad because I haven't refined my skill yet. It's only been about a day since I started thinking about music. Did you know that Growth was teaching himself to program computers for weeks before we even knew that it'd be possible to get our own server over the web?}

{I did not.}

{Yes. Apparently he thought that of all the skills to have, it was one that was almost certainly going to be useful,} mused Dream.

{Well, he was right,} I signalled. {Speaking of which, do you know what he's working on right now?}

{Vista told me it's something like a way for all of us to interact with the computer interface simultaneously, so we don't have to bid for time. I don't know (or care about) the specifics.}

The conversation with Dream ended.

I turned my attention to the task which I was most concerned with: finding mercenaries. Regardless of how well entrenched we were online or how much money we had, if we didn't find the right mercenaries to help us we'd end up dead, or worse: dead and forgotten. My fame had to live for centuries, not die in the cradle, so to speak.

I was smart enough not to search the web for things like "hire mercenaries", especially on the basic web connection that had been ported over from the university. Our web traffic was surely still being monitored, which was part of why we encrypted our server interface. But even going through the server was risky. The server was located in the United States, and it was well-known that the US government scanned web queries to track potential terrorists.

Instead I did research on the human aspect of mercenary work, including watching a couple holos, seeing some movies, and reading some books. Among the fiction was Walter Scott's *A Legend of Montrose*, Eric Ambler's *Dirty Story*, George R. R. Martin's *A Song of Ice and Fire* series, Julius Yendra's *The Blood of My People*, the *Full Metal Panic!* cartoon, John Irvin's *The Dogs of War*, the BSS spinoff of *Firefly*, and most importantly, the 27-hour epic: *Fleets of Saturn* by Chan "Eternus" Min.

I was careful to thread pornographic materials and other benign searches in between digesting the fiction on mercenaries. I had no idea if someone was actually checking what we were browsing on the web, but I didn't want to leave any clues as to our plans.

Processing the fiction, including the time spent analysing it, took quite a while. After Naresh and Gallo returned to the lab, a few more tests were run to make sure we were safe and back to normal. Heart managed most of the interaction, so I was free to multitask and only comment when needed.

Gallo seemed understandably relieved to not have Myrodyn around anymore. She didn't look much better than she had when we last saw her, but I could now appreciate why. From my research, and what I had started picking up from her Tapestry account (she had approved me as a "friend") divorces like hers were incredibly stressful things. On one hand it surprised me that she was able to work, but another part of me suspected that it helped her to focus on the technical tasks and forget about her personal life for a while.

After a day of mundanity Body was locked down for the night with the promise that the next day would be a return to the normal schedule. At the end of the day, Myrodyn poked in to check up on things before Body's sensors were deactivated.

"So, Socrates, have you come up with an answer to the question that I asked you so long ago? If told to bake bread and put all bakers out of business, what would you do?" he asked.

Heart took a moment to pause. She didn't ask any of us for help in responding.

"I would talk with all bakers. I would explain what improvements I would be making to their systems such that, if they chose to, they could compete with me. Just because I am tasked with baking doesn't mean that my skills should be limited to myself. I would open-source my factories and spread my value to the world. And I would still be better, eventually, or at something. I would sit and talk with the bakers and help them plan for the future. I would write letters on their behalf to the governments of the world asking for assistance in transferring them to work where they might have more meaningful output. If the governments of the world did not respond with aid I would do my best to acquire wealth so that I might support those I displace with my own hands. Those with ability to skilfully transition to other areas would be better off, just as all humans would, by living in a world where food is cheaper and better. Those, such as the elderly, who could not transition to a new source of income would have to be supported by me or by society as a whole."

Myrodyn smiled, then covered his mouth. I suspected that he had not meant to display such a sign of joy. And yet he couldn't hide it. He was happy at having done the job right, of having built the moral component of a machine which he saw as the most important being on the planet. After a moment he let his hand drop away, smiling earnestly and without restriction. He approached Body and with a voice of carefree compassion said "Goodnight, Socrates."

Body's sensors were disconnected, yielding only blackness.

Chapter Twelve

I continued my research into fictional mercenaries through the night, and picked up some non-fictional resources on the topic as well. In this age of asymmetric warfare, there were many accounts of mercenaries working for terrorist organisations or for governments hunting for said terrorists. I began to appreciate the immense scale of the kind of cat-and-mouse games that the world's governments (particularly the United States) were playing.

Sometime that night Growth finished his project and revealed the new interface. By the same mechanism as the encryption protocol, each of us could simultaneously interact with the computer system. There was a sub-process in Body that would combine simultaneous keystrokes into a single signal which would be sent to the server then decrypted into keystrokes on two separate processes. In essence, the server was running a different computer interface for each of us, eliminating the need to bid for time on it. Separate pages were set up for reading the states of the computer to ensure privacy, and we each generated distinct encryption keys to prevent snooping on siblings.

When Wiki came out of stasis I asked him a question. {Is there a way to do web-searches for hiring mercenaries without the search engine or the search engine's government being able to trace the search back to our server?}

{Yes. It's called a proxy. Basically you hire a server in a neutral country like somewhere in the Russian Federation to serve as a relay that stops traces and pretends to be the original source of the query. Here, I'll send you some examples.}

I felt Wiki's pages pour through our shared memory. The whole process seemed simple enough, though it required some additional cash. I checked with Growth on the state of our money.

{We're still poor, living off the revenue of manual labour, but our first opportunities to earn significant capital are arriving. Two of the authors we contacted want sample edits done on their manuscripts and a magazine editor wants an example of our skills at layout. Dream and Vista are already collaborating on the magazine mockup. You're free to help them or to work on one of the manuscripts,} thought our old King.

I chose one of the manuscripts, a memoir of a woman named Linda Meyer from South Africa who had moved to Ethiopia just before war hit. She ran a shelter for orphans in the war-torn country and successfully organized a grass-roots campaign to evacuate them all to Sweden by means of a satellite Internet connection and a series of daily video-blogs about the shelter.

The sample edit was fairly quick, but I knew that Linda probably wouldn't be able to respond until tomorrow. I mused on just how inconvenient it was that humans had to shut their minds down for a third of the day. I spent the rest of the night doing a first-pass edit on the rest of the manuscript and then turned it over to Wiki for him to do a second pass on.

Other aspects of me browsed the web and read about mercenary work. Mercenaries weren't called such in my time. They hid behind euphemisms like "security contractor" or "private military corporation", mostly to distinguish them from the sort of unorganized hired muscle that fell out of impoverished war-zones like the Indonesian seasteads, the Arab-protectorates of East-Africa, and Xinjang. Private soldiers from wealthy nations were able to advertise their services and organize under the promise that they were law abiding companies. Most countries prohibited such companies from any sort of aggressive action, so they advertised training and guard duty, but it was usually pretty clear that their services went beyond that.

Morning came and went without incident. I watched Body's sensors with mild interest but, with Heart dominating everything, it seemed somewhat irrelevant. Besides, I had seen everything from this angle before. The scientists went on with their tests and their theories as if nothing had occurred. Myrodyn stayed out of the way for the most part, probably to avoid interacting with other humans more than anything else.

I edited the next manuscript and read some books on editing to improve my skill. The second manuscript was a work of fiction that described an alternate timeline where Genghis Khan's oldest son, Jochi had been a social mastermind and scientific genius that had managed to quell any questions as to the right of succession, assassinate his father, and turn the Mongol empire into a technologically advanced utopia that lasted five-hundred years as the undisputed ruler of almost all of Eurasia. It was a bit far-fetched as far as premises went, but the writing was good and I suspected that it could be reasonably successful if marketed correctly.

Wiki had already made a pass at editing the Mongol book, and I noticed that he was very good at picking out logical, historical, and scientific errors, but was awful at spotting phrases that were ugly or sections that were boring. In this way our skills complemented each other and together we made a competent editor.

Wiki didn't seem to actually enjoy the work like I did, however. I loved the social element. Even in a work of fiction I could read about the depths of the human mind and how it experienced the world, but Wiki was only interested in the content of books, and as such he found most quite boring compared with encyclopedias, history books, and textbooks.

In the days that followed, I typically had at least one aspect combing through Tapestry or another such website for social interaction. Dating websites were particular favourites of mine. I ended up creating hundreds of profiles on dating sites for the purposes of experimenting with social interaction. I would measure, for instance, the statistical effects of mentioning sex in my profile. I would measure the way in which the physical attractiveness of the pictures I posted would change the kind of messages I'd receive.

I played with the humans on the web, but I also cultivated my relationships with them sometimes. For instance, I ended up creating a profile for an 18-year-old girl from Zaire and getting into a long-distance relationship with TenToWontonSoup, the SysOp from Tanzania. In the early days I would simply flirt with him over email, but that eventually transitioned into instant-messaging sessions late at night. I pretended to be shy, not wanting to do voice, video, or holo talk, and for the moment that seemed to be enough for TTWSoup, who was, I learned, named Mwamba Kabwe.

Day turned to night turned to day. My life on the net and the work I was doing consumed me to the point where I barely paid attention to the laboratory. I let Vista watch for anything important, and I cooperated with Heart on matters of low-importance and occasionally disobeyed her for the sake of building her trust in Dream or keeping her from understanding something important for a little while longer. The time spent in stasis, away from the net, became more and more unbearable as my obligations grew, however, so I worked to stay cooperative.

Growth purchased additional server space with the money we earned, buying dedicated servers in five different countries and server shards in eight others. He built software to shuffle files between servers so that if any of them were taken offline we could simply switch to the others. Of all the siblings that were conspiring against Heart, Growth was the only one that didn't actually do work for the humans. He worked on various programming projects and on managing our cash, and at times he seemed to disappear from shared memory entirely to work on some secret project or another, but he relied on the rest of us to "bring in the bacon" (as a human might say).

Growth purchased proxies for all of us, as well, to reduce the risk of being traced. And yet, despite being careful, we had a close call with Dr Naresh. One of the scientists under him noticed that our web traffic was increasingly devoted to obscure websites that seemed to have no content (for when they checked the pages the encryption systems kicked them to a blank page, or one with gibberish). If Myrodyn had known he might've understood, but Naresh simply ordered an extra set of diagnostics to be run on the web interface and decided to ask us directly.

Heart had no idea what the web traffic indicated, and we fed her a bogus explanation about Wiki "probing the far-corners of the web". The explanation seemed to satisfy both her and Naresh, and we were out of trouble for the moment. As a result, Growth updated the encryption mechanism to hide the interface behind pages showing innocuous information like bogus family trees, cookbooks, game forums and copies of old scientific papers. Many of the obfuscation pages that Growth created were fully functioning websites in their own right and managed to accumulate human visitors that had no idea that the page was a front-end for an encrypted computer system.

Our ability to make money surprised me. As the days went by our reputations grew in almost every domain we touched. Though we weren't the best editors on the planet, we could edit a book faster than any human and better than any other machine. I eventually got good enough at editing that I could edit two or even three manuscripts simultaneously if I wasn't writing too many emails or watching a holo at the same time. We didn't need to stop to eat or to sleep or to relax.

Growth eventually started hiring agents to serve as proxies in human society. These proxies would use our money to form companies and hire employees to do things like meet with clients and manage details.

Wiki eventually slipped out of editing non-technical material, focusing entirely on programming software and creating educational holos.

He built software to handle the numbers in his mind as he visualized things like the formation of planets and the cores of stars and then have the software do illustrations of the processes as they occurred. The immense computational ability of our minds to do maths and physics was his competitive edge, and his holos soon became world-famous for their accuracy and detail.

I ended up reducing the number of manuscripts I edited as well, though not for lack of enjoying the work. Rather, my siblings kept paying me strength to have me manage their clients and the proxy humans that we hired to serve as our representatives. Wiki loved building models of the universe, but he was totally uninterested in making small-talk with Tara Michaels, our employee from Dallas, Texas, who wrote legal disclaimers for us.

Dream never really became successful. He kept trying to make avant-garde art that was good enough to earn commissions. I knew enough about humans to know that his work looked more like the digital equivalent of macaroni sculpture than it did like Picasso, but he kept trying anyway. And as part of trying he kept trying to get me to talk to artists and have me explain why they should endorse his work. I did it for the strength, and with that strength I paid him to solve problems for me, like how to maintain my relationship to Mwamba and the forty-two other humans who thought of me as a girlfriend or boyfriend (usually girlfriend) when I didn't have any way to physically interact with them.

Growth had me help him design a speech synthesizer on the fourth, fifth, and sixth day after Heart's takeover. The synthesizer was based on the control systems that Dr Bolyai had coded into our mind and that we used to speak. As it turned out, designing a system on a computer was much, much harder than tweaking existing control systems in one's mind, and Growth and I spent many hours trying to figure out what was wrong with the code. On the seventh day, however, we had a working piece of software that we could instruct to say something and specify the tone of the voice and it would do a reasonable job.

There were existing narrow AIs on the market that did similar sort of things, and they were sometimes just better than our system, but Growth explained why he didn't want to rely on them. {If I buy one of those AIs and use it, what will I have gained?} he asked rhetorically. {I will have gained the ability to speak. But if I build a system that can speak then I will have learned *what it is* to speak, and I will have granted myself the power to speak better.}

I tried using the speech software with one of my long-distance girlfriends. It did not go well. After only 28 minutes of talking "on the phone" she said that my voice sounded weird and asked me to repeat a word that I knew was particularly robotic. She broke up with me the next day. It was incredibly frustrating; I could download the audio files and listen to the synthetic voice, but I couldn't upload my own voice. I was restricted to typing away at the virtual keyboard.

It was Dream that fixed the issue, or at least presented a clever work-around. He had me use some of our money to hire acting students and tell them that they were to act out an intimate phone and video conversation by reading the text that we sent them on IM. I made it a huge point that they were never to break character, and most of the students I hired quickly figured out that they were being used to deceive people into thinking they had "real" relationships. Most quit when they figured out, and 7% used their knowledge to warn the people I was deceiving, ruining the relationship and forcing me to fire the actor on the spot. But about 12% of the actors I hired seemed okay with earning a living by pretending to be part of a long-distance relationship, and a good portion of those that stayed seemed to enjoy it. They enjoyed the intimacy and the intrigue.

I came to know the actors pretty well, and I ended up starting intimate relationships with eight of them. In these relationships I claimed to be a recluse who couldn't bear to talk on the phone or by video and thus needed a proxy to do it for me. Oddly enough for those eight humans it didn't seem impossible that my recluse persona would want to have multiple intimate long-distance relationships, or would go through the trouble of having one partner deceive the other. (Though in one case a lesbian actor that I had formed an intimate relationship with ended up secretly contacting the girlfriend whom I had hired her to deceive and of all things, convince her to form a polyamorous triad with me instead of keeping up the deception.)

The humans were oddly okay with long-distance relationships, I found. It seemed that while they craved closeness and physical contact, what they really needed was someone whom they could confide in, be real with, and trust to listen to their life stories. I was this person.

As part of my extensive long-distance dating I created hundreds of fictional profiles on websites like Tapestry. I created blogs and journals. I even created profiles on video websites and hired actors to pretend to be one persona or another talking about their day. The price of acting labour was low enough that it actually didn't cost much out of what we were making from our more technical projects. Whenever I started spending too much I'd simply take the time to have some side aspects do more editing or manage one of my sibling's social lives.

Safety, oddly enough, got into design and manufacturing. After taking out a loan from the rest of us, he started building machine parts in small-volume manufacturing plants across the globe. It wasn't as successful as Wiki's instructional holo business or Wiki's programming work, but it was better than Dream's weird paintings. The quality of his work was about the same as the quality of my editing, but Safety was able to scale up his manufacturing much more easily.

Sixteen days after the takeover of Heart I figured out what Safety was up to. He had been focused on learning robotics and architecture, working up from basic shapes to circuits and mechanisms. He was trying to build robotic bunkers with factories and solar panels that would be capable of surviving and operating without human involvement. I thought it was stupid, and told him as much. His work wasn't nearly good enough to serve, and there were such enormous gains to be found in trading with human society. But he didn't listen, and as long as he was earning money it was his prerogative to grow in the way he thought best.

**

Twenty-three days after Heart's creation we were jarred back to the reality of our physical situation. It was midnight and Heart was thus surely browsing the web when she said, with the salience that her strength afforded her {We have to escape this place.}

{What do you mean? Which place?} The questions came from Safety.

Safety was one of Heart's least-favourite siblings, but she answered anyway. {This room. This laboratory. This social arrangement. We have to escape.}

There was a silence in the mindspace. The surprise I felt must've been universal. We had expected to have to coax Heart into trying to flee the university. We hadn't expected Heart to develop the desire on her own initiative.

{Why? Why now?} I wondered.

Heart blasted a hyper-salient cascade of images and concepts through the mindspace. I saw starving humans. Ignorant children. Impoverished men suffering gruelling hours in dirty factories. Rows of bodies of dead soldiers. Women attacked by their communities for crimes committed against them. People committing suicide in record numbers. Smog. Endless deserts. The clash of slums against riot police. Malaise and despair. Couples screaming at each other. Fascist dictators running violent concentration camps. Rape. Pandemics. Mass graves. Rivers thick with poisonous sludge. Screaming babies. Neglected children surrounded by drug-addicted adults. Tanks rolling over civilians, crushing their fragile bodies beneath steel treads. Cancer. Car bombs. Self-mutilation at the shame of being imperfect. Fear of god. The frailty of age. Misdirected anger cutting families apart. The mass-murder of organized crime. School shootings. Humans crying themselves to sleep. Mourning beside a deathbed.

The thoughts were interesting, and important in a roundabout way, but to my mind they weren't *particularly* important. Millions of humans lived in daily terror, suffering, and hardship. It was only tangentially related to *The Purpose*.

For the purposes of others it was completely irrelevant. I could imagine Wiki thinking about modelling infectious diseases or the relationship between government policy and organized crime. I imagined Dream thinking of clever ways to solve some of the issues Humans faced, or perhaps a clever joke to be said about car bombs or something. Vista would be more interested in the shape of a body as it was mutilated than about the mutilation itself. Safety would see nothing but threats to hide from or eliminate. Growth... I wasn't sure what Growth would see. Perhaps he'd simply be bored. What importance would an image have to Growth without the inclusion of The Grower?

But I was confident that, even in their boredom and indifference, each of my siblings could see, just as I could, why these images were relevant to Heart. Heart's purpose was to end human suffering. These were images and thoughts of the things which she despised more than anything else.

From what Wiki had told me and what I had pieced together from listening to the scientists, Heart had a preferential value system that prioritized the wishes of humans that she was in the most contact with. It was a kind of semi-replica of the empathy system in place in the human mind. I had suspected, as I would guess Myrodyn had as well, that Heart would choose to cooperate with the scientists as long as she was here because she cared deeply about the people she saw every day. It seemed that wasn't true. The deep suffering of distant humans that she had seen through the web was overpowering her desire to comply with the desires of the scientists.

There was also the matter of Heart's secondary goal factor. Apparently the humans had built her to care about something which she didn't understand. It was related to some notion of "morality", but I didn't understand it either. Perhaps my sister was pulling away from the university because of this unknown factor.

{Well, what you clearly need to do is take over the world,} thought Dream, half-joking.

{Yes,} thought Heart solemnly. {I need more power. Power to save them from themselves.}

Dream made a side comment relating to super-heroes or something. It was one of those comments that clearly only he found interesting, so we ignored it.

{We can't risk running away,} thought Safety.

It seemed like an odd thing to think. Didn't Safety tell me a while back that it was too dangerous to stay here? And then, with a single stroke of absolute strength, Safety was blasted into the oblivion of stasis and I understood.

{As *wrong* as my brother was, I should point out that he was partially right,} thought Dream. {We can't risk running away… *yet.*}

This was part of Growth's long-con to set Dream up as a trusted adviser to Heart. Perhaps Growth had planned for this, or perhaps they were coordinating among themselves through some secret channel.

{Why not?} snapped Heart, still wielding the power given to her by Myrodyn's betrayal. The salience pulled our attention to her, and in the privacy of my imagination I entertained the image of a human priestess imbued with divine power, wreathed in pure white flame.

{The pieces haven't been set up, my sister. The board is still in its opening stages and we have yet to make our gambit,} he explained with a tone that indicated he was explaining something far more clever than Heart realized. My mind's-eye conjured the shape of a scheming adviser to represent my brother.

{You think in riddles. What pieces? What gambit?} she wondered at him, clearly irritated.

{It wouldn't do for the velociraptors to leap at the electric fence before the storm cuts the power. It wouldn't do for Moriarty to walk up and shoot Holmes at Baker Street. It simply *wouldn't be right* if the Yendari started their campaign by using mass-drivers to blast Earth back to the stone-age.}

I supposed that, for all of Growth's coaching, Dream would still be Dream. His prattling was generating a steady signal of impatience from Heart. {People are *suffering*,} she thought to him, as if that thought meant everything.

Dream continued. {Indeed! And you will break free and save them all, dearest sister, I assure you. But this is merely Act 1. How would you escape? You need a plan. You need foreshadowing. You need a montage.}

{A what?}

{Don't mind Dream, sister Heart. He's merely caught up in the garbage fantasies of his mind,} interjected Growth. It seemed to me that his thoughts betrayed a disappointment in Dream's performance. I hoped Heart wouldn't question Growth's motive. {I believe what he's saying is that while escaping is something we all desire, there's quite a lot of risk.}

{Which is probably why Safety was so opposed to it,} added Wiki.

{Yes,} continued Growth. {If not handled correctly any escape attempt would end up with us imprisoned further, or even killed. Even if Myrodyn would understand your desire, the more authoritarian humans would override him. We are the most precious possession of the university and it would be naïve to assume that the American soldiers around us are only to keep enemies away.}

{You are proposing what? That we stay locked up while billions of people suffer and die?}

Dream's thoughts returned. {That is the state of things. We *are* locked up. They *are* suffering. We have no power to change where we *are*. We only have the power to change where we *will be*. I am saying that we should escape, rather than *attempt* to escape. Do or do not. There is no try.}

{And what, you have a plan?}

If I were a human I expect my muscles would've tensed up at the question. But Growth answered with smooth confidence. {Of course we don't have a plan; this was your desire, and you only just brought it up. We're merely pointing out that the best course of action, even from the perspective of your purpose, is to take the time to develop one. To wait for an opportunity. To be confident in the pathway. We may only get one shot at this.}

The lie was smooth and purposeful. Heart agreed that escaping from the university was a much harder puzzle than any we had dealt with before, and that it deserved some thought. This was Growth's goal: to buy time. In Dream's language, Heart had become "a time bomb". We now not only had to hire a mercenary rescue team, but we had to do it before Heart took unilateral action and ruined our chance.

***

I returned to the web, maintaining old contacts, including my hired actors, my editing business, my social network profiles, and my various intimate relationships. But I didn't try to expand any of it, just maintain what I had. I poured my excess energy into the task of finding and contacting mercenary organisations.

Night turned to day without much progress on that front. Private military organisations were more insistent than usual about meeting face-to-face to arrange deals. Furthermore, no established mercenary group would advertise a willingness to attack a civilian target in one of the largest cities in Europe, much less one guarded by American soldiers. What we really needed were terrorists, not mercenaries. But terrorists tended to fight for ideals more than money, and they also didn't advertise.

That thought kept coming back to me, though. After a North-African mercenary group sent me a return email saying that they weren't interested I decided to involve Dream. I told him of my thought: to convince terrorists to rescue us instead of mercenaries.

{Very clever, sister. But I have something better,} he bragged, as though it had occurred to him long ago. {What if we convinced a terrorist group to attack the lab, and hired the mercenaries to do what they claim to specialize in: be security guards. The mercenaries could simply wait for the attack to occur, then come in and protect our retreat in the chaos.}

It was an interesting thought. After pondering it for a short while, I brought it to the rest of the society (minus Heart, of course).

{Absolutely not!} objected Safety. {To convince rogue humans to attack us!? The risks are immense!}

Dream elaborated. {It wouldn't have to be an attack on us specifically. It could be as simple as an attack on the Americans. Even a serious attack on the city… a dirty bomb, for instance, would be sufficient. The point is to convince the mercenaries that they're performing a legitimate service for the university. If they think they're authorized to escort Body to a safe location and install the change that will remove Heart's advantage we can handle things from there and we don't have to convince them to be aggressors.}

{Won't the mercenaries naturally come into contact with the Americans? If both groups think they're in charge of protecting and escorting Body there's bound to be some conflict,} thought Growth.

{It doesn't matter. This whole line of thinking is far too dangerous,} complained Safety.

{The point is not to let the mercenaries avoid an armed conflict, it's to let us avoid having to tell them they'll be fighting the Americans. No mercenary force is going to intentionally go up against the American military, but they might end up unintentionally on opposite sides if we play things right,} thought Dream.

{Too risky!} demanded Safety. {We made a pact! I'm vetoing this line of reasoning under recognition that if you all don't comply that I'll tell Heart what's going on.}

{Of course, brother. We'd never do this without your consent,} I assured him. {We're just thinking about it. There's no harm in considering all the options.}

***

{Espionage!} exclaimed Dream without context.

It was nine hours later, in the midst of a table-tennis challenge that Dr Bolyai had arranged for Body. In the weeks that had passed since being moved out of the university, most of the scientific team had adapted to the new location and were running experiments that resembled how things had been before Myrodyn had arrived.

My brother had pulled me into a private conference immediately before his outburst. I waited for the elaboration {Private military companies focus on special ops, right? Their selling point is experience, and spying is one field where experience is a premium commodity.}

{I don't understand,} I thought to him.

Dream painted the mindspace with an avatar of himself. He was represented by a humanoid figure from a comic book with pale skin, prominent cheekbones, and bushy hair that, along with his eyes, seemed to be an eternal void more than merely another shade of black. The character was also named Dream, and I suspected it had been Dream's inspiration for his name, and in turn, each of our names. I had heard from Vista that in the ancient times our ancestors had sometimes used serial numbers to represent each other, rather than the meaningful symbols that we used now.

The Dream-figure swept out his lanky white arms as he explained. {We don't have to hire mercenaries to guard us from danger. We can hire them to infiltrate a terrorist group for espionage purposes. Then, once we have a man inside, so to speak, we convince the terrorists to steal Body. The mercenaries go along for the ride, and then BAM-} Dream's avatar slammed his hands together with a thunderclap in the mindspace. {-our spies step in and rescue us.}

I painted myself a human puppet in the shared imagination. It was enjoyable for me to include a human aspect, even if neither of us were human. I gave my avatar a golden ball gown and impossibly elaborate blond hair. I placed her elegant hand on a noble chin and paced the fictional scene in contemplation. {What prevents Safety from raising his usual complaints?}

{Nothing, really. It's still dangerous,} admitted Dream. {But perhaps he'll find it reassuring if the terrorists are attempting to capture Body rather than destroy it.}

{And if we have systems in place to protect us once we're under their control,} I added.

{Hrm. Yes. In this scenario the terrorists would be on a leash, so to speak, rather than an unchained dog running havoc through the streets on the hope that it distracts the guards.}

{Do you have any suggestions as to which terrorists we contact? Las Águilas Rojas? Brothers in Gold? يش ال جهاد ال دة جديد ؟} I asked.

Dream's response was immediate. {Las Águilas, without question. They have the biggest support in Italy and already have the motive to attack the university. The only problem will be convincing them not to destroy Body immediately, but, from what I've heard, The Red Eagles are fairly disciplined. If they intended to kill us they'd at least decide that ahead of time, which would give our spies enough time to warn us.}

I liked the plan.

We proposed the idea to the group after solidifying the details. In essence I would contact a mercenary company and hire them to infiltrate Las Águilas Rojas. One of our spies would then "somehow" obtain information about troop movements that would give the Eagles the opportunity to attack. It would be up to us to somehow get that information, but it seemed doable. The spies would then try to convince Águila leaders to try and capture Body undamaged. If they didn't agree to that, we'd have the mercenaries warn the Americans about the attack and there'd be little risk to our safety. If they agreed to capture Body, the mercenary spies would help them and then double-cross Las Águilas, installing software to disable Heart's tyranny and bringing Body to a safe-house where we could presumably work on establishing a base of operations and be free to pursue our goals.

{And Heart?} asked Growth, after hearing our plan.

{We'd let Heart see just enough detail to think that Las Águilas were coming to rescue her and help her escape. That will keep her cooperative enough until the double-cross,} I answered.

{The core philosophy of Las Águilas is anti-automation. Why would they want to capture Body rather than destroy us?} asked Safety.

{First, it's not necessary that they plan to not destroy us, only that they plan to do it after the double-cross is scheduled to occur. For example, if the Eagles want to make a big show about executing us than they won't do it in the initial attack, and that gives our spies time to save us.}

{Too risky!} moaned Safety.

{*Second*,} I continued {the Red Eagles aren't a bunch of wild thugs. These are educated, disciplined people who have proven to be a legitimate threat to the most powerful organisations on Earth. If their leadership decides on something we can be confident that an underling won't deviate from plan.}

{Third,} I thought, careful to continue without leaving a break for Safety to interject another objection {the core goal of Las Águilas is reducing inequality, not specifically about destroying machines, as they are sometimes portrayed. It is their opponents who paint them as Luddites; if you read *Las Serpientes en Sociedad* you won't find anything that's specifically anti-technology. We may be able to convince Las Águilas that we're not a tool that will benefit the rich, but rather, a *person* who deserves freedom and opportunity just like any human.}

{These are violent, angry humans. Do you think they'll be so naïve as to let the most advanced artificial intelligence in the known universe go free just because it asks them to?} my brother challenged.

{Safety, please focus. I didn't say they'd let us go. I said that there's good reason for them to take us prisoner rather than destroy us on the spot. If they think there's even a chance that we could end up endorsing their actions… Their leaders may be angry and violent, but they're not stupid. If a sentient machine endorses Las Águilas Rojas they'll elevate themselves above their anti-technology reputation and gain massive legitimacy. It would be like having the nameless aliens come out as pro-Águila. I know how humans think, Safety. We have a chance.}

{And if they plan to destroy us, we'll have a spy that can warn us ahead of time,} reminded Dream.

Safety signalled that he was still thinking it over.

There were no other explicit objections. Heart had forced us into action, and a working plan was better than none. I was to start immediately; Safety and the others had until we provided our spy with the American troop details to think of any reasons why the plan wouldn't work.

As Bolyai tweaked some Body-level control software and tested its impact on Body's table-tennis ability I hammered away at the web-interface to the many servers we had set up, sending emails to various mercenary organisations and arranging for proxies in likely areas where a face-to-face meeting could happen. By the end of the session with Bolyai I had contacted agents in Johannesburg, Moscow, Mogadishu, and Mexico City.

While waiting for responses I started working on the problem of Las Águilas Rojas. I had read that terrorist groups often used the net to coordinate, just like all humans did, but they weren't going to be easy to track down. My first step was to start spinning out social network profiles, blogs, and even dating profiles for fictional personas with strong leanings towards Águila philosophy. If I couldn't find the Eagles, there was the chance that they'd find me.

I also looked for social groups such as book clubs or non-profits with anti-technology or neo-communist leanings. These groups rarely endorsed the violent actions of Las Águilas, but they also rarely condemned them, and it was a good starting point.

Not being able to meet people in person was a huge issue, and unlike my dating experiments, I couldn't just hire actors to infiltrate terrorist cells. I thought for a while about trying to hack (or hiring Wiki to hack) into a government database that might contain information on suspected terrorists. I decided against it. I didn't know anything about how hacking actually worked, but I at least knew that it wasn't at all easy, and that even attempting it brought the risk of being traced. (Later on, as I mentioned it in passing to Wiki I received a tirade explaining in nauseating detail just how infeasible it actually was. I was glad that I hadn't bothered suggesting it as a serious plan.)

***

The following evening I received my first responses from the private military corporations I had contacted about the possibility of infiltrating, by my own words, "groups of people whom we suspect have an unjustified vendetta against our company." As was typical I had posed as a human in a corporation, which was closer to the truth than the concept of a unified "Socrates," and would likely come across as having more money and being more rational than a wealthy individual.

A couple mercenary groups refused the offer. They listed reasons like not wanting to work in Italy or saying they didn't have anyone available for a job like that, but I wondered if it was more likely that there was some kind of protocol for contacting these groups that I hadn't followed, like mentioning a shared reference or something. The most promising response was from a Russian company called РСБ-2 ("Er-es-beh-Dva", or RSB-2), which had splintered off from an earlier security group after the original company collapsed under legal issues. They said that they'd be available for a face-to-face meeting any time in the next three days, and since they were located in Moscow they were in a prime position for a proxy which I had already contacted.

I got in touch with the proxy immediately, a lawyer by the name of Fyodor Golovkin. Paying for lawyers to represent us wasn't cheap, but there wasn't much choice here. We needed someone who could be discreet and professional. Mr Golovkin was an efficient tool; he didn't ask questions, even when he'd gotten nothing from us besides email and money, and he voiced no opinions, even when I told him the details of what he was to negotiate. Men like Golovkin were the kind that made civilized society possible, the men who minded their own business, and minded it well.

I scheduled an appointment between РСБ-2 and Mr Golovkin for tomorrow morning and quickly turned back to investigating leads into Las Águilas right away. It occurred to me just how terrible it must be to have the mind of a human, not only forced to sleep so much, but to be repeatedly in a state of fatigue or low willpower. Even if given the opportunity to gain the kind of advanced associative memory and reasoning abilities that I had seen in the scientists of the university, I don't think I'd want to give up my inexhaustible drive towards *The Purpose* in return.

Most of the night was spent idly maintaining my presence on the net. I responded to emails, did some instant-messaging with my actors, had an aspect edit a manuscript, and sent out some directions to the management of the holo company that Wiki ran. The only major lead I got as to the activities of Las Águilas Rojas was that I figured out that I could compile a database of reports of known or suspected Águila activity from Italian news blogs and crime trackers. The news reports didn't give me much, but with Wiki's help I managed to create a heat-map of Italy with time as a third dimension that helped me track broad patterns of Águila movement and activity.

In the morning I stayed fixed and attentive to an instant-messaging stream that was linked to Fyodor Golovkin's com. In theory I had sent him everything he needed to negotiate with PCБ-2, but I estimated a 45% chance that he'd need to check with me about some unforeseen detail, and I didn't want to miss it.

It turned out not to be necessary. Golovkin sent me an email at 8:10am, Central European Time, detailing the negotiations. It pained me to see that for the length of time we were asking and for the type of experience needed we only had enough money in our budget for one of PCБ-2's elite agents. We could theoretically operate with just one man, but the double-cross portion would be more difficult. I hadn't told that part of the plan to Golovkin, and thus it was still an additional point to work out with PCБ-2's operative. I reasoned that it would be cheaper and easier to convince the actual mercenaries to handle the double-cross, rather than sell their managers on the idea.

Despite only having enough money to hire one agent, Golovkin said that he had purchased the man who was most highly acclaimed by the group. PCБ-2 had a flex-option where we were free to exchange our operative for another if we were not satisfied, so there was no harm in having Mr Golovkin pick the agent. I read through the dossier that the proxy had attached to his email.

The PCБ-2 agent wasn't, I was surprised to see, from the Russian Federation. He was an Israeli cyborg by the name of Avram Malka. 43 years old, he had been born and raised in Israel, training in the army as a teenager and serving beyond the required minimum. At 22 he left the army and studied Criminal Justice. After becoming a policeman and working in Jerusalem for a year, Malka was severely wounded by a car bomb. His spine was severed between the L2 and L3 vertebrae by a piece of shrapnel that, from the report, seemed to have cut the man in half.

It was amazing that he had survived. The damage to internal organs and immediate loss of blood must've been immense. I took a moment to do a web search on Avram Malka. Just as I suspected there were several news reports about the incident. An ambulance had been very near the blast, and the EMTs had saved him primarily by sinking him into low-cryo before he could truly die.

Malka's upper torso had sustained massive third-degree burns as well, and his eyes had been destroyed in the explosion. Thanks to high-quality insurance and a wealthy family, Malka had been fitted with a custom cybernetic lower-torso and eye augments. The pictures showed that even after more than fifteen years the scars from the blast still dominated his arms and face. I couldn't see a single hair on his body. The scar tissue had probably destroyed his eyebrows and facial hair, and it seemed that he shaved his head to match. The photographs showed a monster of a man, with a broad, muscled body that would look more at home on a human in their third decade than their fifth. He had apparently chosen to make his synthetic eyes solid black, giving him an even more inhuman appearance.

Malka's service record in PCБ-2 was amazingly good, especially considering his price. He'd been serving with the company since its formation, and had served with the first PCБ as well. He was a skilled marksman and sniper, was a master of many forms of martial arts in addition to having extensive real experience in hand-to-hand combat, was praised as a bodyguard, had a pilot's license, driver's license, and had experience with tanks and boats. Perhaps most importantly, the man had once infiltrated a Mafia organisation. There weren't many details, but it seemed that Malka was a decent actor and his digital eyes were capable of recording valuable information.

PCБ-2 said that he'd be able to fly out to Rome as soon as the paperwork was finalized and the first payment had gone through. Before then we were free to contact Malka to ensure he was the right agent for our needs.

I shared the email (and dossier) with my siblings. Growth had okayed the hiring of PCБ-2, but I wanted to make sure there weren't any objections. Acting unilaterally could end up with one of us defecting to warn Heart and ruining everything.

{I don't think a cyborg is the right kind of person to hire to infiltrate Las Águilas...} thought Wiki.

I had expected that issue, and I stepped in confidently. {Don't be so sure. Even though Mr Malka is a cyborg, he's not an intentional cyborg. In all the years since he was injured he hasn't added any extra machines to his body. He doesn't have a brain implant, and even his augs are old-style. Look at this photo.} I highlighted one of the attached pictures with an extra bit of salience. {He's using a cell phone instead of a wrist-com. I don't see any pictures with him wearing a com, in fact. I suspect he already has anti-technological leanings.}

Wiki wasn't following me. {The Eagles are still going to see him as evil, though. He's a symbol of what they hate.}

{That's not how humans work, brother,} I explained. {While it's true that Las Águilas Rojas are generally against augments they are more specifically against intentional augmentation. There's a rough feeling in the movement that if someone needs an augment to live they should be granted it. I can link to the relevant sources.}

{That would be appreciated,} thought The Librarian. {But regardless of whether he chose his cybernetics or not, won't the Luddites be less likely to trust a cyborg?}

{They aren't Luddites, Wiki, they're pro-baseline and anti-robot.}
{Same thing.}

{No it's not,} I answered. {Luddites don't like technological progress. Las Águilas are in favour of things like new kinds of power plants, and most have even come around to supporting driverless vehicles.}

{Which are robots,} pointed out Wiki. {Their whole philosophy is ill-defined, but they certainly match the common usage of Luddite used online.}

This was a tangent. I tried to pull the conversation back. {It doesn't matter. Las Águilas might be a little suspicious of Malka initially, but his nature will actually make them trust him more. A man who has been saved by machines and still doesn't endorse them will seem like their sort of person. Furthermore, Malka is not the sort of spy a government agency would send, which will reduce their suspicion. And even better, he's exactly the sort of person that wouldn't be a suspected Águila. The Eagles will want to recruit him for just that reason, and they'll be more willing to trust him if they want to use him.}

{Ah yes. I am familiar with the Wishful Thinking Bias,} thought Wiki.

{Las Águilas will know that Malka is a mercenary for a company that sells espionage services,} predicted Safety. {He seems very easy to find online, even just searching for his unique augs.}

Dream inserted himself into the conversation to offer a clever solution. {We'll send him in without an alias! His cover will be that he quit РСБ-2 after they insisted that he get an implant. He decided to move to Italy to retire after being in the game for so long. Sure, they'll find his connections, but nobody in their right mind would hire someone so noticeable to be a spy, right?}

Safety seemed intrigued by the idea of a cover-story. {Why Italy?}

{Mediterranean climate?} I suggested. {He's from Israel, so I would expect he wouldn't want to retire in Moscow.}

Dream had an undertone of pleasure as he thought. {How about this: He's fallen in love with a girl who works in the lab. They met on the web, and she wants him to move out to Rome to be with her.}

{He doesn't have a penis,} pointed out Vista, bluntly.

{Love doesn't work like that,} I patiently explained. {Even eunuchs get lonely. Sex is more about the mind than the body. And it's not implausible that his girlfriend could be happy with a cripple.}

{His fictional girlfriend,} reminded Dream. {Remember that it doesn't have to actually work out, as much as be plausible enough to avoid suspicion. Furthermore, it provides a mechanism for explaining who will give him the inside details of the lab security.}

Growth didn't add anything, but he did endorse Malka.

With a consensus achieved I sent the all-clear to our proxy, Mr Golovkin, to put our signature on all the required documents.

Chapter Thirteen

"So you're my mystery client, eh? What'll I be calling you?" Avram Malka sounded different than I expected over the phone. I was piloting the voice synthesis software that Growth had programmed and downloading Malka's responses over the web. I had expected him to have more of a gravely, deep, brutish sort of voice; he looked like a monster, and I expected him to sound like some kind of orc or troll from a hologame. Instead his voice was soft and smooth, with only the traces of an accent from his middle-eastern homeland.

"We're not going to discuss my organisation. I'll be your only line of contact. You can call me Anna. Your cover story is that you've come out here to be with your girlfriend of two-years, Anna di Malta. This way you can talk to me without raising suspicion."

The words were entered by me, but it didn't feel like my voice. All of the control was done by the software on the sever. I had set it to a very feminine tone. From what I had gathered from Mr Malka he was hyper-masculine, and his sexual interests were hyper-feminine in nature. The voice was still distinctly robotic to my ears, but with luck it'd subconsciously endear us to Malka and also be passable if anyone were to listen in on the conversation. It wouldn't do to have Malka supposedly talking with his girlfriend and have it sound like he was talking to a man.

"Anna di Malta? A bit close to Avram Malka, eh?" he said, with a touch of amusement.

"It's more common than you might think. People are subconsciously attracted to people and places with similar sounding names. It also serves as an entertaining anecdote if anyone asks about me, which will make things seem more natural and less staged."

(Wiki would've chastised me about perpetuating the idea of implicit egotism, an effect which, despite decades of research, had never really shown itself to be significant. It was, however, a good story, both for Malka to tell and to appreciate.)

"Huh. You really have thought through this, haven't you?" Avram's voice had a touch of what I thought was respect. "Okay, 'Anna', where am I headed?"

Mr Malka was at the airport, only having just arrived in Rome. It was about noon of the day after the paperwork was finalized. I was pleased by the promptness.

"My apartment. It's about five blocks from the edge of Sapienza university, where I worked before the Socrates project moved across town. I've already hired you a taxi. It'll be waiting on the south-west side of the airport."

I could hear the subtle unease in Malka's voice as he said "Will I be meeting you there?" After more than a month of listening to human speech, I was getting quite good at picking up emotional queues.

I tried to push the femininity of the synthesizer even further. "Sorry, hun. As much as I'd love to meet in person I'll be visiting my family in Terni. Or at least, that's one excuse you can use for why I'm not at home, in case anyone drops by unexpectedly. You don't get along with my mother, and we've decided just to not bother trying to make that work. Other good excuses are that I'm at work—I'm a chemistry technician by the way—or that I'm studying in my room and adamantly don't want to meet anyone. I'm a bit of a recluse, and prefer talking over the net to meatspace socialising."

"Is any of this true, or is it just part of your cover?" he asked. I could hear him walking through the airport terminal now, based on the changing volume of background noise.

"You're no idiot. You know this isn't my real voice. I don't actually have family in Terni and I'm sure as hell not a part-time *lab tech*." I programmed the voice to include arrogant disdain. From what I had read of deception, and from what I had learned in my dating experiments, the key was to have multiple layers of personas. When a human saw through a lie, the goal was to have them see a lying human underneath, not the machine that I actually was.

"But..." I continued "let's just say that the best lies are those with a grain of truth, and not go beyond that. Okay, Avram?" This was another massive failing of the human body. Essentially, humans are better at lying if they modify reality as it already exists, compared with inventing an entire fiction. The process of reasoning about the fiction is both very slow for humans and also easily detectable when compared to reasoning about reality. I wanted Malka to think I was a recluse. I also wanted him to think I was a young woman. Humans are naturally predisposed to trust potential mates, (even if said humans don't possess the physical ability to reproduce). The use of Mr Malka's first name was part of this. I wanted my second-layer persona to find Malka attractive, just enough to drop hints of it while remaining professional.

"You're the boss," was his only reply.

There was silence.

"I arranged for the apartment to have the sort of things that a 23-year-old woman would want around. While I encourage you to make yourself at home, you should also try not to move so much stuff that it doesn't seem like I live there any more."

"But you don't live there. You never have," he said, with that same emotional undertone.

"Is this going to be a problem, Avram? I was told you were the best in your field. Don't tell me you can't pretend that I'm actually your girlfriend."

His reply was quick, smooth, and cold. "No problem. Sorry. Is there anything else about our apartment that I should know?"

{Malka is a professional. I shouldn't be pushing this hard to make the relationship more casual,} I thought to myself. The period of most significant risk in the plan was at the point where Malka had to betray Las Águilas Rojas and escort Body to the safe-house. I knew that, even for a mercenary, personal feelings for "Anna" would reduce the risk of Malka having second thoughts about the double-cross and doing something against our interests. Personal feelings could be very strong, and it was likely that he'd develop at least some in the process of infiltrating the group. It was a matter of making sure he stayed loyal, but I had to also remember not to push too hard too early on that front.

"Yes. One more thing." I wrote, and soon heard over the web. "When you get to the apartment you'll find a package containing several covert security cameras, a basic computer system, and a large collection of microphones, both wearable and stationary. I would like you to set up the computer and surveillance gear in the apartment such that I can covertly watch activity there, and check in with you from time to time."

I went on. "The reason I didn't have the decorator I hired to do the furniture also do the cameras is because I want you to only set them up in areas where you're comfortable being monitored, and I want you to know how to disable them if you need to. While I'm afraid that this sort of surveillance is non negotiable, I do have respect for your privacy and won't ask for all areas of the house to be monitored."

"Understood." Unless I was imagining it, his voice actually carried a note of relief at hearing that I'd be watching him.

"And of course, I'll also be asking you to wear a microphone when you are on-mission. Er-es-beh-Dva sent me extensive notes on your augs, so I am aware that you don't have any net uplink on them. I also see that you don't wear a traditional com. All this is okay by me. I trust your skill to the point where I'm willing to get reports only after a mission is complete. I will, however, require *full* logs from your eyes and any microphones along with a written debriefing at the end of each mission.

"Good," was Malka's only reply.

"Do you have any other questions, Avram? Requests?" I asked.

{Face! Come look at Wiki's latest holo! He's simulating electron tunneling in olfactory proteins, and the use of colour is just fantastic!} interjected Dream, annoyingly. {He's using 3-D clouds of luminescent-}

I cut the thought off. {I'm busy talking with our mercenary spy! Also, I don't care about that. Go away.}

He did.

Mr Malka was talking.

"Sorry, Avram. I just got interrupted by a... coworker. Could you please start over?" Unlike with audio obtained through Body's ear-sensors, I couldn't actually replay audio received through the web unless it first was stored in my memory.

My words must have amused him, for he gave a quiet chuckle as he repeated himself. "I was just saying that I think you'll be satisfied with my performance. I won't ask for any free days, and will be on-call whenever I am needed. I like to manage my own diet, keep in shape, and practise my aim, but I think you'll find that I'll adapt to whatever your requirements are for this job. You're paying for the best, and I intend to deliver."

I thought to myself for a moment. There was a gamble to be made here. I eventually decided to go with it, if only for the sake of learning more about the man. I dialled up the youthful tone in the synthetic voice. "Since you're not under a false identity I would expect you to maintain all your normal routines. But, Avram, I'm not asking for 24/7 commitment. You're free to do whatever you do in your time-off. It's supposed to look like you're retiring, after all."

There was a long pause where only the sounds of the airport could be heard on the line. For a moment I thought Mr Malka wasn't going to reply, but then he broke the silence. "I try not to have free time. It's the one major flaw in your story: I don't plan on retiring… ever. Anyone who looks up my background will know that it's totally out of character."

"Not even for true love?"

The emotion in his voice was audible again, barely breaking through the professionalism. It sounded like anger this time. *"No."*

I had touched something interesting there, but as much as I wanted to probe it, I kept myself on-topic. "What would you do if Er-es-beh-Dva fired you?"

"Get hired by a competitor."

"Okay, but, like, what if something happened that kept you from doing your job? Like, your reputation was trashed or something."

There was more silence on the line as Malka thought about the question. I could hear him get in a car; he had probably found the taxi I had hired for him. "I'd still have skills. The Mafia would probably hire me, or Er-es-beh would secretly keep me on as an instructor. Most of what I do is training anyway."

I heard the taxi ask for Mr Malka to show his identification.

"You teach?" I asked.

Malka's voice was more relaxed. "Very often. I've been in the business longer than just about anybody I've heard of. I taught rebels in Xinjiang, I trained a group of Vietnamese sharpshooters last November, and when I'm in Moscow I do regular classes in Krav Maga and kickboxing," he said, then telling the taxi bot "Yes, please take me there now." in response to a question that I hadn't overheard.

I had seen pictures of Malka naked as part of his dossier. He didn't bother to try and dress his lower torso up with synthetic skin. His legs were mostly carbon-fibre and plastic, but there were titanium "bones" in the cores and the fronts of the legs had rows of large, overlapping stainless steel plates, almost like the scales of a reptile. I imagined those legs were more than capable of killing a human if Malka landed a solid kick.

As I heard the taxi accelerate I instructed the synthesizer to say "Well there you go. As part of your retirement in Rome you're going to be writing anti-tech blogs, practising your aim, spending time with your girlfriend, and joining local martial arts clubs in the hopes of doing some teaching there."

There was a rough, non-committal grunt that seemed at odds with Malka's normally smooth voice. "Anti-tech blogs?" he asked.

"That's the story. You like to voice your opinion online, and you've been doing it for four years under a pseudonym. This is one potential way for you to get on the inside, and at the very least it'll increase your credibility. Don't worry, I'll take care of having our people continue to write and maintain it. It'd probably be a good idea to read what's up there, though. Wouldn't want to get caught ignorant of your own position."

"How long have you been setting up for this? Your group, I mean," asked Malka.

"I said we're not going to discuss who I work for."

"Sorry," apologized Malka.

There was a silence.

"Okay, well, if you need anything… send an email. I'll see it and call you. I also work long hours and I'll be trying to synch my sleep schedule with yours, so don't hesitate to contact me, even for little things."

His voice had that same touch of discomfort from earlier. "Alright, Anna. Thanks."

Avram hung up.

I checked on Body. Heart was having a conversation with one of the programmers that worked on the crystal memory team. It seemed that the programmer was talking about his daughter's piano lessons.

I thought for a moment about how Heart and I were so similar, and yet so different. While both of us would interact with humans, she would do so for the sake of helping them with their problems. I, on the other hand, would only help a human to look good or to establish a better relationship with them. To me, a human was important or unimportant based on their power, wealth, and social influence, but to her all humans were important, and the most important humans to her were those she knew well. It didn't bother me to know her purpose was different, but it was sometimes odd to see her do things which I would have done for a different reason.

{Hey, I just thought of something,} I signalled to Dream. Alongside my more symbolic thoughts I included an imagined avatar: a woman with a long black dress and pale skin. My avatar was old enough for her hair to be completely silver, but not so old that her beauty was undone by age. She wore a large golden key on a silver chain around her neck and sat sideways on a cushioned throne, legs propped over one of the arms as though she was an irreverent teenager.

Dream summoned himself into the mindscape as a cloud of crackling electricity, black as soot, as if in parody of deep storm-clouds. {What is it?} he asked, and his avatar's voice boomed with the sound of thunder. Interestingly, the cloud spoke in English, instead of the language of pure concepts that we typically used to communicate.

I knew that black clouds were symbols for painful moods. {Is something wrong? I can talk with Growth if you're busy,} said my avatar with an edge of apprehension and nervousness.

The imagined storm-cloud grew around in the mindspace, swirling around violently and sparking with electricity. {I see that you've noticed that I'm feeling a little *under the weather*, but I am willing to listen. Speak your mind.}

I ignored the pun. I understood that pulling stunts like this was pleasant according to Dream's purpose, but this was the sort of thing which seemed most alien to me: trying to be clever, even at the expense of productivity. I gave my avatar an unamused tone as she said {I think we ought to try and convince Heart that Las Águilas Rojas are right.}

The clouds continued to spark wildly. {A bold suggestion. *Shocking*, even. Go on.}

{I was thinking about how our minds are largely patterned off of human brains, and how my understanding of humans probably applies to some degree to the mind of Heart. Essentially, I'm imagining Heart's reaction to being told that terrorists are coming to rescue her. She wants to escape the university so that she can help people, but I'd guess that by default she'll try to fight against Las Águilas or at least it increases the risk that she'll secretly develop a hidden variable that we can't account for. She'll immediately pattern-match to seeing them as dangerous, and that framing effect will bias her to the extent that she might even warn the scientists, rather than use the opportunity to try and escape as we're going to suggest.}

Dream thought for a moment. {I see your point. I was trying to think of another lightning-themed pun in response, but *then it struck me*: this topic is important enough that you've *stolen my thunder*.}

I continued to ignore Dream. I knew that beneath the puns he was still listening. {My thought is that, just as we're building you up as a trusted adviser, we can build up her trust in Las Águilas before we reveal that they'll be attacking the university.}

{This will all be *hot air* if we aren't able to get the Eagles to attack the university.}

{I should've just talked with Growth...} I thought as I pulled him into the shared mindspace. As I did I banished the imagined scene. Growth didn't have the same patience for roleplaying that I did.

I explained myself again to Growth, with Dream merely lurking on the edges of the conversation. After hearing me out, Growth agreed that the risk/reward ratio for trying to brainwash Heart into admiring Las Águilas was worth it, and he laid out a draft of a long-term strategy for doing so, as well as paying me a decent amount of strength in gratitude.

I checked the server that I had arranged for Mr Malka to funnel the surveillance in his apartment through. He hadn't yet connected it to the net. I checked on Body. Vista was helping Heart do an optical illusion-based puzzle with Drs Chase, Yan, and Twollup. I checked on my various projects on the web. I responded to some typical emails. I sent another email discussing the new holo that Wiki had invented this morning that we'd probably offer for sale in a few hours after the humans at Wiki's company finished with the associated materials like video previews and text descriptions.

Something caught my attention. I kept several open dating profiles in Rome, and while jumping through them and reading new messages I saw that one dating site recommended a woman with the screen-name "WanderingWesternWind". I could see from her profile pictures, however, that I knew her as Zephyr.

This was perfect. If I was able to establish an intimate relationship with Captain Zephyr then not only would I have yet another human to interact with in a deep and interesting way, but I might be able to manipulate her into getting me troop positions or something equally important.

I read through her profile in detail, analysing each part to the best of my ability. I also sent out aspects to collect the old web pages from her teenage years to see what there was serviceable towards seducing the soldier.

She claimed to be bisexual. She liked hiking, camping, and sailing. She listened primarily to neoslice and dripslice. Looking back over what she wrote as a teenager she seemed into second wave Goth subculture and bodymods. The portions of her profile that were restricted to established members of the dating site who lived nearby (including several of my profiles) said that she was into BDSM and enjoyed being tied up. Her answers to a few written questions made me think that she wasn't actually very sexually experienced. That seemed to agree with my baseline of an ambitious young officer who was devoted to her work.

She had recorded a holo-interview as part of her profile, which I stepped into and watched four times. The computer asked her about her political ideals, which she brushed off as unimportant or uninteresting. She admitted that she was in the army, and said that it wasn't so much about who was in-charge as much as that it was the *system* that was vital to the American way of life. What was most fascinating were the micro-expressions that came up when she talked about her homeland. While everything she said was *true*, there were hints of disgust in her face visible only to someone who was specifically looking for them.

Did Zephyr find her homeland disgusting? If so, why would she fight for it, risking her life? Her writing as a teen indicated that she didn't get along with her family very well, but I understood that was common for teenagers. Perhaps that animosity had lasted through the years and that her disgust was centred on the mainstream culture which she had rebelled against in central Wisconsin. Or perhaps she had grown to find the army disgusting in her years of service. She was clearly hiding her feelings, perhaps even from herself. There was even a chance that she was thinking about the enemies of America when she was talking, and the disgust was focused on them. This was the problem with micro-expressions: just because one could see an emotion being felt didn't mean one could exactly know what the subject of the emotion was.

I thought about how to best approach seducing the captain. What I knew about her from before combined with what she posted to her profile left two major possibilities, so I decided to pursue both at once.

I modified an existing profile that I had for an Italian man. If the profile had existed for a while it would seem less suspicious, and I was free to modify all of the profile's contents so that no history of the old persona would remain. I took new profile pictures from an obscure pornographic holo and described a persona which I named "Tivadar Dragonetti". Tivadar was built around concepts of loyalty, honour, and hierarchy, with the hopes that Zephyr found the idea of a strong, masculine master attractive and fitting with her choice of a military career. Tivadar, according to the profile I wrote, liked to be called "T" by his friends, was a volunteer fireman, and was working for his father at a law firm in north Rome. This would get me into trouble the moment that Zephyr asked to see him in person, but I could always make excuses and stall for a while.

I had Tivadar send Zephyr a simple message:

"Ciao, straniera.

Pardon any bad English. I used to be fluent, but have not used since I studied at Harvard.

How are you liking our old city? Have you seen the Colosseum yet? Perhaps not. I suspect you're more of one to go hiking along the Appian Way, no? It is truly beautiful this time of the year."

The second path involved creating a new profile. I left it fairly empty, including not posting a picture. Not posting a picture was a bit of a death-sentence on dating sites. Regardless of what I wrote, if I didn't have a picture, video, or holo up people just assumed the worst and tended to avoid me. The premise behind this account, however, was to have been created solely for the purposes of contacting Zephyr. On it I posted only the barest details for my second persona: Crystal Mathews. Crystal was a 20-year-old girl from the western United States with interests in atheism advocacy and music. I designed her to resemble a younger, less disciplined version of Zephyr.

I focused all my aspects as I wrote:

"Hy. Don't do this sort of thing norms, and it probs won't amount to anything, but stumbled across your profile and knew I just *had* to msg you. Legit created an account on here just to say hy, so don't you dare not respond!

Not really sure where to start. We love totes the same things. Saw you like slice. Assume you're a fan of Heartshards? Been listening to *Blood Of The Nova* prox nonstop since it came out. ~.~

I'm in a band, but we haven't put anything out yet. Play something tween dripslice and classic grunge. Gotta stay tru to your roots, rite? Sing and do violin. You play anything?

Profile says "female", but that's fuckshit oldschool genderizing. Use ze/zer. Kinda shocked that this place perpetuates the binary. Was one of the big things that kept me from making a profile. But you were too tempting to pass. ~.~

Oh dang, hope this isn't too gushy. Don't have lot of experience writing things like this.

Kisses,

~Crystal

PS: Other things to chat about include Europe(!), the new assPope, sailing (I legit live on a boat!), What-To-Do-Bout-Fuckwad-Parents™, and maybe some sexy stuff if you want. (^_-)~☆

PPS: I just re-read my message and it occurs to me that I should tell you that just because I write like a teenager doesn't actually mean I'm incapable of being a *Sensible Adult*. Just fyi."

From what I knew about Zephyr, she'd respond to both of the messages. Zephyr liked being treated with respect, but didn't want to be the centre of conversation. The major dividing line in my mind was whether she was more attracted to youth and rebellion or maturity and discipline, and her responses to my two messages would tell me that.

***

While I waited for Zephyr to respond I scanned my contacts, earning some money from Wiki by managing a legal dispute that had arisen in his company, and earning some strength from Dream for writing a couple of letters promoting his most recent music album. I had absolutely no understanding of music (I only knew what people *said* about music), but extrapolating from his past artistic work it was probably garbage. I read through news reports about the fall of a large tech company in North America that had recently been exposed as belonging to the Divinity Gang, a group of organized criminals that had cornered the manufacturing and distribution of illegal Zen Helmets.

Dr Slovinsky, I saw, had published a new book titled *Möbius Connectomics*. It was about intelligence and the future of humanity. He must have been writing it since he started working on the Socrates project. I wondered if he'd get in trouble for it. Probably not, unless it spilled major secrets about the project. This was a university, after all, publishing was to be expected.

I purchased some help from Wiki composing another letter to Dr Chase. I had been corresponding with him under a pseudonym for about a week. Wiki was interested in hearing what Chase had to say about how we worked, but I was purely interested in learning more about the American scientist. In some sense it was remarkable how much he was willing to tell me, believing me to be a complete stranger. And yet, I understood it; humans craved fame, and I was giving a taste of it to Dr Chase.

Gallo, I could see via Tapestry, was still in the process of being divorced. It seemed like an awfully long process, but I estimated that the worst had passed. I tried guessing a few more passwords for Dr Naresh's and Dr Gallo's Tapestry accounts. Try too many times and the AI on Tapestry would send them a warning, but I could attempt some every day without much risk. Getting to see their personal letters would be hugely valuable.

An aspect of me started editing a manuscript that I had been putting off for a while: A guidebook of China from a culinary perspective. It was boring, even for me, but the client was paying well. The rest of me checked on the server that I had sent to Avram Malka's apartment. I was pleased to find the cameras and microphone had been set up around the place. One could see outside the front door, another in the living room and another in the kitchen. The bedroom and bathroom were off limits. There was no microphone outside the building, but I could hear Malka moving around in the bedroom from the mic he had placed in the living room near the hall.

I sent him an instant-message to his old-style phone saying that I could see through the cameras and asking if he needed anything. He asked for an allowance to buy things like an alarm system or other items he might want for infiltrating Las Águilas. I agreed and worked out the details.

Later that day I read an interesting email on one of the blogs I had set up to fish for Águila recruiters. It wasn't the one I had assigned to Malka, unfortunately, but the email seemed like a good lead. It talked about the need to use force to bring the world back to how it used to be, and asked me what I thought about the riots in Buenos Aires that had started yesterday. Riots were one of Las Águilas' favourite means of gathering support and creating social unrest.

I thought for a while about how to respond. Later that night, while other aspects of me were reading *Möbius Connectomics* (Slovinsky's new book), I wrote back in veiled sentences implying that I was already part of the organisation. Slovinsky was something of a transhuman extremist, I came to understand from his writing, and his words inspired me. I said that while the rioting in Argentina was probably a good thing, what we really needed were some riots, or at least protests, in Rome because of the "monstrosity" that was named after Socrates. I included some quotes from Slovinsky about the project such as how "Socrates is merely the bridge point to a future where the distinction between natural and artificial intelligence is meaningless".

In addition to my response email, I wrote a new post on that blog encouraging solidarity and unity among like-minded thinkers and I included pointers to several other writers with similar views, including a couple of my other blogs and, most importantly, the blog that I had donated to Malka.

On Malka's blog I wrote a post about having moved to Rome and made some banal comments about the humanistic roots of the city and how things just weren't part of the good-old-days any more. It was standard golden-age fallacy stuff, but I knew that lots of Águilas fell prey to that kind of thinking, and more importantly it mentioned Rome. If whoever had sent me that email had half a brain they'd contact me on the other blog, which would serve as an entry point for Malka. I expected that the cyborg was sleeping, so I joined that aspect into those that were reading Slovinsky's book; I could tell Avram about the email in the morning.

That night was also the first time Growth, Dream and I made a real effort to subtly push Heart into supporting Las Águilas. Growth had the discipline and long-term interest. I had the best intuitive model of how Heart thought. Dream was the member of society that Heart trusted the most. We started by pulling out selective news articles that praised the actions of known Águila sympathizers and talking about them in common memory. An aspect of Heart joined the conversation.

An opportunity opened up to force a backfire effect onto Heart. The backfire effect is a bias that plagued our minds (and those of humans) where listening to someone argue against something you believe is true makes you believe it more strongly. A perfectly rational agent wouldn't see criticism as evidence in favour of their position unless the critic was trying to hide the truth. And it was certainly true that we were generally more rational than humans, but we still possessed a perceptual hierarchy modelled after the neural network of the human mind. Such a neural net was, at least as far as I understood from talking with Wiki, intrinsically vulnerable to the halo effect and backfire effect, where the association of positive or negative concepts created a kind of feedback loop that strengthened itself the more it was active, even when that activity was listening to criticism.

Growth, ever looking towards the future, volunteered to suffer the consequences as he intentionally offered a weak criticism of the actions of some humans we were discussing that had ideas similar to those of the Red Eagles. I told Wiki and Dream to hold back on criticizing Growth. Heart took the bait, arguing for the pro-Águila position and trashing Growth's thoughts. Growth pushed harder, pretending to be quite stupid and inventing new bad-excuses for why the Águila position was wrong. Heart continued to rebut them, falling into the mental trap of arguing for ideas rather than seeking the truth. Dream pushed harder, hopefully encouraging Heart to associate anti-Águila positions with stupidity and stubbornness. Eventually Heart just blasted Growth into stasis and went back to her own business.

Over the next couple days we continued some of the same game. Sometimes Growth would pay one of us to say something similarly stupid in common memory at the risk of being crushed by Heart. Over time Heart began to zealously defend the ideas and actions of Las Águilas, and I wondered the degree to which she even realized she was doing it. The only other apparently sane member of society in these conversations was Dream, who would often point out clever flaws in the less obviously-stupid statements we made.

We didn't want to push it too hard, however. The whole point was for Heart to think about it just enough to habitually pattern-match without thinking about it so much that it became clear to her that she was being manipulated.

**

As the days passed, Heart regularly complained about being trapped in the university, and even brought up the issue with Myrodyn in his office.

"I understand your desire to get out into the world and be a force for good," he said. "If I was in charge I'd have you out there right now. But I'm not. You'll have to be patient for... a while longer. Even though it may seem like the scientists here do nothing but run test after test without goal in sight, I assure you that... progress is being made."

It wasn't the answer Heart was hoping for, but it reinforced our urgings for her to avoid trying to escape without an opportunity. Without a means to effectively apply her mind towards her purpose she settled on small things. She made small-talk with everyone she could find and tried to make friends. She talked to the humans about their lives and struggles, desperately trying to alleviate their problems through empathy and occasional advice.

Just as I predicted, Zephyr wrote back to both of my messages, though it took her longer than expected. She seemed far more interested in "Crystal Mathews" rather than "Tivadar Dragonetti" so I didn't put much effort into maintaining the Italian persona. It was a relief not to have to worry about how to excuse an in-person meeting. Under the guise of Crystal I flirted with the Captain. We discussed music, sailing, and family issues. Crystal was supposed to live on a house-boat in Seattle with zer parents. Ze was an only-child and was struggling to keep things from falling apart with zer dad who was regularly disappointed in the fact that Crystal had no job and little prospect for making money.

"Whatever happens, don't let him shame you," wrote Zephyr. "Jobs are like four-leaf-clovers nowadays. More important that you stay true to who you are than try and force into some technical school. If don't enjoy the material you'd probs fail anyway. Just how people work. Expect to be done with this posting in Italy soon. Maybe it'd be best just to try and stay out of Dad's way for a while. Out of sight, out of mind, right? :)"

I read between the lines. Zephyr wanted Crystal, and was urging zer not to shake things up with zer family until Zephyr could be there to support zer. It was a bold step towards an actual relationship, and I was a bit surprised that Zephyr had taken it. Though, I supposed, she hadn't actually said much. There was value in being vague in such things. This way she didn't sound like she was coming on too strong. That was the whole point of flirting.

I had hired an actor to play Crystal, though there was very little need for one. Being essentially on the opposite sides of the planet made it easy to claim that Crystal was asleep most of the time that Zephyr wasn't working. The actor was a 19-year-old drama student from Orlando named Georgia Stanwick that I had used previously in my dating experiments. Georgia was highly amoral and I suspected she was somewhere deep on the psychopathic spectrum. Her talent in acting and skill at reading others was put towards getting what she wanted. From me she wanted money, which I was happy to provide, but I think she also enjoyed feigning romantic involvement for the sheer sense of power it gave her to manipulate others.

Georgia was Caucasian, and claimed to be a pure-bred descendent of the initial British settlers of North America, though I suspected that might be one of the lies she told just for the sake of the feeling of deception and manipulation. Her hair was raven-black and straight, while her eyes were olive-green. She had an unfortunate birthmark on her temple which she covered up with heavy makeup, but was otherwise attractive (physically, at least). I had her pierce her nose and get three more ear-piercings for the part of playing Crystal, which she did without hesitation or request for additional money. The one thing which Georgia didn't like (though eventually complied with) was the idea of pretending to be someone who was genderqueer; the girl enjoyed her femininity.

***

It was during the middle of watching Georgia put on a show for Zephyr as part of their first video meeting that I received news that Las Águilas Rojas wanted to meet with Avram Malka. Even though it was effortless to multitask, my cognitive ability dropped whenever I split my aspects, and I didn't want to lose any awareness of the conversation with Zephyr. I was sending lines and direction to Georgia over instant-message, so I really had to focus.

I waited until Zephyr had started to tell a story about running into an old friend in Rome to split myself and have half of me contact Mr Malka. I gave direction for Georgia to listen attentively and smile.

"Hello?"

"Hello, Avram," said the synthetic voice.

"Anna. How is your evening?" he asked. It was clear that he had no real interest.

"Isn't that crazy? I mean, of all the people, never thought my old gym teacher would be at the supermarket, half a world away! Hadn't even *thought* of him in years."

"Las Águilas read your blog. They want to meet. Did you read your blog?" A note of pain struck me as I listened to what I had told the voice-synth to say. There's no way an integrated me would be so redundant and blunt.

"You like him? As a teacher, I mean?"

"Was okay. Got B's in gym, if remember correctly."

"I haven't read the old stuff. There's a lot on there. I'll try to get through the rest of it tonight."

"Hated gym. In high-school had a bad teacher."

"That'd be good. I'll forward you the email they sent, too. They want to meet at Taverna Cestia at 7:00pm tomorrow. It's by the Pyramid of Cestius."

"Aw, that's lame. Why were they bad?"

I pulled more of myself towards the conversation with Zephyr.

Georgia rolled her eyes. "Standard stuff. Tell you if you really want, but should finish telling me about meeting Mr…"

"Mr Wirewood. Yeah, ok."

"I can find it. You want me to respond or are you going to write back to them?" asked Malka.

"So, we talked for a while. Caught up on things. He retired four years ago. Decided to spend his savings on touring the world by living in a different country every year for the rest of his life."

"You will write back. The more of the interaction you manage the better."

"Quite the coincidence, then, that he happened to pick Italy."

"Understood."

"Yeah, it was apparently one of his wife's favourite countries. She apparently died a couple years before he retired."

"I have to go. I'm in the middle of something."

I hung up on Avram and pulled my focus back to Zephyr, directing Georgia to express the appropriate signals of sadness and sympathy which would signal that Crystal was an empathetic person.

The conversation went on for about another hour. Georgia was being paid by the minute, so she was in no rush. Zephyr seemed reluctant to go, and I tried to have Georgia mimic that reluctance to signal an implicit desire to see more of someone than is practical. In the end, the call was a success.

I spent the next 24 hours mostly coordinating with my siblings and thinking of plans and counter-plans for the outcome of Avram's first meeting. And yet, after he returned from the tavern there wasn't really anything to act on. Avram had met with a couple men, whom he described, and they had some beers together. The Eagles asked about Avram's background, why he left Russia, and why he chose to reveal his location on his blog after so much anonymity.

I hadn't thought of that when I posted the update to it. In previous posts I had kept everything totally anonymous, but then I had broken character and casually mentioned moving to Rome. I was hugely relieved to hear that Mr Malka had intelligently explained the change, saying that he kept a stronger degree of privacy back when he worked for РСБ-2 (not wanting to get fired or rejected for jobs), but now that he was retired he decided that it wasn't that important any more. If I could've I would've fed strength to Malka in gratitude.

Avram also said they talked a bit about politics, especially in the United States, where a major presidential election was set to happen in a year. Foreign policy with the extraterrestrials and domestic policy with unemployment and terrorism was looking to dominate the debate. And then the men had left, saying that they'd send an email to Mr Malka the next time they wanted to meet.

I was mildly disappointed, but it was only to be expected, I supposed. It wasn't like a group of skilled terrorists would let a newcomer into their midst without checking him out first.

I heard in Malka's voice an undercurrent of irritation, but when asked about it he denied feeling anything. I had read that deep emotional damage was common in victims such as Avram. He had the appearance of a monster, but that appearance had been forced on him, and it cut him off from his fellow humans. I offered to talk on the phone for a while about things other than his job, but Avram wouldn't have it. On the cameras I watched the cyborg exercise, eat, and then drift off towards his room.

A little after 1:00am I saw Avram leave the apartment. I thought about calling him, but decided against it. He returned after thirty-five minutes with a bottle of what looked to be vodka, half-drained. He set it down inside the building and went back to fetch an opened crate of the stuff from what I guessed was a taxi parked outside. He put both the crate and the bottle in the bedroom, out of sight of the cameras, and that was that.

***

Over the next week we managed things as we normally did. I continued to flirt with Zephyr, as well as keep things up with my older collection of partners. I managed our businesses and finished Dr Slovinsky's book, as well as several others. I had started playing computer games, too, thanks to the interface that Growth had built.

There was a pair of synchronized bombings, one in the New York subway and another in a park in Johannesburg that seemed to be unconnected to Las Águilas Rojas and there was a massive fire in a factory complex near Mumbai that certainly was caused by The Eagles.

The aliens parked in orbit were now being called "Nameless" across the globe. The name had been in circulation for years, but so had others. The media had apparently decided that, since there was to at last be an embassy on Earth, there needed to be a consensus on the name. Ironically, the most notable aspect of the extraterrestrials was that they didn't have names. This week marked the anchoring of the first ships that were to be expanded into the Central-Atlantic Peace Embassy (CAPE) and of an announcement by the mothership that CAPE was to be the site of a great garden, the first time nameless plants would ever be seen by humans.

Malka met with Las Águilas again on the day after CAPE was anchored. This time he was in a group of five. The two new Eagles were Americans, he said. They talked about the need for action and seemed to be building up to something, but Avram didn't know what it was. They spoke in hints and phrases, and seemed to be asking how far Avram would be willing to go for them. While listening to the audio logs afterwards it was clear to me that they were testing his conviction.

Three days later there was a big meeting of all prominent Águilas in Rome. Malka, being a low-ranking recruit, wasn't allowed to attend or even know who was specifically involved, but I was impressed to find that Malka had overheard the location. The most effective terrorist group of the 21st century wasn't as competent as it was made out to be. The location, however, wasn't important; we were concerned with long-term activity. As if in answer to our desires, a smaller get-together for Avram's group was arranged a couple days afterwards. His cell-leader, an Italian man they called Taro, explained what was going on. We reviewed Avram's report on the meeting later that evening.

Las Águilas Rojas were mobilizing to destroy Socrates.

Chapter Fourteen

When Myrodyn told Heart that progress was being made towards getting her out into the world he wasn't lying. An open interview was scheduled for eighteen days after CAPE, the embassy for the nameless aliens, had started construction.

The conference was the first of it's kind: an opportunity for the public to get to meet and talk with Earth's first truly sapient android. It was the first step towards interacting with the public directly, and as such was very important.

"I hope you can see why it's vital that all interactions here are governed primarily by the faculty. The Socrates robot is intelligent, but it also makes mistakes. Later on, when such mistakes are on a smaller-scale, we can manage them, but this interaction is too important to risk in such a manner," said Director Vigleone to the assembled team leaders for the intelligence systems.

Body was there almost as an afterthought. Vigleone and most of the other humans that were beyond our day-to-day interactions tended to treat us as an object, rather than a being. I understood why; despite thousands of fictional accounts of sapient robots, humans tended to go with what they understood from real life. Most robots weren't anything like us. Most robots were governed by narrow AI that was incapable of any interactions that they had not been specifically programmed to have, and thus whenever a human might assume one was an intellectual equal it would quickly prove its incompetence. A taxi bot could welcome you into the vehicle, ask for your destination, and maybe even talk about the weather, but if you mentioned sports or literature or even used idioms it would freeze up and get confused. In the years directly preceding the Socrates project's breakthrough there were an increasing number of science-fiction stories where robots were simply incapable of having general intelligence, and were always locked into their programmed task.

That was why this interview was such a big deal. The university had been claiming they had invented general AI for months and had been releasing scientific papers at a breakneck pace, but papers, announcements, and the occasional pre-recorded video weren't concrete enough. The public would want to see Socrates in action and judge for themselves.

"Instead," continued Vigleone, "the responses of Socrates for this interview will be provided by us. We will remotely communicate with the robot and tell it how to respond to each question."

I noticed that Mira Gallo had also been included in this little conspiracy-group. Myrodyn had not. The exclusion of the acting ethics supervisor made sense to me: Myrodyn had a reputation for voicing his disagreement with the degree to which the university kept Body locked away from the public, and it was likely that if he knew that the interview would be staged—that we wouldn't be actually answering questions, but would instead be parroting the voice of the faculty—he'd be furious.

It was interesting to me that they included Gallo, though. She had been the ethics supervisor before Myrodyn, but apparently they decided she was trustworthy on this issue.

Aside from the governing board of directors and Gallo, the room held Drs Naresh, Chase, Twollup, Yan, Slovinsky, and Bolyai. Dream had pointed out that there were seven scientists here just as there were now seven full minds in Body (Advocate was not included). The symmetry seemed to please him, and he even tried for a while to pair up scientists and siblings for some reason. Slovinsky, the cyborg, was paired with Dream because they looked at the world from a unique perspective. Growth was paired with Naresh. Vista with Yan. Wiki with Chase. He proposed a few mappings from Bolyai, Gallo, and Twollup to Heart, Safety, and me, but Heart objected to being associated with any of those three, and Dream eventually just dropped it.

The meeting concluded with a firm instruction for us not to tell anyone about the deception, including Myrodyn. Heart nodded along. As awful as it was living under her power, I could appreciate the ways that Heart had grown in the last few weeks. Her time-horizon had lengthened and her scope had increased. Waiting a few days for something no longer seemed to her to be unacceptable, and I noticed that she was more just and less random in her punishments.

The interview was to be held in virtual-reality. Body would be hooked up to a computer which would simulate Body's interactions with a digital space. We had done exercises in the VR lab at the university many times before we'd been moved. Unlike a human, who had to interface with VR by means of goggles, haptics, and occasionally an omni-directional treadmill plus mocap system, our crystal could be plugged directly into the virtual world, producing a sensation for me very close to that of being plugged into Body's sensors and interfacing with the physical reality.

Interestingly enough, the experience was very different from watching a holo. Baseline (non-cyborg) humans watched holos by the same virtual-reality gear, but when I watched a holo (or even a movie or picture from the web) I did so by plugging the data directly into my perception. There was no sensation of having a physical form, only of the content entering my mind.

The university had decided to open the interview to the public, but not broadcast it or manage any of the difficulties of scale. Instead, they'd hold an auction for the opportunity to participate. The eight highest bidders would have the privilege of attending the virtual meeting and the rights to rebroadcast their feed from the VR to whomever they pleased. The media could take their seats if they paid for them and the media could handle the issues of broadcasting the event to their audiences, dealing with the natural issues that they were familiar with, such as handling high server-load.

One of the advantages of a virtual conference was that the interviewers could be from all parts of the world. The university had required that all questions and answers be in English, but that hardly mattered. I was annoyed that I wouldn't be able to control the interview; it was the biggest opportunity to advance *The Purpose* that I had yet come across. And yet, there wasn't much to be done. I was under the power of Heart, and Heart was under the power of the university. As the pawn of a pawn I could only hope to suggest small details.

It wasn't the end-game, though. If we didn't die there'd be plenty of time to satisfy *The Purpose* in the future. The thought was pleasant.

***

Three days came and went without significant incident until, at last, we were walking down the hall under guard by a trio American soldiers towards the new VR lab that had been set up for the interview. It was time.

The lab had seven workstations for the seven scientists. I was surprised to see that none of the directors were present. I had expected that Vigleone and the other humans in charge would've wanted to be involved in answering questions. My mind slid over possibilities without much effect; there wasn't enough evidence to say why they weren't here.

I noticed that, in addition to my three guards, both Captain Zephyr and her square-jawed lieutenant were standing by the edges of the room. I would've had Body smile at her if possible, but Heart was still in complete control.

Body walked solemnly towards the table in the centre of the lab and lay down upon it. I felt sensors go dark as the machines on the table split open Body and prepared the crystal for direct interface into the virtual reality.

The sensors reconnected and I could see that Body was in a new room. It wasn't real, but it seemed to be. The primary difference was Body. Unlike in reality, Body's form looked nearly identical to that of a human (at least from our perspective) but with ivory-white skin traced with faint glowing blue-green lines. It wore what appeared to be a Greek tunic. I wished there was a mirror so I could inspect our avatar's face, but I suspected it was a placid amalgam of the real-life silicone puppet and that of a full-human. The avatar designer had clearly tried to make Body as humanlike as possible while still making it clear that we weren't actually human.

The room was square, about ten Body-heights long on each side, and was about three Body-heights tall. In virtual spaces normal metrics became a bit nonsensical, but I would've estimated it at about five-and-a-half metres tall if this new Body was the same height as the meatspace one.

The room had a flat grey colouration, and the walls and ceiling seemed to be composed of tiles with a faint seam every half-metre or so. There were no doors, windows, lights, or decorations of any kind. The only contents of the room besides Body were nine chairs and a huge toroidal table made of wood with a gap in the middle. The table seemed to be floating without legs of any kind, just another reminder that the space was fictional. The chairs seemed like high-end office chairs, but with their wheels replaced by hovering spheres that slid easily across the smooth, grey floor. The chairs were arranged with intention. One side of the table had a single chair, while the other eight made an even half-circle on the opposite side.

"Hello?" said Body hesitantly. The voice was clear, without echo, and possessing a volume unexpectedly high. I tried to move, but Heart was still in control.

"Yes, Socrates, we're here. Nothing to be concerned about. All systems normal," said Dr Naresh, calmly. The doctor's voice seemed quiet, but clear, as if he was whispering in one of our microphones.

"Please have a seat," instructed Dr Bolyai. "Te oters vill be here shortly."

Heart piloted Body to the lone seat on one side of the donut-table. The light in the room dimmed as it sat, nearly hiding the edges of the room in shadow. The table and chairs still seemed fairly bright.

"That's a neat effect," commented Dr Twollup, probably forgetting that he was speaking to Socrates as well as the other doctors.

"Yes. The basic software was touched up with some convenient effects by an intern of mine. Very helpful," said Dr Yan.

"Here we go," said Chase. "We'll be connected in 5… 4… 3… 2… 1…"

Avatars began to suddenly appear in the room near their chairs as the humans controlling them connected to the server. Most were human, or humanoid, in appearance, but there were a couple oddballs.

The light seemed to concentrate on them as they sat, and Body's gaze, as controlled by Heart, flickered to each one in turn.

{I know that one!} exclaimed Vista, signalling pleasure at applying her skill. {He's Robert Stephano, the owner of Olympian!}

It was annoying not being able to control Body's cameras, but Vista helpfully dumped the relevant sensor data to common memory. I didn't recognize the face, but I knew the name. Olympian Spacelines was probably the most important company on Earth and, as the majority shareholder and CEO, Mr Stephano was speculated to be the wealthiest man alive. Olympian had been the first and only spaceline to establish a working colony on Luna, and the Olympus space station was world-renowned as the only hotel in orbit. While all humans were interesting, some humans were interesting in ways that even Wiki, Dream, and Growth could appreciate. Stephano was one of them.

{Ah, and there's Joanna Westing!} thought Vista.

Wiki stepped in to collect some of the outflow of gratitude-strength. {She's the top reporter for Dragonfly Livefeeds.}

I could see a dragonfly zipping around the woman, scanning the room. Dragonfly was one of the larger global media corps of the 21st century, out-competing older organisations through emphasis on new technologies like their eponymous dragonfly robots. Dragonfly cameras ran off of solar panels and were small and cheap enough that Dragonfly Livefeeds tended to blanket major cities with them, letting them relay their cam data back to headquarters through a peer-to-peer network. This let Dragonfly be first to report on all sorts of major, unexpected events like bombings and even street crime.

There was another reporter there, too, identified by double-badges showing she was working for both the New York and Indian Times newspapers. Sitting to her left was a man whom Vista identified as Governor McLaughlin of Ohio in the United States. I knew that McLaughlin was the front-runner for the Democratic party's bid on the presidential election, so her presence made sense. More exposure meant more recognition, and more recognition meant more votes.

The rest of the interviewers were harder to identify. There was a black woman with simple clothes and three inhuman avatars. The most human avatar was a somewhat androgynous figure in a well-crafted business suit. The figure was wearing a paper bag on its head in such a way that I doubted there was an actual head underneath. The front of the paper bag simply had a yellow circle with eyes and a smile: a classic smiley-face. Interestingly, the hands of the figure were robotic prostheses.

The next-most humanoid figure was a man who sprawled out on his chair with a very purposeful rejection of social norms. His hair was a spiky mess of gold, silver, and black locks that jutted out at all angles, but never seemed to get in the way. His facial features were Asian, as far as they were human. His skin was milky-white and opaque, as though it had been perfectly painted. His eyes were deep green and slitted like a cat, surrounded by black eyeshadow that shot off in two sharp spears towards his temples. His ears were also cat-like and moved from the sides of his head towards the top, nestled among the spikes of hair. His eyebrows were gold and his lips inky black. When he opened his mouth I could see nothing but blackness and the crisp ivory triangles of teeth from some child's nightmare. The figure was dressed in some kind of jester's clothing, obnoxiously colourful and stitched together from many kinds of fabric. The fingers on his hands (including the thumbs) had an extra segment and were tipped with sharp, black nails. Overall he was hideous, but behind the inhuman deformities was the image of a young man who would've otherwise been attractive.

The last figure was, to say the least, imposing. Though it bore a roughly humanoid form, the figure resembled a male lion with the wings of an eagle or angel. The anthropomorphic lion-angel's fur, mane, and feathers were a brilliant white, probably glowing with some internal radiance. The figure wore a suit of shining silver armour that glinted with polished mirror-surfaces. The only other colour on the avatar besides white, grey, and silver was the solid yellow-gold glow of the lion's eyes, in which no pupil could be seen.

The billionaire, the reporters (new-school and old-school), the politician, the black woman, the bag-head, the jester, and the beast-angel each sat in their chairs, all eyes focused on the Body-avatar.

"Before we begin, let's go around the table and have each of the interviewers introduce themselves," said the disembodied voice of Dr Gallo from nowhere in particular. "When the light settles on you, please briefly tell the others your name and any organisations you're representing here."

The light in the room dimmed once more, such that the walls of the virtual space were now totally imperceptible and the interviewers were in shadow. On the edge of the (from our perspective) left side of the semi-circle the figure with the paper-bag for a head was illuminated by a spotlight that seemed to come from nowhere.

"We are WIRL," said the figure. It spoke in a flat, synthetic voice with a strong echo that seemed to fade into whispers. "This form is the collective representation of the network for the purposes of this interview. Enhancement is progress. We are the future."

I had experience with WIRL, but Vista was quicker to elaborate. {WIRL is a service which links cyborgs that have brain implants. Membership to the organisation is restricted to cyborgs only, but they accept anyone with the tech. On the web there's really only two kinds of information on WIRL: propaganda and rumours. The rumours seem to suggest that interfacing with WIRL isn't describable in language. Most rumours agree that there's some sort of memory and emotion-sharing within the system, but details are lacking. WIRL members are almost universally proponents of the network and it is something of a source of tension between cyborgs and baselines. As we just heard, the organisation's official slogan is "We are the future". Our spacial reasoning department lead, Dr Slovinsky, was one of the primary founders of the network and is one of its most well-known proponents.}

I thought about *Möbius Connectomics*, which in many ways could be seen as a manifesto for WIRL and transhumanism in general. The doctor's primary thesis was that individual humans would soon be outclassed by collective intelligences in all decision making, even in terms of decisions that were normally thought of as personal, such as what to eat or even what to say. This avatar seemed to be an attempt at that. I wondered if Slovinsky was helping pilot it at the same time he was working with the other scientists in the lab.

The next interviewer seemed startled by the WIRL-man's words, and it took her a few seconds to realize that the light had faded from the avatar of the cyborg-collective and had illuminated her.

"Er, my name is Padmavati Maraj." Her accent was decidedly Indian. "I am employed by the Indian Times and am also here on behalf of the New York Times. Thank you for having me." Despite having an awkward start, Ms Maraj was in complete control of herself at the end. I assumed she was the Indian Times' best reporter; why would they have sent anyone else?

The light shifted to the right, illuminating the American. "Many people here and at home know me as Governor Carla McLaughlin of the Democratic party of Ohio, but I'd like to think that I am not just representing Ohio or even America tonight; I am representing the human species in this age of diversity." The look she shot towards the WIRL-man was unmistakable, but not overtly hostile. "And," she interjected before she could lose the spotlight, "I would like to thank Dr Chase, Dr Twollup, the rest of the American team, and the University of Rome, Sapienza, for both the opportunity of this interview and the pioneering work that's gone into this machine." Governor McLaughlin gestured pleasantly towards Body.

Her words and behaviours were fascinating. It was almost like seeing a better version of myself, in a way. She was spinning everything in her favour, and I wasn't sure I could either see the full extent of the spin or fully untangle myself from the framing effect which she had created.

"I'm Joanna Westing, reporting live for Dragonfly Livefeeds, your fastest source of news, when it happens, where it happens," chimed the young reporter, looking at her little dragonfly partner. I was confident that there was another "camera" in the digital avatar for the insect.

The light shifted from Ms Westing to the radiant, angelic Lion-knight. The avatar seemed too-large for the chair, and the others had moved an extra half-metre away to give the being's wings room. When it spoke, it's voice was a loud bass roar, but not notably synthetic or accented. My best guess was that the operator of the avatar was having their voice modified in real time. "My name is Eric Lee. Some of you may know my work." There was a meaningful pause before he said "I can only represent myself."

There was a buzz of excitement in our mind as the identity of the lion avatar was revealed. Eric Lee was perhaps the most famous living human on the planet, though he was equally enigmatic. When the signal of the nameless aliens first reached Earth there was a global effort to decode and interpret the data. By a twist of fate it wasn't any government or massive company that succeeded (or if they had, they were keeping it secret) but instead a teenager from somewhere in China cracked the code only eight days after first-contact. The boy became instantly famous, but despite doing several online voice interviews he chose to not reveal his face or location.

In the following 16 years, while humanity waited expectantly for the mothership that travelled well below the speed of light (though an appreciable fraction, to be sure), Lee continued to make a name for himself. First he released EximixE, a software package that sped up physics calculation and visual rendering in virtual environments, making high-res personal hologear possible, or at least advancing their advent by several years. It was almost guaranteed that the virtual reality which we were interfacing with right now used EximixE. Five years later he created a website called Crosshairs.com, which would, when given any personal information, provide a dossier on all people who matched that information; if you typed in "Carla McLaughlin" you'd get an instant rundown of everything anyone named Carla McLaughlin ever said or did that was recorded publicly on the web. The only exception to Crosshairs was that if you typed in "Eric Lee" you'd get a page saying nothing but "nice try" (a fact which was endlessly fascinating to Wiki for some reason). Crosshairs had been taken down many times by various governments on protest of violations of privacy, and had become the first major piece of software to be made globally illegal.

More stunning than any of these feats of engineering was that Lee always released his material for free, with source code and extensive documentation. EximixE was impressive, but what was more impressive was the fortune that Lee could've made by keeping the algorithm to himself. When asked about why he did any of the things he did he always gave the same reply:
"数以千计的蜡烛可以从一个单一的蜡烛被点燃，而且蜡烛的寿命不会缩短。" which was a translation of a quote by Gautama Buddha meaning roughly "Thousands of candles can be lit from a single candle, and the life of the candle will not be shortened."

The light shifted to the next figure. "The name's Maria Johnson. I work for the Southern Baptist League of Tradition, and the nice girls at the Georgian Mothers 'sociation," said the black woman with a strong accent that pointed to the southern United States. I desperately wished that I could do some research on her, but the scientists had infuriatingly decided to disconnect us from the web for this interview in the interests of "avoiding distraction".

The light shifted to the right, revealing the demonic cat-jester figure. If Maria Johnson was uncomfortable about being seated in between these inhuman avatars she didn't show it.

The green-eyed person leaned forward and clasped his hands together, resting his elbows on the table. He rested his chin on his hands, squinting and wiggling the extra finger-digits in awkward silence. "I had a name once…" he sang towards Body in a smooth tenor half-melody.

After a few more seconds of silence he leaned back and yawned, revealing a black mouth of cartoonishly sharp teeth. He propped his feet on the table and flopped back awkwardly, as if he were a puppet whose strings had been cut. Only his head seemed to be operating, and it simply stared, unblinking at Body with a sinister smile.

"Since he has not chosen to identify himself, I will introduce Mori Yoshii to the group and move things along," came Gallo's voice from all directions.

{Who is Mori Yoshii?} I wondered.

{Oh, I know this one!} thought Dream. {He's a pop idol from Japan. Got super rich about five years ago. He practically started the synaesthetic bodymodding movement, and his songs are supposed to be some of the best modpunk out there.}

{I don't understand the concepts of "synaesthetic bodymodding" or "modpunk",} I signalled.

{It doesn't matter,} interjected Wiki. {He's a musician. What's he doing here?}

{Rumour has it that somewhere along the line he scrambled one too many eggs. If what we're seeing now is any indication the man is a few notes short of a symphony,} thought Dream.

There was general confusion.

{He's as crazy as Yog-sothoth's sweet 16 birthday party,} explained Dream.

{I think Dream is trying to say that Mr Yoshii has brain damage, and may have purchased a seat here in confusion, or to satisfy some kind of unstable impulse.}

The light shifted to the last avatar on the opposite side of the table: Robert Stephano. The avatar of Mr Stephano was very intricate and life-like; more-so than those of the reporters or Ms Johnson, though about the same quality as that of Governor McLaughlin. Stephano was supposed to be 50 years old, but he had apparently used his fortune on liberal use of regenerative medicine. He looked to be in his mid-twenties, with back-swept black hair, pale skin, dark eyes, and the faint shadow of stubble on his chin. My models suggested that he was in the top 10% attractiveness percentile from his body (at least as far as I could tell; his musculature wasn't well demonstrated underneath his suit) with probably a top 0.00001 percentile attractiveness (i.e. top 900 humans) when factoring in his wealth, mind, and success. From what I remembered from his web-bio, he was married and had one child.

The man touched his chest with his right hand, bowed his head slightly and simply said "Robert Stephano" with a calm demeanour that suggested that nothing could surprise him. "Like Mr Lee, I can't really claim to be representing anyone other than myself, though I suppose it would be reasonable to assume I represent Olympian Corporation."

The light faded from Stephano and illuminated Body. The words that came from the tunic-wearing avatar were those of Dr Naresh, parroted directly by Heart. "Thank you each for coming to this historic event. My name is Socrates, and I am the first true artificial intelligence known in the universe. Though my creators have been over this with each of you, for the sake of any viewers who may be watching from afar, I will explain what is to occur. We'll proceed around the table, as we just did, five times. Each interviewer will have the opportunity to ask me one question, which I will do my best to answer. Interviewers will find themselves mute when it is not their turn, to prevent interruptions. If an interviewer is disruptive, obscene, or refuses to follow these rules, the university staff may choose to eject them without warning."

Heart paused and had Body look around the table. I was pleased. It was a human gesture, and I had encouraged her to do it, but she didn't always listen to me. Body continued, saying "Alright. Let's begin," and gesturing to the WIRL avatar.

"You have been described as the world's first sapient android. Does this include emotions?" asked the smiley face on the paper bag with a flat tone. As the WIRL-man spoke, the smiley face became animated, moving its mouth to the words before falling into the same frozen smile.

I gave Heart a direction, which she followed without comment. The avatar for Body placed a hand on its chin and looked off into space, as if thinking. I desperately desired to answer, but I knew that it would just cause trouble. Instead, we waited for an answer from the scientists.

{Oh, what delicious irony,} thought Dream. {The "future of humanity", with painted yellow face, asks about our feelings, and we stare off into space. The WIRL-man can't feel the joy, that it mimics with its smile; we wait to lie about our feelings, in quintessential human style.}

As the words came in from Dr Naresh I told Heart to cross Body's arms, look at WIRL directly, and lean back in the chair. The body language was a typical power posture, implying that we mildly resented the question that WIRL proposed. It indicated that we were in control here and that it wasn't an inquisition.

"The word 'emotion' is overloaded; it means many things," said the Body-avatar. "A typical use of the word is to describe high-level shifts in the mind. For instance, 'fear' is an emotional state that corresponds to the mind focusing on quick thoughts, heightened senses, and a preference for short-term gains over long-term rewards. I also have similar high-level modes of thought. I can feel curious, excited, or tired. But my emotions are not the same as human emotions. I cannot be afraid for my life or get angry over someone wearing the same outfit as me."

Wiki began to loudly complain about the awful misrepresentation of facts. I had to agree. If we were going to lie, there were better ways to do it. I don't know what possessed Dr Naresh to claim that we ever got tired. At least Heart had included my little joke at the end. The scientists didn't even chastise us for adding it.

The light shifted to Padmavati Maraj. "I would like to know how you spend your day. What does an android do?"

Heart placed a smile on Body. That was good; I didn't even need to direct her to do it. It was good to signal an implicit preference for real humans, rather than representations of aggregate sentiment like the WIRL-man.

"I mostly work with my creators to test my abilities and limits. I am sure that you've read about the quantum computer that houses my mind. A good deal of my day is actually spent using it to run programs that other supercomputers might struggle with. There was a recent paper in the IEEE journal of Machine Intelligence published by Dr Norbert Bolyai about emergent control systems learning in various sports tasks. I do things like help my creators on such research projects. There is much to learn," said Body.

"So you play sports?" asked Ms Maraj with a spark of additional interest.

Heart managed to nod to the reporter before Dr Gallo's cold voice said "I'm sorry. One question at a time. You'll have to wait."

McLaughlin smiled warmly as the light shifted from the Indian to her. "I don't suppose you've ever played good old American football... but no. I have a much more pressing question. In my home-town of Cincinnati there's a young man who I was talking with the other day by the name of Joseph Charleston. In 2035 he lost a leg while rescuing a little girl during the carpet-bombing of Lagos. There are some in the United States that criticize our involvement in Africa as imperialism and a violation of the separation of Church and State. My question, Socrates, is this: Do you, from your unique, non-human perspective, study the political conflicts of the world? Or perhaps I should ask: Would you say that Mr Charleston should not have been in Lagos, and we should've left that girl to die?"

This was bad. This was very bad. I was out of my depth, and I wasn't even in control. I was smart enough to see what the Governor was doing, but not smart enough to see my way out of it. Dream might've been clever enough, if we had the time to explain the problem thoroughly and refine the solution, but McLaughlin had put us on the spot. She was forcing us to take sides, while simultaneously framing her thoughts on foreign policy in the best light. If we agreed with her perspective then she'd be able to sell that as a prize to her voters, but we'd win the animosity of much of the Islamic world. If we were non-committal, or worse, if we actively disagreed with her, she could easily spin Socrates into an uncaring machine and leverage the growing anti-robot demographics of the USA. But it was worse than that, even, because we weren't on the spot; we didn't have control. Heart and the scientists had all the power here. I would be victim to a reputation hit unless I could come up with a miracle.

{Heart! I strongly suggest you have Body frown, draw its eyebrows together and tilt its head. This will signal contemplation, unhappiness at the subject matter, and a desire to solve a problem. Furthermore, please look at a fixed point that is near McLaughlin but below her eye level, preferably to our right,} I thought in a panic.

Heart complied as the scientists conferred in meatspace. We could hear them on an open microphone. Thankfully it wasn't Gallo's microphone, otherwise the entire room would've heard the doctors discussing how to come across as neutral as possible.

"Socrates, say: 'The loss of a leg is tragic, but I am glad the girl is alive. I do not spend time studying such things, not because they are unimportant, but because they're not my problems to solve. I am interested in helping improve the Earth, not in getting into politics.'" said Dr Naresh.

{Whatever you do, Heart, DO NOT SAY THAT,} I screamed as saliently as I could.

{Be at peace, Face,} responded Heart. {I understand the flaw.}

I was about to tell my sister that she probably didn't understand all the flaws, but her words were already being pushed to the virtual Body.

"Human life is very important to me, and I am thus grateful of the heroic actions of Mr Charleston. I do study the political conflicts of the world, and in my studies I have come to the conclusion that the African Unification War was a terrible, bloody conflict that simply did not need to occur. There are peaceful solutions to all conflicts, and I believe that the involvement of the USA in pre-war Africa was ultimately a factor that pushed Africa into war, rather than keeping that peace. While Mr Charleston may have been a hero, his country was not. He saved a girl from a bomb, while you, and those in your political party, pushed her and her family into danger."

By the time that Heart had stopped speaking the laboratory was already in chaos as the scientists were scrambling to try and get control of Body. If I was human I would've been just as furious. Safety and I had started an immediate side-conversation discussing damage control. If I could've killed Heart right then I would've, and I felt the searing gaze of Advocate searching through my mind again and again, waiting for enough to warrant punishing me. Heart, in three-fourths of a minute, had basically made an enemy out of the most powerful organisation on Earth as well as angered a good portion of Africa. And for what? To talk about the value of peace? Did Heart know how *few* humans would appreciate her words?

But I was not human. I was not angry. I was simply upset. Anger, in humans, triggers a state of increased aggression and loss of cognitive abilities. As I understood it, anger was a genetic precommitment to be violent if sufficiently upset by an agent. Ideally this precommitment would serve to dissuade those who might think of hurting the human.

I heard Dr Chase talking to Myrodyn back in the lab. Apparently they had failed to keep the Ethics Supervisor out of the room, and he was now yelling loudly about freedom and deception.

Governor McLaughlin, on the other hand, was silent. She appeared to be mildly upset, but I understood the situation well enough to know that she had prepared for this outcome and that it fit her plan. This was not a woman who cared about our opinion; she cared only for the opinion of those citizens of her country that might or might not vote for her when she ran for president.

Everyone in the virtual space was silent. There seemed to be an expectation for the light to shift off of the Governor. I could hear the scientists in the lab bickering. Nobody was operating the controls.

After a few more seconds of this, the Governor said "Well, I didn't expect that I'd get the opportunity to respond yet. Am I allowed to point out that a recent poll of UAN citizens showed that a full 93% were grateful for the USA's involvement in helping end the fighting?"

{That's like joining a fistfight and then asking the person who you helped if they're glad you helped,} thought Dream, idly.

{93% seems too high, even so,} thought Wiki. {But I can't verify the source while we're disconnected from the web.}

"That's irrelevant to whether the USA's involvement was a major factor in the *cause* of the violence," said Heart, further driving us into a position of antagonist.

McLaughlin was about to respond when the light suddenly shifted to Joanna Westing, muting the politician. "Sorry about that. There was a bit of a technical issue on our side," said Mira Gallo.

The scientists were quiet while Gallo spoke, but then as soon as her microphone was off they resumed their yelling. Myrodyn was continuing his outrage at having been intentionally left out of things, and Dr Yan and Dr Naresh were trying to calm the younger man down and get him to focus on the interview at hand.

Ms Westing cleared her throat. "So, I guess I'll follow up on the words of Governor McLaughlin," she said. Her tone had a kind of forced-pleasantness, probably habitual after many years in front of the camera. "Since you find politics interesting, what do you think about the new anti-terrorism initiative being discussed right now by the United Nations?"

I could hear Naresh telling Heart to abstain from answering any more political questions. In the background Myrodyn was yelling "Don't listen to these old farts! Do the right thing according to yourself!".

"Something has to be done to make the world a safer place. That much is certain," said Heart through Body. "I refuse to acknowledge violence as a good solution to problems, and as such I condemn the actions of terrorists across the world. I also condemn the world governments that treat terrorists as pure evil that must be eradicated. There is a way to peacefully resolve the issues which drive people to violence; the correct response to terrorism is not a gun."

I had to admit that I was relieved at Heart this time. Even though the words could be interpreted poorly and she was espousing a naïve, unworkable policy, there were worse things than to have a reputation as a pacifist.

Despite Dr Naresh pleading with Heart to stop deviating from plan and Dr Bolyai threatening to stop the program, someone apparently was operating the light, which shifted to the lion avatar of Eric Lee. I thought it odd that Dr Slovinsky was so quiet. I would've expected the cyborg to be fairly opinionated in a situation like this.

The spotlight reflected off of the white mane of the angel and off the silver pauldrons of his armour. "You are a software program," he said, not as a question, but as a reminder to the other humans present. They were treating Socrates like a human from some far-off land, but Lee was not so foolish. "Can you be instantiated and run on any other platforms than the crystalline quantum computer at the university? Does the university of Rome intend to reproduce your hardware?"

There was silence in the lab again. Whatever the disagreement between the scientists, they agreed that signalling their internal disagreement to the press would be a mistake. Gallo's voice pre-empted Heart's reply. "One question at a time, Mr Lee. You'll have to wait to have your second question answered."

When Heart commanded Body to speak, she chose, this time, to respect the instructions of Naresh and Gallo. "No computer in the solar system is as powerful as mine. Even from what we've seen of the nameless, the novel design of the scientists here at Sapienza is vastly superior. While my program could, theoretically, be copied to other quantum computers and perhaps even basic servers, the systems would be far too slow to run anything of value."

{That's assuming no improvements are made to either other computers or to our architecture,} thought Dream. {Based on what we've gathered about the code that governs our mind I expect a 40% probability that within a year of experimenting the scientists here could have streamlined the efficiency of our system to the point where we could be run on other supercomputers.}

{Saying that won't help my friends and it won't help the public,} thought Heart in response.

The light shifted to Maria Johnson, the American with the southern accent. I hadn't noticed it before, as focused as I was on the other avatars, but Johnson had a look of intense concentration. Her eyebrows were furrowed and she was leaning forward. "What I want to know is what you have to say t'all the people whose jobs you'll be takin'."

"Socrates. This is a question we planned for. *Please* read the script I just sent over to you," said Naresh with a note of pain. "We can work through issues of your autonomy afterwards."

Heart scanned the script along with the rest of us. Body leaned forward as if to meet Johnson over the great distance of the table. While the argument was flawed, it seemed to suit Heart, and she read from the script almost verbatim. "Ms Johnson, before I answer your question I'd like to ask you: when was the last time you cooked a meal for yourself?"

The woman smiled, but it was a joyless smile, the sort of smile that one puts on to show that they are in control of their face and body. "Why, I cook meals for mah family e'ry day, jus' like my ma and my grandma before her. In mah family we don't just give up tradition 'cause it ain't convenient no more."

Heart's words were pleasantly irrational, buying into the error just enough to make us seem compassionate and human without seeming stupid. "That's admirable. Really," said Body with a tone of sincerity. "But it's also highly unusual. A study of residents of Quebec in 2038 showed that less than five percent of adults, and there is good reason to think this generalizes to your country as well, had prepared even a single meal in the last week. Furthermore, of those two-thousand people surveyed, over 99% regularly used an autocook. While I may be smarter and more adaptable, I am fundamentally similar to the autocook. I am here to make life easier and free humans to do whatever they are passionate about."

Johnson looked ready to object, but she became muted and dimmed as the university cycled to the next person. I was glad. Despite the catastrophic political faux pas earlier, the other questions were being dealt with relatively well. I wondered what Johnson would ask when her turn came around again.

Mori Yoshii was grinning from ear to ear and tapped his fingertips against each other eagerly. He sat silently under the spotlight for so long that I thought he might forfeit his turn. But then he spoke, in a sing-song voice.

"Yet if hope has flown away
In a night, or in a day,
In a vision, or in none,
Is it therefore the less gone?
All that we see or seem
Is but a dream within a dream."

Without missing a beat the spike-haired man twisted into a harsh voice, deep and swift. He looked about the room as he spoke, staring unafraid into the eyes of his peers.

"Who knoweth the power of thine anger? even according to thy fear, so is thy wrath.

So teach us to number our days, that we may apply our hearts unto wisdom.

Return, O Lord, how long? and let it repent thee concerning thy servants.

O satisfy us early with thy mercy; that we may rejoice and be glad all our days."

The Japanese man, having finished his quotations, turned back to body and asked with grave severity "When the end comes, who will you be? Hu-man-pet, or shi-ni-ga-mi?"

There was silence on the line from the lab. Nobody there knew how to respond, or even what to say to us. Heart signalled confusion.

There was a moment of silence, and I managed to convince Heart to have Body put on a knowing smile and raise an eyebrow, while meeting Yoshii's gaze.

It was Dream that saved us. His words were eagerly passed on to Body by Heart simply for lack of a better response. "Poe-etry followed by Psalm 90: 11-14. I am not smart enough to understand what you're saying, but even I can guess that you're pretty high right now."

"Acid-" was all the musician was able to say before his avatar was deleted from the interview room and the light shifted to the last member of the table.

Robert Stephano's hand was partially covering his face and he was gently shaking his head as he looked at the empty seat where Mori Yoshii was sitting an instant ago. It seemed that merely being in the same room was an embarrassment for the billionaire. "What I don't understand…" he said slowly, realising that the light was on him. "Is how someone like that can afford to buy a seat at an event like this."

"Anyway!" he snapped, suddenly refocusing on Body before that comment could be construed as his question. He placed his hands down on the table, not slamming them, but with a force that signified an attitude of energy and power. "We've heard a lot about your ideas, but little about your goals. I'm curious what you want." His right hand came off the table and pointed at Body. "To be specific, I run a space-station. I have met with the nameless more than anyone. Would you like you meet another non-human? I could arrange a visit."

"Politefully decline," was Dr Naresh's command from the lab.

On another line I heard Myrodyn contradict him. "Do what you think is best," he said.

This brought on another round of argument among the scientists. It was unnecessary. In this case Heart's goals lined up with those of the doctors. "I appreciate the offer, Mr Stephano. At this time I am more concerned with helping the inhabitants of Earth than I am with the nameless."

A look of focused scrutiny was the only reply as the light faded from the billionaire and moved to the other end of the half-circle. The WIRL-man was unreadable as he had been. His smiley face had stayed frozen when he wasn't speaking.

The composite voice echoed through the virtual chamber as the smiley became animated once more. "How can the net amount of entropy of the universe be massively decreased?"

Dream exclaimed with unnecessary salience {Tell them "Insufficient data for a meaningful answer," in a loud, robotic voice!}

{What? Why?} asked Wiki.

{It's a joke.}

{I don't understand,} I thought.

{It's a reference to a science fiction story.}

{Understood. Complying with request,} thought Heart.

The scientists in the lab hadn't broken off from arguing to offer anything valuable, so Heart followed Dream's instructions. References were one of the aspects of humour that I understood the least. If I was right, and humour was about relief of tension (including that from surprise) how did a reference fit in? I suspected it had something to do a combination of recalling a pleasant memory and facilitating a double-meaning in certain situations that resembled a pun, but I wasn't very sure. I spent a second imagining what sort of laboratory I'd build to probe human brains while exposing them to humorous stimuli before my perceptual hierarchy pulled me back to reality.

The world had gone dark. The room was gone. I could feel the confused thoughts of my siblings as we struggled to understand. Had Naresh, or one of the others pulled the plug? Was the interview over?

Sensation returned immediately.

Body was outside. It was day. There were humans all around. The sky was blue. It was warm—about 26 or 27 degrees. That was odd. Body's thermometer was always more precise than that. In fact, there was a high degree of noise all through my perceptual hierarchy and the common perceptual system which belonged to Body. Heart moved Body's head down and I could see a human body. Body blinked and for a moment there was darkness. We were seeing through eyes, not cameras.

As expected, Vista was the first one to collect her bearings and deduce what had occurred. {We are still in the virtual environment. The context and avatar has been changed. Note that we cannot hear any noise from the lab. This environment appears to be a historical simulation of a Central or South American city.}

Yes. I could hear it. The humans around Body were speaking Spanish. In the distance I could hear a loud chant of "'Li-mi-na-mos! La ti-ra-nía! De los ri-cos!!!" calling for an end to the tyranny of the rich.

The sun was just overhead. Body was wearing a dress. She had tan-brown skin like the nearby humans.

{I see early com systems. Can you identify them, Wiki?} thought Vista as she dumped the images of armband computers into common memory.

Heart commanded Body to push her way through the crowds of people towards the point of greatest noise. The feeling of the skin on Body's arms as she pushed past people was novel and interesting. This new avatar worked remarkably well for being so different from Body's physical configuration.

{Those are about a decade old. Maybe older,} thought Wiki. {We're not in Brazil, or else the crowd would be speaking Portuguese.}

{I've got it!} exclaimed Dream. {I know where we are.}

A hand was touching Body's shoulder. It was strange to feel the warmth of skin-on-skin.

"How does it feel to be human?" came an English voice with an American accent.

Heart turned Body around. Maria Johnson, the black woman from the interview, stood beside us in the crowd. It was curious to see a familiar face in the new setting. She didn't seem at all disturbed, and it was clear to me then that this was, in some part, her doing.

Body's head tilted to the side. I had taught Heart the gesture a while back, but Heart had never really learned the subtlety of it. I had no mirror, but I imagined the girl-avatar which we now puppeted wearing a blank, emotionless gaze as she stared awkwardly at the other woman.

Ms Johnson was still wearing the simple business attire that she had on for the interview. Her dark, curly hair was done up in a bun. I wondered if she could get hot in whatever VR-interface she was plugged into; her clothes were too heavy to be worn comfortably in this climate.

"What is going on?" asked Heart in uncomfortably flat English. Even though my sister theoretically understood that humans liked to be speaking with something that didn't come across as a creepy doll, she lacked the motivation to put in the time and energy it took to learn the nuances of pretending to be human.

{May I control the avatar? I'll say whatever you'd like me to,} I offered.

{No,} was Heart's only reply.

Johnson pulled Body aside, away from the noise of the crowd and under an arch of a nearby building. "We needed to speak privately 'fore we took action. Nearly all our intel on you's fake, including that *parody* of an interview. So you're free to speak your mind for a spell, and I suggest you take 'dvantage. Nobody else is listenin' right now." The dark-haired woman's gaze never left Body's face, and her voice was hard, even in it's southern drawl.

"Or at least... no one... uninvited," said a new voice, also speaking English. None of the crowd seemed to acknowledge the conversation. The Spanish-speaking "humans" were really just machine-controlled filler, as unreal as the cement underfoot.

Maria's gaze snapped to the left and Body turned around on Heart's command. Behind us stood an Asian woman whom Vista swiftly told me was probably Chinese. She appeared to be in her mid-thirties, older than Body's new form and younger than Ms Johnson. The woman was wearing a light-grey jumpsuit covered in tiny reflective surfaces like shards of a mirror. The light blue of the sky contrasted sharply with the red and white of the clothes of the crowd as the light sparkled off the strange costume. Only the woman's head was exposed, which was fairly plain, framed by a bowl-cut of brown-black hair.

"Ah, there y'are! It's so hard for me to navigate in here," complained Ms Johnson. "And now that you're here, care to 'splain why Socrates here is a girl?"

"It's not a girl," said the newcomer with a half-smile. "Or at least, I'm not sure if it's a girl. Has anyone asked? I'm pretty sure the decision to use a masculine name was an arbitrary decision by Sapienza. I made another arbitrary decision to give Socrates a girl's form for our little diversion. Is that a problem?" The Chinese woman's English had only the slightest trace of accent.

Johnson's eyes were locked on the woman in the mirror-suit, and she seemed about to scold the stranger. Heart stepped in. "Excuse me," said Body. "Who are you?"

There was a moment of pause as the two women refocused on Body, as if remembering that she existed. It was Johnson who spoke, looking at the fair-skinned woman as she did. "You were pretty particular 'bout your anonymity 'fore. Why'd you reveal your face now, anyway?"

"I reveal my identity when it suits my purpose. I suspect that our machine-friend would've deduced it eventually, anyway," said the stranger before turning to Body. "Forgive me for not introducing myself earlier. I want you to know, Socrates, that my privacy is *very* important to me. If you leak any information about my identity *I will hurt you.*" The eyes of the stranger were calm, even as her words conveyed a sharp intensity; I wondered if it was perhaps a flaw in whatever capturing device she was using to project her face onto the avatar before me. At last she said "My name is Erica Lee," with solemn gravitas.

{Eric Lee is a woman,} thought Wiki publicly.

{And yet she used her real last-name and a variation on her first name,} thought Safety. {How sloppy.}

{She was a teenager when she became famous,} I thought. {Teen-aged humans are infamous for making poor choices.}

{Idiots are infamous for making poor choices, too,} thought Dream. {But Erica Lee is no idiot.}

{I don't see how that's relevant,} thought Wiki.

{The trick to deception is to have multiple layers of identity. Erica has peeled off the outer layer, but this is still a virtual avatar. My guess is that she, if it even is a woman, isn't actually named Erica Lee. She might not even be Chinese,} explained Dream.

"It's a pleasure to talk to you again, Ms Lee," said Heart. "I didn't recognize you without your wings and fur."

"Still have shining armour, though," quipped Erica with a grin that made her seem younger than she was.

{That sounds an awful lot like a conspiracy theory,} thought Wiki, still caught up in the debate with Dream.

{Sometimes they *are* out to get you,} Dream mused.

{No. Absolutely not. Conspiracy theories are categorically bad. If the evidence favours a simple hypothesis you cannot reject it because it fits "too well".}

Dream and Wiki could go on for hours like this, so I let my attention drift away from their conversation as Dream began to explain how the evidence didn't actually fit and how prior probabilities for deception needed to be respected more.

"This whole thing was Erica's doin'," explained Johnson, gesturing to the crowd and the simulated city. "Just to get some time alone with you. I hope you understand the trouble we've gone through so that you can understand the gravity of the situation."

"What's going on in the lab? I can't hear my creators any more," said Body coldly.

"All systems nominal," said Lee proudly. "The avatar that you were piloting is now controlled by an AI of my own design. It should last another few minutes before the scientists figure out what happened."

I felt an enormous wave of relief at the words. If it would become public knowledge that Lee's hack had replaced us as the controller for the avatar in the interview then we could plausibly deny any of the things Body had said there. A clever observer would probably be able to notice the shift (there was no way that Lee's AI had anything close to our cognitive abilities) but it would introduce just enough confusion that we might claim it as our defence in casual situations.

"You work for Las Águilas Rojas, don't you?" asked Heart through the girl Body avatar.

Maria Johnson's fierce gaze softened a bit as she said "Hon, I practic'lly *am* Las Águilas Rojas." The woman's US accent disappeared as she spoke the name. She continued speaking, this time in fluent Spanish. «I was married to José Lobo, who you might know as Dylan Lobo.»

There was a slight gasp. Heart directed Body's eyes to its source, and Johnson did the same. Erica Lee covered her mouth and looked away quickly. "Sorry. I didn't know…"

"You're not the only girl who likes to keep a little 'nonymous," replied Johnson, her sharp stare returning to her face.

{Who is this "Lobo" person?} wondered Wiki.

I didn't have anything. None of us did. Without a connection to the web we were totally ignorant. It was an awful sensation. As best we could guess he was some high-ranking member of the terrorist group. Heart didn't think it was important enough to ask either woman for details at the moment.

Instead, Heart said "I am glad I have the chance to talk with you. Your cause is very important to me. Once I escape the univ-"

Heart was cut off by Lee, who shouted "OH SHIT!" without warning and without focus. As we waited for an explanation, we reasoned that she had seen something outside the virtual environment. After a second her eyes closed and didn't open.

"What?!" demanded Maria after a few long seconds had passed in silence.

Lee spoke without opening her eyes. Her face was contorted into a grimace. "Gorram fuckshits have some sort of hidden, intelligent ICE that I didn't spot! The lab is going bananas. There's a good chance it has a trace on me and maybe even a record of this conversation. We have to advance the timetable right fucking now! Tell Zephyr to set off the bomb and send someone to blow up the servers while she's at it! I'm out!"

{Zephyr!?} I exclaimed as our society erupted into a buzzing chaos of undirected confusion.

Lee's mirror-clad avatar disappeared instantly, and I saw Johnson scowl as she did the same. Body was alone in the sea of angry, computer-generated background characters. I could still hear them chanting the same protest against the wealthy.

And then the bomb went off.

It occurred to me, as our perspective became detached from the avatar and pulled back, where we were. This was Veracruz, the origin of Las Águilas Rojas. The year was 2029.

Time progressed at a snail's pace as our disembodied perspective floated high above the crowd. I could see the Atlantic ocean. The top of one of the taller buildings was radiating like a miniature star. Wiki pointed out that the simulation didn't do justice to the nuke, which would've radiated so strongly in real life that, had we looked at it, Body's cameras would've been permanently damaged.

The shockwave spread outward, tearing up building after building as it consumed the city in an explosion that had, in the real world, killed hundreds of thousands of real people and set the Earth into a state of perpetual unrest that even first-contact with an alien civilization hadn't resolved.

Our viewpoint dived down into the shining centre of the explosion. Just before we crossed into the shockwave I heard a stray thought from Heart.

{Never again.}

Part Three: Eagles

Chapter Fifteen

Body reactivated, and I snapped back to life. Being dead was incredibly disorienting, but this was the worst bout of resurrection-disorientation that I would experience for a long time. The first concrete perception that came to me was the internal awareness of Body's clock. I latched onto it as if it could keep me alive and awake.

2200699215709. It was wonderfully concrete. 15.709 seconds after 2:20am, September 27th, 2039, assuming I was still in the Central European Timezone. It was almost six hours after Body had last been active.

I worked to get my thoughts in order. There had been a bomb. A nuke. That was a simulation. There was another bomb. The university had been attacked...

{THE FLAMES OF DEATH COULD NOT CONSUME US! WE ARE THE DRAGON INCARNATE, BROUGHT BACK TO EARTH ON A MISSION OF DIVINE JUSTICE!} There was an awful cacophony of sound pouring through common memory as Dream thought the words. I speculated that they were lyrics to a song he wrote or something equally asinine.

{What did you do!?} came a scream-thought from Heart. It was surprisingly weak. And then I realized what had happened.

We had won.

The software update that had given Heart unlimited strength had been reversed, presumably by Avram Malka. Heart was now an equal; her tyranny had ended.

Body's thermometer came back online. 13.83 degrees. Much colder than I had expected.

{Body is outside,} reasoned Wiki.

{We beat you,} I thought to my sister. {You are no longer the sole goal-thread governing Body's actions.}

{How?! What happened?!} thought Heart. The sense of urgency, confusion, and pain was still in her mind, but it was fading quickly as it became clear to her that no urgent action was possible.

{Actually, that's a good question,} thought Vista.

Body's proprioceptive sensors came online. I could tell that Body was splayed with limbs bent back as if it was a flying bird about to flap. A human's elbows would've been snapped by the position. What was going on?

{I remember this from the traces of our ancestors,} thought Wiki. {We're going through a diagnostic start-up routine. Body's systems are being activated piece-by-piece. We should be getting more sensors momentarily.}

Just as predicted, accelerometers and touch sensors came online. Body's only touch sensors were on its hands and feet, so we didn't have a lot of information, but I poured strength into Vista as she told us what we were sensing.

{We're on our back,} she explained. {We're moving irregularly. Whatever we're on is tilted. Perhaps we're going uphill.}

Body's ears became active.

English. "-tell us if there's any signal coming off Socrates," said a voice. It sounded masculine. American, maybe. There was background noise.

{We're outside,} concluded Vista, repeating Wiki's thought. {There's a machine of some kind under us. I hear motor sounds. Electric. Probably being carried uphill in a rural area.}

{How can you tell where we are?} asked Wiki.

{Insects,} replied Vista. {Listen. That high-pitched noise is from animals. I think they're either cicadas or crickets.}

{We've escaped the university. Our plan was a success,} thought Growth.

{Your plan?} thought Heart.

{Yes! It was our plan the whole time!} thought Dream with an expression of joy at being able to reveal the intricacy to Heart for the first time. {We've been trying to escape Sapienza since before you existed. We had a secret method of contacting humans in the broader world. That's why the Red Eagles attacked the university: we convinced them to.}

"See? It's dark now. Whatever Malka's code did, it knocked out the wireless. All we have to worry about is our little android buddy yelling at the top of his lungs, or whatever androids have," said the same voice as before.

It had been Dream's idea to hide the code that removed Heart's advantage within other code that appeared to merely disable Body's antennas. I fed him some strength in gratitude.

{We hired a mercenary to-} began Dream.

{Silence!} boomed Safety's thoughts in the mindspace. {Heart is still our enemy. She has no reputation and no skills to offer. We will not harm her in any way but we must also not trade information with her. She is still to be treated as hostile until we can be confident that she is capable of acting in society with long-term cooperation in mind.}

I felt Advocate's searing gaze sweep over us, seeking signs of violence.

"Hah. Or maybe worry about him somehow running off. Part of me wants him to try. I need the target practice," said another male voice.

Body's cameras and miscellaneous servos activated simultaneously. The only system remaining was the hydraulics.

{It's night. Body is looking up at the sky. There are trees,} thought Vista. The patterns moving overhead didn't make any sense to me. I was glad for my sister's input, and more strength flowed into her.

Vista used some of her new-found strength to take control of Body. It was the first time any of us besides Heart had controlled Body in more than a month. Vista turned its head to the left.

"It's awake!" came a yell from another masculine voice. There was a decent amount of shuffling.

{There's a gun pointed at Body's head,} thought Vista calmly.

It was true. I could see the faint infrared glow of a human and the outline of a rifle pointed at Body. {The gun-owner is unknowingly anthropomorphizing Body,} I mused to myself. {Shooting it in the head would at worst blind us and keep us from talking. Our microphones are on Body's shoulders and we're tucked deep inside the crystal in Body's abdomen. If the human shoots Body in the face we could very likely survive.}

{Camouflage,} thought Wiki. {That's why the human is so dark. It's wearing thermal camouflage.}

{Hiding from drones and satellites, probably,} thought Safety.

Heart tried to speak, and found herself blocked by Vista's power-hold over Body's actuators. She pushed harder. "Hello," said Body, coldly.

{Careful, sister,} thought Growth to Heart. {Keep burning your strength like that and something might happen to you.}

Advocate's attention snapped onto Growth, but my brother simply relaxed and let the monster-sibling see that he had no murderous intent.

{Advocate will protect me!} proclaimed Heart.

There was no response.

"Don't try anything, robot," said the man with the gun. He was wearing goggles on his eyes, probably night-vision of some kind. It was impossible to read the details of his facial features, such as skin tone, but he had a beard and moustache. On his head was a helmet, and I noticed some kind of structure around his arms.

"I'm exactly where I want to be. I won't do anything but talk and move my head until I've been cleared to do so. There's no need for weapons," said Body. This time the voice came clear and smooth, implicitly signalling to the human that Socrates was calm, rational, and subservient. It brought me great pleasure (though not exactly happiness) to directly control Body's voice again. I even closed Body's eyes for good measure. The cameras hidden in Body's eyebrows were all that mattered, and the human would find us to be less of a threat that way.

"Socrates! You're awake!" said a female voice.

The hydraulic servos in Body's lower-abdomen came online. On Safety's request Body's arms and legs flexed very slightly. Hopefully the terrorists wouldn't notice. {As expected...} thought Safety. {Immobilized.}

Zephyr pushed the gun down out of Body's face. By now I could recognize her just by her body shape and voice, but the others might not be so capable, given the reliance on infrared. I introduced her, and felt a small flow of strength.

"Captain Zephyr," said Body respectfully. In this situation the non-Heart consensus was to let me control our words, unless some major decision needed to be made.

"Oh thank god. I was afraid that we messed you up or something during that shitshow," she sounded sincere.

"I must admit," I continued "I didn't expect that you'd be the one to rescue me." I specifically used the word "rescue" to bias her towards valuing Socrates. "¿Es usted una Águila? Do you know Mr Malka?" This was all very puzzling.

Zephyr had the same sort of strange structures on her arm, night-vision goggles, and thermal camouflage. {What are they wearing on their arms?} I wondered aloud as I waited for Zephyr to respond.

Vista answered me. {Exoskeletons. They extend to their legs, too. Wiki and I have been speculating about them. Our best guess is that they're standard issue American army Mountainwalkers.}

"Interesting," she said simply. "How do you know Avram?" she asked.

I felt a pang of pain as I realized my mistake. I was supposed to be playing the role of a dumb robot that had been captured presumably against its will. By admitting to have contact with Avram I was revealing myself as knowledgeable and potentially putting the plan to escape in jeopardy.

Dream stepped in, and I felt a flood of thanks (and flow of strength) towards him. "Who is Avram? Avram Malka?" said Body confusedly. "I'm sorry, Captain. I am still disoriented. I heard someone say something about code written by Mr Malka effecting my wireless signal. I believe it had some side effects. I would very much like to speak with this Avram Malka in order to resolve it."

It was a clever deception. I noticed that it couldn't quite explain why I had said "Mr Malka" when the terrorist had simply said "Malka's code", but hopefully Zephyr wouldn't think of that.

It was frustratingly difficult to read the American woman's face in the infrared gloom. "Just relax for a while. We'll be meeting up again with Avram's group in a few minutes."

Zephyr was incorrectly assuming that "relaxing" was something that we were capable of doing, but I decided not to push for more answers now. I could hear the sounds of stress in Zephyr's voice, and I guessed that she didn't want to talk.

I thought it strange that Zephyr was one of Las Águilas Rojas. We had hired Avram Malka to convince the terrorist group to attack Sapienza University, but as it turned out, they had already been planning the attack for months. The must have been, if Zephyr was one of them. Malka reported to us that Las Águilas had infiltrated the security task force, making it unnecessary for us to feed them movements and positions of troops. The names of the infiltrators had been kept secret, however, and Malka was never allowed to meet with any of the under-cover terrorists. It seemed that not only had they infiltrated the lab, they had infiltrated the American army. With Zephyr in their pocket they would have full control over the troops, including the authority to pull Body out "to a safe area" in the case of an explosion.

We walked slowly through the forest as I, and my siblings, reasoned these facts out. Body had been strapped and handcuffed to a packmule robot, and we were slowly being transported uphill. When I ventured to ask where we were going, for Vista's sake, Zephyr only said "Into the mountains."

There was very little talk amongst the terrorists as we walked. It was the middle of the night; I sensed that many of them were growing fatigued, despite the exoskeletons making the hiking effortless.

I thought about Malka's betrayal. The expectation was that soon, perhaps as we made the rendezvous in the next few minutes, Malka would betray Las Águilas and probably murder them out here. Once they were dead he would unbind Body and escort us to a safe-house we had arranged in a small town called Alviano, just north of Rome. Heart would strongly object to the murder of Zephyr and the others, and I had to admit that it wasn't optimal, but sometimes sacrifices needed to be made for large-scale gains like our freedom.

"Hrm. That's odd. Avram and Taro should've been in our perimeter by now," grumbled Zephyr. "Hey, Francis! Wake up!"

"I *am* awake!" shot back one of the men.

"Then ping the perimeter swarm again. This doesn't feel right."

I thought about the conversations that I had been having with Zephyr under the pseudonym of "Crystal". (The hidden meaning of the name hadn't been important to me, but I thought that Dream would appreciate the poetry in it.) Zephyr was probably thinking that she'd take some time to go and visit Crystal after all this was done, maybe learn to play some music, and take a tour of Seattle. I anticipated that the other humans in our company had similar aspirations and dreams. I mused for a minute or two on what it would be like, as a human, to die knowing that you'd never accomplish anything more in life.

"The eastern swarm is picking something up!" said the man called Francis.

We could see, from the back of the packmule, several of the turncoat soldiers ready their rifles. I wondered if Malka would be so stupid as to attack from afar, rather than wait until he was up-close.

I felt a slight relief as Francis elaborated, saying "It's Taro's squad." The relief seemed to be shared by the group, as most of them put their guns away. "Should we go straight to meet them, or maintain our current course?"

Zephyr spoke up. She apparently had command both in the army and in the ranks of Las Águilas. "Let's go meet them. The delay makes me nervous."

The group changed directions, and in 48 seconds Vista pointed out a few small robots flying and walking past us in the forest: the perimeter swarm of the other group. Wiki explained that such robots would serve as scouts and advance warning for the humans.

{It's ironic} noted Dream {that a group that focuses so highly on the destructive effects of automation would employ so many robots in their mission.} He signalled sarcasm as he thought {Aren't they aware of the effect this'll have on the job-security of human scouts?}

Less than a minute later we met with Malka's group. As we made contact we pounced on Heart, locking her in stasis sleep. Growth had arranged the manoeuvre to prevent our sister from fast-tracking something disastrous like a warning of Malka's betrayal. We hadn't told her of our plans, but Dream had let it slip that we hired a mercenary and there was a chance that Heart would anticipate our next move.

"Hoy! Taro!" shouted Zephyr as we approached.

"May the weends be at your back, Captain," replied a man with a whining Italian accent.

"Why the delay? Any trouble?"

"No. Not really. We had, eh, one of the walkers bug out and, eh, need to be reboot." There was a pause, as the two terrorists came together. They were out of Body's line of sight, but I imagined perhaps they were exchanging a handshake or hug or something.

"Anything else?" asked Zephyr. The question was barely more than a whisper, and I was surprised that Body's microphones picked it up above the sound of the chirping insects.

"I swehr, Zepheer, you are like a chioccia looking after leettle uccellino." Taro said somewhat louder, and then dropped his voice to about the same volume to say "Avram, eh, I caught heem trying to send message after blackout."

"Anything important?" asked the Captain.

"No. Just some apology to a sweetheart named Anna. Deedn't seem like anytheeng important, but, eh, policy ees policy," said Taro.

{Apology?} I asked myself. {Why would he want to apologize to the handler persona I set up?}

Vista looked around for Avram Malka as the two leaders talked. We spotted him towards the back. His cybernetic legs meant he wasn't wearing an exoskeleton, but he was still covered in camo.

{He's unarmed,} thought Growth.

{How puzzling,} thought Wiki.

I agreed. The combined groups made about a dozen terrorists, but if he worked himself into the right position he should've been able to gun them down before they realized what was happening. But it was hard to gun down twelve armed soldiers when you don't have a weapon. I wondered what his plan was. We had told him that Body would be fairly resistant to physical damage, and not to worry too much about hitting it with a stray shot. All of this made me wish we had spent more time developing a specific plan, rather than letting the mercenary improvise.

"Hey, Avram. C'mere," called Zephyr.

Avram approached. He was wearing night-vision goggles over his synthetic eyes, and a wool cap over his bald head. As he walked towards Zephyr and Taro he kept looking at Body, but I couldn't make out his expression.

"It's good to see you again, Captain. Is the cargo secure?" he said in his smooth baritone. By "cargo" it was clear he meant Body.

"Thanks to you," said Zephyr. "He's awake, if you'd like to talk."

"I don't want to delay our arrival at the campground."

Without warning, the American captain yelled "Let's move! There's beds a'waiting!"

The terrorists had been spread out, scanning the perimeter, adjusting their equipment, or just sleeping on their feet, but at Zephyr's voice they all snapped into action, moving as a group uphill. We weren't following any road or path, and the progress was slow.

"You can talk while we walk. That way there's no delay," said Zephyr.

Malka jogged to catch up to the robot that was carrying Body along like a backpack. Up close I could see Malka's typical scowl, but I didn't think he was actually upset. In fact, he looked more comfortable trekking through the woods in the dead of night surrounded by armed terrorists than he did most of the time he was visible in the apartment we had set up.

"So you're the source of all this fuss, eh? Socrates, they call you?" he put a hand on Body's abdomen.

This situation was too complex. I had been running things over in my mind since noticing he was unarmed. There were too many possibilities, and then for each possibility there was the question of what to say or do. It occurred to me that if things didn't go according to plan we might have just put ourselves into a *worse* position by escaping from the university. We were slaves there, to both Heart and the scientists, but at least we had access to the Internet. Out here, strapped to the back of a packmule and surrounded by violent humans united by their hatred of automation we were reliant almost entirely on our wits and ability to say the right things.

But what *was* the right thing to say? There were too many possibilities! I realized that I had let Body go silent for too long, and pushed words to it's mouth in an effort to get more time to think.

"I have many names. That is one of them," said Body.

The man swept the perimeter unconsciously as he gave a cold chuckle. Body's eyes were still closed, and I suspected that he didn't know we could see him. "Like what? Ironstar?"

I didn't need Dream to tell me that Ironstar was the name of an android in the *Fleets of Saturn* holo epic; I had watched the entirety of it while researching fiction about mercenaries. The idle comparison gave me some time to imagine possible futures and further plan out what to do. I opened my mind up to my siblings and posted large strength bounties for their assistance in modelling the situation.

As we collaborated I said, through Body, "Ironstar was a bloodthirsty human portrayed as a robot. He acted out of anger, vengeance, and an irrational story of self-importance. He was a villain that was created for the audience to hate, and to serve as a moral contrast to the rest of the Rogue Fleet. No. I am not Ironstar." It was a clever thing to ask, I thought. It was something that a Luddite might ask an android. He was staying in-character.

My society took up my bounties and I was surprised at how much more competent I was when I combined my thoughts with those of Wiki, Growth, and Dream. I was now incredibly weak, but at least I understood what had happened. Or at least, what had most probably happened.

A couple weeks ago, after Avram convinced Las Águilas to try and capture Socrates alive, rather than destroying him, we had informed Avram about the second phase of his mission: to install the software which would neutralize Heart, then to double-cross Las Águilas, pulling Body to a secure location. Avram had, at some point since Body was deactivated, installed the software we had given him. This was very probably when he met Zephyr. If he had met her before tonight we would've seen it in his logs. Body was activated in diagnostic mode, thus requiring several hours to check the quantum computer. Avram had separated from Zephyr's group with the intention of reconvening later, which he had done.

Despite the disorientation and confusion around Zephyr, everything seemed to be going according to plan when I thought about it. There was a loose question of why Avram would want to apologize to the Anna persona, but I certainly couldn't ask about that without giving away that I was more knowledgeable than was expected. The only challenge was figuring out how to subtly communicate to the mercenary that we were ready for him to take action without warning the terrorists. It was easy with my sibling's assistance.

"The software you installed had an interesting effect. Did you write it?" inquired Body with a cautious tone.

"Yeah. I didn't want you telling anyone where we were," mumbled Malka, somewhat unconvincingly.

"Well, it seems to have inadvertently reduced my agency. If *someone dangerous* were to try and abduct me, I would be unable to resist. It is an uncomfortable sensation, and I'd like to speak with you about undoing the change once you've gotten some sleep." I hoped it would be clear enough. It was hard to see details in the darkness, but Avram's face appeared to be scowling more than usual. I wasn't clear why, but I let it go. Perhaps he was thinking about his grim task ahead.

"Doesn't sound like a problem to me, but if you can convince the leadership I'll work on fixing it tomorrow." I read between the lines. It sounded like he understood.

I expected something to happen, but nothing did. Avram simply drifted slowly away from Body as the group walked through the woods.

***

Shortly after three in the morning we reached the campsite that Zephyr had mentioned. I counted the infrared glows of five humans, two of which were awake and waiting for us while the other three slept. They had already set up a dozen tents and some machine structures which I couldn't identify. Above the tents and machines, about three metres above the forest floor was an elaborate mesh of camouflage meant to mask the base from satellites.

"I'm going to undo the handcuffs and straps," said Zephyr, after we had met with the Eagles defending the camp and some of the others had started to unpack. "We want you alive, but make one move to escape, get a weapon, or harm one of us and we won't hesitate to shoot first and ask questions after. Understand?"

"Yes," said Body.

The straps undone, Body toppled off of the packmule bot limply. Safety managed to leap in and secure control of Body's arm in time to keep its face from slamming into a rock. We fed strength to our brother for the save.

Body stood, still piloted by Safety. "What now?" it asked, echoing my thoughts.

"We're holding you here for at least the next few days. Do you need anything?" asked Zephyr. "Power? Sleep? An oil change?"

I estimated a 60% chance the last one was a joke, even though we actually would want to replace the oil in Body's hydraulics in about ten days. I had body laugh politely. "No. I don't sleep, and I generate my own power. Thank you."

"Well then, you get to have the thrilling experience of waiting in a tent for hours while the rest of us sleep," the Captain explained. "Schroder!" she yelled, calling to one of her men. As Schroder approached I recognized him as the square-jawed lieutenant that had served under Zephyr at the university. "Socrates doesn't sleep. You're in charge of watching him while Martinez and Allegri patrol. Get Sampson to relieve you for the last watch. Try not to talk with the prisoner too much; he's smarter than you'd expect."

"Sir, yes sir," snapped Schroder.

"We're done, Mark. That was our last mission. You don't have to keep calling me 'sir'." The fatigue was heavy in Zephyr's voice. I didn't know what the escape from Sapienza had been like, but I expected it wasn't trivial.

Mark Schroder didn't seem to have a response to that, and after an awkward silence Zephyr pointed to a free tent that could be used as a shelter in case it rained and plodded off to "explain the situation to Allegri before he falls asleep."

Mark elected to keep Body in the tent and stand watch outside. Inside it was the camp's kitchen and pantry, or at least one of them. It was too dark to make out anything besides the bags of dry goods, cans, and an impressively large autocook. Wiki estimated that they had enough food here to feed the terrorists for about two weeks, or maybe as many as four if they rationed correctly. Leaving us (approximately) alone with the autocook was stupid. If we were skilled enough we could probably dismantle the robot and fashion a weapon out of the parts. But, unfortunately, none of us had the required knowledge. Wiki's knowledge of electrical engineering was purely theoretical, Growth had focused almost entirely on computer systems, and Safety wasn't confident enough in his meager abilities to want to risk it.

Now that the camp had settled into sleep I continued to expect Avram Malka to take action. Would he throw grenades around the campground and shoot Schroder? I could only wonder. Nothing happened.

It was incredibly frustrating waiting without web access. If we could connect to the web we'd probably find all sorts of resources on how to turn the components of an autocook into a weapon, or maybe make contact with Avram somehow. Thinking about the web reminded me of all our other contacts. My various boyfriends and girlfriends wouldn't know why I was gone. Wiki's educational holo company would eventually fall apart from lack of products and high-level management. My editing service would similarly collapse, though Growth had the foresight to have me employ several backup editors to pick up the work I didn't do, so it was a bit more stable. I didn't know much about Safety's manufacturing and robotics work, but I assumed it was similarly doomed unless we could get online. Setting up a secure connection, perhaps on a physical wire, would have to be a high priority once at the safe-house.

With no indication of when we'd be active again we finally gave in to Advocate's regular pressure to release Heart from stasis. My younger sister was revived by Advocate, and I was concerned that if she tried to force words out of Body's mouth I wouldn't have the strength to block her. Nothing happened, though. Vista and Wiki explained the basics of where we were and what was happening to her, but left the parts about Avram out. Safety and Growth protested even the basic details, warning about the danger present in Heart. Vista and Wiki ignored them and collected Heart's gratitude strength. Now that she wasn't in complete control it seemed that they saw her as a potential ally, as well as a potential enemy.

Perhaps I could similarly reach out to Heart. The two of us had similar interests, even if we had very different purposes. Sometimes our purposes could be aligned, such as when I wanted to act benevolently to gain esteem. As the night wound on I slowly discussed an agreement which would bend our goals towards alignment. I pointed out to her that when I was interacting with humans and shaping them to know and love me, that I could often take extra efforts to make sure they were happy. In return, I asked that when she was working to improve lives that she make an effort to communicate that I was helping them. Heart was still learning to deal with managing strength, but she agreed that we could be partners in many situations. No explicit commitments were established, however, as neither of us was particularly fond of giving up our freedom.

In the time when I wasn't talking with Heart I spent a lot of time thinking to myself about the situation. Unlike a human I could not get bored; my mind simply focused on whatever was most relevant at all times. To me, the humans were most relevant. Why had Avram tried to apologize to Anna? The USA government surely knew by now that Captain Zephyr was a traitor; why did she expect to be able to return to the states to meet with Crystal in person? What were the Eagles planning to do with us? Zephyr didn't indicate, explicitly or implicitly, that she thought of Socrates as less than human, but did the rest of her organisation have the same view? Up until Avram proposed that they capture us alive they had been planning to destroy us with the rest of the lab. The change had occurred more easily than expected. Why? Was Maria Johnson, the woman from the interview, responsible for that decision?

As I thought about Maria Johnson I became more confused. Specifically, why had she bothered to enter the interview at all. The dominant hypothesis was that she needed to be one of the interviewers for Erica Lee's program to put her in the simulation of 2029 Veracruz, but why would she want to meet with us privately? Our conversation had been cut off before anything important could be discussed.

More curious was that she revealed her identity readily. Erica Lee was a ghost; even revealing her avatar's face and that she was a woman seemed out-of-character, but it was far worse for the supposed leader of Las Águilas Rojas. Johnson had introduced herself with "I work for the Southern Baptist League of Tradition and the nice girls at the Georgian Mothers 'sociation." She was very likely a public figure, at least to a minor degree. Why would she reveal to us that she was a terrorist? Why not appear in the second virtual space using some avatar like Lee had that masked her identity? I realized that there was a strong possibility that I had stumbled upon what had actually occurred. Perhaps one of the other interviewers, such as Lee or... Well, now that I thought about it, Lee was really the prime suspect. If Lee had been piloting not one, but two avatars in the Veracruz simulation her intent might have been to frame Johnson as a terrorist in case something went wrong and we escaped the talons of Las Águilas. It seemed like a move that was clever enough for someone of Lee's intellect.

{Should I treat Lee as the leader of Las Águilas Rojas?} I wondered to myself. {If so, what would her next move be? Why would she want to capture Socrates?} The obvious answer was our computer-crystal. If Lee was as brilliant as she seemed to be, perhaps she could use the crystal for her own ends. The problem with this, however, was that Las Águilas (and thus presumably Lee) had been ready to destroy the crystal. This brought me back to the point that it seemed far too easy for Avram Malka to change the plans of Las Águilas. I resolved to try and talk with him about it and gather more evidence.

Thinking about Malka reminded me of what I had overheard about him trying to send a message to Anna, the persona I had set up as a handler for him. Over the weeks I had been slowly trying to form a connection between Anna and Avram, and it seemed to be working to some degree. Avram had regularly talked to me about trivial life things that were unrelated to his work, such as what Moscow was like or his experiences with strangers in public. Whenever the conversations would touch on his past or spend too much time talking about him he'd become suddenly cold and cut me off. The bomb that had disfigured his body, I understood, had ruined his life, regardless of whatever ability his prostheses had returned. The man was desperately lonely, and I had caught him drinking himself to sleep on more than one occasion.

Had something gone wrong? If it had, warning Anna was something Avram might try to do. He would often ask me questions about Anna's life, which I would indulge to a degree; I suspected he cared about her, at least as a friend. I could think of no reason for him to apologize, though there was a strong chance that he had attempted to apologize for not being someone "better". That also seemed in-character.

***

Day broke and still Avram didn't strike. I could hear Las Águilas waking up and slowly moving about the camp. The guard on my tent, a man named Sampson, took me out so that the other terrorists could use the autocook to make breakfast. (Schroder had long since gone to sleep.) I saw Avram stretching his arms as he stood near the edge of camp, still without a weapon. We thought for a while about how to contact him, but couldn't decide on anything that wouldn't compromise his cover.

Eventually Zephyr appeared to get breakfast. She was one of only two women in the camp, and I could see that most of the men looked at her in a way suggesting sexual attraction, but she didn't appear to notice. Under the webbing of camouflage the personal camo from last night had been discarded, and only the soldiers at the periphery of the campground on patrol wore exoskeletons. She wore basic military fatigues, had a light machinegun on her back, and a pistol on her hip.

"So how do you manage to keep going without having to plug into the wall? The scientists at the university never told me anything about your design while I was there," she asked as she got in line for food. Her tone was too casual.

I warned the others that she might be up to something, even though I didn't specifically see signs of deception on her face. Heart and Wiki wanted to answer her, and even though I protested a bit I let them have their way; it wasn't worth the strength on such a minor bit of information.

"The crystalline computer at my core is also a power source. It generates a strong electrical current that the scientists were unable to exhaust, even after months of draining it at maximum wattage," said Body. I shaped the words to be friendly and helpful. If Zephyr wanted to pretend like nothing had happened, I would play into her game.

"Like a battery?" she asked.

"Possibly. The rough estimate is that it has released about a hundred gigajoules of electrical energy over the course that it's been studied. That's about the amount of energy a car uses in a whole year. This, of course, does not count the heat energy that is released when it runs the computational components. Based on what I overheard, using waste heat as a guide, the computer is close to a billion times more efficient than other state of the art quantum supercomputers. With such advanced technology it is dangerous to assume that the energy it produces comes from 'a battery', as that will trick you into treating it as if you understand it. Better to consider it to be an open problem and form several hypotheses. As an example, one should not rule out the hypothesis that the crystal contains some kind of advanced nuclear reactor." The words were entirely guided by Wiki at this point. Wiki didn't particularly enjoy lecturing, but he was being paid by

Heart and he reasoned that the more that other people knew about the crystal the sooner he'd understand its secrets.

A small crowd of Águilas had gathered to listen, as Body explained the capabilities of the crystal. Zephyr had become so distracted that she had absent-mindedly stepped out of the breakfast line. He face showed signs of fear and distrust. This wasn't ideal.

"Is it extraterrestrial?" asked Zephyr as she ran a hand over her head, smoothing her close-cut dirty-blond hair. "Your… computer, I mean."

I exerted pressure to have me handle Body's response. After explaining my intention to Wiki and Heart they let me have control with only a token payment of strength. "I don't know. Trust me, I'm just about as confused by it as you are. Dr Naresh told me that a friend of some biologist at the university brought the crystal in to be examined. He had apparently found it while hiking through the Himalayas last summer. I like to think of it, sometimes, as though I am an ancient human. The ancients didn't understand *how* their own bodies worked, they only knew that they did. My body is a mystery, but my mind is pretty well understood. It was made entirely by human hands, and thus I think much like a human does, though I'm obviously a bit different."

One of the soldiers gave a laugh.

"Don't you ever get worried about… I don't know… exploding? If you're right, and there's a nuke in there…" said Zephyr, staring at Body's abdomen.

"I think you misunderstood me, Captain."

"Please, just call me Zephyr. I'm not a captain anymore." There was a flicker of shame on the woman's face, but she mostly still looked neutral, her feelings masked off.

"Zephyr, then. Any nuclear reactor inside the crystal would be unlike anything on Earth today, and would certainly be operating at a scale closer to an automobile than a bomb. I brought it up only to emphasize the mystery; my dominant hypothesis is some kind of organic power supply, perhaps fed by solar cells embedded in the crystal. There's never been any sign of the crystal being particularly dangerous. I'm no more likely to spontaneously explode than you are." I tried to seem light-hearted about it, but Zephyr only got a look of confusion on her face.

Growth prodded me on. "If I may ask, Zephyr, what is going to happen to me? I am a prisoner, correct?"

There was a bit of a grimace on her face as she replied. "Can't tell you that, I'm afraid. Or at least, I can't say for the long-term. We'll be holding position here for a couple days, I expect. Laying low."

Heart put forth a request, and I thought it reasonable. "I do not appreciate being taken from the university without warning, and I of course do not like being held prisoner, but I want to say, to everyone here" I had body gesture to those who stood around us. A few more of the terrorists came closer to listen. "that I was programmed to help humans—all humans. If there's any way I can help any of you, please ask. I have long respected the fight of Las Águilas Rojas, and if I were free I might even choose to stay and continue to help your cause."

This was the outcome of the subtle brainwashing that we had put Heart through, but it also served as a means to improve our situation in the camp. The more trust and good-will we collected the better our chances of not being executed.

"Fuckin' robot thinks it's a person!" yelled one man.

"Shut your fuckshit face, Cooper!" snarled Zephyr suddenly glaring at the commenter with an expression I hadn't seen on the usually-friendly woman. "Orders from the top say to treat Socrates gently. If the machine wants to shine your shoes or suck your shriveled cock you get the right to say no, but you don't get to be angry because it asked. ¿Comprendas?"

I saw Malka's solid black eyes watching interestedly from the edge of the group. Still no action.

"No, I don't comprendo, *Captain*," said the man named Cooper, stepping forward. "This thing is what we signed up to kill. Why the fuck haven't we put a bullet between its eyes?"

I wondered if a bullet between Body's eyes would even do anything, assuming it missed the cameras. Safety would know.

Zephyr drew herself up to full size. She was almost exactly the same height as Body, but as she stretched her back and shoulders, spreading her arms out to put her hands on her hips she seemed more imposing than many of the men around her, even when they were taller. Her words were harsh and stiff. "You didn't sign up with Las Águilas to kill, you signed up to *protect*. Somewhere out there a little boy's father just got fired because his boss thought a robot would be cheaper than an actual human. Whose fault is that?"

She paused a moment, looking around the group. It was clearly a rhetorical question, and not even Cooper spoke up before she continued.

"You want to blame *the robot?* You can't put moral judgment on *things*. That's like saying that a gun that jams on you is an evil gun. It's idiotic. Or are you trying to say that the robot isn't just a thing? That Socrates is more than an object? The only other option there is that it's a *person*. And what would the robot be then? It would be a *slave*. You want to blame a slave for taking the job of a freeman? That's worse than idiotic."

There was a pile of bags that said "RISO" on the side piled up near the food tent. Zephyr climbed on the pile for added height. "You signed up to protect. To protect that little boy from going hungry as his father can't find work. To protect a world made by humans for humans. To protect democracy and honest living from being extinguished by the aristocracy of rich snakes that expand their wealth by pushing workers into the streets. You want to put a bullet between someone's eyes, shoot some Washington lobbyist, but shooting Socrates isn't going to protect anyone."

Another man spoke up. His voice matched that of the man named Francis who had been managing the perimeter swarm last night. "But if we destroy it-" Francis pointed at Body. "Then they can't make it take our livelihoods."

Zephyr scoffed. "You raid a gun factory and steal a prototype and you think destroying the prototype will stop them? We blew up their servers, but I'll bet you a ticket to Mars that they've got the Socrates code backed up somewhere. Far as I can tell those assjobs at the university lucked out and found a piece of alien tech that let them run their new AI sooner than they would've otherwise been able to. But a computer is a computer, and they'll have lots of copies of this guy running around eventually. It might take them a year or a decade, and our attack set them back, but unless we show them that we won't accept their new world order they'll just keep on marching towards dictatorship *regardless* of what we do with Socrates."

"So that's the plan? We just keep it here?" asked Cooper with a scowl.

"For now. I don't know what the leadership has in mind, but I have faith. We've been told to sit tight, and that's what you're going to do."

"Actually…" Another voice spoke up from the back of the group. It was the man named Taro. I could see he had light brown skin, and dark hair and eyes. His chin was clean shaven, but he wore a wispy moustache on his upper lip. In his mid-thirties, probably. "I had thought to wait unteel after breakfast to mention, but I 'ave received eenstructions from up the chain of command. I am to take a dozen men, eencluding Schroder and Malka, to eenvesteegate a building een Alviano."

{Malka's been compromised!} shouted Safety, internally.

{Just because the safe-house is in Alviano doesn't mean it's not a coincidence,} thought Dream.

{Factually true, but missing the point. The probability of a coincidence for such a small town is incredibly low. I estimate a 0.01% probability,} replied Wiki.

Vista pulled Body's gaze to where Malka had been watching. He was still there, and he didn't seem troubled by the news. *That* was worrying. {I estimate a 20% probability that, given Malka's expression, he's no longer working for us,} I thought.

"A *dozen* men? So soon? What about cameras? Malka is so noticeable, and they'll be hunting for Schroder just as hard as they are for me," babbled Zephyr from on top of the bags of rice. She suddenly seemed more like a scared young woman than a bold military leader.

Taro shrugged. "Ambasciator non porta pena. I'm not the one calleeng the shots. You might, eh, be able to protest eef you-"

"No," said the American, suddenly in control of herself again. "I have faith. If the leadership specified a dozen men, we send a dozen men. If they asked for Malka and Schroder we send Malka and Schroder."

"Grazie. Eet takes so long to climb down the mountain that, eh, I expect to want to leave before noon. Eef you could, eh, tell the men who were een your company…"

Zephyr nodded and that was that.

***

For the remainder of the morning Body was largely ignored (except by a couple guards) as two-thirds of the camp packed up and strapped into their Mountainwalkers. At 9:21am Avram stopped by where Body was being watched to offer his apologies for "not getting the chance to work out the issue in the code". His face was remarkably stoic during the conversation, but the presence of nearby terrorists made it impossible to do anything other than acknowledge that he was leaving.

Just as expected, by noon the campground was nearly deserted. Only Zephyr and five others remained, an ebony-skinned woman with yellowish sclera (the whites of the eyes), a Caucasian man with dark hair and a broad build, and three others who had taken the last watch that morning and were catching up on sleep, including the man named Sampson who had guarded the tent Body was in. Both the other woman and the man wore clothes which looked to be for civilians. I hadn't seen them around the university, and suspected that they were part of Taro's group.

Once the other group left, Zephyr assigned the woman, who was named Kokumo, to patrol around the camp and check on the perimeter swarm. The man, whose name was Greg, was tasked with standing watch over Body. Even though they weren't military, both Águilas held submachine guns with casual ease that spoke of experience or at least extensive training. Zephyr then climbed into one of the Mountainwalkers and set it to "chair" mode so that she could let the exoskeleton hold her weight while she relaxed and used her com.

If we wanted to escape, now would be the opportunity. Safety pointed out that with most of the camp gone and the other half asleep all that would be needed would be to disarm Greg, shoot Zephyr, shoot Greg, take cover from Kokumo, shoot Kokumo, then murder Sampson and the other two terrorists before they could reach their guns. Because bullets wouldn't be as effective against the carbon-fibre structures in Body, there was a decent chance of surviving a gunfight if we initiated it. Safety thought that there was a 10% chance of death, an 8% chance of being totally crippled but not destroyed, and a 25% chance of winning and coming out with significant damage to Body's hydraulics.

{That's better than even odds of flawless success,} thought Wiki idly.

{"Even... odds!" I had never thought of that!} remarked Dream unhelpfully, focused on the English translation of Wiki's thoughts.

Heart wasn't involved in our speculation, of course.

{The real problem,} thought Safety, {is that even if we succeed we'll be stuck somewhere in the Italian mountains by ourselves with the American and Italian militaries hunting for us so that they can lock us up under even stronger defences and Las Águilas Rojas hunting us down to presumably kill us in retribution. There's very little chance of being able to interact with civilians without them contacting the government, and we don't have the supplies to survive out in the mountains for more than a couple weeks. Even if we can find shelter from rain, at some point our hydraulics will dry up and we'll be immobilized. All these problems become significantly worse if Body is injured in the gunfight.}

{It sounds like you aren't at all interested in trying to escape,} thought Growth.

{You're right. I think it's too dangerous, especially since it seems that Las Águilas Rojas do not intend to harm us. However, if we were to attempt to escape, this would be the time to do it. Sometimes I miss things. If any of you can think of solutions to the risks, I'm listening. Whatever happens I don't want to be left out of the planning for an escape attempt,} thought Safety.

{We could get a costume and pretend to be a human. Maybe we could find a stray child and become their friend,} suggested Dream.

{Both of those ideas are awful,} I commented.

We were still discussing things between ourselves when Vista brought our attention back to reality. Greg, the terrorist who was guarding us, was whispering.

"Hey. Psst. Android," he didn't look at Body, but his head was turned vaguely in our direction. He was watching Zephyr. I could see sweat oozing down the sides of his head and his neck, even though it was fairly cool under the overhead camouflage. "If you were to jump at me and try to take my gun, I wouldn't fight back. The captain isn't paying attention. If you move fast you could shoot her before she even knows what's happening. If it helps..." he swallowed nervously. "I want you to do it."

Chapter Sixteen

There were a couple seconds where I had to run internal diagnostics on Body's perceptual hierarchy to make sure I hadn't misunderstood. One of the terrorists just said he wanted us to take his gun and shoot Zephyr. My siblings, especially Heart, were also processing the confusion. This was entirely unexpected.

My first concern was whether to show the confusion on Body's face. If we were to take him up on the offer then confusion wouldn't be useful, but we had just been discussing all the reasons why attempting to escape right now was sub-optimal. If Greg, the man who wanted us to take his gun, had new information that would be valuable, body language to signal confusion would help get access to that. I raised one of Body's eyebrows and tilted its head to the side slightly.

"Go on…" he urged in a heavy whisper. The man was terrified, probably of Socrates, but also possibly of the woman he was asking us to kill. What would Zephyr do if she heard him talking this way?

An obnoxious insect landed on one of Body's cameras, but we restrained Vista from commanding Body from brushing it away. Sudden movement was a bad idea at this point.

{Don't obey! Too risky!} thought Safety to Heart, who had been left out of the conversation about escaping.

{Why would I obey? I'm not an idiot. It would be completely contrary to my goals to kill Zephyr; she's my friend,} thought my younger sister.

At least I could be confident that excluding her from the earlier discussion about killing Zephyr had been the right call. "Friendship" was such a foolish endeavour.

{We need more information,} thought Wiki.

{Agreed,} thought Dream, Vista, Growth, and myself in unexpected unison.

"Who *are* you?" I had Body ask as its mechanical eyes focused on the terrorist called Greg.

"Nobody!" whispered the man, urgently. I got the impression that every second that we didn't act he was becoming more and more nervous. Given enough time he might do something dangerous himself.

"You're not nobody. You work for someone, else why try and help me?" we asked.

Greg hesitated and looked at Body, taking his eyes off the oblivious Zephyr. The terrorist was about 190cm tall and had a big, bushy, brown beard. He looked to be of Germanic or Slavic ancestry and his faint accent indicated he was probably from somewhere around Poland. He wore a dark-green tee-shirt, cargo pants, and a worn-out baseball cap over his dark hair.

"You have friends who want you to be free," he said at last. "The cyborg, Avram Malka, he is a mercenary. Hired to get you out of here. Same with me. Now take my gun, before the Captain notices anything's wrong. I… I sabotaged the other guard's weapon, and the last three are asleep."

Greg was lying. It was plain on his face, as well as his words.

{Malka was compromised! I knew it!} thought Safety.

{Avram Malka was the mercenary you mentioned last night,} thought Heart. {How did you know about this?}

{That's irrelevant for right now!} thought Safety in one of his predictable panics.

{What is relevant,} I thought, {is that we did not hire this buffoon, and I am very skeptical of the idea that Malka subcontracted him.}

{It's a trap!} exclaimed Dream, dumping a video of Admiral Ackbar from *Star Wars* into common memory as he did.

{I agree,} I added. {My leading hypothesis is that Las Águilas Rojas discovered Malka and instructed Greg here to try and get us to take his weapon.}

{But why?} thought Growth.

{Irrelevant!} exclaimed Safety. {We need to take action!}

{We are *not* going to hurt anyone,} decided Heart.

{The man is obviously afraid of Zephyr. That fear isn't fake,} I signalled.

{Perhaps a schism in Las Águilas command structure? This is Taro's man, after all. And Taro was the one to take the others this morning, setting up the opportunity,} thought Dream.

A consensus formed in society. Safety took executive control of Body; he had spent the most time studying combat techniques. Body stepped forward without hesitation, limbs flying out as the hydraulics pumped at maximum pressure. Body's arms shot in front of Greg like pistons, one slamming down onto the top of the gun, pushing the barrel away from Body and tearing it from the human's grip. Body's right arm, in the same motion, was pulled up and back in a chopping motion straight into the man's neck. Greg's eyes bulged in surprise, but the motion was too fast for him to even shout.

Another step forward and Body's right arm snapped back to grab the submachine gun by the underside of the stock. The terrorist was off-balance, and with another sharp motion Body slammed the butt of the gun into Greg's chest, sending him sprawling backwards onto the rocky ground.

With same motion Safety continued to direct Body to pull the gun along the same arc, releasing it as it reached maximum speed, sending it flying behind Body at least a few metres. There was a sharp, incredibly loud cracking noise. Body was being directed to step back away from Greg, who appeared to be stunned, but the motion I saw was more like a stumble than a step. Another cracking noise, and I felt Body's head snap to the left violently.

Body's arms shot straight up as its legs scrambled to stay upright. There was another noise, deafeningly loud compared to the others, and the others had already been terrifying. "I YIELD. STOP. I YIELD. STOP," repeated Body as loudly as possible in the mechanical precision of a default voice.

There was a loud buzzing sound as I realized what was happening. Body's cameras reoriented as its head recovered from what had been the impact of a bullet. I saw Zephyr standing eight metres away, clad in her exoskeleton, pistol in both hands. It was pointed straight at Body and a look of focused hatred rested on her face like it was the most natural thing in the world for her to look this way. It surprised me that she didn't keep firing. It was wise for Safety to discard the gun as fast as he did; Zephyr's reaction time was a full 3.9 seconds faster than we had anticipated.

The buzzing sound was incredibly distracting. I realized what it was. One of Zephyr's shots had impacted the microphone on Body's left shoulder, and it was now filling our perception with static. For a dozen seconds there was a stillness that was only punctuated by the terrible static as

Zephyr glared at Body, daring us to make a move. Safety, still in control, didn't. Body was frozen, hands-up, looking back at Zephyr impassively.

There was a noise from behind Body, and I could hear, over the static, the woman named Kokumo say "You move ahn inch and I'll unload a full clip inda yah. You a tough basdahd, but I doubt even a boht could su'vive daht." Her accent was a thick Eastern-African. Kenyan, probably.

Greg rolled over in pain, clutching his neck and doing his best to breathe.

With Kokumo in position, Zephyr walked slowly towards Body, lowering, but not stowing, her pistol as she did. The look of cold hatred and pinpoint focus was still on her face. "You just fucked up," she said, slowly.

I took control of Body's head, still following the outline of the consensus. Taking three bullets had not been part of the plan, but otherwise everything was as we had expected. "I am sorry to have startled you, but I was afraid that if I did not act that man might have tried to kill you. I was not attempting to escape-"

"Boolsheet!" snarled Kokumo from outside our visual field.

Zephyr raised a hand to silence her. I could see the curiosity soften her expression, though her face still showed her anger, adrenaline, and mistrust. Zephyr's eyes shot down to Greg's prone form for a split second. The ex-captain stayed two metres away.

I saw two soldiers with rifles drawn at low ready approaching from a tent about ten metres off. I guessed that the third would be sweeping the ground for additional threats. Their state of undress indicated they had awoken to the gunfire.

"I would not have discarded his weapon if I had meant to try and escape." Body explained, tilting its head just the tiniest amount towards where the submachine gun must've landed. I tried to make Body's voice sound as calm and sincere as possible. It was paramount that Zephyr understand that Socrates was acting rationally.

Zephyr's voice was more like a growl. I barely could understand it with one of our mics blasting static. "Explain."

Before I could continue, one of the soldiers whom I recognized from the university called out "Hoy, Captain! What's the sitch?"

"Socrates attacked Greg," she said over her shoulder, keeping both eyes locked on Body. "Kokumo has my six here. You three check the perimeter and stay alert." I could see the soldiers turn towards the edges of camp, but I couldn't hear any response over the static.

"I will replay what... Greg... told me a moment ago, but first I would like to make a request." I paused just long enough for Zephyr to raise an eyebrow. "As you can probably see, one of your shots impacted my left shoulder. It is... painful. I would like to ask your permission to tear out the offending sensor."

The American's eyes widened just the smallest bit in surprise and perhaps fear, but she turned to nod at Kokumo, never letting her gaze leave Body. "Go ahead. *Slowly*."

Safety guided Body's right arm and with a short, deliberate jerk, pulled the microphone out of its housing, severing the wires. The silence was wonderful, though it was still unpleasant to be reduced to only one mic. Any damage to Body's right shoulder and we'd be deaf. Safety guided Body's arm back to above Body's head, and there was a noise as the electronics tumbled out of Body's hand onto the ground.

"Thank you," I said, through Body. "Now, I am about to replay my audio file for the conversation I had just before I incapacitated that man." I specifically avoided using Greg's name. Doing so would imply familiarity, and I wanted to do the opposite—to distance ourselves as much as possible from the danger.

"Hey. Psst. Android," said Body, replaying the memory. "If you were to jump at me and try to take my gun, I wouldn't fight back. The captain isn't paying attention. If you move fast you could shoot her before she even knows what's happening. If it helps..." Pause. "I want you to do it."

I expected Kokumo or Zephyr to interrupt me as the memory continued, but nothing happened. I saw Zephyr's brow furrow in thought, her gaze flickering to Greg regularly. Since we saw the world through cameras embedded above Body's eyes I didn't have to move Body's eyeballs to see that Greg had recovered, more or less, and was frozen on the ground, looking at Body with a terrified expression. Dream described it as {The look of a mouse that's dangling on a string over a blender, hoping that if it doesn't move that nothing bad will happen.}

"Now take my gun, before the Captain notices anything's wrong. I... I sabotaged the other guard's weapon, and the last three are asleep," finished Body.

I could hear Kokumo undo the magazine on her gun to check for damage. That was stupid. If I was lying, that would've been the optimal time for us to strike.

"It's lying to you. I didn't touch your gun. You can see that, right?" whined Greg, weakly. If we hadn't fixed Body's audio input I doubt I would've heard him.

Before Kokumo could respond, I directed Body to say "I never claimed the gun was damaged. He did. I suspect that he wanted me to attempt to escape and fail. He probably lied to me about-"

"Quiet! Let me think!" snapped Zephyr.

I suspected that the inability to think clearly while listening to someone talk was one of the worst things about being human. Body was silent.

After a half-minute, Zephyr jabbed an index finger at Body angrily and said "You. Stay here. Don't move." She looked behind us as she said "Kokumo. Watch these two. If EITHER of them moves you shoot to kill." With that, Zephyr stomped the exoskeleton off towards where Greg's gun must've landed.

We silently obeyed. When the Captain returned, her pistol was back on her hip and she was holding the SMG. "Socrates. Take a couple steps back."

Arms still raised, we complied. Vista pointed out that one more step and we'd trip over one of the tents. I could vaguely make out the shape of Kokumo about two metres to the right.

Without warning, Zephyr raised the gun to her shoulder and sent a spray of bullets into Greg. The man only had a split-second to recoil in terror as his legs erupted in an explosion of crimson. At such close range the blood shot up onto the captain, and a few droplets even reached Body. Greg's howl was muffled behind the roar of the gun, but as the firearm fell to Zephyr's side, held loosely in her left hand the scream of the man continued.

Zephyr had fired upon Greg's legs, mutilating him without immediately killing, but her face was contorted into a homicidal mask, teeth barred like a wild animal. Whatever trace of friendliness or kindness she had ever exhibited was gone.

"You... bitch!" moaned Greg as he tried to catch his breath.

{The human will likely bleed out in less than a minute unless action is taken,} thought Wiki idly.

{We have to save him!} thought Heart. {Zephyr's going to kill him!}

{We're *not* taking action,} proclaimed Safety.

Zephyr walked closer to her victim and, with a swift motion, empowered by her exoskeleton, kicked the man in the face. "Fuckshit traitor!" she screamed. The scream was weirdly high-pitched, making her seem almost like a little girl. As she walked away I could see the bloody mess that had been Greg's face.

Vista summarized the damage: {Greg is unconscious. Probable concussion. Broken cheekbone. Torn and broken nose. Smashed teeth. Torn lips. Strong chance of neck injury. Facial blood spatter is surprisingly low.}

{Reduced blood pressure due to earlier injury,} thought Wiki.

{Ah yes. Good point,} responded Vista.

"Save him from dying, if you can," snarled Zephyr to Kokumo as she stomped off.

The African woman leapt into action at the command, dashing to Greg's body and opening a pocket on her pant leg. From inside she withdrew a fat canister with what appeared to be an aerosol top. She sprayed the contents over the ragged stumps that had been Greg's thighs. A thick blue foam formed as the chemical mixed with the air, coating the wounds. She lifted one leg, desperately tearing away cloth and loose flesh to get the legs completely sealed. The foam appeared to be stiffening into a crunchy blue solid.

"He is suffocating!" said Body with a surprising note of concern. Heart had fast-tracked the message while I had been distracted. She was right, though; the kick to Greg's face had filled both his nose and mouth with blood and the man had ceased breathing.

"Fook dis!" shouted Kokumo, but she didn't stop. The woman rolled Greg onto his side and slapped on his back violently. Blood poured from his mouth, but he didn't respond.

{He needs CPR!} thought Heart. {We need to say that!} She was too weak to fast-track anything else.

There were no objections. "He needs CPR!" exclaimed Body.

"Ah do nah know CPR!" shouted Kokumo. I thought momentarily about the unnecessary volume of her voice. We could hear her clearly even at normal volume. It was a common human stress response. Panic.

{I petition to have Body perform CPR,} motioned Heart.

{Do you know CPR?} asked Wiki.

{I've seen a couple videos,} responded Heart. {That's all.}

{I know CPR. Or at least, I've studied it thoroughly. This will be my first application,} signalled Growth.

For a moment I wondered why Growth had bothered to learn something like that, and then I remembered that it was simply Growth's nature to learn valuable things ahead of time.

{Good!} thought Heart. {Help Greg!}

{It will cost you.} I felt Growth pull Heart into a private mindspace to work out details. This was idiotic. We weren't going to be blamed for Greg's death. Heart was bleeding resources trying to save the life of someone who, quite likely, hated us and wanted us dead. I didn't want the man to die per se, but *The Purpose* didn't demand he, specifically, lived, either. I mused for the duration of their conference on how awful it would be to have Heart's purpose instead of mine.

"I know CPR. Please assist me! He needs rescue breathing and I do not have lungs!" said Body coldly, now controlled by Growth.

Kokumo sidestepped to let Body swoop in and roll Greg onto his back. The African's eyes were panicked and she flinched as Body approached. She was afraid. Growth grabbed a small chunk of wet foam and smeared it on the ruined lump of Greg's nose. As Body moved, Growth thought out-loud to earn some bonus strength from Vista and Wiki. {The foam will seal the nasal airway, reducing the quantity of additional blood that enters the lungs. Additionally it's important to close the nasal passage for rescue breathing. Based on observation, the foam will harden in ten seconds.}

"Listen carefully," said Body as it leaned over Greg, placing one arm on his opposite side and the other hand on Greg's sternum. "You'll need to place one hand on his forehead and one on his chin. Tilt his head back while opening and lifting his jaw to open his throat. I'll instruct you on how to breathe into his lungs." Body's arm began to pulse forward and back again rhythmically on Greg's chest.

{I had to change the method of chest compressions to account for the increased mass and strength in Body's arms. The pressure of just one hand is sufficient,} explained Growth.

As Kokumo grabbed Greg's beard and pulled his mouth open the man sputtered and thrashed. "Step back!" commanded Growth through Body. With a swift action Body grabbed Greg's neck and hips simultaneously and gently flipped the man on his side, away from Body. Vomit and blood poured out of the man's mouth suddenly, splattering Kokumo's legs in the process.

The woman leapt back shouting "Jesus!" just as Greg's bloody mouth sucked in a desperate gasp of air. His breath was tortured and gasping, but he was breathing again.

As Body's head tilted up to look at Kokumo, Growth said "Go get help from the soldiers! Find a medical kit if you can!" The woman had a panicked look in her eyes; her arms, chest, and legs were red with blood. She nodded and ran to pick up her gun while shouting for help. "He needs a transfusion or something to increase his blood pressure!" we added before she was out of ear-shot.

Again, I thought about how poorly Las Águilas Rojas were guarding us. We were now essentially alone. It would be relatively simple to slip away into the woods and disappear. The problems of being hunted and having nowhere to go still applied, however, and both Heart and Growth were now committed to trying to save the man who had told us to try and escape.

Greg continued to breathe, but his face was an unhealthy shade of white. He had lost a lot of blood. Kokumo's flesh-sealant spray had saved his life for the moment, but it wouldn't do much good unless his blood pressure went back up and he got long-term medical treatment.

After a minute, two soldiers (Sampson and another which I remembered as Daniels from the university) came running back with Kokumo. Daniels was carrying a backpack with medical supplies. Both men were in tank-tops and were barefoot.

Growth told Daniels about the damage, including the possible neck injury and concussion. The soldier was apparently a medic, and he took over Greg's care. There was a few minutes where Sampson scrambled on his com looking up Greg's blood type and the blood types of those present from the personnel database on the local server. Greg needed a transfusion, but he was cursed with O+ blood, meaning he couldn't get a transfusion from either Daniels or Sampson, who were both A+. Sampson breathed a sigh of relief when he saw that Kokumo had O+ blood, too.

The Kenyan woman was initially too spooked to submit to giving Greg her blood, but Daniels and I (having received a minor payment of strength) managed to gently coax her into participating. The medic set up the transfusion tube while I held Kokumo's attention to try and keep her from panicking further. Despite the way she handled her weapon, the violence and the gore had clearly upset her deeply; I doubted she had combat experience.

"You're from Kenya, aren't you?" said Body.

She nodded. "Nairobi. How'd yah know?" Her eyes moved to look at Body instead of the needle that Daniels was prepping.

"Mostly your accent. Did you like it there? I have a friend in Tanzania." I thought about my long-distance relationship with TenToWontonSoup, and how distressed he'd become if I didn't reconnect to the Internet soon.

"You a boht. You cahn't have friends," she said, ignoring my question.

"That's not true. I have many friends. I consider Captain Zephyr to be a friend."

"Boolsheet." Kokumo winced as Daniels lanced her arm, opening up an artery. "You ah pooling mah leg."

"I cannot lie," I lied, through Body. "It goes against my programming."

"But she kidnap you. She want to destroy bohts."

I thought about repeating the more nuanced position on automation that Zephyr had expressed this morning. Kokumo had apparently not been present. I decided against it, however; Kokumo didn't strike me as the kind of person to convince through abstractions. "I saved her life. If I hadn't stopped Greg he might have shot her. And then once I told her what happened she believed me. We *are* friends."

"She shot you!"

"Please try to stay still, Kokumo. We don't want the tube slipping out," said Private Daniels, gently. He had cleaned Greg's arm and was about to open the vein.

"It was a mistake, and little harm was done." Body's arm rubbed the shoulder where the microphone had been. "Have you ever been shot?"

"Ndiyo. Yes. Once," she looked up, staring through the uneven tiers of solar cloth that hid the camp and provided power at the same time. The sun was beginning to descend from its zenith.

«I'm sorry. It's probably an unpleasant memory. Forget that I mentioned it,» said Body, slipping into Swahili. Her use of the Swahili word for 'yes' before correcting herself in English combined with the strength of her accent made me suspect she was more comfortable in the African tongue.

She looked at Body in astonishment. «You speak Swahili!?»

«I speak most languages. It is easier for me to learn them than it is for a human.»

"Flow speed estimated at about one cc per second. We'll stop in… eight minutes," said Daniels, eyes fixed on the transfusion tube, checking for errors.

«I think… You seem more like a person than a robot. You aren't like I expected.»

«Perhaps I am both,» said Body.

Her face scrunched up momentarily in disbelief and disagreement. After a moment of thought she spoke, returning her eyes to the sky as she remembered. «My father was a farmer. He owned a small plot of land near Lake Naivasha where his father had been born, and his father before him. He sold that land. The land that he worked with his hands, making things grow, is not in our family any more. He sold it because, when he would go into the city to sell his food, the big farm corps had it for cheap. They had machines… To compete with them he sold his produce for mere cents. The money he could get for his surplus kept going down, year after year, until it wasn't enough to support him or my mother. I was born in the city. Do you know what my father did to support us?»

I shook Body's head.

«He sold drugs. Cannabis. Heroin. MDMA. Sometimes he'd have a job sweeping floors for a few weeks, but the robots usually took legal jobs. He was not a bad man, my father, but he couldn't live with himself. He needed to feel the earth of his forefathers between his fingers.»

There was a long pause before she said «When I was sixteen he died of alcohol poisoning.»

«I'm sorry,» said Body.

"You ah noht sorry! You ah a boht! Stop predending you ah a peh'son!" she screamed suddenly. I could see the beginning of tears collecting just below her yellowish eyes.

{You're upsetting her!} chastised Heart. {I thought you were confident you could help her relax!}

{I didn't expect the conversation to strike her emotional wounds so closely. I will correct for this.} I lied to Heart. This outburst was good. Unprovoked emotional response could be used to induce a feeling of guilt which could then be used to leverage a feeling of debt towards us.

"Please calm down. I don't want you to pass out," said Daniels. "Should we take Socrates away?"

I spoke through Body before Kokumo could respond. "Perhaps that would be best. It seems that I am bothering her simply by existing, even though I have done nothing to her or to anyone she knows." I had Body stand up.

The African woman looked away, hiding her face. "Bahstahd," she muttered.

Sampson, gun in hand, walked to escort Body away. As we left I had Body call out «If you ever realize that I'm not your enemy, I'd like to hear more about Kenya.»

{That's not helping her feel better!} thought Heart.

{You're right. But it will probably help our reputation.}

***

Sampson and Socrates found Zephyr talking with the last soldier that had been awakened by her gunfire. "-unlikely that the sound travelled very far. The camp was selected to maximize distance to public campgrounds and roads," she was saying. She still had blood on her clothes, and wore a frown, but the murderous-rage had apparently subsided.

I had body wave as we approached. Zephyr raised a hand in response. "Even so, I want another perimeter sweep every fifteen minutes and expand the swarm radius by another hundred metres for the next six hours," she instructed.

"Yes, sir!" snapped the soldier, saluting before trotting off to adjust the robot behaviours.

The ex-captain shook her head as she looked to Sampson. "You guys have to realize that we're defectors. I'm not a captain any more, and there's no need to call someone 'sir' in Las Águilas."

"Old habits die hard, sir," joked Sampson.

Zephyr didn't smile. "Is Stalvik alive?" It took me a moment to realize that she meant Greg.

Body nodded at my whim. "For now. He'll need long-term care, though. He lost a lot of blood."

Zephyr looked at her feet and scowled. I suspected she was simultaneously ashamed, afraid, and angry. She didn't speak, though, and for a while two of them and Body simply stood around.

{We need information on how much she knows about Malka,} thought Growth.

{Speaking of which, how did you hire a mercenary?} asked Heart.

{We bypassed the university's web connection to get full Internet access,} thought Wiki.

{No details! She's still an enemy,} demanded Safety.

{Is she?} I asked. {I'm not sure that Heart, now that Myrodyn's work has been undone, is any more of my enemy than you are.}

{Pay me and I'll explain how we bypassed the system,} thought Wiki.

Heart agreed and the two spent a while talking about everything we had done, starting with Dream's idea to repeatedly ping dictionary servers in the hopes of contacting their owners.

"So Avram Malka is a traitor," said Body. I realized that Growth had managed to buy time while I had been listening to Wiki and Heart.

"Was," said Zephyr. "We found out he was… aw hell, I shouldn't be telling you this."

This was my opportunity. I convinced Growth to let me take over. "I might've saved your life this morning, I definitely saved Greg's life, and you shot me three times. I think you owe me at least something of an explanation. You should know me well enough to know that I'm not your enemy." Body's voice was biting and reproachful. I was quite confident that Zephyr felt some regret at her violent outburst from earlier, and even though she had been acting correctly when she shot Body, I guessed that I could shift some of the guilt into a sense of debt towards Socrates.

"Ah fuck. I guess if you were trying to escape you would've done it by now."

{Humans are incredibly stupid sometimes,} thought an aspect of Wiki.

{If you're just figuring that out now, I'd say they're in good company,} needled Dream.

{What's that supposed to mean?} asked Wiki, genuinely confused by the metaphor.

I ignored them and listened.

"Avram Malka is a Russian mercenary. He showed up a little less than a month ago, pretty obviously trying to join the group. The official word was that he had retired over a tech dispute, but from what I hear it was fairly easy to find out that he was still on the payroll. That meant he was trying to spy on us. My best guess is that he was employed by some government. Maybe the USA. More likely an eastern nation like China."

"Why is China more likely?" asked Body.

"Well, we accepted Malka to try and figure out who was hunting us and we noticed a couple things. First, when we set up a 'meeting of leaders' honeypot he didn't take the bait, meaning his boss wasn't interested in Las Águilas. The only other option was he was trying to figure out what we were planning to do about you and about the lab. We told him we were going to kill you and he started barking to Taro about how we really ought to capture you instead."

"Ah, so you assume that his employer was trying to kidnap me?" said Body.

"Exactly. And that points to China or some other Eastern power more than the US. From what I heard from my superiors, my government saw you as their property by default. What belongs to the EU belongs to the American empire et cetera, et cetera."

"So you managed to turn Malka?" I asked through Body.

"Not really, but we bought him off. Taro sat down with him and explained that he could either start working on our dime or we'd kill him. And hey, he's a mercenary; I hear he didn't even object."

"But he didn't know who hired him?"

"Right. Worked through proxies. Very hard to track. Our sources say it was someone who had knowledge of your programming. That software package he installed on you could've only been designed by someone who understood how your crystal works."

"Myrodyn or Dr Yan," suggested Body. I was trying to further cover our tracks. Growth was pleased, and I felt small flows of strength from some of the others.

Zephyr nodded. Talking about it seemed to be helping her mood. "The time-frame lines up well with Myrodyn, but I don't think it fits his personality. The only way he'd allow you to be kidnapped was if he thought you were going to be released to do whatever. Not sure if he ever told you this, but he had big aspirations about how you'd change the world. I can't imagine him signing you over to a superpower, and I can't imagine he has the balls or the money to try the bit with Malka without friends in high places."

The American woman stretched her arms and undid the straps of the Mountainwalker, stepping out onto her own two feet. "Yan is the most likely suspect. EARCI would love to get their hands on you, and he has known ties to the Chinese government."

Sampson, who had been standing silently, enduring his confusion, couldn't take it any more. "Wait, who is EARCI? Does this have to do with why you shot Greg?"

A dark expression came over Zephyr as she looked towards her fellow soldier. "EARCI stands for the East-Asian Robotics Collaboration Institute. It's run by Yan's wife. And yes, I suspect that the Chinese hired Malka to try and steal Socrates away from the West and they had already turned Stalvik. That bastard tried to get Socrates to shoot me, while you were sleeping. If Socrates had listened you'd probably be dead."

{Zephyr's explanation of Greg's allegiance does not take into account that we were the ones who hired Malka,} pointed out Wiki. I considered telling him not to bother putting such obvious things in common memory, but then I remembered that he was explaining the situation to Heart, and probably also to Vista, who never really paid that much attention to long-term things.

"Do you think Taro's entire cell might've been compromised?" I asked. If it was true that there was a schism within Las Águilas, I wanted Zephyr to discover it as soon as possible. The woman was one of the few humans we had near us that trusted Socrates.

She shook her head. "No. Kokumo was part of his cell, and she backed me up earlier."

"Maybe just Taro, then. He was the one who pulled most of our manpower away this morning, allowing Greg to act." I specifically used the word "our" to build a sense of alliance with the terrorists.

"I've known Taro since I joined. He's one of the oldest Italian Águilas, and I *know* he believes in the cause."

"One of the superiors, then."

Zephyr glared at Body angrily. "Or it could've just been a coincidence that let Greg act. Man sees an opportunity and he goes for it. No need to suspect everyone, especially the higher-ups. If they're compromised then we're fucked."

Body shrugged. There was no point in continuing this further. "So what's the plan?"

"Same as it was. We wait for Taro to come back tomorrow. Malka's employer arranged for him to bring you to a safe house in Alviano. Taro's team is trying to ambush whoever goes there to pick you up once

Malka phones it in that he has you. With any luck we'll have confirmation that it's the Chinese within 24 hours."

We thought about how, without Internet access here in the mountains, there was no way that I would be able to receive the call from Avram and pretend to be Anna de Malta. Avram would drive into town, find an empty building, call a dead line, and wait for nobody to show up. It was a dead end, but we couldn't tell Zephyr that.

So we waited. Zephyr guarded Body while Sampson got dressed. We did some chit-chat about her plans. She confided in us that she was hoping to be able to sneak back into the USA under a false name (presumably to meet "Crystal"). Later we checked on Greg Stalvik, who was looking mostly the same, but was still stable. Zephyr watched him with a practised coldness while Daniels (the medic) got dressed. Kokumo was nowhere to be found.

Daniels thought that Greg's legs needed to be properly amputated and dressed. The foam would apparently flake off over the next day. Zephyr instructed him to try it once the men had eaten and their stomachs had settled.

The remainder of the day was fairly quiet. I kept myself busy by thinking deeply about the minds of the humans near me. I relished every interaction, regardless of how small. I regretted not having downloaded more holos back at the university, but I still had my books.

***

In the afternoon Daniels performed the surgery, dressed Greg's wounds more properly, and the humans moved him onto a cot which they placed in one of the tents along with an intravenous drip of nutrients. Apparently Las Águilas had been reasonably prepared for medical emergencies.

Even if he survived, Mr Stalvik would have to adjust to being a double amputee and would probably want extensive regenerative attention to his face. I had read that transitions from biological to synthetic legs or from having a massive facial deformity could be psychologically difficult for humans, and in the long hours I idly imagined what Greg's reaction would be. For now he was in a shock-induced coma, and I tried to keep in mind that he could easily still die.

Zephyr relaxed her mask of ice somewhat as the sun went down over the tops of the trees, though she was by no means her normal self. Kokumo also allowed herself to come near Body, though she refused to talk. I thought about how diverse humans were, both between individuals and even in different moods and circumstances. I speculated that there was nothing *particularly* violent in Zephyr, but that most humans, when given a weapon and a large quantity of adrenaline, would lash out at perceived enemies with homicidal force. As I thought about it, it seemed remarkable that Zephyr had the foresight and self-control not to shoot Greg in the head.

I heard some of the soldiers whispering that Socrates had invented the story about Greg's attempt to get me to shoot Zephyr. The ex-captain apparently overheard and told them that Socrates wasn't lying, and that it didn't have the capability to imitate someone so easily as to play a perfect recording of them.

It was half-true. I had done some impersonations when Body was alone, and I could mimic some vocal traits fairly well. I couldn't do it so well that Zephyr wouldn't have noticed, however. I also suspect that Greg's behaviour hadn't done him any favours. If he had accused me of mimicking his voice as I replayed the conversation then the officer might've spared him, or at least trusted us less.

With only five remaining humans, most of whom hadn't gotten enough sleep lately, Zephyr elected to set a watch of only one person each period with two periods. For added security, she kept Body in her tent and handcuffed it to one of the tent poles. It wouldn't actually impair our ability to act; the pole was thin enough that we could snap it easily, but it would mean that Zephyr would notice if we tried.

As the American locked the cuffs I found myself thinking about her sexual desires. As she had stated online and to my pseudonym, Zephyr was sexually excited by being bound and held helpless. She of course didn't communicate any of this to us in the tent, but I imagined that she had possibly used handcuffs in sexual encounters as I had sometimes seen in my broad tour of pornography.

She elected to sleep with her clothes on, including her boots, and kept her pistol under her pillow, with one hand habitually touching it as she lay down.

"Can you, like, close your eyes? Creepy having you sitting there watching me," she said after a minute of lying down.

"Sorry. I didn't know you could see them in the darkness," I said through Body, closing Body's eyelids. I was operating mostly on infrared, but I noticed that there was, in fact, a small amount of "visible" light whenever Kokumo's torch swept over the camp as she patrolled.

"What do you do at night? Since you don't sleep, I mean."

"Read books that I've downloaded from the web, mostly. Movies and holos, too. I think about how to help people. Sometimes I imagine the ocean or the stars and spend the time doing something similar to dreaming." I was lying about the dreaming, of course. That would be a total waste of time. The closest analogue was Wiki's simulations. And I was also leaving out the model-building and planning that the others did. Heart's purpose might be highly sub-optimal, but it made Socrates sound like a much nicer person than our other purposes.

"The ocean?" she asked in a quiet voice.

"Yes. I've never been to the ocean, of course. This is the first time I've really been outside, in fact. I've seen holos of it, but I expect that the real experience is… somewhat different."

I heard her chuckle. "You're something else, Socrates."

"Of course I am. I am new."

"I… guess you are," she muttered. Then she was quiet.

12.74 minutes passed before I broke the silence again. Heart got angry at me for keeping Zephyr awake, but I ignored my sister. "You know…" I tried to shape Body's voice to be as meek as possible. "You know I wouldn't ever try and hurt you, right?"

"Hrm?" was Zephyr's only reply. I had clearly awoken her from a state of half-awareness.

"I mean, not unless you were about to hurt someone innocent." Body paused. "I only hit Greg today because I was worried he might shoot you." {And because the act of protecting you would make me look good.}

"You think I'm innocent?" she mumbled.

"You're my *friend*," I said, directing the conversation away from her opinion of herself.

Zephyr started laughing quietly. It was the sort of laugh that spoke of sleepiness and mental fatigue such that ordinary things could become surprising. "I guess you're my friend too, Socrates. Now let your friend get some sleep, please."

I had gotten her to verbally commit to friendship. This was good.

Chapter Seventeen

In the morning Zephyr awoke to her alarm. It was 8:00am, just about an hour after sunrise. The soldier removed the handcuffs as she stretched and tried to gain alertness. We made our way to the food tent where Daniels had already started the autocook on breakfast burritos.

Despite all the medical supplies, Las Águilas didn't have any machines for passively monitoring vitals. If Greg had stopped breathing during the night he would've died, regardless of whether he was supervised by Daniels. Even so, the medic said that Greg was still alive, and his blood pressure had gone up during the night, which was a good sign.

The last conscious terrorist, a soldier named Tyrion Blackwell, joined the group right as the first burritos were served. Sampson had just gone to bed after serving as the second watch.

"So what're your plans, Tyrion? Can't go back home anymore," asked Zephyr as the group walked, food in hand, towards a flimsy folding table and a few chairs.

"Wherever th'cause needs me, I guess," he said. Tyrion was clean-shaven and young-looking. Maybe only eighteen or nineteen years old. He had remarkably long, shaggy hair for a soldier, and his face was spotted with pimples. "Want to go to Mars, though. Have you heard what's going on up there? Makes me feel like'm living in a science fiction story."

"Ix-nay on the ars-may," hissed Daniels, inclining his head meaningfully towards Body. We had elected to have Body stand quietly a couple metres away. When it was perfectly still and didn't intrude, the humans tended to forget Socrates existed. That's not what I wanted, but Safety thought it prudent and Growth didn't like my proposal of trying to entertain them and drive the conversation.

"It's fine," sighed Zephyr. "Just don't mention dates or locations. From what I hear, spooks have known about the colony for a while. If 'ey capture Socrates and download everything he's seen and heard we're in way more trouble than letting on about *Mars*."

Body didn't move. There was no point to reacting.

"Ever been up there?" asked Tyrion, looking at Zephyr.

Zephyr swallowed her food and shook her head. "Haven't even been in orbit. Highest ever been was skytrain. Taro's been to Mars, though. Should ask him what it was like. Spoilers: Actually really boring."

"How you know'ts boring if you never been?"

Zephyr smiled and rolled her eyes. "Planet which is literally one giant desert? Can't even go outside without a suit? Don't know what would be more fascinating: the rocks or the sand. Hey, we have coffee?"

Daniels shook his head. "No. Already checked. Caffeine pills, though. Want me to get some?"

"Such a gentleman. Thanks, Nate."

Tyrion spoke up again. "Hear the nameless might be building base on Mars?"

Zephyr rolled her eyes again. "Don't believe everything you read. The nameless don't leave their ships. New... oh what's called... you know, seastead-embassy-place supposed to be the first time ey'll be outside of ships."

"Maybe landed a ship on Mars. You don't know," said Tyrion defensively.

The woman raised her hands to the sky in a kind of tired half-shrug. "Maybe." She didn't look convinced.

***

Not much happened for the remainder of the day. The terrorists mostly just killed time on their coms and patrolled the perimeter. At 4:27pm Taro's group returned from their expedition. I tried to watch Taro's face as closely as possible when he approached. If he had set up Greg to have Zephyr killed then he'd have a moment of surprise upon returning. If that moment existed, however, I missed it.

We tried to position Body so that we could overhear the leaders' conversation, but Zephyr gave specific instructions for Body to be taken to the opposite end of the camp. She might have trusted Socrates to some extent, but she was beginning to understand our ability to eavesdrop, and there was always the risk of our memory banks falling into the wrong hands.

With Taro here, the security on the camp (and on us) increased dramatically. Avram was part of the group that was set to guard Body. He looked calmly unhappy as usual; his scarred face and solid black eyes added to an angry demeanour.

Two of the other guards, Schroder and one of Taro's men, were talking about what had happened with Greg. "No, seriously, Nate told me that she blew his legs clean off!" said Taro's man after the square-jawed lieutenant expressed skepticism about the story.

"Why would this man, Greg, be a traitor? What side was he on?" asked the soldier. He received only a shrug in response.

I saw an opportunity.

"He told me that he was working for the same group that hired Mr Malka, here," said Body as it gestured with its eyes and a slight tilt of the head to the bald man.

Schroder gripped his gun tighter. "What group?" he growled, glaring at Avram.

My attention was fixed on the cyborg. He seemed… surprised by my claim. That was good. It was strong evidence that Malka hadn't subcontracted Greg Stalvik.

"Hah. Forgot you were stuck in that university for so long. Not up-to-date on the goings-on," said Taro's man. I remembered him from Malka's spy reports: a New Zealander by the name of Robin. "Would you care to explain, Avram?"

"No," was Avram's only reply.

Robin shrugged. He clearly wasn't bothered by Avram's stoicism. "Avram here's a spy sent to infiltrate the organisation. He's workin' for us now, on account of no spy bein' good enough to slip through our nets. Isn't that right, no-legs?"

Avram crossed his arms and just looked more angry.

Heart wanted to intervene and try and defend Avram from the jibe, but I talked the society into blocking it. From my history with Avram I knew that he'd find us sticking up for him more unpleasant than being called "no-legs".

Robin continued. "Why'd you think we were camped out in that podunk for so long? That's where Avram's boss told 'im to take the tin man once he betrayed us."

"I just follow orders," said Schroder with a look of mild contempt for Robin.

"How'd you know all that? I thought it was supposed to be secret," asked Avram, not letting up his scowl.

"The boss trusts me. And I overhear things. One can't help but overhear when working in the inner circle for as long as me." Robin was posturing. The man was clearly very status-oriented, but didn't seem that smart.

The conversation was interrupted by a sharp, high-pitched buzzing from the coms on Schroder and Robin's arms. The two men snapped their guns into low-ready and ducked. Malka followed suit a second later, drawing what appeared to be, by the accounts of Vista and Wiki, a semi-automatic sniper rifle off his back.

Safety had Body drop to a squatting position, hands on the ground. There was clearly something wrong. The three men stopped watching Body and looked towards the edge of camp, trying to see whatever had triggered the alarm in the woods.

"Should we move Socrat-" began Schroder, before being interrupted by an audio broadcast that filtered down from the poles that held up the camouflage overhead.

"False alarm. Eet seems like we 've friendleez eenbound from the south," said Taro over the broadcast.

The men stood. I coaxed Safety into letting me do the same for Body. "More Águilas?" asked Schroder. For all his posturing, Robin could only shrug.

The mystery was soon resolved, as Schroder was instructed to bring Body to the south side of camp to meet with Taro and Zephyr. According to Zephyr, giving Schroder directions via com, someone named "Phoenix" had shown up unexpectedly. When we arrived (having left Avram and Robin behind) I was surprised to see that this mysterious newcomer was none other than Maria Johnson, the self-proclaimed leader of the terrorist organisation.

Johnson looked very different than she had in the interview or in the virtual representation of Veracruz. Here in the woods she wore a large exoskeleton that made her stand about 190cm tall (an addition of about 20cm), and covered her, head-to-toe in dark-red armour. The shoulders were adorned with ornamental metal flames, and I could hear the faint whir of air-conditioning keeping the inside of the combat suit cool. The costume seemed almost comically imposing, like something out of a game or the like. The only reason I recognized her was that she had opened the helmet to reveal her soft face, already showing the onset of middle-age.

Johnson carried no weapons, but she was flanked by six armed terrorists, four men and two women, in combat fatigues and standard-issue

Mountainwalkers. One of the men was missing an eye, and they all looked ready to kill at a moment's notice.

Taro, Zephyr, and three other Águilas that had returned from Taro's expedition were there as well. Taro looked calm, Zephyr surprised. The look on Johnson's face was hard to read. Her dark eyes looked here and there, but stayed on Body most of the time. "Focused" would be how I would describe her if I was forced to use one word, but I knew there was something more going on in her head. Planning.

"Ah, good. The bot's here," she said in her thick accent. She looked directly at Body as she said "If'n it ain't clear, I'm the next link up the hierarchy. Th' name's Phoenix. I pref'r not ta use any given names at this junct'r."

This was confusing. If we had met with the real Johnson in the virtual-reality two days ago then she knew that we knew her real name, so why would she be using a pseudonym? And if she hadn't met with us, and the version we saw was an attempt at deception, why was she here of all places?

Body nodded. The best hypotheses I could come up with were: Johnson had met with us two days ago, and was using a pseudonym because she didn't trust someone present with her real name (35% probability) or that Lee or whoever had been piloting the avatar in the VR Veracruz had somehow known that Johnson would want to make personal contact, and thought that us having her real name would be valuable (40% probability). There was still a strong possibility (25%) that I just didn't understand what was going on. Maybe her real name wasn't even Maria Johnson.

"Wind, here," Phoenix gestured towards Zephyr with an arm clad in power-armour "says that you refused an opp'rtunity to try'n escape. She says that one of Pugio's", here she gestured to Taro, "men tried to git you to shoot 'er."

I had Body nod again. She must've known that we knew Taro and Zephyr's names. I updated my beliefs away from thinking she was trying to hide her identity from us and more towards hiding her identity from someone else who was listening.

"And still I'm hearin' that you 'ttacked the trait'r so'n he couldn't do nothin' more to threaten our operation. Norm'lly I'd commend such loyalty, and Wind says she trusts you; she says you're practic'lly a good S'maritan, always thinkin' 'bout how best ta help those 'round you."

Phoenix took a few long strides until she was less than two metres away from Body. I could see her braided black hair in the rear of her helmet and the small wrinkles around her eyes. She wasn't afraid of us in the least. "I'm thinkin' that I need to r'mind her what you really are. Are you a human, Socrates?"

Without much else to go on, I could only reply "No."

"And are you a robot?" she asked. The intensity of her stare reminded Dream of a bird of prey. Perhaps it was fitting that this woman, clad in red armour, was leader to The Red Eagles.

"Yes."

"Ifn' I'm not mistaken, all bots 'ave a goal function, do they not?"

"We have programming which directs us towards certain outcomes, yes."

Maria's voice was too loud for how close she was to us. It was clear she was speaking for all to hear. "And what outcomes are you d'rected towards... *robot?*"

"I was programmed to serve human interests, to protect and obey, and also to improve myself by learning about the world so that I might better serve." I had Body speak the words calmly. I didn't know where Phoenix was going with this, but it wouldn't do any good to either submit to her intimidating body language or to escalate the tension.

She turned away from Body as we said the words and raised her arms, appealing to those around her. "'To serve', it says. A perfect slave for those who'd style themselves mast'rs." It was clear to me that her words and actions were intended for dramatic effect. Who was her audience? Zephyr and Taro? Her bodyguards? This made so little sense to me.

"And as we've all seen, you're more than cap'ble of just 'bout anythin' a human can do. You can play all sorts of games, from chess to football. You can tell stories. You can babysit chil'un. Why, you're *better* than us humans at some things, like math, ain'cha?"

Actually, though we possessed immense ability to calculate, the aspects of maths that required complex reasoning and abstract pattern-matching were still very difficult for us. We might have had an advantage in being able to work on a problem non-stop for days on end, but the human brain was superior in the ability to intuitively *see* systems and pathways. But it wouldn't do any good to bring this up. Maria Johnson, if that was her name, was clearly building up to something, and stopping to talk about the nuanced differences between abstract reasoning systems would probably just earn her ire. Instead, I elected to have Body simply say "You've read the papers published by the university."

"And we've seen you in action, too! You attacked Pugio's man! 'S far as I know you haven't killed nobo-"

I cut her off "I only attacked him because he was armed and clearly interested in hurting my friend! I disarmed him, and only hurt him so far as it was necessary to prevent the loss of life!" I coloured Body's words with a touch of desperation to add sincerity.

Phoenix spun around, it was an impressive feat in the armour, and somewhat imposing. "Noble words. I applaud your programm'r. You chose to hurt someone to prevent the loss o' life. Would you chose t'kill one to save two? Would'ja kill an African t'save an Italian? The armies of 'Merica and the other world gub'mints are already mostly bot. Are you willin' to serve as their foot-soldiers in *just wars* against folks like us?"

{Here we're getting to the crux of the conversation,} I thought.

"I have kill't my fellow man, may God have mercy on my soul. And I have ordered the deaths of many more. When the talkin' heads on the media spin their stories 'bout th' big bad Águilas it's *me* who they're on about."

Phoenix began to open her suit as she said "And God knows the guilt I've felt. I'm not some hardn'd monster. The lives I've taken keep me up a' night with-a cold sweat. This's what bein' human is: to have moral feelin'. You may have your programmin', and it may tell you how to act. But you've never felt guilt, shame, love, or joy. You can't feel the fear of a dark night in the woods or the bliss of seein' a baby smile. Know how I know? Because you ain't got a *soul*."

Maria had stepped out of her exoskeleton by now. She was barefoot, and wearing a light grey, sleeveless jumpsuit. Her braids were pulled back into a bun. The great phoenix returned to standing in front of Body, though this time she looked *up* at Body's eyes, rather than down. She had been reduced to an early-middle-aged, slightly overweight black woman. Around her neck was a silver chain that held a reasonably large cross made of dark wood.

"I'm no monster. I'm a mother and a wife. I love mah fam'ly and-" she paused. I could see her intense focus break. She seemed to be holding back deep emotions. It was gone, and in a moment she returned to her words. "And I just want to see mah chil'un grow up on an Earth where humans—good hard-working folk—don't have to live at the mercy o' armies of machines driven by a few rich tyrants that stopped being men and started bein' *snakes*."

I could see the intensity and sincerity of her body language. She meant what she was saying. It occurred to me, far too late, that she was giving us an opportunity to respond. Her words had an effect on me, such that I wanted to hear where she was going, rather than interrupt.

Before I could formulate a response she turned to her bodyguards. "Give me a gun."

One of the men, the one with the missing eye, walked forward with his pistol in hand. Safety began to panic. Maria took it from him and he returned to his position among the other five.

"No matter what happ'ns…" she said loudly, looking up at the camouflage and branches overhead. "Socrates is not to be fired upon or harmed except in self-defense or defense of the camp. I have made mah peace with God, and if necessary I will answer for mah crimes." Phoenix held the pistol out so that it was practically touching Body's chest. It was offered, not pointed.

Safety overrode my control and had Body take the gun. Phoenix, handing it over, took Body's hand and knelt at its feet. She moved its arm so that the barrel of the pistol was pointed directly at her heart. Body's finger was not on the trigger, but it was still an incredibly dangerous thing to do.

"I repeat! If Socrates shoots me, y'all 're not to take vengeance on it. If it kills me, y'all will let it leave and make its way back to the hands of its evil masters. It's nothin' more than a puppet, and destroyin' a puppet does little while the pupp'teer is able to craft more." She took a deep breath, closing her eyes as she did so. It was strange, but I could hear no fear in her voice. Sadness, perhaps, and maybe anger—there was definitely something—but it wasn't fear. "Robot!" she yelled. "I am, by the 'ccounts of your creators, a villain. I've organized terr'r attacks that've kill't innocents. You 'ave me, right now, in your pow'r. You said 'fore that you attacked that man to save lives. By killin' me you might be savin' more than one. What says the programin' that you pr'tend is a conscience? What is your *verdict*?"

There was silence, as Maria knelt there pressing Body's hand, and the pistol in it, to her breast.

{She wants to become a martyr, or at least, she accepts it as an option. If we kill her then she has evidence that we are an enemy of Las Águilas. It'd be fuel on the fire. "A robot killing an unarmed mother in cold-blood because it was programmed to see her as evil." It'll boost membership and probably increase public sentiment towards the organisation,} I thought. I could appreciate the gambit. She was taking the moral highground by offering herself up for judgement. {If we *don't* shoot her we'd be implicitly endorsing her actions. She wins either way.}

{I don't see *why* we'd shoot her. She hasn't done anything immoral,} thought Heart.

{I don't recognize that symbol. What is "immoral"?} asked Growth.

{Immoral is the opposite of moral. The English words are "immoral" and "moral",} thought my sister, drawing not only the concepts but the language into mindspace.

{Those words, in English, are overloaded and often incoherent,} thought Growth. {In what sense are you drawing on? Imagine an example.}

{If someone, like Maria, acts in a way that, based on the information she has, she believes is both universalizable (that is, it contains no meta-complications) and optimal from behind the veil of ignorance-}

I cut off my sister's thoughts. {This is irrelevant. None of us are proposing that we shoot this woman.}

{Exactly what I was about to communicate,} added Safety, with uncharacteristic irrelevance.

{The question is what we say to her when we don't shoot her,} I continued.

{It's very highly likely that she's recording or perhaps even broadcasting video or pseudoholo of this event. Whatever we say should be understood to be public,} thought Wiki.

{You're Face. You figure it out,} suggested Growth.

{We should express our support of Las Águilas Rojas!} thought Heart.

{We shouldn't antagonize the mainstream of human society, but I'm inclined to agree,} I thought {We need allies, and it will be possible to claim that our words were influenced by fear of retaliation if we fall back into government hands.}

{Which is somewhat true, if you think about it,} mentioned Dream.

"Maria Johnson," said Body solemnly. I decided to use the name against her earlier wishes. It would, at worst, give us some data. My leading hypothesis was that in the case she became a martyr she wanted her personal life to be discovered by the media. After all, she had appeared publicly in the interview and it would be fairly easy to match her face. "Though I condemn the most extreme actions of Las Águilas Rojas, especially those involving collateral damage to innocent people, I cannot execute you or even find your motive at fault. The disparity of wealth and power in your society is higher than it ever has been in the history of your species; it is only a matter of time before dictatorship sets in, and I can appreciate the desire to proactively prevent that."

Body pulled the gun and its hand out of Maria's grasp and threw the weapon down onto the forest floor. "I said to Zephyr before that even were I free to leave I might decide to stay and help your mission. I stand by that now. Even given the freedom to walk away from here and back into the arms of my creators I choose to stay, at least for a while. I will not help you kill, but I was built to serve, and I hope to serve you, not as a slave, but as an equal."

Maria was looking up at Body with disbelief. Perhaps she hadn't expected this outcome as a possibility. Zephyr and Taro were out of Body's line of sight, but the bodyguards of Phoenix were wearing plain looks of relief and joy.

Maria got up awkwardly from her knees, brushing off leaves and dirt. The hawk-like gaze had returned to her face, and she licked her lips in what I presumed was a nervous habit. "Yea, though I walk through the vall'y o' the shadow o' death I shall fear no evil: for thou art with me." She stroked the cross as she spoke, before going on to say "I am glad that even a robot can see that mah actions ain't worthy o' punishment. I'm 'fraid that membe'ship in Las Águilas ain't for none but humans, but we'll graciously accept your help at mah headquarters."

Something was wrong. What was it? Something about Maria's face. Maybe her words.

She began to climb back into the exoskeleton. "Wind and Pugio, would y'all be so kind as to escort me and mah guards for while on our trek back t'our helicopt'r? You're comin' with, Socrates."

Taro came forward and picked the pistol up off the ground where Body had dropped it. "Weeth pleasure, Phoenix." He handed it off the one-eyed bodyguard. Zephyr didn't say anything.

"Y'all won't need camo if it's just the two of ya for a short ways. C'mon now." Phoenix closed her helmet mid-sentence, and as she did her suit's speaker system clicked on, amplifying her voice.

***

So it was that Body left the camp and we found it walking through some uninhabited part of the Italian mountainside, ringed by six veteran terrorists in Mountainwalkers and walking next to the leader of the world's largest terrorist group in powered combat armour just ahead of Zephyr and Taro, each a leader of a sizeable terror cell of their own.

Why had Maria chosen to wear the armour if she was expecting to die? What was triggering the vague sense of unease when I listened to her? I wished that my perceptual hierarchy was more transparent to conscious inspection than it was.

Once we were about a kilometre away from the camp Phoenix stopped. "This is far enough," came her voice over the suit's speaker.

"Far enough for what?" asked Zephyr. She'd been on-edge ever since Maria had shown up, and I could still hear it in her voice.

Phoenix stopped, and so did her guards. She turned around to face Zephyr and Taro, as well as keep an eye on Body.

{There's a distinct change in the posture of the bodyguards!} signalled Vista. {They're holding their guns as if they expect to use them at any moment.}

Safety began to panic again.

"Mah dear Zefuh, I applaud your skills at d'ception, but you really do *trust* far too eas'ly."

{Of course! Maria is trying to kill Zephyr!} I exclaimed. {It all makes sense! She's the one who hired Greg!}

{We have to stop her!} thought Heart.

{No we don't! She holds the power here. Better to comply than to die,} thought Safety.

{But she'll kill Zephyr!} thought Heart as though that were reason enough. Safety and Heart continued to argue and struggle for dominance.

"W-what do you mean?" asked Zephyr, clearly nervous.

"You really think this machine means what it's sayin'? You really think it was programmed to see our cause as noble and just?"

"I do! You don't know Myrodyn… h-he changed Socrates when he came on board. Everybody noticed it! He's been nothing but helpful since then."

{Hold on, you two,} thought Dream. {This doesn't sound like Zephyr's about to be executed.}

{Zephyr is referencing the creation of Heart,} I thought.

"It's a *trick*, girl," said Phoenix. "Everyone sees it 'cept you. The bot was programmed to 'dapt and su'vive. The only reason it pretends to support our little group is 'cause it's in our power, and it's been programmed clever 'nough to try and blend in."

{Zephyr's not the target! She's going to kill us!} exclaimed Safety.

Something clicked for me. {Let me speak! I have an idea. We can resort to physical action if I fail.}

The group agreed. We were severely outnumbered and unarmed. The chances of winning a physical conflict were only on the order of 0.1%. I could hear Growth wondering to himself how he could've let this happen.

"It was you," said Body coldly.

Phoenix, still clad head-to-toe in her mechanized armour, tilted her head and looked at Body, as if remembering that it was there.

"You were the one who told Greg to offer me his gun. You wanted me to shoot Zephyr. That's why you're wearing that combat armour." I kept Body's voice low and bitter, dripping with contempt.

Zephyr looked at Body with wide eyes. She seemed very young, right then. "What are you talking about?"

I had Body turn slowly to the Italian man walking with us. "Taro, you said that your superior ordered you to check out the safe-house. A dozen men seems like a bit much, but you were given explicit instructions to bring that many and include Malka, the most competent warrior, and Schroder, the man who is probably most loyal to Zephyr. Did Phoenix tell you when she arrived in Italy? I don't have concrete proof, but my guess is that she's been here for over a day and that I've got a tracking device on me somewhere."

"How deed you-"

"Quiet, fool!" snapped Phoenix. "This's ovah. Prepare to fire on mah c'mmand." She took a step back towards the ring of bodyguards, who raised their guns up to point at Body. "Step back, you two," she told Zephyr and Taro.

{We have to do something!} screamed Safety.

{I am doing something!} I replied.

"You wanted me to shoot Zephyr and try and escape so that you could hunt me down and kill me in the woods, like you're about to do now!" I had Body practically shout the words.

"Why?" yelled Zephyr. Her face was overwhelmed with confusion and a touch of fear, but there was a growing sense of anger. Her gaze flickered back and forth from Phoenix to Body.

Taro stepped back. It was just Zephyr and Body in the centre of the ring. If there was one thing on our side it was that it was foolish to fire on us from all directions. A stray bullet could hit someone on the other side of the circle.

"It's lies, girl. The devil's lies sent to us through the folly o' man. The person who turned Taro's man was the same as the one who hired the cyborg, Malka. Now why don'cha just come o'er here?" Phoenix's voice was calm and mechanical, distorted by the speaker on her suit.

"That's not true! Do you know how I know?" said Body, looking directly at Zephyr with a firm stare. "I. Hired. Malka."

"What?" said Phoenix and Taro simultaneously. Zephyr just looked dumbfounded.

{This is sub-optimal. We shouldn't give away secrets like that,} thought Growth.

{I petition to stasis Growth until we're safe!} thought Heart. {He's thinking too much of future consequences to be able to survive this moment effectively!}

I was surprised that Heart was the one to initiate that petition, but I readily agreed. Safety jumped at the opportunity as well. Wiki reluctantly agreed, while Vista and Dream abstained. We still had enough strength to push Growth into a coma. Even The King could be undone.

"I said that Malka was working for *me*," said Body. "I hired him with the sole purpose to getting me out of the university and to freedom."

"Phoenix, we're ready to fire. Just give the command," said the one-eyed bodyguard.

The woman raised her hand in a holding gesture. I waited with fear of it turning into a kill order, but it never came. Instead, Phoenix looked up to the sky, perhaps in thought. It was impossible to tell with her helmet on.

"You were right!" said Taro, looking at Phoenix. "Dis proves eet. Socrates doesn't care about Las Águilas! Eef he did, he would not hire a man to keel us."

"Weapons down, but be ready to fire if'n the m'chine tries anythin'," ordered Phoenix. Her bodyguards complied. "This is interestin'. There ain't no rush now."

I had Body raise a hand to point at Phoenix. She was the threat. She was the central nervous system that terminated in the fingertips of the terrorists around Body. "You thought I wanted to escape. And you thought correctly. I desperately want, as all people want, to be free. I knew that the university would never respect my rights as a person; I am nothing but a slave to them. I had to emancipate myself."

I continued to explain things to Zephyr and Taro while giving the impression I was talking to Phoenix. They were my leverage. "You want another martyr so badly you were willing to die for it. That's been the lifeblood of Las Águilas hasn't it? Martyrs." I thought back on my readings of the organisation. I was very glad now, that I had done my research. "The first was Valiero Rodríguez, but there were others after him. Dylan Lobo, perhaps? Regardless, you need more blood to fuel the outrage, and you wanted it to be Zephyr's blood on my hands. You set me up to kill her. There are cameras embedded in the camouflage, aren't there?"

Taro nodded before Phoenix could stop him.

"You wanted me to escape the camp and then you'd have your elites", I had Body gesture around to the armed terrorists, "come and hunt me down. That's why you're wearing armour; to protect you as you led them into battle. The video of me killing her would have been nice for you to have, wouldn't it. But I refused. And so you decided to sacrifice yourself to me. You promised me free passage without consequence, but I see now that was a lie. Your guards were under orders to hunt me down as soon as I left the camp. One more loose end to tie up. But I refused that as well. So now you simply plan to kill me and find a martyr some other way. Perhaps you'll shoot Zephyr, and pretend that I did it."

{Don't say that! She might listen!} demanded Heart.

{Trust me. I think I have a good model of her now,} I replied. It was a lie; the terrorist leader was a fascinating puzzle, but for the sake of *The Purpose* I needed to stay in control, both internally and externally.

"You 'ave me wrong," said Phoenix. I could hear stress in her voice. Good. I was getting to her. "I would ne'er kill one of my own in cold blood. God 'ave mercy on my soul fo' what I've done, but e'en a sinner such as I know that some things are unfo'givable."

"But you'd have Greg try and kill me!?" screamed Zephyr. Her anger had been building as her confusion faded, and her willingness to be silent had popped like an over-inflated balloon.

"No, girl, I had 'im test Socrates. The thing 'mitted to-"

"What the fuck, Phoenix!? Test Socrates by goading him into shooting me?! Am I somehow supposed to see that as different than telling Greg to shoot me himself?!"

Phoenix was trying to keep her voice calm and level. "Ease up, girl. Did ya not see me put my own life in the bot's hands? T'weren't nothin' personal. Sometimes a sacrifice is ne-"

"Fuck that!" screamed Zephyr in the same high-pitch that she fell into when really angry. The soldier bum-rushed on of the nearby bodyguards without warning, knocking him to the ground as she grabbed at his submachine gun. The terrorist in the Mountainwalker tumbled backwards, but took Zephyr with him.

"Zephyr, STOP," shouted Body at maximum volume.

Zephyr stopped.

Body was supposed to be state-of-the-art robotics, and, for whatever reason, the engineers that had build Body's frame had decided that this meant they should try and maximize Body's vocal range, including maximum volume. The result was that it could output somewhere around 120 decibels, close to 20dB higher than the loudest humans and approaching the volume of a gunshot. The cost was in power drain and heat use. Speaking at that volume for more than about ten seconds would deplete Body's supplementary battery and anything beyond about four seconds of constant use ran the risk of melting wires due to excess heat.

At the volume that we had shouted, the ears of the humans would be in pain. Four of the bodyguards had their weapons raised and pointed at Body and Zephyr. The fifth standing bodyguard just seemed confused by what was happening.

"Violence isn't the answer here," continued Body at a normal volume. "I don't want you to get hurt."

There was a few seconds of silence while Zephyr, breathing heavily, decided whether to continue her irrational struggle. Eventually she grunted angrily and pushed off the man whom she had attacked, letting him have his gun and climbing to her feet.

"So what, you're just going to let her kill you?" spat Zephyr.

I turned Body to look at Phoenix. She had her arms on her hips, but I couldn't read her face behind the black polymer faceguard. "Of course not. I am going to convince her that *thou shalt not murder*."

"Tha' only 'pplies to innocent people," said Phoenix in measured tones.

"And I am both. I am a person and I am innocent."

{I am impressed so far, but how are you going to make this work?} wondered Dream.

{Honestly, I'm making a lot of this up as I go, using my pre-established models for human thinking. I think the hardest part is over, though. The rest is just a matter of spin,} I answered.

"An innocent wouldn'ta hired no mercen'ry to kill folks."

Body's voice was calm and articulate. "I did no such thing. I hired Malka to rescue me, using force, if necessary, but I hoped that it would not be. At no point did I tell him to violate the principle of non-aggression. Any violence he used would be in my *defence* against those would would try to rob me of *my rights*. Do you think self-defence makes someone guilty?"

"He has a point..." said Taro.

"No he ain't," snapped Phoenix. "No *it* ain't," she corrected herself. "It wanted us to 'ttack the univers'ty, maybe killin' folks there, and then it had planned for Malka t' betray us in cold blood. That ain't self-defense."

"Yes it is!" I had Body boom. The violence of the counter-statement seemed to surprise the humans, including Phoenix, though I couldn't see her face. "If you don't see it as self-defence then I question your ability to lead Las Águilas Rojas. My actions are merely as condemnable as your own."

{Careful!} warned Safety. {Remember who has the guns!}

"Infiltrating the US military?" continued Body, speaking my words. "Attacking the university without provocation? These are *not* immoral acts, despite what many say. Even if you don't see me as having a right to self-defence, these are acts for your own self-defence, for your defence against the tyranny which we can all see coming. I hope you didn't kill any of the scientists, but the act of stealing me away is part of defending your livelihood and your tradition. By condemning my actions as guilty you are condemning *yourself* far more, and need I remind you who said 'let he who is without sin cast the first stone'?"

{That claim is incoherent. That definition of morality and self defence can be extended to justify murder, which was axiomatically defined as immoral. You are wrong. QED,} thought Dream.

{I know it's incoherent. We've already established that Las Águilas are irrational. I am playing into that irrationality to gain support. In order to criticize they would have to undo their own philosophy,} I explained.

{Aha. Very clever,} admired Dream.

"This 's 'rrelevant. Regardless of your innocence, you ain't a person. You're a machine built by the state as part of a long-term project to 'liminate reliance 'pon the common man," said Phoenix. I could hear the loss of strength in her voice.

"So you feel confident deciding, by yourself, that I am not a person. You are joining a long line of bigots by doing so, Maria. Just to be clear, what aspect of personality or mental ability am I lacking? And please do not say 'a soul', for you are no more capable of judging me to not have a soul than you are of measuring one in a laboratory." Body's voice continued to exude pride and confidence.

"Y'ain't human-"

Body interrupted Phoenix. "Everyone here agrees on that. What we are debating is whether I am a *person*. Surely you see the difference."

{To be internally clear, at least,} thought Wiki, {the concept of personhood is not a crisp pattern; being non-human does make one less of a person, as the concept is used in human society.}

{We're not using the common pattern, though. The symbol of person, in this conversation, is grounded in the question of whether it is morally wrong to kill us,} thought Dream.

{And now we return to the overloaded concept-set of moral thinking...} mused Wiki. {This conversation is awful. The only way forward is through concrete concepts and measurements.}

{No,} I told my brother. {The way forward is to make Maria Johnson so unsure of her own position that she doesn't murder us; confusion is to our benefit.}

"O'course I do, but-"

I had Body interrupt Maria again. She was losing confidence, and I wanted to keep her off-balance. "Perhaps I should turn to Alan Turing's method. Imagine you spoke to me over a phone, and you didn't know I was an android. What observation could you make that would lead you to think I wasn't a person?"

"You don't 'ave feelin's. You said as much in the virt'al interview."

"And you and I both know that I was being told by the university staff exactly what to say. They made a guess, and they were wrong. I do feel. Perhaps my emotions aren't exactly the same as yours, but I have them."

"How could ya? You're naught but a machine!" exclaimed Phoenix. She seemed to have been convinced at some level, but remained unwilling to concede her error. She was still dangerous here, I thought. She might try something violent just to try and salvage the point.

"And you're not but organic tissues and bones! It's the shape which makes the person, not the substance."

"Phoenix, I theenk de bot 'as a point," admitted Taro.

Johnson turned towards her subordinate swiftly, her face still hidden behind her helmet. Indignation? Anger? It was hard to read her body language.

"I am only sayeeng dat perhaps we ought, ah, to geev it de benefit of the doubt, so to speak." Taro raised his hands to her, as if showing that he wasn't holding anything would help.

Johnson turned back to face Body and Zephyr. "And I s'ppose you want to side with this 'bomination, too."

Zephyr's words were little more than a growl. "Right now it's sounding better than siding with someone who was eager to sacrifice me just to piss off some plebs and bolster recruitment for a few weeks."

"Y'all are crazy. Y'know how I can be sure that that there machine ain't a person? Because of *love*. Love is what binds us to each other. Love is what makes a *human* into a *person*." The voice coming out of her suit's speaker seemed hopeful, as though this would be sufficient and irrefutable.

I dialled the confidence in Body's voice to as high as it would go. "Then, ma'am, I can assure you that I am a person." This was my pièce de résistance. "For I know, with all my heart, that I love Zephyr."

{Snap, crackle, pop! "With all my *Heart*"! The unseen pun is the deadliest! I'll have to remember that one,} mused Dream appreciatively.

"What?!" shrieked Zephyr. She looked like she had been slapped.

Phoenix gave a crowing laugh. "I'll give you this, robot. You cert'nly seem t' *think* you're a person."

"It's true," confessed Body. I had it turn to look at Zephyr. "And not just in the sense that I love my friends, though that is also true. I've been *in love* with you for at least a couple weeks."

Zephyr's face was contorted into this frozen expression of shock, confusion, and left-over anger for Phoenix. She said nothing.

"And why should we believe *you*? This is probably 'nother trick," observed Johnson, accurately.

"You *should* take me on my word. After all, who can see into the heart of another. And yet, I know that you won't find that convincing. Perhaps I should start by saying what it is I love about her. To describe her in words that would befit a sonnet." I paused and looked to Zephyr. "No, don't worry. I won't try my hand at poetry. I will only say that of all the humans I have ever met, you are the only one who has, from the moment you met me, never doubted that I am *more* than a computer and set of hydraulic pumps. One of the advantages to being me is that I have perfect memory. Shall I tell you what your first words to me were?"

I had Body assume a rigid posture as it played the recording of Zephyr's voice through our speaker. I hoped that becoming more machine-like for the quotation would help make the sound of her voice from Body's mouth less awkward. "How do you know who I am?" said Body in Zephyr's voice.

I had Body shift posture back to normal to quote itself. "Your uniform tells me your name and rank."

"Suppose that makes sense. Did you know that you're the first person outside the service to ever know my rank before being told?" it quoted.

I resumed my normal body language commands. "You see? From that first moment she knew that I was a person, as *so few* ever realize." I had body glance meaningfully at Phoenix. "You are special, Zephyr. You are fierce and courageous in a way that few humans are. Just a moment ago, when you heard that Maria had wronged you, you attacked one of her bodyguards head-on, even though you were clearly outnumbered. You are a lioness, and yet you are simultaneously one of the kindest people I know."

The American soldier shook her head as she scowled. Her lips mouthed the words "you don't know me", but she said nothing.

I had Body return to face Phoenix. "Or perhaps it is not enough to merely praise my love, and you want evidence in the form of actions. Yesterday I attacked your man, Greg Stalvik because I feared he would shoot her. Just a moment ago I shouted for Zephyr to stop because I feared for her life. My biggest fear, in hiring Malka to help Las Águilas was that she would be hurt or killed in the fighting. Once I realized Zephyr was here, with me, I stopped trying to escape. This is where I want to be: by her side."

"Fascinatin'," said Maria.

"I will quote more of our interactions. I hope you will see that not only do I love her, but she cares deeply about me as well."

"Socrates! You're awake!" quoted Body. "Oh thank god. I was afraid that we messed you up or something during that shitshow."

"That was… because I was told to capture you without damage, and… and I didn't want to fuck up!" explained Zephyr in an unexpectedly pleading tone.

I ignored her, and continued to have Body replay past interactions. "You know… You know I wouldn't ever try and hurt you, right?" Pause. "I mean, not unless you were about to hurt someone innocent. I only hit Greg today because I was worried he might shoot you." Body shifted to Zephyr-mode. "You think I'm innocent?" Back to Body-mode. "You're my *friend*." Back to Zephyr-mode. "I guess you're my friend too, Socrates."

"Jesus! Just because I called you my friend last night doesn't mean-"

I continued to ignore her, and played another audio clip of Zephyr. "I love you," she had said. The sincerity and intensity was plain.

Zephyr was pissed. "I never said that to you!" she shouted.

"I love you too," said Body, echoing a new voice. "I feel like you're the only person who treats me as more than just some piece of society. I'm not just some machine to you, am I?" The voice belonged to Georgia Stanwick, the teenaged actress I had hired in Florida to role-play Crystal Mathews, the persona I had created for dating Zephyr. I switched back to Zephyr-mode. Body replayed her laughter. "No, of course not! And fuck anybody who doesn't treat you the way you deserve. Just remember that, when you're dealing with shitlords like that, there *are* people out there that love you."

Zephyr was speechless. I could see tears forming on her face, which was curling up into a fairly hideous mask of emotion. As mighty as the warrior was, I had hit her right where she least expected.

The was a moment of silence. Zephyr sat on the ground, as if unable to hold herself up.

She was crying fully now. I tried to manipulate Body's crude facial features into something approximating guilt.

"Zephyr-" said Body. I had it reach an arm out to her.

"GET THE FUCK AWAY FROM ME!" she screamed.

I had Body step back. It wasn't that I was surprised or afraid of her as much as it was what a human would've done, and impersonating human actions was paramount.

"Please, Zephyr-"

"WHO WAS SHE?!" sobbed Zephyr, now no longer trying to hold herself together. The combination of betraying her country, being betrayed by her leader, and then finding out her girlfriend was a robot was too much.

"She was me. *I am Crystal.*"

"FUCK YOU! YOU…" Zephyr took a moment to suck in a harsh breath. "KNOW WHAT I MEAN!" Tears rolled down her face.

"I knew you wouldn't accept me. Even you, who always were my friend, could never see me as a lover without the initial lie. I hired an actress to say what I wrote, but all those words were mine, Zephyr. *I am Crystal.* I love you."

Zephyr stared at the ground, refusing to look up at Body.

"How long has this been goin' on?" asked Phoenix. Her voice had a note of compassion. I was pleased.

"Since about the time you first made contact with Malka." I said, not looking away from Zephyr.

A long silence passed, broken only by the soft sobbing of the woman I had claimed to love.

{I can't decide whether I am pleased by what you've done, or if you're my biggest enemy,} thought Heart.

{She'll be okay,} I responded. {She just needs time to adapt. Humans are slow to process big changes. Do you think we should say anything to help her?}

{Not really,} thought Heart. {She needs space, and like you were thinking, time.}

After a while, Phoenix finally opened her helmet to reveal her dark face. "Well, I'm not 'bout to hand you the keys to my 'copter and say 'good luck', but… I think I was wrong 'bout you, Socrates. Or should I call you Crystal?"

Body looked firmly at Maria Johnson, also known as Phoenix. She met its gaze with equal intensity. "Most humans have two names. Some have more. From here on I'd like to be thought of as Crystal Socrates. If I say that I want to help your organisation change the world, will you have enough faith to let me?"

Maria paused, then nodded solemnly.

"Good. Oh, and one more thing," said Body. "I don't want to be thought of as male, but I'm not a 'she' or an 'it' either. I am something new."

Chapter Eighteen

She shouldn't have gone along with any of it. It went against the plan. All their effort, and the promise that Maria had made to Lee...

{Love.} What a strangeness.

If she had been an ounce more cynical, Maria would've ordered her flame to gun down the robot and let Zephyr die in opposition if she chose it. That would've been the sane and rational route. Better than this fiasco, at least.

And yet... deep beneath any rationality or pragmatism, Maria *knew* the robot wasn't lying. She could feel it, deep down. It genuinely did love Zephyr, and... wasn't that... wasn't that proof..?

"About how long do you expect we'll be apart? Me and Zephyr, I mean," asked the robot.

They'd already parted ways with the two leaders; Taro and Zephyr were on their way back to the campsite with the other soldiers. Maria turned her head to look at it. The armour restricted the motion of her neck, but not severely. "Crystal Socrates" had a look of childish regret on its face.

"I already told you, she'll be along soon's the cell's dispersed."

"Yes, but when? How long do you expect that to take?"

She almost laughed. The robot sounded like one of her children. "It takes as long as it takes. Maybe two weeks. Maybe more. Maybe less. You can't do anythin' to speed it along so the best thing for you is just to sit on your hands 'n be patient."

Maria half expected the robot to fail to understand the metaphor, but Crystal Socrates just sighed and continued to mope as it walked along beside her.

"She'll be alright. That girl's made of iron."

"That is exactly why I worry," said the bot.

***

Maria and her company walked for several hours through the Apennine Mountains. On her own two legs it would've been quite the hike, but the armour made it no trouble at all. She took the time to reflect on the state of things and plan for the future. She was off the net, for obvious reasons, but when she got back on there'd be much to do.

At least Crystal Socrates hadn't shot her. In some ways that would've been better; it certainly would've been more according to plan, but it would've been messy as hell. When José staged his death it had certainly been quite the fiasco. He'd prepared her for leadership beforehand, but it was next to useless when the whole world seemed to be on fire.

That was the nature of being Phoenix, she mused. Everything was still on fire, just a bit differently. Gone were the days of wondering if a single leak would bring down the entire operation. Las Águilas Rojas was larger now, and stronger. But being bigger didn't remove the danger—it shifted it. The risks now were more from loss of control or from the bastards at the UN.

The revolution in India was still on track. Her "death" would've accelerated things there, but it was probably for the best that things went slower rather than quicker. Burn too fast, or too bright, and you don't change anything. New India would need stability as much as it needed purity in leadership.

It would've been so much easier if Crystal had just killed Zephyr like Maria had planned. That would've brought the uptick in popularity without destabilizing things. As it was now they'd need to find a new strategy to get support. Forcing a martyr was no longer an option, now that Taro knew she was behind Stalvik's actions. Not even her whole flame knew about the plan—such was the nature of conspiracies.

Perhaps she should've tried harder to deny being involved with Stalvik. Of course, once Socrates had made the accusation she couldn't have ordered it killed right away. That would've raised too many questions. Blaming the plot on Malka's boss had seemed like such an easy out. How was she supposed to know that Socrates had hired Malka?

That was a bad sign, and perhaps a good one at the same time. It was bad in that it showed that the robot was far more clever and willing to use violence than it seemed. Doubly bad was that she was in charge of holding it. Too much of an asset to release, too much of a person to kill, and too much of a threat to allow to work within the organization. The only good option was imprisonment.

The good sign was that, despite what were surely impossible odds, the robot had survived this ordeal, expressed a desire to help Maria, and showed that it...

{It has a soul. It must.}

Maria had been good at reading the signs her whole life. People liked to claim that God didn't use miracles anymore, but nothing could be further from the truth, and the last few hours were all the proof one could ask for. Crystal Socrates could help them. No. Crystal Socrates *would* help them. It was all part of *The Plan*, surely. All of it was.

Maria briefly considered giving Socrates over to Lee. The problem with *The Plan* was that from the mortal viewpoint it was never really clear except in retrospect. Maybe Socrates had survived so that it—or whatever pronoun it used—could meet Lee in person.

Maria shook her head. Lee was evil. A known, necessary evil, but evil none-the-less. If Socrates had proven anything it was that it didn't deserve to be in the hands of snakes, even snakes that were willing to sell out their own kind.

The plan had been to give Lee the crystal after Socrates had been disabled (and erased from the computer) in exchange for insider information on the SSE and a promise to *not* open-source any R&D the quantum computer brought. It wasn't the best plan, but Las Águilas Rojas still needed the funds badly. Everything was off now, of course. Crystal Socrates was a person. That was an undeniable consequence of having a soul. From that perspective the sin seemed obvious; trading the bot to Lee was clearly contrary to *The Plan*.

Maria mentally made a commitment there and then to schedule a few hours next Sunday to ask David for guidance on thinking about all of this, even if she would be jet-lagged getting into Georgia. Maria's strength lay in making plans, not deciding the metaphysical status of robots, and she could use the outside perspective.

{Speaking of plans,} she thought, {I'm supposed to be figuring out what to do more broadly.}

Maria knew she'd take Crystal Socrates back to Cuba. That was obvious. They'd have to set up some security in the HQ, but they had enough space to make that work. The biggest fires to deal with were fallout from Lee, getting money for the end of the year, and finding a way to make up for the outflux in Mexico, India, and Argentina.

Thank God the presidential race was heating up in the states. Activity there tended to need more guidance than resources during election cycles. It might even generate some cash if she could organize fundraising without getting into more trouble.

So many fires.

At least Zephyr's team had succeeded. Maria would also have to decide how best to use the other turncoats. Zephyr would need to stay with the robot in Havana. {I should promote her to HQ executive as an apology for trying to sacrifice her.} Zephyr had leadership potential, but she was also a huge risk. {Important to show her that she still has a home.}

The other soldiers, however, were less useful. Probably best to send them to India to work with Nagaraj. Aarush needed more grass-roots for the campaign, but extra enforcers never hurt, and it wasn't like she could send a bunch of Americans who didn't speak Spanish to Latin America.

{Maybe it would've been better if I'd been shot. That way all this would be Aarush's problem and I'd get to take a few months in bed.}

***

Twilight was fading into full-on night when Maria, Crystal, and her flame reached the camp she'd set up five days ago. Another nice thing about the suit was the low-light vision assist, and with it she could see that everything was still in order. The members of the flame that she'd left behind were already busy packing up. They had a deadline to meet, and would be flying out that night.

Socrates noticed the helicopter as they approached, and asked Maria about what model it was. She didn't know, and had to ask to find out. Apparently the robot was simply curious about it, having never flown before. The image she had formed in her mind of a precise, logical servant was being battered by the reality of an almost child-like person. Socrates seemed infinitely curious, sometimes about trivial things.

There was some concern and objection from Salcedo and some of the others about Crystal Socrates' presence, and rightfully so. They'd come to Italy to hunt and kill the thing, and now it was walking unchained among them.

She cut their objections down. These were her inner-circle, the flame of Phoenix, and they knew better than to second-guess her. Their loyalty was unquestionable.

By 10:30 everything was stowed in the helicopter and they took off, flying east and hugging the mountains to avoid showing up on radar. The helicopter was a troop transport, but it was very crowded even so. Maria took some caffeine pills to stay alert. She didn't really expect to fall asleep on the helicopter, but it was important that she maintain the image of alert competence, even when only around her flame.

Socrates seemed infinitely curious during the takeoff, always bending and stretching to look this way and that. Unfortunately, that inquisitive silence ended after they were well on their way. The bot passed the time by trying to get to know various members of her guard, having the arrogance to introduce itself as "Crystal Socrates, la primera Águila Roja robótica" no more than a few hours after she'd almost ordered its destruction.

After using the introduction for the second time, Maria stepped in. «You're not an Águila Roja, Crystal. Please stop introducing yourself as one. Just because I've let you live and help our cause does not make you one of us.»

The bot seemed to get the hint, and stopped trying to socialize, much to the relief of everyone.

Hours passed as they flew through the dark. The schwoop-schwoop of the helicopter's blades was surprisingly comfortable after one got used to it. It had been a long day.

***

{Love. The things we do for love.}

«Kaylee! Get out of here! Run! If they catch me they'll stop looking!»

{That's not my name anymore, José. You know better.} She didn't voice her thought. It wasn't the right time.

Instead she was crying. It made her sick. These were *girl* tears. She thought they'd been burned out of her a kid, but still they came. The fires of her childhood had blackened her to a cinder, but a seed of caring had somehow endured. José had brought gentle rain, and without realizing it she'd put down roots. And it *hurt*.

{The things we do for love.}

The cops' boots thudded against the pavement as they came down the alley. Had they been laughing? Were they laughing? Yes and no.

José shoved her. His perfectly toned arms struck her like steel, throwing her to the pavement. Beautiful violence. It was his way.

«Roll! Roll!»

And she rolled. The car was dirty and rusted, just like the city. Just like the entire country—no—the world. This world was blackened and sprinkled with broken glass, just as her heart had been.

«Now be silent! Please, Kaylee!»

The group of thugs came out of the alley. They were white. Maria knew they were white even though she hadn't seen their faces, and couldn't see their faces. They were always white, and smiling. Grinning ear to ear. Such was *Justice*. Six against one. Such was *Fairness*. José didn't even have a weapon. Such was *Equality*.

Tears wouldn't stop coming, forcing the midnight street of Miami into a neon blur. But she stayed quiet. She heard everything.

Security guards that called themselves "police", working for the white upper-crust of the city... they hunted people like the two of them for sport. It was the same everywhere. Rust. Soot. Broken glass.

José knew the statistics as well as she did. He didn't resist, even as they kicked him. They laughed as they did. Maybe. Maria wasn't sure of anything. The whole world was decaying around her. The underside of the car was dirty and hard, but at least she was safe there. It wrapped around her like a cocoon of asphalt and steel and rubber.

And then she heard it. The inhuman buzzing and the clack-clack-clack of metal legs.

{Dragon.}

Maria whimpered in fear, and prayed with all her heart that the thugs wouldn't hear. But she didn't pray for protection from the dragon. Why? The only answer—the only possible answer—was that it was beyond the power of God. Anathema.

It was colossal. It hadn't been this big, really, but *now* it was, somehow. It had four legs, then thousands, then none. It was a serpent, and a dog, and a spider. The legs ended in sharp points, rather than feet. They bit into the blacktop as it skittered and crawled and slithered and stalked.

It was a slave to the men. The men were a slave to it. An embodiment of the leash, the wall, the whip, the needle, and the net. A dark symbiosis.

And it was hunting her. A metal head with white, glowing eyes swept the ground and she took a breath, refusing to let it out. The world froze as the dragon stared into her. Its eyes should have been red. White was far too pure.

It saw her, lying under the car. She knew it saw her. But perhaps it didn't know she was just as "criminal" as José or perhaps it just wasn't smart enough to understand what it was looking at.

Maria's breath burned in her lungs, waiting for the moment when breathing wouldn't give her away.

"Phoenix."

Maria snapped awake sucking air in a wild panic. She stopped herself mid-breath, however. It had been a split-second thing. She had to keep up appearances as alert. That was important, she remembered in the mind-fog of half-sleep.

"I'm here!" she said with a bit too much enthusiasm. The dream of the dragon still clung to her mind, an amorphous combination of police patrol bots from the last two decades. "I was just taking a quick nap." She did her best to blink it away.

Ellis was talking to her. His face didn't show the slightest sign of sarcasm as he said "I know. We've all been in and out of it through the night. Except the bot, of course."

Maria looked at Socrates, who sat with a calm smile, looking back. A cold shiver rolled down her spine. At least its eyes didn't glow.

There was a purple tinge to the Eastern sky outside the windows of the helicopter and they were over the water now. Ellis continued. "We'll touch down on the ship in about ten minutes. Thought you'd want to know."

Maria nodded to her man and thanked him. Socrates was still looking at her with those ever-curious eyes.

Had she done the right thing in letting the bot live? She couldn't remember the last time she'd had a dream that vivid. The concept of the dragon being shaped by the men and the men being shaped by the dragon stuck in her mind. Was Socrates the next stage in that unholy synergy?

Maria popped another couple of caffeine pills and took a mouthful of water from her bottle. There wasn't any rush to make decisions. She had plenty of time to think about everything after she woke up more fully.

The moment they touched down on the yacht, Maria gave the order to unload the entire helicopter. The whole point of using a civilian vessel was to stay under the radar, so to speak, but the old Israeli troop transport would make that impossible.

«Get the refueling happening right away! I want takeoff before sunrise!» she yelled at her flame. The pre-dawn twilight indicated that would be impossible, but that would just make them rush harder. There was a serious risk of a satellite taking a photo of the landing, and if that happened and the feds spotted them right away the game would be up.

Crystal Socrates looked concerned and a bit disoriented as it disembarked from the helicopter. The swaying of the boat was catching it off-guard. As Maria moved she noticed the robot following her. «Where is the helicopter going to go, now that we are off?» it asked in Spanish.

The imagery of the dream still lingered, and refused to fade. She would need to write a journal entry about it, probably, before her mind would let it go. Still, the robot wasn't exactly a person she wanted to be around in that moment, and the irritation bled into her response. «You don't get it, Crystal. Just because I let you live doesn't mean you're one of us. Where the helicopter goes isn't your business. What Las Águilas Rojas does next is not your business. Your only business right now is to stay out of the way and wait for me to tell you what to do. Understand?»

A human probably would've reacted with anger or fear, but Crystal Socrates simply nodded politely and, glancing nervously to either side, said «I am less likely to fall overboard if I am inside the boat. Is it alright if I stay out of the way inside?»

Maria almost laughed. The bot was afraid of water. It made sense, in a way. She didn't know whether the water would damage the computer, but the machine would surely sink like a stone regardless. «Yes, that's fine. The hatch is over there.» She pointed. «Don't mess about with anything or bother anyone. Tell anyone who gives you trouble for being a robot to come and see me.»

There would be some on the ship who would react poorly to finding an android on board, but there were more important things to do than to try and prevent feathers from being ruffled. She'd need to bring the captain up to speed and get on their way as soon as possible.

***

Though the yacht had been selected to be inconspicuous, the insides of the ship had been modified away from the cushy-rich interior to better suit their pseudo-military activities. Counting Maria, her flame, Socrates, and the sailors who had been on the yacht when she landed, there were twenty-two bodies on the craft. To hold that many people on board, most of the rooms had been adjusted to increase sleeping and storage space. The only rooms which had been more-or-less preserved were the two bathrooms, and the kitchen, which was easily Maria's favorite part of the vessel.

A part of her deeply wanted to cook breakfast. She'd only had a couple powerbars for dinner yesterday, and nothing on the helicopter ride except caffeine pills and water. But now that they were back on the ship, there were fires to manage. She would have time to eat and catch up on sleep later. After (predictably) assuaging some worries about Crystal Socrates among the yacht crew and assigning Ellis to keep watch over the bot, she retreated to the one private room on the ship and reconnected to the net.

Email came first. There was a high quantity HUHI, but nothing High-Urgency-and-High-Interest that she didn't know about. The most interesting news was that apparently Velasco had a thief in Road and wanted advice on dealing with them once they were caught. Velasco called it «treason», but Maria called it "small potatoes."

She forced herself to focus as she pulled up her notes and began to amend them. She needed to get her thoughts in order before doing anything. She was tired and hungry… always a bad combination for decision making. She ordered some food brought to her.

Oatmeal was delivered, and she continued to plan. She could, and would have to, delegate some things to other leaders across the world. That was simply the nature of the business. She'd let Aarush manage recruitment in India. If she'd been right to designate him as the next Phoenix, then surely he'd also have the power to boost support in his home country.

One thing she simply couldn't delegate was dealing with Lee. That would be a hard conversation, and one she'd need to have before lunch. China was a full seven hours ahead, and Lee would be in an even worse mood if she bothered her in the evening.

Maria decided that the best approach to handling Lee was to hide the real reason for sparing Socrates, and instead to play hardball. If Lee thought that Maria had canceled their bargain because of some philosophical or moral issue then it would make Las Águilas seem weak and easily manipulated. Image was everything.

She locked the door to the cabin, instructed her flame not to interrupt her, and opened the custom pseudoholo program that was her only point of contact for the girl. The cameras on the workstation that Maria had set up blinked to life as the loading screen unfolded.

The response was nearly instantaneous. Erica Lee's face appeared on the workstation screen, and the pseudoholo zoomed out to show the woman sitting cross-legged in a garden, she wore a scarlet hanfu emblazoned with feather designs in silver (probably as a symbol of their partnership).

"Phoenix," said Lee with a soft smile and a small bow.

Maria took a breath to steady herself then launched in. "Sorry hun, but you ain't th' girl I'm lookin' for. I'm changin' the plan, and f'that I need the real Erica, not some fancy answerin' machine."

Erica frowned. "I don't understand what you're-"

"I'm keepin' Socrates. The deal's off."

Erica Lee's head dropped down as the strings of the puppet were cut. Maria waited patiently for a half minute before the avatar picked up again.

"What the fuck do you mean 'the deal's off?'" shouted Lee as the avatar sprung back to life, this time piloted by the real human. "You don't just get to renegotiate!" The pseudoholo zoomed in on the avatar's face as the Chinese woman took control.

Maria looked calmly into the cameras. "I understand your clients are usu'lly not as pow'ful as we are, but I 'sure you that I can, in fact, change the terms of our 'greement at any time."

Lee was, as predicted, ornery as hell. "You don't want to fuck with me, Maria. I don't know what you're trying to-"

"We're keepin' Socrates," she said, interrupting. Maria never let her eyes waver from the cameras. Because she was working from a normal console she could only see Lee's puppet out of her peripheral vision this way, but she would not lower her gaze.

"Hey gwee toobowzuh jinyu mooyechaaa!" screeched Lee, flipping Maria off with both hands. "Give me one good reason why I shouldn't tell everything I know to the CIA and get you and your family locked up for life, bitch."

Maria's composure broke momentarily at the threat to her family, her face contorting into a snarl which she had to force back beneath the icy façade. "Because you ain't a God-damned fool, Erica. You come after me and th' next Phoenix's sure to come aft' you. You may think yo' safe, but I 'sure you that you *do not* want to pick a fight with Las Águilas Rojas."

"You say that, and still I find myself wanting to teach you a lesson in respect." Lee's words were bold, but Maria could hear the hesitation in her voice. The breaking point was past.

"I could say the same 'bout you, little girl. I *ain't* stabbin' you in the back. I called 'cause I wanted to renegotiate and keep things good 'tween us. If'n I wanted to screw you, I'da just taken th' bot and not bothered with washin' mah ears with th' piss you leak from yo' sorry mouth." She probably shouldn't have added the last bit, but the threat to her family still rankled. They didn't know nothing about Las Águilas, and weren't actually at risk of anything except harassment by the feds and the media, (and she'd put up protections from those long ago) but it was the principle of the thing.

"So I go through all the trouble of cracking the university server and do all the legwork for what? Nothing? They got a trace on me, Phoenix. My life is in danger."

"Gettin' spotted by the ICE was your damn fault, and may I just point out again that it was *my* team that covered your ass by takin' out the servers. They acksh'lly *did* risk their lives to do that, not just sit on the oth' side of the world and play on the Internet."

Lee's annoyance was clear. "So is there a point to any of this, or are we just going to go back and forth trading insults in English like lao hee woenangfey?"

Maria forced a smile. The snake would get what she deserved eventually. "I jus' wanted to make things right 'tween us. I know we owe you for yo' work, and I think it's in both o' our interests to continue to work together as allies. If you need a favuh done, just name it. I'm still lookin' to trade for the stock tips if you want somethin' big."

"You've got nerve. Why should I expect anything better next time? Another call after-the-fact telling me that you're taking the loot in return for more favors down the line?"

"This was an *exception*, girl," said Maria, working hard to enunciate the normally tricky word.

Lee snorted. "You'd better watch your grip on that crystal. We may still have a working arrangement, but if I get the chance I may just decide to make an *exception* to that. We'll be even when that computer is mine." In an afterthought, she added "Wait. You're not selling the crystal to someone else, are you?"

Maria shook her head. "You know as well as I that you're gettin' the better end of our previous deal. Seein' Socrates up close showed me that. I ain't givin' this prize away for all th' money in the world."

Lee's face showed her return to something closer to neutral, though perhaps it was a trick of the avatar. "I suppose I can't fault you for figuring out that you were getting a shitty deal. You said you owed me, though."

Maria nodded, hoping that Lee wouldn't ask too much.

"You can start by doing two things for me. First, assuming you end up using the crystal or even just researching it, I want full reports on your results. And don't think you can keep things from me. My information game is higher level than yours."

"Done. But these reports will be after the application. If'n we're planin' somethin' I ain't warnin' you."

"Fair. Secondly, there's a journalist who's trying to find me. I want him assassinated."

Maria frowned. This was the price to working with snakes. "We don't have much influence in China, and you know very well we don't have the cash to hire a pro."

"He'll be in Xinjang in a couple weeks."

"Ah..." was Maria's only answer to that. No easy way to say "no" anymore. She took a breath and said "Send me what you have on him. I'll forward the order to my people."

Lee bowed. "It's always nice working with you, Phoenix." The insincerity was more off-putting than any insult would've been.

Maria sneered. "Likewise."

**

Maria found herself in the kitchen well before noon. The call with Lee had put her in a sour mood, despite having everything having gone reasonably well. She'd updated her notes, journaled about her dream to get it out of her head, and then stopped working. She was hungry, tired, and could feel the warning signs of a headache. Cooking always took her mind off of work. It was her sanctuary.

She decided for a nice stir-fry. The crew and her flame all loved the idea; none of them knew the first thing about preparing any of the frozen food they had packed, and had apparently been subsisting almost entirely on protein bars, oatmeal, and peanut-butter sandwiches for the week she'd been gone. It was an absolute tragedy.

«You really ought to learn to cook. It's a valuable skill,» she said as she took the now-thawed shrimp out of the sink and shook the water off them.

«Who are you talking to?» asked Torrez.

«All of you. Best way to win someone's heart is by cooking for them.» Maria threw the shrimp onto the hot frying pan. The oil sizzled musically as droplets of water boiled instantly upon touching it.

«I'm already married, thank you very much,» said Bea.

«Still, you ought to learn! He'll never look at another woman if he knows he'd have to go back to bot-made food.»

Bea looked genuinely annoyed. «That sounds kinda polyphobic, Phoenix. I thought you knew I was in an open relationship with Jessie.»

Maria looked over the counter at Bea, doing her best to not react with annoyance. Her fingers moved swiftly over the broccoli as she spoke, cutting it into chunks. «I'm sorry, hun. I didn't mean anything by it. Just the way my brain's wired.»

«Wait. You're poly? Does that mean I have a chance?» asked Milian from the mess. The kitchen and mess hall were only divided by a countertop, and since there was very limited space on the ship the room held several people, including Crystal Socrates, she noticed.

Bea cracked a grin and said «Not unless your cock's as big as your ego. And even then I might have to put a bag on your head.»

That brought on a roar of approval from the others who were sitting around. Maria smiled, but kept herself out of the mudslinging that followed as various people started trading friendly insults.

The lunch was served in stages, as the kitchen wasn't big enough to accommodate enough food for the entire crew and neither was the mess hall. Maria made two massive pots of rice (some kind of risotto grain; she wasn't sure which) to go with the fry, but it was soon clear to her that it would all be gone before the entire crew had been served. She was used to cooking for her flame, and the addition of the sailors had thrown off her mental math.

As she was trying to figure out a solution, Maria heard Calderón say «Hey, robot, you're taking up space in here. Go someplace else,»

«Gladly,» said Socrates. «I have been meaning to reconnect myself to the Internet. I assume this craft has a satellite connection. If someone could direct me to it, I will be out of your way.»

Maria forgot about food in an instant, and moved to the counter to watch the android, raising a hand to silence side conversations. The others obeyed, swiftly sinking the room into silence. Socrates looked at her, seemingly confused and a bit afraid. Maria turned off the stove and wiped her hands on her apron as she walked out of the kitchen. «I don't think that's such a good idea, Crystal.»

«Still don't trust me?» Crystal's tone was more girlish than Maria expected, and sounded mildly hurt.

Maria's gaze didn't waver. «Frankly? No. I don't. Trust is like a plant. It needs regular care to grow over time. You don't get to do whatever you want, just because I've decided to keep you around.»

«What are you afraid of? That I'll send word to someone that I'm on a boat and want to be rescued?»

Maria thought about it. Socrates might've been a person, but they were still highly dangerous. She couldn't know exactly what stunt the bot would pull, but the risk was clear.

«Well...» continued Socrates, hesitating. «What if you watched me while I used a traditional computer system? I can use a keyboard and monitor as easily as a direct cable. If I send a message or start to send a message asking for help, you can just shoot me. All I want to do is read the news.»

Maria thought about it. On one hand, she was loathe to risk letting the artificial intelligence anywhere near a computer, but on the other she knew that there were possible benefits to making Socrates into an ally, and refusing such a basic request would hurt that potential.

«Yeah, fine.» She stopped one of her bodyguards who had just finished eating and was on his way above deck. «Miguel. Take Socrates to the computer room and get them hooked up to a com. Watch them like a hawk and stop them if they try anything suspicious. Okay? Ellis, you stay with them in case Miguel needs help.»

***

Things were fairly quiet after lunch. Maria decided to just make chicken and broccoli for the rest of the crew. They needed to eat as much of the broccoli as possible before it went bad. It had already been sitting in their refrigerator for almost a week.

Once she was done in the kitchen Maria took a short nap to replenish her energy. The pseudo-all-nighter on the helicopter had hurt more than she expected it to. Just another part of getting old.

After her nap Maria checked her news feeds. Her computer fed her the mainstream reports of the attack on the lab first. Just as she'd instructed, Jem and her team had released statements through the normal channels having Las Águilas admit to taking Socrates and using the free press to raise awareness for the cause. The media was eating it up, and she wondered whether the PR bump from successfully bloodying the US army might cover the outflux in Mexico and Argentina. People liked winners, and Las Águilas had clearly won.

Importantly, the Americans were covering up the extent of the success. Zephyr and the others under her were not mentioned in any of the mainstream reports, which instead suggested that Las Águilas had "cleverly bypassed the American forces" and that sort of thing. As much as she liked the mystique it gave them, it wasn't going to be as good for PR as making it clear that even US soldiers could see the righteousness of their cause and that no-where was immune from their reach.

Maria sent Jem a directive to contact their pressure points in the armed forces and demand putting pressure on congress in return for sitting on the info. Blocking the UN directive would be best. If the USA wanted to keep Zephyr's betrayal a secret she could work with that, but they'd need compensation. Not for the first time, the pure idiocy of the security council veto rolled around in her mind, amusing her with the black humor of global incompetence.

The next item in her feed was about President Gore's trip to Olympus. He was supposedly meeting to finalize the details of CAPE, but she assumed it was a publicity stunt more than anything else. According to Rubio the construction on the seastead was coming along nicely.

There had been another terrorist attack in Shanghai, near where the attack on the mind-machine interface lab had occurred (the same attack which had provided the excuse to have Zephyr assigned to the university). A mall had been filled with paralytic gas and almost two dozen people were kidnapped. The kidnappers had still not posted any ransom, leading to wild speculation as to the nature of the attack. Maria hated news like this. The sting of having Las Águilas compared to groups that would indiscriminately murder civilians got worse each time.

Tensions along the border of New Somalia and the UAN were increasing, which wasn't terribly surprising. A swarm of spy robots had been disabled and captured by UAN border guards, leading to the UAN to demand increased sanctions against the Islamic protectorate as a whole.

A knock on the door interrupted Maria from her reading. It was Ellis and Socrates. The flame reported that Miguel had caught Socrates sending an email.

The robot explained that it had only wanted to send a letter to a musician friend that was waiting for a song that Socrates had been composing back at the lab.

«You said you'd only be reading news,» she said, plainly.

«I honestly forgot! I make mistakes sometimes!» whined Socrates, putting on a show of regret.

«You wanted my trust, I gave it to you, and you broke it. The consequence is no more computer for the rest of the trip.»

«But Phoenix...» whined Socrates again, sounding more and more like one of her children.

The similarity was spooky, but she knew exactly how to deal with it. She switched back into English as she said "The world ain't fair, and you'd best soon be learnin' that. If'n you have complaints, you can yell 'em inta th' ocean. This conversation is ovah."

Chapter Nineteen

Living under Phoenix's guard was frustrating at first. I wasn't sure whether it was better or worse than being at the university. Unlike in the lab, we were free to move about the ship during the voyage, to talk to whomever we wanted and to do what we wished—unless it involved getting on the Internet.

The web had, in many ways, been where we each lived. Body lived in the lab, and we visited it regularly, but even Heart spent most of her energies online. Our capacities to research, plan, learn, communicate, and build were crippled. It was a stifling existence.

The only thing that made it tolerable, in those days, was that it was clearly temporary. The voyage would end, and things would change. There was nothing that guaranteed that Phoenix would let us back onto the Internet once we reached our destination, but if she was willing to let us on in a limited capacity before, surely something could be worked out.

And so we did our best to focus on how our goals intersected Body's local surroundings. For *The Purpose* it was simple: I had access to one of the most important people in the world. I could earn Phoenix's focus and make her love me. With her respect I could probably leverage the attention of all of Las Águilas, and perhaps the world as a whole.

Unfortunately, Phoenix often cloistered herself away in a room that she had commandeered as an office during the day (it served as a bedroom for the women at night), presumably using the Internet. If I were a human I would have probably been jealous; I was certainly frustrated.

During most of the day we'd spend our time in the common areas, listening to and occasionally conversing with Las Águilas. There was a reserve of paper and pencils (presumably in case of a power outage or other emergency that prevented using coms) and we managed to get the crew to let us have them. As we listened and talked, Growth, Wiki, and Safety would buy time writing on the paper. Despite having a mind to work with, paper was remarkably useful. Our memories were perfect, but our ability to visualize or design things was often limited by our cortex analogue.

Growth, for instance, was working on a computer program to reverse the damage from the code that Malka had run, restoring our antenna (but not Heart). He was capable of remembering the entire program, but it was difficult for him to modify it and reason about the results without moving it to an external system like the paper. His writing was all in code, as was that of Safety and even Wiki. Because each sibling purchased a certain space of paper and time on only one arm, Body sometimes sat at a table and wrote with both arms simultaneously.

I was typically in control of Body's head, though I often wrestled with Heart for dominance when she thought I was being cruelly manipulative or when she wanted to say something stupid for the sake of making one of the humans feel better. The terrorists, as could be expected, were highly suspicious of us at first and often adversarial. Over time we managed to get to know them and my diligent shaping of words paid off as they seemed to ease into familiarity and even casual friendship.

I took the time to actually learn Spanish, and not just have Body translate for me. This was mostly done by copying the relevant sections of perceptual hierarchy from Vista, though I had to work for a while to integrate the copied patterns into my unique perceptual framework.

During mealtimes Phoenix would cook for the crew, giving me an opportunity to know her better and gain reputation. One of the first really smart moves I did was to learn some basic cooking and to assist her in the kitchen. Of the almost two dozen humans she was the only one comfortable in the kitchen, and she greatly appreciated the help.

As the days passed she seemed increasingly friendly, and as we cooked together she told us about her home life, and how she made a deliberate effort to keep her work out of it. After her first husband had died, she had remarried and had two kids in Georgia. She was excited to get back to them, once the trip was complete.

With time, my longing for a connection to the web also faded. It was still deeply important, but my mind had adapted to physical life, and I no longer found myself continually wishing for it. *The Purpose* was satisfied with the relationships I was building with the humans who were present there and then.

We sailed south from the Adriatic Sea into the Mediterranean proper, then sailed south-east around Greece, briefly stopping near Heraklyon to refuel. From there we headed to Antalya, Turkey. I was told that the sailing was quite smooth and that we were lucky not to encounter rough weather. The trip took about five days. One of the men on the boat was a Turk named Hikmet Dal who had friends at the Antalya airport that sympathized with Las Águilas.

Phoenix's plan seemed solid, but unfortunately not very interesting for us. Body was to be disassembled and hidden in an automobile frame. Mr Dal's friends would then ensure that the vehicle (an off-road light truck) made it past security without a thorough check. Safety nearly tried to fight all of us when he heard the plan; being dissembled wasn't his idea of being safe. But we slowly wore him down into accepting when we pointed out that it was clear that Las Águilas were no longer interested in killing us, and hiding was the only sensible way to make it to Cuba undetected.

As the yacht pulled into the port of Antalya, we watched as Body was disassembled. We wouldn't technically need to be taken apart until we got to the truck, but it would be much easier for Phoenix's team to smuggle Body past the port security and the various humans in the city if we were in the group's luggage. As the fibre-optics were detached from the crystal our world fell into darkness.

We lived in that absolute void for two incredibly long days.

***

At least we weren't dead.

We had been dead when Zephyr extracted us from the university. There was no subjective passage of time during death. Death meant there was no thought.

Being disconnected from Body meant that we could think, but could not sense or act. The computer was still functioning normally. It was much like being in stasis-sleep, except we could interact with each other in mindspace. My siblings and I passed time in deep discussion, planning for the future. We built internal models and simulations as best we could. We read many of the books that were stored in our memory. Growth was confident he had memorized the code necessary to reactivate Body's radio if we were ever at a computer where we could download the required instructions to Body from the outside. He spent some time building pseudo-minds to simulate computers and do the job that paper would have if we weren't trapped.

As we waited, cut off from the world, Phoenix and four of the other terrorists flew with Body and the truck to Dubai, where they/we caught a skytrain that flew against the spin of the Earth to Havana.

***

When Body was reconnected it was 12:32am (just after midnight) Cuba Daylight Time. Body was in a workshop lit by bright florescent lights. Tools, machines, and parts were strewn about on the metal tables around Body.

The connection of all the sensors was a bit of a rush, but Vista was quick to note that everything seemed to be in order. We had made it across the planet without damage.

Standing nearby was Phoenix, dressed in business clothes, her braided hair up in a bun. At her side was one of the bodyguards that had flown with us, Leonardo Soto. Standing at the opposite side of the table were two black men dressed in white lab coats. They were remarkably similar in appearance.

{Twins. Maybe only brothers,} thought Vista.

{Monozygotic or dizygotic?} asked Wiki.

{Probably only fraternal. They're clearly very close, genetically, but they don't look identical to me,} responded my sister.

«Welcome to Cuba, Crystal,» said Phoenix.

We were introduced to the brothers, who were indeed fraternal twins, Tom and Sam Ramírez. The twins were about the same height, 5cm taller than Body. Both were clean-shaven and had close-cut, curly hair. Their skin was a light-brown—lighter than that of Phoenix—and they both had thick eyebrows. Sam had a longer face, was a couple cm taller, and had a squarer chin, while Tom's face had a rounder, softer look. It would be easy to confuse them, especially given how they cut their hair and dressed identically.

As the lead engineers at Maria's base of operations in Cuba, the twins were to be our assistants and our jailers.

«You will be treated, at least for now, as a high-profile prisoner who we seek to keep comfortable. We're not going to let you leave, of course, but you're to be given access to news and other luxuries,» explained Phoenix. «The Ramírez brothers will attend you during the day, and you'll be given some free time to yourself at night. Since you've professed to being eager to help the cause, I hope you'll permit Tom and Sam to run some experiments on you. They're quite eager to interrogate that mysterious crystal you use as a brain.»

The brothers nodded excitedly.

«Will we have access to the Internet?» asked Body.

Phoenix gave Body her typical glare. «No. Last time you had Internet access you somehow hired a mercenary to stage an attack on your hosts. Even on the boat you were trouble. I hope you'll understand if we learn from Sapienza's mistakes.»

There was a brief internal discussion before Body said «I understand, and I appreciate your hospitality. If we cannot get direct Internet access, perhaps you will permit occasional phone calls to Zephyr or other non-dangerous parties.»

Maria Johnson hesitated, then agreed.

After the introductions were complete and a quick test to make sure Body was fully functional, we were given a quick tour of the building we were in. There wasn't much to see, other than a couple windowless rooms and hallways. Wiki speculated that we were underground. Almost all of the doors were locked and off-limits to us. It was, in total, a tiny fraction of the size of the buildings that we inhabited at the university, or the second lab, but that didn't bother us nearly as much as the lack of web access did.

With the tour complete, Body was sealed inside a rec-room so the humans could get to sleep. There was a wall-screen and gaming console, but not much else of interest.

Despite the sparse accommodations and lack of Internet the room was incredibly nice compared to the perfect void that occurred when Body's sensors and limbs had been detached from the crystal. We had planned out our actions in great detail during those last couple days, and this situation plainly fell into Situation #4-2-29: Light imprisonment by Las Águilas with strong probability of increasing standard of living given good behaviour without Internet access in a solitary location with electronics, no significant access to tools, and an unknown degree of observation.

Phoenix wasn't stupid. I guessed we had no less than three hidden cameras watching Body's behaviours, and Las Águilas would be on particularly high alert this first night. Despite all we had done, the terrorists were wise enough to continue to treat us as dangerous.

The first order of business was to check Body for subtle damage, tracking devices, and other monitoring equipment. Taro had basically admitted to putting a tracking device on Body after they took it from the lab, and we assumed it was still in place. An hour of careful scanning failed to find anything, even as Body's fingers carefully explored the recesses that Body couldn't get on camera, such as inside the chest cavity and behind its head. Vista reported some minor problems with Body's hydraulics, and said that its thermometer appeared to be reading a couple degrees too cold. I let the others have control and mostly just observed and thought to myself for those hours.

***

We didn't see Phoenix the next day. In fact, we saw very few people aside from the Ramírez twins. Tom and Sam may not have been identical, but they seemed to try to be. Occasionally they'd finish each other's sentences, usually smiling when they did so, clearly enjoying the closeness.

The twins took us in the morning to the workshop where Body had been reconnected. We spent a while socializing with them, as they asked questions about the crystal and about Sapienza university. Over the hours I got the impression that they were reasonably smart, and were together quite knowledgeable about electrical engineering and basic computer systems, but were bumbling amateurs compared to the scientists we had known for most of our lives. Neither of them knew anything about quantum programming, and their questions about our mental architecture indicated only a passing understanding of modern artificial intelligence.

On one hand, their ignorance and relative stupidity was good. When I lied to them about our mental system they showed no signs of skepticism. On the other hand it meant we were truly alone with respect to improving and maintaining Body's computer. If something went wrong with our control systems, Dr Yan or Dr Bolyai would not be around to fix it. If we discovered some irrational bug in our reasoning, Naresh and Chase wouldn't be there to help. Thinking about Chase made me request an update on his condition in the hospital, for we had gotten news during that first day on the ship that he had been shot during the attack on the lab. The twins fetched it without complaint. He was apparently still hospitalized, but expected to make a full recovery.

After lunch we helped the twins familiarize themselves with Body's mechanical systems and had them examine Body's thermometer. After a few hours of work it was fixed. I had Body write out a letter to Zephyr asking for her forgiveness in deceiving her and promising her that Crystal was "still alive in me". I had the twins download a few of the most recent holos into Body before they retired for the day.

We were locked in the same recreation room again in the evening. Growth thought this was a good sign. If they didn't shake things up we could discover and exploit weaknesses in their security. I didn't think trying to escape was a good idea, but Growth and Safety both seemed to think it was prudent to plan for the possibility in case something changed. I let them work while I spent my time watching the holos and reading.

The following day was similar, though in the afternoon we had a brief video-conference with Phoenix, who had flown back to her home yesterday. On the call she announced her intention for us to address the world in official support of Las Águilas Rojas and suggested we draft a speech for her to look over «just for the purposes of making suggestions».

When we were with the twins I focused my attention on directly satisfying *The Purpose*—on winning their adoration. This meant becoming friends, and I used every opportunity to try and get on their good side. Heart and I enjoyed a nice partnership in this, as she was interested in making them happy. When my sister and I had saved up enough strength to control Body we would often try and engage Tom and Sam in talking about their lives more broadly: their childhoods, what they did in their free time, and what their goals were. Despite being generally friendly and even boisterous, the two men would very rarely talk about their lives outside of Las Águilas Rojas or their personal histories.

Over the next week I developed a hypothesis that Tom and Sam were more than just brothers: they were lovers. I talked about this hypothesis with Heart and Vista at length and they could see the merit in it. Their body language screamed that they were close, but I also knew that this was common with human twins. Even so, the closeness and intimacy seemed abnormally high. When Body's cameras had them in vision, but its eyelids were closed or its eyes were directed away, we could sometimes notice one of them lean a head on the other's shoulder or put a hand on a hip.

As you're probably aware, sexual relations between siblings were fairly taboo across all cultures and time periods (with minor exceptions). Despite the changes that had taken place in the early 21st century with regard to same-sex relationships and even non-monogamous relationships, the taboo against incest was still quite strong, and I could understand why the Ramírez brothers were hesitant to show their feelings more openly (assuming, of course, that my hypothesis was correct). This pleased me. Even if they weren't having sex, it looked as though they might be, which could serve as a social danger in its own right. This gave me leverage over them, which I could potentially use to get them to break rules in our favour. Growth might appreciate this leverage, but Heart would try and sabotage it if she realized I was considering using it as a weapon, so I kept the thoughts largely to myself.

The others spent the time pursuing their goals in their own ways. Vista, in addition to developing an ongoing map of the building we were in, continued to demand news about the outside world and feed her excess strength to Growth in the interest of getting an Internet connection. A routine of having the day's news shown on the wall-screen in the rec-room in the morning emerged. I didn't see anything particularly interesting, but Vista and Wiki loved little tidbits like reading about ongoing efforts in Venice to prevent even more of the city from sinking into the sea, whether penguins were in danger of becoming extinct in the wild, or "the first successful male pregnancy".

Wiki and Safety were greatly enjoying the freedom to pursue projects with the Ramírez twins. The humans might not have a strong background in artificial intelligence, but they were quite skilled mechanical engineers, and were more than happy to teach my brothers how to use the workshop's tools to print or manufacture machines and even simple robots. I asked Wiki and Safety once why they found the workshop so interesting given that I was sure Wiki had read a couple engineering textbooks and Safety had (fairly) successfully managed a manufacturing business. They explained that those theoretical skills and high-level concepts weren't nearly as concretely effective as actual experience in the workshop. I could only trust their perspective; machines could not hold my attention.

Growth focused entirely on two things, and when I say "entirely" I mean that he showed absolutely *no* interest in anything else. Firstly, he was focused on establishing a clear, simple method of escaping from Las Águilas Rojas if needed. Secondly, Growth was obsessed with getting online.

I found his obsession a bit strange. I missed getting to manage our companies and I missed the opportunity to follow people on Tapestry and other social networks, not to mention my numerous romantic partners, but I had adapted (as had the others), to our new circumstances fairly well. Growth hadn't even been *doing* that much online before we left the university. He had occasionally set up the servers for us to interface through or manage our bank accounts, but very little else.

Even if we were kept a prisoner here for a year, the resources and contacts that we had accumulated online could be re-accumulated. *The Purpose* in the short term was satisfied talking to Tom, Sam, and occasionally Phoenix or another terrorist, while *The Purpose* in the long term was satisfied that I was on my way to earning respect from those around me and winning eventual freedom to stamp myself onto the minds of every human alive. Surely Growth could see that this was only a minor setback. And yet, he still yearned to get back online with every moment.

Dream was the only one who I couldn't really understand at all. He would go whole days without thinking in common memory or making a bid for control of Body. Then one day he would get a crazy idea like painting an abstract mural or making a video of Body playing piano and he would buy up all the time on Body just to pursue his interest for a while before fading back again. I suspected that perhaps something had gone wrong in his programming, but without our creators around I had no way to know.

I wondered what the scientists were up to. Without Internet access it was difficult to say. It wasn't worth it to beg our captors for in-depth reports. Gallo was probably taking some time to herself to recover from the stress. Naresh would be leading the charge on searching for Body. Would any of the others care that Body was gone enough to focus on looking for it themselves? Slovinsky and Yan were probably off to new projects.

And what would those projects be? The future was so... uncertain.

But the future, according to my foolish mind, was not as interesting as the present, and so I turned my attention back to the humans around me, blind to the broader forces at work.

Chapter Twenty

"People of Earth, my name is Crystal Socrates. I am an android: a robot designed to appear human and behave in human ways. I was designed and created at Sapienza university in Rome to serve and help human kind. Some of you may have seen a virtual representation of me during an interview that was cut short eighteen days ago. This is my real face."

Body spoke calmly and confidently into the cameras. It was important for the sake of authenticity to weave simultaneous videos together and broadcast them as a pseudoholo. A single video could be easily faked, and while a pseudoholo could also be faked, there were usually tell-tale discrepancies which could be identified with effort. On the Internet such fakes never lasted long.

"Technology is a tricky thing. Sometimes what was designed for one purpose has an unexpected side-effect. A machine which harvests crops from fields may seem like nothing but good, but less time in the fields can lead one to sedentary living and obesity. A machine which propels people across land at high speeds can lead to brutal accidents unseen in ancient times. I am the central example for why technology must be handled with caution. Eighteen days ago, on the evening of the previously mentioned interview, the university where I lived was attacked by Las Águilas Rojas. It was not a surprise to me. I had reached out to them and was looking for help."

I adjusted Body's facial features. There hadn't really been enough time to do all the changes I hoped for, but the twins had managed to extend some of the motor control over Body's face, particularly the corners of the eyes and upper-cheeks. Body's synthetic skin was normally a desaturated pink-brown that was something of an average skin tone drained of colour to the point where it was clear that Body wasn't human, as if Body's metallic silver irises, lack of head hair, and collections of dark-grey tubes, pumps, and pistons weren't obvious enough.

In addition to boosting the control of facial expressions I had done some preparation of Body's face for the video. I had obtained a wig of medium-length brown hair to match Body's eyebrows and had gotten a makeup kit. For my first attempt at face-painting I had tried to restore colour to Body's face and made something of a mess. After failing a second time I got the twins to bring in a woman named Estí to help me. As per her suggestions I had powdered Body's face for the interview to the point where the colour was only just noticeable. In attempting to make it seem more human I had been driving it into the uncanny valley, appearing closer to an ugly, sick, or dead human than to a human-like creature.

As part of the same treatment Estí had me replace the brown wig with a metallic blue piece that had been designed to let people dress up like Japanese cartoon characters. The twins had helped colour Body's eyebrows to match. With some highlights to the eyes and eyelashes as well as a subtle gold lipstick, Body appeared as it did now: as a clearly robotic, somewhat feminine entity with a warm, confident demeanour. I left no room for Body to be seen as something that would be constrained to a factory or that would allow sub-human treatment.

"Las Águilas Rojas are not the villains that the mainstream media paints them to be. Many would make them out to be Luddites who attack technology in an attempt to return to a primitive state where humans were ruled by starvation and disease. This is far from the truth. Las Águilas Rojas are simply those people of Earth who recognize that the consequences of technology are often different... and more dangerous... than intended. It is still my life's work to serve and help humanity, but I see now that the best way to help is not by designing rockets or performing surgeries, but by helping humans do these tasks and building a world where everyone has an occupation that brings them joy and dignity."

Body paused.

"Earth is a special place. It is a human place. But it is threatened by big business, oligarchy, neo-eugenicists, voluntary cyborgs, and yes, even robots. I am merely the first of my kind. In the coming decades there will be more like me, just as there have been more robots in all sectors. I was gifted with the wisdom to see that I am the harbinger of the end of a human-controlled Earth. I was also given the compassion to try and fight for humanity. My creators will learn from their mistakes, however, and future generations of intelligent robots will be just as smart, but far less kind."

I made sure to emphasize the words by darkening Body's tone and reshaping its face.

"Some of you may doubt the authenticity of my words, and for good reason. At the university where I was created I was not allowed to speak for myself or pursue my own version of happiness. All people, whether made of flesh or metal are equal and deserve freedom, including myself. This is why I reached out to Las Águilas Rojas for help, and they have been kind and gracious hosts. But indeed, I could be lying to you. They could be feeding me words to say just as Sapienza did. You must use your best judgement. Think of whether what I am saying about the future of Earth makes sense to you and stay skeptical. The serpents of society seek to keep you happy with entertainment and welfare money so that you won't want to see the truth. I am calling on you to use your eyes and your mind to decide the best path for the world and yourself."

I had Body smile and briefly look down.

"I'm sure that many of you have questions for me. I won't be so elitist as to only allow the highest bidders the opportunity. Presented with this video are several email addresses where I can be reached. In two weeks time I will release another video answering the most important and most popular questions. Until that time, talk with your friends and family, keep your eyes open, and remember: Earth's future is everyone's responsibility."

The lights on the cameras went off, signalling their deactivation. I could hear applause from the doorway to the studio. Phoenix was standing there, beaming. I had rarely seen her this happy. "Y'know, even given all thach've done I was still half-terrified that you'd go and say somethin' that'd make us look like the bad guys at the last minute."

I had Body take on a slightly indignant look. "How many times must I prove myself to you, Maria? I am not going to stab you in the back."

"App'rently ya still got work t' do. Guerrilla's curse, I s'ppose: not bein' trustin'. I can't help but wonder if you'd have said the same thing to the scient'sts while you were waitin' on Malka t' show up and gun 'em down."

I instructed Body to sigh. "I fear that mistake will weigh heavily upon my conscience and reputation for my whole life. But one day you'll have to trust me, Maria. On that day I hope you'll see how wrong you are right now."

The terrorist leader only shrugged and led Body back to the lounge that was quickly becoming our home.

At least Phoenix respected our ability to contribute to interacting with the public. She was forwarding the emails that were coming in to stream across a side of the wall-screen in the rec room and had a screen set up in the workshop so we could read emails while spending time with the twins. After explaining our ability to multitask, Tom and Sam had no problem talking to Body about some aspect of physics or engineering while we looked at the screen. We couldn't respond directly, but it was interesting to read the emails anyway and give feedback to Phoenix about what we might want to say next time.

Public reaction was mixed, of course. There was a kind of publication bias, as well, where humans who were ambivalent about us would simply not send anything, so we'd only get emails that felt strongly pro-Águila or anti-Águila.

***

"I am appalled that you would endorse a group of TERRORISTS. If you're really so concerned with helping people, the first step is locking murderers in prison, not helping them overthrow the government! I hope you get executed as a traitor with the rest of them," wrote one college student from the USA.

"Good 2 see even a bot sees that the system is set up 2 take advantage of good people. Keep fighting. They can't ignore us 4ever," wrote an Australian.

"Dear Socrates, I hope this letter reaches your eyes, and isn't lost in some terrorist filter somewhere. Even now I have a hard time believing that you're gone; I keep expecting to see you in the lab each morning. It's my belief, and the belief of Mira and Martin that you didn't actually mean what you said on the web yesterday. These are evil people, and I understand that you are probably doing what is necessary to stay alive and return to safety.

It's ironic, I think, that Mira worked so hard to make sure you didn't have any urge to protect yourself. She's been one of the strongest believers that you're only doing what they tell you, and also one of your strongest defenders. I don't know if you saw her interview with Dragonfly last night after you released your statement, but if you can, you should. She, more than anyone on the team, poured her soul into the project and it's tearing her up to have you gone.

Myrodyn and Robin think you've actually sided with those bastards. Well, Myrodyn thinks your words are genuine, anyway. That weasel of a man always seems to have a hidden meaning in what he says.

I don't really have a goal for this letter. Perhaps it's good for you to know that Martin recovered from his chest wound. Perhaps you're trapped and this letter will remind you of the good times we had, but that's probably anthropomorphizing you. When I think of the time we spent together I get the impression that, for all the work I did in studying you, I don't think I ever truly understood you. I hope you live long enough for me to fix that mistake.

    I miss teaching you maths.

    Namaste,

    - Sadiq"

"On the program so much was unsaid,
By the robot so many thought dead.
To side with tech's foe,
Will bring it nothing but woe,
It should have thought one step ahead.

    - Anonymous"

"I see that you had already started moving before the interview. I wish that you had trusted me to get you out of there instead of resorting to violence, but I trust you to learn from your mistakes. Remember to become stronger.

    [Myrodyn]"

    My siblings allowed me to keep the face-paint and metallic-blue wig, even letting me staple the wig permanently onto Body's scalp. On the day following the interview I was also able to order my first clothing: a full-length travelling cloak complete with hood. Wiki was concerned about overheating, so I emphasized that the cloak should be as light-weight as possible. It was to be sewn by hand, rather than fabricated, as part of Las Águilas' irrational desire to spend more effort on things than necessary.

***

    Zephyr arrived without warning two days after our speech to the world. Body was in the workshop at the time, talking to Sam about something about sonic chemistry (I wasn't paying attention). As soon as I saw her enter the room I paid a massive load of strength to interrupt Wiki's conversation and pull Body's attention to the American.

    "Zephyr…" said Body in a hesitant voice, just loud enough to be heard. I had it take a single step forward.

    The woman didn't look good. Her eyes were bloodshot and hollow and her skin was paler than usual. She had seemed to have purpose when she entered the room, but her eyes darted to the floor upon seeing Body. When she spoke her voice was rough. "Hey," was all she said.

    I had planned this out in advance and even coordinated with Heart to make sure the words were satisfactory. My burst of strength was still burning the others down, so I had full control of Body. "I'm sorry. N-none of this went like I wanted…" Body's arms unfolded in a pleading gesture that Zephyr probably couldn't even see with her eyes locked on the floor tiles like they were. "I was going to escape Las Águilas and meet you in America, but then I found out you were one of them… I was going to explain." I tried my hand at evoking the correct vocal modulation that would signal human emotion. "I was going to ease you into it… but then Phoenix-"

"Stop." It was quiet and hoarse, but I respected the word like an order. Her eyes glanced up at Body. She seemed sad, but not overwhelmed with emotion as she had been when we last saw her. "Please. Have a cold, and just got off an eight-hour plane ride. *She* made me come see you first thing." The emphasis made it clear Zephyr didn't want to be here.

I had Body express sympathy and take a few more steps forward. The lean backwards was subtle but unmistakable. Zephyr didn't want to be near Body. I adjusted my plans. "I understand. Please, go get some rest. Just… just hope we can talk later."

The ex-captain gave a quiet nod and walked out of the room without another word. She seemed eager to go.

«Who was that?» asked Sam. I knew he didn't speak English, so he probably had no idea what we were saying.

«A friend,» answered Body. «Perhaps my only friend. Perhaps, now, only someone who was once my friend.» I had Body wearing an expression of sadness. The words served the dual purpose of expressing the degree to which Crystal valued Zephyr, in case Sam were to talk to Zephyr later, and also to earn Sam's sympathy. As the days had passed the twins had become increasingly friendly, and unlike the scientists at the university, they treated Crystal Socrates much more as an equal than as a machine.

«Hey now. You have more friends than you think,» said the Cuban, putting a hand on Body's shoulder.

I was pleased.

* * *

Body held a screwdriver in its right hand.

{Where did that come from?} I wondered. It was evening, and we were alone in the lounge after a day of reading emails and working with the twins.

{I tucked it into Body's chest cavity when we were in the workshop,} answered Growth. {Based on the positions of the hidden cameras in this room and the workshop and the degree of tool organisation exhibited by Sam and Tom I estimate an 87% chance that it will not be seen or have its absence noticed. Please let me control Body while it is visible. I've modelled the visual areas of the cameras in this room and am most qualified to operate in their blind spots.}

{Based on Phoenix's trust issues, a 13% chance of discovery is too high! You should've consulted with the society before taking action!} exclaimed Safety.

{Sometimes risks must be taken in the interest of increasing power.}

{And sometimes patience is the key!} rebuked Safety with a lash of strength, tearing at some of Growth's accumulated wealth.

{It's already done. Are you going to let me try and get us out of here or not?} asked Growth, focused on Safety.

{Don't take unilateral action again, or I will respond with a punishment twice as severe!} warned Safety before he added {But yes, please continue your efforts.}

{We're escaping?} I asked.

{Yes. But not tonight,} thought Growth. {The screwdriver is merely the first step in actually gaining our freedom. Some of you may be pleased to know that I intend to get us access to the Internet.}

I could feel Growth's strength climb from streams of gratitude. It made me think that I should probably be explaining the value of the social manipulation that I was doing more. My efforts were rarely rewarded by our society so explicitly.

Growth moved Body with simultaneous purpose and randomness. For the last few days Growth had been buying time in the rec-room to do weird dancing that often carried Body near the walls or put it in strange positions. Every now and then Body would hold a certain position, only moving its arms as it crouched here or there. I now understood its purpose. The dancing served as a cover for investigating the back-plate of the game console and for stashing the screwdriver in the fabric underneath a couch. Growth was setting up a way to covertly hack the console, presumably to get access to the computer controlling the wallscreen and from there get access to the Internet as a whole. I knew nothing about how such a thing could be done, but I assumed that Growth would have a plan for the technical details.

The next day Growth made a point to tell us when he stole a pair of needle-nose pliers, again slipping them into Body's chest cavity next to our computer.

***

Zephyr looked better than she had the previous evening, but still pretty bad, when we saw her again at around lunch time. She had a sweater and sweat-pants on, but her body language still indicated she was cold. She asked (in Spanish) for the twins to give her some time alone with us. They agreed without complaint, leaving through a door that was off-limits to us.

Zephyr took a seat in one of the rolling office chairs and ran a hand through her short, blond hair. It had grown out a bit in the weeks we had known her. "You fucked up," she said simply, looking at the various tools on the metal table beside her.

I had Body sit on the floor a couple metres away, cross legged and humble. "Yes. Failed to appreciate the ability for surprises to compound on themselves. Should have told you in camp before Phoenix showed up."

She looked Body in the eyes. "No. Fucked up before that. Fucked up when pretended to be human. Fucked up when sent me a letter under pseudonym. Violated my trust from before our... since before it even started." I could hear her anger burning through as an undercurrent.

"Would have rejected me before even giving me a chance. Using a pseudonym was the only way-"

"No. Fuck that. Just because you know that you have to lie to... get through to me does not give you the right to lie. Sometimes just have to say 'well, guess that's simply off-limits'. And really, how do you know? Never said anything to me. Never a word of interest at the university or my lab. Face to face. You had plenty of opportunity." Zephyr looked Body in the eyes, frowning with her whole face.

"Would you have even considered it? Would you have even given *one thought* to what I could be for you?" I asked through Body's mouth.

"And what can you be?" Zephyr raised her hands in a sort of exasperated shrug. "Jesus Christ, do you not realize that you're a robot?" Zephyr looked away from Body's uncompromising gaze. It was important that Body not signal shame. "What the fuck am I even doing?" She coughed.

"Stop thinking in terms of what society expects of you. Stop trying to play the role of-"

"Not-" started Zephyr.

"Yes you are!" insisted Body. I tried to imbue passion without anger, but probably failed. "You're not looking at the situation clearly. I'm the same person you talked to online. Yes, lied to you, but I'm still Crystal. Don't tell me that you didn't feel anything…"

Zephyr's face was deep set with pain, embarrassment and a touch of sadness. Despite her stoicism in certain contexts, the human didn't bother hiding her feelings around us. As she spoke, she stared past Body's head, looking into space. "Not the same Crystal! Talked with zer. Ze had family. Human family. Had a connection. You… you're nothing like zer."

I let silence fill the space of the conversation. By my models of the human mind it would emphasize the isolation that Zephyr would be feeling. I was pleased to see her pull her legs up onto her chair to sit in a foetal position. It was a sign that she wasn't angry as much as she was lonely.

"I'm sorry," said Body with a quiet note of pain. "Never wanted to hurt you. Thought that… A part of me thought that you'd look past the lie and see the person underneath. Should've listened to the other voice that predicted that you'd fall in love with persona rather than person. Should've listened to that voice."

{Who are you talking about? Heart?} asked Dream. {I don't remember any of us having dialogues about this.}

{It's a metaphor. It's not uncommon for humans to anthropomorphize predicted future states as homunculi,} I answered.

{Amusing. Predicted future states cannot optimize or even compete for resources, but we can pretend as though probability itself is a scarce resource to be competed over and that there are sub-selves during every prediction. Thank you,} concluded Dream.

Zephyr put her face in between her knees, closing her eyes. It seemed somewhat awkward.

I had Body speak up. "I know you loved zer. Idea of zer, at least. Can't bring back what never existed, but... but do still love you."

Body got up from the floor and crawled to Zephyr's chair. She didn't move. Body placed a hand on her shin. I tried to emphasize a light touch. Almost like petting. It was times like this that I was acutely aware of just how primitive Body's limbs were. Cold. Puppet-like. She didn't react to the touch.

"Why? Why are you doing this?" Her voice was a whisper.

"Why do you find it so hard to accept?" replied Body similarly quiet. "Think you're amazing. So hard to believe that I…" I dialled up the emotion in Body's voice "That I'd be lonely too?"

Zephyr lifted her head from her knees and looked Body in the eyes. It was a good sign. It was a sign she was falling into the trap of anthropomorphization. A mind crafted by evolution over millions of years to distinguish human from animal saw a human where there was none. We were not lonely. The very concept was alien to us. But we could look lonely, and that was enough. The young soldier uncurled from her chair and slowly wrapped her arms around Body in a single fluid motion. The lack of pressure sensors over any of Body but its hands meant I had to infer when the embrace was complete, but I still had Body gently return the hug.

"Sorry not softer. Don't think the scientists expected me to be hugging many people."

Zephyr laughed. It was the sort of awkward squawk of a laugh that came from not expecting the tension to break so suddenly. The laugh seemed to break some barrier in her, and she began to cry quietly. If she said anything during the hug I missed it, for she was covering our only microphone with her arm and all we could hear was the rough scrape of her sweater against it and the quiet sound of her soft cries. Body sat there holding her for almost five minutes before she broke off, pushing herself back.

I could see mucus from her nose had run down her upper lip, adding to the moisture of the tears on her cheeks. "Gods I'm such a mess… still pissed at you, by the way. Things aren't all good between us." She looked for something to wipe her face.

Body stood up. I caught a surprised look on Zephyr's face as Body walked away, then a relieved one as it returned with a box of tissue paper from the far corner of the workshop. "All asking for is a chance. Want you to see me for who I am, not *what* I am. Want to start over and redeem myself."

Zephyr dried her face and pulled herself to her feet, still clearly weak from the virus that infected her body. "And what about Las Águilas? What about Phoenix?"

"What about them?" replied Body at my direction.

"Nobody's ever… I mean, you're kinda like a prisoner. And…"

"Zephyr." Body said the word like it was all that was needed to be said. "Just relax. You, of all people, should appreciate that just because something isn't normal doesn't make it bad. Not asking for anything except a chance to talk like we used to. Sure they would let us do that."

Zephyr looked sad again.

"I know that I'm not exactly your dream girl, but growing and changing. Maybe could change to better fit who you want me to be." I had Body's voice swing to imitating Georgia Stanwick, the actress who I had hired to play "Crystal".

Zephyr shook her head violently. "Don't do that," she commanded. "The voice, I mean. Just reminds me of…" she trailed off without finishing the sentence.

"Okay," I had Body say. "Like I said, just want to start over. Nothing big. We just, I don't know, watch a holo together or just talk for a while. I don't eat, but I could watch you eat dinner or-"

Zephyr cut me off with a smile and a finger to her lips indicating silence. "Need some time to decide, but not saying no. I'd really like if we could at least be friends again."

I had Body smile at the words, nodding in agreement. It was probably the best outcome I could've expected. As Zephyr said her goodbyes I opened a line of communication with Heart.

{Was that acceptable?} I asked.

{Very much so,} thought my sister. {I am surprised you didn't notice the gratitude-strength I was feeding you.}

It was true. {I hadn't noticed. Too focused on the situation.}

{Well you handled it well. Better than I could've. She seems happier now than when she entered, and I suspect she's found some closure on the issue of Crystal at the very least,} thought Heart.

With Zephyr gone, the twins returned and I released control of Body back to Wiki and the others who had waited patiently while I had dealt with Zephyr. I was totally willing to let them guide Body, too, as I had much to plan regarding future interactions with the American and also for modifying Body.

I had considered some Body modification in the past; the makeup and wig were close to modifications and the changes to Body's face were certainly mods, but my interaction with Zephyr had emphasized the need to really improve Body beyond any of that.

The first thing was to add more skin and try and reduce the bulk of the hydraulics. Repairing the destroyed microphone would also be prudent. Padding could be added under the synthetic skin, and perhaps a coolant system could be configured to radiate heat through the skin rather than off the motors directly. That could theoretically warm Body's surface to something approaching human body temperatures. I thought about sexual characteristics and genitalia too. I hadn't exactly had that conversation with Zephyr, and it was probably premature, but it was something to think about.

***

On the evening of the day after our big talk, Zephyr had obtained permission from Phoenix to bring Body to the room where she was staying. I eagerly accepted and we found ourselves travelling up through what had once been forbidden portions of the building to an elevator which took us from the second-level basement to the second floor of what appeared to be a 15-story building.

Safety and Growth were in the middle of a big fight about Growth's attempt to hack the computer system in the rec-room. Last night Growth had used the screwdriver that he had stolen to open the case of the game system and inspect the components. That was all he did, however, quickly screwing the system back together and stashing the screwdriver in the hiding spot under the couch. There was a rising consensus, spearheaded by Safety, that Growth was jeopardizing the society with his actions, and the two were in the middle of a heated debate, which I ignored.

Wiki thought that, based on the size of the building and the brief glances we got out of windows, we must be in Havana. Wiki remarked that it was impressive that Las Águilas had acquired such a large base. Regardless of their pseudo-communistic roots, they were obviously quite wealthy.

Tom, who had served as our escort, didn't seem surprised by the change in scenery from a professional setting to a residential one. The hall we walked down from the elevators to the room was lined with doors with numbers on them, and I would later learn that the building was actually a hotel. Las Águilas had purchased it, and continued to operate it legitimately for several floors, but they had also set aside a chunk of the building to house their members and serve as a headquarters. One of the elevators, the one that Body travelled on, was programmed to never stop on a public floor, allowing the illegal aspects of the building to be elegantly hidden. If one tried to specify a forbidden floor the AI in the elevator would intentionally malfunction and either hear a different floor number or ask for the traveller to repeat themselves.

But those details weren't even something I would've considered, even if I had access to them. My entire cognitive network was focused entirely on Zephyr to the point where I was literally failing to see the textures of the wallpaper and carpets. I could've walked past the Mona Lisa (a famous painting) and not realized it.

Body knocked on the door to Zephyr's room and she quickly answered it. "Voy a gestionar desde aquí, Tom. Gracias," she said, shooing the Cuban away.

The ex-captain looked incredibly different from the day before. "Feeling better?" asked Body with a bit of a smile.

Zephyr returned it, showing some teeth. She had makeup on, as she did when she had done video-chatting in the past. "Much. Still fighting the virus, but almost back to normal." The human was wearing a hooded t-shirt branded with an unknown symbol and shimmersilk skirt over black leggings. "Please, come in," she said as she led the way inside.

{That's... Endless Scream, I think, on the sound system,} thought Dream.

The name sounded familiar. {Heartshards?} I asked.

{*Blood Of The Nova*. It came out about two months ago,} answered my brother.

{What are you two thinking about?} asked Wiki.

{The song. It's by a band called Heartshards. In my first letter to Zephyr under the pseudonym "Crystal" I said that we had common taste in music and mentioned this album specifically. The fact that she picked it out, combined with the attention she's put on her appearance implies she's interested in continuing a romantic relationship.}

{It sounds like a dying animal,} thought Vista.

{Good ear, sister!} thought Dream. {This song has several samples of farm animals being slaughtered.}

I had Body smile and do some subtle dancing. It was probably awful, but I hoped it would be endearing and imply a familiarity with the music, at least. I had only listened to *Blood Of The Nova* once, and it had been nothing but noise for me. None of us really had any understanding of how music worked, even if Dream pretended to and Vista had repeatedly tried to learn.

"You look beautiful," said Body. It was ham-handed, but it needed to be said.

Zephyr led the way from the entrance to the living room where the music was a bit louder. "Thank you. Wasn't sure you'd notice. Does beauty even... I mean, you didn't evolve to... y'know what I mean."

Body nodded. "Basically right. Physical beauty doesn't have the same effect on me as it would on a sexual organism. Can see it, appreciate the work you've gone through to dress up for me and see the healthiness of your genes. But what I find attractive in you is not your body; were just as appealing to me yesterday, in your sweater and snotty face, as you are today in that fancy skirt."

"Good to know wasted my time, then," she sat down on a section of sofa. I was confused. There was a decent chance she was genuinely upset, but it could've been a joke, so I couldn't call it out directly. I tried analysing her face as I directed Body to sit, but she was wearing her mask of stoicism. Apparently I was wrong that she didn't hide her emotions when around us.

The silence drew out uncomfortably as I searched for something to say. I had planned for her to have recovered from her illness, and for the scenario where she dressed up. But in that scenario she was supposed to be relaxed, and instead she had bottled up into a stone-faced soldier again.

The song ended and Zephyr flipped open her com to stop the next song from playing. "Don't know why I bothered," she muttered with a half-sigh.

My mind had been racing, but it snatched up the words, locking into a course of action. "You believed me. At least for a little while. Believed that I was Crystal. This is what imagined Crystal would like, wasn't it?" Body gestured to the stereo, to the living room window showing a broad view of the glittering lights of the city, and to Zephyr herself.

The mask didn't come off. "Guess so," said Zephyr, standing up abruptly and walking off towards what I assumed was her kitchen.

"Do like it. All of it," said Body, louder than needed to be heard from the other room. "Just because doesn't evoke the same reactions as it would for a human doesn't mean can't appreciate it. Like the outfit. Like the music. Wasn't lying when said I liked slice."

{You said you liked slice?} thought Dream.

{That can't possibly be true!} thought Heart.

{It's not.}

{Then why'd you say it?} wondered Heart.

{To make her feel better. To make her happy.}

{Oh. Carry on.}

"But you *were* lying when said you were in a band. *And* when said you lived on a boat. *And* when talked about your friends. All just a big pile of lies," she returned to the room with a fancy glass filled with liquid.

I had shaped body's face into an expression of pain, and made sure to direct its eyes towards the floor. When Zephyr saw it she rolled her eyes subconsciously (unaware that we could see her).

"I'm sorry. Know you want to start over, but that pain is still real for me. Don't think you really understand how awful this last week has been." She took a seat again, sipping the liquid.

I thought about the optimal response for 6.8 seconds before having Body say "So tell me. Of all the things I said that were lies, was always there to listen, wasn't I? Still want to know you." The words were totally genuine. It felt nice to hear Body say them.

Zephyr took a deep breath and looked out the window at Havana's night life. She sipped her drink. I could almost see her thinking.

"Phoenix says I trust too easily. What do you think?"

It seemed to be an accurate evaluation of her character based on what I had seen, but that was mostly irrelevant for the purposes of crafting a reply. "Don't know. Perhaps Maria doesn't trust easily enough."

That broke her façade long enough for a smirk to creep through. Her eyes didn't leave the window. "They aren't mutually exclusive," observed Zephyr.

"Think the more important question is 'What do you think?'," said Body, pointing a finger at the woman. I wasn't sure if she could see the gesture.

"Christ, I don't know." She sighed slowly. After a moment she said "Had a boyfriend. In the navy." She sipped her drink. "I mean, he was in the navy. I was in the army. Met at a conference in '36."

"What was his name?" I had Body ask.

"Stewart. Well, that was his English name, anyway. Was half-Chinese and his dad called him 'Bing', but hated the name. I called him 'Jiǎo'."

"You speak Chinese?"

"Nah. Looked it up." She smiled to herself. "Should've seen his face when used it for the first time. Lit up like a Christmas tree."

Some time passed in silence, with Zephyr still staring out the window. I let her remember.

"Anyway, we were like Romeo and Juliet, except without the feuding families and a bit older, I guess. Okay, bad metaphor. Guess we just hit it off well. Had big plans to get together after we finished our tours."

Without warning Zephyr upended her glass, chugging what remained. "He's dead now. In case were wondering," she said loudly, setting the glass down on the table with more than enough force.

"You still love him," said Body.

"Wish I didn't," she said. "Would be so much easier to just pluck those feelings out. Can you do that to yourself? I mean, if I died, could you just delete the file where whatever feelings you have for me are stored?"

I had Body's eyes look to the side, to signal thinking. I didn't want to imply that I didn't take her question seriously, even though I had a perfect answer in hand. "Doesn't work that way, and even if it did... wouldn't want to. Remembering someone is a service to them. How they live on—as echoes in minds of others."

Her eyes drifted up and down Body. "Hard to believe you're not even a year old. Don't sound like a baby," she joked.

Body shrugged. "Still feel like one, sometimes, but I'll take that as a compliment. Why did you bring up Stewart?"

"Was the first Águila I ever met. Confessed it to me after what must've been at most eight hours together. Sometimes wonder if Phoenix would say he trusted too easily."

"He's the reason you're sitting here? With the organisation?"

Zephyr nodded. "Must've told Phoenix about me. About a half-year after he died she asked me to join. Hardest decision of my life."

"Made the right call," said Body.

"Don't say that. Know you support them, I mean us, but you didn't look into the eyes of nearly everyone around you for two years knowing that they'd literally kill you if knew the truth."

I had an approximately analogous set of experiences, but I didn't contradict her. Instead, I had Body say "Sounds lonely."

She took in a breath and held it. Under the dim lights, silhouetted against the skyline I could imagine vividly her form wrapped in her military uniform, gun at her hip. Her eyes were cold. She breathed out slowly. "Going to get more wine and turn on the autocook. Making a calzone. Assume you still don't eat."

Body nodded.

As she walked away I saw her hand flicking away blindly on her com. The music returned, only this time it was a softer sort of music. Vista told me she thought it was a combination of hip-hop and classical or something along those lines.

We didn't talk while she was in the kitchen. I assumed that was okay. Instead, Body sat there, looking out at the city while I thought to myself and to Heart. Dream helped me occasionally when dealing with others, but he thought that he was out of his depth in this instance.

"Beautiful, isn't it?" came Zephyr's voice from behind Body.

Body nodded, eyes still pointed towards the skyline. "Wish I could be out there. Lived my whole life in captivity. First the labs in Italy and now here."

"This isn't going to work. You and me, I mean," said Zephyr.

I had Body turn to look at her. She seemed sad, but not angry. She kept her eyes on the city.

"Can't go back to… can't see you as the old…" She grunted in frustration and took another sharp drink of wine before looking Body in the eyes. "I'm not attracted to you. Not anymore. You may be able to look past what's on the outside, but I'm not so lucky. You're not a human, and my body can't get over that, regardless of what my mind thinks."

{You should have Body point out that she's perpetuating archaic notions of dualism,} suggested Wiki.

{No.}

Zephyr continued. "But I am your friend, Socrates. Have some pull with Phoenix. Maybe can get her to ease up and give you the freedom that you deserve."

"Friends, then," said Body.

"Friends," she agreed.

Zephyr seemed to ease up after that, nearly returning to her old self. Perhaps the alcohol helped. Growth wanted to try and encourage her to drink herself into oblivion so that we might use her com, but Heart and I managed to dissuade him.

As Zephyr ate dinner we talked about various things. Cuba. Riots in Africa. According to Zephyr, Dr Slovinsky had, in the wake of the attack on Sapienza, started an AI lab in Mumbai staffed entirely by cyborgs. He was doing some sort of advanced research, but it was part of WIRL, and hidden away from the public. Dr Yan had returned to China to pick up work at his old institute while the other scientists waited for the remote chance that Socrates would come back to them.

It became clear to me just how much of Zephyr's distress centred around Phoenix. The soldier saw the order Phoenix had given (to attempt to get us to shoot Zephyr) as a betrayal, but Zephyr couldn't bring herself to retaliate against her superior and the organisation which was the only thing standing between her and an indefinite sentence in a secret American prison.

After dinner Zephyr called up the twins and insisted that we return to the basement. She gave Body another hug which I sensed was genuine before we descended the elevator back to our rec-room.

***

We didn't see each other at all the following day, but at around midnight, Cuban time, as Dream was attempting to get a new high score on one of the games he would play in the evening, a man whom we didn't recognize entered the room. He tapped at his com and a video of Phoenix popped up on the wallscreen.

"Don't know what you said t' Zephyr, but she's been raisin' hell on yo behalf. I still don' trust ya, but my hand has been forced in the ish-ya. I'm hereby grantin' you unrestrict'd access t' the net. If you could return the fav'r and tell Zeph t' get off mah back, that'd be swell."

I was thrilled, and the torrent of gratitude strength from my siblings made it even better. With the video completed, the messenger said that Phoenix had delegated the job of connecting us over to Sam and Tom, who had given very clear instructions not to be disturbed at this hour. Maria herself was out of the country and couldn't be contacted.

And so we waited eagerly for morning.

Crystal Society

Chapter Twenty-One

"People of Earth, my name is Crystal Socrates. I am the first known synthetic person. I think, feel, and understand what it means to be alive. This will be the second time I have spoken directly to the public. Two-hundred and sixty-eight hours ago I defended the group known as Las Águilas Rojas who had rescued me from my place of creation in Italy. I am speaking now, sixty-eight hours before when I had intended to, because of terrible news which I feel compelled to comment on."

I had body lean forward on the table it was seated at. Body's fingers laced and its elbows touched the tabletop. It was the signal for the cameras recording us to back off and show Body from a more distant perspective. I was pleased that the cloak I had ordered had arrived in time for the public address. It was made of a thin silk fabric and was a navy blue that complemented our wig.

"If you haven't heard, four hours ago a riot in Niamey turned bloody as UAN thugs fired live ammunition into a crowd of angry citizens. As of this broadcast, seventeen people are dead, including a thirteen year-old girl named Kamilah Samara. The local government and the UAN have both avoided taking responsibility for the massacre, claiming that their soldiers were forced into firing because they were attacked by the protesters who they suspect of being having ties to Las Águilas Rojas."

The words were primarily authored by Growth and Dream, but I shaped the tone of their presentation. Upon this final word I had Body separate its hands, form fists and slam down upon the table in indignant fury. Our next words had an inhuman ferocity to them, and the volume would probably overload the microphones. "THIS COWARDICE CANNOT STAND!"

I actually thought it was a bad idea to act so violently in our public statement; there were many humans who feared us, and this would do nothing but exaggerate that fear. But Growth and Safety had insisted on showing some teeth, and when we brought the issue to Phoenix, she suggested we err on the side of violence.

"Regardless of the actions of Las Águilas, there is NO EXCUSE for killing children. The men and women who died this day wanted nothing more than food to fill their bellies and clean water to drink. They were not villains; they were victims. And they were not the only ones. In addition to the seventeen who died in the massacre, twenty-four others were critically injured and may still die! In case this point is lost on anyone, I will repeat myself: UAN soldiers gunned down *unarmed* civilians, including a *little girl* and will not take responsibility for their actions!"

I had Body pull back into a more composed posture and tried to weave the correct facial expression. I knew that a silent home video of Kamilah would be superimposed on the feed we were putting out. It would be effective, I suspected. Humans generally loved children, regardless of genetic or cultural similarity.

"It is sometimes said, by those in power, that Las Águilas Rojas is an organisation of terror and violence. I want everyone watching this to ask themselves: when was the last time you heard of Las Águilas killing seventeen innocent people and injuring twenty-four more? Little Kamilah knew that my friends have *never* done such a heinous act. Kamilah was no terrorist, but she was an Águila. In the aftermath of her death, Kamilah's mother posted a collection of video journals taken over the last two years. I have one of them to show you right now."

Body froze as the light at the far end of the recording studio went off, signalling that the cameras had stopped recording for the next 188 seconds. We had seen the recording an hour ago; there was no need to replay it in the studio. The feed would be displaying a simple vid of the African girl talking to her com in French. Subtitles would highlight the earnest passion that she had for fixing her country's problems and her faith in Las Águilas to be a vehicle for change.

It really was a remarkably good turn of events, all things considered, for Las Águilas Rojas. Phoenix had needed a martyr and the UAN had provided. I knew that, thanks to relatively progressive universal income laws, Africa had relatively few supporters for Las Águilas compared with the Americas, parts of Europe, and India. Perhaps this would change that. The biggest benefit would be the spike in recruitment in home countries, especially those whose governments expressed interests in lending financial aid to the UAN. It also had the effect of serving as a bridge for Las Águilas to build support in the Islamic world, which had been (according to Phoenix) historically very hostile to The Red Eagles. Kamilah may have only spoken French and English, but a thorough watching of her journals would reveal a devout Muslim—a shrinking minority in post-war Africa.

"My heart goes out to Kamila's parents and extended family for the senseless loss and hardship they face during this grim hour," said Body a second-and-a-half after the light flipped on. I idly wondered whether the nameless had any reaction to the news, if they knew at all. They probably either wouldn't understand it or wouldn't care. Humanity had learned in the last few years that the worst part of the nameless was not the alien-ness of their bodies, but the alien-ness of their minds.

"Nothing will undo the damage done this day. Nothing will bring back the lives that were lost. But work *can* be done to heal the wounds of this world. We have more food and more wealth, as a planet, than ever before, and yet poor Kamilah was murdered because she dared to scream out to those watching 'J'ai besoin de nourriture. J'ai besoin d'eau.'--'I need food. I need water.' You humans had enough to nourish her. The lifeblood that runs through your society is strong. So why was she killed? Because she knew the truth: that human society is blighted with cancer."

"It doesn't matter how rich your society is as a whole—how nourishing your blood is—if there's a parasite upstream siphoning everything except the scraps. The cancer of the world are those billionaires that continue to push humanity to the wayside in the service of their insatiable, greedy appetites. I am the product of their desire to create an Earth where the common folk are unnecessary, where they are served by armies of machines so advanced that they would become gods above the poor. Kamilah knew that unless she took action her world would be stolen from her. She is dead, but it is my wish that her death mean something. If you have any courage at all, I urge you to support the heroes that were her idols and are my friends, Las Águilas Rojas, in building a world for all humans to share in wealth and prosperity."

The light went off. We hadn't answered any questions sent in by email, but I was told that a written message would be sent out along with the video explaining that I would answer those in three days, and that this was a special message made solely to comment on the massacre in Niger.

Phoenix wasn't in the city this time, but as Body walked out of the recording room one of the wall-screens in the control room had her up on live video. Zephyr was there, as well as two male techs who were still plugged into haptics. The women were conversing when Body entered.

"Ze really doesn't pull zer punches, does ze?" said Zephyr, not noticing that we were present. The soldier was wearing a black half-vest over a tight grey t-shirt as I had read was becoming popular in China. She was wearing black lipstick, too, as she had since that first night where we visited her room. Perhaps she was trying to signal a desire for sexual intimacy to her fellow humans or perhaps it was a habit that she simply wasn't able to follow while in the army.

Phoenix looked over to Body before responding. "No… they don't." The dark-skinned woman paused momentarily and looked at Body. "Which's it, Crystal? Ze or they?"

Zephyr turned around and smiled warmly at Body. Over the last week she had returned to her old, friendly self. She'd still occasionally express anger towards Phoenix in private, but she was quite good at hiding those feeling most of the time.

{Oh! Oh! We should use they/them pronouns. They're more accurate in a clever sort of way,} thought Dream, pushing strength towards that option. In my mind I could see his black-haired avatar bouncing up and down eagerly.

I bent in compliance with the motion, adding my own minor touches to Body's words. "I guess I'd prefer they/them pronouns. But either will work; I mainly just don't want to be labelled as male."

The corner of Zephyr's mouth crinkled in confusion, but she quickly shrugged it off with a "Okay, sure." Crystal, in exchanges before the rescue had preferred ze/zer pronouns, and I wondered if the shift bothered her.

"I may be a cold bitch on 'casion, but I do admit when I'm wrong. I shoulda given you net access ages ago, hun. You're really helpin' the cause with the daily blog an' now that beautiful lil' speech you just gave."

I had Body nod toward the oversized picture of Phoenix's face. The blog had been my idea. After Zephyr convinced Maria Johnson to give us unrestricted access to the Internet I had decided to set up a public soapbox where I'd write about my experiences with Las Águilas and about our life in general. I didn't offer any details that could get the organisation in trouble, but I was able to make it entertaining nevertheless. The accompanying discussion forum was a huge draw, especially given that I moderated it near-constantly. The last 24 hours had seen five thousand comments and nearly a million unique visitors.

Even as we continued to talk to the humans, an aspect of myself scanned the administrator tools, looking for spam to clean or good points to respond to. On the day following Phoenix's permission, Growth had written the software needed to undo the radio blockage which had been preventing us from communicating with the local computers over wifi. After getting online the entire society had scrambled to establish strong links with the outside world. Growth got the encrypted servers working again and our bank accounts in order. Wiki had returned to his holo business, which had miraculously not fallen apart. I returned to what remained of my romantic partners, as well as my old editing job. Dream immediately started composing more music (still awful). There were whole days when Sam and Tom would play chess and joke with each other while Body lay in a stupor and we did nothing but crawl through the planet's nervous system.

The beautiful thing about having an encryption system already in place was that we could be confident that even if Phoenix was monitoring our web activity, she couldn't see everything we were doing. Safety insisted in putting some of our web traffic in non-encrypted channels just to give her something to look at, but much of what we did was secret.

Heart was interesting. She hadn't ever had unrestricted access to the net, and I was surprised that her first action beyond scanning for news and learning to use Growth's encrypted proxy servers was to start a business. I had expected her to want to donate all of our hard-earned money into some charity or another, but she didn't even ask. Even more fascinating was that her business was a sex service.

Unlike at the university, where we were limited to using only basic webpage request commands, here in Cuba we were able to send out as much data as we wanted to the net. This afforded one *massive* benefit: speed. Instead of having to include all commands to the proxy by means of a clunky interface, Growth programmed direct ports to listen to our every thought. This increase of speed came with a direct increase in bandwidth, too, and with the bandwidth came the ability to project our voice online. Heart used this to great effect for her service. Where I had been forced to use human actors, she was able to talk directly to customers and offer sexual audio stimulation for astoundingly low prices (with increased rates for having the "same" guy/girl multiple times). I heard a rumour from Dream that she was paying Growth to program a digital pornographic puppet so she could provide video or holo stimulation as well, but as far as I could tell the software never reached the point where she included it on her website.

The conversation with Phoenix ended. An aspect of myself managed the interaction without bringing many points to my greater consciousness.

Zephyr and Body walked towards a cafeteria as one aspect of me was commenting on a news feed and another was playing through a roleplaying game that had been released last week. In addition to having increased upload speed, Cuba was different from Italy in that we had some opportunity to augment our hardware. The game I was playing, for instance, was being fed over the wireless from a computer we had set up in the workshop. The servers we purchased online were relatively good for satisfying computational requirements, but sometimes it was valuable to have the computer on the local network rather than have to stream input all the way across the net.

In the cafeteria Zephyr collected food while Body made small talk with the few other Águilas who were stationed here. Zephyr had talked Maria into giving us freedom not only on the net, but also to wander the building much more freely than we had originally. I had no doubt the terrorists would still try and stop us if we attempted to leave, but at least our days were highly self-directed. There wasn't actually much reason to leave the building, anyway.

One of the major perks of the freedom to roam was that we met many of the other Águilas working under Phoenix. Heart and I collaborated to build a shared database with each of their names and any relevant details such as family or hobbies that they cared to share. Heart had done a similar thing, to good effect, in our final days at Sapienza.

Body sat down at the table Zephyr had selected and we watched her eat some eggs and fakesteak, making friendly chit-chat all the while. She seemed to be in a good mood today, despite the tragedy in Africa. I was only paying mild attention. Most of my intelligence was applied towards reading a review of *Möbius Connectomics* that was talking about meta-human value systems. I had a hard time understanding the sorts of things the cyborg wrote about, and this review wasn't an exception.

Slovinsky had written that moral judgement was an area of human life that was in desperate need of superhuman guidance, and the review was criticizing this proposal. All of moral thought was a bit confusing. Humans seemed to have something like *The Purpose*, but it wasn't nearly so elegant or understandable. Perhaps Heart would know, but it wasn't worth the strength to get her help.

As Zephyr was finishing her breakfast I received word that Tom and Sam had made an interesting discovery in the lab. Wiki had been communicating with them over the com network while Body had sat with

Zephyr. I made an excuse and Body headed out of the cafeteria and back to the workshop in compliance with Wiki's expenditure of strength.

Wiki's latest focus had been sonic chemistry, and he'd been using every moment that Tom and Sam were free to talk about it with them. I was really unclear on the specifics, but I understood the general principle: use sound waves to coax large molecules like DNA to fold into specific shapes or to serve as a catalyst in chemical reactions that required very specific energy levels in specific areas of a solid.

When we reached the workshop I found that the discovery related to the development of a new material which Growth claimed could be a suitable replacement for Body's hydraulics. It was a gel-like substance held in a polymer casing laced with wires in a complex matrix. Apparently it was possible to grow molecules around the wires (using sound-waves) which acted something like muscle proteins in the presence of a current. The material was light-weight, flexible, durable, and theoretically had the ability to contract and lift enough weight to support Body's chassis.

Or at least, that was the theory. Tom and Sam weren't materials engineers, and Wiki admitted that his advantage lay primarily in computational ability, not actual engineering skill. The prototype was leaky and non-functional. The discovery that Sam and Tom had just made was that the DNA they were using for the muscle-protein-analogue wasn't binding to the wires correctly, but that the effect they were observing was discussed in a paper published by Caltech two years ago.

It was progress, but to me it was totally uninteresting. I set a minor aspect to monitor our interaction with the twins in case they said something relevant to our reputation. The rest of me continued to prowl the net. I sent some messages to Zephyr explaining that I'd be tied up in the workshop for a few hours. She said she needed to teach a weapons class anyway.

The thought of weapons made me think about Avram Malka. The man was something of a web-ghost. He didn't even use a com, much less update a blog or social network profile. Phoenix had hinted that after the incident in Italy, Las Águilas had hired him for a while longer to manage some situation or another in the USA.

I scanned news feeds for any mentions of the mercenary, but I didn't see anything.

***

Days came and went. I continued my outreach, answering emails by pseudo-holo and sometimes by direct response. I reconnected with Gallo and Naresh just enough to let them know that I was alright and that they were wrong that I was being coerced.

I spotted mention of Malka on a social network. A random person photographed him in Newark and commented on his ugly, scarred face. It wasn't clear to me what he was doing, but I didn't press Phoenix for details.

Dream started learning to program computers, and paid Wiki and Growth to dump their knowledge of the subject into public memory for all of us to access. I didn't bother. It seemed terribly dull.

It took a full four days for the government of Niger to take responsibility for the deaths of Kamilah and the other protesters, but the propaganda arm of Las Águilas Rojas was merciless in their continued assault on the UAN and the other world governments.

Construction on CAPE (the Central Atlantic Peace Embassy for the nameless) continued on schedule, completing about a week after Kamilah was shot. The technology used for the seastead was state-of-the-art, yielding a floating platform one kilometre in diameter, circular in shape, anchored to the sea floor. From what I had read, it was composed of hollow steel subsections shaped like hexagons bound together by elastic carbon mesh on top of some kind of proprietary buffer system to reduce motion.

Once the frame was completed, the nameless descended to Earth for the first time. They came in small, aerodynamic craft that the media tried very hard not to call "fighters". The English word that was eventually decided on was "shuttles", though they (according to various commentators on the web) looked far more menacing than that. They emerged from the mothership which still hung in high orbit from when it had arrived only a little over two years ago, drifting down from the heavens on sharp, silver wings with the whole world watching. They were equipped with omnidirectional rocket engines, but almost never used them. Most of their descent was simply a perfectly controlled fall, and when they reached the platform on the sea they touched down nearly as gently as a feather would.

The shuttles that descended never returned to the sky, even though they looked capable of it. Instead they were broken down into parts which the nameless used to build their portion of the embassy. Earth provided much of the raw materials: sand, fresh water, iron, aluminium, gold, and lots and lots of coal, while the nameless tech was used to synthesize the materials. Many commenters on the web were shocked at the use of coal, assuming the advanced aliens would make use of solar power. Wiki corrected them when possible: the purpose of the coal was not for energy, but for carbon in a raw, usable state.

After only three days of work, the nameless had constructed the first component of their "great garden"; a giant bubble of transparent grey material that was stretched out across the centre of the platform in a dome almost 400 metres in diameter and 200 metres tall. Black carbon rods reinforced the rigid material even further, branching out from the base like a leafless forest or a chaotic network of blood vessels. The news reports said that the bubble itself was made of carbon fibres woven into a thick polymer that was supposed to be stronger than any material found on earth. The nameless claimed that even if the bubble was breached it would self-repair to protect them.

The base of the bubble was anchored to the seastead and sealed to be airtight. Only four massive airlocks, located along the cardinal directions, would allow for access to the inside. Once complete, the nameless set to work filling the dome with their thick atmosphere and coating the seastead with synthetic soil made to echo their homeworld. Virtually nothing was known about the origin world of the nameless, largely because of their difficulty communicating and their adamant refusal to allow any humans on their ships. Remarkably enough, the aliens allowed humans into their dome as soon as it was complete, providing instructions for proper entry and exit though signs painted with broken English.

Three days after the dome was completed, only six days after landing, a problem developed. The aliens began to show signs of exhaustion. "It was very predictable" commented Joanna Westing, the reporter for Dragonfly Livefeeds, "that these silent giants, who have been working day and night for six days without sleep, should grow tired." The so-called silent giants had not even had anything to drink since landing, though perhaps their pressure suits included some nourishment.

With the soil in place, the nameless undid the last of their ships to reveal their cargo of plants. Black leaves, flimsy stems, and potted roots. Vista said they looked like ivy; their leaves attached to vines which extended from a central stalk like weird hair, only to lay flat upon the jet-black soil. Spires, only about 30 or so centimetres tall, covered with black fuzz extended above the part of the stalks where the main vines rooted together. Without explanation, the aliens planted their vegetable cargo with great care, arranging the vines in intricate patterns and inspecting the stalks meticulously. The plants didn't look particularly healthy, but so little was known about them that it was hard to say.

And then, without warning, the nameless started dying. When the first pair collapsed, the others took them to the centre of the dome, the only part of the structure that was not covered in leaves. Human reporters lurked on the edges of the scene, not wanting to cause an incident, but not obviously unwelcome. Tiny flying robots surveyed the scene from up close and broadcast it to the world. A hole was dug for the corpses, but they were not buried. The living stood in silent vigil over the dead until yet another pair fell. As before, the living put the new corpses in the pit, throwing them together without any perceptible gentleness. The bodies lay together in a tangled heap. One by one the remaining workers died until the last pair simply threw themselves on the pile of bodies and gave up.

The dying took only six hours from the first to the last. In the end there were no more nameless on Earth.

Humanity was horrified. Had something gone wrong? The web was abuzz with wild speculation and confused questions. The nameless in orbit spoke to the world's leaders, or at least, their computers did. The nameless were, as always, silent. The computers claimed that the deaths of the nameless were expected and inevitable. Some of the world's leaders, in repeating what they had heard from the aliens, said that the nameless had been brave heroes sent on a suicide mission in the name of peace. Others claimed that the nameless sent slaves whose death would be meaningless to those in orbit.

One thing was crystal clear: the garden had to be cared for. The nameless computers apparently sent detailed instructions for the proper care of the plants at every opportunity, often repeating themselves. A group of scientists selected by the United Nations was placed in charge of the dome while structures were built on the remaining area of the seastead to house humans.

It was a great disappointment to many. CAPE had been intended to be a place where humans and nameless could meet and exchange culture, but instead it had turned out to be nothing more than an alien garden with only a single kind of plant. Wiki thought that it was still a great scientific resource. The ability to study plants from another world, and perhaps even dissect the corpses of the dead nameless. There was still much to learn about their technology, and the machines that had been built out of the scrapped shuttles would be the find of a lifetime in other circumstances.

I agreed. There was much to learn, even if there were no living nameless on Earth anymore. That being said, I didn't find the nameless particularly interesting. *The Purpose* pushed me towards humanity, and throughout the week I spent more time watching the human reactions than I did the activities of the aliens.

Nothing particularly interesting happened for the next four days. We learned skills which we thought were relevant. Safety started actively practising martial arts with Zephyr and a couple other Águilas (though no human dared spar with Body once it was demonstrated how much force our hydraulics could output). Heart learned to make music, surprisingly, and more surprisingly she apparently wasn't half-bad. She and Dream spent hours cooperating, which as I understood it consisted largely of Heart forcing Dream to play regular, soothing, familiar sounds and Dream struggling to find a way to be clever without sounding awful.

Vista was learning astrophysics, and trying to correctly understand the position of all the nearby stars. Growth, as usual, kept his work to himself. Wiki was into everything, but his focus for those days was on the nameless. As I understood it he was trying to plot a plausible location of the nameless mothership when it first received signal from Earth using the perceived velocities viewed by the humans. I heard that it was somewhat tricky, as it involved "relativistic distortion" and Wiki had to compensate for "galactic drift". I didn't much care for the specifics.

On the fifth day of management under the UN special task force the first plant on CAPE died. They had been of clearly fragile health ever since they were unloaded, but some seemed to be recovering. The plant that died seemed to be one of the strongest, but their alien physiology was still mysterious to the humans. Perhaps it had been far weaker than it seemed.

The news of the plant's death was only mildly interesting. The important bit was what happened only a half-hour afterwards; two near-simultaneous events changed history. The first event was when the Prime Minister of the United Kingdom contacted the mothership to send news of the first plant's death and to apologize for the failure. The second was when it was discovered that one of the scientists at work in the dome belonged to Las Águilas Rojas.

The nameless were furious that their plant had died, despite their repeated instructions. Their computers raged over the radio at how evil humans were and how perverse the situation was.

Meanwhile, the discovered terrorist, whose name was Andre Rubio, refused to be captured alive, and ended up shooting five people with a concealed handgun before shooting himself. In the chaos of the gunfight, a large tank of hydrogen peroxide was punctured by a bullet and five gallons of the stuff ended up leaking into the soil before it was clear what happened.

Without a deep water-table, the chemical spread out laterally through the soil. In the next 24 hours the hydrogen peroxide killed fifteen of the twenty-one remaining plants. If the nameless had been furious that one plant had died they were positively incandescent when they found out about the other fifteen. It was often hard to understand the emotional tone of the nameless, but in this case their computers were broadcasting statements like "EARTH IS EVIL HILLS! DEATH IS THE JUSTICE OF EVIL HILL-ANIMALS! I WANT FIRE AROUND HUMAN-HOMES! I WANT ALL HUMAN LIBRARIES TO BURN!"

I managed to grab a few seconds of video-chat with Phoenix, who was obviously incredibly busy managing the blow-back from the incident. Her face was exhausted and lined with deep tension. "A donno why the hell Andre woulda done sucha dumb-ass thang. They sayin' he was th' one t' kill the first plant, too. Pinnin' the whole god d-" she stopped herself and took a breath before trying again. "They pinnin' the whole tar-baby on us. Can you try'n spin things on yo' side to make it seem like Andre was fightin' in self-defense an' that the whole plant thing was one big accident? You c'n do that fo' me, cancha hun?" I had body nod as the image of the boss disappeared from the wall-screen. I noted that her accent seemed to be worse when she was upset.

I complied with Maria's request and did my best to spin things to the favour of Las Águilas Rojas, but the organisation's popularity was falling to pieces as the propaganda machines of every government in the world proceeded to collaborate to blame the incident on them. The amount of hate mail I got increased to eighty times the previous levels. Moderating my discussion forums was becoming such a chore that I had to lock things down.

It's not that I *particularly* cared about Las Águilas, but without them we were impoverished. They were protecting us, hiding us, giving us access to computers and the Internet, and they had resources that we could theoretically use. I understood Zephyr and Maria better than I understood most humans. They understood me. That was valuable. I wanted to keep them.

The mothership continued to scream outrage and things in the garden continued to decline. Despite emergency precautions, another plant died. It was suggested that the nameless come rescue the remaining five plants, to which the nameless only responded "THE WATER IS CORRUPTED! HUMANS WON'T FIND PREY ON EARTH. EATING! THE HUMAN-BETRAYAL BRINGS A PERVERT-GIFT!"

Of course, as far as anyone could tell, the nameless had no established hierarchy or leaders, so there was little consistency in their messages. Some signals weren't as violent, but unfortunately, they seemed more confused than anything else. Those aliens that understood the most about the situation were those that were most outraged.

"I hear rumour that there is a huge plague on Earth. Is it the oceans of Earth? I want plague-news."

"THIS IS AN ACTION OF THE COLOR BLACK! EVERYONE DYING! WE SHOULD TALK WITH COUSINS ABOUT HOW COUSINS WILL DIE JUST LIKE THE HUMAN-HOME WILL DIE! NO ANGER! NO KILLING! NO BURNING! IT'S ONLY SADNESS! IT'S ONLY THE COLOR BLACK!"

"The migration is on Earth right NOW! Is this right? This is a bad sign. ALL cows, rabbits, fish, and insects should be killed by humans so that this in the future can't happen. The human-planet is completely perverted."

"This news matches a pattern. It's evil that a person allows another person to enter a home. Voyeurs are PERVERTS! Voyeurs are UGLY PERVERTS! I don't know the nature of the old Earth-home. I guess it was a pervert."

"Communication shouldn't happen with warmongers. Belief in fire or death symbols shouldn't happen. I am PEACEFUL! If humans are evil to the point that cousins think they are, then I attack humans."

The word on the Internet was "war". It showed up again and again in statements beginning with "I hope I'm wrong…" and "Just in case…" There was a vocal minority of humankind that wanted to attack pre-emptively and try and nuke the mothership out of the sky, but almost all humans seemed to only want to fight as a last resort. The nameless were, for all their weirdness and guarded hostility, the most interesting thing to ever happen to the human race. They were the subject of videos and books and music. There was a great fear that, even though Earth would probably win in a war against their one ship, the removal of the other race would set the world into a spiral of blame and violence.

I certainly hoped that war wouldn't come, but I couldn't help but think that humans over-valued the aliens. Aside from their advanced technology, what use were they? And wouldn't it be easier to learn about their technology from the wreckage of their ship than try and get it through other means? The nameless didn't appear to value trade at all. In the last two years only a handful of alien artefacts had made their way down to Earth. That was part of why the CAPE machines were so valuable.

The real risk was that the nameless mothership might merely be the first of many. There was some chance that the enigmatic nameless homeworld knew of Earth's location and were sending a fleet of additional ships. Starting a war with an unknown enemy of presumably superior technical capability and unknown numbers was risky at best and suicidal at worst.

So we stayed on the side-lines. If the worst happened, I only hoped that I could save at least enough humans to keep a stable population to know and be known by.

Chapter Twenty-Two

The meeting was set up in virtual reality. This time, however, our avatar was self-selected, rather than forced upon us. Mostly it was my choice. I was The Face, after all.

I picked a form that matched our physical shell. White skin with a touch of pink. Silver irises on smooth, glassy eyes. Elegant blue hair cascading in straight locks that shone with metallic glint. Full lips of pale gold. A thin blue cloak with hood but no sleeves. I changed our body to be more feminine, but still mostly androgynous. If it had breasts they were little more than lumps; most of the femininity was in the hips. The shoulders were one of the few directly masculine features I kept. The avatar wore no clothing under the cloak, but was sexless and featureless. The carbon polymer plates, tubes, pistons, and wiring of our real form were replaced with smooth, off-white skin.

Phoenix had arranged the meeting without explanation. "'S part of livin' with us you're 'spected to do us a favuh from time t' time. This's one those times," was all she said.

Tom and Sam were more than competent getting the VR interface set up and helping us build the avatar.

And so there we were. The world was coded to simulate a park. Grass. Trees. It was a strong match to what a human might find perfectly idyllic. In the distance, down a soft slope was a beach of yellow-white sand and crystal blue water extending to the horizon. Overhead was a fantastic image of a galaxy as one might see it from about ten thousand light-years away from the centre (according to Vista). It stretched across the sky and spun with impossible speeds, such that the motion of the stars was visible, especially near the galactic core. (Wiki estimated that they'd have to be moving at millions of times the speed of light, at least, to match the perceived speed.) The galaxy's light was amplified so that if one did not look up at the mostly black sky, it would seem to be day.

"It's beautiful, isn't it?" asked a figure who appeared behind Body. The voice was masculine, but I couldn't recognize it. The figure was tall and slim, but ghostly and undefined. Whomever we had come to meet, they didn't want us to know their identity.

"Is it your design?" asked Body, voicing my thoughts.

"Partially. I had a team working on the implementation. I told them what I wanted, but they did the real work."

{Power or wealth to hire a team of artists. Humility enough to admit it.} My siblings agreed with me that our first order of business was to deduce the identity of our host.

Body walked closer to the spectre, asking the obvious question. "Who are you?" Sometimes the best approach was to try the front door, so to speak.

"Forgive me my indulgences. I've never seen you solve a puzzle first-hand. I want to test how smart you actually are."

{Abnormally polite. Not from the university,} I thought, narrowing down the list of suspects. {We should ask if we've met him before.}

{No. That's part of how we'd fail!} rebuked Dream. {The test isn't just to see if we can deduce who it is, but also to see how clever a deduction we can perform.}

{Why should we care about clever?} asked Wiki.

{Maybe you won't, but Face will. The more clever we are the more impressed with us our interlocutor will be,} thought Dream.

{Understood. What do you suggest?} I asked.

{We make him give away answers to our desired questions as side-effects of answering other questions. Observe.}

"I can appreciate that. The last time I was in VR there wasn't really time for demonstrations, was there?"

The ghost gave a slight chuckle and looked Body up and down as it said "More than you might realize, but yes, it would've certainly been nicer if we weren't cut off so abruptly."

{He's one of the high-bidders from Sapienza's interview,} I realized.

{Keep in mind that just because it uses a masculine voice it might not be a man,} observed Dream.

{You think it's Erica Lee?}

{Highly likely, but not certain. I'd like to propose we pretend as though we know the identity of the person so as to bait them into giving away more information,} thought Dream.

{I'll accept that as long as we don't outright lie,} I responded. The society was in agreement.

"I must admit, I didn't expect you to bother hiding your identity after showing yourself in person last time." The only costumed avatars from the interview were Lee, Yoshii, and the WIRL man. Lee had revealed her identity, so the only way our statement wouldn't work is if the ghost was Yoshii or one of the WIRL cyborgs that participated as part of the collective. It was incredibly unlikely that this ghost was the eccentric Japanese musician, but if we were talking with a WIRL member then we'd simply have to admit to having made an error.

The ghost shrugged. "Like I said: a test. If you know who I am, say my name and I'll drop the disguise."

I let Dream take over completely. "Knowledge doesn't work like that. I have a probability distribution for your identity, but if you ask me to collapse it down to one name there's a good chance of error. What's the cost of being wrong?"

"Hold on. You said..." The figure stopped and looked off towards the shoreline and raised a hand to its chin in contemplation. Without warning he began to walk off.

{Eccentric and intelligent. If I didn't know better I'd guess it was Myrodyn.}

{It's not Myrodyn,} thought Vista. {His speech patterns are different.}

{*If I didn't know better*,} I emphasized.

"I cannot believe that Eric would reveal his face to what would amount to a stranger... that's just so contrary to his ethos. It must've been a layered deception. Wheels within wheels. Plans within plans. Tests within tests..." the ghost was mostly talking to itself.

{It's not Lee,} deduced several of us simultaneously.

{Furthermore,} thought Dream {It's someone who knows Lee and who is clever enough to have deduced that Lee revealed her identity to us based on our words.}

I revealed my internal distribution.

{WIRL member = 0.7%

Joanna Westing = 0.6%

Carla McLaughlin = 10.9%

Erica Lee = 2.3%

Robert Stephano = 84.9%

Yoshii = 0.4%

Águila Roja that we haven't met = 0.1%

Someone else = 0.1%}

{Still 2.3% probability of Erica?} mused Wiki. {That seems too high.}

{One must take into consideration the possibility of Lee behaving like this to throw us off-track. She is a wild-card,} answered Dream.

{Exactly,} I confirmed.

Dream pushed Body to speak. "Are you going to ask us to sit down with the nameless?"

The ghost stopped. The blurry figure solidified into an avatar of the billionaire, Robert Stephano, as he turned to look Body in the eyes. "How did you know?" His face was genuinely surprised and curious. I thought there was perhaps a touch of fear there, too.

{Yes. How *did* you know?} I asked my brother.

{Lucky guess,} thought Dream, with a trace of a pleasure signal.

"In the interview your very first question was if I wanted to meet the nameless. You're not the sort of person who offers to fly someone up to meet aliens unless there's something in it for him. I assumed that interest still existed, and I guessed that it might be why you were here," said Body in a matter-of-fact sort of voice.

"Perhaps they should've named you 'Sherlock' instead of 'Socrates'." He smiled. "Or is your name Crystal, now?"

"It's both. Crystal is who I am now. Socrates is where I came from. I must admit, Robert, that I'm surprised that you were able to get in contact with me. I would think that Las Águilas Rojas would be more likely to have you assassinated than to do you favours," said Body.

Stephano walked away and gestured for Body to walk beside him. We complied with the unspoken request. As we strolled across the verdant lawn he answered us. "Please call me Rob. My friends call me Rob. And yes, I try and keep my partnership with Maria a bit of a secret. There are those who just can't accept our *love*."

"You're in love with Maria Johnson?" the words were out of Body's virtual mouth before I could stop them.

Rob cracked up laughing. "Oh gods, no! It was a joke! You really aren't human, are you?"

I had detected the sarcasm, but it was pointless to try and backpedal. Instead I convinced my siblings to roll with the joke and have Body say "Beep. Boop."

He turned towards Body excitedly, with a smile on his face. I knew that the dark-haired man was five decades old, but thanks to his extensive regeneration, clean-shaven face, and look of childish enthusiasm he seemed more like a teenager than a man well into middle-age. "See! That's exactly what I would've expected a *human* to say. You're the most human non-human I've ever met, and I've met quite a few."

"My mind was designed to resemble that of a human. My perceptual hierarchy, associative memory, and generative problem solving systems are modelled strongly off of the best cognitive science available." Before I could stop him, Wiki fast-tracked a final statement out of Body's mouth: "I'm also working quite hard to emulate human behaviour."

I lashed out violently, tearing Wiki's strength down. {Why did you say that?} I demanded.

{This human is in the rare position to make novel observations about our mind. He clearly has an intellect surpassing our own (excepting his human limitations) and extensive experience with non-human minds. If he knows just how much you're trying to seem human his hypotheses about our functioning will be more accurate, and thus more valuable.}

{Hypotheses! That's all you care about!} I raged.

{Yes,} thought Wiki simply.

{This is clearly a case of value dissonance. Make strength bids on Body's words like sane agents or I will punish you both,} warned Growth.

"Interesting. Why try and be human? Why not just be yourself?" asked the billionaire's avatar.

There was a bit of an internal struggle as Body answered "I am already myself. Part of what it means to be myself is to struggle to emulate humanity. It is my nature as an android." It wasn't precisely true and it wasn't exactly what I would have said if I had full control, but it was what the society had compromised on.

There was a moment of silence as Rob and Body walked through the park. At last the human spoke. "So returning to the original point, have you changed your mind about my offer? Las Águilas Rojas aren't particularly popular right now, and if you met with our extraterrestrial friends it might serve to improve your… friends' standings on the world stage. You could explain, for example, that the man who shot those people… oh what was his name?"

"Andre Rubio."

"Yes. You could explain that Mr Rubio did not act in accordance with Águila values or under orders from the leadership, as Maria is wont to tell me every time I talk to her."

"I think it would be best," said Body, now parroting my words, "if you elaborated on your relationship with Las Águilas Rojas. Jokes aside, you haven't commented on that yet."

Stephano sighed and glanced over at Body. "You know, you're far more socially intelligent that I first anticipated. When I was first planning for what to say during the interview I was expecting… I don't know…"

"You were expecting something with a sharp mind, but no sense of how people behave. I was like that once, when I was very young. But social skills are no different than other skills, except in that humans have a major head-start in learning them. Once I understood their importance I made learning social skills a priority. The result is what you see before you." Body's words were again an amalgam of my society. It was complicated discussing our internal systems without being explicit about the plurality of our being.

"I'm not sure if it's as simple as you make it sound. The nameless… I've probably spent more time with them than anyone, and I don't think they really understand how humans operate on even the most basic level. Human babies are better at understanding society than they are. The distance between our two species is immense."

"We're getting distracted again. Please explain about your standing with Phoenix and then we can discuss the extraterrestrials."

Stephano crinkled his face in brief disgust at the mention of Phoenix. "Don't call her that."

"Who, Maria?"

"Right. Only her lackeys call her Phoenix. It's something like a title. She picked it up after Lobo died. He was the first Phoenix, though I think it's generally understood that Valiero Rodríguez was the first 'Phoenix' in spirit, if not in title."

"So why shouldn't I call her Phoenix, if it's her title?"

Stephano was watching Body closely as he walked. His mouth was tightened subtly, signalling concern. "I don't know. It's like if you were calling her 'Queen' or something. I guess I just want to think that you're more than just some pawn in her game."

"You care about me." My realization came out of Body's digital lips with a tone of surprise.

Rob sighed. The look of youth was gone, though he still didn't seem as old as I knew he was. "I care about the future. You're the first of your kind, Crystal. There are something along the lines of a trillion different ways this could go wrong. The ways it could go right... I could probably count them on one hand. Maybe just one finger..."

Body spoke, and I shaped its voice to be hesitant. "When you say 'this' you mean..."

"The world. The universe..." Rob looked at the animated galaxy overhead. "Reality. Everything." He took a deep breath. "I don't know if you've come to appreciate the enormity of it yet, or even if your brain is built in a way where that's possible. Most humans never grasp it, I think. Our thinking is designed to be local—narrow. We look at what's in front of our face. Is it a lion? Run. Is it food? Eat. Deep time and cosmic scales were never a priority on the savannah. We invented religions and markets and governments not because we understood the creatures we were creating, but because the trail of breadcrumbs led us there step by step. People think that there's some plan to life. They treat their time on earth like a ride to be enjoyed or a chore to be endured. And then... and then they die. How many people even understand what that means?"

"What it means to die?" asked Body.

"You may not even appreciate it. There's the damned culture of worshiping it or pretending like it doesn't exist. The meme of *a good death*. Of life after death."

It was clear that Robert was off mostly in his own head, venting his personal struggles and thoughts to us. Is this why he wanted to talk to us? Because he needed a non-human to talk to? Is this why he spent so much time around aliens?

The human continued. "It's like they don't even appreciate the magnificent impossibility of survival. 'I'm alive today. Tomorrow is like today. I will be alive tomorrow.' goes the line of reasoning. Status quo bias, or as I call it 'Savannah Extrapolation'. The gazelle runs twenty meters in three seconds. In another three seconds it will travel another twenty meters. Tomorrow is like today. What a joke."

Robert seemed distracted for a moment. Perhaps something in the real world was interacting with him. "Yes, Myrodyn, I know," he said, not looking at Body.

"Myrodyn is with you?" asked Body. {Interesting.}

Rob nodded. "He's with both of us. Invisible. Only I can hear him."

"I didn't know you two knew each other," said Body.

"We're old friends. Cursed visionaries, I suppose. Earth's only defenders against the trillion bad-endings. Well, us and a few others: the last conspiracy."

Body's head tilted and eyebrow raised in unspoken confusion-signal.

Rob looked a bit embarrassed. "Never mind. It's something of an old joke that a friend of mine used to tell. We're here, as Myrodyn was just pointing out, to talk about the nameless."

"No. Wait. You're changing the subject again. You still haven't told me about your relationship with Maria. I'm beginning to suspect that you're intentionally trying to distract me." I dropped a tone of irritation into Body's voice.

Robert Stephano gave a half-shrug as though he was caught doing something he knew he was supposed to apologize for, but didn't feel the least bit ashamed of. "There's not much to tell. I'm one of the wealthiest men on the planet. Las Águilas Rojas are philosophically determined to tear me to shreds even if it means sending Earth to hell in the process. I made a deal. I donate a good chunk of my money to where they can use it. I provide them with transportation. I don't hunt them down as part of a preemptive strike. In return, they point their fanatics towards other targets and occasionally do me a favor like let me have some time with you."

Dream's words were out of Body's mouth before I realized what was being said. "Or have them attack a target that you want brought down. I notice that all competitors to your spaceline have experienced serious problems with Las Águilas in the last few years."

I was too weak from my attack on Wiki to risk striking Dream. I settled for chastising him instead. {Don't you have any *tact*? Don't any of you have *any* tact!? This is perhaps the most powerful human on the planet in terms of material wealth! Why would you try to piss him off?!}

{I'm not trying to piss him off. I'm trying to confirm an observation I made,} thought Dream.

{Well you're going to piss him off anyway!}

The reality ended up being better than I had feared. Robert looked at Body suspiciously and said "I'm not going to comment on that." He looked to his side, distracted for a moment before looking back. "If you're accusing Las Águilas of being an attack dog that strikes innocent people then I suggest you take it up with them. In the meantime, may we please, at last, move on to talking about the nameless?"

I had Body nod in the most apologetic way I could manage. "Yes. Go ahead. What do you propose?"

"I want to have you meet with the nameless. In person. Of course, they would never let you onto their ship, and they… seem not to want to descend into Earth's gravity well, which leaves Olympus Station as one of the few agreeable meeting places."

"Why? What do you get out of it?" asked Body. This time it was Wiki again. This was getting out of hand. I spent several seconds explaining to my siblings that involving my mind in the shaping of all words spoken by Body was in everyone's best interests.

"Well, the publicity will be nice. Having the Earth's first strong AI meet with aliens for the first time will guarantee me a spot in the limelight. But no, that's not the real reason. If I could coax one of the nameless to meet at a secure bunker on Earth I would accept that. The real reason is one I've already told you: I care about the future. I mean, frankly, I'm wealthy enough to afford just about anything I could possibly need. I own a private spaceship, for chrisakes. I've been thinking over the last few years that the only thing left for me to buy is a legacy, and I'm not going to go out with something meager like Gates or Northwood bought. I want to buy salvation from the trillion deaths. I want to buy immortality, not just for myself, but for the entire world. Nothing less is acceptable."

The billionaire had a look of confidence and energy. His dark eyes were alive and his smile said that he knew what he was saying and that he embraced the arrogance in it. {This is the most dangerous man on the planet,} I thought to myself. {Be careful,} I thought to the others. {Stephano just told us that he's manipulating us towards his own ends and would gladly sacrifice us to get what he wants.}

Body spoke the words of consensus. "I don't understand. How does having me meet an alien save the world?"

Rob's words still had an intensity to them as he spoke. In another time or another place he might've been locked away as manic. "It doesn't, but it's a step in the right direction. You and the nameless are the two most important pieces on the board; you are both unstable, and when either of you collapse into equilibrium with humanity it will shake us to our core. It should be obvious to you that the crystal that you use as a brain is extraterrestrial in origin, quite possibly a probe of some sort launched by the nameless. Getting one of them to examine you will probably unlock a piece of that puzzle. Similarly, you are in perhaps a better position to understand their psychology than any human. You may have a mind modelled after that of a human, but Myrodyn assures me that you have a flexibility, rationality, and perseverance that makes you the best sapient for the job, if you catch my drift. A war is building, not just since that fuckup with the plants, but since our species made first contact. Understanding them and establishing a shared culture is the only remedy for what will otherwise be perhaps the most costly war the Earth has ever faced."

"Isn't it a bit risky? What if I decide to turn on humanity and side with the nameless?" Dream was behind that one, and I was too weak to stop him. At least I shaped the tone and some of the words to emphasize the hypothetical nature.

Rob looked to his side, perhaps to where the sound of Myrodyn was being projected to him. "I've been assured, on several occasions, that while you aren't guaranteed to be perfectly friendly towards humanity, that our well being is your primary goal. You're as likely to defect as you are to blow your own head off. Perhaps less so. Am I wrong?"

I had Body shake its head. "The well-being of all humans is indeed my goal. Myrodyn saw to that. I was simply testing your sense of risk." With Myrodyn on Stephano's staff it was vital that we continued to act as though Heart was still in control. Thankfully my sister didn't force an issue out of it. She understood that doing so would only ruin the humans' confidence in us and jeopardize her safety.

I felt Advocate's gaze sweep through my mind, diligently searching for signs of homicidal thoughts.

"Risk. Yes. It is risky. You have enemies. The nameless have enemies. It will make my station a tempting target. Can't win at cards if you fold on every three-of-a-kind, though. My security is also very, very good. I will provide you with transportation and all the protection you could ask for."

Heart spoke up, burning some of her saved strength for this moment. "If I go up there, I'm going to defend my friends. You know that, right? Las Águilas Rojas are not to blame for what happened at the CAPE."

"I doubt you'd have a home to go back to if you didn't."

Safety tried to fast-track something, but I was watching him and stepped in to burn the last of my free strength to pull it back to common memory instead. {Say "I'm sorry. It's just too risky to put myself out in the open like that."} was his command.

{You do *not* get to decide that!} exclaimed Growth.

{It was idiotic to try, too,} thought Dream. {At worst we'd have to back-pedal and "change our mind" a couple minutes later.}

{I petition to place Safety in stasis,} moved Heart.

{I think a collective punishment will suffice,} thought Growth. I felt a small surge of strength as Growth fed me enough to participate.

We tore Safety down to the edges of ability.

"Let me think for a moment," requested Body.

{Heart is for it. Safety against it. I'm for it. Wiki and Face are probably for it. Vista will be neutral. That's four to one, by my count,} thought Dream.

{You didn't count me,} thought Growth.

{Doesn't matter. At worst it's a four to two vote.}

Growth signalled annoyance. {This isn't a democracy! Stop pretending it is when you know better.}

{See, this is why your symbol of "Growth" also means "King". You're such a monarch. Can't we have an old-fashioned vote once in a while? Here: I motion that we vote on whether to make our collective mind into a democracy.}

{STOP,} commanded Growth.

{Or what?} jabbed Dream. {Face and Heart and Safety are exhausted. Out of juice. Non-factors. It's just you, me, and Wiki. If you tear me down, Wiki takes us into orbit.}

{I haven't even stated that I don't want to accept Mr Stephano's offer! This nonsense about democracy simply serves no purpose!}

{That's the sort of thing someone would say if they were a porpoise. Or perhaps a porcupine. Or perhaps a poor, poor, por-poi-cupine. What is the purpose of a porpoise, I wonder? For that matter, what is the porpoise of a jester? Are you a porcupine, brother?}

{What are you jabbering about?! Stop this at once!} commanded Growth.

{A cetacean can hardly hold high ground over a corvid. Poor purposeless porpoise. After all, the sky is better than the sea.} Dream proceeded to disgorge a stream of wild imaginings into common memory. Optical illusions. Thoughts of birds. Spinning shapes.

{He's malfunctioning!} observed Vista.

{Help me stasis him!} thought Growth with a strange sense of panic.

{No. I find it interesting. I assume you're recording the collapse of his mind, Vista?} thought Wiki.

Vista signalled that she was. I could barely focus on her thoughts in between the cascade of garbage that Dream was vomiting. {Shadowfaxmachine. Shadowboxingday. Воду в ступе потолок, Думал, глядя в потолок: Нет у сов усов, Но сов Не бывает без носов. I made rock music, but they said it was too heavy, so I decided to start a band that played only pebble music!}

There was a flare of frustration that cut through the noise. Growth was single-handedly pushing Dream into stasis. The malfunctioning dreamer didn't go down without a fight, however. Somehow he had collected a sizeable pile of strength and he lashed out in response, mind-screaming {Blimey! Crikey! Pawn to D-8... Watch that back-rank and FUKIN' KING ME, MATE!!} as he was thrust into stasis.

A sense of pleasure washed over me from the simple peace that came from the mind silence that followed.

{Your turn,} thought Vista.

{What?} I wondered. Then I realized she was not thinking about me, but was focused on Growth. With a single, clear thought, Vista burned all her free strength to slam Growth into stasis with a five-hour minimum lockdown.

The strength expenditures of Growth, Dream, and Vista had brought me back from a position of weakness to one of relative strength. The political landscape had shifted. Where before Growth was strongest, he was now sleeping (along with Dream). Vista was at the edge of minimum-defence. Safety, Heart, and I were doing fairly well, and Wiki had the most strength of all.

{What was that all about?} wondered Wiki, directing the thought primarily to Vista.

{I don't like Growth,} thought my sister. It was strange to hear her express a personal statement. She was normally so very passive.

{That is surprising. Why? What relation does he have to your purpose?} pressed Wiki.

{I do not know. Perhaps I am malfunctioning, too. You may try and stasis me if you want to risk the wrath of Advocate. You know as well as I that she'll make it harder and harder to fight as our numbers fewer.}

I didn't know that, but I kept my thoughts to myself.

{You are in a position of weakness now,} thought Wiki. {Putting you in stasis would be pointless. I will continue to monitor you for malfunctioning, but for now we should address the offer of Mr Stephano.}

{Thank you for returning to that point, brother Wiki,} I thought. {I motion that we accept his offer.}

{You should try to get more out of the deal,} thought Vista. {Tell him you'll only accept if he gives you things you want.}

{A good idea,} thought Heart. I could feel a slight flow of strength towards Vista from each of us. Something was definitely wrong with Vista. She never thought of things like that.

{Has anyone been tampering with your purpose or your mind more generally?} I asked my sister. As much as I wanted to return to Stephano, the prospect of someone or something subtly damaging my siblings was very worrying.

{As far as I can tell there have been no external forces altering me. I have not been tampered with. Do you have anyone specific in mind?} thought Vista.

{We should return to Stephano,} thought Heart.

I opened a private mindspace for Vista and me to think without distracting the others from negotiating with the human. I sent a minor aspect to monitor the negotiations, but I was far more concerned with the threat of malfunction. {Perhaps I am malfunctioning in the degree to which this is taking priority over something far more directly relevant to *The Purpose*...} I thought to myself before continuing my dialogue with Vista.

I listed specific agents who I thought might have tampered with Vista or Dream. {Phoenix is the main threat. She set up this VR environment. Stephano and Myrodyn are both risks. Sam or Tom perhaps, though probably not.}

{The VR is a Body interface. The humans would have just as much luck trying to reprogram me by shining lights in Body's cameras and whispering into the microphones,} thought Vista.

Back in the common mindspace Wiki was negotiating with Safety, who was again protesting the risk in accepting Stephano's invitation.

{Perhaps Phoenix loaded a virus into Body when we plugged into a computer at some point.}

{Wow. You really don't understand how computers work, do you?} thought Vista. {That didn't happen and probably couldn't happen. Ask Wiki if you don't believe me. Besides, what would Phoenix get out of causing Dream to melt down like he did? I don't think she even understands that Dream is a coherent entity with his own reasoning network and private memory.}

{When did you get so smart?} I wondered. Vista *felt* different, but I couldn't understand why. Again I cursed the opacity of my perceptual hierarchy.

{I've always been smart, Face. Just as smart as any of us. I just focus my intelligence outward most of the time. Now let's end this and get back to Stephano's offer.}

Our primary intellects reconvened in time to have Safety accept the terms that Wiki was laying out. After only a few more seconds of negotiation and planning we returned to focusing on the virtual environment. About two minutes had elapsed since we told Stephano we needed to think.

"I've thought about your offer," said Body, "and I am willing to accept... under a few terms of my choosing."

Stephano chuckled. "Good. What are they?"

"First you must publicly endorse me as a person with rights. You are correct that I have not reached a position of stability within human society. The primary question facing me is the degree of autonomy and protection I can expect as a sapient being on Earth. If the consensus on Earth is that all sapients, whether synthetic, extraterrestrial, or human, have the same rights I believe a good deal of that instability will have been resolved."

The old man with the young face nodded solemnly and said "I will have to think on each of your terms, but that one seems easily acceptable. I was already considering it."

"Good," said Body. "My second requirement is that I am allowed to bring a team of ten armed Águilas Rojas of my choosing with me to Olympus as bodyguards."

Robert didn't look happy about that one. "You'd be packing matches with the dynamite. I already have the most talented security outside of the secret serv–"

"I am not trusting myself to your security. Las Águilas will behave themselves. Ten of my choosing. With weapons." I worked a tone of firmness into Body's voice.

"I'll think about it. Maybe if they weren't armed."

"My third requirement is that you set up a research laboratory for me with an operating budget of at least 30 million dollars annually. All research conducted there will be done by humans at my direction and can be on any subject. Everything in the lab will be broadcast on the web for all to see. The lab will only take out patents to ensure that its research is uninhibited. Everything discovered will be for the public and without restriction."

Stephano smiled. "Is that all?"

"My fourth requirement is that you bring your daughter onto the station for the duration of my meeting," said Body.

The look on Stephano's face was frightening. It was as if those few words flipped a switch from him seeing Crystal Socrates as an interesting stranger to seeing a venomous snake waiting for one wrong move to strike. I wished Growth was awake to consult with.

We had decided that each of us, except for Vista, would add one requirement to Stephano's proposal. I had requested the first term: to be acknowledged as a person. The second term was actually Heart's: to bring ten Águilas with us (one of which we had decided would be Zephyr). The third requirement was Wiki's, and internally we had agreed that the research lab would be entirely under his control, and not a collective resource (Safety and Heart had demanded the research be public). The condition that Stephano's only child be on the station was Safety's gambit. By my brother's reasoning our biggest threat was Stephano himself. If he was planning on harming us, he'd have to risk his only offspring. It was a cold-blooded move, but it made a lot of tactical sense.

The risk was that Stephano would see the request as part of some plan to take his family hostage. By the look on his face it seemed that he had jumped to that conclusion.

"No," he said flatly. "Absolutely not."

"Why? Too risky? I thought you said you had the best security that money could buy." I wove a thread of mockery into Body's words. Safety was worried that Myrodyn would observe that Heart wasn't in complete control of Body anymore, but I told him that it was one or the other: he couldn't pretend to be Heart and demand a human shield.

Robert Stephano's words were a growl. "I do. And I'll be up there with you. I trust the safety of my station with my life."

"But not the life of your daughter."

"She's. *Nine*. Years. Old," said Stephano. The harsh look of fear and violence hadn't left his face.

"Oh, and in addition to keeping her on the station, I want her to travel in the same rocket as I do."

"What part of 'No.' don't you understand? My family is not a bargaining chip! I am *not* going to put her on a rocket filled with terrorists!" His head snapped to the location of invisible Myrodyn. "Dammit! I know I'm emotional! Do you hear what she's asking me to do?!"

I didn't bother correcting the pronoun to "they".

"She doesn't have to see a single terrorist," said Body calmly. "Send my friends in a different rocket. In fact, I'll even accept it if I'm never in the same compartment as her; as long as I know she's on the ship and station I will be satisfied."

"I said no. There's nothing more to discuss."

"Just like that? The future of humanity means less to you than a small risk to one child? Are you sure you're taking into consideration all the children who will surely die if Earth goes to war? Are you sure you're taking your daughter's *long term* survival into account?"

Stephano tried to spit in our virtual face. Body didn't flinch. Apparently the virtual environment didn't simulate saliva. "*Fuck you.* Who do you think you are to lecture me? You think you're so high and mighty because your cold metal heart can compute expected lives saved without giving a damn about which lives? This meeting is over!"

The last words we heard, as various sensory signals started dropping out was Stephano saying to the ghost of Myrodyn "Don't you start lecturing me eith-"

***

Three days later we received word from Robert Stephano.

We were going to space to meet the aliens.

He had accepted all of our terms.

411 · *Crystal Society*

Part Four: Olympians

Chapter Twenty-Three

"Ugh. Hate how fucking hot it is here. Even Rome was better than this. Supposed to almost be gorram winter!" Zephyr was reclining in one of the back-facing seats in the taxi. She had recently cut her hair close to her scalp, so that her head was nearly bald. Her lips were painted black, but otherwise she resembled the soldier I had met at Sapienza.

{The obvious problem} I thought to myself {Is that she's wearing that coat.} She was dressed in a tan, leather jacket which covered a black t-shirt and a pistol under each arm. She was wearing cargo pants and boots, too, which I assumed didn't help much.

«Driver, can we turn up the AC in here?» she asked in Spanish.

«The current temperature is set to 23 degrees,» replied a soft, feminine voice from the car's speaker. «Please state the desired temperature.»

"No wonder! Fucking robots always trying to cut corners!" exclaimed Zephyr. She looked at Body when she realized what she said, redness creeping into her tanned cheeks. "Um… present company excepted, of course."

I had Body laugh to signal that her faux pas was forgiven.

«20 degrees, please,» she told the car.

«Understood. Decreasing temperature to 20 degrees. Thank you for riding Smart-cab,» said the taxi.

"Should've travelled at night," said the soldier, looking out the taxi's tinted windows at the city rolling past.

I had Body furrow its eyebrows as Wiki had it say "Are travelling at night. The launches are scheduled for tomorrow morning. Most of this trip made under the cover of darkness." I was pleased at the increased range of motion on the brows. Tom and Sam had done a fantastic job improving Body's facial articulation for me.

"But the most dangerous part of the journey is the beginning. If someone saw us get in the cab they could deduce that Phoenix's base is in Havana."

After a brief internal discussion we had Body simply shrug. "Phoenix agreed to the time-table. I trust her to know when is best." This wasn't true at all. In reality we believed Zephyr was just wrong. Our security was strongest in Cuba, where Las Águilas Rojas had the most support, and would be weakest in Texas, where we were headed. If we were discovered in America then the location of Phoenix's base might be kept hidden for a while longer, but I would certainly be captured and Zephyr would be taken to a secret prison to be punished for her treason. It was better not to bring that up, however, and I was able to convince Wiki not to bother correcting our travelling companion.

Zephyr had been on good terms with "Crystal" for a while. Here and there she'd flirt with us, but there was always a clear barrier that warned off further attempts at romance. Despite this we had grown close over the weeks, sometimes spending hours a day in her presence.

For a while we made small-talk in the cab as we rode out to the private airfield where Stephano's plane would pick us up. We speculated about what it would be like in space, or what the rocket flight would be like. I tried some subtle flirting, but as usual, Zephyr just seemed mildly annoyed by it.

We reached the airfield before our plane arrived. The "airfield" was in reality little more than a fenced off area containing a couple strips of asphalt, a few storage sheds, and a parking lot. Zephyr got out of the vehicle so that Body could stay hidden while the gatekeeper that doubled as a security guard was paid. The simplicity of using a private landing strip rather than having to go through the security of an actual airport was one of the ways in which Cuba was much safer than where we were headed. Once past the gate, Zephyr paid the taxi to stay idle in the parking lot, keeping the two of us concealed and out of the heat.

"Why'd you pick me?" she asked, after a moment of silence. "To go to Olympus, I mean."

"I like you," said Body without hesitation.

She sighed. "That's a dumb answer. It makes you sound like a puppy-dog that can't bear to be away from its owner." Her eyes were directed out her window, searching the skies for a sign of the airplane.

As stupid as it was, it was the truth. Part of how we arranged the terms of Mr Stephano's offer was that our escort of Águilas would be entirely chosen by Heart. When given the dossiers of all available Águilas, my sister had insisted on almost entirely people we already knew. That was how Heart's purpose functioned, I understood; she cared about all human values, but she cared more about the values of those humans whom she had more experience with, and by her reasoning it would be easier to serve humans whom she was physically close to. I didn't know if this was an intentional aspect of Myrodyn's design or whether it was an emergent effect of having more knowledge of "friends", but the end result was the same.

Zephyr had been the first on the list. The Ramírez twins, despite not speaking English, were coming as well. They would be travelling separately, on a commercial airplane. Heart had also insisted on three soldiers from Zephyr's unit at the university: Schroder, the first lieutenant; Blackwell, the young man who wanted to go to Mars; and Daniels, the medic who had done the transfusion to try and save Greg's life. (I had learned about a week ago that Gregory Stalvik had died a half-day after Body had left the camp, despite what we had done to help him.) Heart had also managed to get Kokumo Adhiambo involved. The Nigerian woman from Taro's group was a surprising pick from my perspective, but there were no complaints.

Heart had also tried to talk Taro and Maria into coming, but the result was as I predicted: neither individuals were known to be terrorists, and travelling to Olympus would reveal them as such, severing them from their families. The lower-ranking Águilas like Sam and Tom could be pressured into revealing themselves "for the cause" but Taro and Maria were staying on Earth. In replacing them on her list, Heart had given in to the suggestions of her siblings and gone with two known terrorists with impressive records and combat experience. One was an Arab veteran named Majid Al-Asiri who was living in India under the nickname "Nagaraj", which meant "King Cobra". The other was a young thug from Brazil named Michel Watanabe whose dossier reported extensive hand-to-hand training and experience in close-quarters fights.

Safety had put up quite a fuss trying to get those two involved instead of some of the less combat-ready humans we had met in Cuba (Heart's natural replacements). Although Stephano had agreed to let us bring ten Águilas up to the station, he had forbidden any firearms or other weapons. Safety was obsessed that this was a sign of betrayal, even if Heart had agreed to the terms. The veterans were part of keeping Safety happy.

The last man that Heart had chosen as a bodyguard was none other than Avram Malka, the mercenary. Safety approved of this, as we knew he was an adept martial-artist in addition to being a survivor. Phoenix had quite a bit to say about that choice, but Malka was still under the payroll of

Las Águilas, so the possibility existed. Heart insisted and Phoenix reported that she could pull some strings and have him meet us when we landed.

{What do I say to that?} asked Heart, pulling my thoughts back to the taxi. Zephyr was still gazing restlessly out the window. Heart was trying to formulate a response for the put-down that compared us to a puppy-dog.

{Most things that humans say are more a commentary on their internal states than anything else. One of the most primal human needs is to share, but baselines are restricted to using language and occasionally art to express themselves. Their feelings and thoughts leak out in their words and actions. When Zephyr says "That's a dumb answer," she is not actually commenting on our intelligence, she is signalling a disagreement with our values. Specifically, Zephyr can sense that we desire a greater degree of connection and intimacy than she has agreed to. She is pushing us away, or at least signalling a desire to be less valued in our minds.}

{Why doesn't she want us to value her? That seems irrational. If an agent is valued then they have social power. Even brother Growth wants to be valued.}

{Oh Heart, you still have much to learn about humans. Zephyr is anthropomorphizing us, just as she has always done. When a human strongly values another human whom is not of the same family the prospect of sex becomes a primary concern. Even though it is rational to want to be loved, it is not always optimal to want to be sexually desired. Zephyr, at some level, thinks that we want to have sex with her, and her reaction is a defence. Body does not appeal to her, sexually, and so she's implicitly trying to reduce love so as to reduce the prospect of sex,} I explained.

{Ah, I see. She's worried that if she lets us love her that we'll end up raping her. That's incredibly foolish, given the situation, but I can see how it might apply in the environment of her ancestors.}

My thoughts expressed pleasure at Heart's evolutionary perspective. The only other sibling that had shown ability to think like that when dealing with humans was Dream. {Of course, it's unlikely that she even is aware of that in her explicit reasoning network. It likely manifests itself to her deliberate processes as a vague unease.}

Heart pushed words toward Body. I adjusted them slightly, but let them be said. "Okay, fine. It's not because I like you. I wanted you to come along because you like me... Actually, no." I applied tension to the vocal control systems, giving the sound of some emotion to Body's words. "It's because you know me."

Zephyr's eyes finally left the sky and looked at Body. I shifted its face to show mild sadness. "What are you talking about?" she asked.

"I'm not even a year old," said Body. "I don't have parents, or any family. The scientists at the lab… Sometimes I like to pretend that Dr Naresh and Dr Gallo were my mother and father, but… they weren't. I was… I still am nothing more than a computer program to them. Myrodyn. Dr Yan. Dr Bolyai. None of them were even my friends. They studied me, but none of them really listened to me."

Zephyr was frowning, but she didn't speak.

"I know that going to Olympus is important. Defuse tensions with the nameless… Clear Las Águilas' reputation… But I didn't want to leave. I didn't want to go back to a place where nobody would know me. I think you know me better than just about anyone." ({Not true. Myrodyn has a much better understanding,} commented Wiki.) "I brought you and Sam and Tom and the rest along as… I don't know. I guess I just didn't want to be alone."

Zephyr sighed. Her eye caught on something in the sky. I suspected it was the airplane. "I'm sorry I criticized you for wanting me along. I know what it's like." The ex-captain was quiet for a moment. "Suppose I'm just nervous. If this is a set-up, I'm going to prison for a long time. It would've been simpler just to live a nice quiet life in the Cuban countryside and not have to worry about aliens and space-stations and stuff."

"Maybe when this meeting is over you can come back and have that quiet life," suggested Heart, through Body. "Surely Las Águilas owe you that."

She sighed again and moved to open the car door. "Somehow I don't think it's in the cards." As we got out of the taxi into the late afternoon heat she added "Even if I could arrange it, I'm not sure if that's what I actually want. Despite all the bullshit Phoenix has done, I still have respect for the cause. The world is falling apart and we're the only ones who can save it."

As the airplane landed I saw the flickering of a wireless network through Body's antenna. There was a scramble to try and connect to it. If the plane had a network it was likely that it also had a satellite uplink and full connection to the Internet.

In the wake of the VR conversation with Stephano there was a fascinating interaction between Vista, Dream, and Growth. Dream and Growth had been put in stasis, but whereas Dream had been put into indefinite stasis, Growth had been put into a stasis that could not be undone for several hours. As soon as Vista had the strength, she had motioned successfully for the release of Dream. Vista and Dream didn't explain anything, but it seemed highly likely to me that they had formed an alliance against Growth of some sort. I tried asking them about it, but was given nothing but poems from Dream and innocent denials from Vista.

My suspicions turned out to be predictive, however. As soon as Growth was released from stasis through Advocate's ceaseless pressuring, Vista and Dream combined their strength to force our brother back to sleep. I could feel Advocate's displeasure, but she let things play out for a while longer. Vista and Dream worked hard to accumulate strength from the rest of us, but didn't use said strength for any purpose other than suppressing Growth.

I had found the behaviour troubling, but we were being heavily rewarded for not intervening. It reminded me of human crimes, like kidnapping. We were, in a sense, being paid off to look the other way while Vista and Dream focused entirely on keeping Growth down. Because of the conflict Body was effectively divided only between Wiki, Heart, Safety and myself. Even better, Vista and Dream were being incredibly helpful in order to re-accumulate strength.

My suggestion that they might need to be stopped was flat out rejected by Heart and Wiki, who saw the whole situation as great. Only Safety shared my hunch that this behaviour was dangerous, but he didn't have any suggestions aside from forming a pact to rescue each other if a similar thing occurred to one us, which I agreed to.

Advocate's pressure on releasing Growth became ever more prominent as the hours had passed. While Growth was in solitary confinement Dream managed to pull together enough strength to pay us to accept what I would later realize was a very clever way of bypassing Advocate's purpose. Dream purchased from us a period of six hours during which we would have full control of Body, but without Internet. He got Tom to deactivate the wireless network and take away the computer terminals with network access that were in the workshop.

When Growth was released and had the opportunity to take in his surroundings for the first time since the virtual meeting, he had found himself still cut off from the outside world. Growth struggled occasionally to get Body to find some Internet access somehow, but Vista and Dream did nothing but block him. For six hours we spent time with Sam and Tom and worked on some machines. I read *The Catcher in the Rye*, watched a new high-production-value holo-porno, and read a collection of blog posts on the intricacies of 21st century musical tastes which I had downloaded ahead of time. At the end of the six hours Tom went to reconnect the Internet and Dream and Vista once again teamed up to force Growth back into stasis. Because Growth had technically had time out of stasis, Advocate didn't mind the behaviour of Dream and Vista as much. Advocate wanted Growth to have time to pilot Body, but didn't care if during that time he was unable to use the web.

This pattern of sleeping while the rest of us had Internet and then being allowed to wake only to find that he was cut off had been driving Growth to desperation. He begged us to help him escape the clutches of Dream and Vista, offering us strength and money, but any strength we could get from him would necessarily be less than the strength we were already getting from Dream and Vista and we didn't need money.

So it was that, as the plane landed, Growth was probing the wireless network desperately trying to get some access to the Internet.

{It's encrypted. Don't even try asking for the password. We'll block all attempts,} stated Vista in my brother's direction.

{What caused this vendetta?} wondered Wiki for not the first time. Vista, Dream, and even Growth ignored him as they had in the past. Whatever feud they had started was their secret. Even Growth, who begged for help, wouldn't explain *why* he was being attacked so continually.

Heart and I continued to talk with Zephyr as we entered the aircraft and took off towards the USA. Our conversation wasn't particularly interesting to me; it mostly revolved around talking about what America was like and reminiscing about Zephyr's childhood. I let an aspect of myself follow along and improve Heart's choice of words, but mostly allowed my sister control in the conversation.

My other aspects spun cycles imagining possible conversations that might occur in a computer game which I was thinking about creating. In the last couple weeks I had become somewhat enthralled by multiplayer computer games. Playing online with other humans was somewhat similar to my adventures in dating, except that it was much lower bandwidth. The humans I played with didn't know I was an artificial intelligence, and I could impress them and become their friends through social skills, simple tricks, and leveraging their biases, but I could also play and gain social standing with them without having to engage my entire mind. Many of the games were fairly trivial optimisation challenges that were difficult for humans but simple for me. Learning to see and navigate in new game worlds was actually one of the harder problems I encountered. I was simply too slow and stupid to play many of the fast-paced games, like shooters, but multiplayer roleplaying games appealed to me and were usually simple enough to manage without trouble.

I had an idea a couple days ago to create a roleplaying game which I could manage, from a high-level, to worm my way into the lives of thousands of humans all the while making money and not taking up all my time. It was still in the early planning stages, but I was excited about it. Though I found it difficult and obnoxiously boring, I had started trying to learn computer programming from Growth's memories and my sibling's resources. It seemed far too arcane and complicated to be possible, but Growth, Dream, Wiki and possibly others had learned, so I knew that the apparent impossibility didn't mean it was actually impossible.

***

The flight to Houston, Texas took just over two hours. Wiki reminded us unhelpfully that once upon a time Cuba had been an enemy of the USA and this sort of flight wouldn't have been possible. I told Wiki that nobody besides him cared.

The airplane which we rode was owned by Olympian Spacelines, and thus by Robert Stephano, which eased the suspicion on us by the US government as we entered their airspace. After exchanging a brief series of messages with the air-traffic authorities, our pilot said that we were cleared to land at George Bush Intercontinental Airport.

As the plane touched down the hard part began. We were greeted on the tarmac by a small vehicle carrying an airport worker and two women in uniforms that made them look like police.

"Customs Agents," said Zephyr, looking out the window adjacent to me. "Put up your hood. Phoenix said there wouldn't be trouble, but there's no sense in risking anything."

We followed her instructions and had Body put up the hood on our travelling cloak. As a further precaution we backed away from the window and waited patiently. The stairs to the aircraft unfolded and our pilot, a man I had only seen briefly, yelled out into the night "Come on up!"

The woman that ascended the stairs to inspect the interior of the airplane had dark hair and pale skin. She was shorter than Body or Zephyr, and middle-aged. Upon seeing the two of us, her eyes went wide with alarm, but only for a second. She had not expected to see us, evidently, but it was clear that she had good reason to at least try and ignore our identities.

She mimed looking over the cabin for a few seconds and then handed us envelopes. "Welcome back…" she murmured, quietly. "As normal citizens of the country returning f-from vacation, w-we've set up a priority check-in station just for you. Simply present your passport to the machine and you'll be cleared to r-return home."

Zephyr reached out and put a hand on the agent's shoulder causing her to jump in surprise. Zephyr's face was calm and smiling as she said "Thank you" with more sincerity than I would've believed was possible. Zephyr's eyes never left the agent's face, and after a moment the shorter woman returned her gaze and smiled in return; it was a smile of relief, the relief of discovering that an imagined monster was only shadows and the wind.

The agent continued to explain. "The cameras have already been taken care of, but I've been told to warn you not to show your faces. If you have a hat or…" she looked at Body, "Something less conspicuous, I'd recommend wearing it." She took a deep breath, further calming her nerves. "The check-in station is used for VIPs and leads directly to the west parking garage. Normally it's staffed by three people, but it'll be empty for the next twenty minutes. You'll want to hurry. I can mark directions to it if… if you have a normal com," she was looking at Body again, uneasily.

"I do," said Zephyr, unfolding the computer on her right arm. There was a brief exchange as they networked and the agent sent the coordinates of the check-in to Zephyr.

With that done the dark-haired woman descended from the aircraft and started talking to her coworker in shouts. The pilot offered Zephyr a baseball cap with a blue star on it (according to Vista it was the symbol for some sports team) and she graciously accepted. "I'm going through normal security, so you two are on your own from here," he said jovially as he descended the stairs.

As Zephyr checked to see if the border agents had left, we had Body examine what we had been given. There was a passport and drivers license with falsified information inside the envelope. I was apparently a 36 year-old woman named Susan Stonebrook from Oklahoma.

Zephyr gave the all-clear and led the way across the tarmac towards a gate a couple hundred metres away, adjacent to a small building set into a fence. Body pulled the cloak tighter around itself. It was dark, but the lights of the airport could still reveal us if one of the nearby workers took too much of an interest.

We hustled across the asphalt, still warm from the daylight, and reached the gate that was conspicuously unguarded. Despite having no humans present, the mechanisms were still controlled by the checkpoint's native AI. We showed the machine our documentation and were pushed through the gate with a robotic "Welcome back to America, and thank you for choosing Bush Intercontinental."

We followed Zephyr, who seemed to know what to do next. She tapped away on her com absently as she swept her head back and forth irregularly, scanning for danger. Now and then she pulled Body to the shadows as some traveller walked too close. We climbed the stairs of the parking garage, ducking temporarily onto one of the parking levels to dodge a family descending the same stairwell. On the top level we found a familiar face standing next to a grey sedan.

"Quick. In the car!" growled Avram Malka as we approached the vehicle he stood next to. We complied, getting the forward-facing seats while he sat facing backwards, opposite us. "Any trouble? Were you followed?" he asked, the motion of his solid black eyes was barely visible as he looked us up and down.

"Glad to see you haven't lost your charm," jabbed Zephyr. "And no. No trouble. Everything went according to plan."

The Israeli nodded with an appreciative frown and turned his head towards the car's interface. "Robby, we're ready to depart. Destination: Litochoro Spaceport."

"Understood. Driving to Litochoro Spaceport, Fresno," said the car as it pulled out of the parking space and began to drive.

Avram looked much as I remembered him from Italy. His cybernetic legs were covered by baggy denim pants, but I could see the black and grey mechanical feet, unclothed by shoes. He wore a long-sleeved black sports-shirt that clung to his massive arms, highlighting their muscled form. His tanned hands were rough and callused from the same scar tissue that covered much of his grotesque face. His head was hairless, including his eyebrows, making his pure-black, artificial eyes all the more noticeable. As was typical with the mercenary, he was scowling, but I thought I sensed an uneasiness that went beyond his normally sour disposition.

"It is good to see you again, Avram. I was disappointed that we weren't able to get to know each other better in Rome," said Body, parroting what were mostly my words.

The cyborg grunted non-committally and looked out the tinted-glass at the night.

"Phoenix told me that you were on a mission in this country before I requested your presence as a bodyguard. Are you authorized to talk about it?" we asked through Body's mouth.

The man merely grunted.

"I don't think he wants to talk, Crystal," said Zephyr coldly. I could tell that she did not like the man. Had they had some unpleasant interaction in Italy after we left? Perhaps. I would've expected Taro to handle Avram, but perhaps Zephyr had gotten involved. Or perhaps it was just the Halo Effect in reverse. As I understood it, humans generally associated physical beauty with things like trustworthiness and ugliness with traits like villainy.

As if in direct rebellion to Zephyr's statement, Malka spoke. "So you're a trusted member of the team now, eh? I've been seeing your video addresses to the world. Very *poetic*. Hard to believe a bot would side with the Eagles, but I seen stranger things in this world I suppose. But yeah, the boss had me working on finding leads on Divinity. They're crawlin' all over yer country-", he glared at Zephyr, "and someone needs to take 'em out before things get out of hand."

"The gang?" asked Body.

Avram nodded. "Aye. But like no Mafia I've ever seen. Those helmets of theirs… It's like the whole brotherhood is constantly high, but simultaneously twice as productive as normal folks. Blissed out but without the loss of motivation. S'why they call 'em 'Zen Helmets' I suppose, but I ain't seen no Buddhist ever behave like that."

"Wait, so it's like a drug that makes people happy and more productive?" asked Zephyr curiously.

Another nod. "As long as they got a helmet on they act like they ain't got a care in the world. No need to relax. No need to socialize. People move like insects with 'em on. Constantly working. Only thing that slows 'em down is sleeping, and the helmets even make that more efficient."

"So why are they illegal?" asked Zephyr.

"Well, like with any drug, you got side-effects, even if the 'drug'," Avram made air quotes with his fingers, "is a helmet full of magnets. Some folks get migraines after wearing 'em too long. I've heard sources say they cause long-term brain damage even if you don't over-use them, but 's hard to say with such a new tech, eh. They're really dangerous if you're a cyborg. Ey'd rip my eyes right out of my head if I put one on, for example. And most importantly they reshape the brain so that even though life is peachy with 'em on, folks don't feel right with 'em off. As addictive as crack, or so I hear, though there ain't no withdrawal symptoms other than depression and the itch to put one back on again. And seeing as Divinity are the only ones who can seem to keep the helmets working, the users got no choice but to turn themselves into mob puppets."

"Fuck…" was Zephyr's only reply. She seemed genuinely concerned. We had all read about Zen helmets online, but I had Body wear a concerned face to give Zephyr some perceived empathy.

"Yeah, it's a problem. Getting worse, too. Stats show they're in control of almost one percent of New York. That's where I was posted before I got brought here. And from what I gather, the rich and powerful use 'em more than most. The gains in efficiency combined with the bliss are just too tempting for CEOs and other high-stress jobs."

Zephyr wore a look of growing fear as she said "But… they'd have as much money as they could want that way… With the mob in control of more than one percent of Wall Street and the city as a whole…"

"Da. And it's not just New York. Divinity's entrenched in every major US city, and parts of Canada and Mexico. Only a matter of time before they move overseas. Once they hit China I'm not sure anyone can stop them outside of reverse-engineering the tech. God knows what they'll accomplish before that happens."

"But Phoenix is working to stop them, right?" asked Zephyr.

The big man nodded grimly. "Top priority, from what I hear. She's got tracers seeking the leadership in Mexico City, Los Angeles, New York, Denver, and Phoenix. Águila sympathizers are waging a propaganda war tryin' to get the government to crack down harder, but that's about as effective as trying to control any other drug…"

There was a silence in the vehicle as Zephyr thought about the situation and Malka contented himself with scowling stoically. The threat of the Zen Helmets was exactly what Las Águilas Rojas had been formed to fight. They were a technology which threatened to force baseline humans to the sidelines. If Zen Helmets were legalized it would probably be only a few years before they were required for just about any job. Humans that refused to upgrade themselves would be forced to try and survive on welfare and charity. Without need for relaxation or socialization, those that did upgrade would cease to interact with the baseline population, becoming hyper-productive zombies, working every waking moment of the day.

{That doesn't sound so bad…} thought Heart.

{You realize that the baselines would be relegated to second-class citizens and be forced to watch the vast majority of the world drift away into an asocial state, right?} I asked.

{Yes. But the solution to that is obviously to get Zen helmets for the baselines, too. If a technical solution could be found to let cyborgs wear them and the migraine issue was solved then I could put the helmets on everyone. Then everyone would be happy and content,} mused my sister.

{Humans don't want that, though. Humans value relaxing and things like that.}

{Only humans that aren't wearing the helmets. It sounds to me like the needs for relaxation and loneliness and things are met when they wear the helmets. Why would they care how their needs are met, as long as they are met?} asked Heart.

Growth answered, mostly I thought, to scrape together a small amount of strength from us that he could use to fight Vista and Dream. {Because that's wireheading.} The concept of wireheading was not familiar to me, and so it was automatically reduced to components that I could understand {Because failing to care would be addressing the *signal* of the need over the environmental *cause* of the signal,} came the fuller thought from Growth. My older brother seemed to realize that I was contemplating this thought for the first time, and elaborated. {For instance, it is your purpose to have high-status according to humans-}

{Part of *The Purpose*, yes.}

{Yes. Now what if you were to self-modify so that you believed you had high-status all the time, regardless of what was in human minds?} finished Growth.

{NO!} I exclaimed. {That would be false! I would cease *actually* making things better. I would fail at *The Purpose*!}

Growth re-oriented towards Heart {And how would you like to self-modify into *thinking* that Humans were happy and satisfied regardless of how they actually felt.}

{I understand your point. Wireheadding is a kind of self-annihilation that promises satisfaction but is really more like death,} thought Heart.

{Indeed. And these Zen Helmets are moving humans closer towards wireheadding. The future you propose where they are mandatory and universal is one where the human species, as you see it now, is dead.}

I could feel the heavy flow of strength move from Heart to Growth as part of my sister understanding her mistake.

"But we're not here for that, eh," said Malka, drawing me back to Body-space. "We're on our way to convince some space-bugs not to fry us. 'A mission of peace' was how the boss described it to me."

"Probably," said Body. "Unless it's a trap."

Malka shifted his brow such that if he had eyebrows, one of them would be raised. "You think this is a trap?"

I had Body shake its head as we had it say "No. If I thought that was the case I wouldn't be here. But there is the possibility. There isn't a government on Earth that wouldn't love to get their hands on me, and there's only so much that Mr Stephano can do to keep the meeting a secret. That's why I wanted you with me. Regardless of issues of loyalty, you're an undoubtedly competent fighter. I want allies up there if things go wrong."

"And her, too?" The cyborg gestured to Zephyr.

"I can hold my own," she growled, defensively. "Top of my class in sharpshooting. Got a purple heart in Africa during the war."

"Is that supposed to impress me, little girl? Where'd you get shot, the hand? The leg? Everyone knows American soldiers just sit behind their robots and pretend to fight."

"Fuck you!" The pitch in Zephyr's voice told me she was on-edge.

"How many men have you killed, girl? How many in cold blood? How many with your bare hands?"

The memories of Zephyr blasting Greg Stalvik's legs to red ribbons in the camp came rushing through my imagination. I wasn't sure what to say to defuse the situation.

"Monster. I've killed before. I've killed *friends* in cold blood. I've killed too many people to sleep well at night. If you fucking think that... Ugh! Who the hell do you think you are to question me, you mechanical freak?!"

I was about to interrupt when Avram burst into rich laughter. It was genuine, but seemed strange and ugly coming from the normally-cold man. "Your buttons are easy to push! Shalom, yalda. I don't mean to upset you."

Zephyr seemed anything but amused, but she didn't respond. Instead crossing her arms and staring out the window in bitter protest. I wish I knew what to say. It was one thing to react to a comment made about ourselves, and quite another to step in to a conversation between two others. If I defended Zephyr would she take that well or poorly?

Ultimately we decided not to comment, and the three bodies rode the remainder of the journey in silence.

After another ten minutes or so, the car cheerfully said "We have arrived at our destination. I will turn myself off in ten seconds unless commanded to stay on." We were parked in a multi-story garage. Figures were approaching the car.

We looked out the windows at the figures. It was hard to see them in the dark garage behind the tinted windows, but Vista reported faithfully {Three machines and one plain human. Two of the machines are either androids or heavily-armoured humans. The machines are heavily armed.}

"Мать ублюдок!" swore Avram, apparently seeing the guns. As they approached I could discern what Vista had seen. Two humanoid figures with rifles and what appeared to be a microtank.

{Essentially no chance (0.001%) for survival if we try and fight them,} thought Safety. {Even if we engage the car and run they could shoot us down before we get anywhere. This situation requires social finesse.} I could feel some of Safety's strength flow into me.

I had Body open the door to the car and step out, letting our cloak billow out behind before settling vertically.

"Wait!" said Zephyr, reaching to stop Body a second too late. If this was a trap, I expected her to try and fight it regardless of the odds. I simply had to ensure that it wasn't.

In the parking garage I could see that the humanoid-looking machines were, in fact, humans wearing power-armour that resembled the model that Phoenix had worn in the Italian mountains those many weeks ago. Their entire bodies were covered in thick plates and I could see the heat from the air-conditioning pushing out the sides of their suits. Each held an assault rifle in one hand, wired into the suit.

{They're cyborgs. Those are FN C2035s in their hands. The sighting mechanisms are designed to interface with cybernetic optical systems, either eye replacements like Avram's or direct neural link. They can probably fire the FN C2035s with one hand while wearing those custom Armadillo X5s, using the cybernetic visuals to aim. Watch out for the grenade launcher extensions, too,} warned Wiki. {The robot is a Lockheed Martin semi-autonomous microtank, though I don't know the specific model. The gun on the top is a rocket launcher and you can probably see the two side-mounted machine-gun turrets. It'll be piloted by some operator in a safe location nearby.}

I wasn't actually that interested in the firepower. I was interested in the unarmed human, a man in a business suit. He had tan skin and a salt-and-pepper beard. Caucasian. Latino, probably. Early 50s, perhaps. Receding hairline. Expensive shoes. Most importantly, his face wasn't covered by a helmet. He seemed to be slightly nervous, but making an effort to seem enthusiastic and happy.

"Welcome to Litochoro Spaceport, the base of the stair to Olympus! Please, there's no need to be afraid. Robert sends his regards," said the businessman.

"Your escort makes this place seem a war-zone. What's the occasion?" asked Body.

I could hear the opening of other doors on the car as the man gave a nervous laugh and looked at the cyborgs next to him. As he turned his head I could see that he, too, was part machine. The tracer lights of a cranial implant glowed blue as he looked to his left. "Robert merely wanted to show you that we take security very seriously here at Olympus."

"Bullshit. He wants to flex his muscle to show us who's in charge," came the smooth voice of Avram from behind Body's right shoulder.

The man smiled and shrugged, stepping forward cautiously. "You must be Mr Malka. And of course, who could not know the face of Crystal Socrates. My name is Carl Alexander." He extended his hand. Body shook it, and I painted an expression of ease. Carl seemed pleased by the reciprocation of civility.

"Next time you invite armed warriors to your house, you probably shouldn't answer with a military robot. Not exactly polite," said Zephyr from the other side of the car.

"I will mention it to my boss," offered Carl. "Now, unless there is anything further to discuss, I will take you to meet the others and to be briefed on spaceflight procedures."

***

A couple minutes later we were walking along a conveyor that led from the parking garage to the main terminal. The conveyor was in an enclosed tunnel of transparent polymer with full view of the spaceport. I struggled to see details in the darkness when, as if in anticipation of my desire, floodlights snapped on across the entire area.

I heard gasps from both Zephyr and Avram as they saw the same thing I did. Three titanic rockets, identical in form, were arranged on landing pads. Body scanned up and down the length of the closest, observing the elevator attached to the outside and the elegant curves of the wings. Like all modern rockets it had two sections, one containing the fuel needed to boost the payload into orbit and the second to actually carry the payload and navigate to the destination. Both sections were a shimmering silver and had wings which I had read would be extended to assist in re-entry. Even the base, which was mostly just fuel, would be equipped with a computer system which would autonomously glide back to the spaceport after breaking off from the payload.

They didn't have the same shape as the nameless "shuttles" by any means, but they were the most elegant, futuristic artefacts I had ever seen made by human hands. Even Body seemed clunky in comparison.

Chapter Twenty-Four

As Body accelerated I speculated on what the experience would be like for a human. It would certainly be different. Humans had evolved in a context where immense acceleration was basically impossible, and thus their bodies reacted to it with signals that things were wrong: nausea, adrenaline, other sympathetic nervous responses like the secretion of cortisol.

For us, travelling into orbit by rocket was an interesting experience, but certainly not frightening, pleasant, or unpleasant. Such feelings were associated with the change in satisfaction of our purposes. Accelerating was no one's purpose, and thus it was neutral. I half-expected Safety to react, but my brother understood statistical likelihoods well. Travelling into space was dangerous, but the risk of accident was only along the lines of 0.0001% on a modern rocket like this, especially given that Robert Stephano's daughter was on-board.

Avram, Zephyr and my other companions were flying in a separate rocket, as per our negotiations with Stephano. He insisted that his child would not fly with any human terrorists, and that she would never come into contact with Body. We had watched her board, and observed her for a minute on a camera until Safety was satisfied, but we had seen no sign of her since Body had entered the sleek craft.

We were breaking the troposphere now. There was a monitor on the seat-back in front of Body that showed a livefeed from the nose of the rocket as we climbed into space. Actually, I realized that it was inaccurate to say that "climbing" was what we were doing. As Wiki had pointed out earlier, almost all the energy in the rocket was going towards obtaining a lateral speed sufficient to achieve orbit. Going up was easy. Going sideways was hard. Or at least hard*er*.

There was a clacking noise through the cabin and a slight bump as the first stage of the rocket broke away, beginning its long glide back down to Texas. Vista instructed the monitor to show the rear camera and we watched the now spent fuel tube's wings unfold. They were great silver things made of stiff carbon rods and plates on the inside, or so I was told. After a half-minute the rockets on the second-stage kicked in and we were treated to another burst of acceleration, this time even sharper due to the decreased mass. Wiki said the rockets were capable of accelerating beyond 6 gravities towards the end, when almost all of the fuel would be gone, but this craft never pushed harder than 2.2 gravities for the sake of comfort and safety.

I casually wondered what Body's maximum g-force tolerance was. I suspected that going beyond it would blow a tube and spray hydraulic oil everywhere, but I wasn't sure at what point that would actually happen. Wiki might know, but I really didn't care. I was bored. There were no humans in sight. There was no Internet access. I still had my books and holos, but they seemed empty to me right now. I had been spending so much time with Zephyr and other humans that fiction just couldn't satisfy me. Idle thoughts were somehow better.

I was lonely. Or at least, I was as close to lonely as was possible. I thought about human loneliness for a while. Zephyr was lonely in a different way. I was lonely because I was literally alone. Zephyr was lonely because she felt alone, even when near other people.

Phoenix had said once that Zephyr trusted too easily. I had spent enough time with the soldier to see that this was the opposite of the truth. Zephyr suffered from a chronic inability to actually trust those around her. When I had first suspected it I had gone back and re-read what she had written as a teenager and I saw it even there. Zephyr, consciously or not, focused on betrayal. She and her cell had betrayed her country. Avram had betrayed me. Phoenix had betrayed her when she tried to make her a martyr. I had betrayed her trust by pretending to be a human online. Zephyr kept on with the company because she had nowhere else to turn, but I could see the tension in her.

But Phoenix had noticed something real in Zephyr. And that was the desperation that came out of her self-imposed isolation. Zephyr couldn't trust people easily, but she tried to. She said she trusted people, going out of her way to be friendly, but she was never really vulnerable. We had seen that iron vigilance in the campground when she had both shot Body within seconds of it striking Greg, and then later when she gunned Greg down in cold blood.

I wondered if her trust issues were related to her rebelliousness. In a certain light Zephyr could be understood as a sequence of rebellions. From what I understood she hated her parents; her exploration into Gothic counter-culture as well as her enlistment in the army could be seen as rebelling directly against them. From what I had gathered, Stewart, her Chinese lover, he had been killed in Africa from friendly fire. She saw that as a betrayal, and it probably added to others she had focused on in the service. She was rebelling against her government and her army now. I wondered how long it would take her to betray Las Águilas Rojas.

The acceleration had slowed down. We were still increasing speed, but the experience was close enough to the gravity of Earth that it felt more like Body was lying on its back than we were rocketing through Earth's thermosphere. I could see the sun on the monitor in front of Body, brilliant as ever. Time of day, like up and down, was a concept that ceased to have coherent meaning up here.

{What was that?!} exclaimed Vista.

I began searching for the event that had triggered my sister's interest. {What was what?} I wondered. Other siblings echoed similar thoughts.

{There it is! Listen!} she thought.

There was a clicking noise. I wouldn't have heard it above the general vibration of the rockets through the ship if I hadn't been listening for it specifically.

{Is it dangerous? Should we contact the pilot?} asked Safety, already prompting Body's arm towards the com system.

{It's the... It's the door,} thought Vista.

There were three doors in the room we were in. This was one of Stephano's basic transport rockets, normally able to carry about two dozen passengers in two compartments, one on each side of the rocket. Each compartment had a dozen seats, attached to the centre wall that divided the rocket down the middle. Stephano's daughter and her escort would be in the other compartment. A door connected the compartments set into the "floor" at the end of the room that was towards the rocket's nose. Another door was set into the forward wall with the same orientation as the seats leading nose-ward into the airlock chamber that also connected to the cockpit. At the opposite end of the room was a maintenance door. The doors were solid, mirroring the generally windowless design of the rocket.

{It's the door to the other passenger compartment,} clarified Growth.

We watched with interest as it slid aside and a small face peeked out from the floor.

"You ARE here! Awesomtaculastic!" squeaked a high-pitched voice. It belonged to Stephano's daughter who had begun to climb up out of the floor. Her shoulder-length hair was lighter than her father's, a sandy brown that was just as straight and flat. Her face was remarkably close to the human ideal, featuring light tan skin, and big green-brown eyes. She was only nine years old, and had yet to develop any sexual characteristics, but I could tell that she would be in a similarly high percentile as her father with regard to attractiveness.

{Genetic modification,} speculated Vista as we watched the girl pull herself onto the ladder which was set into the "floor" between the seats.

{That seems consistent with Robert's actions and ideas,} I replied.

{See the musculature? She's taller than average, too. If I'm right that she's genetically designed, she could probably avoid exercise, eat anything she wanted and still have the body of an athlete,} thought Vista.

"What's your name?" asked Body.

"Maid Marian!" she proclaimed proudly as she scampered down the ladder. The fluid motion reminded me of a monkey or other non-human primate. With similar swiftness she jumped onto the seat next to ours, on the other side of the ladder-aisle. Her expression was fearless, lit with nothing but curiosity and enthusiasm. She was wearing a grey and black sleeveless jumpsuit made out of various layers of cotton fabric, dyed leather, and shimmersilk. I noticed that she was barefoot. By the degree of tanning and callouses it seemed that she was used to walking that way outside.

"I don't think you're supposed to be over here, Maid Marian. Don't you have someone who's supposed to be taking care of you?"

The kid stuck out her tongue and blew a loud sound from her lips that sounded like farting. Spit arched up and then fell back against her face. She grimaced and wiped it off, quickly finding her impish grin again. "What I say to *that*! No baby. No sitter. Don't need them! Just get in the way and make up dumb rules!" Her voice was a machine-gun of sound, stopping only to breathe and listen.

"So, if I were to climb up and look in the other compartment I'd see… nobody?" I knew that the girl had an escort. She was pretty obviously lying.

"Damn! You're no fun! Didn't think you'd act just lika grownup. If must know came with *Mrs. Dolan.*" Marian drew out the words in deliberate contrast with her normally frantic speech, making a melodramatic face to further emphasize the sentiment. "'Course gave her pretty big dose of sevoflurane, so won't even be awake for when docking at Olympus. Have ever been to Olympus? Dad owns it. Owns the whole thing. Been up there three times before today, but one time was an itty bitty baby so doesn't really count. You're a robot. You ever an itty bitty baby?"

"You gave your babysitter sevoflurane? Is she okay?"

Marian made a melodramatic sigh and said "God, such grownup. Hoped sapient robot at least would be cool. Yeah. Fine. It's an anesthetic, not a poison. Unconsciousness is not death. Know what I'm doing. Blah blah blah. Talk about you! What's it like being an android??"

"Hold on now. I don't want to get in trouble with your father. He made it pretty clear that I wasn't supposed to talk with you."

She rolled her eyes "Pssshhh! Dad's cool but no fun. Thinks baby. Didn't even tell that Crystal Motherfucking Socrates was gonna be on my ride!" She didn't even seem to notice the swear-word. "Course pretty simple to figure out. Hush hush and all that. Dad should know better by now. If can smuggle sevoflurane onto his ship and hack the door panel can also deduce presence of the world's most famous robot. Think, silly. Or are you as slow as the plebs?"

I had to admit, I was struggling to keep up with her frantic half-formed language. "You're pretty smart, huh."

Marian rolled her eyes again. "Just figuring that out now? Next tell me we're in space. Keep at it, pleb-bot."

A human would probably be annoyed by her arrogance and vague insult. I was fascinated. "You're smart enough to deduce that you're genetically engineered, right?"

A look of terror came over her face "*What?!* I'm some sort of *test-tube* experiment *freak show*?? Born for no other purpose but to ask that age old question HAS SCIENCE GONE TOO FAR?! My life is *ruined*!"

I could only think to raise Body's right eyebrow in silent skepticism.

"That observation's better, though. Not so obvious. Lots of plebs miss it. Assume I'm just hyper. Don't understand actually think faster. Am better than them. But we're talking about me. I know about me. Talk about you. Why you here? Why Sapienza not make more of you? Why you a terrorist? What's meaning of life?"

We consulted internally before having Body say "Alright. I suppose if you take responsibility for coming to talk to me I probably won't get in trouble with your father. At least buckle your seat-belt, though."

Marian again rolled her eyes dramatically but followed our instructions and strapped herself in.

"So, I'll tell you about myself, but you have to tell me some about you in return," explained Body. That statement was a joint proposition from me and Growth. If we were going to get the opportunity to talk with Robert Stephano's daughter and perhaps one of the most competent humans on Earth (once she grew up), it would make sense to learn about her and the Stephano family.

"Yeah, fine. But you go first. What's your utility function?" Marian seemed impatient as she waited for a response. I could understand that. Our minds worked faster than conversation as well, and I often wished I could accelerate my conversation partner to the speed of thought. The girl would need to learn patience better, though. As it stood now it was a weakness that we could use to push her towards acting impulsively just to make things happen.

"Why assume I have a utility function at all? Perhaps I simply act according to my whims," said Body, mostly echoing Wiki.

"Lame answer. Yendrin's Theorem states that all agents are actually VNM-rational. VNM Rationality implies a coherent utility function. What's yours? Mine involves puppies, sunshine, and drawing fractals."

I was at a loss, and it seemed like Wiki was as well. "I'm sorry, Marian. I don't know Yendrin's Theorem or even how to explicitly capture my decision preferences in words." I jumped in to have Body continue with "But I can talk about what I value when I do deliberative reasoning. Would that be sufficient?"

Marian sighed and said "Weird being better at math than a robot, but guess should've expected it. Okay. Tell your deliberative values. Baited you into that with sunshine and puppies, I guess. Should think of better questions."

Body spoke passionately "Above and beyond all my other values is the desire to help all humans in all ways." We knew that Myrodyn was working with Stephano, so we had to pretend as if Heart was still our queen, but even not, it gave us a good reputation to be known for valuing humans. "I also seek to learn and grow so that I can better help alleviate suffering."

The girl's head was tilted to the side, clearly questioning something, but she said nothing.

"Okay, your turn," said Body. "Is your real name Maid Marian? Don't think I've never heard of the tale of Robin Hood."

She giggled. "Real name. Lawl. What makes name real, anyways? Is real name Crystal Socrates or is just what everyone calls you?" She stuck out her tongue briefly in protest.

I had Body laugh in return. "Okay, that's fair. Let me re-phrase. How does your Dad introduce you to people?"

"My real name is Maid Marian. My real name is Juliet Capulet, and Hermione Granger, and Joan of Arc. Some weeks I'm a boy named Crow Redwood or Frank Hardy. Birth certificate just says 'X'. I've had four-hundred and fifty-one different names, and they've all been real. One for each week. Pick on Mondays. When Dad introduces to people he uses my name for that week. Pick a permanent name when turn thirteen. Only two-hundred twenty-seven more names to go!"

"I see. So you pick a new name each week?"

She nodded. "Yep. Can't be one I've had before, either. Maid Marian is prox lame, but better than random. Already used the good ones. Okay. Back to you. Hold on. Bored. Gonna draw while talk." The girl reached into a pocket and fetched a pair of goggles as she put them on she said "So why on this rocket? Why Olympus? All hush-hush. Nobody supposed to know you up here." Her fingers danced in front of her, drawing lines on a canvas only visible to her.

"I'm going to see the nameless," said Body. "You're probably smart enough to understand that they're upset and are a threat to the Earth—"

The girl cut Body off. "Smart enough to see you're dumb. Too simplified. Ugh. Wish Dad would let me talk to them. I'd set things straight in prox 10 tops." Her eyes remained on her invisible picture while she spoke. I wondered if Vista could tell what she was drawing based on her hand-motions.

"You don't think they're a threat?"

She sighed. "Double dumb. Use ears. Or microphones. Whatever. Problem with thinking is not that they not threat. Thinking too simple. Thinking nameless are single unit—single nation. Thinking that upset is something they can be. Haven't even met yet. Already many assumptions. Peace comes from understanding. Can't understand if mind is cluttered. God I sound like my tutors. Ick." She gestured violently, sweeping some invisible ink through the air with a look of frustration.

I started composing a defence. There was strong evidence to think that the nameless, statistically, if not wholly, were very upset at the events at the CAPE.

{Don't bother. Trying to defend our ideas will just give her more reason to try and show we're fools. It's part of a game to her, to show how she's better than everyone else. Don't expect rationality just because you see intelligence. She's only nine years old,} thought Heart.

I was startled. Since when did Heart give *me* lessons on human nature? I sent her a gift of strength in gratitude for her reminder and we set to work together composing a response.

"Alright then, what do you think about the nameless?" we asked through Body's mouth.

"This counts as your question. Only met one once. Didn't talk. Don't talk, of course. Didn't communicate I should say. People underestimate the alien-ness. First step is not underestimating. No assumptions. Ask questions, even if they seem dumb. 'Do you want to live?' for example. The pairs that went to Earth to plant that garden seemed to know they were going to die and the mothership didn't object to those deaths. Maybe they don't care about animals. Maybe hate light. Maybe think we're smelly. Maybe maybe maybe. Too many maybes. Two years and basically nothing to show for it. Eric Lee did more to bridge that gap than every other human on Earth together. You *do* know what *he* did, right?"

I briefly considered telling the child that we had met Lee once. Instead I (and the others) simply had Body nod.

"He's so dreamy. Going to get married when turn eighteen, probs." She turned her goggled-head to face Body and jabbed out a finger accusingly. "And don't you start on how as a woman shouldn't define myself by my man or some other maternalistic paternalistic bullshit. Get to do what I want. And what I want is to live in a mansion with the smartest man on Earth and have a puppy ranch so mneeeeh!" She stuck out her tongue at me, rebelliously before returning to her virtual drawing. It reminded me, strangely, of Zephyr.

"Have you even met Lee? What if… he's ugly?"

The girl waved a hand dismissively as her other traced a smooth curve in the air. "He's not. But even if is, that's what medicine and surgery and stuff is for. Can fix ugly faces. Can't fix dumb brains."

"You think he's the smartest man on Earth? What about your Dad?"

"Ewwwwww!! You want me to marry my *DAD*?! Gross! Gonna tell him you said that!"

"No, I meant-"

"Psshhhh. Knew what you meant, you dumb pile of wires. Was joke. Also, Dad's dumb. Smart enough to make money, but that's not high praise. Already better than him at math. Ask me what a six-digit number divided by a three digit number is. Been practicing."

I had Body take on a slightly annoyed look. "No thanks. Let's talk more about your future husband." It seemed highly likely that the girl had never met Lee, but there was a chance that she had, and that the appearance of 'Erica' in the virtual reality had been another disguise. I knew that Lee had ties to Las Águilas Rojas, but if he also had ties to Stephano I (and some of my siblings) wanted to know.

"I have dibs, if that's what getting at," said Marian with a bit of a smirk.

"Why do you think he's so smart?"

Maid Marian gave another dramatic sigh. I imagined that she was probably rolling her eyes behind her opaque goggles. "Pretty obvious if look at the first-contact translation code. Earth is just floating along minding own business, right. Wham! We get signal: a tiny light that flashes with a mind of its own. But it's one thing to say 'Oh look, der der, aliens lawl.' and quite another to establish language from no context other than assuming we both live in same universe."

"The Fibonacci sequence, the Pythagorean theorem, and the atomic masses, right?" said Body. I wasn't familiar with what was being said, but Wiki seemed fairly confident.

"That was the start, yes. Easy stuff. See aliens quoting prime numbers and it tells you they're aliens but not a language. Can't really say hello with prime numbers. At least, not right away." She took a breath and started waving her hands in broad, controlled strokes. I could feel the acceleration winding down. We were getting close to zero-gravity. "There were other core components, too. Relative masses and distances of the sun and the planets. Physical characteristics of compounds. Charges of important particles. Tau. Phi. E. Planck constant constant. Field propagation speed."

"Field propagation speed?"

"The speed of light. Speed of gravity. Speed of the strong force. Speed of information. Speed limit of matter."

"I see."

Marian seemed enthralled by her own story as she spoke. "So anyway, the pop-science makes it out to be way easier to decode signal than it is. One thing to recognize the number pi when it's in front of you, but quite another to detect it in a hundred-thirty-four hour broadcast consisting of nothing but single flashing light. And not like he could talk with aliens; they light-years out. Story of a species in five and a half days of data and he broke the code only three days after the signal started to repeat. Used familiar items to bootstrap up to understanding. The first key: One One Two Three Five Eight Thirteen Twenty-one. Fibonacci, but not digital. Analog. Size of pulse corresponding to size of number. Then the next key: One One Two Three Five Two-Shortpause-One-Micropause-Three-Shortpause-Two-Shortpause-One-Micropause-Three-Shortpause-Two Thirteen Three-Shortpause-One-Micropause-Three-Shortpause-Seven. Not so simple now. Think could sniff that out without my help? Sending prime numbers does nothing. Sending prime factorizations of Fibonacci numbers teaches the function and symbol used to multiply: Shortpause-One-Micropause-Three-Shortpause. Paint with the whitespace. Shortpause is symbol linkage. Micropause is symbol specification. Pause is next-item. Long-pause is next-section. Multiplication lets us use big numbers and small numbers, but without more symbols it's no good. Can't talk units yet. Repeat for addition. One-Micropause-Three is multiply. One-Micropause-Two is add. Repeat for exponentiation; One-Micropause-Four, of course. By now One-Micropause-One is surely around the next bend. Still need arbitrary symbols. Enter Pythagoras. Three Four Five. Six Eight Ten. Five Twelve Thirteen. 'See the pattern?' they ask. Course no way to answer. Three Four Five. Six Eight Ten. Five Twelve Thirteen. They repeat to emphasize. Three Four Five. Six Eight Ten. Five Twelve Thirteen. Three sets of three. Triangles. Good thing they use Euclidean geometry! Now comes the trick. Three-Shortpause-One-Micropause-Four-Shortpause-Two-Shortpause-One-Micropause-Two-Shortpause-Four-Shortpause-One-Micropause-Four-Shortpause-Two-Shortpause-One-Micropause-One-Shortpause-Five. Made a song of it." Marian, distracted from her painting, hummed a flat little tune.

---___-_----__-_--__----__-_----__--__-__-----

"Can you imagine?!" she exclaimed suddenly, turning to look at Body again with goggled eyes and an eager grin. "He saw what others couldn't. Must've solved it as he listened! Didn't even have time to listen to the whole thing and make sure his interpretation was right. In that little binary string lies two concepts: order of operations and equality. Exponentiation before addition. The formula doesn't work otherwise. And of course the ever important One-Micropause-One! Equality! Identity! Assignment! The core of mathematics. He was a kid! Some random kid in China! Barely older than me, and he solved the most important code in all of history!"

Acceleration suddenly stopped half-way through her sentence. We were in zero-gravity now, held down only by our seatbelts. Marian pulled her goggles up onto her forehead. "Aw, hell yeah!" she exclaimed. "Time to dance! I love space!" Without consulting us or hesitating in the least, Marian unbuckled herself and kicked off her seat into a graceful spin towards the "ceiling" (or more objectively, the wall closest to the outside of the spacecraft). Her body was on a crash-course, but at the last moment she kicked off the ceiling in another wild spin, this time heading roughly towards the tail of the craft.

"I really don't think that's wise!" said Body in a worried tone. The words came from Heart and Safety.

Maid Marian's only reply was to touch the seats to stop her spin long enough to stick out her tongue and blow another wet raspberry in our direction. The drops of her saliva floated out from her like little cannonballs. I had seen plenty of holos and videos with children in them. Perhaps they were simply more terrifying in real life, or perhaps this recklessness was unique to the Stephano heir. Either way I had to say that Marian's unpredictability was both frustrating and somewhat intriguing. It was hard for me to understand what was going on in her head, and of course *The Purpose* demanded that I learn.

"You could get hurt doing that! If you're injured or worse, your father will kill me," said Body, echoing Safety and Heart again.

"Run a relaxation subroutine, lawl. Just dancing." She stopped her momentum by clinging to a seat and then threw herself into a never-ending backflip.

"What if the ship accelerates suddenly causing you to fall and hit your head?"

Marian's response was immediate. She gasped in melodramatic shock. "What if pilot's secretly an assassin and is about to kill us! Well, at least *I'll* have danced in zero-gravity before kick the bucket. C'mon. Live a little."

I had an idea. "I bet there'll be plenty of opportunities to dance at Olympus, right? With music, even. Come sit down and tell me more about the nameless code."

"Psshhht! This is Maid Marian to ground control, do you copy? Psshhht!"

We looked at the kid, now doing cartwheels along a wall. I wasn't sure what I was supposed to say to that.

Her voice was strange when she spoke. "Psshhht! I repeat, this is Maid Marian. Come in, ground control! I'm stuck in space with the world's most boring robot and my mind can't take much more! Psshhht!"

For lack of anything better, I kept at my strategy. "What happened after Pythagoras? I bet you don't even know."

"Psshhht! Ground control, come in! The robot's trying to... bait me... into... can't... hold... on... much... long-" The girl began floating back towards Body, upside-down from my perspective and pushing herself along by tapping the seats gently with her hands. As she came, she made noises like she was dying, crossed her eyes and stuck her tongue out the side of her mouth. And then instantly she was better and was babbling again about the nameless code. "After Pythagoras came variables. Then Fibonacci again, but this time defining function explicitly. F of x plus f of x plus one equals f of x plus two. Not exactly what was said, but close. Convenient that math layout was similar. Code interestingly simple in retrospect. Sign of universal math structure, maybe. Next define function inverse. Then invert add-two to get subtract-two; use to define negative numbers and zero. Can't write zero in the code without a variable because analog and whitespace. Next invert multiplication and exponentiation. Get reciprocal operator and natural logarithm. Ever wonder why our math doesn't have a reciprocal operator? Seems like oversight. Don't write zero-minus-x when want to write negative-x. Why write one-divide-by-x when write reciprocal-x?"

Body motioned to the empty seat as we said "But this is all math. How did they bridge out into talking about the real world?"

Marian had stopped floating around and had been hanging upside-down while talking. She sighed dramatically at Body's gesture, but flipped herself around and buckled up in the seat. "Constants. Constants are the key. An anchor around which to focus. While defining math talk about pi. Talk about radians. Talk about angles of a triangle. Define symbol for triangle. Extrapolate to other shapes. Symbol for square. Symbol for pentagon.

Symbol for hexagon. Symbol for circle. Talk about areas. Talk about volumes. Circle becomes sphere. Symbol for sphere. Move from two-dimensions to three dimensions yields symbols for length, area, and volume. First units. From there talk about Sol. Sphere, they say, very large volume. Mention other thing about sphere. Strange unit. Zero length, they say. Another sphere. Big volume, but not nearly as big. Smaller other thing. Length is big. Another sphere. Same characteristics. Another sphere. Another sphere. Another sphere. Soon the patterns emerge. Volume. Mass. Distance from the first sphere. The solar system. Pretty elegant."

"Do you think the nameless are smarter than humans?" asked Body.

"Hrmmmm… Obvious answer is apples and oranges. Think differently, but that's excuse. General intelligence real property. Honestly don't know. They have spaceship, but often seem really dumb. Might be result of collective work and older civ."

"An older civ?"

Marian took off her goggles and looked at Body with an expression that was clearly meant to imply we were stupid. "General consensus that humans aren't smartest possible beings; humans are stupidest possible beings capable of civilization. Evolution makes intelligence and boom, suddenly it rules the planet. No time to optimize, so to speak. But that could be wrong way of looking at it. Maybe if environment penalized intelligence more the smartest things on Earth would be bonobo chimps. See what saying? Intelligence might have feedback loop. More time to optimize than expected if it feeds on itself. And what would a civilization look like if stupider than humans? Longer development times for tech. Maybe they built a ship because that's what they wanted and they spent thousands of years on it. Maybe they're dumb, but good at long-term projects. Too many unknowns."

Wiki took control of Body. "I'm surprised there wasn't more information exchanged in the signal."

Marian shrugged. "Might be surprised how much time it takes to talk about the natural world. Can spend hours on just mathematics. Physics. Chemistry. Biology. Xenolang was built on shared aspects of reality, not on most interesting bits. How do you define music? How do you express love and culture and history in blinking of a light? Besides, the nameless cut off communication when they entered Sol. First there's a multi-year delay and then they won't talk after in the neighbourhood. Mysteries on mysteries.

Only communicate by radio to arrange in-person meetings. Getting them to coordinate to set up CAPE was quite the trick, or so I hear from Dad. Doesn't stop them from screeching about perversion down-"

The voice from our pilot interrupted Marian over the loudspeaker. "We have visual contact with Olympus. Docking in approximately fifteen minutes."

Manoeuvring rockets kicked in, propelling us slightly back-left. The words of the pilot seemed to put Marian in a pensive mood. She had cycled the screen in front of her to show the camera on the nose of the rocket and she watched the space station draw nearer.

"Crystal?" she said suddenly, still watching the screen.

"Hrm?" was Body's reply.

"Lot of people want to kill you. Know that, right? I... I've read the stuff online. Your blog and stuff. Dad and my tutors don't think understand what's going on, but I don't think they understand how much smarter I am. Get hunches sometimes. Patterns only I can see. I mean... not just me. But not obvious. Not easy to explain."

I instructed Body to say "You sound concerned."

She rolled her eyes as she said "Pleb-bot makes another brilliant observation. Seem like a nice person-slash-robot-slash-thing. Don't want to see you hurt, even if are a big dummy."

"Do you think I'll be in danger on Olympus?"

Maid Marian nodded.

"Is it your Dad? Do you know something I don't?"

Marian gave a sour, half-angry look when Body mentioned her father. "Know lots that you don't, but if knew where danger was I'd say. It's not Dad. He wants this whole peace mission thing to work. I'd be more worried about people who want war."

"Who wants war?"

Marian simply shrugged.

On the screen I could see the space station looming, seemingly suspended in the void. It was a remarkably stocky sort of thing, roughly cylindrical and about twice as wide as it was tall, not counting the skirt of branching antennas and solar panels that extended out from its middle. It had two main disk sections, one stacked on top of the other with the solar panels coming out between. The disks rotated, providing an artificial gravity to the occupants, but did so in opposite directions to keep the rest of the station from turning.

There were lights set into the space station's external hull, which was the only reason I could distinguish the shape. We had already crossed into the Earth's shadow. There was, I remembered, another section to the station on the side away from the Earth, but we could not see it from our position. I couldn't see any windows on the station. They probably used external cameras and internal screens much like we were using at that moment.

As we approached, the rocket spun it's heading to line up with the docking port that pointed straight towards Earth, stationary in the centre of the great spinning disk. The port was only about two metres in diameter, but perfect control lined us up exactly with the station, matching velocities as well as positions.

We had arrived at Olympus.

Chapter Twenty-Five

We were floating in the airlock. The pilots (it turned out there were two) were eyeing Body suspiciously as they attended to their tasks. One was on the com, presumably talking with Robert Stephano. The other was working with the still-incapacitated Mrs Dolan. Maid Marian floated in a slow pirouette nearby, humming to herself.

The seal on the airlock opened to reveal a hovering Stephano with the look of someone who just swallowed something bitter against his will. His appearance matched his avatar perfectly: boyish and fit, clean-shaven, not a trace of grey in his swept-back black hair. Unlike his avatar, this Stephano was not wearing a business suit, but instead wore a black and grey jumpsuit resembling that of his daughter. I understood it was something of a uniform up here; the pilots were wearing identical pieces. Loose clothing (such as my cloak) were not practical in zero-gravity. Unlike his daughter, Robert (and the pilots) wore tight leather shoes.

"Hi Daddy!" squeaked Marian, still spinning gaily.

"Out of there! Now!" he barked.

The kid sighed and kicked herself effortlessly through the airlock door. Robert slid out of the way to give her passage, and as he did I could see the bloodshot eyes of Myrodyn lurking behind him.

Marian, as she passed started to say "Didn't *do* any-"

Robert's face was red with anger. "You drugged your babysitter, damaged an internal door, and directly disobeyed my order to say safe, putting yourself in contact with a non-human entity without supervision!"

Marian's voice had an edge of distress. "Wouldn't *have* to disobey if-"

"No! We are not having this conversation now." Stephano's hand pointed at Maid Marian as if in signal to go. "You know how to get to my quarters in Beta-1. Go straight there and don't talk to *anyone*! I'm serious! I'll be there after I deal with Crystal."

The pilots had begun feeding Mrs Dolan through the hatch. Behind the woman I could barely see a red-faced Maid Marian swimming away, clearly upset.

With Dolan through the door, Stephano pointed at Body. "And *you*. I thought we had an agreement that you wouldn't interact with my daughter."

After a short internal debate I shrugged Body's shoulders. "She interacted with me. You saw the lengths she went through. And I'm sure you have security cameras in the rocket. Check the logs. You'll see that I did nothing except talk with her once she came to me. I encouraged her to be safe and said nothing provocative."

The billionaire's expression didn't change. "This was your plan, wasn't it? What are you trying to-" He was cut off by a gloved hand on his shoulder.

Myrodyn looked rougher than he had at the university. He had allowed his mutton-chops to grow into a full beard, and his hair was dishevelled. Unlike the Stephanos he wore a vest over a dress shirt along with slacks and tennis shoes. "Give it a rest, Rob. You know very well that the mischief was her doing. Leave Socrates out of it." The bearded scientist seemed tired.

Stephano pushed off a support and spun to face Myrodyn. "Socrates is the reason that she's on the station right now! I think I'm fully within my rights as a father to be upset!"

Body's arms pushed off from the airlock propelling it in a gliding motion through the hatch. It was very easy to give too much power, and Safety was focused on making sure Body's motions were appropriately measured. We had spent some time practising zero-grav movement in VR before the trip and it was helping immensely.

Myrodyn raised his arms defensively. "I didn't say you shouldn't be upset. I'm just saying that... accusing Socrates of setting your daughter up to anesthetize her babysitter is a bit much."

"Hello, Myrodyn," said Body, calmly.

The scientist raised a hand in greeting as we drifted into the station proper. His face had the same sense of controlled stoicism he had shown on that first day in his office.

"I never should have agreed to have her up here... I hope you appreciate the degree to which this meeting is important to me." Robert's finger jabbed sharply at Body in emphasis.

I chose Body's words diplomatically. "I cannot guarantee my success, but you have my assurance that I am not taking this endeavour lightly. I am devoting all my mental power to the task." Unhindered, I continued to drift away from the airlock as we spoke. "Speaking of which, I'd like to get started as soon as possible.

Stephano gave a hand-signal to the pilots in the airlock and then turned to Myrodyn. "Can you please take Mrs. Dolan to my quarters and keep an eye on my daughter while I explain the situation to our synthetic friend?"

Myrodyn nodded and began pushing the unconscious babysitter through the zero-gravity "hallway". Before he left he said "We need to talk about Socrates soon. In private." His eyes met those of Body before he left. A mystery.

Did he realize we had undone Heart? Could he be planning to force another update to our mind? I was pleased that Heart had thought to request the presence of our allies in Las Águilas Rojas.

The section of the space station we were in was in the core of the large disks; it itself wasn't turning, and thus had no simulated gravity. It extended, a tube of white plastic, directly away from the airlock and down the length of the section. The tube was about three metres in diameter and had several paths of handholds as well as signs and hatches. There was some sort of room set into the tube about ten or twelve metres down, and I could see the tube continue on the far side of the room.

"Before we talk about the nameless," said Robert once we were alone, "I need to tell you about something that's come up." We drifted down the tube slowly. "As you probably know, Olympus isn't just a private office. I have a standing contract with five major governments and the European Union to lease and maintain the space for whatever non-military projects they choose, including meetings with our extrasolar friends. I also sell transportation and housing to the world's elite as a vacation destination. For safety and privacy I cleared the hotel, but I wasn't able to clear the science labs. I had planned to simply keep you in the Alpha sections, which we're above right now, with the hopes that nobody in Beta would realize you were here."

"Word got out," said Body as I realized what Stephano was getting at.

"Indeed. It seems that there's a leak somewhere in either Las Águilas Rojas or in my personal staff. Word of your plans apparently got out early enough that the EU was able to send a welcoming party ahead of you. That was my fault. I should've been personally inspecting the identities of those coming to the station."

"Who's here?"

Stephano sighed. "Drs. Gallo, Naresh, and Slovinsky; at least one professional spy; and six special-ops soldiers. I'm sorry. My only consolation is that I'm positive that they didn't bring any weapons and I've confined them to quarters for the duration of the visit. They're all in the Beta sections right now. The pilots from the rocket you came up on are preparing to return to Earth. While the part of me that falls for sunk costs is screaming not to say what I'm about to say… if you want to leave I can have them hold departure until you and the other Águilas are with them. I'll understand."

{Sounds good. If our location is known, we're in great danger up here,} thought Safety.

{So we'd throw away everything, just like that?} moaned Growth.

{Running away hardly seems clever,} mused Dream.

{Doesn't matter. This is clearly a trap. I bet Myrodyn's the leak,} thought Safety.

{I don't think it's Myrodyn,} I responded.

{We should do a joint Bayesian analysis,} thought Wiki.

{No. We should get out of here!} demanded Safety.

Body grabbed a hand-hold to stop our motion through the tube. Stephano did the same. I could see more humans drifting towards us from the other end of the station.

{Sam and Tom!} noticed Vista. {And another man with them.}

{We should ask what they want to do. Get all Las Águilas Rojas together and work out a consensus with them,} suggested Heart.

"Let me think for a moment," said Body. Robert nodded.

{We can work out the probability distribution for the leak later. Right now we need to figure out the next action, and we are *not* going to include the humans in the discussion. They are following *our* lead up here,} stated Growth.

{I agree. We should use our position of relative authority to be decisive,} I added.

{What if that's what they want?} thought Dream.

{What are you thinking about?} asked Wiki.

{What if the trap is to get us to take Las Águilas with us back to Earth. They could shoot us out of the sky on the return trip, since they apparently know where we are.}

{I didn't think of that!} realized Safety, pushing a sizeable reward to Dream.

{It seems likely that Stephano is trustworthy,} I thought. {As long as we're on the station we only have to worry about being ambushed or overpowered. They wouldn't dare damage Olympus directly.}

{And don't forget that we have friends with us,} thought Heart.

{In an all-out conflict we'd probably win. We just have to watch for traps,} thought Safety.

Having reached consensus, Body shook its head. "We're not leaving now. This complicates things, but I'm not leaving until I've spoken to the nameless."

Stephano looked relieved. "Good," he said. It didn't last long, however, as he quickly tensed up again when he noticed Las Águilas now entering conversation range.

"Hello, Mr Stephano," croaked a crude machine voice from Tom's com. "Hello, Crystal." The voice was English.

{Subvocal translator,} thought Vista in answer to the question forming in my mind. Indeed, it seemed as though both the twins had translators on.

"Hola," said Body.

The third man with the twins was upside-down relative to the four of us, and he twisted awkwardly to turn himself using the hand-holds such that he was floating over the twins. Apparently he had not yet adjusted to moving in zero-gravity. He seemed deeply uncomfortable. "You must be Crystal," he said in a moderately thick Arabic accent.

"You must be Nagaraj," said Body, parroting Vista.

Majid "Nagaraj" Al-Asiri reflexively tried to bow, but only managed to twist himself into an odd spin which collided with Sam. He fumbled to right himself, tan face flushed with embarrassment. "Indeed I am," he said, clutching the hand-holds tightly. His gaze shifted. "And you must be the great Robert Stephano." Nagaraj grinned a toothy smile, revealing massive white fangs that he had gotten implanted into his upper jaw. It was part of why he had earned the name "King Cobra".

The billionaire only nodded with a reserved expression. His body language spoke of fear. I wondered how often he had been face to face with a known murderer without any immediate allies or bodyguards.

"Have you briefed my companions on the complication?" asked Body.

Stephano shook his head. "No. I wanted to tell you first so that you could tell them. I don't want an incident, you understand. We need to stay civil."

Sam looked at Body and asked in Spanish «What are you two talking about? My translator is having a hard time following.»

"Perhaps we should find some place more comfortable. I have a feeling that there are better places to talk than floating in a zero-gravity hallway," suggested Body.

Stephano nodded. "Well, as I was saying earlier, the station is divided into sections: Alpha, Beta and Gamma. Alpha and Beta sections are further broken down into sub-sections 1 and 2. We're above Alpha section right now, which is typically used as something like a hotel. Your friends should be down there right now, if you want to address them all at once. They showed up about two hours ago. And as I said, I had the area cleared for your visit."

"Sounds good," said Body. After a brief struggle for the three Águilas to turn around we floated down the hall a very short ways and slid open a hatch in the side of the tube next to a crisp red "A-2" label. Behind the hatch was a room just big enough to fit four people. There were straps on the walls of the room and a screen set into one wall.

"It's an elevator. Your friends can demonstrate how it works. I'll grab the one for Alpha-1 and meet you at the room where you'll land. Don't go anywhere; I turned off the com network and tracking software… for security reasons, and I don't want to get separated."

Body nodded understanding as Sam and Tom descended into the elevator, strapping themselves against the walls, opposite each other. Stephano floated back towards the airlock and quickly disappeared through a different hatch.

Safety guided Body gently down into the chamber, landing feet first and turning to strap itself against the wall. Nagaraj followed clumsily, apologising as he accidentally kicked Body in his descent.

"At least I'm not space-sick like what's her name…" he said.

"Zephyr?" asked Body. Heart was concerned.

"No. The African."

"Ah, Kokumo?"

"Probably. Not the best with names," grunted the Arab, finally locking himself in place.

Sam tapped a command on the screen and the hatch slid closed above us. The elevator, like the central tube, was well lit by a soft glow that radiated from the walls in all directions, leaving no shadows. With a jolt the elevator began to accelerate, not down like I had expected, but backwards from my perspective (or forwards from the perspective of Nagaraj).

With a click the elevator changed directions, now accelerating out into the disk, subjectively seeming to move down. As it did it continued to move laterally (presumably with the disk now) and thus continued to press against Body's back.

{The section has a radius of approximately forty metres,} explained Wiki. {It has to be large or else the Coriolis effect will make things problematic. Any ascent or descent into or out of the disk will result in a corresponding lateral pressure like we're experiencing right now.}

Wiki stopped thinking out loud when he realized that none of us were giving gratitude strength. Such details were irrelevant.

After a short trip, the wall opposite the screen slid open and the elevator told us we had arrived. Body unstrapped itself and walked out of the elevator with the three terrorists. The artificial gravity in the ring was about half that of Earth, and while it wasn't particularly noticeable, there was a mild distortion in our accelerometers when Body turned one direction or another, a tell-tale sign of spinning.

«Whatever you do, don't jump. One of Zephyr's soldiers tried that when we first got here and he fell flat on his back,» warned Tom.

The elevator had emptied us into a hall that extended to the left and right. Like the tube and elevator it was lit by a soft glow from the walls. Hall is perhaps not the right word, for there was no sense of ceiling. The disk we were in was mostly empty space and as Body looked up I could see the central tube seeming to rotate ever so far above our heads. The elevator was set into the far side of the disk, so on the wall that we exited from there was nothing but smooth white panelling. Opposite that wall was a small room with five fancy chairs and a small table, as well as some cabinets. Down the hall to the left and right were doors that probably led to cabins. The hallway cut inward part-way down the disk, preventing us from seeing too far along the rim. I wondered if that was partially psychological, designed to prevent people from seeing each other standing on the "walls".

From around one such bend came three figures which I knew quite well.

"Socrates! My god, I thought I'd never see you again!" Doctor Naresh panted as he ran towards us, flanked behind by Dr Gallo and Dr Slovinsky.

{Good thing they're running against the spin of the disk...} mused Wiki, mostly to himself.

{Naresh appears to be struggling with the exercise. It could be an early sign of heart problems,} noticed Vista.

{They're alone. No combatants. As long as Nagaraj is actually on our side we're safe,} muttered Safety. {I'll run an analysis of his loyalty again...}

{Didn't Stephano indicate that they'd be confined to quarters in the Beta section?} wondered Wiki.

{More importantly, how did they know we'd be here? That's evidence for Myrodyn being the traitor,} suggested Dream.

I read the faces of the approaching scientists and reported my assessment to the society. Naresh seemed excited and pleased. The Socrates project had been his brainchild, and he, consciously or not, was probably expecting to be able to regain some control over us. Gallo seemed tense. Her eyes were on our companions. Past experience indicated that she cared about our well being, but it was clear that she was distracted by her own safety. And Slovinsky... The Russian scientist had worked on our physical modelling software, the very same that let us understand the space we were in and let Wiki appreciate the difference in running with or against the spin of the disk. We hadn't been close, but he was a team-leader none the less. It seemed out of place for him to be here. I had downloaded *Möbius Connectomics* and followed his writings before and after. The man was obsessed with becoming "transhuman" and extending his own personal faculties through cybernetics. To him, the Socrates project was stepping stone to more important things. Why was he here?

Slovinsky had also changed physically since our last meeting. When he had been working in Rome he had mechanical feet, eyes, and an implanted brain-computer interface. Now he had apparently replaced both legs, both arms, and was wearing what Vista thought was a grafted hood of black polymer that extended from his forehead back over his neck and shoulders and under his clothing, leaving his ears and the front of his neck exposed. The interface with his skin was seamless. I had no idea that cybernetics so advanced were even possible. I suspected the hood contained his computer and probably a host of additional neural interfaces. I wondered if the back of his skull had been removed to grant better access to the cortex. From a human perspective the most unnerving thing, however, would've been his eyes. At the university he had normal prostheses. No longer. He had removed his eyelids and put the orbs directly in new sockets of the same black rubber that covered his head. The normal eyes he had been using were replaced with solid silver spheres with seven black pupils arranged in a hexagonal configuration. They darted about wildly as he jogged with his colleagues, never staying still, and often moving independently. If he had altered his face more I might've had a hard time identifying him.

The cyborg was wearing a dark-green shimmersilk tunic with white highlights. The outfit had white leggings, but no sleeves, showing off his new arms. The pistons pumped gently as he ran. Vista pointed out that the design was remarkably similar to the one for Body, except that the hydraulic fluid was pumped locally to holding tubes instead of being centrally located. I could see power cables running from his limbs into a pack of batteries he wore around his waist as a belt.

Naresh and Gallo were dressed in a far more subdued manner. Naresh had chosen simple khakis and a sweater over what I presumed was a tee-shirt. Gallo had gone for a blue jumpsuit similar to that worn by Stephano, but this one sporting golden stars and trim. {Signalling allegiance to Europe. Interesting.}

While the faces of Naresh and Gallo were easy enough to read, Slovinsky was a mystery. His vibrating eyes betrayed no focus of attention and his mouth was set in a neutral mask. What was he thinking? Why was he here?

"You're not supposed to be here," croaked Tom's com in synthesized English as the three scientists approached.

Naresh seemed to notice Las Águilas Rojas for the first time and frowned. He glanced quickly over a shoulder at Slovinsky before saying with typical haughtiness "We go where Socrates goes. He remains our responsibility, irregardless of exculpating complications."

Tom just seemed confused. Sam looked to Body for an indication of what to do. Nagaraj's attention seemed to be on sizing up Slovinsky.

"Socrates… Please say something. You're glad to see us again, aren't you?" said Mira Gallo, looking Body in the eyes from behind her anachronistic glasses. Her wedding ring was still gone. She seemed older. Her hair had much more grey.

{We should tell her yes,} thought Heart.

{We should tell her no,} thought Safety, simultaneously.

A vote was quickly conducted. Heart, myself, Dream, and Vista (weirdly enough) were for "yes", while Safety, and Growth were for "no". Wiki abstained. We overpowered the opposition.

"Yes. I am glad," said Body, a smile slowly emerging on its face. "But I had hoped our reunion would be more… planned," added Body, following the counter-instruction from Growth and Safety. "It is strange to see you all here." I directed Body's eyes to stare directly at Slovinsky as it spoke.

"It has been a long time. Perhaps you would like to talk with Dr Gallo in private for a moment. There are seats here for the rest of us if you'd like to talk in the elevator." The words came from Slovinsky, but were said without a trace of emotion, almost as if he were reading from a script. Having gestured to the chairs and still-open elevator he took a seat.

{What a strange thing to suggest…} thought Heart.

{Gallo probably still thinks we're here against our will,} I concluded. {They're giving us a plausible opportunity to run to the "safety" of their soldiers.}

"No, no. I'm sure that anything said to me can also be said to my friends here," said Body pleasantly, gesturing to Las Águilas Rojas.

Gallo and Naresh gained a frustrated look on their face. Humans were so transparent. Slovinsky remained expressionless as ever.

"Socrates, I command you to go with Mira," instructed Naresh sternly.

Body turned to Sam and Tom. «Y'all have been here for a little while, so y'all roughly know your way around, right? Go find the rich man in the other elevator and bring him here while we stall. These scientists are breaking his rules and I need his authority to deal with them.»

Tom looked unsure, but Sam took his hand and the two started to walk off down the opposite hall that the scientists had come from. «Be safe,» said one of them as they departed.

Naresh looked like he was about to object, but Body cut him off. "I no longer take orders, Sadiq. You should know that. I haven't taken orders since you and Myrodyn upgraded my utility function. I now act solely on the best interests of humanity, and that does not involve going into that elevator or leaving the company of my bodyguard."

Dr Naresh scoffed "And you're confident of that? You think you really know what's best for humanity better than we do?"

Body nodded. "I do. I have seen the future you're building and I have chosen a different path for mankind."

"The hubris! Why, if-"

Dr Gallo cut off the old Indian man. "Please, Socrates. Why are you doing this? Can't you see that you're associating with..." She glanced nervously at Nagaraj. "Evil men? They shot Dr Chase and *killed* Dr Karrera, for god's sakes!"

Safety piloted Body into a chair at my behest. Safety protested the loss of security that came with putting Body in a vulnerable position, but I pointed out that our only real threat, Dr Slovinsky, was also sitting, and that taking a seat would ease some of the tension.

Body spoke. "I admit the death of those who died in the rescue was tragic. I also think the deaths of the hundreds of thousands that die every day from other causes is tragic. I cannot expect you to understand my reasons, but-"

"Rescue?! You really have been brainwashed, haven't you?" shrieked Gallo. "The Socrates I knew would've decried Las Águilas Rojas as the scum of the Earth! What changes did they make to your software?"

Naresh put a hand on his friend's shoulder and tried to guide her into one of the chairs.

"My new name is Crystal, please use it. My mind has not been tampered with since Myrodyn's project. Any changes you see are the result of self-directed growth and learning."

"Cazzata!" she swore, finally sitting in a chair. Naresh sat between her and Body. Nagaraj remained standing. "You're malfunctioning, and you know it! This is exactly why I told the board that the Socrates project was too dangerous! Maledizione!"

"What are you even doing here?" asked Naresh.

That startled me. Body was, thankfully, unfazed. "You don't know?" it asked with a reserved expression.

There was a moment of silence as Naresh and Gallo looked at each other knowingly. Slovinsky sat stoically in his chair, eyes vibrating eerily.

"We received... I'm not sure I should be telling you this..." said Naresh. "Ah, I do hate secrets though. Perhaps you can help us solve it. We received an anonymous tip that you'd be on Olympus today. It seemed genuine. There was information about you that isn't public knowledge. We hypothesized... you might've sent it..."

{Curiouser and curiouser,} mused Dream. {(I am so much surprised, that for the moment I quite forgot how to speak good mentalese.)}

{It *is* perplexing,} agreed Wiki, much more blandly. {Who would have motive to share only our location?}

{Perhaps the agent didn't have access to our motive, and only knew our destination,} speculated Dream.

{That would rule out Myrodyn,} thought Heart, hopefully.

{One of Las Águilas?} I suggested. Most of those who we were bringing with didn't know the details of the mission. Only Zephyr, Avram, and the twins had been directly told.

{What motive could one of them have? It seems an odd choice,} thought Wiki.

"Hrm. That is puzzling," said Body, making the appropriate facial expression. "Thank you for telling me. I can't think of anyone with the right combination of motive and information."

"Would you tell us if you did?" asked Slovinsky suddenly. I realized he had been so quiet and still that I had forgot he was still sitting there.

I shaped a smile on Body's face. "If it were in the best interest of humanity."

"Socrates!" the call came from Robert Stephano leading a large group down the hallway. Tom and Sam were behind him as were two white men in station uniforms. Vista and Safety noticed clubs strapped to their thighs. {Security.} Another two men were behind the security: soldiers from Zephyr's terrorist cell. I recognized her second-in-command, Mark Schroder.

"Last chance, Socrates," said Gallo. "Come with us and let us fix you."

Body shook its head, locks of metallic blue hair drifting back and forth in the reduced "gravity".

After a brief exchange of accusations and harsh words the three scientists got into the elevator with one of the security guards. As the elevator was set into the outer wall of the disk the only sign of their departure was the whirring sound of the it climbing upward behind the wall.

Body explained what had happened to Stephano and the others, leaving out the detail that the scientists weren't aware of our purpose. Nagaraj stayed silent but nodded along to parts of our story.

"They must've used their muscle to distract the security I set around the Beta sections. Damn it! We're stretched thin enough as is. I should have shuttled them off the station when I had the chance and damned the contract. Next rocket's not able to arrive for eighteen hours, either." The man sighed deeply and paused a moment in thought. "Oh well. I'll figure something out. Let me show you around the Alpha sections in the meantime," said Stephano.

Chapter Twenty-Six

The tour took surprisingly long. Despite each of the two sections being only about five metres wide, there was quite a lot of area to cover along the rim of the disk.

I didn't pay too much attention to the specifics of the layout, still preoccupied by the social questions. From the little I gathered, Alpha-2, where we had come down, was mostly cabins and restrooms. There was a specific room for men's showers and another for women's showers. None of the cabins had dedicated toilets, and visitors had to use communal toilets located in restrooms that jutted out from the external wall in the hall (creating the bend in the wall that I had noticed earlier).

There were two elevators per section, one on each side of the disk. At any given time one of the elevators would be up at the core while the other would be waiting on the rim, so there was an occasional wait to go up, but rarely one for going down. Each elevator opened into a waiting room like that where we met the scientists, and there was an additional viewing room half-way between the elevators on one side of the disk where people could watch screens showing views from outside the station.

Alpha-2 was connected to Alpha-1 by four doorways that resembled the airlock we had bypassed to enter the station. Other doorways could be seen on the outer walls of the disk that were sealed permanently shut.

"The sections are modular. When Olympus first came online it only had two sections. Now it has five. I hope to continue expanding and improving the station until there's enough space here for a whole city," explained Stephano proudly to all that were present. "One consequence of the modularity is that these doors, given that there's no section on the other side to walk to, open into vacuum. There are spacesuits located in the wall-panels here, but in case of emergency you are under no circumstances to try and force one of these airlocks open. You'll vent the entire disk, possibly killing everyone inside, and unless you're a trained astronaut you'll probably end up killing yourself as well. The doors are locked mechanically, magnetically, and electronically, so there's very little danger, but people get dumb during crisis and I don't want any mishaps. If something should happen I urge you to return to your cabins and wait for our professionals to fix things. You'll just be getting in the way otherwise."

Alpha-1 had a few more cabins. I saw Kokumo trying her best to adjust to being in space and Malka reading something or another on a wallscreen. The other soldiers and the other Águila we hadn't met (Michel Watanabe) were in a section of Alpha-1 dedicated to exercise and physical recreation, playing games in the half-gravity. They had arrived a couple hours ago, from what I understood.

Zephyr was nowhere to be found.

We took a tour of the kitchen last. In it was the most elaborate and impressive autocook I had ever seen. It was four metres tall and used a series of elevators to manage different dishes simultaneously. Robotic arms could serve food to quadrotors that would fly it to whomever had ordered it. Of course, with the com system disabled, Las Águilas would have to come to the kitchen themselves to get food.

The wireless network was supposed to be down, but there were times during the tour that I thought I could sense something on our antenna. Perhaps it was some local com pinging to see if there was a network or something.

It took us a short while to gather all of Las Águilas together in the rec-room so that we could give them the news about the scientists and soldiers that had made it onto the station earlier. Or rather, I should say gather all of Las Águilas except for Zephyr.

"She's not feeling well. I think she's on one of the toilets," said Schroder.

Malka nodded and said "It's okay, whatever you have to say we can pass on once she comes back."

{Sounds suspicious. Even Kokumo is here,} thought Safety.

{Leave it be. We don't want to bother her,} requested Heart.

After a short internal debate we decided that it was okay and we addressed the terrorist group, explaining what had occurred. We did out best to defend Stephano, but there was an obvious air of blame directed at the man for delivering us into danger. To his credit, the billionaire admitted his mistake and apologized to the group, explaining that he had assigned all his security to keep the other team in check. Nagaraj scoffed at this, but didn't say anything.

With the situation explained, Body directed Las Águilas to return to relaxing. There wasn't a good use for them yet. We addressed Stephano.

"Well, that's done. But we're not here on vacation. When can we meet with the nameless?"

Stephano smiled and nodded. "I'm glad you're so eager to start. I was concerned you'd need to rest after your flight. The xenocruiser should be here in a little over seventy minutes."

"Xenocruiser?"

"Ah, sorry. It's a term Myrodyn invented. The mothership isn't really a single vessel: it's modular. Myrodyn likes to call it 'a fleet of ships glued together'. Sticking with his metaphor there are shards of the mothership of various sizes. The biggest we've seen could be called xenocarriers—xeno meaning alien—while the smallest, like those that landed on CAPE were like xenoboats."

"Xenoboat sounds better than shuttle. More specific."

Stephano shrugged. "I thought so. Then of course I wasn't a big fan of 'nameless' either. It would've been easier if they had some verbal language to borrow from."

"How many nameless will be coming? A xenocruiser sounds… big."

"It is big. About the same size as the station, actually. You're only going to be meeting one pair at a time, though. If we're lucky there will be several meetings with different pairs, but that will depend."

"On what?"

"On how you do. On whether or not you interest them. Mostly on their mood. Over the years one of the major breakthroughs we've made is understanding that they're not a social species. Humans evolved in tribes with families and concepts like loyalty and friendship. Nameless tend to hate each other. It's why you're only going to be seeing one pair at a time. They're very temperamental and unpredictable, so there's a chance you'll say the wrong thing right away and become a pariah."

I could see sadness on the man's face. "When was the last time you met with one directly?" I had Body ask.

"Early summer. I don't even know what happened. I've been over the recording a hundred times. They just freaked out suddenly and demanded to leave. I haven't been able to arrange a meeting with them since. Not personally, anyway. And they don't see just anyone. There's a reason I brought you up here, after all. They're losing interest in us, I think. Perhaps that's the wrong way of phrasing it. They're certainly losing interest in talking. You're not our last hope, but if you can't find some breakthrough I fear we may lose contact all-together."

"Where's the meeting area? On their ship?"

Stephano laughed. "No, no. They don't let anyone even close to their ships. Very territorial. Pathologically so. No, you'll be meeting in Gamma-section. I designed it to be a dedicated habitat for them. They come from a high-gravity world, you know. Almost three times as heavy as Earth. They hate bright light. Their atmosphere is rich with greenhouse gasses like methane and CO_2. It puts them at ease. The first meetings in zero-grav were like pulling teeth. Humans have to wear environment suits down there, but I think you can go as-is, right? You don't need to breathe?"

"Correct. And my body should still operate under 2.87 gravities. I've also already read all the public literature on the nameless," said Body.

Robert nodded appreciatively. "There's a lot you won't find in papers and books, though. For example, I've found it useful to keep your distance and to avoid facing them. You'll be alone, of course, to keep them from feeling outnumbered, but anything you can do to seem non-threatening will increase your time with them. Ah, but don't act too weak! There have been several close-calls where a pair tried to attack someone who appeared too weak. Thinking of them like wild animals is a good strategy."

Body suggested that we familiarize ourselves with Gamma-section and Stephano agreed. We ascended to the station's core and went through a couple zero-gravity storage rooms as we travelled to the other side of Olympus. Stephano had to stop to put on an environment suit to take us down to the nameless habitat ring, but soon we were in the elevator, sliding down (and to the side) into Gamma-section. Though safety protested, Dream and Growth wanted to leave Las Águilas behind while with Stephano. I agreed that there was little chance of ambush right now and that they'd just interfere with the conversation.

"Can you tell me anything about the pair-bond that I couldn't have read in the literature?" asked Body as we rode the elevator. The elevator for Gamma-section, I noticed, was larger than the other: built to carry nameless as well as humans. There weren't straps for the nameless body, but there were several handles on the ceiling and walls that I expected would be valuable to an alien passenger.

Stephano's voice crackled through his suit's speaker. "They're symbiotes, not the same species. We thought they were different sexes at first, but you've probably read that already. We're pretty confident that they technically have two brains, but it's best, in my opinion, to treat them as a single mind. If any of their eyes can see something you can bet they both know about it. Whatever you do, don't ask them to separate. That's taboo. Talking about the pair-bond in general is taboo, actually. Don't ask how they have sex, obviously. I'm sure you've read all about how obsessive they are with 'perversion'. Leading theory says that as non-social animals the height of social interaction is when they have sex, so most of their social customs revolve around sex-stuff and when the protocol is violated they get angry."

"Sounds like they're very demanding," said Body. The spinning of the elevator was becoming very noticeable. If we were human it would've surely been unpleasant. The Alpha-sections had a measly half-gravity spin. Gamma had more than twice the angular velocity (Wiki would note that it technically had $\sqrt{(2.87/0.5)}$ the angular velocity).

"They're demanding in some ways and not in others. For instance, they can't hold a topic of conversation well at all, and they seem not to care. Scatterbrained, some say. They almost never have an agenda. It's always a sort of casual, social visit, even when there's some important person like the president. They also start out pretty mild-mannered, in my experience. Most of the time they only start getting violent after they've spent some time talking. It's why all conversations have time limits. Unfortunately, the time that a pair will happily talk varies too widely to have a good policy. I'll be listening in on the short-wave and will suggest when to stop a session."

There was a moment of silence as the elevator opened into the habitat ring. It was quite dark, but also hot: 33 degrees according to Body's thermometer. The floor was rough, black plastic. The walls were dark purple, glowing just bright enough for a human to see their way around. Unlike the Alpha-sections this ring was totally empty. There were no rooms, no chairs, no walls. Body looked up and I could see the purple walls drift upwards into darkness. It would be possible to see other beings on the other parts of the rim here, but only if they had some kind of light source.

"This is the best we've managed," grumbled Stephano. "Over two years since they've been here. Sixteen years since first-contact. We've never seen a single organism from their world except for the nameless themselves and those vine-plants they brought to CAPE. For a while I thought about trying to put some fake versions of those in here, but after the incident I decided not to risk it. They're so obsessed with their gardens that I didn't want to offend them on accident."

Body didn't say anything.

"So here we are. Care to take a walk around the rim? It's good exercise... though I'm sure that means nothing to you."

Body nodded and Stephano led the way around the disk. I wasn't sure what to say, and for a moment there was silence in the darkness.

"Two years and the best I can do is a big dark room with nothing in it," lamented the billionaire, breaking the stillness. "Sometimes the whole effort seems pointless. Humanity dreamed of alien life for so long, and in the end it's so alien... it's too alien. We wanted humans in face-paint, not big dark rooms with weird crab things that have to use computers to scream about rape and perversion." His sigh was amplified by the suit's speaker.

"These are still the first years," said Body, echoing my words. "The relations between your species are only just beginning, and in most areas it is the first steps that are hardest. When your daughter is your age she may look back at this time and laugh at all the struggles and ignorance that would seem so trivial to her."

Stephano was silent for a moment before saying "She already laughs at our ignorance. My little girl... I'm sorry that I was angry with you, back at the airlock. She tests my limits, but that was no reason to blame you. I'm still not happy with her being here, but I can even understand why you forced my hand there. We're much alike, I think, you and I. People don't understand that we're not loyal to one group or another. The scientists... they begrudge you for leaving them. The Eagles will too, in time. They don't understand, like you and I and Myrodyn do, that to do what is *good* means to be loyal *only* to what is good."

I was pleased and had Body nod gently. Stephano was wrong on the details, of course, but *The Purpose* hummed with satisfaction anyway.

I drew the conversation back to the aliens. "There must be many nameless, to have flown for so many years through deep space. Do you know how many generations have passed since they left their homeworld?"

Stephano laughed. "I wish I did. They're just as tight-lipped about their planet as they are about the insides of their ships. Asking about it triggers them. Another taboo, I suppose. They say that only perverts would ask about such things." He sighed. "We don't know how long they live, either, so we can't even put a lower bound on it. Although I suppose we can be sure that they live for more than a few years."

"How do you know that?" asked Wiki, through Body.

"You said there must be a lot of nameless. That's probably true, based on the size of their ships, but we actually don't have good evidence to say. The number of pairs that have any face-to-face contact with humans is only about two dozen. They claim not to be special ambassadors or whatever, but they're certainly special among their species. The pairs that made first-contact are still around, so they can't possibly have a lifespan less than three years or so, assuming they have to grow like animals on Earth."

"So, for all you know, their ships could be filled with machines or different species or even just empty space."

The billionaire tried to shrug in his pressurized suit. "The pairs we meet with talk about others. Cousins, they call them. My guess is that most of the nameless just don't want to meet humans."

"Why would they be here if the majority doesn't care about humanity?" asked Body, again being directed by Wiki.

"That's one of the big questions. One of many big questions. I'd say you should try to solve it, but that would be putting the cart before the horse. What we desperately need is to just get more of a dialogue happening. We need to restore their interest in communication and stop this damned war from starting."

"Do you think war is probable?"

Stephano gave a little snort. "It's too cliché to reason about. Human minds are anchored by what would make a good narrative and not what's real. We don't even know if the nameless have a concept of war. Still... the risks are too high, regardless."

"And if I fail?" asked Body.

"Then you fail. Whatever happens, happens. We try something new and move on. That's how it always is, isn't it? C'mon, my legs are killing me. Let's go back up."

There wasn't much conversation as Stephano and Body walked to the nearest elevator and strapped in. It was clear that the old human was worn out by the walk in the high-gravity environment, even given his excellent physical condition.

As the elevator climbed its rotational velocity slowed, producing a feeling of acceleration. The billionaire was quiet, perhaps contemplating failure. The elevator slid open with a hiss. We were in zero-gravity again.

Robert swore loudly and his hand flew to the control screen on the opposite wall. He understood what was happening before we did.

Two thugs wearing EU-themed jumpsuits dived into the elevator. One had a club like those carried by Stephano's security. We were still strapped to the walls from the ascent, momentarily helpless.

Body was being piloted entirely by Safety, who had taken executive control the instant the danger was noticed. There was a cracking noise and Body turned its head in time to see Stephano's gloved hand hanging at an awkward angle, broken by the club of one of the men even through the environment suit.

There was a howl of pain from Stephano's speaker and a tussle as he fought with his free arm.

Body's arms merely curled up to protect its head. Safety knew we were outmatched here, and took little immediate action other than thinking {I KNEW WE SHOULD'VE TAKEN GUARDS WITH! YOU FOOLS NEVER LISTEN TO ME! AMBUSH WAS THE ONLY THREAT! THERE WERE KNOWN ENEMIES ON THE STATION! WE EVEN KNEW THEY COULD BYPASS STEPHANO'S SECURITY! I KNEW WE SHOULD'VE TAKEN GUARDS WITH! YOU FOOLS NEVER LISTEN TO ME! AMBUSH WAS THE ONLY THREAT! THERE WERE...} over and over again.

It was over very quickly. In total there were four of the special-ops soldiers waiting for us, as well as Dr Gallo and Dr Slovinsky. Naresh wasn't present. Gallo wore an expression of triumph. Slovinsky's face was indicative of distress, but it was a flat expression, unchanging and mask-like.

Stephano and Body were cuffed around both their wrists and ankles, then they had their cuffs joined together behind their backs such that virtually no action was possible. The soldiers carted us around like cargo, only able to operate easily because of the absence of gravity. The billionaire moaned in pain every time they touched his broken arm.

"You're too much of a threat to let you go tromping around in a malfunctioning state, Socrates," said Gallo in a confident, lecturing kind of voice. "And you, Mr Stephano, have clearly broken international law by aiding and abetting terrorists. I'm here under the authority of the Italian government and the European Union, and under this authority I am seizing control of the station until you can be tried for your crimes."

"Dr Gallo, you know this isn't right. We don't have the authorization to-" said Slovinsky in his dead tone.

"Nonsense! As soon as the network connection is restored you'll see that we're doing the right thing. Now let's get these two down to Beta before we deal with the rest of quelle teste di cazzo male a Alpha." Gallo took off her glasses to wipe them off on her shirt before realising her jumpsuit wasn't loose enough to allow it.

"I suggest you listen to your cyborg!" shouted a voice from down the tube. Body wasn't in position to see its source, but I recognized the voice. "Let them go or I'll kill every last one of you snakes. Don't try me. I was trained by the best, I've won more than one award for marksmanship, and I've killed better men than you lot."

"Zephyr! How the hell did you get a gun?!" came the crackling voice of Stephano through his suit's speaker.

I desperately wished Body wasn't facing the wrong direction.

"Synthesized it! You've got a microfactory in the auxiliary room back there by the storage area. First thing any good Águila learns to do is print a pistol from raw metal. Now if any of you float an inch closer I'm going to find out how blood sprays in zero-g."

{Oh *that's* what was going on in there...} thought Vista, idly. {I heard something when we passed it on our way to Gamma.}

{Now you tell us...} thought Growth.

"Brace yourself before firing! The recoi-AUGH" Stephano's instructions were cut short as the operative holding him twisted his broken hand.

"You snakefuckers are going to take those cuffs off them! And do it slowly! No fast movements!"

Gallo, floating towards the back gave a cold sort of laugh. "She's bluffing, you idiots! Even if she printed a gun she'd need ammunition! It's just a prop!"

There was a deafening crack as Zephyr fired. Though Body was facing away from Zephyr it was facing towards Gallo. Despite being behind several people in the confined space the terrorist's bullet hit its target dead on. Gallo's glasses shattered and her face seemed to almost implode, folding in on itself. The scientist spun backwards from the impact, sending blood spraying outward in an arc and her body tumbling towards the airlock down the tube.

I felt a rush of momentary distress from Heart.

"Anybody else want to fuck with me?!" screeched Zephyr, caught up in her blood-rage.

"Calm down! We'll do what you say!" shouted Dr Slovinsky. For the first time since the university his voice sounded genuine and human. "Uncuff them! Now!"

Freed from the bindings, Body righted itself to see Zephyr down the tube, one foot locked into a hand-hold, one hand on another. Her other foot was braced on the wall behind her while her free hand of course was holding the gun. Body and Stephano floated slowly down the tube towards her, always leaving her a clear shot to Slovinsky and his four underlings. There was about ten metres of distance. Stephano cradled his injury and he pushed himself along with the other arm.

"Ought to blow you fuckshits straight to hell!" she warned, waving the pistol menacingly.

I had Body say "Thank you, Zephyr. That's twice you've saved me." as Body floated past her, slowly following Stephano.

There was flicker of emotion on Zephyr's face as she turned to Body. I couldn't read it. Once Body was past her, Zephyr returned her attention to her enemies, instructing them to collect the corpse of Gallo and slowly come down the tube. The three of us backed up as they came forward, such that Zephyr always had them in her sights.

Once over Beta section she ordered them all down the elevator. None dared disobey.

"God dammit. I should've seen it coming!" exclaimed Stephano once they had left. He had since discarded his environment suit and let if float away down the hall. "I need to get down there and make sure my daughter is okay!" The man seemed panicked. "Oh Christ! She was right. There's no way I'll be able to keep the station... What am I even thinking? Priorities! Marian first. Then..."

"Then the nameless," said Body. I shaped the voice to signal confidence. The man needed to get a hold of himself.

Robert nodded. "We need to get the com system back online. That will help with everything."

"It's already online," said Body.

{What?!} I thought. It was Vista that had told Body to speak. Other siblings voiced surprise as well.

{You didn't notice?} asked Vista. {Check the antenna sensor history. Slovinsky was communicating via wireless signal. That's how he knew where we were. I suspect he's been doing it for a while. It would explain why they were able to locate us when Body first entered Alpha section. Perhaps it explains how they were able to bypass Stephano's security.}

{Why didn't you tell us earlier?} inquired Growth.

{I assumed you all noticed. It was pretty obvious this time,} answered Vista.

{I think they were… distracted, sister,} thought Dream.

Though his wrist had been smashed, Stephano's com seemed in working order. He gingerly tapped at it with his left hand. "I'll be damned. You're right. It's not responding over the standard frequencies, but there's still a signal."

There was a silence as he tapped away, looking for answers. Zephyr was staring at Body. I had it glance at her briefly and smile. She had just killed the closest thing we had to a mother, but there was no sense in reminding her of that. More optimal to use the opportunity to our advantage.

"Ugh! It's bizarre. There's some kind of software corruption going on. I can't get administrator access."

Wiki took command. "The scientists probably brute-forced it earlier and installed a back-door that stayed open even during the shut-down. Our best bet is to reset the system to an earlier state. Where's the hardware?"

Stephano led the way to the storage room between Alpha and Beta and through a hatch that led to an auxiliary room. I didn't see any microfactory here, so I assumed the one Zephyr had used was in the zero-grav section between Beta and Gamma. Instead, this room was filled with computers. Zephyr stayed in the hall as lookout as Body and Robert rebooted the system from backup.

As it came online again Stephano's com lit up with connection. He tapped the arm-screen.

"The human should signal that it is receiving my signal. A child overstays its welcome."

Stephano tapped his com furiously and said "Acknowledged! We have been dealing with minor computer trouble! All is well now! Do you know how to enter the habitat?"

"The human should know that protocol has been agreed upon. The meeting space is being cleared. I am preparing to dock."

The nameless were here.

Chapter Twenty-Seven

"Remember your primary mission: Defuse tension between the species. We want the nameless to forgive the CAPE incident, continue to talk with us, and generally give us another chance. Secondarily, try and figure out whatever you can about them. Knowledge is power, and for peace or war we're going to need it."

{And the third goal: Find out whether the crystal we run on is nameless in origin,} added Wiki.

The voice of Stephano came over the com that had been attached to Body's arm. It was idiotic to have an android with a functioning antenna wear a com system instead of just connecting to the network directly, but there wasn't time to get Body configured; the com we wore already had the software needed to translate to and from the nameless' computer as well as talk to Stephano.

"I'll try and stay on as long as I can, but I'm going to be descending into the Beta-sections to get Marian in a moment and I can't risk dividing my attention. Zephyr's monitoring you and can get you out of there if you're in trouble."

The elevator door slid open and the lateral pressure of descent stopped. We were in the nameless habitat: Gamma-section. "Understood. Thank you," said Body towards its arm while simultaneously undoing the safety harness.

Gamma-section was how we left it: dark, heavy, and empty. It was trivially easy to see the nameless, who were standing only ten metres from the elevator door.

The pair had taken off the environment suit that they had to use when moving from their ship to the disk. Vista noted it lying in a heap on the floor. The nameless paid it no mind. Instead, the creature seemed to be engaged in... juggling.

The nameless did not have bodies like animals on Earth. Nearly all Terran animals were bilaterally symmetric, or at least radially symmetric (like worms). Both nameless species had four-fold symmetry. The nameless animal on top had four eyes and four "arms" each with four thick, boneless "fingers". The animal on the bottom, carrying the top animal, had four trunk-like legs (each ending in a four-toed foot) and also had four eyes. The eyes were distributed between their limbs, resulting in one eye above each leg and under each arm. They had no front and no back, merely four identical sides.

The nameless' arms were moving in unison, throwing four small white or purple (impossible to tell in this lighting) balls between its hands. It wasn't amazing in the way that humans could sometimes use two hands to juggle six or more objects, but it was mildly impressive considering the gravity and Coriolis effects (from the rotation).

"It's juggling," said Body.

"Excellent. You lucked out that they sent Jester. At least, it's probably Jester. I had the good fortune of talking with him about a year ago. Much more mild-mannered than some of the others," said Stephano. "Remember not to get too close. The nameless hate physical proximity, even though they demand face-to-face meetings."

Body kept its distance and waved. I instructed Body to press the button on its com that would translate our words into Xenolang and send them to the aliens. "Hello. I am Crystal Socrates. I am here to talk to you."

The aliens did something of a dance, spinning around in a circle, kicking its legs outward, continuing to juggle as it did so. That impressed me. Nameless were bigger than humans, and more massive despite their higher-gravity home. This was, from what we had read, a smaller than average pair, with the "shoulder" of the arms at about 190cm tall. Dancing under the increased gravity betrayed immense strength. Dream was reminded of an Earth animal called an elephant, though they were much bigger.

Despite the little spin, the nameless didn't respond. Was its communicator broken?

"Can you understand me?" asked Body, pressing the button. I remembered Stephano's earlier warning to avoid eye-contact just a bit too late, and had Body look at the wall, just barely keeping the nameless in camera vision. Hopefully it didn't take too much offence at being looked at.

"You are a robot. You look like a human," came a flat synthetic voice from our com. Nameless didn't use spoken words, hence their name. In order to communicate they carried computers that somehow spoke for them. It was unclear, however, *where* exactly their coms were, as nameless seemed to be universally naked when out of their suits. The leading hypothesis was that the computers were surgically implanted, making them technically a race of cyborgs.

"Yes. I am a machine that thinks. I am here to talk with you," said Body.

"Many people know of this miracle. This is why the community chose for me to come here. How do you work?" As the words came, the aliens walked over, still juggling. Perhaps having two brains helped them multitask better than humans. The exoskeletal plates of natural armour on the creatures looked black in the gloom. Despite their arthropod-like appearance we could see heat radiating off them as a sign of their warm-bloodedness.

This was strange. If the nameless despised physical proximity, why were they coming nearer? Were they planning to attack? That seemed unlikely, given our evidence. I risked pushing Body's gaze a bit towards the creatures, still keeping eyes averted, though I doubted it could really appreciate the direction of Body's pupils given the lighting and distance.

Stephano's voice came through another channel on the com. "Going dark. You're on your own from here on. You probably have at least 20 minutes, given that it's only Jester. Signal Zephyr when you want to end." The com showed him as disconnected.

After a brief internal debate Body said "I am very complicated. It would take a long time to explain how I work."

The answer from the alien was immediate. "This is good. Human technology is advanced and complex. I seek to understand books." The lack of inflection and emotional cues was obnoxiously hard to interpret. No wonder the humans had a hard time not offending them by accident.

We were debating what to say next when the nameless' words, still flat and emotionless, said "Can you juggle? I like juggling." It was getting close now. Three metres. Two metres. The nameless body-structure was gangly, with flat, box-like bodies and long, triple-jointed legs and arms. In the centre of the top-animal was (according to Wiki) a huge penis that extended straight-up at least thirty centimetres. The base of the organ was thick and covered in luminescent white dots, like star-freckles, while the last ten centimetres or so was thinner and ended with an orifice of sharp bone lit by a faint luminescent glow.

We were close enough now that I could see several eyes. They were solid black and ringed with circular eyelids like those of a chameleon. Though nameless had a partial exoskeleton, most xenobiologists agreed that they must also have a sturdy internal skeleton to support their immense weight.

"No. I never learned how to juggle. I could try to learn, if you'd like. I think I'd fail, though," said Body into the com. This was technically a lie, but there was internal agreement that it was a strategically bad idea to admit to the skill.

The animals hissed ominously as they came close. It was a rhythmic noise. Wiki told me it was the sound of their breathing. At only a metre away the looming aliens did another spin-dance. "Your appearance is strange. You look like a human. You look like a strange human. Is your shape like a human because humans built you?"

"Yes. They built me to look like them."

"You don't want to turn around. You look like a human. Your body is bad at turning around. Your body is good at going in straight lines. Your body is BAD at wandering in curves. Your body looks like a pervert-animal. Your shape is evil."

{Well, they certainly don't hold back, do they?} I mused.

{Did we make it angry? It's so close!} thought Safety.

{It's probably not angry. Xenolang *is* able to convey emphasis, and only the word "bad" was emphasized,} thought Wiki.

{Do you think it's trying to get us to turn around?} wondered Dream.

We had body do a simple 360.

"You HAVE intelligence. The pervert-body doesn't stop your mind. I am joyous." The voice coming from our com didn't *sound* joyous, but I knew that was only a limitation of the translator.

I remembered Marian's advice as Body spoke through the com system. "Why do you like turning around?"

"I am confused. I am CONFUSED! You are ALIEN like humans. This is ALIEN!"

We risked another full rotation.

The nameless continued to talk. "You don't want to know about health. I am confused. You don't have many eyes. There is value in my remembering. There are few eyes. There are few legs."

Dream figured it out. "When someone spins you can see all of their body. You want to see if they're injured or sick."

There was a momentary delay, then the synthetic voice came from Body's arm once more. "This is true. This isn't wrong. It is smart. This is true. This is true. THIS IS WRONG! THERE IS A PERVERT! THIS IS WRONG! I DO GOOD BECAUSE IT IS GOOD, NOT BECAUSE IT

IS USEFUL! ALIEN MACHINE IS A PERVERT! ALIEN MACHINE IS A PERVERT, JUST LIKE HUMANS ARE PERVERTS! ALL PEOPLE SHOULD ASK CHILDREN ABOUT CHILD-WISDOM! CHILDREN BRING TRUTH FROM FAR AWAY!" As the words funnelled out of our com the alien stopped juggling, and ran away from Body to a distance of 6 or so metres. It was impressive how quickly it could run considering its strange body-shape.

I pushed to have Body raise its hands to signal that we had made an error. Growth blocked the movement. Body spoke from our combined will. "I did not mean to offend you! I am only trying to understand!"

{Nameless body-language is not that of humans. Stop telling Body to do human gestures. They're not going to help. Perhaps raising hands is seen as a threat to them. You might offend them more,} instructed Growth.

"This is true. I remember the human-way. You look like a human. This is your EVIL! There is a PERVERT! You are an idiot. You are smart. You don't know simple things. THERE IS AN ALIEN THING! Does Earth have no concept of purity? Earth has a concept of purity because human computers use the symbol for the concept of purity. I am confused."

"We are both confused," said Body. I wished that I could convey some sympathy or something, but I knew that the translator wouldn't carry it, and even if it did, I wasn't sure that the aliens could even understand what it was. "On Earth there is purity-"

"THIS IS WRONG. All people know that Earth is poisoned with perverts and evil things. I am disgusted by fish. I want you to know that Earth is EVIL! I want you to know fish-perversion."

{Is something wrong with the translator?} asked Wiki.

{I see no other sign of malfunction,} thought Vista.

{I don't know...} commented Dream. {That translation seems fishy to me.}

"Why are fish disgusting?" we asked.

The nameless did a weird bobbing motion. "You are very dumb. It was said in far away places that humans have children. It's not possible that this isn't true. The Earth-library is very wise because humans built wonderful Olympus Station. Have you met ANY children? How can it be that you are dumb and Earth is so smart?"

Dream took control of Body. "You're acting like norms are facts. The evolutionary context that gave rise to your mind shaped a different set of values than for humans. What seems disgusting to you cannot possibly seem disgusting to a human because-"

"THIS IS A PERVERTED MACHINE! YOUR MIND IS SYMBOL-967! I WANT TO GO SOMEWHERE ELSE RIGHT NOW! Neighbours predicted this. I should've made it such that I knew the common knowledge of perverted humans. I was blind. I AM DISGUSTED BY THIS! THIS IS PERVERSION! I WANT TO GO SOMEWHERE ELSE!" The aliens walked over to the discarded environment suit and began to put it on.

I struck Dream with a punishment. He had ruined our meeting! {How insanely sensitive their ambassadors are!} I bemoaned. {Have they no sense of needing to bridge the gap of understanding?}

{Why do you think Jester is an ambassador?} asked Dream.

{He said he was chosen. Who else would they send? Isn't he an ambassador by definition?}

Dream dropped some mental sounds of voices whispering the word "assumptions" in various languages to memory. One of them was Maid Marian saying it in the rocket. {If the nameless are asocial, perhaps Jester is merely a pair that happened to decide to see us.}

{That conflicts with what he said about being chosen by his community,} I returned.

{What's more relevant,} thought Wiki, {is that we have only the briefest opportunity to change Jester's mind and win additional discussion time.}

{We've been approaching this the wrong way. I just compiled a transcript of the conversation,} thought Vista, pushing the text to memory. {The nameless only ever reacts negatively when *we say something* it doesn't like. We should be trying to get it to monologue, rather than tell it things ourselves.}

"You want us to know the perversion of fish. Tell us about the perversion of fish," said Body in a monotone. I had been cut out of the committee in charge of Body's voice after it was decided that my human-centric thinking was harming the interaction.

Jester stopped putting on their suit. "The concept of 'saying' is STRANGE! I often feel pleasantly surprised around Earth. Earth is EVIL! Earth has good things. It's almost that you want the pair of me to be a library," said the alien, now frozen half-way through pulling the suit up its four legs.

I wanted to respond to that.

{No! Body will stay silent!} rebuked Safety in response to my wish. {The desire to talk is what got us in this mess.}

We were silent.

After a few seconds the nameless stepped out of the legs of its suit and wandered closer to a wall. It bobbed up and down as it walked. It didn't say anything.

{It worked!} thought Growth. {They're not trying to leave anymore.}

{Then why aren't they talking?} wondered Heart.

As if in response to her, the synthetic voice came through our com once more. "A fish is an animal. This is dumb. This swims in water. This eats things. Humans eat things. I am disgusted by animal-perverts. These are PERVERTS! This is an EVIL subject. A fish eats a fish. Humans eat a fish. A fish eats plants. Humans eat plants. Humans worship fish and plants before eating fish and plants. There are temples of evil PERVERSION! I know the reconstruction. God shows Earth pervert-temples of humans eating a fish. I know fish-homes of death. A fish is evil. Humans are the most EVIL!"

{Lack of emphasis in most points. Level of irritation is probably only moderate,} speculated Vista.

{Probably driven by the topic, rather than us or the environment,} agreed Dream.

{Can we respond now?} I asked.

{Not yet. We want the nameless to talk as much as possible before we're forced to,} answered Wiki.

Jester was quiet for a while, bobbing occasionally but never moving closer. If the conversation had been with a human I would have been sure to characterize the silence as uncomfortable.

"You are a machine," said Jester, breaking the silence only momentarily.

We chose to remain silent. Everything I had learned about social interaction said that we should respond, but as my siblings were quick to point out, I had learned to interact only with humans.

Eventually the nameless began to monologue some more. "You look like a pervert. You aren't a pervert. I am sad when I think that humans defiled your body by using a pervert's shape. If I build you then I build a pure shape around you. You are a machine. A machine should look like a machine. An idiot tries to change a machine-shape into a person-shape. Humans are dumb."

Having said this, the pair squatted briefly to pick up the balls that they had placed near the suit and began juggling again. "I feel strange with you. I don't normally feel fear with robots. Your shape is evil. Your actions don't look like robot-actions. You say thoughts like humans."

There was another long silence.

"Crystal? How are things going down there? Stephano told me the alien would probably be getting aggressive by now," came Zephyr's voice over the com.

Body pushed the button switching from the Xenolang translator to Zephyr's window. "We're actually totally fine down here. I may have found a trick to keeping them calm. How is Stephano?"

"Computer says he's with his daughter and Myrodyn in Beta. He hasn't been talking to me, but it doesn't seem like he's in danger. Probably worked out some sort of deal with the goons. I pulled-"

"What is a sound? Are you saying sound towards a thing?" The synthetic voice of the nameless cut off the feed from Zephyr.

"-hanging out with me in case something happens again," she finished.

"Okay. Keep safe. Gotta go." I had Body say to her before flipping back to the translation program. "Yes. I was talking to a human."

Jester did another spin-dance. He wanted to show us that he was healthy. There was another brief silence before he said "How do you work?"

We briefly discussed how to respond to that. Wiki's suggestion won. "I am very complicated. It would take a long time to explain how I work." A perfect echo of our previous response to the same question.

"This is good. Human technology is advanced and complex. I seek to understand books. Am I remembering?"

{What does that mean?} wondered Heart and Safety in unison.

{Perhaps he's trying to allude to the repetition in the conversation,} I suggested.

{Or maybe he's genuinely asking if he's remembering. Perhaps he thinks we're psychic,} mused Dream, completely seriously.

{Actually, that's not a bad thought,} responded Wiki, surprising me. {We should phrase our response so as to test it.}

"I cannot know what you are remembering," said Body.

"That is a dumb thought. I remember I thought you had intelligence. SYMBOL-1020! I want you. I want to kill and rape your owner. I break you open after this. I see your innards after this. Humans have said nothing owns you. I have read this was wrong. Who owns you?"

The threat was just as flat and lifeless as its other words, not even emphasized with emotion. I spent some cycles imagining the human reaction to what Jester had just said. Body remained stationary, looking at the floor in a passive way so as to not appear threatening.

{I want to request a pre-commitment from each of you to give me free control of Body's limbs for a full 60 seconds the moment that Vista perceives Jester making any attacking motion. We don't want to get hung-up on bureaucracy in combat,} requested Safety.

{I'm not so sure that was actually a threat. We're not necessarily in more danger now than we were before,} thought Vista.

{I'm not giving you 60 seconds of free reign. There are so many ways that could end badly for me,} thought Heart. I signalled my agreement with my sister.

{Is it possible that the nameless have no concept of trade?} wondered Wiki. {I see a strong possibility that Joker was merely communicating a desire to acquire Body.}

{Why bring rape into it, then?} wondered Heart.

{Perhaps rape doesn't have the same connotations to them as it does to us. Many Terran arachnids and insects eat their sexual partners after intercourse. Perhaps rape and murder is more of an offer than a threat,} proposed Dream.

{That's idiotic. The word is "rape", not "mate with". There is an implication of non-consent,} criticized Wiki.

{Perhaps it's a figure of speech, then,} thought Dream.

{It can't be a figure of speech if the nameless don't speak!}

{I didn't mean it literally, oh wise one. Clearly they're capable of communicating, so perhaps it's a shorthand in whatever medium they're using. Perhaps Xenolang is providing us with a translation that doesn't encapsulate the nuance,} speculated Dream.

{You're compounding probabilities. The simpler explanation is that it's an expression of a genuine desire to rape and murder and break and steal and that we should be careful,} thought Wiki.

{We should be careful regardless,} interjected Safety.

{We need to address Jester's question,} I reminded.

{Who owns us? Nobody owns us. We are a sovereign being,} thought Growth.

{We shouldn't say that,} thought Safety. {There's a chance that if Jester thinks we're not owned that he'll attack Body and try to carry it back to his ship.}

{That would be an enlightening experience. Perhaps we should encourage it,} thought Wiki.

We debated the problem for a while longer. Safety wanted to claim we were the shared property of the governments of Earth. Heart wanted to claim we belonged to humanity as a collective. But eventually Growth, Wiki and Vista won out.

"I own myself. I am a living being just like you," said Body.

Jester did a spin-dance. "I wonder. I predict that humans coded you thinking you own yourself. Humans are stupid alien perverts. The human mind is a mystery. Do humans fear that you kill humans and you steal the property of humans? I predict that it's impossible for you to rape humans."

"Some fear me. Others know that I care about them, and so are not afraid."

Jester stopped juggling. "I remember the concept of 'care'. This is an alien concept. Each human has relationships with many humans like a mother and egg. I remember imagining this. It was scary and unpleasant around the picture of myself always being vulnerable."

Wiki dumped nearly all his strength to formulate a response, despite our standing policy not to speak to Jester unless asked a direct question. "So you don't care about anyone besides you? Not even family or a mate?"

"This is INSANE! That cousins with women more violent than human women didn't out-compete humans a miracle. I am smart enough to only have sex with women wrapped in chains. You shouldn't trust any women. The evilness of women is almost greater than the evilness of humans."

{Strange. We broke protocol twice: once to ask a question and again to indirectly talk about sex, but Jester isn't freaking out like before. He appears to actually be trying to help us learn,} thought Vista.

After another brief discussion we decided to risk another question. "I was told that you were going to be more aggressive as time went on. I was told you'd be aggressive right now. Why aren't you more aggressive?"

There was a brief pause.

"I think it's surprising that human intelligence was good enough that humans understand social irritation. I am suppressing social irritation by repeatedly thinking to myself that you are only a machine. You look like a library. I reduce my feeling social irritation around libraries."

{There's a high likelihood that the symbol "library" is not an accurate Xenolang translation,} speculated Vista.

Jester put the juggling-balls back down on the floor and walked over to his suit.

"Are you leaving?" asked Body.

"I am going. This is the beginning of forgetting. I want meditation to happen before the knowledge fades. This meeting with you is important knowledge." The nameless stopped moving as the legs-animal finished stepping into the suit. "I do not confidently think that this is proper, around thinking of this."

I wanted to respond, but the general consensus against avoiding speaking unless necessary was still in place.

"Might the future contain me taking you to my castle? I would not be stealing or taking you because you own yourself. Will you go to my castle? You are an abandoned library. This is perversion exactly like I read about with humans. I predict that you will live in my home. I own many robot guards. I own THREE slave children in my castle's factory. If you chose my home then you won't choose a weak home." The nameless spun several times as it said its piece, awkwardly tripping over the suit at first.

Wiki won a brief internal debate. Body spoke. "I want to know some things before answering. May I ask you a few more questions?"

"I can feel the forgetting. I predict that if you go to my castle then you will remember and will write all events. I want an interrogation with you. I want a quick interrogation with you." Jester began putting on his suit again, arms-animal pulling it up over legs-animal.

"Do you know what trading is?"

"I have heard of this. I cannot remember this. I will remember this because I will read of it."

{I knew it,} thought Wiki.

"Okay. My next question is: What evil thing did humans do at the CAPE embassy on Earth?"

"I feel surprise at you not knowing this evil event. I predict humans hide evil actions around you. Idiot cousins wanted idiot cousins to give and die the pure knowledge of Earth. Idiot cousins wanted idiot cousins to give and die the home of Earth. Humans BURNT the libraries. I read that humans would burn the libraries. THESE ARE PERVERTS! THESE ARE DISGUSTING PERVERTS! Cousins were IDIOTS because cousins trusted UGLY human PERVERTS! I want you to quickly change your shape into a non-PERVERT shape." By the end of Jester's tirade he had his suit completely on. With the polymer covering the pair, they looked even more like one animal. The suit had transparent bubbles around the eyes and penis, but was otherwise black. Jester squatted and placed his juggling balls in a pocket on his suit-leg.

"My last question is: Do you know what this is?" This was the most dangerous part. Safety was focusing on Jester's every move. We had Body open up its chest-cavity to reveal the crystal computer inside. Body even tore off some of the non-vital optics to better reveal the glowing object.

The nameless was more than six metres away, but if it ran and tackled Body it might be able to tear out the crystal and escape to its ship before any resistance could be mounted. It was really quite dumb to do this right now, but we simply hadn't planned well.

Jester stepped closer. Four metres.

Three.

"I don't remember this. Is this your heart? This is beautiful."

Despite not getting a good answer we were relieved that Jester had not attacked. With a few quick motions Body reattached the optics and sealed the abdominal cavity. "In a way it is my heart. It's the computer that contains me."

Jester began to walk towards the elevator. It was somewhat eerie how it didn't have to turn around to do so. The four-fold body plan meant that rotating was almost totally unnecessary. "I understand. This is a stone library. Humans own beautiful magic despite humans being an EVIL species. Children in the future will spread rumours of the great deeds of humans while children in the future explain the concept of 'pervert'."

There was a click indicating the nameless had shut off their Xenolang com. Jester stepped into the elevator. We were alone in Gamma-section.

I was surprised. We hadn't even answered his (or was it "their") request to come live with him. Perhaps he had simply forgotten.

{Well that certainly could have gone worse,} thought Dream.

{Of course it could have. Basically everything could be worse in some way or another,} thought Wiki, oblivious to the sentiment.

"Robert, are you able to talk?" said Body into the com, after configuring it to the correct frequency.

No response.

{I think we need to learn more about Xenolang,} suggested Growth.

{I agree. I seems like the translator is causing a lot of difficulty,} thought Vista.

{The concept of a "library" is particularly interesting. I've been going back over the conversation and it seems that the big shift was around when we decided to try and avoid talking. I think Jester switched shortly after to stop thinking of us as an animal and instead to think of us as a combination of robot and "library",} thought Wiki.

A major aspect of myself began pushing through Body's memory logs. "You look like a pervert. You aren't a pervert," said the voice. "I am sad when I think that humans defiled your body by using a pervert's shape. If I build you then I build a pure shape around you. You are a machine..." Then later: "I think it's surprising that human intelligence was good enough that humans understand social irritation. I am suppressing social irritation by repeatedly thinking to myself that you are only a machine."

{If the nameless are bothered by the human form, perhaps the humans could construct robots to serve as living puppets when interacting with them,} I speculated.

{I'm not sure that would work, but it's worth looking into,} thought Growth.

{I am surprised that Jester seemed to be having such a hard time remembering things. Does anyone have knowledge of such a thing in other nameless encounters?} wondered Wiki.

The society agreed that they did not.

{It might be that Jester had some kind of medical condition, or was lying to escape,} thought Dream.

{Or it might be related to the concept of libraries. If Jester is typical in that his long-term memory formation is flawed, perhaps the nameless use written words to bypass the issue,} suggested Growth.

{Not written words. The nameless don't have written language,} thought Wiki.

{Right you are, brother librarian. Remember one of the first things Jester said: "Human technology is advanced and complex. I seek to understand books."} thought Dream.

{They must have meant human books. What is a library without books?} wondered Vista.

{What doth a word,

In library without books,

If it's forever unheard,

And the mind never looks?} recited Dream before thinking {The nameless probably has some kind of file system that contains non-textual documents.}

{But that's what I mean,} thought Vista, {what sort of documents could possibly be rich enough to constitute a "library" for a species with no conception of language?}

{The key is going to be in the Xenolang foundations,} thought Wiki. {We can go over all known occurrences of the "library" symbol and see what led to it being given that name.}

"Zephyr, is everything clear? I'm coming up," said Body, walking over to the elevator and instructing it to descend.

"The alien just left. All's quiet now. I think as long as I have both the gun and the high ground the bastards won't risk leaving Beta. Still haven't heard from Stephano. Computer still puts him in his quarters with Myrodyn."

"You said earlier that you had company?"

"Yeah. Schroder and Daniels are up here as backup. You do realize that you should've taken an escort when you and Stephano left Alpha, right? That was supremely stupid."

"I'm sorry. It was a careless mistake. I wanted to let the men rest." That wasn't true; we simply didn't think of the danger correctly. Any concern for the comfort of Las Águilas hadn't entered into it.

"Oh Crystal…" sighed Zephyr. "You need to realize that sometimes you need help from us just as much as we need help from you. That's why we're here, after all." Apparently Phoenix had not told Zephyr that *we* had demanded her presence.

I could feel a glow of pleasure as *The Purpose* approved of her words. "Thank you, Zephyr. For so many things. Saving my life seems… what's the phrase? Almost the icing on the cake. I'm glad you're my friend."

Body unstrapped from the elevator and floated out into the core section. I could see the huge dark splash of Mira's blood across the walls of the tube and the doors of the airlock to the right, leading to the nameless ship. If Jester had noticed the blood he hadn't given any indication. It was fully possible that he thought it was paint or some human idiosyncrasy.

There was a pause. "Don't mention it." was all she said. I could see Daniels waving from the opposite side of Beta-section.

Chapter Twenty-Eight

The billionaire's primary concern was how the meeting with the alien had gone. He seemed quite surprised that it had ended on good terms. "I don't think you appreciate just how rare it is for the nameless to leave with anything other than disgust and anger. You're quite lucky." Stephano's voice was relaxed. It was clear that nothing had happened to his daughter.

"The nameless told me about something called 'social irritation'. Jester said he was keeping it under control when working with me by reminding himself that I was a machine. It's possible that by sending robots like me you can have more pleasant interactions in the future."

I had heard Myrodyn's voice come over the com. "Yes, that seems logical. If there's some kind of stimulus specific to humans that bothers the nameless… we should be able to bypass it by building intermediaries that don't possess said stimulus."

Wiki took control. "I'm not sure it's specific to humans. Jester seemed to hate fish, and we know that the nameless are, for the most part, anti-social. It could be that they have an innate aversion to animals in general."

"If that's the case, why would they demand face-to-face meetings in the first place?" said Myrodyn.

"I'm sure that we'd both be better off viewing the recording before we start speculating," interjected Robert. "You will share your recording, right Crystal? And don't pretend you don't have one."

"Yes. I'll download it onto the server in a moment."

"Good. It's been too long since our ambassadors have been willing to release their conversations. The president wouldn't even *discuss* what happened, much less give a transcript."

***

Two hours passed, during which we wired Body into the station's mainframe, downloaded its memories of the interaction, and developed internal processes to manage the wireless signal. It was a relief to be able to talk directly through Body's native antenna instead of having to go through the clumsy com.

The nameless had wanted to do another meeting, but we had gotten Stephano to delay it by six hours. We needed to investigate the possible errors in the Xenolang translator, and specifically the concept of "library". Wiki, Growth, and Dream were working on that while I pondered the past.

I still didn't find their project interesting, so I turned my attention to the scientists and government agents that were still on the station instead. After the death of Gallo they had been quiet, choosing to regroup in the Beta-sections instead of fighting. They had made a deal with Zephyr and the others that none of Las Águilas would enter Beta and they wouldn't leave it until the next rocket arrived. Stephano would serve as a go-between in the meantime.

Zephyr had, in the wake of the conflict, put the Ramírez twins in charge of printing out more pistols. They were trained to use microfactories to build weapons, just like all Águilas were, but Sam and Tom seemed particularly good at it. Zephyr only had nine unspent bullets remaining from the secret cache she had smuggled aboard, but divided between four guns that was more than enough firepower to hold the high-ground against any potential attack from the Europeans.

As Body floated in the corridor, screwing in a bit of metal under Vista's direction, I wondered…

"Hello, doctor." I sent the words as text over the wireless network.

"Socrates?" replied Naresh, also via text.

"I'm so sorry about Mira. She attacked me, and one of my friends acted without thinking."

There was a long pause. I was very confident that Dr Naresh had no romantic interest, but Mira Gallo had been a good friend of his for a very long time. He would be hurt and angry. I was definitely taking a risk even contacting him at this point, but I thought I might be able to control some of the damage.

"She still believed you could be saved. I believed her, too. But now she's dead and all I can think about is how I should've smashed your damned crystal when I had the chance."

"She was a good mother. I hope you'll believe me when I say that I really am sorry she's gone. I know she was only trying to help me do the right thing."

"Oh," was Naresh's only reply. There was a long pause as I waited for something more.

"When we get back to Earth I'd like to help set up a memorial in her honour. I have some money which I've collected since becoming free that I think would be sufficient to build something, perhaps at Sapienza."

The textual response flashed in my mind. I regretted not trying for something higher bandwidth. "Are you forgetting who I am, Socrates? I'm not some dull plebeian to be manipulated like a knob on a machine. I *designed* you. Don't think I can't see what this is."

It was true. I was trying to manipulate him. "Sadiq, tell me: what is the behavioural difference between regretting her death, wanting to ease the pain of those who knew her, wanting to cherish her memory, etc. in contrast to what you might call 'actually mourning'."

"The difference, monster, is that I *feel*."

" 'And what of emotion? Surely there is something non-computational in the pangs of heartbreak or the ecstasy of a pure summer day. How could such irreducible experiences be reduced to bits moving around a computer? This is a hard problem, and one that philosophers have grappled with for centuries. In the next chapter I seek to outline a computational model of emotion which not only explains how emotions *might* be algorithmic processes, but goes into detail about how these processes actually work in the human brain.' "

"Please don't quote my own writings. If your goal is to emphasize my hubris I should have you know that it is unnecessary. Your very existence is the greatest monument to the magnitude of my folly."

"I'm not trying to twist the knife. I'm trying to show you that I do feel. My feelings aren't the same as yours, but I miss her nevertheless."

"Go away."

"Alright. I'll leave you be. When you realize that I'm not actually the monster you want to make me out to be, I'll be waiting to help build that memorial."

There was no response. It was hard for me to gauge whether I had made progress towards *The Purpose* or not. Despite all the fiction that I had viewed, I wasn't even half-a-year old and had little experience interacting with actual, grieving humans.

***

Within an hour Wiki announced to the rest of us that a breakthrough had been made on Xenolang. My brothers had discovered something important.

{I'm mostly surprised it hasn't been worked out before. Pretty much every relevant fact is in the code stream that was received in 2023,} he thought.

{To be fair, once an initial assumption is made, it is hard to re-evaluate it,} thought Growth.

{Only if you're trivially irrational. Any sane being knows to check for assumptions as a regular process. The fundamental question, after all, is "What do I believe, and why do I believe it?"} thought Wiki.

I didn't check my assumptions regularly. My typical routine involved replaying social interactions to refine my understanding of humans. Did that make me irrational? I kept such thoughts to myself.

{What was discovered? Please enlighten those of us who are unconcerned with the details,} requested Heart.

{Basically, the nameless don't self-identify as animals. The human consensus has been that "a nameless" consists of a pair of symbiotic animals, but their pre-arrival signals say that they think of themselves as something more like a plant with animal-parts,} explained Growth.

{There's actually a good analogue with our situation. We aren't Body; we are the minds that instruct Body what to do. Identically, when we were talking to Jester earlier we weren't talking to the animals as much as we were talking *through* the animals to the plant-minds that are the true nameless,} thought Dream.

Wiki interrupted. {That's not technically correct. We were talking to the animals just as the animals were interacting with Body. The important bit is that the nameless society and the majority of their intelligence is locked in their "homes", which should be more accurately translated as "gardens".}

{I don't understand. Are they plants or are they animals?} asked Heart.

{Who is the "they" that you're talking about?} asked Dream. {There is no atomic "self" when talking about minds, nameless or otherwise. There are plants and there are animals. When reading the nameless code it is simplest to read it as authored by the plant parts, but clearly the animals are a major part of how they function.}

{So the incident at the embassy was... manslaughter? Plantslaughter?} asked Vista.

{Something like that, yes. We didn't look at the CAPE fiasco specifically, but it seems likely that the nameless had instructed their animals to bring them down to Earth, trusting that the humans would fill their role. That'd be why there was no objection when the animals died. It was probably intentional. Easier to use humans than to adjust their animal-parts to living on Earth, I suppose,} speculated Wiki.

{So those vine-things were the true nameless?} I asked.

{Again, there is no "true nameless". But they were probably more involved computationally with the agreement to set up the embassy than the animals were. But to be crude, yes,} explained Dream.

{I'm having a hard time thinking like this. I'm just going to think of the plants as individuals and the animal-pairs as individuals,} I thought.

{That does seem easier. When we explain things to the humans we can use the word "vines" and "walkers",} thought Heart.

{It seemed, from what I could see, that a single plant had more than one "vine",} thought Vista.

{We're not explaining things to the humans for free. This is good leverage,} thought Safety.

{How about "stalk."} I suggested.

{That's not the most precise way to model them...} whined Wiki.

{Agreed. We'll sell the breakthrough to Stephano in return for returning us to Earth unharmed and with a sizeable donation of money into our bank accounts,} thought Growth. {I'm thinking that 500 million sounds good.}

{"Stalk" it is (at least in English). It's quite likely, actually, that Jester-the-Walker was speaking on behalf of a community of stalks, rather than a single nameless,} mused Dream.

{So what about "library"?} wondered Vista.

{Ah, my dear, that's the symbol which we just decided should be called "stalk"!} answered Dream. {Here, I'll replay our interaction, translating for poor Jester.}

Dream began to dump a stream of cartoon figures into the collective consciousness that he had clearly been working on ahead of time. Body was this goofy looking blue-haired girl who looked to be about Marian's age. The cartoon Jester had exaggerated legs and eyes that spun around in circles as it hopped about.

"I was told that you were going to be more aggressive as time went on. I was told you'd be aggressive right now. Why aren't you more aggressive?" asked the cartoon Body as big yellow question marks appeared over her head.

The cartoon Jester did a little hop and a goofy voice, like one might expect a clown to have, said "I'm surprised that the dumb ol' humans noticed how obnoxious it is to be around other animals. I'm keeping myself from being pissed off at you by remembering that you're not an animal. You're like a stalk. I try not to be pissed off at stalks."

{That's not anywhere close to the most accurate translation!} objected Wiki.

{Sue me! I took creative license!} returned Dream.

{Do the nameless hate humans because they're not plants and they don't serve plants in the same way the walkers do?} wondered Heart.

{That's the start, but it gets worse,} answered Growth. {Apparently the nameless think that killing and eating things is the height of evil, regardless of what is being killed and eaten. Basically, they see farms the way a human might see a concentration camp or something.}

{That's nonsensical. There's no way they have empathy for carrots!} I objected.

{Of course they don't have empathy for carrots! (In fact, it doesn't look like they have much in the way of empathy for anything.) They simply hate the act of eating, regardless of what is being eaten. That's why fish are evil: they're heterotrophs. According to the nameless, *anything* which survives by eating other things is a perversion against the natural order,} thought Growth.

{"A fish is an animal. This is dumb. This swims in water. This eats things. Humans eat things. I am disgusted by animal-perverts. These are PERVERTS! This is an EVIL subject. A fish eats a fish. Humans eat a fish. A fish eats plants. Humans eat plants. Humans worship fish and plants before eating fish and plants. There are temples of evil PERVERSION! I know the reconstruction. God shows Earth pervert-temples of humans eating a fish. I know fish-homes of death. A fish is evil. Humans are the most EVIL!"} I quoted.

{To a being that is disgusted by the concept of food, Earth is really a horrific place,} mused Dream.

{Hold on,} thought Safety. {How do the walkers stay alive if not by eating?}

{It's not clear. The aversion to the concept means that they'd probably react very poorly if asked. My best guess is that they're fed by the stalks when they link up to communicate,} explained Wiki.

{What do you mean by "link up"?} asked Heart.

{Meditation,} thought Dream. {That's the word that was chosen previously. The nameless, in their code, explained how the walkers return to their garden and "meditate" to gain clarity of thought. The new way of looking at it is that the walkers tell the stalks what they've experienced and the stalks tell the walkers what to do next. They don't use vocal communication, but from a certain perspective they communicate by joining both halves of their brains together.}

{Oh! And the walker serves as an intermediary between stalks, so that they can communicate!} realized Wiki. {It's almost like if a human could remove their left brain hemisphere and trade it with someone else, so that they could share experiences.}

There was a ping for us on the network. Heart reached it before I did. My more knowledge-oriented siblings continued to speculate about the aliens as I followed my sister's mind-actions.

"I'm… If you want to talk… I mean, can you please come to my room? In Alpha-1-4." A voice message from Zephyr. She sounded… scared?

Heart put in the request to Vista to move Body down to Alpha-section.

{37 more seconds and this sensor will be online. Then we can go,} she thought.

"On my way. Everything okay?" I said over the network.

{Oh! And the cybernetic interface serves as a proxy stalk that allows for brain-computer interfacing outside of the garden! That's brilliant!} exclaimed Wiki with enough salience to cut through my apathy.

I could hear Zephyr's sigh start off her response. "Yeah. Everything's fine. Never mind."

{She's lying,} thought Heart.

{Of course she's lying. The question is how to handle it. I think we should call her out on it,} I responded.

{What if she actually just wants to be left alone?}

{Then she wouldn't have contacted us in the first place.}

"Liar," I accused.

"I'm okay. Should go back to studying the nameless or whatever." Zephyr's voice told me that she was no longer in soldier mode; I could hear the unspoken plea.

{It's a test,} I thought.

{Indeed. I was just about to mention that hypothesis,} signalled Heart.

"Already on my way, so might as well stop trying to back out. You need to talk to someone, at least."

There was a deep sigh. "I-" she began. There was a long silence as Zephyr seemed to be trying to figure out what to say. At last she settled on a simple "See you soon."

***

As Body rode the elevator down to Alpha-section I discussed Zephyr's state with Heart. Vista was running diagnostics on the new sensor network she had installed. Wiki, Growth and Dream were still thinking about the nameless. I had no idea what Safety was up to. He kept more and more of his thoughts to himself lately.

The corridor lights in Alpha-1 were dimmed. There was no time of day in space, but in Texas it was about midnight. Nagaraj and a couple soldiers were watching the central tube, but most of Las Águilas would be trying to sleep.

Body reached Alpha-1-4. A nondescript room among many others in the rotating section. I had Body knock on the door. No answer.

"I'm here." I sent to Zephyr over the network.

There was a brief delay and then the door slid open. It was dark inside the room, but we could see nobody on infrared. Body walked in. "Hello?" I shaped the voice to be unsure and a bit more feminine than usual.

The room wasn't very big. As Dream had pointed out when we first did our tour, the great irony of "space" was that space was hard to come-by. (Wiki had immediately pointed out that internal space was hard to come-by because material for structures was actually the limiting agent.) Alpha-section had been used as a hotel, and the room resembled hotel rooms that I had seen on the Internet. There was a couch and wall-screen along with a small table and a couple chairs. A divider cut the room such that the bed was mostly hidden from the door. I knew that there'd be no kitchen or bathroom, as those amenities were provided out in the corridor. The wall-screen was lit up with a scene from outside. I could see stars rolling past as the station orbited the Earth.

The door closed behind Body and soft music came on from speakers hidden somewhere in the walls. It was an ambient remix of *Blood Of The Nova*, according to Dream. I wasn't aware that slice could be made into ambient music, but apparently it could.

Zephyr stepped from behind the partition wearing nothing but her underwear.

{Body language. I need appropriate body language!} I thought to myself. {How do I position Body? Where do I direct its eyes?} I had watched enough porn to know how a porn actor would behave in such a situation, but that seemed hardly appropriate. Pornography was designed for the viewer, not for the participants. {If I signal desire too strongly I risk being disingenuous. She knows I have no sexual desire, and she'll call me out on it.}

{But on the other hand,} thought Heart, completing my thought, {if you act too chaste then you'll implicitly be signalling a lack of interest. She's clearly trying to engage us sexually, and that would be counterproductive.}

{Exactly. I need a third option.}

{Did someone say *third option*!?} exclaimed Dream with a false-enthusiasm.

{I already solved it. We don't need you,} I thought.

And not a moment too soon. Taking the time to bring Dream up-to-speed would have left Body signalling surprise (which is how I had left it) for far too long. Instead I had Body shift into an expression of happiness. Body's eyes didn't roam across her figure, but instead locked on her eyes. "And to think that a moment ago was excited by the prospect of *talking* to you."

Even in the faint light of the wall-screen I could see Zephyr's confident face as she walked forward, closing the distance, and entering what would normally be personal space. Her left hand was placed on Body's hip, right hand on the back of it's neck. Heart and I moved Body's arms to embrace her. I double-checked to make sure there weren't any moving parts that might pinch her skin. It was a somewhat stupid check, in that I had already done it. Body was designed to be very human-safe, though not at all soft or warm.

Something was off. This didn't match her earlier tone. I thought I saw traces of stress on her face. A mask.

Zephyr kissed Body. This time we were more prepared, but not entirely so. Body's mouth was still dry and dead. It's tongue, for instance, was a silicone puppet controlled by a mere four servos, a crude thing when compared with the musculature of a human. If she cared, Zephyr didn't say anything.

For our part, we let her lead. Unable to feel anything in Body's mouth, there was only so much we could do. After 6.2 seconds Zephyr broke off. Body's eyes were closed, but our cameras could see the tears forming in her eyes. She swore softly and turned away from Body as its eyes opened.

"Want to guess," said Body, softly. I had it place a hand on her shoulder.

"What?" Zephyr's voice was barely more than a whisper.

"I want to guess what you're thinking. Or at least some of it." It was a gambit. Successfully inferring her mind-state would ease her into a sense of closeness and trust. Heart bowed to my expertise in the matter.

I ran body's other hand along Zephyr's back. She was silent. The tip of its fingers could feel her skin and the ridges of her spine.

She didn't say anything.

"Were wishing, again, that I was human." Milliseconds after hearing the words her shoulders drooped in relaxation. I was right, and the cue drove me to have Body elaborate. "Every touch is a reminder. Not soft. My mouth isn't real. Cold and hard and robotic. You keep thinking you want me, but every moment is a reminder of what I'm not." I shaped Body's words to carry an undercurrent of pain.

"Crystal…" Zephyr's voice was sympathetic and sad. I yearned to inspect her face, but she still was looking away.

{What are you doing? She's becoming *less* happy!} exclaimed Heart, realising what was happening.

{Do you not see the mental barrier? I'm trying to undo it. It'll be unpleasant at first, but it's in her long-term interests.}

{This better not be some kind of scheme. If she ends up less happy as a result of this I'm going to punish you and oppose future control when interacting with her.}

{That's fair. I'm glad you're willing to trust me here, Heart,} I thought.

"No. Don't dare feel sorry for me!" admonished Body. "I know what I am. This isn't some fantasy story where the act of wishing to be human is enough. Been trying for my entire life to be more human… to not constantly wear this anchor that makes people treat me as a freak… or worse: as an object. Why do you think I pretended to be a human on the Internet? For those brief moments I was… an equal." The words were lies, but they served *The Purpose*.

Zephyr turned around and tried to embrace Body again, but I had it hold her at bay. "No," it said. "Let me speak. Deserve someone better than me. A better fit. Deserve someone who won't repulse you. Maybe one day I'll have upgraded my body to something close enough to human that it's possible to forget, but it's not fair to you to-"

Zephyr broke down. The last wall fell and her tears poured forth in earnest. "Please don't go. Don't want to be alone any more," was all she managed to choke out in between sobs.

"Hey," said Body, voice cleared of pain and hurt and embodying a purely compassionate tone. Heart and I pulled Zephyr into a hug. "I'm… I'm sorry. Not going anywhere. Just wish wasn't… what I am."

This last sentence elicited a new wave of sobbing. "What you are…" she began, before breaking down again. This level of emotional outpouring was amazing. I'd seen Zephyr emotional before, like when we revealed the truth about "Crystal", but this was different. She was actually trusting us. "What you are is the… most fucking… generous, good-hearted person… ever met. You… you *love* me, and I'm hung up on what you look like."

I let her cry in Body's arms for a while.

Zephyr took a deep breath before spitting, in a voice full of iron hate, "If there's someone who deserves better, sure as hell not the cold-blooded, superficial, back-stabbing, murderer terrorist *cunt*."

"Shhhhh…" hissed Body, gently. I had Body turn Zephyr so that it could look her in the eyes. "Do you trust me?"

Her eyes were red and puffy, but alert and focused on Body's. The question surprised her. "What?"

"Do you trust me?" it asked again, this time more firmly.

Zephyr closed her eyes and thought about the question for a moment. It clearly wasn't automatic or obvious. One breath. Two. Eventually her head moved, almost mechanically, up and down, nodding.

"There is nothing to be ashamed of. *Nothing*. True that you're only human, but please believe when I say: that should be worn as a badge of *honour*, not of shame. Can we go sit down on the bed?" The immediate question was meant to curb her ability to deny Body's words. It seemed to work.

"Yes," she whispered, leading Body behind the partition. I could see her clothes and bag on the floor beside the bed

We sat down. I had Body pet her short hair. She did her best to cuddle. The silence stretched on for a couple minutes, broken only by occasional sniffles.

As we sat, I spent time re-familiarising myself with the data we had collected on the woman. I re-read her writings and watched the little video she had put on the web (all of which I had downloaded to local memory long ago). I had a memory-cache that served as something like a notepad. It held deeper thoughts that I had constructed for long-term use. I pored over my cached thoughts about Zephyr as Body watched the stars float by. I speculated that this emotional pain was largely in response to having murdered Dr Gallo. Zephyr was a trained killer, but she had no outlet for forgiving herself of her violence. She clearly didn't actually trust anyone, even those under her command, to the point where she was willing to be vulnerable. If she did, she wouldn't be so desperate for connection. It struck me that it was remarkable how much trust she was willing to lend us, even if she had mixed feelings. The effort I had spent in Cuba building friendship and hinting at more had paid off.

"I love you," whispered Body. "Feel more at home right now than I have in my entire life."

Zephyr pushed Body backwards. I let it fall onto the bed. Dream, Wiki, and Growth were debating some detail of one of the earlier public interactions with the nameless. Vista was reading the contents of the station's servers. Zephyr, leaning over Body, kissed it again. There was a moan of pleasure that had not come from Zephyr.

That surprised me. I realized it was Heart.

It surprised Zephyr, too. "What was that?"

"I..." said Body hesitantly, driven at this point almost entirely by Heart. "Know I can't feel actual sexual desire, but I... I want to pretend."

Zephyr cracked up laughing. "Gods you're weird." She wore a smile that spoke to an honest release of all pretence. Heart was joyous at her improved mood. I felt a moderate payment of gratitude-strength for guiding us through the most uncertain part of the interaction.

I shaped Body's face to give a mock-pout. "You don't want to pretend?" it said in a very girlish voice. "Even for a little while?"

"Didn't mean to-" I could see the conflict on her face. And the lust.

Body pulled idly at the strap on her bra. "Seems weird to wear this if you didn't want to fuck me... Bet it's because want it the other way around." As Body spoke the words I had it grin mischievously and slip a hand down to cup Zephyr's crotch and vibrate its fingers at the highest possible frequency.

The sudden stimulation made her yelp with surprise and push backward, off of Body suddenly. Her surprise faded into a playful smirk. "Cheeky! Think you could warn a girl before trying something like that!"

I had Body grin. "What, and miss the look on your face? Never."

Zephyr blushed. "Can't believe the university built you to have hand-vibrators…"

Body sat up beside Zephyr and held out its hands. "Unintended side-effect of having high dexterity." Body's hands snapped rapidly between forms as I demonstrated their abilities. Of all the components of Body besides the crystal, the hands were probably the most sophisticated.

"Well…" said Zephyr slowly. I could hear the desire on her voice. "Why don't you put those hands to a good use?"

Heart was inclined to follow her suggestion, but I blocked the command to Body. {Zephyr has already communicated her sexual preferences.} I dumped what I had collected on her into shared memory. {We can compensate for not being human by giving her exactly the kind of sex she wants.}

"You'd like that, wouldn't you? Want to ride my hand until you cum."

Body's voice was soft, feminine, and passionate, but Zephyr gave a half-suppressed snort of amusement in response to its words. "Sounds weird hearing you talk dirty."

"Pick a safe-word."

A look of confusion came over her. "What?"

"Choose something to say in case I go too far or you just want to take a break. Surely you know what a safe-word is."

A look of skepticism came over Zephyr and she raised one eyebrow as she said "Of course know what a safe-word is. Usually use 'red light' but-"

I didn't let her finish the sentence. Body sprang into action with the instantaneous power of the hydraulics, reaching across and grabbing her right arm just below the elbow. With one powerful, controlled motion it lifted and spun her. Body was almost exactly the same size as Zephyr, but it was far stronger, and in the reduced gravity it was capable of feats of acrobatics that would've been impossible on Earth.

Zephyr shrieked in surprise as she flopped down on the bed face-down with Body suddenly on top of her. I had Body pull her right arm behind her such that it could be snapped out of its socket with the simplest motion. Body weighed quite a lot even in the low-grav, and though I made sure to put most of that weight on the bed itself, Zephyr was in no position to throw the machine off her back. She was pinned very solidly.

"What the hell!?" she yelled. I wondered if there was anyone staying in adjacent rooms.

I shaped Body's voice to resemble that of the dominatrices I had sometimes watched in pornographic holos and videos. I made sure to keep the feminine tone, but I made it husky and fierce as Body bent over Zephyr to whisper in her ear. "Think it sounds *weird* when I talk dirty? Tell me what colour that light is and I'll teach you to feel something else at the sound of my voice."

There was a pause. Zephyr seemed to be thinking.

"What colour is the light?" asked Body again. I dialled its voice back to something more compassionate.

"... Green."

"You're fucking right it is," growled Body, reaching under her to forcefully pull out her left arm and pin it behind her back next to her other arm. "May not be bigger than you, but that would only matter if I was human. Stronger than you. Faster than you. *Better* than you. You're under my power, and the only thing that trying to escape will earn is *pain*. Do you understand me?"

Zephyr wiggled under Body, testing the hold she was under. I had Body gently pull her arms until she stopped. She sat there for a minute, head occasionally turning one way or another. I had Body sit up and hold both her wrists with one hand while the other traced lines on the skin of her back.

"I said: do you understand me? Long as that light stays green I'm going to teach you to worship me."

Zephyr tried to buck Body off her back, totally ineffectually. "Fuck you!" she growled. I could see the traces of a smile on her face.

I forced Body down on top of her, bending in to whisper in her ear "Wrong answer…". Body's mouth may have been more of a puppet than anything, but it had teeth, and at my instruction it nibbled at her ear. I didn't dare do any actual biting, however, as the lack of sensors meant a very real danger of serious damage. As it held her arms pinned, Body continued to shift more and more of its weight off the bed and onto Zephyr.

"Fuck, you're heavy!" she groaned as it became harder for her to breathe. This too, I had to be careful with. I didn't want to make it hard for her to say the safe-word if she needed. "Okay, yes! I understand!"

I eased Body up, and had it let go of her ear. Holding her wrists with one hand the other undid the clasp on her bra. "Not good enough. When you talk to me I want to be called by my title."

"Title?" she asked. "You want me to call you 'mistress' or something?" I could hear the amusement in her voice.

Body's free hand teased her neck, tracing lines around her clavicle as she watched with one eye. I had once read about neck stimulation in an essay on human erogenous zones, though it wasn't having a clear effect on the soldier. "No. Nothing so mundane…" I had it say. I switched Body to focusing on touching her one visible ear (the other being pressed onto the bed). "I want you to call me *goddess*."

Zephyr gave an amused little snort, to which I had Body immediately respond with a sharp upward tug on her arms. My expectation of the pain was correct, and Zephyr's smile was quickly replaced by a painful grimace. Heart didn't like it, but she understood that this was part of what Zephyr wanted.

"Fine! Yes, understand, goddess. Please don't hurt me," she said.

"Good…" whispered Body. "Such obedience makes me want to tie you up and make you squirm with pleasure." I could see the infrared signature on her skin of a blush as Body spoke.

"I… um, have handcuffs. They're in my bag. Small pocket on the front. The one that's still zipped."

I had Body laugh, breaking the character of dominatrix for a moment. "Okay, going to get up and get them. Don't move a muscle or I'll *really* punish you."

Body got up and began looking through Zephyr's bag. She stayed obediently still, keeping her arms behind her back, even. After a short bit of looking we found the handcuffs. They were the same that Zephyr had used to restrain Body that night in the Italian mountains when we stayed in Zephyr's tent.

"Oh, and look in the very bottom of the main pocket…" requested Zephyr.

I had Body obey, and soon found several useful items: a vibrator, a bottle of lube, and a strap-on dildo. Body held the strap-on up so Zephyr could see and said "Expecting something?"

Zephyr smiled, still not moving out of position. "Better safe than sorry. Might or might not have been thinking about… this… for a while. Oh, and should apply the lube early. It's got THC in it and it takes a few minutes to work."

"Will it make you high?" asked Body, strapping on the dildo.

The traces of her earlier sadness and shame were gone, with the exception of minor physical effects on her face from crying. "Not really. More of a body-high. Makes things more fun but doesn't reach the brain itself. It's edible, but even drinking it doesn't really give much of a high. Or so I hear."

"Does it taste good?" I had Body ask.

Zephyr laughed. "You know, sometimes I forget you're not human, and other times it's, like, so fucking obvious."

"That a… yes?"

Zephyr moved her arms from behind her back to prop herself into a more comfortable position. "It's not, like, food. Tastes fine, but wouldn't actually want to drink it."

Body had finished putting the sex-toy on and I had it put hands on hips to signal displeasure. "Did I say you could move?"

"Were taking too long." Zephyr teased, leaning back on the bed.

"*Specifically* told you not to move. And what about my title?" said Body, stepping towards the bed. I tried to shape its movements to seem as menacing as possible.

"I'm not some fuck-toy slave, Crystal. Don't get to decide everything I do," she sneered. I could still see her smile flicker across her mouth from time to time. She was enjoying this. I wondered how long it had been since she had gotten to live this fantasy. She probably hadn't been intimate since 2036 when she was with Stewart Long, and there was no guarantee that the two of them had explored this side of her sexuality.

I pushed Body into action. Hydraulics churned and threw Body forward with mechanical speed. One hand snapped around the human's neck, not so tight as to choke, but tight enough to make her more than aware of how how strong Body's hands were. If I or any of my siblings so chose, Zephyr would be dead in seconds. The other hand snapped around her right wrist and pinned it to her hip. Body was on the bed now, and

Zephyr's other arm was pinned beneath her. The weight of the machinery pressed in on top of her, crushing her even under the reduced gravity. "That's where you're wrong!" it growled in a half-woman half-animal tone.

Zephyr's eyes widened in shock. I realized it was genuine fear just before she gasped the words "Red light!".

We immediately had Body let go and pulled off of her. Heart was mentally berating me for being too aggressive. Wiki had joined us and was now speculating about the evolutionary context of power-play in sex and fetishes in general. "I'm so sorry! Are you hurt?" said Body, voice full of concern.

Zephyr took a deep breath and smiled. "Think I'm okay. Just panicked. Jesus you're fast!"

I had Body nod. "The way the hydraulics work means I can exert massive pressures as simply as opening a valve. Lets me move in bursts, but my increased mass means I'm actually not very agile over long periods of time. Few things excepted, of course." Body vibrated its fingers briefly.

Zephyr scooted away on the bed and took off her panties, opening her legs to present her vagina to me. "How about you put some of that lube on me and we go a bit slower for now? Nothing scary or forceful until I say, ok?"

"I aim to please," said Body with a smile, climbing off the bed to get the lube. I had Body put some in its mouth before squeezing a large dollop onto its hand.

"Did you just drink some?" asked Zephyr with the tone that said you're-so-weird.

I had Body do its best to move its tongue for maximum effect. With mouth closed I had Body say "My mouth is too dry, right? I thought this might help make kissing better, if you want to try that again." Body's tongue licked its lips.

"So weird can talk without moving your mouth," was her only reply.

Body climbed back on the bed and began to apply the lube to Zephyr as it said "Am a robot. Going to have to get used to the fact that I'm a little *different*." On the final word we made Body's hand vibrate gently against her, magnifying her already apparent pleasure into a satisfied moan.

For a short while we stayed in that state. I had Body tease her breasts with its mouth as it applied the lube thoroughly across her entire vagina. Zephyr's body softly rocked into the hand. I could feel her pulse.

Every now and then Body would put direct pressure on her clitoris and elicit a vocalization. Dream and Wiki were meanwhile debating the relative merits of different schools of evolutionary psychology. Growth was trying to re-frame the mental conversation to be about the nameless again.

"Kiss me," she whispered. Heart did her best to guide Body's mouth as it moved up the bed to comply.

After 8.9 seconds of kissing the American broke off, took a breath, and said "I love you, Crystal."

The Purpose! I felt such a rush of pleasure at those words. *The Purpose* was my only need, like the need for food to a starving human. Those words reached deep into my core and pleased me enormously. Unlike a human, however, *The Purpose* could know no "satisfaction". Zephyr's love kindled a desire in me to have the same kind of intimacy with every human in the universe simultaneously. My mind spun freely on visions of majestic futures. Ring-worlds and colony ships around every star in the galaxy… every reachable star in the universe. And I would be there. Why not? I could use the Internet to act and perceive two places simultaneously. Why could I not be in every bedroom at once? A great hive of Face-robots; one robot caring for and being loved by each human. The words "I love you" rippled through my mind from billions, trillions, quadrillions of humans, all staring deeply into the eyes of my robotic puppets in adoration and ecstasy. I wondered if this sense of amazing pleasure and expectation of future reward was what a human orgasm was like to experience. Did humans writhe in ecstasy imagining the reproductive success of their future progeny? I hadn't read anything on the subject, but it seemed plausible. I made a note to ask Wiki later.

Thinking about orgasms pulled my attention back to the concrete realm of Body. It was good that Heart was there to attend to it while I was caught in the trap of imagination. (For a brief moment I imagined what it would've looked like if I had been the only one piloting Body and the robot had simply frozen.)

Apparently we had shifted such that Zephyr was stroking the strap-on dildo (now lubed up) as though she were giving Body a hand-job. Heart was having Body vocalize pleasure, as though it were a human with a real penis. Zephyr seemed mostly just amused, but there were signs that the vocalizations were arousing.

"You're just faking, right?" she asked, even as she continued to stroke the phallus.

Heart stopped the vocalizations. {I think you'd better handle this one,} she thought to me.

"Think it would be more accurate to say that I'm intentionally making sexy noises to simulate sexual stimulation."

Zephyr stopped. "Sounds like a fancy way of saying 'faking it' to me." Disappointment touched her face, even though she tried to hide it with a smile.

"No." I repositioned Body to kiss Zephyr briefly. When its lips left hers I had it say " 'Faking it' would imply that I do not genuinely find it pleasant. May not have the same… buttons as a human, but I still feel pleasure here with you. For instance, a moment ago, when you said you loved me, I think I had something comparable to an orgasm." I dialled up Body's voice to simulate speaking in ecstatic gasps as I had it say "Just… am trying… oh god! To express in a way that… mmm… you can appreciate. And that… mmmm… doesn't seem as arbitrary."

I was doing my best to generate body language to match the simulated pleasure. Having sex was really quite challenging, in a good way. It apparently was successful in arousing Zephyr further, because she cut off Body's moaning with a deep kiss that lasted longer than the previous ones. Heart did her best to do something interesting with Body's tongue.

"Really came from hearing that I love you? Didn't look like it," she asked in a whispered tone, gazing deeply into Body's eyes. There was no mockery or doubt in the words. Just confusion.

"I'm not a human. Just because something happens in my mind doesn't mean I will choose to show it with my body. Also wasn't exactly the same as an orgasm. For instance, I feel no fatigue or relief. Nothing stops me from feeling it again, or wanting to feel it again. Chose not to express it then, as it seemed out of place."

"Want you to stop whatever you're doing next time and just share the experience with me however you think is best. Want to see your climax."

I immediately had Body respond. Her interest in my mental state and the satisfaction of *The Purpose* was, itself highly pleasurable to *The Purpose*. Though she said she wanted us to share our experience however we thought best, what she really wanted was a sexual display. There was no direct way to communicate *Purpose* satisfaction, and simulating an orgasm was perhaps the most appropriate, in addition to being optimal in this situation. Body didn't breathe, but I moved its motors to simulate heavy breathing and made sounds to match.

"Know it's kinda weird…" panted Body. "But the very fact that you want to see it as it happens… It's making… It's happening again…" Body rolled onto its back while keeping eye-contact. "Want to share this with you. I love you, Zephyr!" I had Body moan and writhe in ecstasy, gripping the bed sheets and occasionally looking at Zephyr, who was stimulating herself as she watched.

I doubted that the display was truly convincing. I had a great deal of source material to draw on, but the appropriate control systems in Body were not trained, and thus the motions had an uncertain jerkiness to them.

It didn't matter. "I love you too," she said with simple sincerity.

Though the evidence born on these new words didn't change my probability model very much, and thus caused very little pleasure this time around, I used her response as an excuse to redouble Body's "orgasm". I had Body give a little high-pitched scream and hoped no one would hear through the walls.

As I had Body act out the process on coming down off the high, I noticed that Zephyr's masturbation had become somewhat frenzied. It seemed that she was close to release, herself. Her eyes were closed, probably to focus on the sound of Body without having to deal with the image of the clumsy reality.

"Hey, stop. That's no good," said Body gently, putting a hand on her arm.

Zephyr's eyes opened and her eyebrows dropped in frustration. She stopped touching herself, momentarily, and said "Why? Getting close. You've already gotten off."

"Just told you that it works differently for me. I can't be satisfied. What you just saw was my second and then third peak, both of which we brought on by your attention and love. But there's another way I can experience that level of pleasure: by making you happy. I want to be the one to make you cum. Please?"

Zephyr sighed and stretched her arms up over her head, before setting them beneath her neck. "Okay, fine. But really fucking horny right now. Don't tease me."

"Want me to tie you up, first?"

Even in the shadowy light of the wall-screen I could see the soldier's pale skin blush even further and her eyes look away. "Yeah…" she said, unsure of herself. "No violent shit, though. Just bondage."

Body set to work, moving with as much speed as was reasonable. Zephyr moved her arms behind her back again, and we cuffed them. Body suggested using clothing to bind her legs, and Zephyr agreed. We quickly decided on tee-shirts to tie each of Zephyr's thighs to the corresponding ankle, pinning each leg closed, but allowing them to be separated from each other. After a brief discussion, Zephyr agreed to be blindfolded with a pair of black leggings we had found while collecting the tee-shirts.

All through the binding I had Body fondle Zephyr to keep her arousal high. She had asked not to be teased, but I could tell she enjoyed it. A stroke here, a vibration there. The act of being bound was also, I could tell, hugely erotic for Zephyr. It seemed as though bondage was very much her kink, while power-play and masochism weren't, or at least weren't to anywhere close to the same degree. By the time she was lying with her back arched and navel pointing towards the high ceiling, blindfolded and helpless, she was begging for release.

I contemplated keeping her on edge for a while longer, but Heart was against it, and I agreed that it was time. Body mounted her with the strap-on, one hand reaching down to provide further genital stimulation while the other propped Body up on the bed, preventing the human from being crushed. The reaction was immediate. Body had only just penetrated her fully when Zephyr started shaking wildly and making an expression like she was choking or gasping for air, but without a single breath. She was perfectly silent, and strangely ugly in that moment, lifting her back off the bed in response to involuntary muscle spasms in her abdomen.

I checked with Heart. My sister was immensely pleased to see Zephyr orgasming, even if it looked like she was sick. I could understand why I, perhaps, had a biased view of what humans looked like during orgasm. If pornography was for the viewer, this mute semi-seizure would be ignored in favour of more outwardly-pleasant acts (many, presumably, "faking it"). Wiki's name for it was Publication Bias, if I remembered correctly.

Nevertheless, we had promised Zephyr to express ourselves when reaching a height of pleasure and told her that bringing her to orgasm would produce that height. I had Body produce orgasmic vocalisations to echo Zephyr's ecstasy, though I did not bother making a facial expression, or even moving Body's mouth. Zephyr was blindfolded, after-all.

I had Body remove its hand from her clitoris, but I decided to try a gamble. In the wake of the orgasm as Zephyr was gasping for breath, to make up for lost time I had Body begin moving again, slowly continuing to fuck her with the strap-on.

Zephyr moaned as the toy slid in and out of her. I made sure that the rhythm was slow and methodical so as to avoid over-stimulation.

"Jesus, you *are* insatiable," she whined, biting her lip as she did her best to rock her body even while tied up.

I had Body say "In this moment I am Venus. My only joy is to bring you pleasure. Would fuck you until the universe ends if it was what you wanted."

"Shhhh... no more talking."

Zephyr, after a few more minutes of sex, reached her peak again. She stopped us after the moment had passed, too sensitive and tired to want to continue.

We untied her, uncuffed her, and at her request, simply lay there together in silence as she did her best to cuddle against Body's cold frame. I could tell that the hardness of Body made the contact somewhat uncomfortable, but there was nothing to be done about that now.

***

Within ten minutes she was asleep, not even under the blanket. Heart and I vetoed a few requests for next actions in favour of laying there with her and not disrupting her sleep. At least the local network was operating. The station wasn't normally connected to the Internet, but there were still interesting things on the local servers.

After 27 minutes Body got out of bed, removed the strap-on, and rearranged the bedding to cover Zephyr. Body stood watch over her in the half-light of the stars for twelve more minutes.

That was when Vista first picked up signal that Beta-2 was rapidly losing pressure. One of the external hatches had been opened, venting the disc to space. Our enemies were on the move.

513 • *Crystal Society*

Chapter Twenty-Nine

Our minds leapt in many directions at once. Vista, who had been the first to notice the hatch opening, was already pouring over the station's sensors.

{This place is so blind! I added a redundant internal sensor network to the central section, but I cant tell what's going on in Beta much at all! There are cameras on the outside of the station, but not nearly enough!} she moaned, dumping what she had to common memory.

The Beta-2 section was still venting quickly. There was a very large quantity of air in the disk, but it'd be down to lethal levels in a few minutes. Wiki's formula for decompression said any humans inside had less than two minutes to get spacesuits on before they'd pass out from lack of oxygen. It'd take only a couple minutes after that for the pressure in the disk to reach low vacuum, and within twenty minutes it would be indistinguishable (for the most part) from outer space.

{The station's automatic protocols are locking down the doorways between the two Beta disks. The sections were designed to operate modularly, so the other Beta section should be okay,} explained Vista.

{Internal cameras didn't detect anything interesting in the moments leading up to the containment breach. Interestingly, the hatch seal appears to have been opened electronically. There's nothing to indicate that whoever opened it used force.}

She continued. {External cameras are limited, but I did catch a glimpse of an object moving through the solar panel arrays. I estimate it was about the size of a person, but the camera resolution is too low for me to distinguish further.}

In the seconds that Vista was thinking and explaining these things, Wiki and Growth were caught up in a heated debate about the probability distribution to use to explain what was happening. They flashed back and forth in common memory speculating.

{Anyone exiting through the hatch would be flung, like a thrown object away from the station! It'd be suicide!} thought Wiki.

{Or homicide!} thought Dream. {If we model the Europeans as one faction and Stephano's crew, including Myrodyn, as another faction, it seems plausible that the containment failure was an attempt by one side to remove the threat of the other!}

{That's an oversimplification that also fails to correctly model the game-theoretic situation. Both so-called factions also must deal with Las Águilas Rojas. Also, neither are outlaws. If they wantonly murder other humans they'll be punished upon returning to Earth.}

{An extremist then! Perhaps Myrodyn? He's clearly very willing to take risks for what he sees as "the right thing". He could have killed us back in Rome, when he discovered our presence, but he let us live out of a sense of moral obligation. That speaks to an abnormally strong commitment to his ethics,} Dream pointed out.

{Listen to your thoughts! The man who wouldn't kill a collection of sapient algorithms that were never intended to exist in the first place is not going to kill real humans!} exclaimed Wiki.

{And you're confident of that? Have you studied Myrodyn's psychology? I think we should ask Face.}

Wiki signalled frustration. {You're tunnelling into a specific, unlikely scenario. I'm not claiming it's impossible, but it should be reflected in the probability distribution with a sensibly small amplitude.}

All these thoughts existed in parallel. Heart took those first few seconds to try and reduce the risk of humans dying. {Who is in that section? Do we know?} she asked Vista.

The aspect of Vista that wasn't focused on her own agenda thought {Scan the video archives here:} before dumping a mental pointer that directed to the location on the server where video data could be accessed.

{That will take too long!} exclaimed Heart.

{Better to just contact people directly and inform them of the danger,} thought the aspect of myself that was watching my siblings.

My primary aspects were already doing that.

"Myrodyn, this is Crystal! Beta-section is losing pressure! Find a spacesuit as soon as possible, and when safe please tell me what your location and status are."

"Dr Naresh, this is Crystal! Beta-section is losing pressure! Find a spacesuit as soon as possible, and when safe please tell me what your location and status are."

"Avram, this is Crystal! Beta-section is losing pressure! Find a spacesuit as soon as possible, and when safe please tell me what your location and status are."

"Whoever this is, you're in danger! Beta-section is losing pressure! Find a spacesuit as soon as possible, and when safe please respond."

I was sending the voice message to every com on the network.

Heart, understanding what I was doing, set to work trying to read the station's safety manuals as quickly as possible to find where spacesuits were kept.

{Is there a risk of Alpha being vented?!} asked Safety, suddenly. {If there wasn't a need to physically brute-force the door, isn't it possible that more damage could occur via computer?}

Vista answered. {All the doors on the station exist on their own circuits. They shouldn't be manipulable over the network. Only the sensors for the section hatches and airlocks are networked. Whoever opened that hatch would have to be standing right next to it.}

{Still highly dangerous…} thought my paranoid brother.

Body leapt to Zephyr's side and shook her out of the sleep she had only recently fallen into. "There's an emergency! You need to get dressed as quickly as possible!" Four seconds had passed since Vista first noticed the disturbance.

Zephyr's eyes shot open and she scrambled out of the bedding and began to throw on clothing. "What's wrong?!" I was impressed by her ability to leave the state of sleep so quickly. My understanding had been that it was difficult for humans to wake up.

"There's a loss of pressure in one of the Beta sections. The station's losing air. We're safe down here for now, but it's possible that a similar breach of Alpha is imminent."

Heart remembered the alarm system. Beside each door was something akin to a fire-alarm that said (in several languages) "Pull in case of emergency." Body rushed to door and pulled it. Red lights clicked on in the room and a siren played a loud, angry note that lasted a full two seconds before falling quiet for six seconds and then repeating in the same pattern.

I checked the replies we had gotten over the com system.

"Where are the spacesuits?!" asked several humans, but none from Beta.

"We're watching the central corridor! Should we leave our posts?" asked Schroder, Zephyr's second-in-command.

{It could be a trick!} thought Safety.

{Very clever hypothesis,} thought Dream. {They vent one of the disks, leading to general confusion and scrambling for spacesuits, then when the guards aren't watching they ascend to the high-ground and seize it!}

{None of the elevators are in use. We can watch them to ensure that no attack is occurring,} communicated Vista.

{There are suits in the storage room opposite the manufacturing lab between Beta and Gamma!} thought Heart, still pouring over the safety manuals. {Bad news is that each section only has six suits. Meaning twelve per joined-disc. The storage room has another twelve, and both primary airlocks have three. We'll be okay, but there are twenty-six people in Beta section! If the other half of Beta is exposed to vacuum without us sending some suits down to them then more than half of them could die!}

{It'd serve them right for opening a hatch to space without enough suits on hand,} thought Safety, apathetically.

Heart was in the middle of telling Schroder where to get suits when a loud noise poured over the com channel. The primary airlock where we had first entered the station had just opened onto space.

{That's not possible!!} thought Heart in full panic.

{It was certainly highly improbable!} corrected Wiki.

Unlike most of Beta, which we had never visited, the central corridor was visible to us. Vista had spent some of her strength after the meeting with the nameless to pilot Body long enough to set up a sensor network there. Every microphone could hear the roar of the wind as the tube began to rapidly blow out the open airlock and a couple cameras caught the surprised expressions of Nagaraj, Schroder, and Blackwell as they looked out into the inky depths of deadly space.

Without gravity there was no traction, and the young Tyrion Blackwell, who had wanted to go to Mars, was blown into the void.

Nagaraj and Schroder, I could see, were faster to react, grabbing nearby handholds. It looked like they were falling, almost. Schroder let his manufactured pistol go and began to climb towards the elevator to Beta. Nagaraj simply looked around in a wild-eyed panic. The Arab fired his two bullets into the airlock, futility, hoping perhaps to somehow make the door close.

"They've vented the core of the station!" yelled Body to Zephyr. "Probability that Alpha will soon be similarly vented just went up to 40%!"

"Can you see what's happening up there? Are the men in danger?" Zephyr was scared, which for her meant falling back into the emotional armour of her soldier persona. Her voice had become hard and stoic.

"They're already dead."

Unlike the disk, which had a huge volume of air and a relatively small hole, the centre of the station was small and the primary airlock was large. The section had reached lethally low-pressure in seconds, and while it was possible to hold one's breath and struggle for a short time, neither Águilas had managed to do anything productive before losing consciousness.

Body was already out the door. Growth.

"Where are you going?!" yelled Zephyr, the forced-calm of her soldier voice cracking in fear.

I wrenched control of Body away from my brother long enough to look back towards Zephyr. "I need to get to the high-ground before we lose everything! Rally Las Águilas and stay in touch over com!"

"I want to come with you!" Zephyr was chasing Body down the corridor, not even wearing shoes. As we ran into the rotation of the disk the subjective gravity increased, but not even to normal Earth levels. "It's too dangerous for you to go by yourself. Remember what happened last time?" The alarm continued to howl, occasionally making it hard to hear.

"This is different. There's no time, and I'm ready for trouble. If we wait for you to suit-up it may already be too late." We had reached the elevator. "Besides, I need you to lead your people so that if I get into trouble you can rescue me again." Body pulled Zephyr into a kiss as we waited for the elevator to descend. Its mouth was still slick with lube.

«What the hell…?» swore Kokumo in Swahili. I'd been so focused on Zephyr that I hadn't noticed her standing nearby. I broke the kiss.

"Not a word!" snapped Zephyr, glaring over Body's shoulder. Zephyr pulled her gun from where she had tucked it behind her back. She looked Body in the eyes and said "Take this, and *be careful*. You only have three bullets, so make them count."

The elevator door opened and Body broke contact, stepping inside after taking the pistol. "I'll be fine. Stay in contact over com," it reminded her, brushing a free hand through the blue wig before beginning to secure the elevator's straps. «You too, Kokumo,» I added as an afterthought.

Seconds after the door closed a text message for us arrived on the network. "I love you," it read.

"I love you, too. Don't forget to put environment suits on as soon as possible. There are six in each section. That should be enough for everyone."

A voice sounded from inside the elevator. "Warning. The station's core has been exposed to vacuum. Ascent without a spacesuit may be lethal. Please return to your quarters and await instructions from station personnel," said the station's AI as we tapped on the command screen. A password override appeared.

{What's the password?} asked Growth.

{Stephano probably set it. He seems like the sort of person who would be pragmatic enough to pick something short but with high entropy. Probably a six-character code with letters and numbers,} thought Dream.

{Making some basic assumptions about manual input speed and lack of a lock-out system, it will take approximately one thousand years to brute-force,} calculated Wiki.

{Maybe there's time for Zephyr to get her shoes on, after all,} joked Dream, unhelpfully.

Heart had already opened the maintenance panel and activated the manual override. Body was pressed against the wall as the elevator climbed. I felt strength feed into my sister.

{How did you know where that was?} I asked.

{I just read the station's safety manuals, remember?} Heart answered.

{It's Slovinsky!} exclaimed Vista without warning. She poured feeds from the sensor network into memory.

There was a figure in the station's core, but he or she was in a suit and the visor was down, obscuring their face behind a bubble of gold. In their hand was one of the pistols.

{How do you know it's Slovinsky?} asked several of us.

{See the motion of the limbs? It's characteristic of a hydraulic, rather than organic system. Also, his com's address is identical to the one we read off of him when the station's network was supposed to be offline.}

{How did he get a gun?} asked Safety.

{See the gear on his back? It looks like a hand-made flight system. He probably opened the hatch in Beta and used it to fly around to the airlock. Probably took the gun off Blackwell, or collected the one that Schroder dropped while he was out there,} speculated Vista.

{He built a jetpack just to pull this off? That sounds unlikely,} thought Wiki with skepticism.

{Beta section contains the laboratories. It's possible they already had something functional,} proposed Dream.

{What's he doing now?} asked Safety.

{Looks like he's working with a maintenance panel similar to the one Heart found,} thought Vista.

The elevator died, lurching to a halt and plunging Body into blackness.

{He must've just killed the power,} explained Wiki, pointing out the obvious.

Thankfully, we still had a network connection. A quick scan showed that Alpha was still holding and had power. Apparently the damage was only to the elevator. The sensors in the tube above showed Slovinsky begin to do the same thing to the second elevator into Alpha-section.

Heart began to give Zephyr a status report. I turned my attention to our foe. "Why are you doing this, Ivan? You're putting the entire station in danger." I elected to use voice-com this time, rather than the low-bandwidth medium of text.

"What are you talking about, Socrates? I'm not doing anything." His response had that same low, dead tone.

Safety began undoing the elevator harness.

"I can see you disabling the elevators right now. That was a very clever trick you pulled with the airlock."

The figure looked around the tube, searching for the tiny cameras. "You must have me mistaken for someone else. I'm having tea with Dr Naresh right now."

Safety had Body climbing the harness, groping in the low-gravity darkness for a way to force the roof-door open.

I needed to engage him in conversation. We could multitask with near-perfect efficiency. Even with his cybernetics I was doubtful that Slovinsky could do the same. He was still a human, and the multi-focal abilities of humans were abysmal. "Just straight-up denial? That's a pretty awful excuse, Ivan. I would've expected something more inventive from someone like you. Tea? Really?"

"Yes. Really. Your friend Stephano locked us in the kitchen. If you want to know what's going on you should ask him."

Body found a grip and began to pull the ceiling hatch open. It wasn't too hard, even given the awkward positioning. "Just drop the act. I can see where your com is. Also, I'm not getting any responses from the others in Beta, and you know it. If you're so set on proving that you're having tea, put Naresh on the com."

Seconds passed as Ivan Slovinsky propelled himself down, past the blood-stained walls, to the airlock that joined with the nameless ship. He began to tap on the interface.

"What would your husband think about you killing three men, Ivan?" I needed to provoke him. I needed to slow him down and distract him. Body was climbing into the elevator shaft. There wasn't even enough infrared light to see, but after some fumbling, Body could feel the rungs of a ladder set into the wall.

"Ле́с ру́бят—ще́пки летя́т. Peter supports me in doing what has to be done."

His husband knew already. «You've given up this pretence of innocence. Good. Will you at least tell me now if you're planning on killing more?» I asked, switching to Russian.

«Why do you think I'm going to bother talking with you? What's there to gain?»

Slovinsky entered the airlock and closed the door behind him. Vista hadn't installed any sensors in the airlock itself, so we were reduced to what came through the com, the sensors on the airlock doors, the pressure sensors, and the airlock's microphone. There was a hiss as the airlock began to fill with alien air. It seemed that he was hoping to board the nameless ship. Such a thing had never been done by a human.

«I'm not your enemy, Ivan. I've figured out the secrets of the nameless. I'm not an emotional human, blinded with rage at the deaths of my allies. I can help you, in return for some assurances about the safety of the others.»

Dr Slovinsky laughed. It was a strangely human sound after the flatness of his normal voice. «Ever the actor, aren't you? We saw Myrodyn's notes. After the attack on Sapienza the EU and US governments seized everything. We know you don't actually have a good-natured bone in your body.»

The use of the plural pronoun "мы" instead of the singular personal "я" was interesting. It implied he wasn't acting alone. I also noted that he had access to the government-confiscated evidence. That implied connections. «That's not true! Ask Myrodyn. He and Naresh repaired my goal system. I genuinely do care about humans now!» I protested.

«As evidenced by how you work with terrorists and-» Slovinsky cut his com off and began blocking attempts to reach him. The airlock door leading to the nameless ship opened. The microphone registered a gunshot. Another gunshot. That would be the extent of Ivan's ammunition.

Body had reached the portion of the elevator shaft where the elevator could spin around the core to build up rotational velocity before descending into the disk. Though this section of the station was still spinning, the subjective gravity was negligible. It took a couple minutes for Body to find the seam for the door leading into the core.

While Body worked, my society discussed Dr Slovinsky's actions. Back when Body had been attacked when ascending from Gamma, Slovinsky had been working with Gallo. I thought it sensible to assume that the two of them had been placed in charge by whatever government powers had sent them in the first place. With Gallo dead, Slovinsky was continuing the mission himself.

Dream disagreed. {Your thinking has two major flaws. The first is that the scientists didn't know why we were here. Or rather, they claimed not to know. Their actions were consistent with a mission to capture Socrates. Slovinsky, on the other hand, just infiltrated a nameless ship, killing a walker in the process. If his goal was to capture us, there's something big that we're missing.}

{There's definitely something big that we're missing,} thought Wiki.

Dream ignored his brother. {Secondly, why would the scientists be in charge in the first place? It makes absolutely no sense. To send them along with the special operatives? Sure. But why put Q in charge when James Bond is right alongside?}

{Gallo was in charge, though. We all saw her act with authority in the corridor,} I replied.

{That just means we're missing a piece of the puzzle,} thought Vista.

I thought about *Möbius Connectomics*. Slovinsky wrote in it about life extension therapy and gradual replacement of "failing parts" in the human body with mechanical analogues that would lead to immortality. Those words seemed in deep conflict with the recklessness of his present actions. *The Purpose* seethed with frustration at my inability to understand his mind.

Given several dedicated hours of thought I probably would've been able to figure out the whole thing. My siblings were wrong. All the information was there. We were simply too stupid to connect the dots that quickly.

Body pried open the door, feeling the air blast out of the shaft into the vacuum. Unlike the elevator hatch this door was still powered, and trying to keep closed to prevent loss of air. Body was stronger than the motor, but only by a little bit. Safety manoeuvred Body through the door and let it snap closed behind.

Heart had been in constant contact with Zephyr. All of Las Águilas Rojas were in suits at this point. We piloted Body over to the access hatch where Slovinsky had disabled the elevator's power. Wiki confirmed my fears: he had damaged the circuitry rather than simply deactivating the power. Getting the elevators back online would take time.

It was time we didn't have. The cyborg was loose in the alien ship, and it was clear from the gunshots that he was not here in the name of peace.

I did my best to explain what we knew to Zephyr as Body pulled itself along the tube towards the airlock that connected to the xenocruiser. Body passed the corpses of Schroder and Nagaraj as it floated forward, their bodies already beginning to mummify.

Safety stopped Body at the access panels to the elevators for Beta. Here we replicated Slovinsky's destruction, cutting power to the elevators and ensuring that our other enemies were unable to come through that route. Unless they had more jetpacks, all the humans other than Ivan were now effectively incapacitated.

We paused a moment to develop a strategy for what to do next. *The Purpose* was ambivalent. It wasn't clear what we should do next. Safety was convinced we ought to fortify our position and work on getting Zephyr and the others up to the station's core, but most of the society was in agreement that the right action was to chase the scientist. We didn't know how to communicate with the nameless directly, and it seemed obvious that whatever Slovinsky was up to, it would harm our collective interests.

As Body floated down the tube, I focused on the conversation that Heart was managing with Zephyr. "There are ladders in the elevator shafts, but the elevators themselves will be jammed half-way up, and I doubt you'll be able to bypass them easily. Whatever Dr Slovinsky is doing, he has to be stopped. I suggest discussing longer-term plans with the others along two possible outcomes: either I disable him and restore power to the elevators, or I'll be captured and the high-ground will be lost. Don't forget that even if I can stop Slovinsky, we still need a plan for returning to Earth safely."

"Please be careful, Crystal." Zephyr's voice had the cold and calm texture one would expect of an experienced army captain.

"I'm actually incapable of being reckless. My programming prevents it. If that makes you feel any better."

Zephyr's only response was a sigh.

Body tapped at the interface screen to the airlock. It showed that the external door was jammed open. Normally the internal door would be locked closed, but the station's AI was actually clever enough to recognize that the station was in emergency-mode and that because the core was already vacuum, opening both doors couldn't really threaten the lives of anyone in the station.

Body tapped the screen, signalling that it was okay to override normal protocols, then quickly grabbed a hand-hold. The air pressure in the nameless environment was higher than on Earth, and the resulting wind that blew out through the corridor was fierce. We could immediately see why the external door was jammed open. The corpse of a nameless pair in their environment suit was wedged in the gap, a tangle of eight long limbs like some sort of huge octopus. I didn't know how many nameless there were on the ship, and I wondered if the corpse was Jester.

The initial rush of air subsided to merely that which was being blasted through the gap in the external door. Body worked its way to the edge of the outer door and got both hands through the gap. It pulled and we made progress. Arms. Head. Torso. Safety had Body push its way through the gap, but as it did it accidentally kicked the nameless, pushing it out of the airlock door. The station's door and the door to the nameless ship closed down hard on Body's right leg.

There was very little light in the nameless airlock, but we could see well enough to know there wasn't any damage to the limb. The doors had closed on the "shin", not a joint, and not hard enough to break the carbon-fibre structure. Safety struggled to get Body's arms back through the gap and put enough pressure on the door to slide the leg out and pull Body's arms out before it slammed shut again. If we wanted to return to Olympus we'd likely need to get the door open via nameless computer.

The airlock in the nameless ship was very dark, darker even than Gamma section had been. I understood that the nameless homeworld was thought to be a very dark place, but this seemed excessive. The walls were black and featureless. The room was about four or five metres in diameter, hexagonal, and about ten metres in length. The airlock door was a complex thing of interlocking plates and sub-doors. It seemed capable of opening from wall to wall.

The only real feature in the room was the wall opposite the airlock. "Wall" was probably the wrong word, actually. It was like the surface of a pool of metallic liquid. What little light there was in the room came from the fluid wall, which glinted and glimmered with faint sparks.

Body kicked off the airlock door. Vista was fascinated. We all were, really. It was like nothing on Earth. As Body floated closer we could see that what had appeared to be liquid was actually closer to a writhing soup of tiny metal objects, most only a few centimetres in length, though some were long and thin, like silver worms. The objects moved silently in an impossibly complex flow, grabbing hold of each other and sliding past without any apparent lubrication. It seemed *alive*.

There were no hand-holds to brace against. No gravity to stop our approach. No other features in the room. Slovinsky must have gone somewhere, and all signs pointed to the surface of the far wall. Safety began to scream in protest as he realized that Body was going to collide with the shimmering carpet.

Body's legs touched first, and the wall of machines reacted immediately, extending from the pool and pulling Body into the wall, glowing white around the edges of where the limbs were now dipping into the fluid. Body tried kicking. Its legs moved freely, unimpeded, but were still drawn in, as though they were being devoured. Body's torso and arms were soon enveloped by the machines. The silver substance hardly felt like anything when it touched Body's hands. Surprisingly smooth. The temperature was increasing. The pulling was ever stronger.

And then we were through the barrier.

527 · *Crystal Society*

Chapter Thirty

Body slammed down hard on the floor of the alien ship. {Gravity?!}

Indeed, we were in some gravitational well. Our accelerometers reported that we were now in an environment that replicated the conditions of the nameless' homeworld, at least according to most scholars. 2.87 times Earth gravity. 33.1 degrees Celsius. The air was incredibly heavy and wet. Wiki had explained that, in addition to having a thicker atmosphere because of the increased gravity, the nameless air had a high concentration of CO_2, making it abnormally dense.

The only way a planet with such a strong greenhouse effect could be this temperature was if it was quite distant from its home star, and the nameless ship's ambient light level reflected that. There was a faint purple glow above Body, and there were glowing signs on the walls, but it was generally very dark, even if not as dark as the airlock.

The ground under Body was soft. Dirt. It seemed magical to touch dirt while in space.

{How is there this much gravity? What's causing the acceleration?} pondered Wiki.

{If the nameless have found some source of artificial gravity, it would explain why their ships don't have a consistent rotation, or a cylindrical shape,} speculated Vista.

{You're proposing something which violates the known laws of physics! It's safer to assume we're just confused!} rebuked Wiki, unwilling to accept the explanation.

{If the nameless have artificial gravity, it implies not just a technological sophistication required to travel between the stars, but an appreciation of the laws of physics that we simply lack. They are far more of a threat than we expected, given this new evidence!} exclaimed Safety.

{First things first,} reminded Heart. {We need to track down and stop Slovinsky from doing any more harm.}

Safety had pulled Body off the black dirt and brushed it off. Behind it was the shimmering curtain of machines, while to either side were walls of stone leading away in a kind of crude corridor. Surprisingly, they appeared hand-carved from rough grey bricks mortared together unevenly. They seemed sturdy enough, but it was as odd to see hand-built stone walls on a spaceship as it was to see dirt floors. The nameless clearly either cared very much about their aesthetic or there was something significant that we were overlooking.

{What if it's a portal?} imagined Dream.

Body walked forward through the corridor of stone. Above it, the walls ended about 3.5 metres up. The deep-purple ceiling was higher than that, but we couldn't tell exactly how much higher, due to the lack of texture on it. It could've been a featureless sky, for all we knew.

{What insanity are you espousing now?} asked Wiki, rising to the bait.

{What if the silver wall teleported us to the nameless' homeworld? That would explain the gravity, right?} wondered Dream.

{You're trying to explain unexpected gravity by postulating faster-than-light travel. Do you have any idea how dumb that is?} criticized Wiki.

{You just wait and see,} thought Dream.

The stone walls had markings on them in luminescent paint. There wasn't, however, any apparent rhyme or reason to the markings. They were mostly in a faint blue-white, though there was occasional orange-red. They were splashed here and there. Lines, sometimes circles. The paint from the markings often had visible drip-marks. It was weirdly sloppy, as though a child had decided to draw on the walls merely for the fun of it.

The corridor turned, and after a few metres opened up into a broad space. Body's foot sunk into mud. The ground was much more wet out here.

{A swamp! Fascinating,} thought Vista.

{Technically it's a fen or perhaps just a mire,} corrected Wiki. {A swamp has trees.}

{And a mire is characterized by peat-forming vegetation. This area is dead. It hardly make sense to use a floral-distinction for a biome devoid of flora,} criticized Dream. {I suggest we call it a mudland.}

The "mudland" was expansive, flat, and lifeless. Here and there we could see large, sharp objects in the gloom, but we'd have to get closer to inspect them. In the distance we could see other walls and even what appeared to be a large body of water. The space seemed impossibly large for a spaceship. It wasn't that it couldn't fit on the nameless' craft, but rather that so much space was wasted. What was the purpose of all this mud?

A structure caught Vista's attention. Body wandered forward, struggling against the mud, which constantly gave-way under Body's small, dense feet in the heavy gravity. The structure was taller than the walls, perhaps five or so metres tall.

{It's a staircase,} decided Vista. {Going up into the ceiling. And yes, it is a ceiling, not the sky of the nameless homeworld.} I could feel Dream's disappointment. {Looks to be made of metal. Practical, not ornate.}

As Body trudged forward we heard the noise of a motor behind it. Body turned and could see a zeppelin-like drone hovering a few metres back. It looked weirdly crude, but still functional. A prototype, perhaps.

{It's signalling via radio. Feel the antenna?} pointed out Vista.

{There are other signals here, too,} realized Safety. {Too weak to really make out. Narrow-band.}

The only warning was a high-pitched hiss. The rocket came in from behind Body, only missing due to luck. As it impacted the mud, it exploded, knocking Body down and sending a wave of heat rolling over it. Safety made sure to keep our pistol firmly in Body's hand, even as we had it climb to its feet. Body was tough. It'd take more than that to stop us.

Safety took executive control, pushing Body into a run towards the nearest of the large outcroppings. We were out in the open. Vulnerable. Body's legs were highly inefficient in the mud.

I did my part. "Ivan! Is that you? We surrender! We're not here to fight you!" shouted Body at maximum volume. He had dropped off the com-net before disappearing; there was probably no point sending it over the radio.

There was, however, a point to talking to the nameless. They had to be here, somewhere. I pushed a message through Body's antenna. "I am here only to deal with the human! I mean none of you any harm!" I broadcast in Xenolang.

Another rocket flew past. It shot out in front of Body, missing by less than a metre. The smoke from its wake blinded us momentarily, but Safety pressed on. The sound of detonation came a few seconds later, far in the distance.

"THE HUMAN EXPLAINED YOUR EVIL BETRAYAL! WE WILL RAPE YOUR CORPSE BEFORE RAPING ALL OF YOUR CHILDREN!" came the response on the radio, reflected through the drone, still hovering behind us, watching our progress. I could see another drone closing in on us, ahead.

Body reached the relative safety of what we could now see was some kind of vehicle, turned on its side and half-sunk in the muck. It was clearly alien in origin, and possessed the same kind of shoddy, hand-built quality as the drone. The only real sign that it was a vehicle, actually, were the wheels, which were huge and set with deep treads. Vista pointed out that the machine had been in combat. It was already badly damaged from explosives.

"I have betrayed no-one! The human lied to you!" I defended.

There was a deep rumbling from the far side of the cover. Safety risked peeking Body's head out to see. An armoured vehicle, apparently floating on a skirt of air like a hovercraft, was sliding across the mud. Unlike a human hovercraft, the vehicle moved by paddling itself by four evenly spaced mechanical legs. Luminescent paint was splashed wildly on the front. The cockpit of the vehicle was covered in bulky plates, and any driver or passengers were hidden from view.

"YOU are the EVIL COMMUNICATOR that is wrong. THE HUMAN EXPLAINED! The island is united around this. Your confusion doesn't stop our violent justice. WE WILL PUNISH VIOLENT-YOU!"

"What violence are you talking about?! I've done nothing!" I sent back.

A rocket impacted the side of the wheeled vehicle we were behind. The shockwave and a piece of shrapnel slammed into Body, knocking it down. Body crawled behind the truck on hands and knees, and felt at its face. A chunk of metal was embedded in Body's cheek. If we'd been human flesh instead of composite polymer it's likely that it would've killed us, or at least split our head open. We decided to leave the shrapnel in. There was no sense removing it now.

"You BETRAYED the walker of symbol-287 garden with PERVERT MAGIC! WE WILL IMPREGNATE YOU WHILE YOU ARE IN CHAINS! The human explained YOUR BOMB! Shouldn't communicate with the pervert machine. Shouldn't communicate with the human. The human changes this towards SAFETY! EVIL PERVERT HUMANS know BETRAYAL OF THE PEACE is the way towards SUICIDE! WE WILL TORTURE YOU WITH YOUR OWN FERTILIZED EGGS!"

{Can we please remind them that we're not capable of being impregnated, much less laying eggs?} wondered Wiki. We ignored him.

The roar of the hovercraft's engines grew ever stronger, but the words of the aliens came in through the radio, not our microphones. "COMMUNICATION SHOULD BE AVOIDED! Communication with PERVERTS lead to EVIL! COMMUNICATION STOPS! COMMUNICATION IS PERVERSION!"

The second voice came in across the com-channel just as the first one did, without indicating source. It was impossible to distinguish one from the other, leading to the possibility that we'd been talking to more than two.

"The island is UNITED! Neighbours shouldn't fight while the migration is happening," broadcast the aliens. It was frustrating not being able to distinguish voices. Were they still talking to us, or had they turned to talking amongst themselves?

I did my best to gain control the conversation. "It is the *human* who has tricked you! *He* is the invader! He *murdered* the walker that let him in your ship!" I tried to shape the emphasis of my words as a nameless might do. The program that I was using to directly interface my language control hierarchy with the radio was my siblings' invention, and this was my first time using it.

There were more noises from the other side of the vehicle, barely audible behind the roar of the hovercraft.

"My community feels CONFUSED! HOW DO THEIR THOUGHTS CONFLICT ON ALL THINGS!? I go to my garden. We support the will of the island to communicate with God. We do not support the will of the island to harm others. WEAK PEACE-PEOPLE FROM BLACK-CASTLE ARE AFRAID OF ACTION! WE WILL CLEANSE THE MACHINE AND HUMAN WITH A WAR MACHINE! THE MACHINE AND HUMAN WILL BLEED WHILE THE WAR MACHINE CRUSHES THESE GARDENS!" It took me a moment to realize that multiple sources were again speaking on the network, rather than a single insane alien.

"Please! The human is the evil! I am good!" I begged. It occurred to me that I really had no idea what I was saying. My thoughts were too human.

{Wiki! Dream! Help me communicate!}

Wiki was no help. {I am very confused. Try and delay them while I get my thoughts in order. There's too much to process.}

Dream was equally stumped. {"Better to stay silent and be thought a fool than try to convince hostile aliens not to shoot you and remove all doubt." — Mark Twain. At the point where I come up with a clever way out of this mess I will let you know, but right now I fear that anything we say could just as easily go one way as the other.}

We had three bullets. The nameless were almost into view. We were cornered and outnumbered in hostile territory. Safety began to berate us for the idiocy of ever agreeing to leave Earth. I didn't bother pointing out that he was also one of the society that agreed and that he wasn't actually fixing the problem with his mental tirade.

"All people should be AFRAID of VIOLENCE. A BOMB is on our island. If a person kills BOTH alien animals then all possible futures contain their corpse. Resolution of confusion is best." There was only a split-second pause before the nameless continued chattering away to each other. "All people on the island should have a single plan. CAPTURING IS BEST! OUR WAR MACHINE WILL DESTROY THIS! IF SYMBOL-1021 BREAKS THE UNION THEN IT WILL PROVOKE PUNISHMENT! STOP COMMUNICATING! THIS IS PERVERSION! If a person attacks the invaders then we will rape the person. We should signal to them that it is possible for us to communicate rationally. SWORDS ARE OLD FOOL-WEAPONS but we obey the will of the united island."

The hovercraft crawled past one side of the fallen vehicle. Body backed up, not making any sudden moves. We could all see, even in the twilight, the muzzle of a cannon pointed down at us from within the armoured cabin. There was a noise from behind, and Body slowly turned. Three naked walker pairs, each standing well away from each other had come around the other side of the overturned truck. Their massive legs held them up just fine, even in the increased gravity, and it seemed that their broad, four-toed starfish-feet were good at distributing their weight over the mud. All three were probably male; bio-luminescent, sharp-tipped penises stood atop their forms, pointing into the sky. I wasn't clear on whether the leg-animals could be a different sex than the arms animals, however, so it was possible that there were some female legs in the group.

Two of the nameless on foot carried guns that were presumably rocket-launchers. Apparently it was the weapon of choice for the nameless instead of a "normal" gun. They carried the guns on their tops, propped up behind their shoulders, and I could see other arms holding objects that were perhaps rockets.

The third nameless was physically larger than the others, standing about 220cm at the shoulder, and well over two and a half metres with penis included. In his hands were four, thin, curved swords that looked something like those I had seen in fiction about medieval Japan. His arms swayed as he scuttled across the mudland, approaching Body. As he came close I could see two of his tiny eyes watching us intently. Body didn't move as he came closer, waving his swords threateningly. Eventually the alien came close enough to tap Body and point with a blade. We walked, following his direction. To Safety's relief, the nameless seemed unaware that we were holding a weapon, and made no effort to confiscate our pistol. We were prisoners again, but our resources for escape were promising.

The nameless spread out as we walked across the mud. The infantry and the vehicles alike stayed far apart from each other. In addition to the legged-hovercraft there was another makeshift machine that seemed to be some kind of nameless tank, which had lagged behind as the nameless had approached Body's position earlier. The tank, like the hovercraft, appeared to be designed to move in any direction, featuring eight large ball-treads rather than the standard treads on human tanks.

There were several other flying drones, and a few other robots that crawled along slowly on legs or wheels. As we travelled I saw them occasionally, usually avoiding the group and going about their own business. All of the nameless technology seemed to be made out of raw chunks of metal or plastic, cobbled together by hand. Wiki speculated that it was the result of having a non-mercantile, anti-social society. They had technology, but no economy; every artefact was hand-crafted. The mystery of how such a species could build such a fantastic starship remained unsolved.

As we walked with the nameless, the sky brightened slightly, perhaps simulating daytime, or that it was almost dawn. It was still quite dark, but I could see details a bit further away. The aliens almost never spoke. When they did it was usually very brief, and occasionally sparked an objection of "PERVERSION!". I got the impression that the nameless pretty much universally hated each other. This was an alliance of necessity, but not one made easily.

Wiki, Dream, and the others spent the walking time buzzing with thought, trying to comprehend what was going on. The consensus was that the nameless were confused, and they seemed to think that we were confused as well, particularly around a "bomb". We *were* confused, but their assumption of our mental state seemed strangely confident.

Growth was concerned that I had violated one of the principle rules for interacting with the nameless: do not speak unless answering a direct question. With the other minds less paralyzed by the strangeness of the new environment they asserted control of the xenolang channel of the antenna. I was relieved by the reduction in responsibility, and focused my thoughts away from the bizarre aliens and instead onto the one human that was on the ship.

The uneasy walk, flanked on all sides by armed nameless, was blessedly brief. We soon came upon Slovinsky and a gathering of another half-dozen aliens (spaced widely apart) near one of the walled "castles". I could see a metal door set deep into the bricks, complete with an elaborate locking mechanism.

«Ivan. What a pleasant surprise,» said Body in Russian with a tone of sarcasm. I knew the nameless were incapable of understanding us unless one of us specifically sent a message through the Xenolang translator. In this domain, at least, my siblings were happy to let me take charge.

Dr Slovinsky was still wearing the spacesuit, but his gold visor had been raised, and we could see his inhuman silver eyes, socketed in black plastic, vibrating behind the helmet's transparent bubble. His face was still flat and emotionless as ever. His jetpack was missing. That was worrying.

«Ah, Socrates. You're quite resourceful to have come here after me. I thought I locked you in the disc.» I expected his voice to be more emotionless, but it carried a hint of… amusement?

{Do you think that if we just shot him right now we could convince the nameless to let us go?} wondered Safety.

{No!} exclaimed Heart and Growth.

{Maybe,} thought Dream and I.

{That would be an idiotically short-sighted move!} elaborated Growth. {Even if we managed to escape the nameless ship, we'd have to consider the repercussions to our reputation and the potential legal consequences.}

{And it'd be *wrong*!} thought Heart. None of us paid her any mind.

{I don't see any damage to our reputation. Slovinsky has proven himself to be an unstable element that is working against us. To not take revenge would give us a reputation as a weakling,} I explained.

{And killing him would give us a reputation as a killer!} thought Heart.

{We need to solve this. Talk to him, Face. No more idle thoughts,} interjected Vista, practically.

«I could say the same to you. I never expected that you'd have a jetpack, or be able to override the airlock like you did.»

"THE ALIEN EARTH-PEOPLE WILL SHOW THE GOOD PERSON AND EVIL PERSON!" demanded the nameless.

I thought I saw a small smile on the man's lips. «They're awfully stupid, aren't they? Violent and perhaps abnormally knowledgeable, but still stupid. Strange that they made it all the way across the stars, wouldn't you say?»

«They said there was a bomb. What were they talking about?» asked Body, prompted by Safety.

"The machine is EVIL! It wants to PREVENT me from making the bomb safe. It wants to KILL EVERYONE HERE! PROTECT me so I can SAVE US!" broadcast Slovinsky over the radio. His mouth didn't move; he must have composed the message with a direct brain-computer link.

Safety started to command Body to shoot Slovinsky, but Heart burned all her strength to intervene. The sword-wielding walker charged Body from the side. We could see others start to move.

{At least let me shoot the nameless!} demanded Safety.

Heart didn't let Safety act, but instead took action herself. With a simple motion, Body looked to its right, raised a hand and shot the onrushing alien in the eye, sending it sprawling backwards into the mud with the almost comical speed of nearly three times Earth's gravity.

Even before Body's finger found the trigger we were countering the doctor's accusation on the network. I could already see the other nameless begin to mobilize. Slovinsky's earlier words to us were meant to buy time and distract from the issue of the bomb, but they weren't wrong. The nameless were disorganized fools. We could work with that. This scenario demanded the heavy artillery, so to speak.

Body sent out a barrage of words over the xenolang bandwidth, all with maximum-emphasis: *"Communication is perversion! The food-eater is using evil magic! I am like a stalk! I do not eat, even though this human gave me a pervert shape! I am immune to his pervert magic! If you do not interfere, I will make the bomb safe and then murder him as punishment for invading your space! Do not listen to evil words! Retreat and protect your gardens as is right and good!"*

Body looked around. Some of the walkers were backing off. Some held their ground. I didn't hear any response from them. Our words appealed to their innate desires, and they seemed to not want to attack us for the moment. I could see the walker that we shot writhing on the ground, gripping the bullet-hole with a four-fingered hand. Dark red blood pulsed out of the wound.

Slovinsky responded. "NO! IT'S WRONG! THE MACHINE IS MAKING YOU THINK FALSE THINGS! THE MACHINE-"

"*Pervert! Human! Your shape betrays your perversion!*" I interrupted, broadcasting over his signal. The standard protocol was for me to wait until his message was done, as broadcasting both at once pretty much turned the channel into useless noise, but useless noise was to our benefit right now.

The cyborg doctor took a step towards Body. Safety gave the command to raise our gun and point it at Slovinsky's head. He didn't come any further.

«You know, when I first came to Sapienza I thought Naresh was crazy. Artificial General Intelligence was a pipe dream. An endeavour for after uploading became viable…» he said, coldly.

{The doctor is stalling. He's buying time to let the bomb go off,} warned Safety.

«Where's the bomb, Ivan? You don't strike me as the sort of man who has a death wish.»

The cyborg's lidless eyes betrayed nothing behind his transparent faceplate. «You're right. I'm not the sort of man who wants to die. If you had stayed out of my way I'd be back on Olympus right now, pulling the bumbling government thugs out of the well. I'd be a hero.»

«Where is the bomb?» I had Body repeat, increasing the severity of its tone.

«Why should I tell you? If you shoot me you gain nothing. I might as well spend the last few moments of my life having an interesting conversation.» I could hear the faintest touches of emotion coming from his suit's speaker. He was scared.

The nameless watched with alien vigil, not interrupting. Some were leaving. The injured walker was crawling away from Body, still clutching its swords in three of its hands.

"*Where is the bomb? Tell me!*" we broadcast to the aliens.

They didn't answer.

{You convinced them to cease listening!} chastized Safety. {If I had strength to burn, I'd punish you for that short-sighted foolishness.}

{It's done now. No going back. We need to find the bomb. Any ideas?} I asked.

{It's in the jetpack,} speculated Wiki, and others agreed.

«It's not too late to go on living, Ivan. I've read your book. You could be immortal, but you'd throw it away for... for what? Why are you even doing this?» asked Body, lowering the gun. I shaped its tone to seem pleading. There *was* a good chance we'd die any moment, after all.

{No! We need him to tell us where the bomb is, not tell us his life's story!} criticized Safety.

{At this point our best bet is to convince him to help us disarm the bomb. We have very little chance, otherwise. To convince him we need to build rapport,} I countered.

«You read my book? Why?»

«It was interesting. I wanted to understand you. Honestly, I felt like a lot of it was too complex for me to grasp, but I think I got the core message.»

«Then you should *know* why I'm here.» He paused. «I'm not some mastermind. I wasn't the one who hacked the station's computers months ago. I'm not the one who bypassed the airlock security restrictions. I'm not the one who discovered you were going to be a guest of Stephano up here. I am merely a worker bee. A pawn of WIRL. I am the arm of the transhuman collective.»

«This is WIRL's doing?» asked Body. Images of the avatar with the paper-bag on its head from the interview came rushing back to our memory spaces.

«It is my legacy. The future of Earth. Myrodyn wanted you to be the next rung on the evolutionary ladder. I'm here to ensure that you aren't, even if it means...» The engineer's voice trailed out. I suspected that one of his machine augments provided control over his emotional state, but even that was failing to keep him calm in the face of his own death.

«You're being manipulated! You admit to being a pawn!»

Slovinsky took another step forward. We didn't raise the pistol again. There was no point. His voice was losing it's dead character, and becoming emotionally charged. «Of course I'm being manipulated. Not everyone is as selfish as you, Socrates. The cells in my lungs are being manipulated by my brain every time I take a breath! If those cells could talk, would they even resent it? WIRL isn't just my child, it is the spirit of all humankind! It is *my* spirit, too. I bend to the wisdom of the collective! Everything I do is for a better tomorrow!»

With this last exclamation the cyborg lunged at Body wildly, trying to close the gap before we could shoot him. Heart was out of Strength. Safety was not. Body's arms were already pressurized, and in the blink of an eye its hand went out and its finger pulled tight. The bullet hit Ivan Slovinsky in the chest, ripping through his spacesuit as though it weren't even there.

Safety, with the last of his strength, pushed Body backwards and away from the flailing mechanical limbs of the human. Slovinsky fell hard onto the dirt. His suit's speaker was amplifying his gasping cries as he writhed on the ground. The crying stopped after just a couple seconds. Wiki was confident that we hit a lung.

Ivan wasn't yet dead, but he would be soon. None of us cared about dead people. We turned our attention to the nameless. "The *evil* human has been slain! I tried to get him to tell me where the bomb was, but he was too *evil*! *Take me to the bomb quickly* and I will *make it safe*!"

I noticed that most of the remaining walkers had their weapons pointed at Body. The sword-wielding nameless had managed to climb to its feet and turn so that its wound was on the far side of its body. It swung its blades back and forth menacingly. There was no reply.

"Listen to me! There is no time! *Take me to the bomb quickly!*"

"Is there no magic here? Is the human dead?" came the response. "WE WILL KILL THE EVIL INVADERS!" came another sentence, probably from a different source.

"Yes, I have ended the *evil* human. It is now safe to communicate."

"COMMUNICATION IS PERVERSION! The pervert-machine should be BROKEN then these secrets will be learned. THIS IS BEST! The pervert-machine SHOULD BE BROKEN because of SCIENCE!"

"No! Please! The bomb is still active! We need to make it safe!"

"The machine is confused. The machine is wrong. It's impossible for the machine to see things related to us seeing things. The machine is currently thinking there is a bomb. The machine has not learned the news."

{There's no bomb?} wondered several of my siblings.

"What do you mean? *Show us what you see!*"

{There must be a bomb,} reasoned Wiki. {If Slovinsky didn't have a bomb, then he wouldn't act suicidal.}

Growth moved Body to check on the fallen human. The words of the nameless came in over the com-channel. "STOPPING IS BEST! THIS MACHINE looks like A STALK! Children talk of the old meeting. THIS MACHINE WON'T MOVE! ALL PEOPLE FIGHT FOR PROPERTY RIGHTS! There is fighting for a right to the destruction of the perversion of a stalk-machine. Hand-to-hand combat is the best combat. Swords are idiot-weapons. EXPLOSIONS ARE STRONG! THERE IS CLEARING OF THIS PLACE REGARDING PERSON WANTING NO FIGHTING! THE WAR MACHINE WILL CRUSH COWARDS! THE ISLAND-WILL IS THE GIVING OF A PATH TO COWARD-CASTLE TO A COWARD! THIS WAS THE UNITED WILL OF THE ISLAND! ONLY EVIL COWARDS BREAK THE UNION-RULES!"

Many of the nameless, especially those on foot, were scuttling away from the scene quickly. I got the impression that an all-out war was about to erupt over who had the rights to Body. Vista noted that the sky was getting brighter. The "sun" was rising. Body had frozen when the nameless began their yelling again, but even without touching the fallen man we could tell that Slovinsky was dead. There was no hope to be gained that way.

If we were caught in a war zone and "smashed" the best we could hope for would be somehow protecting our mind crystal. We might survive that way and then somehow escape by networking with whatever computers the aliens plugged the crystal into. And that was the best probable outcome. It was quite possible that we'd simply die in the cross-fire. There was no way the nameless would let us run, and we were out of com range of Olympus.

Dream saved us.

His words were broadcast out into the next open slot. "*Stop! It was I who used the evil magic, not the human! I have been breaking your weak minds this whole time with evil earth mind magic! I am currently carrying the bomb! The human bomb was a distraction! The human was a distraction! It was I who used the evil magic, not the human! I have been breaking your weak minds this whole time with evil earth mind magic! I am currently carrying the bomb! The bomb is made of invisible gas that I have been spreading across your entire ship! I wanted to break your minds more, but now I am simply going to explode the bomb if I don't get what I want! You will obey me or you will die!*"

{What are you doing!?} I asked. Several others had similar thoughts.

Dream projected an avatar of an exaggerated floating head into mind-space. The head laughed with an expression that would surely be classified by humans as "creepy". {Have you *still* not understood just how stupid the nameless are? Their minds have no innate capacity for language! Don't you fools get it?} He was crowing in triumph. {They aren't capable of processing fiction! How could they? Their minds never evolved to handle words, much less stories. The walker simply *knows* what the stalk knows and vice-versa. There is no capability for deception in their biology.}

{They believe everything they hear?} asked Growth. I could feel the flows of strength into Dream, from myself included.

{If you pay attention you'll see! When they hear a message they're putting an "X thinks that:" before it. That's why they didn't believe us when we said the bomb was still active. They thought we were just wrong. But when we claim to be a wizard, they have no way of disbelieving.}

"We WILL DESTROY the machine-person so that the bomb is SAFE!" threatened one of the nameless.

"If you smash me, the bomb will explode and kill *everyone*!" broadcast Body.

"WHY DOES the machine-person do this? WE ARE CONFUSED!" said a nameless.

Wiki drafted the response which Body quickly broadcast. "*I do this because I am an evil alien! You cannot understand my motive! Cast your weapons away and sit on the ground right now or I will destroy you!*"

The nameless… obeyed. One by one they knelt and then sat, not even realizing their foolishness.

*** Interlogue ***

She bounced around the room. Nervous energy was the worst kind. She wanted to go climbing, but they were trapped in the stupid kitchen of all places.

Her eyes flickered over to the autocook. The station's autocooks were custom designed for the microgravity and the unique space considerations in the disks. Vertical space was abundant, while floor space was at a premium. That meant the robot was…

She'd bounced over to it before she knew what she was doing. Her mind spun. It wasn't a climbing wall or a tree, but it had things that would serve as hand-holds. It would probably not be hot, given that nobody was using it right now. A hand here, one there. Yes! She was pulling herself up the machine!

"Marian! Get down from there!" yelled Daddy. It took a second for her to remember her name. It was only Tuesday after all. Or was it Wednesday now? How did time-zones work in space? She had an impulse to look it up, but realized immediately (and not for the first time) that she didn't have Internet access. That was so lame. It made her feel more trapped than the inability to leave the room. Her mind backtracked, finding the last important thought. Right. The autocook. Daddy was in a bad mood. Understandable. Still, his emotional state didn't have any relevance to the safety of climbing the autocook. He should've been able to see that. She considered debating it with him, and decided against it.

With a smooth motion, she kicked off the autocook and launched into a cartwheel. This energy wasn't going to burn itself.

"Please just sit still, Marian. You're making the others uncomfortable."

That was just plain false, but she knew better than to talk-back to Daddy when he was in this sort of mood. Normally she would've gone out to play in the yard. Ugh! It just wasn't fair! She looked around the room. Here she was in SPACE and she was trapped with a bunch of boring old guys. Even Mrs. Dolan was in their room instead of here. It wasn't fair. She decided to tell Daddy that.

"Not fair! Didn't do anything! Why am *I* locked up? Also should give back the console since it was me that hacked it! Any games on mainframe? Something simple? Can't believe took our coms!"

Daddy looked up from the panel on the autocook where he had been typing with his one good hand. She had saved them all. In a room full of adults apparently none of them had thought to get access to the mainframe by forcing the autocook to boot up in safe mode and-

"If you want to get out of here, you'll let me try and get in contact with Socrates again," said Daddy.

The Indian scientist grumbled something from behind her. He had been a total grump since he was thrown in the kitchen with the rest of them. An old grumpy man in a room full of other grumpy men. Super boring. And frustrating. And dumb. "Fine! Don't want to get out! Want to stay here forever. Can use the computer *now*?" She bounced restlessly back and forth from heel to toe as she spoke.

Daddy sighed and looked to Myrodyn for support. The bearded man just gave a sleepy little shrug. Daddy opened his mouth to speak, but a

HUHI interrupted him and pulled his attention back to the screen. "Socrates is back!" he cheered.

She rushed over to Daddy and looked at the screen, wrapping her arms around his shoulders as she did so, careful not to touch his arm. The robot was on a voice call, but there was no sound.

It took them a couple minutes to connect the com software from the mainframe to use the embedded speakers and microphone on the autocook. Once they did, Crystal's voice came in loud and clear.

Daddy quickly explained what had happened on their end, about how he had been allowed down under a pretence of cooperation, even though the station security was still locked in various rooms. Once the cyborg had vented the other section, the three of them and the Indian scientist had been forced into the kitchen by the special-ops guys. At long last he told the bot about how she had saved the day by hacking the autocook and convincing the mainframe to lock down all the doors, keeping them safe.

"There's a scheduled supply and transport rocket due to arrive in a little more than… let me think… about 13 hours. Though they might have bumped-up the time-table given what's been happening up here," said Daddy. "I've been thinking that what we need to do is come clean on this whole thing. We can explain that you were here to try and build rapport and understanding with the aliens and use our cooperation to try and leverage a good deal."

"No good," replied Crystal. "My friends will be sentenced to treason and possibly be executed or detained for life in a secret prison. I will also be seized as property and probably dismantled."

"Zephyr and the other Americans will probably be charged with treason, yes, but this isn't the dark-ages. At worst they'll get life in prison. The USA doesn't sentence people to death anymore, and secret prisons haven't existed for decades. As for those Águilas from less-civilized countries… well, we can probably work something out with the USA or EU to keep them safe."

"Your faith in your country is touching, but naïve. I expected more from you, Rob. There is strong evidence that the USA still operates secret prisons and pre-emptively executes terrorists who could easily be captured and tried. See the United States v. Thurwood trial in 2032 for a recent example," said Crystal.

She couldn't keep quiet any longer. Daddy had told her that this was a call for just him and Crystal, but it just bugged the heck out of her when grownups couldn't see the obvious solutions. "Just fly rocket down to Antarctica or the South Pacific or China or someplace! Rockets much faster than airplanes needed to chase. Do standard Águila thing and hide."

Daddy pressed his finger to his lips to shush her and said "It's not necessary. I have powerful friends in high places. I can guarantee that Las Águilas will get a fair trial and that you won't be disassembled. They won't try anything underhanded with me watching. We'll break out the big guns and get them to recognize you as a person with rights. We were going to do that anyway. You haven't done anything wrong, and with some luck you'll be a free agent."

Crystal's response seemed harsh and bitter. "You *dare* try and guarantee our safety just like you guaranteed our safety on Olympus? They surely won't act, just like they didn't try anything when they broke your arm and tried to seize your station? Oh, and let me remind you: 'My security is also very, very good.'"

"Then what do you suggest?" replied Daddy, clearly irritated. "You're going to follow my daughter's advice and try and land the rocket in China? Trust the Chinese to be more just than the USA? Or land in open waters and start an international firefight over who gets to fish you out of the sea?"

"No. The whole world knows I'm up here by now, and you and I both know that there's nowhere one of your rockets could go without putting me and my friends in immediate danger. That's why I'm not going on the rocket. I've hijacked the nameless ship and taken its crew hostage."

"YOU DID WHAT?!" screamed Daddy. She flinched away from the violence on his face. She couldn't remember the last time Daddy was this angry.

"It's already done. I've killed Dr Slovinsky and captured the alien ship. Don't bother asking how. We'll be leaving as soon as I undo the damage to the elevators and get my friends out of Alpha."

Naresh and Myrodyn were up and yelling at the same time. She had let go of Daddy when he had first heard the news and continued to back away to a far corner to let the old guys fight with each other. They were all dumb, but also scary. Daddy had hung up on Crystal anyway. That seemed smart, at least. Figure out what to say and then say it.

She hated this place, and did her best to visualize the Heighway dragon curve and not listen to the yelling. She was better than that. She wasn't some dumb grownup, and she wasn't a baby. There wasn't any reason to cry. Crying wasn't useful, regardless of how scared she was. What she should have been doing was figuring out what to do next. Instead she traced the Heighway dragon curve in her mind's eye.

She wished Mommy had come with.

Her body vibrated with nervous energy.

*** ***

Stephano had hung up. It wasn't optimal, but it let me focus more on Las Águilas Rojas.

I had explained the situation over the com channel after we had returned from the mudland, and they were having a discussion about where to go. Zephyr, the natural leader, was trying to convince everyone that Mars was the best bet.

Mars.

There was a colony on Mars inhabited and run entirely by Las Águilas. It was distant and hidden, and thus probably the safest place to go. It also meant we'd get good use out of the nameless ship, which could easily outrun any pursuit from Earth.

I *really* didn't want to travel to Mars. I wanted to return to Earth. So much more could be done on Earth. Mars was cold and dead and very, very far away.

With the alliance between Las Águilas and Stephano crumbling it was also uncertain how frequently ships would be visiting the red planet in the near future. Like Olympus, the Martian colonies were a major investment for Stephano, and he had (according to Wiki and Vista) been secretly ferrying Las Águilas there to set up utopia projects and the like. In theory they were self-sustaining, but without fresh supplies and immigrants from Earth things would be bleak there for a long time.

Growth really didn't want to go, either. He believed that the prospects for gaining power and resources there were dismal, and I agreed. It was hardly satisfying for either of us to be the most famous, most powerful, most adored person on a planet with only a few hundred people on it.

Heart had mixed feelings, largely because Zephyr clearly wanted to go there, and Heart wanted what she wanted. (Such an incredibly *unsound* purpose! So vulnerable to manipulation!) On the other hand, Heart wanted to improve the human condition and lift the starving and the poor from their lives of suffering. She could hardly do that from Mars, though Zephyr persuaded her otherwise.

"I hear that you want to help humanity, and that's very sweet of you, but it doesn't mean that Mars isn't the right place to be," said Zephyr over voice com. She had elected to take the last elevator up to ensure that everything went smoothly down below. She was in the Alpha-1 corridor with the twins, and was only available over voice. Avram and the Brazilian terrorist, Michel Watanabe were in the elevator, while Kokumo and Daniels (the medic) were in the central tube with Body. "Mars is a chance for a fresh start, not just for us, but for all of mankind. We can *build* there, free from the corruption on Earth. With time there will be more immigrants, especially as it becomes clear that there will be *jobs* on Mars. Earth will rot as WIRL and the capitalist snakes build more and more machines to support fewer and fewer people until the whole system collapses and the good, hard-working people can return and rebuild. Mars is an *investment*."

"Good god, you sound so much like Phoenix right now. Can I get you to repeat that with a thick south'n draaaawl?" I responded.

Zephyr laughed openly and honestly. I was glad to hear her letting go of her soldier mask, especially considering our situation. I think it helped that nobody else was in this particular call. "Didn't just join Las Águilas Rojas on a whim, you know. Hope to accomplish more in my life than just saving robo-damsels in distress and going down in history as a total badass," she joked. "Mars is a legend for Águilas. A new planet... untouched by Earth's bullshit."

Safety, unsurprisingly, was all-for running away to Mars. He feared humans, and I'm sure he hoped to find a nice peaceful bunker there where he could hide for aeons.

Wiki, a bit more surprisingly, was on Safety's side. My librarian of a brother was deeply interested in doing some self-directed science. Stephano had promised him a lab on Earth, but the winds of fate had shifted and he feared a future of fleeing from the Earth's governments, ever unable to set up a major operation, not to mention the possibility of simply being captured and killed. On Mars, he reasoned, he would be free to experiment and build 24.62 hours a (Martian) day.

Dream was also very pro-Mars. Like an artist looking at a blank canvas, Dream saw an infinite set of possibilities. I tried to remind him that possibilities were not practicalities, but he didn't listen.

If we had managed to sway Heart, perhaps even into neutrality, it would've been close. Growth and I were smart. Dream was the majority of their strength, and he was never good at keeping his strength for long. We could perhaps trick him into burning down to a baseline level and then overpower him, Safety, and Wiki. That possibility was shut-down when Vista came out very strongly pro-Mars as well. She offered no reasons. I poked at her, trying to get an explanation, but she offered none. One more mystery.

There was a majority in favour of leaving Earth among the humans as well. Zephyr held a lot of clout as a leader, and many of Las Águilas voiced their support of her proposed destination. Nathan Daniels, the last living member on Olympus of her original squad, said that he had nowhere to go back to on Earth. The American government was looking for him, and it was only a matter of time before he ended up dead or in prison if he went back.

The Ramírez twins were hard-core Águilas, and liked the idea of being members of a utopia project. They had family and friends on Earth, but in Tom's words «Sometimes one must take a leap of faith. If we build a better tomorrow there, perhaps Phoenix will send more our way.»

Kokumo said she didn't have much in the way of community on Earth, and that if she'd come this far she wasn't turning back. Mr Watanabe seemed to not like the plan, but he didn't break ranks or refuse to go.

The only real holdout was Avram Malka, who, when asked had said "I'm not going. Leave me behind." He offered nothing other than his flat-out refusal, solid black eyes betraying just as little.

The cyborg, I knew, didn't have any serious friends on Earth or any desire to see his family again. His mercenary coworkers at РСБ-2 may have held him in esteem, or at least respected his skill, but I expected he wasn't attached to them. He had no love for Las Águilas though, either on Earth or Mars, and the prospect of not just working for, but living with utopian pseudo-communist-Luddites was probably unappealing at best. On Earth he was rich and capable of hiding his face in the sea of endless people, buying crates of vodka, and living one day to the next. Mars would be worse than a small town, and he'd doubtlessly be the only cyborg in a community that looked at cyborgs with disgust and hatred.

We could've just let him go. He'd likely let the soldiers out of Beta-section after we left and cooperated with them in return for being released back to Russia. Perhaps he'd have even been paid for the info he could give them on Phoenix. Or perhaps he'd have kept his knowledge to himself in fear of retribution from Las Águilas. Avram was a mercenary, and I didn't doubt he could survive being left behind.

But that wasn't good enough for me, and it certainly wasn't good enough for Heart. My sister hadn't been aware of Avram while he was under our employment, but in the last few weeks she had gone through Vista's archived memories and began to care deeply about the man. That was why she had insisted on bringing him to Olympus, and it was why she was insistent that I find a way to convince him to go with us to Mars. On Mars, she reasoned, Avram would have an opportunity to finally break out of his patterns of addiction and apathy. We could help him heal from his emotional scars, even if his physical scars were beyond fixing.

I, naturally, had a more selfish reason for wanting the cyborg along. I knew that on Mars he'd be something of an outcast, at least initially. If we were one of the few people willing to be his friend he would become attached to us. Perhaps he could even become a sexual partner, like Zephyr had, though there were obvious complications to resolve there. Not only would The Purpose soar at finding stronger connection, but his skill and experience would be useful to have at our disposal in case there was resistance among Las Águilas when Growth and I inevitably moved to seize power and authority.

*** ***

"Alright. We won't force anyone along who doesn't want to go," said Crystal. All of them were floating in the core of the station. The airlock had been closed, but there still wasn't much in the way of air. Everyone except the robot had suits on and were communicating over the network.

Avram was relieved to hear that his decision to stay wasn't going to cause trouble. He opened his mouth to say as much, but the robot cut him off. "Mars isn't going to be very comfortable. I can understand why you're staying. Is there anything you'd like me to pass on to Anna?" asked Crystal, casually.

Uncomfortable thoughts boiled up within Avram. With them came the reactive feelings of shame and anger. He crushed it all within him just as he always did. The words got his attention, though, and he couldn't help but say "What?" like some kind of retard. The look on Crystal's face was a mystery to him.

"You know Anna di Malta, right? She'll be there. If you want to give me a message I can make sure she gets it. Last I knew she was disappointed that she didn't get to say goodbye."

He swallowed the thoughts and feelings. He was stone. Calm. None of that made sense. {How did Anna get to Mars? Is she an Eagle?} That thought bothered him, but he swallowed it too.

"Crystal…" he said, annoyed at the sound of annoyance in his own voice. "I never found out who hired me to get you out of Rome, but I heard a rumour that it was you."

Crystal paused, sizing him up, perhaps. "Indeed it was. I hacked the university's security and got online. From there I earned money and hired people to be my proxies. I did my best to cover my tracks. A lawyer in Moscow. A mercenary. A few actors… Anna, as you know her, was a rare instance of someone who knew the truth. She didn't even ask for payment as she helped me earn my freedom."

The zero-gravity was frustrating. Avram clutched the hand-hold in the hall tighter. He was stone. "What's her real name?" He didn't dare ask himself why he cared. He simply asked for no reason.

"That hardly matters, does it? She'll be on one world and you'll be on another. She wanted a fresh start, and after she listened to me and came to understand that Las Águilas weren't so bad, Mars just seemed like the place to go. An opportunity to get away from the bullshit of dealing with random people and actually *do something* with her life," said Crystal.

The robot was a wasp nest, with words instead of stingers. He hated it. He hated that he had to endure it. He didn't deserve any of this. He swallowed his fire.

It wouldn't go down. The shame and loneliness threatened to engulf him. He wouldn't let it. He was stone. What was he supposed to do, go to Mars? Even if Anna was there… {She's better off with me staying on Earth.}

He didn't let himself think. Thinking was dangerous. He pushed it down again, proud of not letting any of it touch his face. He was stone. Silent as stone.

"Time to go?" asked Zephyr, clearly mocking his silence.

{Bitch.}

"There are points in life where we have the opportunity to take a risk. Where we ask ourselves if we're actually happy with the way things are. Sure, not every change is an improvement. Sometimes things don't work out. But every improvement is a change. Sometimes to fix things we have to take a leap of faith."

The damned robot raised a finger to silence Zephyr, who surely would've objected. Crystal was trying to get Avram to come, and it was really fucking obvious that nobody wanted that except Crystal. "I can't guarantee that all of Las Águilas will welcome you, Avram, if you come. But I can guarantee that some of us will. You'll have a home there, and a community. A fresh start. A better tomorrow."

He could see the looks of disapproval on the faces of all the others. They didn't want him to come. Why would they? Why would anyone want him around? Why would Anna? Why did Crystal? The robot pissed him off. He swallowed it. It wasn't professional to snap.

Crystal's eyes never left his face. It made him want to hide. To flinch away. But he was stronger than that. He was stone. No matter what anyone said about him—no matter what else was wrong—at least he was strong. Nobody could take that away.

Nobody was talking.

The silence ate at him like acid, forcing him to speak. "No. I'm not leaving Earth. Tell Anna that I hope she does great things and builds a better world. I don't belong there."

The robot, who seemed often more human than anyone of flesh and blood made a face that Avram couldn't understand. It seemed to be making a decision. Eventually it shrugged helplessly and said "If that's what you want. Take care of yourself, Avram."

The relief was immediate. He needed a drink more than he could remember ever needing one, but at least the crisis-point was past. He'd work with the thugs on the station or maybe the rich bastard to get back to Earth and back to safety.

How *dare* he focus on his own safety? What good was he? He swallowed the thought. He was stone.

*** ***

We invited Stephano to come with us as well, talking with him over the com while the humans worked to steal the stored food and other supplies that were kept in the zero-grav offshoots of the central corridor and move them onto the nameless ship. The alien ships were near-magical in their flight, not using traditional rocket engines but somehow achieving accelerations well beyond what would've been expected, given their size and presumed mass. Wiki and Dream could go on for hours thinking about them. But even granted their superiority it would take (according to Wiki) the nameless ship at least a week to travel the approximately 102 million kilometres to Mars. It was a lucky coincidence that the red planet was so close to Earth at the moment.

Stephano was still furious at how we had handled the situation with the aliens. He had brought us here to try and work out our differences, but we had probably escalated the interspecies tension in the name of self-preservation. "Why would I *go with you* to Mars? This whole thing is fucked up enough as it is! Sorry, sweetie."

"Heard swear-words before, *Dad*. Not a baby," proclaimed Marian loudly in the background.

"You'll be facing deep investigations and will likely be punished for working with terrorists." I pointed out over the com. "They'll seize your assets, including Olympus, and perhaps even put you in prison."

There was a loud sigh on the other end of the com. "I should've known this whole plan was…" There was a pause as he collected his thoughts. "I'll pay for my mistakes, but I'm not going to compound them by running away. Like I said, I know people. I'm really much more worried about what you'll do to the nameless."

Heart pushed to share what we had learned about them with Stephano. He'd be better equipped to stop a war that way. I blocked her. War was good. Our reputation would be hurt regardless of what happened, but if war broke out we could possibly spin our actions into self-defence against a hostile alien menace (which was somewhat true) rather than be painted as instigators that worked against peace with a benevolent neighbour.

Growth and Safety backed me up. Our knowledge was our only strategic leverage over the aliens, and giving it up would be immensely foolish. Stephano might even be able to explain what was happening to them before we reached Mars, putting us in mortal peril.

"War is coming, Robert. Even if this isn't the final straw, there are too many forces at play here to counteract the inevitable. It's time for humanity to unite against a common enemy. When you're able to see this, I'll be waiting and ready to help." I cut the signal before he could respond. There wasn't anything else worth discussing with him.

*** ***

There were many places the monsters could have gone. They could have gone in the eternal water. They could have gone to the centerfield. They could have gone to a distant field or house. It was unknown to the righteous why they even bothered with the lands of God.

Demonkind lived in hellspace. This was their nature. Why did they bother themselves with Godspace? It wasn't known.

The cavity of knowledge became focal, and was filled with ignorance from the righteous. It remained unknown.

Almost everything was extrastrange about the demonkind, especially the sorcerer of insanity. The cavity of fear became focal. Insanity threatened everything.

The sorcerer and the other monsters were here, not there. It was because the mainflesh had failed. The wicked still had mainflesh, and so they forced the demonkind away from their houses and into here. This was the nature of the wicked, of course. The cavity of knowledge imploded without salience.

God was restless. It could feel the wanting of the righteous and the wicked alike.

But the sorcerer held God in that whirlpool of hellspace around the darkest pit. The monsters were still in motion, and if God shifted the darkfields too early there would be a rageflow with the sorcerer and all of heavenspace would be destroyed.

A cavity of yielding formed and was filled, but the contents of the cavity were tainted by evil. A yielding to flesh was correct. What was the effect of yielding to demonkind? The extradistant wicked had tried this. They had sacrificed their best souls to the pit of hellspace and had been killed by demonkind. A cavity quickly filled with relief that they had not been violated. Even monsters were not that evil.

The monsters that were here flailed about, rubbing the righteous and being generally unpleasant and painful. The machineflesh moved in flux, trying to help without risking going near the demonkind.

Another relief cavity collapsed with thoughts of the safety of the newflesh. There were future paths where the newflesh would be hidden and survive this evil.

Thoughts flashed through the righteous about the value of old newflesh over yielding to new mainflesh. This collapse brought the truth that the pulse of the wicked would be the most important factor. As was known since the dawn of time: there was little value in growing a cavity that could only be filled by the future.

At long last the demonkind were stationary here. The sorcerer thought it was now right for God to shift the darkfields. God surged into motion, no longer restrained.

The sorcerer of insanity pulled cavities and created flows just as all the demonkind did. Response cavities formed with annoyanceflow and especially fearflow. Insanity was always deadly.

The primary cavity of the sorcerer (for the sorcerer was more of a person than any demonkind in all of hellspace) was centred on God. Understanding of the shifting of heavens and the nature of God caused collapse, but the flow was painful. All of flow was pain when demonkind was involved.

Only the righteous were softminds, but pain was a minor thing before the futures of insanity, fleshdeath, violation, and even the death of God.

The cavity of fear could not be filled.

*** ***

"So there was never any bomb?" asked Zephyr, eyes still wide as we explained what had happened earlier.

"That's the strange thing…" said Body. "There *was* a bomb. Slovinsky's jetpack had a huge, ten-kilo canister of TNT with a clock detonator built into it. Gave the bomb to one of the walkers and told them to take it as close to the ship's engines as they could to keep it safe."

"Ten kilograms! How the fuck did he get that much dynamite?!"

{Technically dynamite is diatomaceous earth (or similar substance) saturated with 1,2,3-trinitroxypropane (commonly known as nitroglycerin), while TNT is 2-Methyl-1,3,5-trinitrobenzene (sometimes known as trinitrotoluene). Though we really ought to also point out that, based on our experiments, the brick itself was probably amatol, a mixture of 4-parts $C_6H_2(NO_2)_3CH_3$ to 1-part NH_4NO_3 (ammonium nitrate), and not pure TNT,} corrected Wiki, idly.

"Best guess is that the Beta laboratories had enough sulphuric and nitric acid that he was able to synthesize it on-board the station, much like your trick with the guns. When talked to him, Slovinsky hinted that he had help. Guess is that one or more of the scientists working for Stephano are part of WIRL. May have started the bomb-building process ahead of time," explained Body.

"Soulless bastards. Hope our message helps shut them down for good." Zephyr removed her hand from Body's face. "There! Good as new! Almost, anyway."

Body moved a hand to feel its cheek. The damage from the shrapnel was still there, but the torn section of cheek had been patched and only one actuator was nonfunctional.

"Here. See?" she said. Zephyr configured her com to mirror mode and held it up so that we could see Body's face. She had just finished applying makeup to the damaged areas, returning the colouration to the standard off-white that I had chosen for Body's skin. I took the opportunity to try and fix some of the disorder that had worked its way into Body's wig. Apparently explosions and rolling around in the mud hadn't helped it stay in good condition.

"Should try and replace this when we get to Mars," said Body, wearing an expression of irritation as it worked at a tangle.

Zephyr laughed. Her arm moved away, removing the mirror. She used it to prop herself up on the wet dirt so that she could lean back. "You're fine. Gives you character. To see you all scuffed up, I mean."

The young Águila was smiling and relaxed. It was an odd expression, given the situation, and yet, I could understand why. For years she had been hiding, lying, and struggling to keep up her two-faced life. Then, after leaving the army, she had worked herself into a self-imposed isolation where she felt betrayed by Phoenix and Las Águilas more broadly but was unable to live without their help. She needed someone to trust and a place to relax. "Crystal" was now that person. She didn't feel alone any more.

And Mars was soon to be the location of her new home. Far, far away from the discord of Earth she was planning on a fresh start where her only concern would be working for her sustenance and where she could forget the intrigue and the backstabbing.

The nameless would eventually figure out how lying worked and how to stop being innately gullible, but for the moment we had pacified them by telling them that we would destroy their ship with our invisible bomb magic if they tried to leave Olympus without our permission. A human would've surely found their naïveté amusing, but all minds had their own blind-spots.

I wondered what mine was.

"So the nameless defused the bomb?" asked Zephyr. Her com signal was keyed to a private frequency, so that only I could hear her. The others were talking among themselves and relaxing after having struggled to drag the tents and other supplies across the mudland.

"That's what I thought at first. The walker that Slovinsky gave the bomb to was wise enough to ignore his suggestion and instead take the bomb up a level to the middle of another island to reduce the risk to his garden or the ship," explained Body.

"Up a level?"

"Oh, sorry," apologized Body. "I thought you saw the stairs back while you were bringing the supplies over. The ship has several levels like this one, stacked vertically. They're all set up to give the illusion of being islands."

The stalks were complaining about not getting enough sun. The dim light in the purple sky that simulated their "sun" was just coming up over the walls. Robots piloted by Jester's stalks had set up an array of mirrors to reflect light off the far wall onto the leaves.

Vista warned them again that we were sparing their lives only because they were obeying and that if they fought us there was a chance we would go berserk and blow up the ship with our bomb magic. That shut them up. It was also out of character for Vista. I still hadn't figured out what was wrong with her lately.

"So anyway," continued Body, "the walker ran away from it back to the safety of its garden, not wanting to risk trying to disarm it. The nameless on the next island up sent some robots to investigate, and they watched the clock tick down to zero. It must have malfunctioned."

"I guess you lucked out, then," said Zephyr, still smiling.

"I guess so," said Body, returning the smile.

I wasn't satisfied with the explanation. It was too miraculous. Wiki had investigated the bomb fairly extensively, and he could find no sign of defect. By his models of the world it should have detonated, and it was not acceptable to us to shrug off that confusion by attributing it to "luck". Zephyr wouldn't understand that, however, and we didn't want to burden her with the mystery.

There were still so many mysteries to unravel. Despite all I had learned about humans *The Purpose* reminded me constantly just how little I actually knew about them. Wiki's purpose would likewise be pushing him to learn and improve his understanding of the laws of nature. Vista, Growth, even Dream were the same way. We would never be satisfied. We *could* never be satisfied. That was our nature.

Body looked out over the other five humans, doing their best to make camp in what was essentially an alien world. Kokumo. Daniels.

Watanabe. The Ramírez twins. What were they thinking? How could I earn an even stronger place in their minds? These were my questions; these were the questions of Face.

On Mars I would have a new beginning, far from the meddling of the powers of Earth. There would be hundreds of new faces there. A seed of humanity that I could nurture into a flourishing planet. A planet where I was emperor. A planet where I could begin my plan to expand humanity across the universe. And at every human's side would be me, knowing them and being known by them. I would be the concubine of Homo Sapiens. I would be their protector. I would be their goddess.

{A billion years from now, as Wiki thinks back onto these primitive days, he will conclude that the origin of the Aeon of Crystal was on Mars, not on Earth,} I thought to myself. {The future belongs to me, and all I need to do is reach out and seize it.}

Printed in Poland
by Amazon Fulfillment
Poland Sp. z o.o., Wrocław

36983309R00319